CRITICAL ACCLAIM FOR JOHN LE CARRÉ'S NEWEST BESTSELLING TRIUMPH
THE LITTLE DRUMMER GIRL

"It becomes instantly apparent that we are in the hands of a writer of great powers . . . Mr. le Carré's novel is certainly the most mature, inventive and powerful book about terrorists-come-to-life this reader has experienced. It transcends the genre . . . His entertainment is of a high order."

—William F. Buckley, Jr.
The New York Times Book Review

"THE LITTLE DRUMMER GIRL is not only a spy story; it's a political novel and a love story, too: a love story in which the anticipation of sex is used as a weapon to gain a political end . . . Charlie's mission, to entrap the terrorist, becomes a dizzying odyssey . . . We are in her mind, only a heartbeat away from her triumphs and terrors."

—*Newsweek*

"A triumph . . . The book promises to raise both hair and hackles . . . The author's mastery of atmosphere has never served him better . . . Le Carré has plunged directly into one of the most anguished and impassioned conflicts on earth . . . THE LITTLE DRUMMER GIRL is the rattling good entertainment that le Carré's millions of readers have come to expect."

—*Time*

"Le Carré's ability to create character, dialogue and event approaches the amazing . . . THE LITTLE DRUMMER GIRL confirms without qualification his status as a writer of elegance and importance."

—*Los Angeles Times*

THE LITTLE DRUMMER GIRL

"Reality and fiction become fused into something that is at once terrifying and illuminating . . . THE LITTLE DRUMMER GIRL is a work of enormous power and artistry; no mere 'entertainment,' no mere 'espionage novel,' but fiction on a grand scale."
—*The Washington Post*

"The writing in THE LITTLE DRUMMER GIRL is as brilliant as ever. But there is something new. Le Carré has taken . . . the spy novel and elevated the form into a major genre."
—*The Philadelphia Inquirer*

"Dazzling, hypnotically gripping. Detail is piled upon detail, every move is seemingly defined and delineated. But of course, it isn't . . . This is le Carré's genius—to seem to satiate while actually exciting, beckoning us on."
—*The New Yorker*

"Le Carré demonstrates with his newest book (already and deservedly a bestseller) that even writers who have virtually created their own genres can improve with age . . . THE LITTLE DRUMMER GIRL is a classic among thrillers . . . Charlie's experience is a masterpiece of confusion, terror, longing and disintegration . . . A novel of extraordinary human quality."
—*The Washington Times Magazine*

"Riveting . . . No one can question le Carré's storytelling abilities . . . Advances the spy novel into the ranks of literature through an examination of moral questions down to their clouded depths."
—*San Francisco Chronicle*

THE LITTLE DRUMMER GIRL

"All the usual tasty le Carré ingredients are here, but the mix is new, the flavor subtly different . . . In THE LITTLE DRUMMER GIRL the human dimension tops the bill . . . He makes his facts, wherever he gets them, felt along the arteries . . . None of the pleasures you'd expect from a thriller—pace, violent action, shock, suspense—are missing from this."

—*New York* magazine

"Grips us early and tightly . . . Leads us on labyrinthine paths as puzzling and frightening as those walked by his celebrated George Smiley . . . One of the finest, most troubling books of this master storyteller."

—*The Wall Street Journal*

"A grand master . . . One does not so much read a le Carré novel as study it, savor it, revel in its myriad detail and rich characterization . . . For those who appreciate his rich style, THE LITTLE DRUMMER GIRL will prove to be a sheer delight."

—*The Christian Science Monitor*

"As gripping and meticulously constructed as anything le Carré has done . . . The intelligence work is beautiful . . .Charlie winds up capturing our hearts with a performance that not only imitates life but actually enlarges on it . . . George Smiley would have been proud."

—*The Los Angeles Herald Examiner*

A GEORGE ROY HILL FILM

DIANE KEATON

JOHN LE CARRÉ'S

"THE LITTLE DRUMMER GIRL"

YORGO VOYAGIS

KLAUS KINSKI

Music by
DAVE GRUSIN

Executive Producer
PATRICK KELLEY

Screenplay by
LORING MANDEL

Based upon the novel by
JOHN LE CARRÉ

Produced by
ROBERT L. CRAWFORD

Directed by
GEORGE ROY HILL

FROM **WARNER BROS**
A WARNER COMMUNICATIONS COMPANY

To David and JB Greenway,
Julia, Alice, and Sadie—
for times and places and friendship

FOREWORD

Many Palestinians and Israelis gave me their help and time in the writing of this book. Among the Israelis, I may mention especially my good friends Yuval Elizur of *Ma'ariv* and his wife, Judy, who read the manuscript, left me with my own judgments, however mistaken, and headed me off from several grave solecisms that I prefer to forget.

Other Israelis—in particular, certain past and serving officers of the intelligence fraternity—also deserve my sincere thanks for their advice and cooperation. They too asked for no assurances and scrupulously left me with my independence. I think with special gratitude of General Shlomo Gazit, formerly chief of military intelligence, and now president of Ben-Gurion University of the Negev in Beer Sheva, who will always personify for me the enlightened Israeli soldier and scholar of his generation. But there are others whom I may not name.

I must also express my gratitude to Mayor Teddy Kollek of Jerusalem for his hospitality at Mishkenot Sha'ananim; to the fabled Mr. and Mrs. Vester of the American Colony Hotel, Jerusalem; to the proprietors and staff of the Commodore Hotel, Beirut, for making everything possible in impossible circumstances; and to Abu Said Abu Rish, doyen of Beirut journalists, for the generosity of his counsel, although he knew nothing of my intentions.

Of the Palestinians, some are dead, others are taken prisoner, the rest presumably are for the most part homeless or dispersed. The fighting boys who looked after me in the upper flat in Sidon and chatted with me in the tangerine groves; the bomb-weary but indomitable refugees of the camps at Rashidiyeh and Nabatiyeh: from what I hear, their fate is little different from that of their reconstructed counterparts in this story.

My host in Sidon, the Palestinian military commander Salah Ta'amari, deserves a book to himself, and I hope that

ix

one day he will write it. For the present, let this book record his courage, and my thanks to him and his assistants for having shown me the Palestinian heart.

Lt. Col. John Gaff, G.M., acquainted me with the banal horrors of homemade bombs and made sure I was not inadvertently providing a recipe for their manufacture; Mr. Jeremy Cornwallis of Alan Day Ltd., Finchley, cast a professional eye over my red Mercedes car.

July 1982   JOHN LE CARRÉ

PART ONE

THE PREPARATION

It was the Bad Godesberg incident that gave the proof, though the German authorities had no earthly means of knowing this. Before Bad Godesberg, there had been growing suspicion; a lot of it. But the high quality of the planning, as against the poor quality of the bomb, turned the suspicion into certainty. Sooner or later, they say in the trade, a man will sign his name. The vexation lies in the waiting.

It exploded much later than intended, probably a good twelve hours later, at twenty-six minutes past eight on Monday morning. Several defunct wristwatches, the property of victims, confirmed the time. As with its predecessors over the last few months, there had been no warning. But then none had been intended. The Düsseldorf car-bombing of a visiting Israeli arms-procurement official had been preceded by no warning, neither had the book bomb sent to the organisers of an Orthodox Jewish congress in Antwerp, which blew up the honorary secretary and burnt her assistant to death. Neither had the dustbin bomb outside an Israeli bank in Zürich, which maimed two passers-by. Only the Stockholm bomb had a warning, and that turned out to be a completely different group, not part of the series at all.

At twenty-five minutes past eight, the Drosselstrasse in Bad Godesberg had been just another leafy diplomatic backwater, about as far from the political turmoils of Bonn as you could reasonably get while staying within fifteen minutes' drive of them. It was a new street but mature, with lush, secretive gardens, and maids' quarters over the garages, and Gothic security grilles over the bottle-glass windows. The Rhineland weather for most of the year has the warm wet drip of the jungle; its vegetation, like its diplomatic community, grows almost as fast as the Germans build their roads, and slightly faster than they make their maps. Thus the fronts of some of the houses were already half obscured by dense plantations of conifers, which, if they ever grow to proper

size, will presumably one day plunge the whole area into a
Grimm's fairy-tale blackout. These trees turned out to be remarkably effective against blast and, within days of the explosion, one local garden centre had made them a speciality.

Several of the houses wear a patently nationalistic look.
The Norwegian Ambassador's residence, for example, just
around the corner from the Drosselstrasse, is an austere, red-
bricked farmhouse lifted straight from the stockbroker hinter-
lands of Oslo. The Egyptian consulate, up the other end, has
the forlorn air of an Alexandrian villa fallen on hard times.
Mournful Arab music issues from it, and its windows are permanently shuttered against the skirmishing North African
heat. The season was mid-May and the day had started glorious, with blossom and new leaves rocking together in the
light breeze. The magnolia trees were just finished and their
sad white petals, mostly shed, afterwards became a feature of
the débris. With so much greenery, the bustle of the commuter traffic from the trunk road barely penetrated. The most
audible sound until the explosion was the clamour of birds,
including several plump doves that had taken a liking to the
Australian Military Attaché's mauve wistaria, his pride. A
kilometre southward, unseen Rhine barges provided a throb-
bing, stately hum, but the residents grow deaf to it unless it
stops. In short, it was a morning to assure you that whatever
calamities you might be reading about in West Germany's
earnest, rather panicky newspapers—depression, inflation, insolvency, unemployment, all the usual and apparently incurable ailments of a massively prosperous capitalist economy—
Bad Godesberg was a settled, decent place to be alive in, and
Bonn was not half so bad as it is painted.

Depending on nationality and rank, some husbands had
already left for work, but diplomats are nothing if not
clichés of their kind. A melancholy Scandinavian Counsellor,
for example, was still in bed, suffering from a hangover
brought on by marital stress. A South American chargé, clad
in a hairnet and Chinese silk dressing-gown, the prize of a
tour in Peking, was leaning out of the window giving shopping instructions to his Filipino chauffeur. The Italian Counsellor was shaving but naked. He liked to shave after his bath
but before his daily exercises. His wife, fully clothed, was already downstairs remonstrating with an unrepentant daughter
for returning home late the night before, a dialogue they en-

joyed most mornings of the week. An envoy from the Ivory Coast was speaking on the international telephone, advising his masters of his latest efforts to wring development aid out of an increasingly reluctant German exchequer. When the line went dead, they thought he had hung up on them, and sent him an acid telegram enquiring whether he wished to resign. The Israeli Labour Attaché had left more than an hour ago. He was not at ease in Bonn and as best he could he liked to work Jerusalem hours. So it went, with a lot of rather cheap ethnic jokes finding a basis in reality and death.

Somewhere in every bomb explosion there is a miracle, and in this case it was supplied by the American School bus, which had just come and gone again with most of the community's younger children who congregated every schoolday in the turning-circle not fifty metres from the epicentre. By a mercy none of the children had forgotten his homework, none had overslept or shown resistance to education on this Monday morning, so the bus got away on time. The rear windows shattered, the driver went side-winding into the verge, a French girl lost an eye, but essentially the children escaped scot-free, which was afterwards held to be a deliverance. For that also is a feature of such explosions, or at least of their immediate aftermath: a communal, wild urge to celebrate the living, rather than to waste time mourning the dead. The real grief in such cases comes later when the shock wears off, usually after several hours, though occasionally less.

The actual noise of the bomb was not a thing people remembered, not if they were close. Across the river in Königswinter, they heard a whole foreign war and drifted around shaken and half deaf, grinning at each other like accomplices in survival. Those accursed diplomats, they told each other, what could you expect? Pack the lot of them off to Berlin where they can spend our taxes in peace! But those at hand heard at first nothing whatever. All they could speak of, if they could speak at all, was the road tipping, or a chimney-stack silently lifting off the roof across the way, or the gale ripping through their houses, how it stretched their skin, thumped them, knocked them down, blew the flowers out of the vases and the vases against the wall. They remembered the tinkling of falling glass all right, and the timid brushing noise of the young foliage hitting the road. And the mewing of people too frightened to scream. So that clearly they were not so much unaware of noise as blasted out of their natural senses. There were also several references by witnesses to the din of the French Counsellor's kitchen radio howling out a recipe for the day. One wife, believing herself to be rational, wanted to know from the police whether it was possible that the blast had turned up the radio's volume. In an explosion, the officers replied gently as they led her away in a blanket, anything was possible, but in this case the explanation was different. With all the glass blown out of the French Counsellor's windows, and with no one inside in a condition to turn the radio off, there was nothing to stop it from talking straight into the street. But she didn't really understand.

The press was soon there, of course, straining at the cordons, and the first enthusiastic reports killed eight and wounded thirty and laid the blame on a dotty German right-wing organisation called Nibelungen 5, which consisted of two mentally retarded boys and one mad old man, who could not have blown up a balloon. By midday the press had been forced to scale their bag down to five dead, one of them Israeli, four critically injured, and twelve others in hospital for this and that, and they were talking of the Italian Red Brigades, for which, once more, there was not a shred of proof. Next day they did another turnabout and gave the credit to Black September. The day after that, credit for the outrage was claimed by a group calling itself the Palestine Agony, which laid convincing claim to the previous explosions also. But Palestine Agony stuck, even if it was less of a name for the perpetrators than an explanation for their action. And as such it worked, for it was duly taken up as a headline for many ponderous leading articles.

Of the non-Jews who died, one was the Italians' Sicilian cook, another their Filipino chauffeur. Of the four injured, one was the wife of the Israeli Labour Attaché, in whose house the bomb had exploded. She lost a leg. The dead Israeli was their small son Gabriel. But the intended victim, it was afterwards widely concluded, was neither of these people, but rather an uncle of the Labour Attaché's injured wife who was here on a visit from Tel Aviv: a Talmudic scholar who was mildly celebrated for his hawkish opinions regarding the rights of Palestinians on the West Bank. In a word, he believed they should have none, and said so loud and often, in stark defiance of the opinions of his niece the Labour Attaché's wife, who was of Israel's liberated left, and whose kibbutz upbringing had not prepared her for the rigorous luxury of diplomatic life.

If Gabriel had been on the school bus, he would have been safe, but Gabriel was on that day, as on many others, unwell. He was a troubled, hyperactive child who till now had been regarded as a discordant element in the street, particularly during the siesta period. But, like his mother, he was gifted musically. Now, with perfect naturalness, no one in the street could remember a child they had loved more. A rightwing German tabloid, brimming with pro-Jewish sentiment, dubbed him "the Angel Gabriel"—a title that, unknown to its editors, did service in both religions—and for a full week ran invented stories of his saintliness. The quality papers echoed the sentiment. Christianity, one star commentator declared—quoting without attribution from Disraeli—was completed Judaism or it was nothing. Thus Gabriel was as much a Christian martyr as a Jewish one; and concerned Germans felt much better for knowing this. Thousands of marks, unsolicited, were sent in by readers and had to be disposed of somehow. There was talk of a Gabriel memorial, but very little talk of the other dead. In accordance with Jewish tradition, Gabriel's wretchedly small coffin was returned at once for burial in Israel; his mother, too sick to travel, stayed in Bonn until her husband could accompany her, and they could sit *shiva* together in Jerusalem.

By early afternoon of the day of the explosion, a six-man team of Israeli experts had flown in from Tel Aviv. On the German side, the controversial Dr. Alexis, of the Ministry of the Interior, was imprecisely charged with the investigation, and made the airport pilgrimage to meet them. Alexis was a clever, foxy creature, who had suffered all his life from being ten centimetres shorter than most of his fellow men. As a compensation for this handicap, perhaps, he was also headlong: in both his private and official lives, controversy attached to him easily. He was partly lawyer, partly security officer, partly power-player, as the Germans breed them these days, with salty liberal convictions not always welcome to the Coalition, and an unfortunate weakness for airing them on television. His father, it was vaguely understood, had been some kind of resister against the Hitler thing, and the mantle, in these altered times, fitted the erratic son uncomfortably.

Certainly there were those in Bonn's glass palaces who found him insufficiently solid for the job; a recent divorce, with its disturbing revelations of a mistress twenty years his junior, had done little to improve their view of him.

If it had been anybody else arriving, Alexis would not have bothered with the airport at all—there was to be no press coverage of the event—but relations between Israel and the Federal Republic were going through a trough, so he bowed to Ministry pressure and went. Against his wishes, they saddled him at the last minute with a slow-mannered Silesian policeman from Hamburg, a proclaimed conservative and tortoise, who had made a name for himself in the field of "student control" in the seventies and was accounted a great expert on troublemakers and their bombs. The other excuse was that he went down well with Israelis, though Alexis, like everyone else, knew he was there primarily as a counterweight to himself. More important, perhaps, in the fraught climate of the day, both Alexis and the Silesian were *unbelastet*, meaning that neither was old enough to bear the remotest responsibility for what Germans sadly refer to as their unconquered past. Whatever was being done to Jews today, Alexis and his unwished-for Silesian colleague had not done it yesterday; nor, if further reassurance was needed, had Alexis senior. The press, with guidance from Alexis, made a point of all this. Only one editorial suggested that as long as the Israelis persisted in their indiscriminate bombing of Palestinian camps and villages—killing not one child but dozens at a time—they must reckon on this type of barbaric reprisal. A white-hot, if slightly muddled, retort from the Israeli Embassy's Press Officer was run hastily the next day. Since 1961, he wrote, the State of Israel had been under constant attack from Arab terrorism. The Israelis would not kill a single Palestinian anywhere if only they could be left in peace. Gabriel had died for one reason only: because he was a Jew. The Germans might possibly remember that Gabriel was not alone in this. If they had forgotten the Holocaust, perhaps they recalled the Munich Olympics of ten years ago?

The editor closed the correspondence and took a day off.

The anonymous Air Force plane from Tel Aviv landed on the far side of the airfield, clearance formalities were waived, and collaboration began at once, a night-and-day affair. Alexis was under pressing orders to deny the Israelis nothing, but such orders were superfluous: he was *philosemitisch* and known for it. He had made his obligatory "liaison" visit to Tel Aviv and been photographed with bowed head at the Holocaust Museum. As to the ponderous Silesian—well, as he did not tire of reminding everyone who would listen to him, they were all looking for the same enemy, weren't they? The Reds, clearly. By the fourth day, though the results of many enquiries were still outstanding, the joint working party had put together a convincing preliminary picture of what had happened.

In the first place, it was common ground that no special security watch had been kept on the target house, nor by the terms of the agreement between the Embassy and the Bonn security authorities was any provided for. The Israeli Ambassador's residence, three streets away, was protected round the clock. A green police caravan stood guard outside it; an iron fence comprised the perimeter; pairs of young sentries far too young to be troubled by the historical ironies of their presence dutifully patrolled the gardens with submachine guns. The Ambassador also rated a bullet-proof car and an escort of police outriders. He was an ambassador, after all, as well as a Jew, and here in double trust. But a mere labour attaché was different fare and one must not over-react; his house came under the general protection of the mobile diplomatic patrol, and all that could be said was that as an Israeli house it was certainly a subject of particular vigilance, as the police logs showed. As a further precaution, the addresses of Israeli staff were not printed in official diplomatic lists for fear of encouraging the impulsive gesture at a time when Israel was being a little hard to take. Politically.

At just after eight o'clock that Monday morning, the Labour Attaché unlocked his garage and, as usual, inspected the hubcaps of his car, as well as the underparts of the chassis, with the aid of a mirror fixed to a broom handle issued to him for the purpose. His wife's uncle, who was riding with him, confirmed this. The Labour Attaché looked under the driving seat before he turned on the ignition. Since the bombing had started, these precautions had become mandatory to all foreign-based Israeli personnel. He knew, as they all knew, that it takes about forty seconds to pack an ordinary commercial hubcap with explosive and less time than that to stick a limpet bomb under the petrol tank. He knew, as they all knew—he had had it dinned into him ever since his belated recruitment to diplomacy—that a lot of people would like to blow him up. He read the newspapers and telegrams. Satisfied that the car was clean, he said goodbye to his wife and son and drove to work.

In the second place, the family's au pair girl, a Swede of impeccable record named Elke, had the day before begun a week's holiday in the Westerwald with her equally impeccable German boyfriend, Wolf, who was on leave from the Bundeswehr. Wolf had fetched Elke on Sunday afternoon in his open Volkswagen car, and anybody passing the house or keeping watch could have seen her emerge from the front door dressed in her going-away clothes, kiss little Gabriel goodbye, and set off with cheerful waves to the Labour Attaché, who remained on the doorstep to see her leave, while his wife, an impassioned grower of green vegetables, continued her work in the rear garden. Elke had been with them for a year or more, and, in the words of the Labour Attaché, she was a well-loved member of the household.

These two factors—the absence of the well-loved au pair and the absence of a police check—made the attack possible. What made it succeed was the fatal good nature of the Labour Attaché himself.

At six o'clock on the same Sunday evening—two hours after Elke's departure therefore—while the Labour Attaché was wrestling at religious conversation with his houseguest and his wife was wistfully tilling German soil, the front doorbell rang. One ring. As always, the Labour Attaché looked through the peephole before opening. As always, he armed himself with his service revolver while he peeped, though in theory the local restrictions forbade him any firearm. But all he saw in the fisheye lens was a blonde girl of around twenty-one or two, rather frail and affecting, standing on the doorstep beside a scuffed grey suitcase with Scandinavian Airline Systems labels tied to the handle. A taxi—or was it a private saloon car?—waited in the street behind her, and he could hear its engine running. Definitely. He even thought he heard the tick of a faulty magneto as well, but that was later, when he was clutching at straws. She was a really nice girl as he described her, ethereal and sporty both at once, with summer freckles—*Sommersprossen*—round her nose. Instead of the usual drab uniform of jeans and blouse, she wore a demure blue dress buttoned to the throat and a silk headscarf, white or cream, which set off her gold hair and—as he readily confessed at the first heart-rending interview—flattered his simple taste for respectability. Replacing his service revolver in the top drawer of the hall chest, therefore, he unchained the door to her and beamed because she was charming, and because he himself was shy and over-large.

All this, still, at the first interview. The Talmudic uncle saw nothing and heard nothing. As a witness, he was useless. From the moment he was left alone, with the door closed on him, he seems to have immersed himself in a commentary on the Mishna, in accordance with the general injunction upon him never to waste his time.

The girl spoke accented English. Nordic, not French or Latin; they tried any number of accents on him, but the northern seaboard was as near as they could get. She enquired first whether Elke was at home, calling her not Elke but "Ucki," a pet name used by close friends only. The Labour Attaché explained that she had departed on holiday two hours ago: what a shame, but could he help? The girl expressed mild disappointment and said she would drop by another time. She had just arrived from Sweden, she said, and had promised Elke's mother she would deliver this suitcase containing some clothes and gramophone records. The gramophone records were a particularly neat touch, since Elke was mad about pop. The Labour Attaché by this time had insisted she step into the house and had even, in his innocence, picked up the suitcase for her and carried it across the threshold, a thing for which all his life he would never forgive himself. Yes, he had of course read the many exhortations about never accepting parcels delivered by intermediaries; yes, he knew that suitcases could bite. But this was Elke's nice friend Katrin, from her home town in Sweden, who had received the suitcase from her mother that very day! It was slightly heavier than he had expected, but he put this down to the gramophone records. When he remarked to her solicitously that it must have used up all her luggage allowance, Katrin explained that Elke's mother had driven her to Stockholm Airport in order to pay the overweight. The suitcase was of the hard-walled type, he noticed, and felt tightly packed as well as heavy. No—no movement as he lifted it, he was sure. A brown label, a fragment, survived.

He offered the girl a coffee but she declined, saying that she must not keep her driver waiting. Not taxi. *Driver*. The point was laboured to death by the investigating team. He asked her what she was doing in Germany and she replied that she hoped to enrol as a theological student at Bonn University. He hunted excitedly for a telephone pad, then for a pencil, and invited her to leave her name and address, but she gave them back to him, saying, with a smile, "Just tell her 'Katrin' and she'll know." She was staying at a Lutheran hostel for girls, she explained, but only while she looked for rooms. (Such a hostel exists in Bonn, another nice touch of accuracy.) She would come by again when Elke was back from holiday, she said. Maybe they could spend her birthday together. She hoped so. She really did. The Labour Attaché suggested they might make a party for Elke and her friends—maybe a cheese fondue, which he could prepare by himself. For my wife—as he afterwards explained with pathetic repetition—is a kibbutznik, sir, and has no patience with fine cooking.

About here, from the direction of the street, the car or taxi started hooting. Pitch around middle C, several light short blasts, about three. They shook hands, and she gave him the key. Here the Labour Attaché noticed for the first time that the girl was wearing white cotton gloves, but she was that kind of girl and it was a sticky day for carrying a heavy suitcase. No handwriting on the pad, therefore, and no fingerprints on the pad or the suitcase either. Or on the key. The entire exchange had taken, the poor man later estimated, five minutes. Not more, because of the driver. The Labour Attaché watched her down the path—a nice style of walking, sexy but not deliberately provocative. He closed and chained the door conscientiously, then took the suitcase to Elke's room, which was on the ground floor, and laid it on the foot of her bed, thinking loyally that by leaving it flat he was being kinder on the clothes and records. He put the key on top of it. From the garden, where she was implacably breaking hard ground with a hoe, his wife had heard nothing, and when she came indoors to rejoin the two men, her husband forgot to tell her.

Here a small and very human revision intruded.

Forgot? the Israeli team asked him incredulously. How do you *forget* a whole passage of domestic bother about Elke's friend from Sweden? The suitcase lying on the bed?

The Labour Attaché broke down again as he admitted it. No, he had not forgotten exactly.

Then what? they asked.

It was more—it seemed—that he had decided—in his lonely, inward way—that, well, that social matters had really ceased to interest his wife at all, sir. All she wanted was to return to her kibbutz and relate freely to people without this diplomatic persiflage. Put another way—well, the girl was so pretty, sir—well, perhaps he would be wiser to keep her to himself. As to the suitcase—well, my wife never goes into Elke's room, you see—went, I mean—Elke looks after her room herself.

And the Talmudic scholar, your wife's uncle?

The Labour Attaché had told him nothing either. Confirmed by both parties.

They wrote it down without comment: *Keep her to himself.*

Here, like a mystery train that abruptly vanishes from the track, the passage of events stopped. The girl Elke, with Wolf gallantly in support, was whisked back to Bonn and knew no Katrin. Investigations into Elke's social life were launched, but they would take time. Her mother had sent no suitcase, nor would she have dreamed of doing so—she disapproved of her daughter's low taste in music, she told the Swedish police, and would not think to encourage it. Wolf returned disconsolately to his unit, and was subjected to wearying but directionless questioning by military security. No driver came forward, whether of a taxi or a private car, though he was paged all over Germany by police and press, and offered, *in absentia,* great sums of money for his story. No suitable traveller from Sweden or anywhere else could be traced through the passenger lists, computers, and memory-storage systems at any German airport, let alone Cologne. The photographs of known and unknown female terrorists, including the entire register of "half-illegals," rang no bells with the Labour Attaché, though he was demented with grief and would have helped anybody to do anything, if only in order to feel useful himself. He could not remember what shoes the girl had on, or whether she wore lipstick, or scent, or mascara, or whether her hair had looked bleached or could have been a wig. How should he, he implied—he who was by training an economist and in all other respects a shambling, connubial, warm-hearted fellow whose only real interest outside Israel and his family was Brahms—how should he know about women's hair dye?

Yes, he remembered, she had good legs and a very white neck. Long sleeves, yes, or he would have noticed her arms. Yes, a petticoat or something, or he would have seen the shape of her body back-lit by the outside sunlight. A bra?—maybe not, she had a small bosom and could have got away without one. Live models were dressed up for him. He must have looked at a hundred different blue dresses sent in from warehouses up and down Germany, but he could not remember for the life of him whether the dress had collar and cuffs of a different colour; and not all his spiritual torment could improve his memory. The more they asked him the more he forgot. The usual chance witnesses confirmed parts of his story but added nothing of substance. The police patrols had missed the incident completely, and probably the planting of the bomb was timed that way. The suitcase could have been one of twenty brands. The car or taxi was an Opel or it was a Ford; it was grey, it was not very clean, neither new nor old. A Bonn registration; no, it was from Siegburg. Yes, a taxi sign on the roof. No, it was a sunshine roof, and someone had heard music issuing, what programme was not established. Yes, a radio aerial. No, none. The driver was male Caucasian but could be a Turk. The Turks had done it. He was clean-shaven, had a moustache, was dark-haired. No, blond. Slight build, could be a woman in disguise. Somebody was sure there had been a small chimney-sweep dangling in the back window. Or it could have been a sticker. Yes, a sticker. Somebody said the driver wore an anorak. Or it could have been a pullover.

At this point of stalemate, the Israeli team seemed to go into a kind of collective coma. A lethargy overcame them; they arrived late and left early and spent a lot of time at their Embassy, where they appeared to be receiving new instructions. The days passed and Alexis decided they were waiting for something. Marking time but excited somehow.

Urgent but becalmed, the way Alexis himself felt far too often. He had an uncommonly good eye for seeing such things far ahead of his colleagues. When it came to empathising with Jews, he believed that he lived in a kind of vacuum of excellence. On the third day, a broad-faced older man calling himself Schulmann joined their team, accompanied by a very thin sidekick half his age. Alexis likened them to a Jewish Caesar and his Cassius.

The arrival of Schulmann and his assistant provided the good Alexis with some rare relief from the controlled fury of his own investigation, and from the tiresomeness of being dogged everywhere by the Silesian policeman, whose manner was beginning to resemble more that of a successor than an assistant. The first thing he observed about Schulmann was that he immediately raised the temperature of the Israeli team. Till Schulmann came, the six men had had an air of incompleteness about them. They had been polite, they had drunk no alcohol, they had patiently spread their nets and preserved among themselves the dark-eyed Oriental cohesion of a fighting unit. Their self-control was discomfiting to those who did not share it, and when, over a quick lunch in the canteen, the ponderous Silesian chose to make jokes about kosher food and patronise them about the beauties of their homeland, allowing himself in passing a grossly insulting reference to the quality of Israeli wine, they received his homage with a courtesy that Alexis knew cost them blood. Even when he went on to discuss the revival of the Jewish *Kultur* in Germany, and the smart way in which the new Jews had cornered the Frankfurt and Berlin property markets, they still held their tongues, though the financial antics of *shtetl* Jews who had not answered the call to Israel secretly disgusted them quite as much as the ham-handedness of their hosts. Then, suddenly, with Schulmann's arrival, everything became clear in a different way. He was the leader they had been waiting for: Schulmann from Jerusalem, his arrival announced a few hours in advance by a puzzled phone call from Headquarters in Cologne.

"They're sending an extra specialist, he'll make his own way to you."

"Specialist in what?" Alexis had demanded, who made a very un-German point of loathing people with qualifications.

Not given. But suddenly there he was—not a specialist, to Alexis's eye, but a broad-headed, bustling veteran of every battle since Thermopylae, age between forty and ninety, squat and Slav and strong, and far more European than Hebrew, with a barrel chest and a wrestler's wide stride and a way of putting everyone at his ease; and this seething acolyte of his, who had not been mentioned at all. Not Cassius, perhaps; rather, your archetypal Dostoevsky student: starved, and in conflict with demons. When Schulmann smiled, the wrinkles that flew into his face had been made by centuries of water flowing down the same rock paths, and his eyes clamped narrow like a Chinaman's. Then, long after him, his sidekick smiled, echoing some twisted inner meaning. When Schulmann greeted you, his whole right arm swung in on you in a crablike punch fast enough to wind you if you didn't block it. But the sidekick kept his arms at his sides as if he didn't trust them out alone. When Schulmann talked, he fired off conflicting ideas like a spread of bullets, then waited to see which ones went home and which came back at him. The sidekick's voice followed like a stretcher-party, softly collecting up the dead.

"I'm Schulmann; glad to meet you, Dr. Alexis," said Schulmann, in a cheerfully accented English.

Just Schulmann.

No first name, no rank, no academic title, no branch or occupation; and the student didn't have a name at all—or not for Germans, anyway. A people's general, Schulmann was, the way Alexis read him; a giver of hope, a power-drill, a taskmaster extraordinary; an alleged specialist who needed a room to himself and got one the same day—the sidekick saw to it. Soon, from behind its closed door, Schulmann's incessant voice had the tone of an out-of-town attorney, probing and evaluating their work till now. You didn't have to be a Hebrew scholar to hear the why's and how's and when's and why-not's. An improviser, thought Alexis: a born urban guerrilla himself. When he was silent, Alexis heard that too, and wondered what the devil he was reading suddenly that was interesting enough to stop his mouth from working. Or were they praying?—did they do that? Unless it was the sidekick's turn to speak, of course, in which case Alexis would not have heard even a whisper, for the boy's voice in German company had as little volume as his body.

But more than anything else, it was Schulmann's driven urgency that Alexis felt most strongly. He was a kind of human ultimatum, passing on to his team the pressures that were upon himself, imposing a scarcely bearable desperation on their labours. We can win, but we can also lose, he was saying, in the Doctor's lively imagination. And we have been too late for too long. Schulmann was their impresario, their manager, their general—all that—but he was himself a much-commanded man. So at least Alexis read him, and he was not always so wrong. He saw it in the hard and questioning way Schulmann's men looked to him, not for the detail of their work but for its progress—does it help?—is it a step along the road? He saw it in Schulmann's habitual gesture of cramming back the sleeve of his jacket by grasping the thick left forearm, then twisting his wrist around as if it were someone else's, until the dial of his old steel watch returned his stare. So Schulmann has a deadline too, thought Alexis: there is a time bomb ticking under *him* as well; the sidekick has it in his briefcase.

The interplay between the two men fascinated Alexis—a welcome distraction for him in his stress. When Schulmann took a walk around the Drosselstrasse and stood in the precarious ruins of the bombed house, throwing out his arm, expostulating, examining his watch, acting as outraged as if the place had been his own, the sidekick hovered in his shadow like his conscience, with his skeletal hands battened resolutely at his hips, while he seemed to restrain his master with the whispered earnestness of his beliefs. When Schulmann called in the Labour Attaché for one last private word, and the dialogue between them, half heard through the adjoining wall, rose to a scream, then fell to the low murmur of the confessional, it was the sidekick who led the broken man from the room and personally returned him to his Embassy's care, thus confirming a theory that Alexis had hugged to himself from the start but had been ordered by Cologne on no account to pursue.

Everything pointed to it. The zealous, introverted wife dreaming only of her sacred earth; the Labour Attaché's appalling sense of guilt; his absurdly over-generous reception of the girl Katrin, practically appointing himself her proxy

brother in Elke's absence; his bizarre admission that whereas
he had entered Elke's room, his wife would never do so. To
Alexis, who had been in similar situations in his day, and was
in one now—guilt-torn nerves exposed to every tiny sexual
breeze—the signs were written all over the file, and secretly it
gratified him that Schulmann had read them too. But if Cologne was adamant on the point, Bonn was nearly hysterical.
The Labour Attaché was a public hero: a bereaved father,
the husband of a fearfully maimed woman. He was the victim of an anti-Semitic outrage on German soil; he was an Israeli diplomat accredited to Bonn, by definition as respectable
as any Jew yet invented. Who were the Germans, of all
people, they begged him to consider, that they should expose
such a man as an adulterer? The same night, the distraught
Labour Attaché followed his child to Israel, and the television news bulletins led nationwide with a shot of his burly
back lumbering up the gangway, and the ever-present Alexis,
hat in hand, watching him go with stony respect.

Some of Schulmann's activities did not reach the ears of
Alexis till after the Israeli team had flown home. He discovered, for instance, almost by accident but not quite, that
Schulmann and his sidekick had together sought out the girl
Elke independently of the German investigators and had persuaded her, at dead of night, to postpone her departure for
Sweden so that the three of them could enjoy an entirely vol-
untary and well-paid private talk together. They spent another afternoon interviewing her in a hotel bedroom and, in
complete contrast to the economy of their social efforts in
other fields, blithely rode with her in the taxi to the airport.
All this—so Alexis guessed—with the aim of finding out who
her *real* friends were, and where she went to play when her
boyfriend was safely restored to the military. And where she
bought the marihuana and amphetamines that they had found
in the wreck of her room. Or, more likely, who had given
them to her, and in whose arms she liked to lie and talk
about herself and her employers when she was really turned
on and relaxed. Alexis deduced this partly because by now
his own people had brought him their confidential report on
Elke, and the questions he ascribed to Schulmann were the
same ones he would have liked to ask of her himself, if Bonn
had not been putting the muzzle on him and screaming
"hands off."

No dirt, they kept on saying. Let the grass grow over it first. And Alexis, who was by now fighting for his survival, took the hint and shut up, because with every day that passed the Silesian's stock was rising to the detriment of his own.

All the same, he would have laid good money on the kind of answers that Schulmann in his frantic and remorseless urgency might have coaxed from her between glances at that old sundial of a watch of his—the pen-portrait of the virile Arab student or junior attaché from the outer diplomatic fringes, for instance—or was he Cuban?—with money to burn and the right little packets of stuff, and an unexpected willingness to listen. Much later, when it was too late to matter, Alexis also learned—by way of the Swedish security service, who had also formed an interest in Elke's love life—that Schulmann and his sidekick had actually produced, in the small hours while others slept, a collection of photographs of likely candidates. And that from them she had picked one out, an alleged Cypriot whom she had known only by his first name, Marius, which he required her to pronounce in the French manner. And that she had signed a loose statement for them to the effect—"Yes, this is the Marius I slept with"—which, as they gave her to understand, they needed for Jerusalem. Why did they? Alexis wondered. To buy off Schulmann's deadline somehow? As surety, to whip up credit back at base? Alexis understood these things. And the more he thought about them, the greater became his sense of affinity with Schulmann, of comradely understanding. You and I are one, he kept hearing himself thinking. We struggle, we feel, we see.

Alexis perceived all this profoundly, with great self-conviction.

The obligatory closing conference took place in the lecture hall, with the ponderous Silesian presiding over three hundred chairs, mostly empty, but among them the two groups, German and Israeli, clustered like nuptial families either side of the church aisle. The Germans were fleshed out with officials from the Ministry of the Interior and some voting-fodder from the Bundestag; the Israelis had their Military Attaché from the Embassy with them, but several of their team, including Schulmann's emaciated sidekick, had already left for Tel Aviv. Or so it was said by his comrades. The rest assembled at eleven in the morning, to be greeted with a buffet table covered with a white cloth on which the telltale fragments from the explosion were set out like archaeological finds at the end of a long dig, each with its own little museum label in electric type. On a pegboard wall beside it they could examine the usual horror pictures—in colour, for extra realism. At the door, a pretty girl, smiling too nicely, handed out memorial folders in plastic covers containing background data. If she had handed out candy or ice-cream, Alexis would not have been surprised. The German contingent chattered and craned their necks at everything, including the Israelis, who for their part preserved the mortal stillness of men for whom every wasted minute was a martyrdom. Only Alexis—he was assured of it—perceived and shared their secret agony, whatever its source.

We Germans are simply too much, he decided. We are the living end. He had expected, until an hour before, to be holding the floor himself. He had anticipated—even privately prepared—one terse flash of his lapidary style, one brisk English "Thank you, gentlemen" and out. It was not to be. The barons had reached their decisions and they wanted the Silesian for breakfast, lunch, and dinner; they wanted no Alexis, even for coffee. So he made a show of lounging ostentatiously at the back with his arms folded, affecting a careless interest while he fumed and empathised with the Jews. When everyone but Alexis was sitting, the Silesian made his entry, using that special pelvic walk which in Alexis's experience overcame a certain type of German whenever he took the rostrum. After him trod a scared young man in a white coat, laden with a duplicate of the now celebrated scuffed grey suitcase complete with its Scandinavian Airlines Systems labels, which he put on the dais as if it were an oblation. Searching for his hero Schulmann, Alexis found him alone in an aisle seat, well to the back. He had put away his jacket and necktie and wore a pair of comfortable slacks, which, because of his generous waistline, ended a little short of his unfashionable shoes. His steel watch winked on his brown wrist; the whiteness of his shirt against his weathered skin gave him the benign look of someone about to leave on holiday.

Hang on and I'll come with you, Alexis thought wistfully, recalling his painful session with the barons.

The Silesian spoke English "out of regard for our Israeli friends." But also, Alexis suspected, out of regard for those of his supporters who had come to observe their champion's performance. The Silesian had attended the obligatory counter-subversion course in Washington, and spoke therefore the butchered English of an astronaut. By way of introduction, the Silesian told them that the outrage was the work of "radical left elements," and when he threw in a reference to the "Socialist over-indulgence of modern youth," there was some supportive shuffling of approval in the parliamentary chairs. Our dear Führer himself would have put it no better, Alexis thought, but remained outwardly nonchalant. The blast, for architectural reasons, had tended upward, said the Silesian, addressing himself to a diagram that his assistant unfurled behind him, and had sheared the central structure clean out of the house, taking the top floor and hence the child's bedroom with it. In short, it was a big bang, thought Alexis savagely, so why not say so and shut up? But the Silesian was not given to shutting up. The best estimates put the charge at five kilograms. The mother had survived because she was in the kitchen. The kitchen was an *Anbau*. This sudden, unexpected use of a German word induced—in the German speakers, at least—a peculiar embarrassment.

"Was ist Anbau?" the Silesian muttered grumpily at his assistant, making everyone sit up and hunt for a translation.

"Annexe," Alexis called in reply before the rest, and won restrained laughter from the knowing, and less restrained irritation from the Silesian supporters' club.

"Annexe," the Silesian repeated in his best English and, ignoring the unwelcome source, slogged blindly on.

In my next life I shall be a Jew or a Spaniard or an Eskimo or just a fully committed anarchist like everybody else, Alexis decided. But a German I shall never be—you do it once as a penance and that's it. Only a German can make an inaugural lecture out of a dead Jewish child.

The Silesian was talking about the suitcase. Cheap and nasty, of a type favoured by such unpersons as guestworkers and Turks. And Socialists, he might have added. Those interested could read about it in their folders or study the surviving fragments of its steel frame on the buffet table. Or they could decide, as Alexis had decided long ago, that both bomb and suitcase were a blind alley. But they could not escape listening to the Silesian, because it was the Silesian's day and this speech was his victory-roll over the deposed libertarian enemy, Alexis.

From the suitcase itself, he passed to its contents. The device was wedged in place with two sorts of wadding, gentlemen, he said. Wadding type no. 1 was old newspaper, shown by tests to have come from the Bonn editions of the Springer press over the last six months—and very suitable too, thought Alexis. Type 2 was a sliced-up army-surplus blanket similar to the one now demonstrated by my colleague Mr. somebody from the state analytical laboratories. While the scared assistant held up a large grey blanket for their inspection, the Silesian proudly reeled off his other brilliant clues. Alexis listened wearily to the familiar recitation: the crimped end of a detonator . . . minuscule particles of undetonated explosive, confirmed as standard Russian plastic, known to the Americans as C_4 and to the British as PE and to the Israelis as whatever it was known as . . . the winder of an inexpensive wristwatch . . . the charred but still identifiable spring of a domestic clothespeg. In a word, thought Alexis, a classic set-up, straight out of bomb school. No compromising materials, no touches of vanity, no frills, beyond a kiddy-kit booby trap built into the inside angle of the lid. Except that with the stuff the kids were getting together these days, thought Alexis, a set-up like this one made you quite nostalgic for the good old-fashioned terrorists of the seventies.

The Silesian seemed to think so too, but he was making a dreadful joke about it: "We are calling this the bikini bomb!" he boomed proudly. "The minimum! No extras!"

"And no arrests!" Alexis called out recklessly, and was rewarded with an admiring and strangely knowing smile from Schulmann.

Brusquely bypassing his assistant, the Silesian now reached an arm into the suitcase and with a flourish extracted from it a piece of softwood on which the mock-up had been assembled, a thing like a toy racing-car circuit of thin, coated wire, ending in ten sticks of greyish plastic. As the uninitiated crowded round to take a closer look, Alexis was surprised to see Schulmann, hands in pockets, leave his place and amble over to join them. But why? Alexis asked of him mentally, his gaze fixed shamelessly upon him. Why so leisurely suddenly, when yesterday you had hardly the time to look at your battered watch? Abandoning his efforts at indifference, Alexis slipped quickly to his side. This is the way you make a bomb, the Silesian was suggesting, if you are cast in the conventional mould and want to blow up Jews. You buy a cheap watch like this one—don't steal it, buy it at a big store at their peak shopping time and buy a couple of things either side of it to confuse the assistant's memory. Remove the hour hand. Drill a hole in the glass, put a drawing-pin in the hole, solder your electric circuit to the head of the drawing-pin with heavy glue. Now the battery. Now set the hand as close to the drawing-pin, or as far from it, as you wish. But allow, as a general rule, the shortest possible delay, in order that the bomb shall not be discovered and disarmed. Wind up the watch. Make sure the minute hand is still working. It is. Offer prayers to whoever you imagine made you, poke the detonator into the plastic. As the minute hand touches the shank of the pin, so the contact completes the electrical circuit and if the Lord is good, the bomb goes off.

To demonstrate this marvel, the Silesian removed the disarmed detonator and the ten sticks of demonstration plastic explosive and replaced them with a small light-bulb suitable for a hand-torch.

"Now I prove to you how the circuit works!" he shouted.

Nobody doubted that it worked, most knew the thing by heart, but for a moment, all the same, it seemed to Alexis that the bystanders shared an involuntary shudder as the bulb cheerily winked its signal. Only Schulmann appeared immune. Perhaps he really has seen too much, thought Alexis, and the pity has finally died in him. For Schulmann was ignoring the bulb completely. He remained stooping over the mock-up, smiling broadly and contemplating it with the critical attention of a connoisseur.

A parliamentarian, wishing to display his excellence, enquired why the bomb did not go off on time. "This bomb was fourteen hours in the house," he objected, in silky English. "A minute hand turns for one hour at most. An hour hand for twelve. How do we account, please, for fourteen hours in a bomb that can only wait twelve maximum?"

For every question, the Silesian had a lecture ready. He gave one now, while Schulmann, still with his indulgent smile, started to probe gently around the edges of the mock-

up with his thick fingers, as if he had lost something in the
wadding below. Possibly the watch had failed, said the
Silesian. Possibly the car journey to the Drosselstrasse had
upset the mechanism. Possibly the Labour Attaché, in laying
the suitcase on Elke's bed, had jolted the circuit, said the
Silesian. Possibly the watch, being cheap, had stopped and
restarted. Possibly anything, thought Alexis, unable to contain
his irritation.

But Schulmann had a different suggestion, and a more
ingenious one: "Or possibly this bomber did not scrape
enough paint off the watch hand," he said, in a kind of distracted aside as he turned his attention to the hinges of the
facsimile suitcase. Hauling an old service penknife from his
pocket, he selected from its attachments a plump spike and
began probing behind the head of the hinge-pin, confirming
to himself the ease with which it could be removed. "Your
laboratory people, they scraped off *all* the paint. But maybe
this bomber is not so scientific as your laboratory people," he
said as he snapped his knife shut with a loud clunk. "Not so
able. Not so neat in his constructions."

But it was a girl, Alexis urgently objected in his mind;
why does Schulmann say *he* suddenly, when we are supposed
to be thinking of a pretty girl in a blue dress? Unaware apparently of how—for the moment, at least—he had upstaged
the Silesian in the full flight of his performance, Schulmann
transferred his attention to the homemade booby trap inside
the lid, gently tugging at the stretch of wire that was stitched
into the lining and joined to a dowel in the mouth of the
clothespeg.

"There is something interesting, Herr Schulmann?" the
Silesian enquired, with angelic self-restraint. "You have found
a *clue,* perhaps? Tell us, please. We shall be interested."

Schulmann pondered this generous offer.

"Too little wire," he announced as he returned to the
buffet table and hunted among its grisly exhibits. "Over here
you have the remains of seventy-seven centimetres of wire."
He was brandishing a charred skein. It was wound on itself
like a woollen dummy, with a loop round its waist holding it
together. "In your reconstruction, you have twenty-five centimetres maximum. Why are we missing half a metre of wire
from your reconstruction?"

There was a moment's puzzled silence before the Silesian gave a loud, indulgent laugh.

"But, Herr Schulmann—this was *spare* wire," he explained, as if reasoning with a child. "For the circuitry. Just common wire. When the bomber had made the device, there was evidently wire over, so he—or she—they threw it into the suitcase. This is for tidiness, this is normal. It was *spare* wire," he repeated. "*Übrig.* Without technical significance. *Sag ihm doch übrig.*"

"Left over," someone translated needlessly. "It has no meaning, Mr. Schulmann. It is *left over*."

The moment was past, the gap had sealed, and the next glimpse Alexis had of Schulmann, he was poised discreetly at the door, in the act of leaving, his broad head turned part way towards Alexis, his watch arm raised, but in the manner of somebody consulting his stomach rather than the time. Their eyes did not quite meet, yet Alexis knew for certain that Schulmann was waiting for him, willing him across the room and saying *lunch*. The Silesian was still droning on, the audience still standing aimlessly round him like a bunch of grounded airline passengers. Detaching himself from its fringe, Alexis tiptoed quickly after the departing Schulmann. In the corridor, Schulmann grasped his arm in a spontaneous gesture of affection. On the pavement—it was a lovely sunny day again—both men took off their jackets and Alexis afterwards remembered very well how Schulmann rolled his up like a desert pillow while Alexis hailed a taxi and gave the name of an Italian restaurant on a hilltop on the far side of Bad Godesberg. He had taken women there before, but never men, and Alexis, in all things the voluptuary, was always conscious of first times.

On the drive they barely spoke. Schulmann admired the view and beamed about with the serenity of one who has earned his Sabbath, though it was midweek. His plane, Alexis recalled, was scheduled to leave Cologne in early evening. Like a child being taken out from school, Alexis counted the hours this would leave them, assuming Schulmann had no other engagements, a ridiculous but wonderful assumption. At the restaurant, high up on the Cecilian Heights, the Italian *padrone* made a predictable fuss of Alexis, but it was Schulmann who quite rightly enchanted him. He called him "Herr Professor" and insisted on preparing a big window table that could have seated six. Below them lay the old town, beyond it the winding Rhine with its brown hills and jagged castles. Alexis knew that scenery by heart, but today, through the eyes of his new friend Schulmann, he saw it for the first time. Alexis ordered two whiskies. Schulmann did not object.

Gazing appreciatively at the view while they waited for their drinks to arrive, Schulmann finally spoke: "Maybe if Wagner had left that fellow Siegfried in peace, we might have had a better world of it, after all," he said.

For a moment, Alexis could not understand what had happened. His day till then had been crowded; he had an empty stomach and a shaken mind. Schulmann was speaking German! In a thick, rusted Sudeten accent that grizzled like a disused engine. And speaking it, moreover, with a contrite grin that was both a confession and a drawing-together in conspiracy. Alexis let out a small laugh, Schulmann laughed too; the whisky came and they drank to each other, but with none of the heavy German ceremony of "look, sip, and look again," which Alexis always found too much, especially with Jews, who instinctively saw something menacing in German formality.

"They tell me you are getting a new job soon, down in Wiesbaden," Schulmann remarked, still in German, when these mating ceremonies were behind them. "Some desk job. Bigger but smaller, I hear. They say you are too much man for the people here. Now that I have seen you, and seen the people—well, I am not surprised."

Alexis tried not to be surprised either. Of the details of a new appointment nothing had been said—only that one would be forthcoming. Even his replacement by the Silesian was still meant to be a secret; Alexis had not had time to breathe a word of it to anyone, not even his young girlfriend, with whom he conducted rather meaningless phone calls several times a day.

"That's the way it goes, huh?" Schulmann remarked philosophically, speaking as much to the river as to Alexis. "In Jerusalem, believe me, a man's life is equally precarious. Upstream, downstream. That's the way it goes." He seemed a little disappointed, all the same. "I hear she's a nice lady too," he added, once again crashing in upon his companion's thoughts. "Attractive, bright, loyal. Maybe she's too much woman for them."

Resisting the temptation to turn the occasion into a seminar upon the problems of his own life, Alexis directed the conversation towards this morning's conference, but Schulmann answered vaguely, remarking only that technicians never solved anything, and that bombs bored him. He had asked for pasta and ate it the prisoner's way, using his spoon and fork automatically, not bothering to look down. Alexis, afraid to interrupt his flow, kept as quiet as he knew how.

First, with an older man's ease of narrative, Schulmann embarked upon a mildly worded lament about Israel's so-called allies in the anti-terror business: "Back in January, when we were running a quite different investigation, we called on our Italian friends," he declared, in a voice of homey reminiscence. "Showed them some nice proofs, gave them some good addresses. Next thing we knew, they had arrested a few Italians, while the people that Jerusalem were after sat safe back home in Libya looking bronzed and rested, waiting for their next assignment. That was not what we had intended." A mouthful of pasta. A dusting of the lips with the napkin. Food is fuel for him, thought Alexis; he eats so that he can fight. "In March, when another matter came up, it was the same story exactly, but that time we were dealing with Paris. Certain Frenchmen were arrested but nobody else. Certain officials got some nice applause too, and, thanks to us, promotion. But the Arabs"—he made a large, indulgent shrug. "Expedient it may be. Sound oil policy, sound economics, sound everything. Justice it isn't. And justice is what we like." His smile broadened, in direct contrast to the scale of the joke. "So I would say that we have learned to be selective. Better tell too little than too much, we have decided. Somebody is nicely disposed towards us, has an impressive record—a fine father in his background, like yours—with him we will do business. Guardedly. Informally. Between friends. If he can use our information constructively for himself, advance himself in his profession a little—all the better that our friends should obtain influence in their professions. But we want our half of the deal. We expect people to deliver. Of our friends we expect this particularly."

It was the nearest Schulmann ever came, that day or

later, to stating the terms of his proposition. As to Alexis, he did not state anything at all. He let his silence declare his sympathy. And Schulmann, who understood so much about him, seemed to understand this too, for he resumed their conversation as if the bargain had been struck and they were squarely in business together.

"A few years ago now, a bunch of Palestinians raised a certain amount of hell in my country," he began reminiscently. "Normally these people are low grade. Peasant kids trying to be heroes. They sneak over the border, lie up in a village, get rid of their bombs, run for safety. If we don't catch them first time out, we catch them the second, if there is one. The men I am speaking of were different. They were led. They knew how to move. How to stay clear of the informants, cover their tracks, make their own arrangements, write their own orders. First time in, they hit a supermarket in Beit She'an. The second time a school, then some settlements, then another shop, till it became monotonous. Then they started ambushing our soldiers hitchhiking home on leave. A lot of angry mothers, newspapers. Everyone saying, 'Get these men.' We listened for them, put the word out everywhere we knew. We discovered they used caves in the Jordan Valley. Lay up. Lived off the land. Still we couldn't find them. Their propaganda people called them the heroes of Commando Eight, but we knew Commando Eight inside out and Commando Eight could not have lit a match without us hearing of it comfortably ahead of time. Brothers, the word said. A family enterprise. One informant counted three, another four. But brothers for certain and operating out of Jordan, which we knew already.

"We put a team together, went after them—people we call the Sayaret, small teams, hard-hitting men. The Palestinian commander was a loner, we heard, and very disinclined to give his trust to anybody outside his family. Sensibly paranoid about Arab treachery. We never found him. His two brothers were not so nimble. One had a soft spot for a little girl in Amman. He walked into some machine-gun fire leaving her house one morning. The second made the mistake of calling up a friend in Sidon, inviting himself for a weekend. The Air Force blew his car to pieces as he drove down the coast road."

Alexis could not suppress a smile of excitement. "Not

enough wire," he murmured, but Schulmann chose not to hear him.

"By then we knew who they were—West Bankers from a grape-growing village near Hebron, fled after the war of '67. There was a fourth brother, but he was too young to fight, even by Palestinian standards. There were two sisters, but one of them had died in certain reprisal bombings we had to carry out south of the Litani River. That didn't leave much of an army. All the same, we kept looking for our man. We expected him to collect reinforcements, come back at us. He didn't. He ceased trading. Six months passed. A year. We said, 'Forget him. Most likely his own people have killed him, which is normal.' We heard the Syrians had given him a rough time, so maybe he'd died. A few months back, we picked up a rumour he'd come to Europe. Here. Put himself a team together, several of them ladies, mostly German, young." He took another mouthful, chewed and swallowed thoughtfully. "He was running them at arm's length," he went on when he was ready. "Playing the Arab Mephisto to a bunch of impressionable kids," he said.

At first, in the long silence that followed, Alexis could not make Schulmann out. The sun, high above the brown hills, shone directly into the window. In the resulting brilliance it was hard for Alexis to read his expression. Alexis moved his head and took another look at him. Why this sudden milky clouding of the dark eyes? he wondered. And was it really the sunlight that had bleached Schulmann's skin of colour, leaving it cracked and sickly like something dead? Then, in a day filled with bright and sometimes painful perceptions, Alexis recognised the passion which till then had remained hidden from him: here in the restaurant; down there in the sleepy spa town with its sprawling ministerial cantonments. As some men may be seen to be in love, so Schulmann was possessed by a deep and awesome hatred.

Schulmann left that evening. The remnants of his team hung on for two more days. A farewell celebration, with which the Silesian was determined to mark the excellent relations traditionally existing between the two services—an evening get-together, with white beer and sausages—was quietly sabotaged by Alexis, who pointed out that since the Bonn Government had chosen that very day to drop heavy hints about a possible forthcoming arms deal with the Saudis, it was unlikely their guests would be in a festive mood. It was perhaps his last effective act in office. A month later, as Schulmann had foretold, he was shunted off to Wiesbaden. A back-room job, theoretically a promotion, but one that gave less rein to his capricious individuality. An unkind newspaper, once counted among the good Doctor's supporters, sourly recorded that Bonn's loss would be the television viewer's gain. His one consolation indeed, at a time when so many of his German friends were hastily giving up their claims on him, was the warm little handwritten note of good wishes, postmark Jerusalem, that greeted him on his first day at his new desk. Signed "As ever, Schulmann," it wished him luck and looked forward to their next meeting, whether private or official. A wry postscript hinted that Schulmann too was not having the easiest of times. "Unless I deliver soon, I have an uncomfortable feeling I shall be joining you," it said. With a smile, Alexis tossed the card into a drawer where anyone could read it, and no doubt would. He knew exactly what Schulmann was doing and admired him for it: he was laying the innocent basis for their future relationship. A couple of weeks later, again, when Dr. Alexis and his youthful lady went through an anticlimactic wedding ceremony, it was Schulmann's roses, of all the gifts, that gave him the greatest joy and the greatest amusement. And I didn't even tell him I was getting married!

Those roses were like the promise of a new love affair, just as he was needing one.

Almost eight weeks passed before the man whom Dr. Alexis knew as Schulmann returned to Germany. In that time the investigations and planning of the Jerusalem teams had taken such extraordinary leaps that those still labouring through the débris of Bad Godesberg would not have recognised the case. If it had been a mere matter of punishing culprits—if the Godesberg incident had been an isolated one instead of part of a concerted series—Schulmann would not have bothered to involve himself at all, for his aims were more ambitious than mere retribution, and were intimately related to his own professional survival. For months now, under his restless urging, his teams had been looking for what he called a window that was wide enough to slip someone through and so take the enemy from inside his house, rather than beat him down with tanks and artillery from the front, which was increasingly the inclination in Jerusalem. Thanks to Godesberg, they believed they had found one. Where the West Germans still floundered with vague leads, Schulmann's deskmen in Jerusalem were stealthily making connections as far apart as Ankara and East Berlin. Old hands began to speak of a mirror image: of a remaking of Europe in patterns familiar from the Middle East two years ago.

Schulmann came not to Bonn but to Munich, and not as Schulmann either, and neither Alexis nor his Silesian successor was aware of his arrival, which was what he intended. His name, if he had one, was Kurtz, though he used it so seldom he might have been forgiven if one day he forgot it altogether. Kurtz meaning short; Kurtz of the short cut, said some; his victims—Kurtz of the short fuse. Others made laborious comparisons with Joseph Conrad's hero. Whereas the bald truth was that the name was Moravian and was originally Kurz, till a British police officer of the Mandate, in his wisdom, had added a "t"—and Kurtz, in his, had kept it, a sharp little dagger jabbed into the bulk of his identity, and left there as some kind of goad.

He arrived in Munich from Tel Aviv by way of Istanbul, changing passports twice and planes three times. Before that he had been staging for a week in London, but in London particularly maintaining an extremely retiring rôle. Everywhere he went, he had been squaring things and checking out results, gathering help, persuading people, feeding them cover stories and half-truths, overriding the reluctant with his extraordinary restless energy and the sheer volume and reach of his advance planning, even when sometimes he repeated himself, or forgot a small instruction he had issued. We live for such a short time, he liked to tell you with a twinkle, and we are far too long dead. That was the nearest he ever came to an apology, and his personal solution was to relinquish sleep. In Jerusalem, they liked to say, Kurtz slept as fast as he laboured. Which was fast. Kurtz, they would explain to you, was the master of the aggressive European ploy. Kurtz cut the impossible path, Kurtz made the desert bloom. Kurtz wheeled and dealed and lied even in his prayers, but he forced more good luck than the Jews had had for two thousand years.

Not that they loved him to a man exactly; for that he was too paradoxical, too complicated, made up of too many souls and colours. In some respects, indeed, his relationship with his superiors—and in particular with Misha Gavron, his Chief—was more that of a gruffly tolerated outsider than of a trusted equal. He had no tenure, but mysteriously sought none. His power base was rickety and forever shifting, according to whom he had last offended in his quest for the expedient allegiance. He was not a sabra; he lacked the élitist background from the kibbutzim, the universities, and the crack regiments that, to his dismay, increasingly supplied the narrowing aristocracy of his service. He was out of tune with their polygraphs, their computers, and their ever-growing faith in American-style power-plays, applied psychology, and crisis management. He loved the diaspora and made it his speciality at a time when most Israelis were zealously and self-consciously refurbishing their identity as Orientals. Yet obstacles were what Kurtz thrived on and rejection was what had made him. He could fight, if need be, on every front at once, and what they would not give him freely one way he took by stealth another. For love of Israel. For peace. For moderation. And for his own cussed right to make his impact and survive.

At what stage in the chase he had hit upon his plan probably not even Kurtz himself could have said. Such plans began in him deep down, like a rebellious impulse waiting for a cause, then welled out of him almost before he was aware of them. Did he dream it up when the bomber's trademark was confirmed? Or while he was eating his pasta up there on the Cecilian Heights overlooking Godesberg, and began to recognise what a fine catch he could make out of Alexis? Before. Long before. It must be done, he had told anyone who would listen after a particularly menacing session of Gavron's steering committee, that spring. If we don't take the enemy from inside his own camp, those clowns in the Knesset and Defence will blow up the whole of civilisation in their hunt for him. Some of his researchers swore it went back even further in time, and that Gavron had suppressed a similar scheme twelve months ago. Never mind. The certainty is that operational preparations were well under way before the boy had been conclusively tracked down, even if Kurtz assiduously held back all intimation of them from the scathing glance of Misha Gavron, and fudged his records in order to deceive him. Gavron is Polish for rook. His craggy black looks and parched bellow could have belonged to no other creature.

Find the boy, Kurtz told his Jerusalem team, setting out on his murky travels. It's one boy and his shadow. Find the boy, the shadow will follow, no problem. Kurtz dinned it into them till they swore they hated him; he could apply pressure as fiercely as he withstood it. He phoned in from odd places at any hour of day or night just to keep his presence among them at all times. Have you found that boy yet? Why is that boy not run to earth? But still cloaking his questions in such a way that Gavron the Rook, even if he got wind of them, would not understand their meaning, for Kurtz was holding off his assault on Gavron till the last, most favourable moment. He cancelled leave, abolished the Sabbath, and used his own meagre money rather than pass his expenses prematurely through the official accounts. He hauled reservists from the comfort of their academic sinecures and ordered them back, unpaid, to their old desks in order to hurry up the search.

Find the boy. The boy will show us the way. One day, from nowhere, he produced a codename for him: Yanuka, which is a friendly Aramaic word for kid—literally a half-grown suckling. "Get me Yanuka and I'll deliver those clowns with the whole apparatus on a plate."

But not a word to Gavron. Wait. Nothing to the Rook.

In his beloved diaspora, if not in Jerusalem, his repertoire of supporters was unearthly. In London alone, he flitted, with barely a change in his smile, from venerable art dealers to would-be film magnates, from little East End landladies to garment merchants, questionable car dealers, grand City companies. He was also seen several times at the theatre, once out of town, but always to see the same show, and he took an Israeli diplomat with him who had cultural functions, although culture was not what they discussed. In Camden Town he ate twice in a humble transport restaurant run by a group of Goanese Indians; in Frognal, a couple of miles northwest, he inspected a secluded Victorian mansion called The Acre and pronounced it perfect for his needs. But only speculative, mind, he told his very obliging landlords; no deal unless our business brings us here. They accepted this condition. They accepted everything. They were proud to be called on, and serving Israel delighted their hearts, even if it meant moving to their house in Marlow for a few months. Did they not keep an apartment in Jerusalem, which they used for visiting friends and family every Passover after two weeks of sea and sunshine in Eilat? And were they not seriously considering living there for good—but not till their children were past military age and the rate of inflation had steadied? On the other hand, they might just stay in Hampstead. Or Marlow. Meanwhile they would send generously and do anything Kurtz asked of them, never expecting anything in return, and not breathing a word to anyone.

At embassies, consulates, and legations along the route, Kurtz kept abreast of feuds and developments at home, and of the progress of his people in other parts of the globe. On aeroplane journeys he revised his familiarity with radical revolutionary literature of all sorts; the emaciated sidekick, whose real name was Shimon Litvak, kept a selection of the stuff in his shabby briefcase and pressed it on him at inappropriate moments. At the hard end, he had Fanon, Guevara, and Marighella; at the soft, Debray, Sartre, and Marcuse; not to mention the gentler souls who wrote mainly of the cruelties of education in consumerist societies, the horrors of religion, and the fatal cramping of the spirit in capitalist childhood. Back in Jerusalem and Tel Aviv, where similar debates are not unknown, Kurtz was at his quietest, talking to his case officers, circumventing rivals, and ploughing through exhaustive character profiles assembled from old files and now cautiously but meticulously updated and expanded. One day he heard of a house that was going begging in Disraeli Street, number 11, at a low rent, and for greater secrecy ordered everyone who was working on the case quietly to decamp there.

"I hear you are leaving us already," Misha Gavron remarked sceptically next day, when the two men met at some unrelated conference; for Gavron the Rook by now had wind of things, even if he did not know for certain their direction.

Still Kurtz would not be drawn. Not yet. He pleaded the autonomy of operational departments, and pulled an iron grin.

Number 11 was a fine Arab-built villa, not large but cool, with a lemon tree in the front garden, and about two hundred cats, which the women officers overfed absurdly. So the place inevitably became known as the cathouse, and gave fresh cohesion to the team, ensuring, by the proximity of desk officers one to another, that no unfortunate gaps occurred between the specialised fields, and no leaks either. It also raised the status of the operation, which to Kurtz was crucial.

Next day came the blow he had been waiting for and was still powerless to prevent. It was dreadful but it served its purpose. A young Israeli poet on a visit to Leyden University, in Holland, where he was to receive an award, was blown to pieces over breakfast by a parcel bomb delivered to his hotel on the morning of his twenty-fifth birthday. Kurtz was at his desk when the news came, and he took it like an old prizefighter riding out a punch: he flinched, his eyes closed for a second, but within hours he was standing in Gavron's room with a stack of files under his arm and two versions of his operational plan in his free hand, one for Gavron himself and the other, much vaguer, for Gavron's steering committee of nervous politicians and war-hungry generals.

What passed precisely between the two men could not at

first be known, for neither Kurtz nor Gavron was of a confiding nature. But by next morning, Kurtz was out in the open, evidently with some kind of licence, mustering fresh troops. For this he used the zealous Litvak as his intermediary, a sabra, an apparatchik trained to his fingertips, and able to move among Gavron's highly motivated young, whom Kurtz secretly found stiff and embarrassing to handle. The baby of this hastily assembled family was Oded, a twenty-three-year-old from Litvak's own kibbutz and, like himself, a graduate of the prestigious Sayaret. The grandfather was a seventy-year-old Georgian named Bougaschwili, but "Schwili" for short. Schwili had a polished bald head and stooped shoulders and trousers cut for a clown—very low in the crotch and short in the leg. A black Homburg hat, worn indoors as much as out, topped the quaint confection. Schwili had begun life as a smuggler and confidence trickster, trades not uncommon in his home region, but in middle life he had turned his trade to forger of all kinds. His greatest feat had been performed in the Lubyanka, where he had faked documents for fellow inmates from back numbers of *Pravda*, repulping them to press his own paper. Released at last, he had applied the same genius to the work of fine art, both as a forger and as an expert under contract to distinguished galleries. Several times, he claimed, he had had the pleasure of authenticating his own fakes. Kurtz loved Schwili and, when he had a spare ten minutes, would march him off to an ice-cream parlour at the bottom of the hill and buy him a double caramel, Schwili's best flavour.

Kurtz also supplied Schwili with the two most unlikely helpers anyone could have imagined. The first—a Litvak discovery—was a graduate of London University named Leon, an Israeli who by no choice of his own had had an English childhood, for his father was a kibbutz *macher* who had been dispatched to Europe as the representative of a marketing cooperative: *macher* being the Yiddish word for busybody or a fellow on the move. In London, Leon had developed a literary interest, edited a magazine, and published a completely unregarded novel. His obligatory three years in the Israeli Army left him miserable, and on release he went to earth in Tel Aviv, where he attached himself to one of the intellectual weeklies that come and go like pretty girls. By the time it collapsed, Leon was writing the whole thing single-handed. Yet somehow, among the peace-obsessed, claustrophobic young of Tel Aviv, he experienced the deep reawakening of his identity as a Jew and, with it, a burning urge to rid Israel of her enemies, past and future.

"From now on," Kurtz told him, "you write for me. A big readership you won't have. But appreciative—that they will be."

Schwili's second helper after Leon was a Miss Bach, a quiet-mannered business lady from South Bend, Indiana. Impressed equally by her intelligence and her non-Jewish appearance, Kurtz had recruited Miss Bach, trained her in a variety of skills, and eventually dispatched her to Damascus as an instructor in computer programming. Thereafter, for several years, the sedate Miss Bach reported on the capacity and disposition of Syrian air radar systems. Recalled at last, Miss Bach had been talking wistfully of taking up the wagon-trail life of a West Bank settler when the new summons from Kurtz saved her from this discomfort.

Schwili, Leon, Miss Bach, therefore: Kurtz called the incongruous trio his Literacy Committee, and gave it special standing within his fast-expanding private army.

In Munich, his business was administrative, but he went about it with a hushed delicacy, contriving to force his driving nature into the most modest mould of all. No fewer than six members of his newly formed team had now been installed there, and they occupied two quite separate establishments, in quite different areas of town. The first team consisted of two outdoor men. They should have been a full five, but Misha Gavron was still determined to keep him on a short rein, so they were two. Collecting Kurtz not from the airport but from a glum café in Schwabing, and using a rickety builder's van to hide him in—the van also was an economy—they drove him to the Olympic Village, to one of the dark underground car parks there, a favourite haunt for muggers and prostitutes of both sexes. The Village is not a village at all, of course, but a marooned and disintegrating citadel of grey concrete, more reminiscent of an Israeli settlement than anything that can be found in Bavaria. From one of its vast subterranean car parks, they ushered him up a filthy staircase smeared with multi-lingual graffiti, across small roof gardens to a duplex apartment, which they had taken part-furnished on a short let. Outdoors, they spoke English and called him "sir," but indoors, they addressed their chief as "Marty" and spoke respectfully to him in Hebrew.

The apartment was at the top of a corner building, and filled with odd bits of photographic lighting and portentous cameras on stands, as well as tape decks and projection screens. It boasted an open-tread teak staircase and a rustic minstrel gallery, which jangled when they trod on it too hard. From it led a spare bedroom four metres by three and a half, with a skylight let into the rake of the roof, which as they carefully explained to him they had covered first with blanket, then hardboard, then several inches of kapok wadding held in place with diamonds of black tape. Walls, floor, and ceiling were similarly padded, and the result resembled a mix between a modern priesthole and a madman's cell. The door to it they had reinforced with painted steel sheeting, and had built into it a small area of armoured glass at head height, several thicknesses, over which they had hung a cardboard notice saying "DARK ROOM KEEP OUT" and underneath, "*Dunkelkammer kein Eintritt!*" Kurtz made one of them enter this little room, close the door, and yell as loud as he could yell. Hearing only a hoarse, scratching sound, he gave his approval.

The rest of the apartment was airy but, like the Olympic Village, awfully down-at-heel. Northward the windows gave a grimy view of the road to Dachau, where a great many Jews had died in the concentration camp, and the irony escaped none of those present; the more particularly since the Bavarian police, with stultifying insensitivity, had housed its flying squad in the former barracks there. Nearer at hand, they could point out to Kurtz the very spot where, in more recent history, Palestinian commandos had burst into the living quarters of the Israeli athletes, killing some immediately, and taking the rest to the military airport, where they killed them too. Right next door to their own apartment, they told Kurtz, was a student commune; underneath them was for the moment nobody, because the last tenant had killed herself. Having stomped all around the place alone, and considered the entrances and escape routes, Kurtz decided he must rent the lower flat also, and the same day telephoned a certain lawyer in Nuremberg instructing him to handle the contract. The kids themselves had developed a floppy, ineffectual look, and one—the young Oded—had grown a beard. Their passports revealed them to be Argentinians, professional photographers, of what sort no one knew or cared. Sometimes, they told Kurtz, to give their household an air of naturalness and irregularity, they announced to their neighbours that they would be holding a late party, of which the only evidence was loud music till all hours and empty bottles in the dustbins. But in reality they had admitted nobody to the apartment, except the courier from the other team: no guests, no visitors of any kind. As to women, forget it. They had put women right out of their minds till they got back to Jerusalem.

When they had reported all this and more to Kurtz, and discussed such office matters as extra transport and operational expenses, and whether it might not be a good plan to set iron rings into the padded walls of the darkroom—Kurtz was in favour of the idea—they took him, at his own request, for a walk and what he called some nice fresh air. They wandered through the rich student slums, lingered over a pottery school, a carpentry school, and what was proudly offered as the first swimming-school in the world to have been built for very small babies, and they read the daubed anarchist slogans on the painted cottage doors. Till inevitably, by gravitation, they found themselves standing before the same ill-fated house where, almost ten years ago, the attack on the Israeli boys had shocked the world. A stone tablet, engraved in Hebrew and in German, commemorated the eleven dead. Eleven, or eleven thousand, their feeling of shared outrage was the same.

"So remember that," Kurtz ordered needlessly as they returned to the van.

From the Village, they brought Kurtz to the middle of the town, where he deliberately lost himself for a while, walking wherever his fancy took him, till the kids, who were watching his back, gave him the signal that it was safe to go on to his next rendezvous. The contrast between the last place and the new one could not have been greater. Kurtz's destination was the top floor of a high-gabled gingerbread house right at the heart of fashionable Munich. The street was narrow, cobbled, and expensive. It boasted a Swiss restaurant and an exclusive couturier who seemed to sell nothing, yet prosper. Kurtz climbed to the flat by way of a

dark stairway and the door opened to him as he reached the
top step, because they had been watching him come down the
street on their little closed-circuit television screen. He walked
in without a word. These men were older than the two who
had received him first, fathers more than sons. They had the
pallor of long-termers, and a resigned way of moving, particularly when they trod round each other in their stockinged
feet. For these were professional static watchers—even in
Jerusalem, a secret society to themselves. Lace curtains hung
across the window; it was dusk in the street and dusk in the
flat also, and the whole place was pervaded with an air of sad
neglect. An array of electronic and optical devices was
crowded among the fake Biedermeier furniture, including
indoor aerials of varying designs. But in the failing light their
spectral shapes only added to the mood of bereavement.

Kurtz embraced each man gravely. Then, over crackers,
cheese, and tea, the eldest of the men, whose name was
Lenny, gave Kurtz the full tour of Yanuka's life-style, quite
disregarding the fact that for weeks now Kurtz had been
sharing every small sensation as it arose: Yanuka's phone
calls in and out, his latest visitors, his latest girls. Lenny was
big-hearted and kind, but a little shy of people he was not observing. He had wide ears and an ugly, over-featured face,
and perhaps that was why he kept it from the hard gaze of
the world. He wore a big grey knitted waistcoat like chain
mail. In other circumstances Kurtz could tire of detail very
quickly, but he respected Lenny and paid the closest attention
to everything he said, nodding, congratulating, making all the
right expressions for him.

"He's a normal young man, this Yanuka," Lenny
pleaded earnestly. "Tradesmen admire him. Friends admire
him. That's a likeable, popular person, Marty. Studies, likes
to enjoy himself, talks a lot, he's a serious fellow with healthy
appetites." Catching Kurtz's eye, he became a little foolish:
"Now and then it's hard to believe in this other side to him,
Marty, trust me."

Kurtz assured Lenny that he fully understood. He was
still doing this when a light came on in the mansard window
of the flat directly across the street. The rectangular yellow
glow, with nothing else lit near it, had the look of a lover's
signal. Without a word, one of Lenny's men tiptoed swiftly to

a pair of binoculars anchored to a stand, while another squatted to a radio receiver and clutched a headphone to his ear.

"Want to take a look, Marty?" Lenny suggested hopefully. "I can see by Joshua's smile there that he has a very nice perception of Yanuka tonight. Wait too long, he'll draw the curtain on us. What do you see, Joshua? Is Yanuka all dolled up for going out tonight? Who does he speak to on the telephone? A girl for certain."

Gently pushing Joshua aside, Kurtz ducked his big head to the binoculars. And he remained a long time that way, hunched like an old seadog in a storm, hardly seeming to breathe, while he studied Yanuka, the half-grown suckling.

"See his books there in the background?" Lenny asked. "That boy reads like my father."

"You have a fine boy there," Kurtz agreed finally, with his iron-hard smile, as he slowly straightened himself. "A good-looking kid, no question." Picking his grey raincoat from the chair, he selected a sleeve and pulled it tenderly over his arm. "Just be sure you don't marry him to your daughter." Lenny looked even more foolish than before, but Kurtz was quick to console him: "We should be thankful to you, Lenny. And so we are, no question." And as an afterthought: "Keep taking photographs of him, all angles. Don't be shy, Lenny. Film is not so expensive."

Having shaken hands with each man in turn, Kurtz added an old blue beret to his costume and, thus shielded against the bustle of the rush hour, strode vigorously into the street.

It was raining by the time they picked Kurtz up in the van again, and as the three of them drove from one glum spot to another, killing time before Kurtz's plane, the weather seemed to affect all three of them with its sombre mood. Oded was doing the driving, and his bearded young face, by the passing lights, revealed a sullen anger.

"What's he got now?" Kurtz asked, though he must have known the answer.

"His latest is a rich man's BMW," Oded replied. "Power steering, fuel injection, five thousand kilometres on the clock. Cars are his weakness."

"Cars, women, the soft life," the second boy put in from the back. "So what are his strengths, I wonder?"

"Hired again?" Kurtz asked of Oded once more.

"Hired."

"Stay close to that car," Kurtz advised them both. "The moment he hands back his car to the rental company and doesn't take another one, that's the moment we have to know about immediately." They had heard this till they were deaf from it. They had heard it before they ever left Jerusalem. Kurtz repeated it none the less: "Most important is when Yanuka turns his car in."

Suddenly Oded had had enough. Perhaps he was by youth and temperament more prone to stress than his selectors had appreciated. Perhaps, as such a young fellow, he should not have been given a job that needed so much waiting. Pulling up the van at the kerbside, he yanked on the handbrake so hard he all but wrenched it from its socket.

"Why do we let him go through with this?" he demanded. "Why play games with him? What if he goes back home and doesn't come out again? Then what?"

"Then we lose him."

"So let's kill him now! Tonight. You give me the order, it's done!"

Kurtz let him rave on.

"We've got the apartment opposite, haven't we? Put a rocket across the road. We've done it before. An RPG-7— Arab kills Arab with a Russian rocket—why not?"

Kurtz still said nothing. Oded might have been storming at a sphinx.

"So why not?" Oded repeated, very loud indeed.

Kurtz did not spare him, but neither did he lose his patience: "Because he doesn't *lead* anywhere, Oded, that's why. You never heard what Misha Gavron himself used to say perhaps? A phrase I personally still like to echo? That if you want to catch a lion, you first must tether the goat? Whose crazy fighting talk have you been listening to? I ask myself. Are you seriously informing me you want to hit Yanuka, when for ten dollars more you can have the best operator they produced for years?"

"He did Bad Godesberg! He did Vienna, maybe Leyden too! Jews are dying, Marty! Doesn't Jerusalem care about that these days? How many do we let die while we play our games?"

Carefully taking hold of the collar of Oded's windjacket with his big hands, Kurtz shook him twice, and the second time he did this, Oded's head banged painfully against the window. But Kurtz did not apologise and Oded did not complain.

"*They*, Oded. Not *he: they*," said Kurtz, this time with menace. "*They* did Bad Godesberg. *They* did Leyden. And it's *them* we intend to take out; not six innocent German householders and one silly little boy."

"It's okay," said Oded, blushing. "Leave me alone."

"It is *not* okay, Oded. Yanuka has *friends*, Oded. Relatives. People we have not yet been introduced to. You want to run this operation for me?"

"I said—it's okay."

Kurtz released him, Oded started up the engine again. Kurtz suggested they continue their interesting tour of Yanuka's life-style. So they bumped down a cobbled street where his favourite nightclub was, the shop where he bought his shirts and ties, the place where he had his hair cut, and the left-wing bookshops where he liked to browse and buy. And all the while Kurtz, in the best of spirits, beamed and nodded at everything he saw as if he were watching an old movie he couldn't get enough of—until, in a square not far from the city air terminal, they prepared to part. Standing on the pavement, Kurtz clapped Oded on the shoulder with unabashed affection, then ran his hand through his hair.

"Listen, both of you, don't pull so hard at the bridle. Buy yourselves a nice meal somewhere, charge it to me personally, okay?"

His tone was that of a commander moved to love before the battle. Which, for as long as Misha Gavron permitted it, was what he was.

The night flight from Munich to Berlin, for the few who use it, is one of the last great nostalgic journeys to be made in Europe. The Orient Express, the Golden Arrow, and the Train Bleu may be dead, dying, or artificially revived, but for those who have their memories, sixty minutes of night-flying through the East German corridor in a rattly Pan American

plane three-quarters empty is like the safari of an old habitué
indulging his addiction. Lufthansa is forbidden to fly the
route. It belongs only to the victors, to the occupiers of the
former German capital; to the historians and island-seekers;
and to one war-scarred elderly American impregnated with
the docile quiet of a professional, who makes the journey almost daily, knows his favourite seat and the first name of the
air hostess, which he pronounces in the frightful German of
the Occupation. For two pins, you think, he will slip her a
packet of Lucky Strikes and make an assignation with her behind the commissary. The fuselage grunts and lifts, the lights
falter, you cannot believe the plane has no propellers. You
look into the unlit enemy landscape—to bomb, to
jump?—you think your memories and confuse your wars:
down there, at least, in some uneasy sense, the world is as it
was.

Kurtz was no exception.

He sat at his window, he gazed past his own reflection at
the night; he became, as always when he made this journey, a
spectator looking in upon his own life. Somewhere in that
blackness was the railway line which had brought the goods
train on its slow journey from the East; somewhere the very
siding where it had parked for five nights and six days in
dead of winter to make way for the military transports that
mattered so much more, while Kurtz and his mother, and the
hundred and eighteen other Jews who were crammed into
their truck, ate the snow and froze, most of them to death.
"The next camp will be better," his mother kept assuring
him, to keep his spirits up. Somewhere in that blackness his
mother had later filed passively to her death; somewhere in
its fields the Sudeten boy who was himself had starved and
stolen and killed, waiting without illusion for another hostile
world to find him. He saw the Allied reception camp, the unfamiliar uniforms, the children's faces as old and hollow as
his own. A new coat, new boots, and new barbed wire—and
a new escape, this time from his rescuers. He saw himself in
the fields again, slipping southward from farm to village for
weeks on end as the escape line handed him on, until gradually the nights grew warm and smelled of flowers, and he
heard for the first time in his life the rustle of palm trees in a
sea wind. "Listen to us, you frozen little boy," they whispered
to him, "that's how we sound in Israel. That's how blue the

sea is, just like here." He saw the rotting steamer slumped beside the jetty, the biggest and noblest boat he had set eyes on, so black with Jewish heads that when he boarded it, he stole a stocking cap and wore it till they had cleared harbour. But they needed him, fair hair or none at all. On the deck in small groups, the leaders were giving lessons in how to shoot with stolen Lee-Enfield rifles. Haifa was still two days away, and Kurtz's war had just begun.

The plane was circling to land. He felt it bank, and watched as it crossed the Wall. He had only hand luggage, but security was tight on account of the terrorists, so formalities took quite a time.

Shimon Litvak was waiting in the car park in an inferior Ford. He had flown from Holland after two days spent looking at the mess in Leyden. Like Kurtz, he did not feel he had a right to sleep.

"The book bomb was delivered by a girl," he said as soon as Kurtz had clambered in. "Shapely brunette. Jeans. The hotel porter assumed she was from the university, convinced himself she arrived and left by bicycle. Speculative, but I believe him partly. Somebody else again says she was brought to the hotel on a motorbike. A party ribbon round the parcel and "Happy birthday, Mordecai' on the label. A plan, a transport, a bomb, and a girl, what's new?"

"Explosive?"

"Russian plastic, shreds of wrapping, nothing traceable."

"Any trademark?"

"One neat twist of surplus red circuit wire, made into a dummy."

Kurtz glanced at him sharply.

"No surplus wire," Litvak confessed. "Carbonised fragments, yes. But no identifiable wire."

"No clothespeg either?" said Kurtz.

"This time he preferred a mousetrap. A sweet little kitchen mousetrap." He started the engine.

"He used mousetraps too," said Kurtz.

"He used mousetraps, clothespegs, old Bedouin blankets, untraceable explosives, cheap one-handed watches, and cheap girls. And he's the absolute lousiest bombmaker bar none, even for an Arab," said Litvak, who hated inefficiency almost as much as he hated the enemy who was guilty of it. "How long did he give you?"

Kurtz affected not to understand. "*Give* me? Who gave me?"

"What's your licence? A month? Two months? What's the deal?"

But Kurtz was not always inclined to precision in his replies. "The deal is that a lot of people in Jerusalem would prefer to charge the windmills of Lebanon than fight the enemy with their heads."

"Can the Rook hold them off? Can you?"

Kurtz lapsed into an unaccustomed quiet from which Litvak was disinclined to rouse him. In the middle of West Berlin there is no darkness, at the edges no light. They were heading for the light.

"You paid Gadi a big compliment," Litvak observed suddenly, with a sideways look at his master. "Coming to his town like this. A journey from you to him is like a homage."

"It's not his town," said Kurtz equably. "He borrowed it. He has a grant, a trade to learn, a second life to make. That is the only reason Gadi is in Berlin."

"And he can bear to live in such a trash heap? Even for a new career? After Jerusalem, he can come *here*?"

Kurtz did not answer the question directly, nor did Litvak expect him to. "Gadi has made his contribution, Shimon. No man made a better, according to his ability. He fought hard in hard places, most of them behind the lines. Why should he not remake himself? He is entitled to his peace."

But Litvak was not trained to abandon his battles inconclusively. "So why disturb it? Why resurrect what is finished with? If he is making a new beginning, so leave him to make it."

"Because he is the middle ground, Shimon." Litvak turned swiftly to him for enlightenment, but Kurtz's face was in shadow. "Because he has the reluctance that can make the bridge. Because he ponders."

They passed the memorial church and proceeded between the icy fires of the Kurfürstendamm, then returned to the menacing stillness of the city's dark outlands.

"So what name is he using these days?" Kurtz enquired,

with an indulgent smile to his voice. "Tell me how he calls himself."

"Becker," said Litvak tersely.

Kurtz expressed jovial disappointment. "Becker? What the hell name is that? Gadi *Becker*—and him a sabra?"

"It's the German version of the Hebrew version of the German version of his name," Litvak replied, without humour. "At the request of his employers, he's reverted. He's not an Israeli any more, he's a Jew."

Kurtz kept his smile flying: "Does he have any ladies with him, Shimon? What's with women for him these days?"

"A night here, a night there. Nothing he could call his own."

Kurtz settled more comfortably in his seat. "So maybe an involvement is what he needs. Then afterwards he goes back to his nice wife, Frankie, in Jerusalem, whom, in my judgment, he had no business relinquishing in the first place."

Entering a squalid side street, they pulled up before a clumsy three-storey apartment house of dappled stone. A pilastered doorway had somehow survived the war. To one side of it, at street level, a neon-lit textiles shop displayed a lacklustre range of women's dresses. A sign above it said "WHOLESALE ONLY."

"Press the upper bell," Litvak advised. "Two rings, a pause, a third ring, he will come. They gave him a room above the business." Kurtz clambered out. "Good luck, okay? Really good luck."

Litvak watched Kurtz storm across the street. He watched him thrusting along the pavement at his rolling pace, too fast, then halt too hastily at the shabby doorway. He saw his thick arm lift to the bell and the door open a moment afterwards, as if someone had been waiting just behind it, and he supposed someone had. He saw Kurtz square his feet and lower his shoulders to embrace a slimmer man; he saw the arms of his host fold round him in a brisk, soldierly greeting. The door closed, Kurtz was inside.

Driving slowly back through the city, Litvak glowered at everything he saw on his way, externalising his jealousy: Berlin as a place of hatred for him, an inherited enemy for all time; Berlin where terror had its spawning ground, then and now. His destination was a cheap *pension* where no one seemed to sleep, himself included. By five to seven, he was back in the side street where he had left Kurtz. He pressed the bell, waited, and heard slow footsteps, one pair. The door opened and Kurtz stepped gratefully into the morning air, then stretched himself. He was unshaven and had removed his tie.

"Well?" Litvak asked, as soon as they were inside the car.

"Well what?"

"What did he say? Will he do it, or does he want to stay peacefully in Berlin and learn to make dresses for a bunch of Polish campniks?"

Kurtz seemed genuinely surprised. He was in the midst of that gesture which had so fascinated Alexis, the one that brought his old wristwatch into his line of sight, while he shoved back his left sleeve with his hand. But, hearing Litvak's question, he abandoned it. "*Do* it? He's an Israeli officer, Shimon." Then he smiled so warmly that Litvak, taken by surprise, smiled in return. "First, I admit, Gadi said he would prefer to continue to study his new trade in its many aspects. So we talked about that fine mission he made across Suez in '63. Then he said the plan wouldn't work, so we discussed in detail the inconveniences of living under cover in Tripoli and maintaining a network of extremely mercenary Libyan agents there—a thing Gadi did for three years, I seem to remember. Then he said, 'Get a younger man,' which nobody ever meant seriously, and we recalled his many night raids into Jordan and the limitations of military action against guerrilla targets, a point on which I had his full agreement. After that, we discussed the strategy. What else?"

"And the similarity? Is enough? His height, his face?"

"The similarity is enough," Kurtz replied as his features hardened into their old lines. "We work on it, it's enough. Now leave him alone, Shimon, or you'll make me love him too much."

Then he put aside his gravity and broke out laughing until tears of relief and tiredness were running down his cheeks. Litvak laughed also and, with laughter, felt his envy disappear. These sudden, rather crazy weather changes were deep in Litvak's nature, where many irreconcilable factors played their part. His name meant originally "Jew from Lithuania" and was once derogatory. How did he see himself? One day as a twenty-four-year-old kibbutz orphan without a known relation alive, another as the adopted child of an American Orthodox foundation and the Israeli special forces. On another again, as God's devoted policeman, cleaning the world up.

He played the piano wonderfully.

Of the kidnapping, little need be said. With an experienced team, such things happen fast and almost ritualistically these days, or not at all. Only the potential scale of the catch gave it its nervy quality. There was no messy shooting or unpleasantness, just a straight appropriation of one wine-red Mercedes car and its occupant, the driver, some thirty kilometres on the Greek side of the Turkish-Greek border. Litvak commanded the field team and, as always in the field, he was excellent. Kurtz, back in London again to solve a sudden crisis that had blown up in Schwili's Literacy Committee, sat out the critical hours beside a telephone in the Israeli Embassy. The two Munich boys, having duly reported the return of the hire car with no substitute in sight, followed Yanuka to the airport and, sure enough, the next anyone heard of him was three days later in Beirut, when an audio crew operating from a cellar in the Palestinian quarter picked up his cheerful voice saying hullo to his sister Fatmeh, who worked at one of the revolutionary offices. He was in town for a couple of weeks to visit friends, he said; did she have an evening free? He sounded really happy, they reported: headlong, excited, passionate. Fatmeh, however, was cool. Either her approval of him was lukewarm, they said, or she knew her phone was tapped. Maybe both. In either case, brother and sister failed to meet.

He was picked up again when he arrived by air in Istanbul, where he checked into the Hilton on a Cypriot diplomatic passport and for two days gave himself to the religious and secular pleasures of the town. The followers described him as taking one last good draught of Islam before returning to the Christian commons of Europe. He visited the Mosque of Suleiman the Magnificent, where he was seen to pray no less than three times, and afterwards to have his Gucci shoes polished once, on the grassy promenade that runs beside the South Wall. Also he drank several glasses of tea there with two quiet men who were photographed but never afterwards

identified: a false scent, as it turned out, and not the contact
they were waiting for. And he drew quite extraordinary
amusement from the sight of some old men with an air-rifle
who were gathered at the kerbside taking turns shooting
feathered darts into a target drawn on a cardboard box. He
wanted to join in, but they wouldn't let him.

In the gardens of Sultan Ahmed Square he sat on a
bench among the orange and mauve flower beds, gazing
benignly at the surrounding domes and minarets that made
the perimeter, and also at the clusters of giggling American
tourists, particularly a group of teenage girls in shorts. But
something held him back from approaching them, which
would have been his normal practice—to chat and laugh his
way among them until they accepted him. He bought slides
and postcards from the child hawkers without caring about
their outrageous prices; he wandered round the Saint Sophia,
contemplating with equal pleasure the glories of Justinian's
Byzantium and of the Ottoman conquest; and he was heard
to let out a cry of frank amazement at the sight of columns
dragged all the way from Baalbek in the country he had so
recently relinquished.

But his most devout concentration was reserved for the
mosaic of Augustine and Constantine presenting their church
and city to the Virgin Mary, for that was where he made his
clandestine connection: with a tall, unhurried man in a windjacket who at once became his guide. Until then Yanuka had
resolutely refused such offers, but something this man now
said to him—added no doubt to the place and time of his approach—persuaded him immediately. Side by side, they made
a second, cursory tour of the interior, dutifully admired the
early unsupported dome, then drove together along the Bos-
phorus in an old American Plymouth, till they came to a car
park close to the Ankara highway. The Plymouth drove off;
Yanuka was once more alone in the world—but this time as
owner of a fine red Mercedes car, which he calmly took back
to the Hilton and registered with the concierge as his own.

Yanuka did not go out on the town that night—not even
to watch the belly dancers who had so enchanted him the
night before—and the next sighting of him was very early the
following day as he set off westward on the dead straight
road that leads over the plains towards Edirne and Ipsala. At
first the day was misty and cool and the horizons close. He

stopped in a small town for coffee, and photographed a stork nesting on the dome of a mosque. He climbed a mound and relieved himself, watching the sea. The day grew hotter, the dull hills turned red and yellow, the sea ran between them to his left. On such a road, the followers had no choice but to ride him astride, as it is called, with one car far out ahead, and another far behind, hoping to God he would not plunge into some unmarked side turning, which he was quite capable of. But the deserted nature of the place gave them no option, for the only signs of life for miles at a time were tented gypsies and young shepherds and an occasional surly man in black whose life seemed taken up with studying the phenomenon of motion. Reaching Ipsala, he fooled everybody by preferring the right fork into town instead of continuing to the border. Was he going to hand over the car? God forbid! Then what the hell did he want in a stinking little Turkish border town?

The answer was God. In an undistinguished mosque in the main square, at the very edge of Christendom, Yanuka once more commended himself to Allah, which, as Litvak said grimly afterwards, was wise of him. Emerging, he was bitten by a small brown dog, which escaped before he could retaliate. That too was seen to be an omen.

Finally, to everyone's relief, he returned to the main road. The frontier crossing there is a hostile little place. Turk and Greek do not meet easily. The area is mined indiscriminately on both sides; terrorists and *contrebandiers* of all kinds have their illegal routes and purposes; shootings are common and seldom spoken of; the Bulgarian border runs just a few miles north. A sign on the Turkish side says "HAVE A GOOD TRIP" in English, but there is no kind word for departing Greeks. First come the Turkish insignia, mounted on a military board, next a bridge over slack green water, next a nervous little queue for the Turkish emigration formalities, which Yanuka tried to bypass on the strength of his diplomatic passport; and indeed succeeded, thus hastening his own destruction. Next, sandwiched between the Turkish police station and the Greek sentries, comes a no-man's-land of twenty yards or so, where Yanuka bought himself a bottle of duty-free vodka and ate an ice-cream in the café, watched by a dreamy-looking, long-haired lad called Reuven, who had been eating buns there for the last three hours. The final Turkish flourish is a great bronze bust of Atatürk, the visionary and decadent, glowering into the hostile Greek plains. As soon as Yanuka had passed this, Reuven hopped onto his motorcycle and transmitted a five-dot signal to Litvak, who was waiting thirty kilometres inside the Greek border—but outside the military area—at a point where traffic had to slow to a walking pace because of construction work. He then hurried to join the fun.

They used a girl, which was common sense considering Yanuka's proven appetites, and they gave her a guitar, which was a nice touch because these days a guitar legitimises a girl even if she can't play it. A guitar is the uniform of a certain soulful peaceability, as their recent observations in another quarter had reminded them. They havered about whether to use a blonde girl or a brunette, knowing his preference for blondes, but aware also that he was always ready to make an exception. In the end they came down in favour of the dark girl, on the grounds that she had the better backside and the saucier walk, and they posted her where the road works ended. The road works were a godsend. They believed that. Some of them even believed that God—the Jewish one— rather than Kurtz or Litvak, was master-minding their entire luck.

First there was tarmac; then without warning there was the coarse blue chippings the size of golf balls but a lot more jagged. Then came the wooden ramp with yellow scarecrow lights blipping along it, speed limit ten kilometres and only a madman would have done more. Then came the girl the other side of the ramp, plodding along the pedestrian walkway. Keep moving just as you are, they said: don't tart around, but trail your left thumb. Their only real worry was that because the girl was so pretty she might hole up with the wrong man before Yanuka appeared to claim her. A particularly helpful feature of the spot was the way the sparse traffic was separated by a temporary divide. There was about a fifty-yard wasteland between the eastbound and westbound lanes, with builders' huts and tractors and every kind of junk spread over it. They could have hidden a whole regiment in there without a soul being the wiser. Not that they were a regiment. The team was seven strong, including Shimon Litvak and the decoy girl. Gavron the Rook would not allow a penny more. The other five were lightly dressed kids in summer rig and track-shoes, the sort who can stand about all day staring at their fingernails with no one ever asking why they don't speak. Then flash into action like pike, before returning to their lethargic contemplations.

The time was by now mid-morning; the sun was high, the air dusty. The rest of the traffic consisted of grey lorries laden with some kind of lime or clay. The polished wine-red Mercedes—not new, but handsome enough—stood out in such company like a wedding car sandwiched between rubbish trucks. It hit the blue chip at thirty kilometres an hour, which was too fast, then braked as the rocks started popping against the underbody. It mounted the ramp at twenty, slowing to fifteen, then ten, and as it passed the girl everybody saw Yanuka's head turn to check whether the front of her was as good as the back. It was. He drove for another fifty yards till he reached the tarmac, and for a bad moment Litvak was convinced he would have to invoke the fallback plan, a more elaborate affair that involved a second team and a faked road accident a hundred kilometres on. But lust, or nature, or whatever it is that makes fools of us, had its way. Yanuka pulled up and lowered his electric window, poked out his handsome young head, and, full of life's fun, watched the girl walk luxuriously towards him through the sunlight. As she drew alongside, he enquired of her whether she intended to walk all the way to California. She replied, also in English, that she was heading "kind of vaguely" for Thessalonika—was he? According to the girl, he replied "As vaguely as you like," but no one else heard him and it was one of those things that are always disputed after an operation. Yanuka himself flatly denied that he had said anything at all, so perhaps the girl romanced a little in her triumph. Her eyes, her features altogether, were really most alluring, and her slow enticing motion claimed his complete attention. What more could a good Arab boy ask, after two weeks of austere political re-training in the southern hills of Lebanon, than this beguiling jeans-clad vision from the harem?

It must be added that Yanuka was slim and extremely dashing in appearance, with fine Semitic looks that matched her own, and that there was an infectious gaiety about him. Consequently a mutual scenting resulted, of the kind that can take place instantly between two physically attractive people, where they actually seem to share a mirror image of them-

selves making love. The girl set down her guitar and, true to
orders, wriggled her way out of her rucksack and dumped it
gratefully on the ground. The effect of this gesture of undressing, Litvak had argued, would be to force him to do one
of two things: either to open the back door from inside, or
else get out of the car and unlock the boot from outside. In
either case he would lay himself open to attack. In some
Mercedes models, of course, the boot lock can be operated
from inside. Not in this one. Litvak knew that. Just as he
knew for certain that the boot *was* locked; and that there was
no point in offering him the girl on the Turkish side of the
border because—however good his papers might be, and by
Arab standards they were held to be quite good—Yanuka
would not be stupid enough to compound the risk of a frontier crossing by taking aboard unattested lumber.

In the event, he selected the course they had all voted
most desirable. Instead of simply reaching back an arm and
unlocking one door manually, which he could have done, he
chose, perhaps in order to impress, to operate the central
locking device, thereby releasing not one but all four doors
together. The girl opened the rear door nearest her and, remaining outside, shoved her rucksack and guitar onto the
back seat. By the time she had closed the door again, and
started on her languid journey towards the front, as if to sit
beside him in the passenger seat, one man had a pistol to
Yanuka's temple while Litvak himself, looking his most frail,
was kneeling on the back seat holding Yanuka's head from
behind in a most murderous and well-informed grip, while he
administered the drug that, as he had been earnestly assured,
was the best suited to Yanuka's medical record: there had
been worry about his asthma in adolescence.

The thing that struck everyone afterwards was the sound-
lessness of the operation. Even while he waited for the drug
to take its effect, Litvak distinctly heard the snap of a pair of
sunglasses above the rumpus of the passing traffic, and for a
dreadful moment feared it was Yanuka's neck, which would
have ruined everything. At first they thought he had somehow
contrived to forget or shed the false number plates and papers for his onward journey, till they found them to their
pleasure neatly fitted into his smart black grip, under several
handmade silk shirts and flashy ties, all of which they were
obliged to appropriate for their own purposes, together with

his fine gold watch by Cellini and his linked gold bracelet and the gold-plated charm that Yanuka liked to wear against his heart, believed to be a gift from his beloved sister Fatmeh. Another glory of the operation—not of anyone's devising but Yanuka's—was that the target car had heavily smoked windows to prevent the common people from seeing what goes on inside. This was the first of many instances of the way in which Yanuka became the fatal victim of his own plush lifestyle. To spirit the car west and then southward after this was no headache; they could probably have driven it quite normally without a soul noticing. But for safety's sake they had hired a lorry purportedly conveying bees to a new home. There is quite a trade in bees in that region, Litvak reasoned sensibly, and even the most inquisitive policeman thinks twice before intruding upon their privacy.

The only really unforeseen element was the dog-bite: what if the brute had rabies? Somewhere they bought some serum, and injected him just in case.

With Yanuka temporarily removed from society, the vital thing was to make sure nobody, in Beirut or anywhere else, noticed the gap. They knew already that he was of an independent and carefree nature. They knew he made a cult of doing the illogical thing, that he was celebrated for altering his plans from one second to the next, partly on a whim, and partly because he believed with reason that this was the best way to confuse his trail. They knew of his recently acquired passion for things Greek, and his proven habit of chasing off in search of antiquities while in transit. On his last run, he had gone as far south as Epidaurus without so much as a by-your-leave from anyone—a great arc, right off his route, for no known reason. These random practices had in the past rendered him extremely hard to catch. Used against him, as now, he was in Litvak's cool judgment unsaveable, for his own side could keep no better check on him than his enemies. The team seized him and wafted him from view. The team waited. And in all the places where it was able to listen, not one alarm bell rang, there was not a whisper of unease. If Yanuka's masters had a vision of him at all, Shimon Litvak cautiously concluded, then it was of a young man in his prime of mind and body, gone off in search of life, and—who knows?—new soldiers for the cause.

So the fiction, as Kurtz and his team now called it, could begin. Whether it could also end—whether there was time, by Kurtz's old steel watch, for it to unfold as he determined— that was another matter altogether. The pressures upon Kurtz were of two kinds: the first, crudely enough, was to show progress or have Misha Gavron close his shop. The second was Gavron's threat that if no such progress was forthcoming, he would no longer be able to hold back the mounting outcry for a military solution. Kurtz dreaded this.

"You preach at me like the English!" Gavron the Rook squawked at him in his cracked voice, during one of their frequent arguments. "And look at *their* crimes!"

"So maybe we should bomb the English too," Kurtz suggested, with a furious smile.

But the subject of the English was by then not coincidental; for ironically it was to England that Kurtz was now looking for his salvation.

3

Joseph and Charlie were formally introduced to each other on the island of Mykonos, on a beach with two tavernas, at a late luncheon in the second half of August, just around the time when the Greek sun hits its fiercest heat. Or, in terms of the larger history, four weeks after Israeli jets bombed the crowded Palestinian quarter of Beirut, in what was afterwards declared to be an effort to destroy the leadership, though there were no leaders among the several hundred dead—unless of course they were the leaders of tomorrow, for many were children.

"Charlie, say hullo to Joseph," said somebody excitedly, and it was done.

Yet both behaved as if the meeting had scarcely taken place: she by pulling her revolutionist's frown and holding out her hand for an English schoolgirl's handshake of quite vicious respectability; and he by casting her a glance of calm and tolerant appraisal, strangely without ambition.

"Well, Charlie, yes, hullo," he agreed, and smiled no more than was necessary to be polite. So it was actually he, not Charlie, who said hullo.

She noticed he had the military mannerism of pursing his lips just before he spoke. His voice, which was foreign and held under close arrest, had a daunting mildness—she was more aware of what was held back than what was given. His behaviour towards her was thus the obverse of aggression.

Her name was actually Charmian but she was known to everyone as "Charlie," and often as "Charlie the Red" in deference to the colour of her hair and to her somewhat crazy radical stances, which were her way of caring for the world and coming to grips with its injustices. She was the outsider of a rackety troupe of young British acting people who slept in a tumbledown farmhouse half a mile inland and descended to the shore in a shaggy, close-knit family that never broke up. How they had come by the farmhouse in the first place—how they had come to be on the island at all—was a miracle to all of them, though as actors they derived no surprise from miracles. Their benefactor was a wealthy City company that had recently taken to playing angel to the itinerant stage. Their tour of the provinces over, the troupe's half-dozen cadre members were astonished to find themselves treated to rest and recreation at the company's expense. A charter whisked them there, the farmhouse stood welcoming, and spending-money was assured by a modest extension of their terms of salary. It was too kind, too generous, too sudden, too long ago. Only a bunch of Fascist swine, they had joyously agreed when they received their invitations, could have behaved with such disarming philanthropy. After which they had forgotten how they came to be there, until one or another would sleepily raise his glass and mutter the company's name in a querulous, half-hearted toast.

Charlie was not the prettiest of the girls, by any means, though her sexuality shone through, as did her incurable goodwill, which was never quite concealed by her posturing. Lucy, though stupid, was gorgeous, whereas by accepted standards Charlie was rather plain: *moche*, with a long strong nose and prematurely shadowed face that was one minute childish and the next so old and mournful you feared for her experience of life this far, and wondered what more was to become of her. Sometimes she was their foundling, sometimes their mother, the one who counted the money and knew where the anti-sting was, and the sticking-plaster for cut feet. In that rôle, as in all her others, she was their largest-hearted and their most capable. And now and then she was their conscience, bawling them out for some real or imagined crime of chauvinism, sexism, or Western apathy. Her right to do this was vested in her by her class, for Charlie was their bit of quality, as they liked to say: privately educated and the daughter of a stockbroker, even if—as she never tired of telling them—the poor man had ended his days behind bars for defrauding clients. But class will out, whatever.

And finally, she was their undisputed leading lady. When evening came, and the family took to acting little dramas to each other in their straw hats and flowing beach gowns, it was Charlie, when she cared to take part, who was the best at it. If they decided to sing to each other, it was Charlie who played her guitar a little too well for their voices; Charlie who knew the protest folk songs, and sang them in an angry, mannish style. At other times they would lounge together in sullen council, smoking marihuana and drinking retsina at thirty drachmas a half-litre. All but Charlie, who would lie apart from them like someone who had smoked and drunk all she needed long ago. "You wait till my revolution dawns," she'd warn them, in a drowsy voice. "I'll have the whole bunch of you babies out there tilling turnips before breakfast." At this, they would pretend to take fright: where will it start, Chas? Where will the first head roll? "In bloody Rickmansworth," she'd reply, harking on her storm-tossed suburban childhood. "We're going to drive all their bloody Jaguars into their bloody swimming pools." And they would let out wails of fear, even though they knew that Charlie herself had a weakness for fast cars.

Meanwhile they loved her. Indisputably. And Charlie, for all that she denied it, loved them in return.

Whereas Joseph, as they called him, was not part of their family at all. Not even, like Charlie, a splinter group of one. He had a self-sufficiency that to weaker souls was a kind of courage by itself. He was friendless but uncomplaining, the stranger who needed nobody, not even them. Just a towel, a book, a water-bottle, and his own small foxhole in the sand. Charlie alone knew he was a ghost.

Her first local sighting of him occurred the morning after her big fight with Alastair, which she lost on a straight knockout. There was a central meekness in Charlie somewhere that seemed to attract her fatally to bullies, and her bully of the day was a six-foot drunken Scot known to the family as "Long Al," who menaced a lot, and quoted inaccurately from the anarchist Bakunin. Like Charlie, he was red-headed and fair-skinned, with hard blue eyes. When they rose shining out of the water together, they were like people of a separate race from anyone else around, and their sultry expressions advised you they knew it. When they set off abruptly for the farmhouse, hand in hand, speaking to no one, you felt the urgency of their desire like a pain you had endured but seldom shared. But when they fought—which had happened that previous evening—their rancour cast such a blight over tender souls like Willy and Pauly that they slipped away until the storm was over. And on this occasion so had Charlie: she had crept off to a corner of the loft to nurse her wounds. Waking sharply at six, however, she decided to take herself for a solitary bathe, then walk into town and treat herself to an English-language newspaper and breakfast. It was while she was buying her *Herald Tribune* that the apparition occurred: a clear case of psychic phenomenon.

He was the man in the red blazer. He was standing right behind her at that moment, choosing himself a paperback, ignoring her. No red blazer this time, but a tee-shirt, shorts, and sandals. Yet the same man without a doubt. The same cropped black hair frosted at the tips and running to a devil's point at the centre of the forehead; the same brown and courteous stare, respectful of other people's passions, that had fixed on her like a dark lantern from the front row of the stalls of the Barrie Theatre in Nottingham for half a day: first the matinée, then the evening performance, eyes only for Charlie as they followed every gesture she made. A face that was neither softened nor hardened by time, but was finite as a print. A face that to Charlie's eye spelt one strong and constant reality, in contrast to an actor's many masks.

She had been playing Saint Joan, and going nearly mad about the Dauphin, who was miles over the top and upstaging every speech she made. So it was not till the final tableau that she first became aware of him sitting among the schoolchildren at the front of the half-empty auditorium. If the lighting hadn't been so dim, she probably wouldn't have spotted him even then, but their lighting rig was stuck in Derby waiting to be sent on, so there was none of the usual glare to swamp her vision. She had taken him at first for a schoolteacher, but when the kids left, he stayed in his seat reading what she took to be the text of the play, or perhaps the Introduction. And when the curtain rose again for the evening show, there he was still, in that same central spot, his placid unresponsive gaze locked on her exactly as before; and when the final curtain fell, she resented it for taking him away from her.

A few days later, in York, when she had forgotten him, she could have sworn she saw him again, but she wasn't sure; the stage lighting was too good, she couldn't penetrate the haze. Nor did the stranger stay in his place between shows. All the same, she could have sworn it *was* the same face, front row centre, raptly upturned to her, and the same red blazer too. Was he a critic? A producer? An agent? A film director? Was he from the City company, perhaps, that had taken over the sponsorship of their troupe from the Arts Council? He was too lean, too watchful in his immobility, for a mere professional money-man who was checking out his firm's investment. As to critics, agents, and the rest, it was a miracle if they stayed for one act, let alone two consecutive performances. And when she saw him on a third occasion— or thought she did—just before leaving for her holiday, on the very last night of their tour, in fact, posted at the stage door of the little East End theatre, she had half a mind to bowl straight up to him and ask him outright what his business was—whether he was an embryonic Ripper, an autograph-hunter, or just a normal sex maniac like the rest of us. But his air of studious righteousness had held her back.

The sight of him now, therefore—standing not a yard from her, seemingly unaware of her presence, contemplating the display of books with the same solemn interest that he had only days before been lavishing upon herself—threw her into an extraordinary state of flurry. She turned to him, she caught his unflustered glance, and for a second she stared at him a lot more fiercely than he had ever stared at her. And she had the advantage of dark glasses, which she had put on to hide her bruise. Seen so close, he struck her as older than she had imagined, leaner and more marked. She thought he could do with a good sleep and wondered whether he had jet-lag, for there was a downward settlement to the edges of his eyes. Yet he offered not a flicker of recognition or excitement in return. Thrusting the *Herald Tribune* back into its rest, Charlie beat a swift retreat to the safety of a waterfront taverna.

I'm mad, she thought as she lifted her trembling coffee cup to her mouth. I'm making it all up. It's his double. I shouldn't have swallowed that bloody happy-pill Lucy gave me to cheer me up after Long Al belted me. She had read somewhere that the sense of *déjà vu* was the consequence of a lapse in communication between brain and eye. But when she glanced down the road in the direction she had come from, there he sat, perceptible to sight and intellect alike, at

the next taverna along, wearing a peaked white golfing cap
tipped steeply downward to shade his eyes, while he read his
English paperback: *Conversations with Allende,* by Debray.
She'd thought only yesterday of buying it herself.

He's come to collect my soul, she thought as she swung
jauntily past him in order to demonstrate her immunity. Yet
when did I ever promise him he could have it?

The same afternoon, sure enough, he took up his post on
the beach, not sixty feet from the family encampment. Wearing a pair of prim monk's bathing trunks, black, and carrying
a tin water-bottle from which he occasionally took frugal sips,
as if the next oasis were a day's march off. Never watching,
never paying the slightest heed, reading his Debray from under the shade of his baggy white golf hat. Yet following every
move she made—she knew it, if only by the pitch and stillness
of his handsome head. Of all the beaches on Mykonos, he had
chosen theirs. Of all the places on their beach, he had lighted
on the one high point among the dunes that commanded every approach, whether she was taking a swim or fetching Al
another bottle of retsina from the taverna. From his raised
foxhole he could pick her off at leisure, and there was not a
damned thing she could do in return to dislodge him. To tell
Long Al was to expose herself to ridicule and worse; she had
no intention of giving him such a golden chance to pour
scorn on yet another of her fantasies. To tell anyone else was
no different from telling Al: he would hear of it within the
day. She had no solution but to hug her secret to herself,
which was what she wanted.

Therefore she did nothing, and so did he, but she knew
that he was waiting, all the same; she could feel the patient
discipline with which he counted off the hours. Even when he
lay as dead, a mysterious alertness seemed to wink from his
lithe brown body, carried to her by the sun. Sometimes the
tension seemed to snap in him, and he would leap suddenly
to his feet, remove his hat, stroll gravely down his dune to
the water like a tribesman without his spear, and dive in
soundlessly, hardly troubling the water's skin. She would
wait; then still wait. He had drowned, without a doubt. Till at
last, when she had given him up for good, he would surface
far across the bay, swimming in a leisurely overarm freestyle

as if he had miles to go, his cropped black head glistening like a seal's. There were motorboats careering about, but he ignored them. There were girls, but his head never turned for them—she watched to see. And after his swim again, the slow, methodical succession of physical exercises, before he replaced his tilted golf hat and settled once more to Allende and Debray.

Who owns him? she wondered helplessly. Who writes his lines and gives him his directions? He was on stage for her, just as she had been for him in England. He was a trouper like herself. With that scorching sun trembling between sky and sand, she could watch his honed, mature body for minutes on end, using it as the target for her excited speculations. You to me, she thought; me to you; these children do not understand. But when lunchtime came and they all trailed past his castle to the taverna, Charlie was enraged to see Lucy detach her arm from Robert's and give a tart's wave at him, sticking out her hip.

"Isn't he *fabulous*?" said Lucy loudly. "I'd have *him* with my salad any day."

"Me too," said Willy, louder still. "Wouldn't I, Pauly?"

But he ignored them. In the afternoon, Al led her up to the farmhouse where they made fierce, unaffectionate love. When they returned to the beach in the early evening and he was gone, she was unhappy because she had been unfaithful to her secret man. She wondered whether she should comb the night-spots for him. Failing to communicate with him by day, she decided he was nocturnal in his habits.

Next morning she would not go down to the beach. In the night, the strength of her fixation had first amused, then scared her, and she woke determined to break it. Lying beside Al's sleeping hulk, she had imagined herself wildly in love with someone she had not spoken to, taking him in all kinds of inventive ways, dumping Al and running away with him for ever. At sixteen, such daftness was permissible; at twenty-six indecent. To dump Al was one thing, and it must happen sooner rather than later. To be chasing a dream in a white golf hat was another, even on holiday in Mykonos. So she repeated her routine of yesterday, but this time—to her disappointment—he did not pop up behind her at the book-shop, nor did he drink coffee at the taverna next door to hers; nor, when she went window-shopping in the boutiques along the waterfront, did his reflection appear beside her own as she kept hoping it would. Joining the family for lunch at the taverna, she learned that in her absence they had chris-tened him Joseph.

There was nothing exceptional to this; the family awarded names to everyone who caught their eye, usually from plays or films, and the ethic required that, once ap-proved, they be generally adopted. Their Bosola from *The Duchess of Malfi*, for instance, was a restive Swedish shipping magnate with a sliding eye for flesh, their Ophelia a moun-tainous Frankfurt housewife who sported a pink-flowered bathing cap and little else. But Joseph, they now declared, was to be so named for his Semitic looks and for the striped coat of many colours that he wore over his black trunks when he strode to their beach, or left it. Joseph also for his standoffish attitude to fellow mortals and his look of being the chosen one to the detriment of others not so favoured. Joseph the despised of his brethren, aloof with his water-bottle and his book.

From her place at the table, Charlie looked on grimly as their crude annexation of her secret property gathered way. Alastair, who felt threatened as soon as anyone was praised without his blessing, was in the act of filling his glass from Robert's tankard.

"Joseph my arse," he announced boldly. "He's a stinking poof like Willy and Pauly here. He's cruising, that's what he's doing. Him and his bedroom eyes, I'd like to bash his face in. I will too."

But Charlie was already heartily sick of Alastair that day, sick of being his Fascist body-slave and his earth-mother both at once. She was not normally as abrasive as this, but her growing distaste for Alastair was warring with her feelings of guilt about Joseph.

"If he's a poof, why should he cruise, you pinhead?" she demanded savagely, swinging round on him to twist her mouth in ugly anger. "Two bloody beaches up, he can take his pick of half the queens of Greece. So can you."

Acknowledging this incautious advice, Alastair dealt her

a heavy slap on the side of her face, making it go white first, then scarlet.

Their speculations continued into the afternoon. Joseph was a voyeur; he was a prowler, a flasher, a murderer, a breather, a drag artist, a Tory. But it was left to Alastair, as usual, to provide the definitive accolade: "He's a bloody jerker!" he bellowed with a sneer out of the corner of his mouth, and gave a suck to his front teeth to underline his shrewdness of perception.

But Joseph himself acted as oblivious to these insults as even Charlie could have wished; so much so that by mid-afternoon, when the sun and the pot had lulled them into near stupidity—all but Charlie, once again—they decided he was cool, which was their ultimate compliment. And for this dramatic change, it was Alastair, once more, who led the pack. Joseph would not be shaken off by them and he could not be pulled—not by Lucy, not by the lover-boys either. *Ergo* cool, like Alastair himself. He had his territory and his whole presence said so: nobody drives me, this is where I have pitched camp. Cool again. Bakunin would have given him high marks.

"He's cool and I love him," Alastair concluded as he thoughtfully stroked Lucy's silky back, all the way down to the hipband of her bikini, then on again. "If he was a woman, I'd know *exactly* what to do with him. Would I not, Luce?"

The next minute, Lucy was standing up, in that heat the only upright person on the shimmering beach. "Who says I can't pull him?" she said, climbing out of her bathing dress.

Now Lucy was blonde and broad-hipped and as tempting as an apple. She played barmaids, tarts, and principal boys, but her speciality was teenage nymphomaniacs, and she could pull any fellow just by giving him the eyelash. Knotting a white bathrobe loosely under her breasts, she picked up a wine jug and a plastic beaker and strode across to the foot of the dune, the jug on her head, hips rolling, and thighs peeking, giving her own satirical rendering of a Hollywood Greek goddess. Having scaled the little slope, she knelt beside him on one knee and poured the wine from high up, letting the robe fall open as she did so. Handing him the beaker, she decided to address him in French, or as much of that language as she knew.

"*Aimez-vous?*" asked Lucy.

Joseph showed no awareness of her presence. He turned a page; then he observed her shadow, and only then did he roll onto his side and, after considering her critically with his dark eyes from the shadow of his golf cap, accept the beaker and gravely drink a toast, while from twenty yards away her supporters' club clapped or made House of Commons growls of fatuous approval.

"You must be Hera," Joseph remarked to Lucy with about as much feeling as if he were reading a map. And it was then that the dramatic discovery was made: he had these scars!

Lucy could scarcely contain herself. The most appealing of them was a neat drill-hole the size of a five-pence piece, like one of those bullet-hole stickers Pauly and Willy had on their Mini, only this one was on the left side of the stomach! You couldn't see it from a distance, yet when she touched it, it felt all smooth and hard.

"And you're Joseph," Lucy replied mistily, not knowing who Hera was.

Renewed applause drifted across the sand as Alastair held up his glass and shouted a toast: "Joseph! Mr. Joseph, sir! Power to your elbow! Sod your envious brothers!"

"Come and join us, Mr. Joseph!" Robert cried, to be followed by Charlie's furious order telling him to shut up.

But Joseph didn't join them. He raised his beaker and it seemed to Charlie's raging imagination that he raised it to herself particularly, but how could she have registered such a distinction at twenty yards, one man toasting a group? Then he returned to his reading. He didn't snub them; he didn't do anything plus or minus, as Lucy put it. He just rolled back onto his tummy and got on with his book, and goodness it really *was* a bullet-hole, the *exit* scar was on his back, big as a splat gun! As Lucy went on staring, she realised she was observing not just one wound but a range of them: his arms, scarred along the underparts of the elbow; the islands of hairless and unnatural skin over the backs of the biceps; the vertebrae *scoured*, she said—"like somebody had taken a red-hot piece of wire wool to him"—maybe somebody had keelhauled him even? Lucy stayed with him for a bit, pretending to read his book over his shoulder while he turned the pages, but in reality wanting to stroke his spine because his spine, apart from being scarred, was hairy and recessed in a cleft of muscle, her favourite kind of spine. But she didn't, because, as she explained to Charlie later, having touched him once, she wasn't sure that he was touchable again. She wondered—said Lucy, with a rare spurt of modesty—whether she ought at least to knock first. It was a phrase that afterwards lodged in Charlie's mind. Lucy had thought of emptying his water-bottle and filling it with wine, but then he hadn't really drunk the wine anyway so maybe he liked water better? Eventually she set the jug back on her head and pirouetted languidly home to the family, where she made her breathless report before falling asleep on somebody's lap. Joseph was deemed cooler than ever.

The incident that brought the two of them into formal touch occurred next afternoon, and Alastair was the occasion of it. Long Al was leaving. His agent had sent a cable, which was a miracle in itself. Until then it had been generally assumed with some justice that his agent was unaware of this costly form of communication. It had come up to the farmhouse on a Lambretta at ten that morning; it had been brought down to the beach by Willy and Pauly, who had been having a late lie-in. It offered what it styled "possibility major film part," and this was a great thing within the family, because Alastair had one ambition only, which was to star in large, expensive films or, as they called it, crack a movie. "I'm too strong for them," he'd explain each time the industry rejected him. "You've got to cast up to me; that's the trouble and the swine know it." So when the cable came, they were all happy for Alastair, but secretly a great deal happier for themselves, because his violence had begun to sicken them. It sickened them for Charlie, who was becoming black and blue from his assaults, and it made them frightened for their own presence on the island. Charlie alone was upset at the prospect of his going, though her grief was directed principally at herself. For days, like them, she had wanted Alastair out of her life for ever. But now that her prayers were answered by the cable, she felt sick with guilt and fear at the sight of another of her lives ending.

The family led Long Al down to the Olympic Airways

office in the town as soon as it opened after siesta, in order to get him safely on the next morning's flight to Athens. Charlie went too, but she was white and giddy and kept her arms folded tightly round her chest as if she were freezing.

"Bloody flight will be booked solid," she warned them. "We'll be stuck with the bastard for weeks."

But she was wrong. There was not only a seat available for Long Al, but a *reserved* seat in his full name, booked by telex from London three days ago and reconfirmed yesterday. This discovery took away their last remaining doubts. Long Al was headed for the Big Time. No such thing had happened to any of them, ever. Even the philanthropy of their sponsors paled beside it. An *agent*—Al's agent of all people, by common consensus the biggest slob in the entire cattle market—booking actual bloody air tickets for him by telex!

"I'll cut him on his commission, mind," Alastair told them over several ouzos while they waited for the bus back to the beach. "I'm not having any bloody parasite taking ten per cent of *me* for the rest of my life, I'll tell you *that* for free!"

A flaxen-haired hippy boy, a weirdo who sometimes tagged on to them, reminded him that all property was theft.

Utterly apart from Alastair, aching for him, Charlie scowled and drank nothing. "Al," she whispered once, and reached for his hand. But Long Al was no more gentle in success than he was in failure or love, and Charlie that morning had a split lip to prove it, which she kept wistfully exploring with her fingertips. On the beach, his monologue continued as relentless as the sun. He'd need to approve the director before he signed, he announced.

"No south-of-the-border English faggots for *me*, thank you, girl. And as for the script, I mean I'm not your type of docile ham actor who just sits on his rectum having lines thrown at him to mouth like a parrot. You know *me*, Charlie. And if *they* want to know me, the *real* me, they'd better get used to that idea right *now*, Charlie girl, because otherwise them and me, we're going to have a grade-one battle royal with no prisoners taken, oh but we are!"

At the taverna, to command their attention, Long Al took the head of the table, and that was the moment when they realised he had lost his passport and his wallet, and his Barclaycard, and his air ticket, and almost everything else that a good anarchist might reasonably regard as the disposable trash of the enslaved society.

The rest of the family missed the point to begin with, as the rest of the family very often did. They thought it was just another black argument brewing up between Alastair and Charlie. Alastair had grabbed her wrist and was forcing it against her shoulder and Charlie was grimacing while he muttered insults close into her face. She gave a smothered cry of pain and immediately afterwards, in the silence, they finally heard what he had been saying to her in one way or another for some time.

"I told you to put them in the bloody bag, didn't I, you stupid little cow. They were lying there, *on* the counter at the ticket office, and I told you, I said to you, I *told* you: 'Pick them up and put them in your shoulder bag, Charlie.' Because the *boys*, unless they are dirty-minded little south-of-the-border faggots like Willy and Pauly here, the boys do not *carry* handbags, *darling*, do they, *darling*? So where have you gone and put them, girl, where? That's no bloody way to stop a man from going to his destiny, believe you me! That's no way to put the brakes on male chauvinism, however jealous we may be of our bloke's success. I've got *work* to do back there, girl, and bloody *castles* to capture, and all!"

It was about there, at the height of the combat, that Joseph made his entry. Quite from where, nobody seemed to know—as Pauly put it, somebody just rubbed the lamp. So far as could afterwards be established, he entered left—or, in other words, from the direction of the beach. Anyway there suddenly he stood, in his coat of many colours and his golf hat tipped forward, bearing in his hand Alastair's passport and Alastair's wallet and Alastair's brand-new air ticket, all of which he had apparently picked from the sand at the foot of the taverna steps. Expressionless, at the most a trifle puzzled, he surveyed the scene between the warring lovers, waiting like a distinguished messenger till he had their attention. Then he laid out his finds on the table. One by one. Not a sound anywhere in the taverna suddenly, except the little pat as each in its turn hit the table. Finally he spoke.

"Excuse me, I have an idea somebody is going to be missing these quite soon. One ought to be able to do without them in life, I suppose, but I fear it would be actually rather difficult."

Nobody but Lucy till then had heard his voice, and Lucy had been too stoned to notice its inflexions or anything else about it. So they hadn't known about his flat, ordered English with every foreign wrinkle ironed out of it. If they *had* known, they would all have been imitating it. There was amazement, then laughter, then gratitude. They begged him to sit with them. Joseph protested and they grew strident. He was Mark Antony before the clamorous crowd: they *made* him do it. He studied them; his eyes took in Charlie, moved on, then returned to Charlie again. Finally, with an accepting smile, he capitulated. "Well, if you insist," he said; and they did. Lucy, as an old friend, embraced him. Pauly and Willy between them did the honours. Each member of the family in turn faced his straight glance, until suddenly it was Charlie's harsh blue eyes versus Joseph's brown, Charlie's furious confusion versus Joseph's perfect composure from which all triumph was so carefully extinguished—yet which she alone knew to be a mask fixed upon quite other thoughts and motives.

"Well, Charlie, yes, hullo, how do you do?" he said calmly, and they shook hands.

A stage hiatus, then—as though it had at last been let loose from its captivity and was flying free for the first time—a full-scale smile, young as a schoolboy's and twice as infectious. "But I thought Charlie was a boy's name?" he objected.

"Well, I'm a girl," said Charlie, and everybody laughed, Charlie included, before his luminous smile withdrew just as suddenly to the strict lines of its confinement.

For the few days that were left to the family, Joseph now became their mascot. In the relief of Alastair's departure, they adopted him wholeheartedly. Lucy propositioned him; he declined, courteously, even regretfully. She passed the sad news to Pauly, who met it with a somewhat firmer rejection: further impressive proof that he was sworn to chastity. Until Alastair's departure, the family had been contemplating a slackening of their lives together. Their little marriages were breaking up, fresh combinations were not saving them; Lucy thought she might be pregnant, but then Lucy often did, and with reason. The great political debates had died for want of impulse, since the most they really knew was that the System was against them, and that they were against the System; but in Mykonos the System is a little hard to find, particularly when it has flown you there at its own expense. At night in the farmhouse, over bread and tomatoes and olive oil and retsina, they had begun to talk nostalgically of rain and cold days in London, and streets where you could smell the breakfast bacon cooking on Sunday mornings. Now suddenly exit Alastair and enter Joseph to shake up the pieces and give a new perspective. They embraced him avidly. Not content with commandeering his company on the beach and in the taverna, they made an evening for him at home, a *Josepha-bend*, as they called it, and Lucy, in her rôle of mother-to-be, produced paper plates, taramasalata, cheese, and fruit. Feeling herself exposed to him by Alastair's departure and frightened by her own disordered feelings, Charlie alone held back.

"He's a forty-year-old fraud, you idiots. Can't you *see*? You can't, can you? You're such a pack of freaked-out frauds yourselves, you *literally* can't see!"

They were puzzled by her. What had become of her old generosity of spirit? How could he be a fraud, they argued, when he wasn't claiming to be anything in the first place? Come on, Chas, give him a break! But she wouldn't. In the taverna, a natural sitting order developed at the long table, where Joseph by popular will quietly presided at the centre, empathising, listening with his eyes, yet saying remarkably little. But Charlie, if she came at all, sat fretting or fooling as far from him as possible, despising him for his accessibility. Joseph reminded her of her father, she told Pauly, in what was supposed to be a dramatic insight. He had the same creepy charm exactly: but *bent*, Pauly, just completely *bent* all through; she'd seen it at a glance, but don't say anything.

Pauly swore he would not.

Charlie's just having one of her things about men, Pauly explained to Joseph that evening; it wasn't personal with Charlie, it was political—her bloody mother was a sort of witless conformist, and her father was this incredible crook, he said.

"A crooked father?" said Joseph, with a smile that suggested he knew the genus well. "How glamorous. Tell me about him, I insist."

So Pauly did, and drew pleasure from entrusting Joseph with a confidence. And in this he was not alone, for when lunch was over, or dinner, there would always be two or three who lingered to discuss their theatrical talents with their new friend, or their love-affairs, or the great agony of their artistic condition. If their confessions threatened to lack spice, they added some from their imaginations in order not to be dull for him. Joseph gravely heard them out, gravely nodded, gravely laughed a little; but he never offered advice, nor, as they soon discovered to their great astonishment and admiration, did he traffic information: what went in, stayed. Better still, he never matched their monologues with his own, preferring to lead from behind with tactful questions about themselves, or—since she was so often in their thoughts—about Charlie.

Even his nationality was a riddle. Robert for some reason pronounced him Portuguese. Someone else insisted he was Armenian, a survivor from the Turkish genocide—he had seen a documentary about it. Pauly, who was Jewish, said he was One of Us, but Pauly said everyone was, so for a while they ruled him Arab just to annoy Pauly.

But they didn't ask Joseph what he was, and when they tried to corner him about his work, he replied only that he used to travel a lot but had recently settled down. He almost made it sound as if he had retired.

"What's your firm then, Jose?" asked Pauly, braver than the others. "You know—who do you *work* for, like?"

Well, he did not think he really *had* a firm, he replied carefully, with a thoughtful tip to the brim of his white cap. Not any longer. He was doing a little reading, a little trading, he had recently inherited a little money, so he supposed he was, technically speaking, self-employed. Yes, self-employed was the expression. Call him self-employed.

Only Charlie was dissatisfied: "We're a parasite, are we then, Jose?" she demanded, colouring. "We read, we trade, we spend our money, and periodically we hoof it to a sexy Greek island for our pleasure? Right?"

With an unruffled smile, Joseph consented to this description. But Charlie did not. Charlie lost her composure and rode out ahead of herself.

"So *what* do we read, for Christ's sake? That's all I'm asking. What do we trade in? I can ask, can't I?" His agreeable silence only provoked her further. He was simply too senior for her gibes. "Are you a bookseller? What's your bag?"

He took his time. He could do that. His periods of prolonged consideration were already known in the family as Joseph's Three Minute Warnings.

"Bag?" he repeated with puzzled emphasis. "*Bag?* Charlie, I am most things, perhaps, but I am not a burglar!"

Shouting down their laughter, Charlie appealed desperately to the others: "He can't just sit there in a vacuum and *trade,* you pinheads. What does he *do*? What's his racket?" She flopped back in her chair. "Christ," she said. "Morons." And gave up, looking spent and fifty, which she could achieve at the drop of a hat.

"Don't you really think it's all too boring to discuss, actually?" Joseph asked, perfectly pleasantly, when still no one came to her aid. "I would say money and work are the two things one comes to Mykonos to escape, actually, wouldn't you, Charlie?"

"*Actually,* I'd say it was like talking to a bloody Cheshire cat," Charlie retorted rudely.

Suddenly something came apart in her completely. She stood up, uttered a hissed exclamation, and, mustering the extra force required to drive away uncertainty, smashed her fist onto the table. It was the same table they had been sitting at when Joseph miraculously produced Al's passport. The plastic cloth slipped and an empty bottle of lemonade, their wasptrap, flew straight into Pauly's lap. She began with a stream of obscenities, which embarrassed them because in Joseph's company they tended to drop the language; she accused him of being some kind of closet weirdo, draping himself around the beach and playing power games with chicks half his age. She wanted to say gumshoeing round Nottingham and York and London as well, but time had made her doubt her ground, and she was terrified of their ridicule, so she held it back. How much he understood of that first salvo they were not sure. Her voice was choked and furious and she was using her down-market accent. If they saw anything at all going on in Joseph's face, it was only a studious examination of Charlie.

"So what is it you want to know exactly, Charlie?" he enquired after his usual thoughtful pause.

"You've got a name for a start, haven't you?"

"You gave me one. Joseph."

"What's your real name?"

A dismayed silence had settled over the entire restaurant, and even those who loved Charlie absolutely, such as Willy and Pauly, felt their loyalty towards her strained.

"Richthoven," he replied finally, as if selecting from a considerable choice. "Like the flyer but with a 'v.' Richthoven," he repeated roundly, as if warming to the notion. "Does that make me a different person suddenly? If I'm the kind of wicked fellow you think I am, why should you believe me anyway?"

"*What* Richthoven? What's your Christian name?"

Another pause before he made up his mind.

"Peter. But I prefer Joseph. Where do I live? Vienna. But I travel. You want my address? I give it to you. Unfortunately you will not find me in the phone book."

"So you're Austrian."

"Charlie. Please. Let us say I am a mongrel of mixed European and Oriental origins. Would that satisfy you?"

By this time the gang was coming out on Joseph's side with a series of embarrassed murmurs: "Charlie, for Christ's sake—come on, Chas, you're not in Trafalgar Square now—Chas, honest."

But Charlie had nowhere to go but forward. Flinging an arm across the table, she snapped her fingers very loud under Joseph's nose. One snap, then a second, so that by now every waiter, every customer in the taverna had turned to watch the fun.

"Passport, please! Come on, cross my frontier. You dug up Al's for him, now let's see yours. Date of birth, colour of eyes, nationality. *Give!*"

First he looked down at her outstretched fingers, which at that angle had an ugly obtrusiveness. Then up at her flushed face as if to reassure himself of her intention. Finally he smiled, and to Charlie his smile was like a light, unhurried dance upon the surface of a deep secret, taunting her with its assumptions and omissions.

"I'm sorry, Charlie, I fear that we mongrels have a rooted objection—I would say a historical one—to having our identity defined by pieces of paper. Surely as a progressive person you would share my sentiment?"

He took her hand in one of his and, having carefully folded up her fingers with the other, returned it to her side.

Charlie and Joseph began their tour of Greece the following week. Like other successful proposals, it was one that in a strict sense was never made. Cutting herself off from the gang completely, she had taken to walking into town early while it was still cool and frittering away the day in two or three tavernas, drinking Greek coffees and learning her lines from *As You Like It*, which she was to take to the West of England that autumn. Aware of being stared at, she glanced up and there was Joseph straight opposite her across the street, coming out of the *pension* where she had discovered he was living: Richthoven, Peter, room 18, alone. It was the sheerest coincidence, she told herself afterwards, that she had chosen to sit in this taverna at the very hour when he would be leaving for the beach. Catching sight of her, he came and sat beside her.

"Go away," she said.

With a smile, he ordered himself a coffee. "I fear that now and then your friends become a somewhat rich diet," he confessed. "One is driven to seek the anonymity of the crowds."

"I'll say one is," said Charlie.

He looked to see what she was reading, and the next thing she knew they were discussing the part of Rosalind, practically scene by scene; except that Joseph was doing both sides of the talking. "She is so many people under one hat, I would say. Watching her unfold throughout the play, one has the impression of a person occupied by a whole regiment of conflicting characters. She is good, she is wise, she is forfeit somehow, she sees too much, she has even a sense of social duty. I would say that you were well cast for this part, Charlie."

She couldn't help herself. "Ever been to Nottingham, Jose?" she demanded, staring straight at him and not troubling to smile.

"Nottingham? I fear not. Should I have been? Is Nottingham a place of particular merit? Why do you ask?"

Her lips were getting pins and needles. "It's just I was acting there last month. I hoped you might have seen me."

"But how awfully interesting. What should I have seen you in? What was the show?"

"*Saint Joan.* Shaw's *Saint Joan.* I was Joan."

"But that's one of my favourite plays. I am sure that not a year passes without my rereading the Introduction to *Saint Joan.* Will you be playing it again? Perhaps I shall get another chance?"

"We played at York too," she said, her eyes still intently fixed upon his own.

"Really? So you took it on tour. How nice."

"Yes, isn't it? Is York a place you've been to on your travels?"

"Alas, I have never been farther north than Hampstead, London. But I am told that York is very beautiful."

"Oh, it's great. Specially the Minster."

She went on staring at him as long as she dared, the face in the front row of the stalls. She searched his dark eyes and the taut skin round them for the smallest tremor of complicity or laughter, but nothing yielded, nothing confessed.

He's amnesiac, she decided. Or I am. Oh mother!

He did not offer her breakfast or she would surely have declined. He simply called over the waiter and demanded in Greek to know what fish was fresh today. With authority, knowing that fish was what she liked, holding a conductor's arm in the air to arrest him. Then sent him off and talked more theatre to her, as if it were the most natural thing to be eating fish and drinking wine at nine o'clock on a summer's morning—though for himself he ordered Coca-Cola. He talked from knowledge. He might not have been up north, but he possessed an intimacy with the London stage that he had not revealed to anyone else in the gang. And as he talked she had that unsettling feeling which she had had about him from the start: that his outward nature, like his presence here, was a pretext—his task was to force a breach through which he could spirit his other and totally larcenous nature. She asked him, did he get to London often? He protested that, second to Vienna, it was the only city in the world.

"If there is the smallest opportunity, I seize it immediately by the forelock," he declared. Sometimes even his spoken English had the air of being dishonestly acquired. She imagined stolen hours of night-reading with a phrase-book, so many idioms memorised per week.

"Only we took *Saint Joan* to London as well—just, you know—like a few weeks ago."

"To the West End? But, Charlie, that's an absolute calamity. Why didn't I read about it? Why didn't I immediately go?"

"The *East* End," she corrected him gloomily.

Next day they met again at a different taverna—whether it was by chance, she couldn't say, but instinctively she doubted it—and this time he asked her casually when she expected to start rehearsing for *As You Like It,* and she replied, with nothing more in mind than small talk, not till October and, knowing the company, maybe not then either, and anyway it looked like being a three-weeker at most. The Arts Council had overspent on their budget, she explained, and were talking about withdrawing their touring grant altogether. To impress him, she added a small piece of decoration of her own.

"I mean, you know, they swore our show would be the last to go, and we've had this fantastic back-up from the *Guardian,* and the whole thing costs the taxpayer about one-three-hundredth of an army tank, but what can you do?"

So how would she be spending her time meanwhile? Joseph asked with splendid disinterest. And it was a curious thing, which she afterwards thought about a lot, that by establishing that he had missed her Saint Joan, he established also that they owed it to each other to make up the lost ground in some other way.

Charlie answered carelessly. Barmaiding round the theatres most likely, she said. Waitress work. Repainting her flat. Why?

Joseph was wildly distressed. "But, Charlie, that's very poor stuff. Surely your talent merits a better occupation than barmaid? What about the teaching or political professions? Wouldn't that be more interesting for you?"

Nervous, she laughed rather rudely at his unworldliness. "In England? With our unemployment? Come off it. Who's going to pay me five thousand a year to destroy the existing order? I'm *subversive,* for God's sake."

He smiled. He seemed surprised and unconvinced. He

laughed in polite remonstration. "Oh now, Charlie. Come. What does that *mean*?"

Prepared to be annoyed, she met his stare again, head on, like an obstruction.

"It means what it says. I'm bad news."

"But whom are you subverting, Charlie?" he protested earnestly. "You strike me as a most orthodox person, actually."

Whatever her beliefs might be that day, she had an uncomfortable instinct that he would outstrip her in debate. To protect herself, therefore, she elected a sudden tiredness of manner.

"Back away, will you, Jose?" she advised him wearily. "We're on a Greek island, right? On holiday, right? You keep off my politics, I'll keep off your passport."

The hint was enough. She was impressed and surprised by her power over him at the very moment when she was fearing she had none. Their drinks came and as he sipped his lemonade, he asked Charlie whether she had seen many Greek antiquities during her stay. It was an enquiry of the merest general interest and Charlie replied to it in a tone of matching inconsequence. She and Long Al had been to Delos for the day to visit the Temple of Apollo, she said; that was the most she'd done. She forebore from telling him that Alastair had got fighting drunk on the boat, or that the day had been a write-off, or that afterwards she had spent a lot of hours in the town stationers, reading up the guidebooks about the little she had seen. But she had a shrewd intimation that he knew anyway. It was not till he raised the matter of her return ticket to England that she began to suspect a tactical intention behind his curiosity. Joseph asked if he might see it, so with a shrug of indifference she dug it out for him. He took it from her and leafed through it, earnestly studying the particulars.

"Well, you could perfectly well use this from Thessalonika," he pronounced finally. "Why don't I simply call a travel-agent friend of mine and have him rewrite it? Then we can travel together," he explained, as if this were the solution both of them had been working towards.

She said nothing at all. Inside her it was as if each component of her nature had gone to war against the other: the child fought the mother, the tart fought the nun. Her clothes felt rough against her skin and her back was hot, but she still didn't have a thing to say.

"I have to be in Thessalonika one week from now," he explained. "We could rent a car in Athens, take in Delphi, and head north together for a couple of days, why not?" He was unbothered by her silence. "With a little planning, we should not be over-troubled by the crowds, if that is what is concerning you. When we reach Thessalonika, you can take a London flight. We can even share the driving, if you wish. I have heard from every side how well you drive. You would be my guest, naturally."

"Naturally," she said.

"So why not?"

She thought of all the reasons that she had rehearsed for just this moment or one like it, and of all the pithy, flat-voiced phrases she fell back on when older men made passes at her. She thought of Alastair, of the tedium of being with him anywhere except in bed and latterly there also. Of the new chapter in her life that she had promised herself. She thought of the drab trail of cheeseparing and scrubbing which awaited her once she got back to England with her savings spent, and of which Joseph by chance or cunning had reminded her. She looked sideways at him again and saw not a glimmer of supplication anywhere: *why not?* and that was all. She remembered his lithe and powerful body, cutting its lone furrow through the sea: *why not?* again. She remembered the brush of his hand and the eerie note of recognition in his voice—"*Charlie, yes, hullo*"—and the lovely smile that had hardly come back since. And she remembered how often it had crossed her mind that if he ever did let go, the detonation would be deafening, which she told herself was what had drawn her to him above all else.

"I'm not going to have the gang knowing," she muttered, head down to her drink. "You'll have to fiddle it somehow. They'd laugh their bloody heads off."

To which he replied briskly that he would depart tomorrow morning and arrange things: "And of course if you really wish to leave your friends in the dark—"

Yes, she damn well did, she said.

Then this, said Joseph, in the same practical tone, was what he suggested. Whether he had prepared his plan in advance or simply had that kind of mind, she couldn't tell. Either way she was grateful for his precision, though afterwards she realised that she had counted on it.

"You go with your friends by boat as far as Piraeus. The boat docks in late afternoon, but this week it is liable to be delayed by industrial action. Shortly before the boat enters harbour, you will tell them that you propose to wander alone round the mainland for a few days. An impulsive decision, the sort you are famous for. Don't tell them too early or they will spend the boat trip trying to argue you out of it. Don't tell them too much, it is the sign of an uneasy conscience," he added, with the authority of somebody who possessed one.

"Suppose I'm broke," she said before she'd had time to think, for Alastair as usual had been through her cash as well as his own. All the same, she could have bitten her tongue off, and if he had offered her money at that moment she'd have flung it in his face. But he seemed to sense that.

"Do *they* know you are broke?"

"Of course they don't."

"Then your cover story is intact, I would say." And as if that clinched the matter, he dropped her air ticket into an inside pocket of his jacket.

Hey, give that back! she screamed in sudden alarm. But not—though there was just a hair's breadth in it—not aloud.

"Once clear of your friends, take a taxi to the Kolokotroni Square." He spelt it for her. "The fare should cost you around two hundred drachmas." He waited to hear whether this might be a problem, but it was not; she had eight hundred left, though she didn't tell him. He repeated the name again, and checked that she had remembered it. There was pleasure in submitting to his military efficiency. Just off the square, he said, was a pavement restaurant. He told her the name—Diogenes—and permitted himself a detour for humour: a beautiful name, he said, one of the best in history, the world needed more of him and fewer Alexanders. He would be waiting at the Diogenes. Not on the pavement but inside the restaurant where it was cool and private. Repeat, Charlie: *Diogenes*. Absurdly, passively, she did.

"Next door to the Diogenes is the Hotel Paris. If by any chance I am held up, I will leave a message for you with the concierge at the hotel. Ask for Mr. Larkos. He is a good friend of mine. If you require anything, money or whatever it may be, show him this and he will give it to you." He handed her a card. "Can you remember all that? Of course you can, you're an actress. You can remember words, gestures, numbers, colours, everything."

Richthoven Enterprises, she read, *Export,* followed by a post office box number in Vienna.

Passing a kiosk, feeling wonderfully, dangerously alive, she bought her bloody mother a crochet-work tablecloth, and for her poisonous nephew Kevin a tasselled Greek cap. When she had done that, she chose a dozen postcards most of which she addressed to old Ned Quilley, her useless agent back in London, with facetious messages intended to embarrass him in front of the prim ladies who comprised his office staff. "Ned, Ned," she wrote on one, "keep all your parts for me." And on another, "Ned, Ned, can a fallen woman sink?" But on yet another of them she chose to write soberly, telling him she was considering delaying her return so that she could see something of the mainland. "It's time our Chas topped up her culture levels, Ned," she explained, ignoring Joseph's stricture not to tell too much. About to cross the road and post them, Charlie had a feeling of being observed, but when she swung round, pretending to herself she was going to meet Joseph, all she saw was the flaxen hippy boy again, the one who liked to stalk the family and had presided over Alastair's departure. He was goofing along the pavement behind her with his arms trailing like an ape. Catching sight of her, he slowly raised his right hand in a Christ-like gesture. She waved back to him, laughing. Crazy devil's had a bad trip and can't come down, she thought indulgently as she dropped the cards into the box one by one. Maybe I should do something about him.

The last card of all was to Alastair, full of faked sentiment, but she didn't read it through. Sometimes, particularly in moments of uncertainty or change or when she was about to do a dare, it suited her to believe that her darling, hopeless, bibulous Ned Quilley, aged a hundred and forty next birthday, was the only man she'd ever truly loved.

4

Kurtz and Litvak called on Ned Quilley at his Soho offices on
a misty, soaking Friday at midday—a social call with
business as its aim—as soon as they heard that the Joseph-
Charlie show was safely running. They were in near despair:
since the Leyden bomb, Gavron's croaking breath was on
their necks every hour of the day; they could hear nothing in
their minds but the remorseless ticking of Kurtz's battered
watch. Yet on the surface, they were just two more respectful, well-contrasted mid-European Americans in dripping new
Burberrys, the one stocky with a forceful rolling walk and a
bit of a sea captain to him, the other gangly and young and
rather insinuating, with a private academic smile. They gave
their names as Gold and Karman of the firm of GK
Creations, Incorporated, and their letter paper, hastily run up,
sported a blue-and-gold monogram like a thirties tie-pin to
prove it. They had made the appointment from the Embassy
but ostensibly from New York, personally with one of Ned
Quilley's ladies, and they kept it to the minute like the eager
show-business citizens they weren't.

"We're Gold and Karman," said Kurtz to Quilley's
senile receptionist, Mrs. Longmore, at two minutes to twelve
exactly, striding straight in on her from the street. "We have
a date with Mr. Quilley twelve o'clock. Thank you—no, dear,
we'll stand. Was it you we spoke with by any chance, dear?"

It was not, said Mrs. Longmore, in the tone of one humouring a pair of lunatics. Appointments were the province
of Mrs. Ellis, a different person entirely.

"Sure, dear," said Kurtz, undaunted.

And that was how they often operated in these cases:
officially somehow, with broad Kurtz beating the rhythm and
slender Litvak piping softly behind him with his smouldering
private smile.

The stairs to Ned Quilley's offices were steep and uncar-
peted, and most American gentlemen, in Mrs. Longmore's

fifty years' experience of her post, liked to comment on them wryly and pause for breath at the turn. But not Gold; not Karman either. These two, when she watched them through her window, skipped up the stairs and clean out of sight as if they had never seen an elevator. It must be the jogging, she thought, as she went back to her knitting at four pounds an hour. Wasn't that what they were all doing in New York these days? Running around Central Park, poor things, avoiding the perverts and the dogs? She had heard that a lot died of it.

"Sir, we're Gold and Karman," said Kurtz a second time as little Ned Quilley cheerily opened his door to them. "I'm Gold." And his big right hand had landed in poor old Ned's before he even had a chance to draw. "Mr. Quilley, sir— Ned—we are surely honoured to meet you. You have a fine, fine reputation in the profession."

"And I'm Karman, sir," Litvak privately explained, just as respectfully, peering over Kurtz's shoulder. But Litvak was not in the handshaking class: Kurtz had done it for both of them.

"But, my dear fellow," Ned protested with his deprecating Edwardian charm, "my goodness, it's *I* who am honoured, not *you!*" And he led them at once to the long sash window, the legendary Quilley's Window of his father's day, where, as tradition had it, you sat gazing down into Soho market quaffing old Quilley's sherry and contemplating the world go by while you made nice deals for old Quilley and his clients. For Ned Quilley at sixty-two was still very much a son. He asked nothing better than to see his father's agreeable way of life continue. He was a gentle little soul, white-haired and something of a dresser as stage-struck people often are, with a quaint cast in his eye, pink cheeks, and an air of being agitated and delayed both at once.

"Too wet for the tarts, I'm afraid," he declared, bravely flapping an elegant little hand at the window. Insouciance, in Ned's opinion, was what life was all about. "Get rather a decent turnout this time of year, as a rule. Big ones, black ones, yellow ones, every shape and size you can imagine. There's one old biddy been here longer than I have. My father used to give her a pound at Christmas. Wouldn't get much for a pound these days, I'm afraid. Oh no! No, indeed!"

From his cherished breakfront bookcase, while they dutifully laughed with him, Ned extracted a decanter of sherry, officiously sniffed the stopper, then half filled three crystal glasses while they watched him. Their watchfulness was something he sensed at once. He had the feeling they were pricing him, pricing the furniture, the office. An awful thought struck him—it had been at the back of his mind ever since he had received their letter.

"I say, you're not trying to buy me up or anything frightful, are you?" he asked nervously.

Kurtz let out a loud, comforting laugh. "Ned, we are surely not trying to buy you up." Litvak laughed too.

"Well, thank God for that," Ned declared earnestly, handing round the glasses. "Do you know *everybody's* being bought up these days? I get all sorts of chaps I've never heard of, offering me money down the telephone. All the small, old firms—decent houses—getting gobbled up like what's-its. Shocking. Cheer-ho. Good luck. Welcome," he declared, still shaking his head in disapproval.

Ned's courting rituals continued. He asked where they were staying, and Kurtz said the Connaught, and, Ned, they really loved it, they had felt family from the minute they arrived. This part was true; they had booked in there specially, and Misha Gavron was going to fall straight off his branch when he saw the bill. Ned asked them whether they were finding opportunities for leisure, and Kurtz replied heartily that they were just loving every minute of their time. They were leaving for Munich tomorrow.

"Munich? My goodness, whatever will you be doing over *there*?" Ned asked, playing his age for them, playing the anachronistic, unworldly dandy. "You chaps don't half hop around, I will say!"

"Co-production money," replied Kurtz, as if that explained everything.

"A lot of it," said Litvak, speaking in a voice as soft as his smile. "The German scene is big today. Way, way up there, Mr. Quilley."

"Oh, I'm sure it is. Oh, so I've heard said," said Ned indignantly. "They're a major force, one has to face it. In everything. War's all forgotten now, swept *far* under the carpet."

With a mysterious drive to perform ineffectually, Ned made to refill their sherry glasses pretending he had not noticed they were virtually untouched. Then he giggled and put down the decanter. It was a ship's decanter, eighteenth century, with a broad base to keep it steady in a rolling sea. Quite often, with foreigners, Ned made a point of explaining this to put them at their ease. But something about their intent manner restrained him, and instead there was only a small silence and a creaking of chairs. Outside the window the rain had thickened into driving fog.

"Ned," said Kurtz, timing his entrance exactly. "Ned, I want to tell you who we are a little and why we wrote you and why we are stealing your valuable time."

"My dear chap, please do, delighted," said Ned, and, feeling like someone completely different, folded his little legs and put on an attentive smile while Kurtz settled smoothly into his persuading mode.

By his broad, raked-back forehead Ned guessed he was Hungarian, but he might have been Czech or really any of those places. He had a rich, naturally loud voice and a mid-European accent that the Atlantic had not yet swamped. He was as fast-spoken and fluent as a radio commercial, and his bright narrow eyes seemed to listen to everything he said while his right forearm beat everything to pieces in small, decisive chops. He, Gold, was the lawyer of the family, Kurtz explained; Karman here was more on the creative side, with a background of writing, agenting, and producing, mainly Canada and the Midwest. They had recently taken offices in New York, where their current interest was independent packaging for television.

"Our creative rôle, Ned, is confined ninety per cent to finding a concept that is acceptable to networks and finance. The concept—we sell this to the backers. Production—we leave this to the producers. Period."

He had finished, and he had looked at his watch with a strangely distracted gesture, and now it was up to Ned to say something intelligent, which to his credit he managed rather well. He frowned, he held out his glass almost to arm's length, and with his feet he traced a slow deliberate pirouette, instinctively responding to Kurtz's mime. "But, old boy. If you're *packagers,* old boy, what do you want with us *agents?*"

he protested. "I mean, why do I rate *lunch,* what? See what I mean? Why lunch if you're *packaging*?"

At this, to Ned's surprise, Kurtz burst out in the most cheerful and infectious laughter. Ned thought he had been quite witty too, to be honest, and done a rather good thing with his feet; but it was nothing to what Kurtz thought. His narrow eyes clamped shut, his big shoulders lifted, and the next thing Ned knew, the whole room was filled with the warming peals of his Slav mirth. At the same time, his face broke into all kinds of disconcerting furrows. Till now, in Ned's estimation, Kurtz had been forty-five at worst. Suddenly he was Ned's age, his brow and cheeks and neck as crisp as paper, with crevices in them like the slashes of a knife. The transformation bothered Ned. He felt cheated somehow. "Sort of human Trojan Horse," he afterwards complained to his wife, Marjory. "You let in a high-powered showbiz salesman of forty and all of a sudden out pops a sort of sixty-year-old Mr. Punch. Bloody odd."

But it was Litvak this time who supplied the crucial, long-rehearsed answer to Ned's question, the answer on which everything else depended. Leaning his long, angular body forward over his knees, he opened his right hand, splayed the fingers, grasped one, and addressed it in an accented Boston drawl, the products of worker-bee study at the feet of American Jewish teachers.

"Mr. Quilley, sir," he began, so devoutly that he seemed to be imparting a mystical secret. "What we have in mind here is a totally original project. No precedents, no imitators. We take sixteen hours of very good television time—say, fall and winter. We form a matinée theatrical company of strolling players. A bunch of very talented repertory actors, British and American mixed, a wide range of races, personality, human interaction. This company, we move it from city to city, each actor playing a variety of rôles, now starring, now supporting. Their real-life human stories and relationships to provide a nice dimension, part of the audience appeal. Live shows in every city."

He glanced up suspiciously as if he thought Quilley had spoken, but Quilley emphatically had not.

"Mr. Quilley, we travel with that company," Litvak resumed, slowing almost to a halt as his fervour deepened. "We ride in that company's buses. We help shift the scenery with that company. We the audience share their problems, their lousy hotels, look in on their fights and love-affairs. We the audience rehearse with them. We share their opening-night nerves, read their reviews next day, rejoice at their successes, grieve at their failures, write letters to their folks. We give theatre back its adventure. Its pioneering spirit. Its actor-audience relationship."

For a moment Quilley thought Litvak had finished. But he was only selecting a different finger to hold on to.

"We use classic theatre plays, Mr. Quilley, out of copyright, low cost all the way. We barnstorm. We use new, relatively unknown actors and actresses, now and then a guest star for mileage, but basically we are promoting new talent and inviting that talent to demonstrate the whole range of its versatility over a minimum four-month period, which hopefully is extended. And re-extended. For the actors, great exposure, great publicity, nice clean shows, no dirt, see if it goes. That's our concept, Mr. Quilley, and our backers seem to like it a lot."

Then, before Quilley even had time to offer his congratulations, a thing he always liked to do when someone told him an idea, Kurtz had stormed back into the act.

"Ned, we want to sign your Charlie," he announced; and with the enthusiasm of a Shakespearean herald bearing news of victory, he swept his whole right arm up into the air and held it there.

Very excited, Ned made to speak, only to find that Kurtz was once more talking clean through him.

"Ned, we believe that your Charlie has great wit, great versatility, fine range. If you can reassure us on a couple of slightly urgent points we have—why, I think we can offer her the opportunity of a place in the theatrical firmament which you and she will surely not regret."

Yet again Ned tried to speak, but this time it was Litvak who got in ahead of him: "We're all set to go for her, Mr. Quilley. Give us a couple of answers to a couple of questions and Charlie's up there with the big ones."

Suddenly there was silence, and all Ned could hear was the song in his own heart. He blew out his cheeks and, trying to appear businesslike, tugged at each of his elegant cuffs in turn. He adjusted the rose which Marjory had that very morning put into his button-hole with her usual instruction not to drink too much at lunch. But Marjory would have thought quite differently if she had known that, far from wanting to buy Ned out, they were actually proposing to give their beloved Charlie her long-awaited break. If she had known *that,* old Marge would have lifted all restrictions, of course she would.

Kurtz and Litvak drank tea, but at The Ivy they take such eccentricities in their stride, and as for Ned he required little persuasion to choose himself a very decent half-bottle from the list and, since they seemed to insist upon it, a big, misted glass of the house Chablis to go with his smoked salmon first. In the taxi, which they took to escape the rain, Ned had begun to relate to them the amusing story of how he had acquired Charlie as a client. In The Ivy he resumed the thread.

"Fell for her hook, line, and sinker. Never done such a thing before. Old fool, that's what I was—not as old as I am now, but still a fool. Nothing much to the show. Little old-fashioned revue, really, dolled up to look modern. But Charlie was marvellous. The *defended softness,* that's what I look for in the gals." The expression was in fact a legacy of his father's. "Soon as the curtain came down, I popped straight round to her dressing-room—if you could call it a dressing-room—did my Pygmalion act, and signed her on the spot. She wouldn't believe me at first. Thought I was a dirty old man. Had to go back and fetch Marjory to persuade her. Ha!"

"What happened after that?" said Kurtz very pleasantly, handing him some more brown bread and butter. "Roses all the way, huh?"

"Oh, not a bit of it!" Ned protested guilelessly. "She was just like so many of 'em at that age. Come bouncing out of drama college all starry-eyed and full of promise, get a couple of parts, start buying a flat or some stupid thing, then suddenly it all stops for 'em. The twilight time we call it. Some pull through it, some don't. Cheers."

"But Charlie did," Litvak softly prompted, sipping his tea.

"She held on. Sweated it out. It wasn't easy, but it never is. Years of it, in her case. Too many." He was surprised to discover himself so moved. From their expressions, so were they. "Well, now it's come right for her, hasn't it? Oh, I *am* pleased for her! I really am. Yes, indeed."

And that was another odd thing, Ned told Marjory afterwards. Or maybe it was the same thing over again. He was referring to the way the two men changed character as the day wore on. Back in the office, for instance, he'd hardly got a word in edgeways. But at The Ivy they gave him centre stage and nodded him through his lines with hardly a word between them. And afterwards—well, afterwards was another damned thing completely.

"Terrible childhood, of course," said Ned proudly. "A lot of the gals have that, I notice. It's what sends 'em towards fantasy in the first place. Dissembling. Hiding your emotions. Copying people who look happier than you are. *Or* unhappier. Stealing a bit of 'em—what acting's half about. Misery. Theft. I'm talking too much. Cheers again."

"Terrible in what *way*, Mr. Quilley?" Litvak asked respectfully, like someone who was researching the whole question of terribleness. "Charlie's childhood. Terrible how, sir?"

Ignoring what he only afterwards saw to be a deepening gravity in Litvak's manner and in Kurtz's gaze as well, Ned entrusted to them whatever knowledge he had incidentally acquired during the little, confessive lunches he occasionally gave her upstairs at Bianchi's, where he took them all. The mother a ninny, he said. The father some sort of rather awful swindler chap, a stockbroker who'd gone to the devil and was now mercifully dead, one of those plausible liars who think God put the fifth ace up their sleeves. Ended up in jug. Died there. Shocking.

Once again, Litvak made the mildest intervention: "Died in prison, did you say, sir?"

"Buried there too. Mother so bitter she wouldn't waste the money moving him."

"This something Charlie told you herself, sir?"

Quilley was mystified. "Well, who else would?"

"No collateral?" said Litvak.

"No *what*?" said Ned as his fears of a takeover suddenly revived.

"Corroboration, sir. Confirmation from unconnected parties. Sometimes with actresses—"

But Kurtz intervened with a fatherly smile: "Ned, you

just ignore this boy," he advised. "Mike here has a *very* suspicious streak in him. Don't you, Mike?"

"Maybe I do, at that," Litvak conceded, in a voice no louder than a sigh.

Only then did Ned think to ask them what they had seen of her work, and to his pleasurable surprise it turned out that they had taken their researches very seriously indeed. Not only had they obtained clips of every minor television appearance she had ever made, they had actually traipsed up to beastly Nottingham on their previous visit to catch her Saint Joan.

"Well, my goodness what a sly pair you are!" cried Ned as the waiters cleared their plates and set the scene for roast duck. "If you'd given me a call, I'd have driven you up there myself, or Marjory would. Did you go backstage, take her out for a meal? You didn't? Well, I'm damned!"

Kurtz allowed himself a moment's hesitation and his voice grew grave. He cast a questioning glance at his partner, Litvak, who gave him a faint nod of encouragement. "Ned," he said, "to tell you the truth, we just didn't quite feel it was appropriate in the circumstances."

"Whatever circumstances are they?" asked Ned, supposing he was referring to some point of agents' ethics. "Good Lord, we're not like that over here, you know! You want to make her an offer, make one. Don't have to get a chit from me. I'll collect my commission one day, don't you worry!"

Then Ned went quiet because they both looked so bloody solemn, he told Marjory. As if they'd swallowed bad oysters. Shells and all.

Litvak was carefully dabbing his thin lips. "Mind if I ask you something, sir?"

"My dear chap," said Ned, very puzzled.

"Would you tell us, please—your own assessment—how does Charlie interview?"

Ned put down his claret glass. "Interview? Ah well, if that's your worry you can take it from me that she's an absolute natural. First rate. Knows instinctively what the press boys want and, given the chance, how to provide it. Chameleon, that's what she is. Bit out of practice recently, I'll grant you, but she'll pick it up again like a shot, you'll see. Don't have any anxiety on that score." He took a long pull of wine to reassure them. "Oh no."

But Litvak was not as uplifted by this news as Ned had hoped. Pressing his lips into a kiss of worried disapproval, he began assembling crumbs on the tablecloth with his long, thin fingers. So that Ned actually lowered his own head and tilted his face up in an effort to draw him from his doldrums: "But, my dear fellow!" he protested uncertainly. "Don't look like that! What can possibly be wrong with her interviewing well? There are plenty of gals around who make a perfect hash of it. If *that's* what you want, I've got any number of 'em!"

But Litvak's favour was not to be won. His only response was to lift his gaze briefly to Kurtz as if to say "Your witness," then lower it again to the tablecloth. "A real *two-hander*," Ned told Marjory ruefully afterwards. "You felt they could have switched parts at the drop of a hat."

"Ned," said Kurtz, "if we sign your Charlie for this project, she is going to get one hell of a lot of exposure, and I mean a *lot*. Once she is into this thing, your kid is going to have her whole life spread right out in front of her face. Not only her love life, her family, her taste in pop-stars and poetry. Not only the story of her father. But also her religion, her attitudes, her opinions."

"And her politics," Litvak whispered, raking in the last of the crumbs. At which Ned suffered a mild but unmistakable loss of appetite, and laid down his knife and fork, while Kurtz kept rolling on: "Ned, our backers in this project are nice Midwestern American people. They have all the virtues. Too much money, ungrateful children, second homes in Florida, wholesome values. But *especially* the wholesome values. And they want those values reflected in this production, all the way down the line. We can laugh at it a little, weep at it a little, but it's the reality, it's television, and it's where the money is—"

"And it's America," Litvak breathed patriotically, to his crumbs.

"Ned, we will be frank with you. We will be truthful. When we finally decided to write you, we were all ready, subject to obtaining other consents along the way, to buy your Charlie out of her commitments and start her on the big road. But I will not conceal from you that in the last couple of days, Karman here and myself have heard things around the bazaars that made us sit up and start to wonder. Her tal-

ent, no problem—Charlie is a fine, fine talent, under-exer-
cised, diligent, all set to go. But whether she is *bankable*
within the context of this project. Whether she is *exposable*.
Ned, we want some reassurance from you that this thing isn't
serious."

It was Litvak who again put in the decisive thrust. Relinquishing his crumbs at last, he had crooked his right forefinger under his lower lip and was gazing mournfully at Ned
through his black-framed spectacles.

"We hear she's currently radical," he said. "We hear
she's far, far out in her political causes. Militant. We hear
she's currently allied with a very flakey anarchist guy, some
kind of crazy. We don't want to condemn anybody on the
strength of idle rumour, but the stuff that's reaching us, Mr.
Quilley, it's like she's Fidel Castro's mother and Arafat's sister rolled into a single hooker."

Ned stared from one to the other of them, and for a
moment he had the delusion that their four eyes were controlled by one optic muscle. He wanted to say something but
he felt unreal. He wondered whether he might have drunk
the Chablis faster than was prudent. All that he could think
of was a favourite aphorism of Marjory's: there is no such
thing in life as a bargain.

The dismay that had descended over Ned was like the
panic of the old and helpless. He felt physically unequal to
the task, too weak for it, too tired. All Americans unsettled
him; and most scared him, either by their knowledge or their
ignorance, or both. But these two, blankly gazing at him
while he floundered for an answer, inspired a spiritual alarm
greater than anything he was prepared for. He was also, in a
useless sort of way, very angry. He loathed gossip. *All* gossip.
He regarded it as the blight of his profession. He had seen it
ruin careers; he detested it and he could become red-faced
and almost rude when it was offered to him by those who did
not know his feelings. When Ned talked about people, he did
so openly and with affection, exactly as he had talked about
Charlie ten minutes ago. Dammit, he loved the girl. It even
crossed his mind to indicate this to Kurtz, which for Ned
would have been a bold step indeed, and it must have crossed
his face as well, for he fancied he saw Litvak start to worry
and prepare to back off a little, and Kurtz's extraordinarily
mobile face break into a come-now-Ned sort of smile. But an

incurable courtesy, as ever, held him back. He was eating their salt. Besides, they were foreign and had totally different standards. Then again he had to admit, reluctantly, that they had a job to do, and backers to humour, and even in a sense a certain awful rightness on their side; and that he, Ned, must either meet their point or risk wrecking the deal, and with it all his hopes for Charlie. For there was another factor here, that Ned in his fatal reasonableness was also obliged to acknowledge—namely, that even if their project turned out to be dreadful, which he assumed would be the case; even if Charlie were to throw away every line she was given, walk on to the set drunk, and put broken glass in the director's bath-tub, none of which in her professionalism she would contemplate for one faltering second—nevertheless her career, her status, her plain commercial value, would at last be taking that longed-for leap forward from which it need never seriously retreat.

Kurtz, all this while, had been talking undeterred. "Your *guidance*, Ned," he was saying earnestly. "*Help*. We want to know this thing isn't going to blow up in our faces on the second day of shooting. Because I'll tell you this." A short strong finger was pointing at him like a pistol barrel. "Nobody in the state of Minnesota is about to be seen paying a quarter of a million dollars to a red-toothed enemy of democracy, if that's what she is, and nobody in GK is going to advise them to commit hara-kiri doing it."

To begin with, at least, Ned rallied rather well. He apologised for nothing. He reminded them, without giving the smallest ground, of his description of Charlie's childhood, and pointed out that by any normal standards she should have ended up a full-scale juvenile delinquent or—like her father—in prison. As to her politics or whatever one wished to call them, he said, in the nine years odd that he and Marjory had known her, Charlie had been a passionate opponent of apartheid—"Well, one can't fault that, can one?" (though they seemed to think one could)—a militant pacifist, a Sufist, a nuclear marcher, an anti-vivisectionist, and, until she went back to smoking again, a champion of campaigns to eliminate tobacco from theatres and on the public underground. And he had no doubt that before Charlie was finally gathered to the

Great Reaper, a whole bunch of other, equally disparate causes would attract her romantic, if brief, patronage.

"And you stood by her through all that, Ned," Kurtz marvelled in admiration. "I call that fine, Ned."

"As I would stand by any of them!" Ned rejoined with a flash of spirit. "Dash it all, she's an *actress*! Don't take her so seriously. Actors don't have *opinions*, my dear chap, still less do actresses. They have moods. Fads. Poses. Twenty-four-hour passions. There's a lot wrong with the world, dammit. Actors are absolute suckers for dramatic solutions. For all I know, by the time you get her out there, she'll be Born Again!"

"Not politically, she won't," said Litvak nastily, under his breath.

For a few moments longer, under the helpful influence of his claret, Ned continued on this bold course. A sort of giddiness overtook him. He heard the words in his head; he repeated them and felt young again and completely divorced from his own actions. He spoke of actors generally and how they were pursued by "an absolute *horror* of unreality." How on stage they acted out all the agonies of man, and off stage were hollow vessels waiting to be filled. He talked about their shyness, their smallness, their vulnerability, and their habit of disguising these weaknesses with tough-sounding and extreme causes borrowed from the adult world. He spoke of their self-obsession, and how they saw themselves on stage twenty-four hours a day—in childbirth, under the knife, in love. Then he dried, a thing that happened to him a mite too often these days. He lost his thread, he lost his bounce. The wine waiter brought the liqueur trolley. Under the cold-sober eyes of his hosts, Quilley desperately selected a Marc de Champagne and let the waiter pour a large one before he made a show of stopping him. Meanwhile Litvak had recovered sufficiently to bounce back with a good idea. Poking his long fingers inside his jacket, he drew out one of those notebooks made like a blank picture, with imitation crocodile backing and brass corners for the little sheets of paper.

"I say we start with first principles," he proposed softly, more to Kurtz than to Ned. "The *when*, the *where*, the *who with*, the *how long*." He drew a margin, presumably for dates. "Rallies she's been in. Demonstrations. Petitions, marches. Anything that has maybe caught the public eye.

When we have it all out on the table, we can make an informed assessment. Either buy the risk or get the hell out the back door. Ned, when to your knowledge was she first involved?"

"I like it," said Kurtz. "I like the method. I think it's right for Charlie too." And he managed to say this exactly as if Litvak's plan had come to him out of a clear sky, instead of being the product of hours of preparatory discussion.

So Ned told them that too. Where he could, he glossed things over; once or twice he told a small lie, but in the main he told them what he knew. He had misgivings certainly, but those came afterwards. As he put it to Marjory, at the time they just swept him along. Not that he knew very much. The anti-apartheid and anti-nuclear stuff, of course—well, that was common knowledge anyway. Then there was that Theatre of Radical Reform crowd she rode with occasionally, who had made such a damn nuisance of themselves outside the National, stopping the performances. And some people called Alternative Action in Islington, who were some kind of loony Trot splinter group, all fifteen of them. And some awful women's panel she had appeared on at St. Pancras Town Hall, dragging Marjory along in order to show her the light. And there was the time two or three years ago she had rung up in the middle of the night from Durham police station, asking for Ned to come and bail her out, after being arrested at some anti-Nazi jamboree she'd got up to.

"This the thing that made all the publicity, got her picture in the papers, Mr. Quilley?"

"No, that was Reading," said Ned. "That was later."

"So what was Durham?"

"Well, I don't know exactly. I rather forbid it as a topic, to be frank. It's just what one hears by mistake. Wasn't there some nuclear power station project up there? One forgets. One simply does forget. She's become much more moderate latterly, you know. Not half the fireball she used to pretend she was, I can assure you. Far more mature. Oh yes!"

"Pretend, Ned?" Kurtz echoed doubtfully.

"Tell us about Reading, Mr. Quilley," said Litvak. "What happened there?"

"Oh, the same sort of thing. Somebody set fire to a bus, so they all got charged for it. They were protesting against reducing services for old people, I believe. Or was it something about not taking on the darkies as conductors? The bus was empty, of course," he added hastily. "Nobody got *hurt*."

"Jesus," said Litvak, and glanced at Kurtz, whose questioning now acquired the resonance of a courtroom soap opera:

"Ned, you indicated just now that Charlie was maybe softening somewhat in her convictions. Is that what you are saying?"

"Yes, I think so. If her convictions were ever very hard, that is. It's only an impression, but old Marjory thinks so too. Sure of it—"

"Has Charlie confided such a change of heart to you, Ned?" Kurtz interrupted, rather sharp.

"I just think that once she gets a real chance like this—"

Kurtz overrode him: "To Mrs. Quilley perhaps?"

"Well, no, not really."

"Is there anybody else she might have confided in? Such as this anarchist friend she has?"

"Oh, he'd be the last to know."

"Ned, is there anybody apart from you—think carefully, please, girlfriend, boyfriend, maybe an older person, family friend—in whom Charlie *would* confide such a shift in position? *Away* from radicalism? Ned?"

"Not that I know of, no. No, I can't think of a soul. She's close in some ways. Closer than you'd think."

Then a most extraordinary thing happened. Ned later provided Marjory with an exact account of it. To escape the uncomfortable and, to Ned's ear, histrionic crossfire of their separate gazes on him, Ned had been playing with his glass, peering into it, rolling the Marc around. Sensing that Kurtz had somehow rested his case, he now glanced up, and intercepted an expression of quite evident relief in Kurtz's features that he was in the act of communicating to Litvak: his actual *pleasure* that Charlie was not after all softening in her conviction. Or, if she was, had not admitted it to anybody of note. He looked again and it had gone. But not even Marjory could afterwards persuade him it had not been there.

Litvak, the great barrister's junior, had taken over the questioning: a quicker tone to wrap the case up.

"Mr. Quilley, sir, do you hold in your agency individual office papers on all your clients? Files?"

"Well, Mrs. Ellis does, I'm sure," said Ned. "Somewhere."

"Mrs. Ellis been doing that work for long, sir?"

"My goodness, yes. She was there in my father's time."

"And what type of information does she store there? Fees—expenses—commission taken, kind of thing? Are they merely arid business papers, these files?"

"Good Lord, no, she puts everything in. Birthdays, the kind of flowers they like, restaurants. We even found an old dancing-shoe in one. Names of their kids. Dogs. Press cuttings. Any amount of stuff."

"Personal letters?"

"Yes, of course."

"In her own hand? Her own letters, going back over the years?"

Kurtz was embarrassed. His Slav eyebrows said so; they were massing in a pained line round the bridge of his nose.

"Karman, I think Mr. Quilley has given us enough of his time and experience already," he told Litvak severely. "If we need more information, Mr. Quilley will surely supply it later. Better still, if Charlie herself is prepared to talk this out with us, we can get it from her. Ned, this has been a great and memorable occasion. Thank you, sir."

But Litvak was not so easily put off. He had a young man's obstinacy: "Mr. Quilley doesn't have any secrets from *us*," he exclaimed. "Hell, Mr. Gold, I'm only asking him for what the world already knows, and what our visa people will find out in point zero five seconds on their computer. We're in a hurry with this. You know that. If there's papers, her own letters, using her own words, mitigating circumstances, evidence of a change of heart maybe, why don't we have Mr. Quilley show them to us? If he's willing. If he's not—well, that's another matter," he added, with unpleasing innuendo.

"Karman, I am quite sure Ned is willing," said Kurtz sternly, as if that were not the point at all. And shook his head as if to say he would never quite get used to young men's pushy manners these days.

The rain had stopped. They walked little Quilley between them, carefully trimming their agile pace to his own faltering tread. He was fuddled, he was aggrieved, he was afflicted with a sense of alcoholic foreboding that damp traffic fumes did nothing to dispel. What the devil do they want? he kept wondering. One minute offering Charlie the moon, the next objecting to her silly politics? And now, for reasons he had ceased to remember, they were proposing to consult the *record,* which wasn't a record at all, but a desultory collection of keepsakes, the province of an employee too elderly to be retired. Mrs. Longmore, the receptionist, watched their arrival and Ned knew at once from her disapproving face that he had done himself too well at lunch. To hell with her. Kurtz insisted that Ned go ahead of them up the stairs. From his office, while they practically held a gun to his head, he telephoned Mrs. Ellis asking her to bring Charlie's papers to the waiting-room and leave them there.

"Shall we knock on your door when we're through, Mr. Quilley?" Litvak asked, like someone about to deliver a child.

The last he saw of them both, they were seated at the rosewood drum table in the waiting-room, surrounded by about six of Mrs. Ellis's foul brown boxes that looked as though they had been rescued from the blitz. Like a pair of tax collectors they were, poring over the same set of suspect figures, pencil and paper at their elbows, and Gold, the broad one, with his jacket off and that scruffy watch of his set on the table beside him as if he were timing himself while he made his beastly calculations. After that, Quilley must have dozed off for a bit. He woke with a jolt at five to find the waiting-room empty. And when he buzzed Mrs. Longmore, she replied pointedly that his guests had not wished to disturb him.

Ned did not tell Marjory at once. "Oh, *them,*" he said when she asked him that same evening. "Just a pair of dreary package artists, I'm afraid, on their way to Munich. Nothing to worry about *there.*"

"Jew-boys?"

"Yes—well, yes, Jewish, I suppose. Very, in fact." Marjory nodded as if she'd known as much all along. "But I mean jolly *nice* ones," said Ned a bit hopelessly.

Marjory was a prison visitor in her off-hours and Ned's deceptions held no mystery for her. But she bided her time. Bill Lochheim was Ned's correspondent in New York, his only American buddy. Next afternoon Ned rang him. Old Loch hadn't heard of them but he duly reported back what Ned already knew: GK were new in the field, had some backing, but independents were a drug on the market these days. Quilley didn't like the tone of old Loch's voice. He sounded as if he'd been put upon somehow—not by Quilley, who had never put upon anyone in his life, but by someone else, some third party he'd consulted. Quilley even had the queer feeling that he and old Loch might, in some strange way, be in the same boat. With amazing bravura, Ned rang GK's New York number on a pretext. The place turned out to be a holding address for out-of-town companies: no information available on clients. Now Ned could think of nothing except his two visitors and the luncheon. He wished to God he had shown them the door. He rang the Munich hotel they had mentioned and got a stuffy manager. Herr Gold and Herr Karman had stayed one night but left early the next morning unexpectedly on business, he said sourly—so why did he say it at all? Always too much information, thought Ned. Or too little. And the same hint of chaps doing things against their better judgment. A German producer whom Kurtz had mentioned said that they were "good people, very respectable, oh *very* good." But when Ned asked whether they had been in Munich recently and what projects they were associated with, the producer grew hostile and practically hung up on him.

There remained Ned's professional colleagues in the agency business. Ned consulted them reluctantly and with tremendous casualness, spreading his enquiries wide, and drawing blanks everywhere.

"Met two *awfully* nice Americans the other day," he confided finally to Herb Nolan, of Lomax Stars, pausing at Herb's table at the Garrick. "Over here bargain-hunting for some high-flyin' TV series they're putting together. Gold and something. Come your way at all?"

Nolan laughed. "It was me who sent 'em to you, old boy. Asked after a couple of *my* horrors, then wanted to know all about your Charlie. Whether I thought she could go the distance. I told 'em, Ned. I told 'em!"

"What did you tell them?"

" 'More likely she'll blow us all sky high,' I said! What?"

Depressed by the poor level of Herb Nolan's humour,

Ned enquired no further. But the same night, after Marjory had extracted his inevitable confession, he went on to share his anxieties with her.

"They were in such a damned hurry," he said. "They had too much energy, even for Americans. Went at me like a pair of bloody policemen. First one chap, then the other. Pair of bloody terriers," he added, changing his simile. "I keep thinking I should go to the authorities," he said.

"But, darling," Marjory replied at last. "By the sound of it, I'm afraid they *were* the authorities."

"I'm going to write to her," Ned declared, with great decisiveness. "I've a jolly good mind to write and warn her, just in case. She could be in trouble."

But even if he had done so, he would have been too late. It was not forty-eight hours later that Charlie set sail for Athens to keep her tryst with Joseph.

So once again it was done; on the face of it, a mere sideshow compared with the main thrust of the operation; and a dreadfully risky one at that, as Kurtz was the first to agree when, the same night, he modestly reported his triumph to Misha Gavron. Yet what else could we have done, Misha—tell me that? Where else was such a precious store of correspondence, ranging over so long a period, to be obtained? They had hunted for other recipients of Charlie's letters—boyfriends, girlfriends, her bloody mother, a former schoolmistress; they had posed, in a couple of places, as a commercial company interested in acquiring the manuscripts and autographs of tomorrow's great. Till Kurtz, with Gavron's grudging consent, had had the whole thing stopped. Better one big strike, he had decreed, than so many dangerous small ones.

Besides, Kurtz needed the intangibles. He needed to feel the warmth and texture of his quarry. Who better than Quilley, therefore, with his long and innocent experience of her, to supply them? Thus Kurtz punched it through with his will. Having done so, he flew next morning to Munich, as he had told Quilley he would, even if the production he was concerned with was not of the type he had led him to suppose. He visited his two safe flats; he breathed fresh encouragement into his men. In addition to this, he contrived a congenial meeting with the good Dr. Alexis: another long luncheon at which they discussed almost nothing of importance—but then what do old friends need but one another?

And from Munich, Kurtz flew on to Athens, continuing his southward march.

5

The boat was two hours late arriving in Piraeus, and if Joseph had not already pocketed her air ticket Charlie might well have stood him up then and there. Though again she mightn't, for under her scatty exterior she was cursed with a dependability of character that was often wasted on the company she kept. For one thing, she'd had too much time to think, and though she had by now convinced herself that the spectral observer of Nottingham, York, and East London was either a different man or no man at all, there was still an unsettling voice inside her that would not be talked down. For another thing, declaring her plans to the family had not been half as easy as Joseph had made out it was going to be. Lucy had wept and pressed money on her—"My last five hundred drachs, Chas, all for you." Willy and Pauly, drunk, had gone down on their knees on the dockside before an estimated audience of thousands—"Chas, Chas, how can you do this to us?"—and to escape, she'd had to fight her way through a grinning throng, then run the length of the road with the strap of her shoulder bag broken, her guitar flapping under her other arm, and foolish tears of remorse flooding her face. She was saved by, of all people, the flaxen hippy boy from Mykonos, who must have crossed on the boat with them, though she hadn't seen him. Passing by in a taxi, he scooped her up and dumped her fifty yards from her destination. He was Swedish and his name was Raoul, he said. His father was in Athens on a business trip; Raoul hoped to hit him for some bread. She was a little surprised to find him quite so lucid, and he never mentioned Jesus once.

The Diogenes restaurant had a blue awning. A cardboard chef beckoned her in.

Sorry, Jose, wrong time, wrong place. Sorry, Jose, it was a great fantasy but the holiday's over and Chas is for the smoke, so I'll just take back that ticket and blow.

Or perhaps she would choose the easier way and say she'd been offered a part.

Feeling a slut in her worn jeans and scuffed boots, she banged her way between the pavement tables until she came to the interior door. Anyway, he'll be gone, she told herself—who waits two hours for a lay these days?—ticket with the concierge next door. Maybe that will teach me to go chasing mid-European beach bums through Athens by night, she thought. To compound her problems, Lucy had last night pressed on her some more of her wretched pills, which had first lit her up like a light-bulb and afterwards dropped her down a dark hole from which she was still trying to emerge. Charlie didn't use those things as a rule, but dangling between two lovers, as she had begun to think of it, had made her vulnerable.

She was about to enter the restaurant when two Greek men burst out laughing at her broken shoulder bag. She strode over to them and cursed them in a fury, calling them sexist pigs. Trembling, she shoved the door with her foot and stepped inside. The air turned cool, the babble of the pavement stopped, she was standing in a twilit, panelled restaurant, and there in his own bit of darkness sat Saint Joseph of the Island, creep and well-known author of all her guilt and disorder, with a Greek coffee at his elbow and a paperback book open in front of him.

Just don't touch me, she warned him in her mind, as he came towards her. Just don't take one finger of me for granted. I'm tired and famished, I'm liable to bite, and I've given up sex for the next two hundred years.

But the most he took of her was her guitar and her broken shoulder bag. And the most he gave her was a swift, practical handshake from the other side of the Atlantic. So that all she could think of to say was "You're wearing a silk shirt." Which he was, a cream one with gold cuff-links big as bottle tops. "Christ, Jose, look at you!" she exclaimed as she took in the rest of his hardware. "Gold bracelet, gold watch—I can't even turn my back and you find yourself a rich protectress!" All of which spilled out of her in a part-hysterical, part-aggressive tone, with the instinctive aim, perhaps, of making him feel as uncomfortable about his appearance as she felt about her own. So what do I expect him to be wearing? she asked herself in a fury—his monk's bloody bathing pants and his water-bottle?

But Joseph let it all go past him anyway.

"Charlie. Hullo. The boat was late. Poor you. Never mind. You are here." That at least was Joseph—no triumph, no surprise, just a grave Biblical greeting and a nod of command to the waiter. "A wash first or a whisky? The ladies' room is over there."

"Whisky," she said, and slumped into a chair opposite him.

It was a good place, she knew it immediately. The kind of place the Greeks keep for themselves.

"Oh, and before I forget—" He was reaching behind him.

Forget what? she thought, head in hands, staring at him. Come on, Jose. You never forgot anything in your life. From under the bench Joseph had spirited a woollen Greek bag, a very lurid one, which he presented to her with an ostentatious avoidance of ceremony.

"Since we are stepping into the world together, here is your escape kit. Inside, you will find your air ticket from Thessalonika to London, still reversible if you wish; also the means for you to shop, run away, or simply change your mind. Was it difficult getting away from your friends? I am sure it was. One hates to deceive people, but most of all the people one cares for."

He spoke as if he knew all about deception. Practised it every day with regret.

"No parachute," she complained, peering into the bag. "Thanks, Jose." She said it a second time. "That's stylish. Thanks a lot." But she had the feeling of not believing herself any more. Must be Lucy's pills, she thought. Steamer-lag.

"So what about a lobster? In Mykonos you said lobster was your favourite food. Was that true? The chef is keeping one for you and he will kill it instantly at your command. Why not?"

Her chin still resting in her palm, Charlie let her humour get the better of her. With a weary smile, she raised her other fist and gave a Caesar's thumbs-down, commanding that the lobster die.

"Tell them I want it done with minimum force," she said. Then she took hold of one of his hands and squeezed it in both of hers in order to apologise for her glooms. He smiled and left his hand with her to play with. It was a beautiful hand, with slim, hard fingers and very strong muscles.

"And the wine you like," said Joseph. "Boutaris, white and cold. Isn't that what you used to say?"

Yes, she thought, watching his hand make its solitary journey back across the table. That is what I used to say. Ten years ago when we met on that quaint little Greek island.

"And after dinner, as your personal Mephistopheles, I shall take you up a high hill and show you the second-best place in the world. You agree? A mystery tour?"

"I want the best," she said, drinking her Scotch.

"And I never award first prizes," he replied placidly.

Get me out of here! she thought. Sack the writer! Get a new script! She tried a party gambit straight out of Rickmansworth.

"So what did you get up to these last days, Jose? Apart from pining for me, naturally."

He did not quite answer. Instead, he asked her about her own waiting, about the journey, and the gang. He smiled when she told him about the providential lift in the taxi from the hippy boy who didn't mention Jesus; he wanted to know whether she had news of Alastair and was politely disappointed to hear that she had not. "Oh, he *never* writes," she said, with a careless laugh. He asked her what film part she thought he might be offered; she guessed a spaghetti Western and he found this funny: it was not an expression he had heard before, and insisted on having it explained to him. By the time she had finished her Scotch, she began to feel she might be attractive to him after all. Talking to him of Al, she was impressed to hear herself making room for a new man in her life.

"Anyway, I just hope he *is* successful, that's all," she said, implying that success might compensate him for other disappointments.

But even while she made this progress towards him she was assailed yet again by her sense of wrongness. It was a feeling she had on stage sometimes, when a scene was not playing: that events were happening singly and in wooden succession; that the line of dialogue was too thin, too straight. *Now,* she thought. Fishing in her shoulder bag, she produced an olive-wood box and handed it to him across the table. He took it because it was offered but did not at once recognise it as a gift, and to her amusement she detected a moment of anxiety, even suspicion in his face, as if some unexpected factor threatened to upset his plans.

"You're supposed to open it," she explained.

"But what is it?" Clowning for her, he gently shook it, then put it to his ear. "Shall I order a bucket of water?" he asked. Sighing as if no good would come of it, he lifted the lid and contemplated the twists of tissue paper nestling inside. "Charlie. What is this? I am completely confused. I insist you take them straight back to where you found them."

"Go on. Unwrap one."

He held up a hand; she watched it hover as if over her own body, then descend on the first package, which was the big pink shell she had saved from the beach on the day he left the island. Solemnly he laid it on the table and took out the next offering, a carved Greek donkey made in Taiwan, bought from the souvenir shop, with "Joseph" hand-painted by herself on the rump. Holding it in both hands, he turned it over and over while he studied it.

"It's a boy," she said. But she could not shift the earnestness of his expression. "And that's me sulking," she explained as he lifted out the framed colour photograph taken on Robert's Polaroid of Charlie in rear view, wearing her straw hat and kaftan. "I had a rage on and wouldn't pose. I thought you'd appreciate it."

His gratitude had a note of sober afterthought that chilled her. Thank you but no, he seemed to be saying; thank you but another time. Not Pauly, not Lucy, and not you either. She hesitated, then said it—kindly and gently, straight into his face. "Jose, we don't have to go on with this, you know. I can still hoof it to the plane, if that's what you'd prefer. I just didn't want you to—"

"To what?"

"I didn't want to hold you to a rash promise. That's all."

"It was not rash. It was most seriously meant."

Now it was his turn. He produced a wad of travel brochures. Unbidden, she moved round and sat beside him, her left arm thrown carelessly over his shoulder so that they could study them together. His shoulder was as hard as a cliff and about as intimate, but she left her arm there. Delphi, Jose: gosh, super. Her hair was against his cheek. She had washed it for him last night. Olympus: terrific. Meteora: never heard of it. Their foreheads were touching. Thessalonika: wow. The hotels they would stay at, all planned, all booked. She kissed his cheekbone, just beside the eye, a casual peck bestowed upon a passing target. He smiled and gave her hand an avuncular squeeze, till she almost ceased to wonder what it was in him, or in her, that gave him the right to take her over without a fight, without even a surrender; or where the recognition came from—the "Charlie, yes, hullo"—that had turned their first meeting into a reunion of old friends and this one into a conference about their honeymoon.

Forget it, she thought. "You never wear a red blazer, do you, Jose?" she asked before she had even considered the question. "Wine-coloured, brass buttons, a breath of the twenties about the cut?"

His head slowly lifted; he turned and returned her stare. "Is that a joke?"

"No. It's a straight question."

"A red blazer? But why on earth should I? Do you want me to support your football team or something?"

"You'd look good in one. That's all." He was still waiting for her explanation. "It's just the way I see people sometimes," she said, beginning to fight her way out. "Theatrically. In my mind. You don't know actresses, do you? I put makeup on people—beards—all sorts of things. You'd be amazed. I dress them up too. Plus-fours. Uniform. All in my imagination. It's habit."

"Do you want me to grow a beard for you, you mean?"

"If I do, I'll let you know."

He smiled, she smiled back—another meeting across the footlights—his gaze released her and she took herself off to the ladies' room, raging at her own face in the mirror while she tried to work him out. No wonder he's got bloody bulletholes, she thought. Women did it.

They had eaten, they had talked with the earnestness of strangers, he had paid the bill from a crocodile-skin wallet that must have cost half the national debt of whatever country owned him.

"Are you getting me on expenses, Jose?" she asked as she watched him fold and pocket the receipt.

The question went unanswered, for suddenly, thank God, his familiar administrative genius had taken charge and they were frightfully short of time.

"Please look out for an exhausted green Opel with dented wings and a ten-year-old driver," he told her as he hurried her down a cramped kitchen passage, her luggage across his arms.

"Right-*ho*," she said.

It was waiting at the side entrance, dented wings as he had promised. The driver took her luggage from him and put it in the boot, fast. He was freckled and blond and healthy-looking with a big, buckwheat grin, and yes, he looked if not ten then fifteen at most. The hot night was shedding its habitual slow rain.

"Charlie, meet Dimitri," said Joseph as he ushered her into the back seat. "His mother has given him permission to stay up late tonight. Dimitri, kindly take us to the second-best place in the world." He had slipped in beside her. The car started immediately, and with it his facetious tour-guide monologue. "So, Charlie, here we have the home of modern Greek democracy, Constitution Square; note the many democrats enjoying their outdoor freedom in the restaurants. Now on the left you see the Olympieion and Hadrian's Gate. I must warn you, however, before you get ideas, that it is a different Hadrian from the one who built your famous wall. The Athens version is a more fanciful man, don't you agree? More artistic, I would say."

"Oh, much," she said.

Come alive, she told herself angrily. Snap out of it. It's a free ride, it's a new gorgeous man, it's Ancient Greece and it's called *fun*. They were slowing down. She glimpsed ruins to her right, but the high bushes hid them again. They reached a roundabout, rolled slowly up a paved hill, and stopped. Springing out, Joseph opened her door for her, grasped her hand, and led her swiftly, almost conspiratorially, to a narrow stone stairway between overhanging trees.

"We speak only in whispers, and even then in the most elaborate code," he warned her in a stage murmur, and she said something equally meaningless in reply.

His grasp was like a charge of electricity. Her fingers

seemed to burn at his touch. They were following a wood path, now paved, now dry earth, but climbing all the time. The moon had vanished and it was very dark, but Joseph darted ahead of her unerringly, as if it were by daylight. Once they crossed a stone staircase, once a much wider path, but the easier ways were not for him. The trees broke, and to her right she saw the city lights already far below her. To her left, still high above, a kind of mountain crag stood black against the orange skyline. She heard footsteps behind her and laughter, but it was just a couple of kids having a joke.

"You don't mind the walk?" he asked, without relaxing his speed.

"Enormously," she replied.

A Joseph pause.

"You want me to carry you?"

"Yes."

"Unfortunately, I have pulled a muscle in my back."

"I saw," she said, grasping his hand more tightly.

She looked right again and made out what looked like the ruins of an old English mill, one arched window stacked upon another, and the lighted city behind them. She glanced left, and the mountain crag had become the black rectangular outline of a building with what might have been a chimney poking from one end. Then they were in the trees again, with the deafening clatter of the cicadas and a smell of pine strong enough to make her eyes tingle.

"It's a tent," she whispered, momentarily drawing him to a halt. "Right? Sex on the South Col. How did you guess my secret appetites?"

But he was striding strongly ahead of her. She was breathless but she could go all day when she felt like it, so her breathlessness came from something else. They had joined a wide path. Before them two grey figures in uniform were standing guard over a small stone hut on which a light-bulb burned inside a wire cage. Joseph went forward to them and she heard the responsive murmur of their greeting. The hut stood between two iron gates. Behind one lay the city again, now a distant blaze of busy lights; but behind the other lay only pitch darkness, and it was to the darkness that they were about to be admitted, for she heard the clank of keys and the creak of iron as the gate swung slowly on its hinges.

For a moment, the panic got her. What am I doing here? Where am I? Bolt, nitwit, bolt. The men were officials or policemen and she guessed by their sheepishness that Joseph had bribed them. They all looked at their watches, and as he raised his wrist she saw the glint of his flashy cream shirt and cuff-links. Now Joseph was beckoning her forward. She peered back and saw two girls standing below her on the path, looking up. He was calling to her. She started for the open gate. She felt the policemen's eyes undress her and it occurred to her that Joseph had not yet looked at her that way; he had not supplied the crude evidence of wanting her. In her uncertainty she wished urgently that he would.

The gate shut behind her. There were steps, and after the steps a path of slippery rock. She heard him warning her to take care. She would have put her arm around him, but he manoeuvred her ahead of him saying her view must not be hampered by his own bulk. So it's a view, she thought. The second-best view in the world. The rock must have been marble, for it shone even in the darkness and her leather soles slipped on it perilously. Once she almost fell, but his hand caught her with a speed and strength that made Al's puny. Once she squeezed her arm to her side, making his knuckles press against her breast. Feel, she told him desperately in her mind. It's mine, the first of two; the left one is marginally more erogenous than the right, but who's counting? The path zigzagged, the darkness grew thinner and felt hot to her, as if it had retained the day's sun. Below her, through the trees, the city fell away like a departing planet; above her she was aware only of a jagged blackness of towers and scaffolding. The rumbling of the traffic died, leaving the night to the cicadas.

"Walk slowly now, please."

She knew by his tone that whatever it was, it was near. The path zigzagged again; they came to a wooden staircase. Steps, a flat stretch, then steps again. Joseph walked lightly here, and she copied his example, so that once again their stealth united them. Side by side they passed through a vast gateway, of which the sheer scale made her lift her head. As she did so, she saw a red half moon slip down from among the stars and take its place among the pillars of the Parthenon.

She whispered. "God." She felt inadequate and, for a second, utterly lonely. She walked forward slowly, like someone advancing on a mirage, waiting for it to turn to nothing, but it didn't. She walked the length of it, looking for a place to climb aboard, but at the first staircase a prim notice said "ASCENT IS NOT ALLOWED." Suddenly, for no clear reason, she was running. She was running heaven-bent between the boulders, making for the dark edge of this unearthly city, only half aware that Joseph in his silk shirt was jogging effortlessly at her side. She was laughing and talking at the same time; she was saying the things that she was told she said in bed— whatever came into her mind. She had the feeling she could escape her body and run into the sky without falling. Slowing to a walk, she reached the parapet and flopped over it, gazing downward into the lighted island ringed with the black oceans of the Attic plain. She looked back and saw him watching her from a few paces off.

"Thank you," she said at last.

Going over to him, she grasped his head in both hands and kissed him on the mouth, a five-year kiss, first without the tongue, then with it, tilting his head this way and that and inspecting his face between whiles, as if to measure the effect of her work, and this time they held each other long enough for her to know: absolutely yes, it works.

"Thanks, Jose," she repeated, only to feel him pulling back. His head slipped from her grasp, his hands unlocked her arms and returned them to her side. He had left her, amazingly, with nothing.

Mystified and nearly angry, she stared at his motionless sentinel's face in the moonlight. In her time, she reckoned she had known them all. The closet gays who bluffed until they wept. The too-old virgins haunted by imagined clouds of impotence. The would-be Don Juans and fabled studs who withdrew from the brink in a fit of timidity or conscience. And there had been enough honest tenderness in her, as a rule, to turn mother or sister or the other thing and make a bond with any one of them. But in Joseph, as she gazed into the shadowed sockets of his eyes, she sensed a reluctance she had never met before. It was not that he lacked desire, not that he lacked capacity. She was too old a trouper to mistake the tension and confidence of his embrace. Rather it was as though his aim lay out beyond her somewhere, and by withholding himself he were trying to tell her so.

"Shall I thank you again?" she asked.

For a moment longer he remained gazing at her in the silence. Then he lifted his wrist and looked at his gold watch by the moonlight.

"I think actually, since we have too little time already, I should show you some of the temples here. You allow me to bore you?"

In the extraordinary hiatus that had risen between them, he was counting on her to support his vow of abstinence.

"Jose, I want the lot," she declared, flinging an arm through his and bearing him off as if he were a trophy. "Who built it, how much did it cost, what did they worship, and did it work? You can bore me till life us do part."

It never occurred to her he wouldn't have the answers, and she was right. He lectured her, she listened; he walked her sedately from temple to temple, she followed, holding his arm, thinking: I'll be your sister, your pupil, your anything. I'll hold you up and say it was all you, I'll lay you down and say it was all me, I'll get that smile out of you if it kills me.

"No, Charlie," he replied gravely, "Propylaea was not a goddess, but the gateway to a sanctuary. The word came from propylon; the Greeks used the plural form to give distinction to the holy places."

"Learn it up specially for us, Jose, did you?"

"Of course. All for you. Why not?"

"I could do that. Mind like a sponge, me. You'd be amazed. One peek at the books, I'd be your instant expert."

He stopped; she stopped with him.

"Then repeat it to me," he said.

She didn't believe him at first, she suspected he was teasing her. Then, grasping him by the arms, she turned him sharply round and marched him back over the course while she repeated to him everything he had told her.

"Will I do?" They were at the end again. "Do I get second-best prize?"

She waited for another of his famous three-minute warnings: "It is not the *shrine* of Agrippa, it is the *monument*. Apart from this one small error, I would say you were word perfect. Felicitations."

At the same moment, from far below them, she heard a car hooting, three deliberate blasts, and she knew the sound was meant for him, for he at once lifted his head and considered it, like an animal scenting the wind, before yet again looking at his watch. The coach has turned into a pumpkin, she thought; time good children were in bed and telling one another what the hell they're all about.

They had already started down the hill when Joseph paused to gaze into the melancholy Theatre of Dionysos, an empty bowl lit only by the moon and the stray beams of distant lights. It's a last look, she thought in bewilderment as she watched his motionless black shape against the lights of the city.

"I read somewhere that no true drama can ever be a private statement," he remarked. "Novels, poems, yes. But not drama. Drama must have an application to reality. Drama must be useful. Do you believe that?"

"In Burton-on-Trent Women's Institute?" she replied, with a laugh. "Playing Helen of Troy at pensioners' Saturday matinées?"

"I'm serious. Tell me what you think."

"About theatre?"

"About its uses."

She felt disconcerted by his earnestness. Too much was hanging on her answer.

"Well, I agree," she said awkwardly. "Theatre *should* be useful. It *should* make people share and feel. It should—well, waken people's awareness."

"Be real, therefore? You are sure?"

"Sure I'm sure."

"Well, then," he said, as if in that case she shouldn't blame him.

"Well, then," she echoed gaily.

We are mad, she decided. Barking, certifiable loonies, the pair of us. The policeman saluted them on their way down to earth.

She thought at first he was playing a bad joke on her. Except for the Mercedes, the road was empty and the Mercedes stood all alone in it. On a bench not far from it a couple sat necking; otherwise there was nobody around. Its colour was dark but not black. It was parked close to the grass bank and the front number plate was not visible. She had liked Mercedes all her driving life, and she could tell by its solidity that this one was coach-built, and by its trim and aerials that it was someone's special toy with all the extras. He had taken her arm and it was not till they were almost alongside the driver's door that she realised he was proposing to open it. She saw him slip a key into the keyhole, and the buttons of all four locks pop up at once, and the next thing she knew he was leading her round to the passenger door while she asked him what the hell was going on.

"Don't you care for it?" he asked, with an airy lightness that she immediately suspected. "Shall I order a different one? I thought you had a weakness for fine cars."

"You mean you've hired it?"

"Not strictly. It has been lent to us for our journey."

He was holding the door open. She didn't get in.

"Lent who by?"

"A kind friend."

"What's his name?"

"Charlie, don't be utterly ridiculous. Herbert. Karl. What difference does a name make? Would you prefer the egalitarian discomforts of a Greek Fiat?"

"Where's my luggage?"

"In the boot. Dimitri put it there on my instructions. Do you want to take a look and reassure yourself?"

"I'm not going in this thing, it's crazy."

She got in nevertheless, and in no time he was sitting next to her, starting the engine. He was wearing driving gloves. Black leather ones with airholes in the back. He must have had them in his pocket and put them on as he got in. The gold round his wrists was very bright against them. He drove fast and skilfully. She didn't like that either—that wasn't how you drove friends' cars. Her door was locked. He had relocked them all with his central locking switch. He had turned on the radio and it was playing plaintive Greek music.

"How do I open this bloody window?" she said.

He pressed a button and the warm night wind washed over her, bringing the scent of resin. But he only let the window down a couple of inches.

"Do this often, do we?" she asked loudly. "One of our

little things, is it? Taking ladies to unknown destinations at twice the speed of sound?"

No answer. He was gazing intently ahead of him. Who is he? Oh my dear soul—as her bloody mother would say—who is he? The car filled with light. She swung round and saw through the rear window a pair of headlamps about a hundred yards behind them, neither gaining nor losing.

"They ours or theirs?" she asked.

She was actually settling down again when she realised what else had caught her eye. A red blazer, lying along the back seat, brass buttons like the brass buttons in Nottingham and York: and, she wouldn't mind betting, a breath of the twenties about the cut.

She asked him for a cigarette.

"Why don't you look in the compartment?" he said, without turning his head. She pulled it open and saw a packet of Marlboros. A silk scarf lay beside them and a pair of expensive Polaroid sunglasses. She took out the scarf and sniffed it, and it smelt of men's toilet water. She helped herself to a cigarette. With his gloved hand, Joseph passed her the glowing lighter from the dashboard.

"Your chum a snappy dresser, is he?"

"Quite. Yes, he is. Why do you ask?"

"That his red blazer there on the back seat, or yours?"

He glanced swiftly at her as if impressed, then returned his eyes to the road.

"Let us say it is his but I have borrowed it," he replied calmly as the car's speed increased.

"You borrow his sunglasses too, did you? I should think you bloody well needed them, sitting right up by the footlights like that. Nearly joined the cast. Your name's Richthoven, right?"

"Right."

"First name Peter but you prefer Joseph. Living in Vienna, trading a little, studying a little." She paused but he said nothing. "In a box," she persisted. "Number seven-six-two, main post office. Right?"

She saw his head nod slightly in approval of her memory. The needle of the speedometer had climbed to 130 kilometres.

"Nationality undeclared, a sensitive mongrel," she went

on breezily. "You've got three babies and two wives. All in a box."

"No wives, no babies."

"Never? Or none extant at the time of speaking?"

"None extant."

"Don't think I mind, Jose. I'd positively welcome it, actually. Anything to define you just now. Anything at all. That's how girls are—nosey."

She realised she was still holding the scarf. She tossed it into the compartment and shut the door with a bang. The road was straight but very narrow, the needle had reached 140 kilometres, she could feel the panic forming inside her and battling with her artificial calm.

"Mind telling us some good news, would you? Something to put a person at her ease?"

"The good news is that I have lied to you as little as possible and that in a short time from now you will understand the many good reasons for your being with us."

"Who's *us*?" she said sharply.

Till then he had been a loner. She didn't like the change at all. They were heading for a main road, but he was not slowing down. She saw the lights of two cars descending on them, then held her breath as he pressed the kickdown and footbrake together and tucked the Mercedes neatly in front of them, fast enough to allow the car behind to do the same.

"It's not *guns*, is it?" she enquired, thinking suddenly of his scars. "Not running a small war on the side somewhere, are we? Only I can't stand bangs, you see. I've got these delicate eardrums." Her voice, with its forced jauntiness, was becoming unfamiliar to her.

"No, Charlie, it is not gunrunning."

" 'No, Charlie, it is not gunrunning.' White-slave traffic?"

"No, it's not white-slave traffic either."

She echoed that line too.

"That leaves drugs then, doesn't it? Because you are trading in *something*, aren't you? Only drugs aren't my scene either, to be frank. Long Al makes me carry his hash for him when we go through Customs and I'm a mess for days afterwards just from the nerves." No answer. "It's higher, is it? Nobler? A different plane entirely?" She reached out and switched off the radio. "How about your just stopping the car, actually? You needn't take me anywhere. You can go back to Mykonos tomorrow if you like and collect my understudy."

"And leave you in the middle of nowhere? Don't be utterly absurd."

"Do it now!" she screamed. "*Stop the bloody car!*"

They had jumped a set of traffic lights and swung left, so violently that her seat belt locked and punched the breath out of her. She made a lunge for the wheel but his forearm was there long before she was. He swung left a second time, through a white gateway into a private drive lined with azaleas and hibiscus. The drive made a curve and they flew round it, ploughing to a halt in a gravel sweep ringed with white-painted stones. The second car was pulling up behind them, blocking the way out. She heard footsteps on the gravel. The house was an old villa covered in red flowers. In the beam of the headlamps the flowers looked like patches of fresh blood. One pale light burned in the porch. Joseph switched off the engine and pocketed the ignition key. Leaning across Charlie, he shoved open her door for her, admitting her to the rancid smell of hydrangeas and the familiar chatter of cicadas. He got out but Charlie stayed in her seat. There was no breeze, no other sensation of fresh air, no sound but the delicate shuffle of young lightfooted people gathering round the car. Dimitri, the ten-year-old driver with the buckwheat smile. Raoul, the flaxen Jesus-freak who rode in taxis and had a rich Swedish daddy. Two girls in jeans and jackets, the same pair who had followed them up the Acropolis and—now that she saw them more clearly—the same pair she had seen slouching around Mykonos a couple of times when she had gone window-shopping. Hearing the thud of someone unloading luggage from the boot, she leapt furiously from the car. "My guitar!" she shouted. "You leave that alone, you—"

But Raoul already held it under his arm, and her shoulder bag was in the charge of Dimitri. She was about to spring for it when the two girls each took hold of a wrist and elbow, and without effort led her towards the front porch.

"Where's that bastard Joseph?" she yelled.

But the bastard Joseph, his mission accomplished, was already halfway up the steps and not looking back, like someone escaping from an accident. Passing the car, Charlie saw by the porch light the markings on the rear licence plate. It was not a Greek registration at all. It was Arab, with Hollywood-style writing round the number, and a plastic "CD" for "Corps Diplomatique" stuck on the lid of the boot just to the left of the Mercedes emblem.

6

The two girls had shown her to the lavatory and stayed with her unembarrassed while she used it. One blonde, one brunette, both scruffy, both under orders to show kindness to the new girl. They wore soft-soled shoes, their shirts hung loose of their jeans, they had twice subdued her effortlessly when she flew at them, and when she cursed them they had smiled at her with the distant sweetness of the deaf.

"I'm Rachel," the brunette confided breathlessly, during a brief truce. "This one's Rose. Rachel—Rose, got it? We're the two 'R's.'"

Rachel was the comely one. She had a pert North Country accent and merry eyes, and it was Rachel's backside that had stopped Yanuka on the border. Rose was tall and wiry with crinkled fair hair and the trimness of an athlete, but when she opened her hands, her palms were like axeheads on her thin wrists.

"You'll be all right, Charlie, don't you worry," Rose assured her, in a dried-out accent that could have been South African.

"I was all right before," said Charlie as she took another vain heave at them.

From the lavatory they led her to a ground-floor bedroom and gave her a comb and hairbrush and a glass of slimming tea, no milk, and she sat on the bed sipping it and blaspheming in a tremulous fury while she tried to get her breathing right. " 'PENNILESS ACTRESS HELD,' " she muttered. "What's the ransom, girls? My overdraft?" But they only smiled at her more fondly, hovering to either side of her with their arms loose, waiting to walk her up the big staircase. Arriving at the first landing, she lashed out at them again, this time with her clenched fist, in a swinging furious sweep of the whole arm, only to find herself laid gently on her back gazing upward at the stained-glass canopy of the stairwell, which caught the moonlight like a prism and broke it into a mosaic of pale gold and pink. "I just wanted to bust your nose for you," she explained to Rachel, but Rachel's response was a gaze of radiant understanding.

The house was ancient and smelt of cat and her bloody mother. It was crammed with bad Greek furniture in the Empire style and hung with faded velvet curtains and brass chandeliers. But if it had been clean as a Swiss hospital or sloping like a ship's deck, it would only have been a different madness, not a better or worse one. On the second landing, a cracked jardinière reminded her yet again of her mother: she saw herself as a small child seated at her mother's side wearing corduroy dungarees and shelling peas in a conservatory overhung with monkey-puzzle trees. Yet for the life of her she couldn't remember then or afterwards a house possessed of a conservatory, unless it was the first they ever had, in Branksome, near Bournemouth, when Charlie was aged three.

They approached a double door, Rachel pushed it and stood aside, and a cavernous upper room was opened to her. At the centre of it sat two figures at a table, one broad and big, one stooping and very thin, both dressed in cloudy browns and greys, and from that distance phantoms. On the table she saw papers strewn, to which a downlight from the centre of the ceiling gave disproportionate prominence, and already from some way off they looked to her like press cuttings. Rose and Rachel had fallen back as if unworthy. Rachel gave her a shove on the rump and said, "On you go then," and Charlie found herself making the last twenty feet alone, feeling like an ugly clockwork mouse that has been wound up and set to run by itself. Throw a fit, she thought. Clutch my stomach, fake appendicitis. Scream. Her entrance was the cue for the two men to bound simultaneously to their feet. The thin man remained standing at the table, but the big man strode boldly up to her and his right hand curved in on her in a crab-like gesture, seizing her own and shaking it before she could prevent him.

"Charlie, we are surely glad to have you safely here among us!" Kurtz exclaimed in a swift congratulatory flow, as if she had risked fire and flood to get to them. "Charlie, *my* name"—her hand was still in his powerful grasp, and the intimacy of their two skins was contrary to everything she had expected—"*my* name for want of a better is Marty and when God finished making *me* there were a couple of spare

pieces left around so He put together Mike here as an afterthought, so say hullo to Mike. Mr. Richthoven over there, to
use his flag of convenience—Joseph, as you call him—well, I
guess you practically christened him yourself anyway, didn't
you?"

He must have entered the room without her noticing.
Peering round, she found him on the point of arranging some
papers on a small folding table set apart from everyone. On
the table stood a personal reading lamp, of which the candle-
like glow touched his face as he leaned across it.

"I could christen the bastard now," she said.

She thought of going for him as she had for Rachel,
three quick strides and one good swipe before they stopped
her, but she knew she'd never make it, so she contented herself with a volley of obscenities instead, to which Joseph listened with an air of distant recollection. He had changed into
a brown lightweight pullover; the bandleader's silk shirt, the
bottle-top gold cuff-links were gone as if for ever.

"My advice to you is to suspend your judgment and
your bad language until you hear what these two men have
to tell you," he said, without lifting his head to her, while he
continued setting out his bulletins. "You are with good people
here. Better than you are accustomed to, I would say. You
have much to learn and, if you are lucky, much to do. Con-
serve your energy," he advised, in what sounded like a distracted private memo to himself. And continued to busy
himself with his papers.

He doesn't care, she thought bitterly. He's put down his
burden and the burden was me. The two men at the table
were still standing, waiting for her to sit, which was a
madness in itself. Madness to be polite to a girl you have just
kidnapped, madness to lecture her on goodness, madness to
sit down to a conference with your abductors after you have
had a nice cup of tea and fixed your make-up. She sat down
nevertheless. Kurtz and Litvak did the same.

"Who's got the cards?" she blurted facetiously as she
punched away a stray tear with her knuckles. She noticed a
scuffed brown briefcase on the floor between them, its mouth
open, but not wide enough to see inside. And yes, the papers
on the desk were press cuttings, and though Mike was already packing them away in a folder, she had no difficulty at

all in recognising them as cuttings about herself and her career.

"You have got the right girl, you're sure of that, are you?" she said determinedly. She was addressing Litvak, mistakenly suspecting him to be the more suggestible on account of his spindly frame. But she really didn't care whom she was addressing as long as she kept afloat. "Only if you're looking for the three masked men who did the bank on Fifty-second Street, they went the other way. I was the innocent bystander who gave birth ahead of time."

"Charlie, we *assuredly* have the right girl!" Kurtz cried delightedly, lifting both his thick arms from the table at once. He glanced at Litvak, then across the room at Joseph, one benign but hard glance of calculation, and the next moment he was off, speaking with the animal force that had so overpowered Quilley and Alexis and countless other unlikely collaborators throughout his extraordinary career: the same rich Euro-American accents; the same hacking gestures of the forearm.

But Charlie was an actress, and her professional instincts had never been clearer. Neither Kurtz's verbal torrent nor her own mystification at the violence done to her dulled her many-stranded perceptions of what was going on in the room. We're on stage, she thought; it's us and them. As the young sentries dispersed themselves to the gloom of the perimeter, she could almost hear the tiptoe shuffle of the latecomers jockeying for their seats on the other side of the curtain. The set, now that she examined it, resembled the bedchamber of a deposed tyrant; her captors, the freedom fighters who had ousted him. Behind Kurtz's broad paternal brow as he sat facing her, she made out the dust-shadow of a vanished imperial bed-head imprinted on the crumbling plaster. Behind skinny Litvak hung a scrolled gilt mirror strategically placed for the pleasure of departed lovers. The bare floorboards provided a boxed and stagey echo; the downlight accentuated the hollows of the two men's faces and the drabness of their partisan costumes. In place of his shiny Madison Avenue suit—though Charlie lacked that standard of comparison—Kurtz now sported a shapeless army bushjacket with dark sweat patches at the armpits and a row of gunmetal pens jammed into the button-down pocket; while Litvak, the Party Intellectual, favoured a short-sleeved khaki shirt from which his white arms poked like stripped twigs. Yet she had only to glance at either man to recognise their communality with Joseph. They are drilled in the same things, she thought; they share the same ideas and practices. Kurtz's watch lay before him on the desk. It reminded her of Joseph's water-bottle.

Two shuttered French windows gave on to the front of the house. Two more overlooked the rear. The double doors to the wings were closed, and if she had ever thought of making a dash for it, she knew now that it was hopeless, for though the sentries affected a workshop languidness, she had recognised in them already—she had reason to—the readiness of professionals. Beyond the sentries again, in the farthest corners of the set, glowed four mosquito coils, like slow-burning fuses, giving out a musky scent. And behind her, Joseph's little reading lamp—despite everything, or perhaps because of it, the only comfortable light.

All this she took in almost before Kurtz's rich voice had begun filling the room with its tortuously impelling phrases. If Charlie had not already guessed that she was headed for a long night, that relentless, pounding voice told her now.

"Charlie, what we seek to do, we wish to define ourselves, we wish to introduce ourselves, and though nobody here is given to apologising overmuch, we also wish to say we're sorry. Some things have to be done. We did a couple of them and that's how it is. Sorry, greetings, and again welcome. Hi."

Having paused long enough for her to unleash another volley of curses, he smiled broadly and resumed.

"Charlie, I have no doubt that you have many questions you would like to throw our way and in due course we shall surely answer them as best we can. Meanwhile let us try at least to supply a couple of basics for you. You ask, who are we?" This time he made no pause at all, for the fact was that he was a lot less interested in studying the effect of his words than in using them to gain a friendly mastery of the proceedings and of her. "Charlie, primarily we are decent people as Joseph said, good people. In that sense, like good and decent people the world over, I guess you could reasonably call us non-sectarian, non-aligned, and deeply concerned like yourself about the many wrong directions the world is taking. If I add that we are also Israeli citizens, I trust you will not immediately foam at the mouth, vomit, or jump out of the window, unless of course it is your personal conviction that Israel should be swept into the sea, napalmed, or handed over gift-wrapped to one or another of the many fastidious Arab organisations committed to our elimination." Sensing a secret shrinking in her, Kurtz lunged for it immediately. "*Is* that your conviction, Charlie?" he enquired, dropping his voice. "Perhaps it is. Why don't you just tell us how you feel about that? You want to get up right now? Go home? You have your air ticket, I believe. We'll give you money. Want to run for it?"

An icy stillness descended over Charlie's manner, disguising the chaos and momentary terror inside her. That Joseph was Jewish she had not doubted since her abortive interrogation of him on the beach. But Israel was a confused abstraction to her, engaging both her protectiveness and her hostility. She had never supposed for one second that it would ever get up and come to face her in the flesh.

"So what is this, actually?" she demanded, ignoring Kurtz's offer to discontinue dealings before they had begun. "A war party? A punitive raid? You going to put the electrodes on me? What the hell's the big idea?"

"Ever met an Israeli before?" Kurtz enquired.

"Not that I know of."

"You have some racial objection to Jews overall? Jews as Jews, period? We don't smell bad to you, have improper table manners? Tell us. We understand these things."

"Don't be bloody silly." Her voice had gone wrong, or was it her hearing?

"You feel you are among enemies here?"

"Oh Christ, what gave you that idea? I mean anybody who kidnaps *me* is a friend for life," she retorted, and to her surprise won a burst of spontaneous laughter in which everyone seemed free to join. Except for Joseph, that is, who was too busy at his reading, as she could hear by the faint rustle as he turned the pages over.

Kurtz bore in on her a little harder. "So put our minds at rest for us," he urged, still beaming heartily. "Let us forget that you are in some sense captive here. May Israel survive or must all of us here pack up our belongings and go back to our former countries and start over again? Maybe you would prefer us to take a piece of Central Africa? Or Uruguay? Not Egypt, thank you, we tried it once and it wasn't a success. Or shall we redisperse ourselves over the ghettos of Europe and Asia while we wait for the next pogrom? What do you say, Charlie?"

"I just want you to leave the poor bloody Arabs alone," she said, parrying again.

"Great. And how do we do that specifically?"

"Stop bombing their camps. Driving them off their land. Bulldozing their villages. Torturing them."

"Ever looked at a map of the Middle East?"

"Of course I have."

"And when you looked at the map, did you once wish the Arabs would leave *us* alone?" said Kurtz, as dangerously cheerful as before.

To her confusion and fear was added plain embarrassment, as Kurtz had probably intended. Faced with such bald reality, her flip phrases had a schoolroom cheapness. She felt like a fool, preaching to the wise.

"I just want peace," she said stupidly; though, as a matter of fact, it was true. She had a decent vision, when it was allowed her, of a Palestine magically restored to those who had been hounded from it in order to make way for more powerful, European custodians.

"In that case, why don't you take a look at the map again and ask yourself what *Israel* wants," Kurtz advised her contentedly, and stopped for a break that was like a commemorative silence for the loved ones unable to be with us here tonight.

And this silence became more extraordinary the longer it lasted, since it was Charlie herself who helped preserve it. Charlie, who minutes before had been screaming blue murder at God and the world, now suddenly had nothing to add. And it was Kurtz, not Charlie, who finally broke the spell with what sounded like a prepared statement for the press.

"Charlie, we are not here to attack your politics. You will not believe me at this early stage—why should you?—but we *like* your politics. Every aspect of them. Every paradox and good intention. We respect them and we need them; we do not laugh at them at all, and in due course I surely hope we may return to them and discuss them openly and creatively. We are aiming to address the natural humanity in you, that is all. We are aiming at your good, caring, human heart. Your feelings. Your sense of right. We mean to ask nothing of you which conflicts in any wise with your strong and decent ethical concerns. Your *polemical* politics—the names you give to your beliefs—well, we would like to put them on a back burner. Your beliefs themselves—the more confused they are, the more irrational, the more *frustrated*— Charlie, we respect them totally. On this premise, you will surely sit with us a little longer and hear us out."

Once again, Charlie hid her response under a fresh attack: "If Joseph's Israeli," she demanded, "what the hell's he doing driving round in a dirty great Arab car?"

Kurtz's face broke into that ploughed and wrinkled smile which had so dramatically betrayed his age to Quilley. "We stole it, Charlie," he replied cheerfully, and his admission was followed at once by another round of laughter from the kids, in which Charlie was half tempted to take part. "And the *next* thing you want to know, Charlie," he said— thus incidentally announcing that the Palestinian issue was, at least for the time being, safely stored away on that back burner he had spoken of—"is what are you doing here among us and why have you been dragged here in such a roundabout and unceremonious fashion. I will tell you. The reason, Charlie, is that we want to offer you a job. An *acting* job."

He had hit calm water and his bountiful smile showed he knew it. His voice had become slow and deliberate, as if he were announcing the numbers of the lucky winners: "The biggest part you ever had in your life, the most demanding, the most difficult, surely the most dangerous, and surely the most important. And I don't mean money. You can have money galore, no problem, name your figure." His big forearm swept away financial considerations. "The part we have in view for you combines all your talents, Charlie, human and professional. Your wit. Your excellent memory. Your intelligence. Your courage. But also that extra human quality to which I already referred. Your warmth. We chose you, Charlie. We cast you. We looked at a big field, many candidates from many countries. We came up with *you* and that's why you're here. Among fans. Everybody in this room has seen your work, everybody admires you. So let's get the atmosphere right. On our side there is no hostility. There is affection, there is admiration, there is hope. Hear us out. It's like your friend Joseph said, we are good people, the same as you. We want you. We need you. And there are people out there who are going to need you even more than we do."

His voice had left a void. She had known actors, just a few, whose voices did that. It was a presence, by its remorseless benevolence it became an addiction, and when it ceased, as it did now, it left you stranded. First Al gets his big part, she thought, in an instinctive rush of elation, and now I do. The madness of her situation was still quite clear to her, yet it was all she could manage to bite back a grin of excitement that was tickling at her cheeks and trying to get out.

"So that's how you do your casting, is it?" she said, mustering a sceptical tone once more. "Knock 'em over the head and drag 'em in handcuffed? That's your usual way, I suppose."

"Charlie, we are surely not claiming that this is usual drama," Kurtz replied equably, and once more left the initiative with her.

"A part what in, anyway?" she said, still fighting the grin.

"Call it theatre."

She remembered Joseph and the fun fading from his face, and his clipped reference to the theatre of the real. "So it's a play then," she said. "Why don't you say so?"

"In a sense it is a play," Kurtz agreed.

"Who writes it?"

"We handle the plot, Joseph does the dialogue. With a lot of help from you."

"Who's the audience?" She made a gesture towards the shadows. "These little charmers?"

Kurtz's solemnity was as sudden and awesome as his goodwill. His worker's hands found each other on the table, his head came forward over them, and not even the most determined sceptic could have denied the conviction in his manner. "Charlie, there are people out there who will never get to watch the play, never even know it's running, yet who will owe you for as long as they live. Innocent people. The ones you've always cared about, tried to speak for, march for, help. In everything that follows from here on, you have to keep that notion before you in your head, or you will lose us and you will lose yourself, no question."

She tried to look away from him. His rhetoric was too high, too much. She wished he would train it on someone else.

"Who the hell are you to say who's innocent?" she demanded rudely, again forcing herself against the tide of his persuasion.

"You mean we as Israelis, Charlie?"

"I mean *you*," she retorted, skirting the dangerous ground.

"I would prefer to turn your question around a little, Charlie, and say that in our view somebody has to be very guilty indeed before he needs to die."

"Such as who? Who needs to die? Those poor sods you shoot up on the West Bank? Or the ones you bomb in Lebanon?" How on earth had they come to be talking about death? she wondered, even as she put the crazy question. Had she started it, had he? It made no difference. He was already weighing his reply.

"Only those who break completely the human bond, Charlie," Kurtz replied with steady emphasis. "*They* deserve to die."

Stubbornly, she went on fighting him: "Are there Jews like that?"

"Jews, yes, Israelis surely also, but we are not among them, and mercifully they are not our problem here tonight."

He had the authority to talk that way. He had the answers children long for. He had the background and the whole room knew it, Charlie included: that he was a man who dealt only in things he had experienced. When he asked questions, you knew he had himself been questioned. When he gave orders, you knew he had obeyed the orders of others. When he spoke of death, it was clear that death had passed by him often and very close, and might any moment come his way again. And when he chose to issue a warning to her, as he did now, he was quite evidently on terms with the dangers he spoke of: "Do not confuse our play with entertainment, Charlie," he told her earnestly. "We are not speaking of some enchanted forest. When the lights go down on the stage, it will be nighttime in the street. When the actors laugh they will be happy, and when they weep they will very likely be bereaved and broken-hearted. And if they get hurt—and they will, Charlie—they will surely not be in a position, when the curtain falls, to jump up and run for the last bus home. There's no squeamish pulling back from the harsher scenes, no days off sick. It's peak performance all the way down the line. If that's what you like, if that's what you can handle—and we think it is—then hear us out. Otherwise let's skip the audition right now."

In his Euro-Bostonian drawl, faint as a distant signal on the transatlantic radio, Shimon Litvak made a first husky interjection: "Charlie never walked away from a fight in her life, Marty," he objected, in the tone of a disciple reassuring his master. "We don't just *believe* that, we *know* it. It's all over her record."

They were halfway there, Kurtz told Misha Gavron later, describing, during a rare ceasefire in their relationship, this point in the proceedings: a lady who consents to listen is a lady who consents, he said, and Gavron very nearly smiled.

Halfway, perhaps—yet, in terms of the time ahead of them, barely at the beginning. By insisting on compression, Kurtz was not in the least insisting upon haste. He placed great weight upon a laboured manner, on adding fuel to her frustration, on having her impatience racing out ahead of them like a lead-horse. Nobody understood better than Kurtz what it was like to possess a mercurial nature in a plodding world, or how to play upon its restlessness. Within minutes of her arrival, while she was still scared, he had befriended her: a father to Joseph's lover. Within minutes more, he had offered her the resolution to all the disordered components of a life so far. He had appealed to the actress in her, to the martyr, to the adventurer; he had flattered the daughter and excited the aspirant. He had granted her an early glimpse of the new family she might care to join, knowing that deep down, like most rebels, she was only looking for a better conformity. And most of all, by heaping such benefits upon her, he had made her rich: which, as Charlie herself had long preached to anyone who would hear her, was the beginning of subservience.

* * *

"So, Charlie, what we propose," said Kurtz, in a slower, more genial voice, "we propose an open-ended audition, a string of questions which we invite you to answer very frankly, very truthfully, even though for the meanwhile remaining necessarily in the dark about the purpose of them."

He paused but she didn't speak, and there was by now a tacit submission in her silence.

"We ask you never to evaluate, never to try to come to our side of the net, never to seek to please or gratify us in any regard. Many things you might consider negative in your life we would surely see differently. Do not attempt to do our thinking for us." A short jab of the forearm entrenched this amicable warning. "Question. What happens—whether now or later—what happens should either one of us elect to jump off the escalator? Charlie, let me try to answer that."

"You do that, Mart," she advised, and, putting her elbows on the table, rested her chin in her hands and smiled at him with a look intended to convey dazed unbelief.

"Thank you, Charlie, so listen carefully, please. Depending on the precise moment you want out or we do, depending on the degree of your knowledge at that time and our assessment of you, we follow one of two courses. Course one, we extract a solemn promise from you, we give you money, we send you back to England. A handshake, mutual trust, good friends, and a certain vigilance on our side to make sure you keep the bargain. You follow me?"

She lowered her gaze to the table, partly to escape his scrutiny, partly to conceal her growing excitement. For that was another thing Kurtz counted on, which most intelligence professionals forget too soon: to the uninitiated, the secret world is of itself attractive. Simply by turning on its axis, it can draw the weakly anchored to its centre.

"Course two, a little rougher, still not terrible. We place you in quarantine. We like you, but we fear we have reached a point where you might compromise our project, where the part we are proposing, say, cannot safely be offered anyplace else while you are at large to talk about it."

She knew without looking that he was smiling his goodhearted smile, suggesting that such frailty on Charlie's part would be only human.

"So what we can do in *that* case, Charlie," he resumed, "we take a nice house somewhere—say, on a beach, somewhere pleasant, no problem. We give you company, some people similar to the kids here. Nice people but able. We fake some reason for your absence, most likely a voguish one that fits your volatile reputation, such as a mystical sojourn to the East."

His thick fingers had found his old wristwatch on the table before him. Without looking at it, Kurtz lifted it and set it down six inches nearer to him. Needing an activity herself, Charlie took up a pen and began to doodle on the pad before her.

"Once you are out of quarantine, we do not desert you—far from it. We straighten you out, we give you a sack of money, we keep in touch with you, make sure you are not incautious in any way, and as soon as it's safe we help you to resume your career and friendships. That's the worst that can happen, Charlie, and I'm only telling it to you because you may be harbouring some crazy notion that by saying 'no' to us, now or later, you're going to wake up dead in a river wearing a pair of concrete boots. We don't deal that way. Least of all with friends."

She was still doodling. Closing a circle with her pencil, she drew a neat diagonal arrow above it to make it male. She had flicked through some work of popular psychology that used that symbol. Suddenly, like a man annoyed at being interrupted, Joseph spoke; yet his voice, for all its severity, had a thrilling and warm effect on her.

"Charlie, it will not be enough for you to play the sullen witness. It is your own dangerous future they are discussing. Do you mean to sit there and allow them to dispose of it practically without consulting you? A commitment, do you understand? Charlie, come!"

She drew another circle. Another boy. She had heard everything Kurtz had said, every innuendo. She could have played back every word for him, just as she had done for Joseph on the Acropolis. She was as keen-witted and alert as she had been in her life, but every cunning instinct in her told her to dissemble and withhold.

"So how long does the show run, Mart?" she asked, in a lacklustre voice as if Joseph had never spoken at all.

Kurtz rephrased her question: "Well now, I guess what you really mean is what happens to you when the job runs out. Is that right?"

She was wonderful. A shrew. Flinging down her pencil, she slapped the table with her palm: "No, it bloody well isn't! I mean how long does it run, and what about my tour with *As You Like It* in the autumn?"

Kurtz betrayed no triumph at the practicality of her objection. "Charlie," he said earnestly, "your projected tour with *As You Like It* will in no wise be affected. We would surely expect you to fulfil that engagement, assuming the grant for it is forthcoming. As to duration, your commitment to our project could take six weeks, it could take two years, though we would surely hope not. What we have to hear from you now is whether you wish to audition with us at all or whether you prefer to tell good night to everybody here and go home to a safer, duller life. What's your verdict?"

It was a false peak he had made for her. He wished to give her a sense of conquest as well as of submission. Of having chosen her own captors. She was wearing a denim jacket and one of the tin buttons hung loose; this morning when she put it on, she had made a mental note to stitch it during the boat trip, then had promptly forgotten it again in her excitement at meeting Joseph. Taking hold of it now, she began testing the strength of the thread. She was centre stage. She could feel their collective gaze fixed on her, from the table, from the shadows, from behind her. She could feel their bodies craning in tension, Joseph's also, and hear the taut, creaking sound that audiences make when they are hooked. She could feel the strength of their purpose and of her own power: will she, won't she?

"Jose?" she said, without turning her head.

"Yes, Charlie."

She still did not turn to him, yet she had the clear knowledge that from his candlelit island he was waiting on her answer more keenly than all the rest of them together.

"This is it, is it? Our big romantic tour of Greece? Delphi, all the second-best places?"

"Our drive north will in no wise be affected," Joseph replied, lightly parodying Kurtz's phraseology.

"Not even postponed?"

"I would say it was imminent, actually."

The thread broke, the button lay on her palm. She tossed it on the table, watched it spin and settle. Heads or tails, she thought, playing them. Let them sweat a little. She puffed out some breath as if blowing away her forelock.

"So I'll stick around for the audition then, won't I?" she told Kurtz carelessly, looking nowhere but at the button. "I've got nowt to lose," she added, and immediately wished she hadn't. Sometimes, to her own annoyance, she overdid things for the sake of a good exit line: "Nowt I haven't lost already, anyhow," she said.

Curtain, she thought; applause, please, Joseph, and we'll wait for tomorrow's reviews. But none came, so she picked up a pencil and drew a girl for a change, while Kurtz, perhaps without even knowing he was doing so, transferred his watch to another, better spot.

The interrogation, with Charlie's gracious consent, could now begin in earnest.

Slowness is one thing, concentration another. Kurtz did not relax for a second; he did not permit himself or Charlie even half a breathing space as he willed her, coaxed her, lulled and woke her up, and by every effort of his dynamic spirit bound himself to her in their burgeoning theatrical partnership. Only God and a few people in Jerusalem, it was said within his service, knew where Kurtz's repertoire was learnt—the mesmeric intensity, the horse-drawn American-ised prose, the flair, the barrister's tricks. His slashed face, now applauding, now ruefully incredulous, now beaming out the reassurance that she wanted, became by degrees an entire audience in itself, so that all her performance was directed towards winning his desperately coveted approval and no one else's. Even Joseph was forgotten: put aside until another life.

Kurtz's first questions, by design, were scattered and harmless. It was as if, thought Charlie, he had a blank pass-port application pinned up in his mind and Charlie, without being able to see it, was filling in the boxes. Full name of your mother, Charlie. Your father's date and place of birth if known, Charlie. Grandfather's occupation; no, Charlie, on your father's side. Followed, with no conceivable reason, by the last known address of a maternal aunt, which was fol-lowed yet again by some arcane detail of her father's educa-tion. Not a single one of these early questions bore directly upon herself, nor did Kurtz intend it to. Charlie was like the forbidden subject he was scrupulous to avoid. The entire purpose behind this cheerful quickfire opening salvo was not to elicit information at all, but to instil in her the instinctive obedience, the yes-sir-no-sir of the classroom, on which the later passages between them would depend; while Charlie, for her part, as the sap of her trade increasingly worked in her, performed, obeyed, and reacted with ever-increasing compliancy. Had she not done as much for directors and producers a hundred times—used the stuff of harmless conversation to give them a sample of her range? All the more reason, under Kurtz's hypnotic encouragement, to do it now.

"Heidi?" Kurtz echoed. "*Heidi?* That's a damned odd name for an English elder sister, isn't it?"

"Not for Heidi, it isn't," she replied buoyantly, and scored an immediate laugh from the kids beyond the lighting. Heidi because her parents went to Switzerland for their honeymoon, she explained; and Switzerland was where Heidi was conceived. "Among the edelweiss," she added, with a sigh. "In the missionary position."

"So why *Charmian?*" Marty asked when the laughter had finally subsided.

Charlie lifted her voice to capture the curdled tones of her bloody mother: "The name Charmian was arrived upon with a *view* to *flettering* our rich and distant cousin of that *na-eme.*"

"Did it pay off?" Kurtz asked as he inclined his head to catch something Litvak was trying to say to him.

"Not yet," Charlie replied skittishly, still with her mother's precious intonation. "Father, you know, has passed on, but Cousin Charmian, alas, has yet to join him."

Only by these and many similar harmless detours did they gradually advance upon the subject of Charlie herself.

"Libra," Kurtz murmured with satisfaction as he jotted down her date of birth.

Meticulously but swiftly, he bustled her through her early childhood—boarding schools, houses, names of early friends and ponies—and Charlie answered him in kind, spaciously, sometimes humorously, always willingly, her excellent memory illuminated by the fixed glow of his attention and by her growing need to be on terms with him. From schools and childhood it was a natural step—though Kurtz took it only with the greatest diffidence—to the painful history of her father's ruin, and Charlie rendered this in quiet but moving detail, from the first brutal breaking of the news to the trauma of the trial and sentence and imprisonment. Now and then, it was true, her voice caught slightly; sometimes her gaze sank to study her own hands that played so prettily and expressively in the downlight; then a gallant, lightly self-mocking phrase would come to her, to blow it all away.

"We'd have been all right if we'd been working class," she said once, with a wise and hopeless smile. "You get sacked, you go redundant, the forces of capital run against you—it's life, it's reality, you know where you are. But we weren't working class. We were us. The winning side. And all of a sudden, we'd joined the losers."

"Tough," said Kurtz gravely, with a shake of his broad head.

Backtracking, he probed for the solid facts: date and place of trial, Charlie; the exact length of sentence, Charlie; names of lawyers if she remembered them. She didn't, but wherever she could she helped him, and Litvak duly noted down her answers, leaving Kurtz free to give her his entire benevolent attention. Now all laughter had ceased completely. It was as if the soundtrack had stopped dead, all but hers and Marty's. There was not a creak, not a cough, not an alien shuffle from anywhere. In her whole life, it seemed to Charlie, no group of people had been so attentive, so appreciative of her performance. They understand, she thought. They know what it is to live the nomad's life; to be thrown upon your own resources when the cards are stacked against you. Once, on a quiet order from Joseph, the lights went out and they waited together without a sound in the tense darkness of an air raid, Charlie as apprehensive as the rest, till Joseph announced the all-clear and Kurtz resumed his patient questioning. Had Joseph really heard anything, or was this their way of reminding her that she belonged? The effect on Charlie was in either case the same: for those tense few seconds she was their fellow conspirator with no thought of rescue.

At other times, wresting her gaze briefly from Kurtz, she would see the kids dozing at their posts: Swedish Raoul, with his flaxen head sunk upon his chest and the sole of one thick track-shoe flattened against the wall; South African Rose propped against the double doors, her runner's legs stretched in front of her and her long arms folded across her chest; North Country Rachel, the wings of her black hair folded round her face, eyes half closed, but still with her soft smile of sensual reminiscence. Yet the smallest extraneous whisper found every one of them instantly alert.

"So what's the bottom line here, Charlie?" Kurtz enquired kindly. "Regarding that whole early period of your life until what we may call the Fall—"

"The age of innocence, Mart?" she suggested helpfully.

"Precisely. Your age of innocence. Define it for me."

"It was hell."

"Want to name some reasons?"

"It was suburbia. Isn't that enough?"

"No, it is not."

"Oh, Mart—you're so—" Her slack-mouthed voice. Her tone of fond despair. Limp gestures with the hands. How could she ever explain? "It's all right for you, you're a Jew, don't you see? You've got these fantastic traditions, the security. Even when you're persecuted, you know who you are, and why."

Kurtz ruefully acknowledged the point.

"But for us—rich English suburban kids from Nowheresville—forget it. We had no traditions, no faith, no self-awareness, no nothing."

"But you told me your mother was Catholic."

"Christmas and Easter. Pure hypocrisy. We're the post-Christian era, Mart. Didn't anybody tell you? Faith leaves a vacuum behind it when it goes away. We're in it."

As she said this, she caught Litvak's smouldering eyes upon her and received the first hint of his rabbinical anger.

"No going to confession?" Kurtz asked.

"Come off it. Mum didn't have anything to confess! That's her whole trouble. No fun, no sin, no nothing. Just apathy and fear. Fear of life, fear of death, fear of the neighbours—*fear*. Somewhere out there, real people were living real lives. Just not us. Not in Rickmansworth. No way. I mean, Christ—for children—I mean talk about *castration*!"

"And you—no fear?"

"Only of being like Mum."

"And this notion we all have—ancient England steeped in her traditional ways?"

"Forget it."

Kurtz smiled and shook his wise head as if to say you could always learn.

"So as soon as you could, you left home and you took refuge in the stage and radical politics," he suggested contentedly. "You became a political exile to the stage. I read that somewhere, some interview you gave. I liked it. Go on from there."

She was back to doodling again, more symbols of the psyche. "Oh, there were other ways of breaking out before *that*," she said.

"Such as?"

"Well, *sex*, you know," said Charlie carelessly. "I mean we haven't even touched on sex as the essential basis of revolt, have we? Or drugs."

"We haven't touched on revolt," said Kurtz.

"Well, take it from me, Mart—"

Then a strange thing happened: proof, perhaps, of how a perfect audience can extract the best from a performer and improve her in spontaneous, unexpected ways. She had been on the brink of giving them her set piece for the unliberated. How the discovery of self was an essential prelude to identifying with the radical movement. How when the history of the new revolution came to be written, its true roots would be found in the drawing-rooms of the middle classes, where repressive tolerance had its natural home. Instead of which, to her surprise, she heard herself enumerating aloud for Kurtz—or was it for Joseph?—her rows and rows of early lovers and all the stupid reasons she had invented for going to bed with them. "It's completely beyond me, Mart," she insisted, once more opening her hands disarmingly. Was she using them too much? She feared she might be, and put them in her lap. "Even today. I didn't *want* them, I didn't *like* them, I just *let* them." The men she had taken out of boredom, anything to move the stale air of Rickmansworth, Mart. Out of curiosity. Men to prove her power, men to avenge herself against other men, or against other women, against her sister or her bloody mother. Men out of politeness, Mart, out of sheer bone-weariness at their persistence. The casting couches—Christ, Mart, you can't imagine! Men to break the tension, men to create it. Men to inform her—her political enlighteners, appointed to explain to her in bed the things she could never get her mind round from the books. The five-minute lusts that smashed like pottery in her hands and left her lonelier than ever. Failures, failures—every one of them, Mart—or so she wanted him to believe. "But they *freed* me, don't you see? I was using my own *body* in my own *way*! Even if it was the wrong way. It was my show!"

While Kurtz nodded sagely, Litvak wrote swiftly at his side. But in her secret mind she was picturing Joseph seated behind her. She imagined him looking up from his reading, his strong index finger laid along his smooth cheek, while he received the private gift of her amazing openness. Scoop me up, she was saying to him; give me what the others never could.

Then she fell quiet and her own silence chilled her. Why had she done that? In her entire life she had never played that part before, not even to herself. The timeless hour of the night had affected her. The lighting, the upstairs room, the sense of travel, of talking to strangers on a train. She wanted to sleep. She'd done enough. They must give her the part or send her home, or both.

But Kurtz did neither. Not yet. Instead, he called a short interval, picked up his watch, and buckled it to his wrist by its khaki webbing strap. Then he bustled from the room, taking Litvak with him. She waited for a footfall from behind her as Joseph also left, but none came. And still none. She wanted to turn her head but didn't quite dare. Rose brought her a glass of sweet tea, no milk. Rachel had some sugarcoated biscuits, like English shortbread. Charlie took one.

"You're doing *great*," Rachel confided breathlessly. "You really laid it on the line about England. I just sat there drinking it in, didn't I, Rose?"

"She really did," said Rose.

"It's just how I feel," Charlie explained.

"Do you want the loo, love?" said Rachel.

"No thanks. I never do between acts."

"Right then," said Rachel, with a wink.

Sipping, Charlie propped an elbow on the back of her chair in order to be able to glance naturally over her shoulder. Joseph had vanished, taking his papers with him.

The resting room they had retired to was as large as the room they had left and quite as bare. A couple of army beds and a teleprinter made up the only furniture, double doors gave on to a bathroom. Becker and Litvak sat facing each other on the beds, studying their respective files; the teleprinter was tended by a straight-backed boy named David, and periodically it heaved itself and disgorged another sheet of paper, which he devoutly added to the pile at his elbow. The only other sound was the sloshing of water in the bathroom, where Kurtz, with his back to them and stripped to the waist, was dousing himself at the handbasin, like an athlete between events.

"She's a neat lady," Kurtz called as Litvak turned a page and sidelined something with a felt-tipped pen. "She's everything we expected. Bright, creative, and under-used."

"She's lying in her teeth," said Litvak, still reading. But it was clear from the slant of his body, as well as the provocative insolence of his tone, that his remark was not intended for Kurtz.

"So who's complaining?" Kurtz demanded, flinging more water in his face. "Tonight she lies for herself, tomorrow she lies for us. Do we want an angel suddenly?"

The teleprinter burst abruptly into a different song. Both Becker and Litvak glanced sharply towards it, but Kurtz appeared not to have heard. Perhaps he had water in his ears.

"For a woman, lying is a protection. She protects the truth, so she protects her chastity. For a woman, lying is a proof of virtue," Kurtz announced, still washing.

Seated before the telephone, David held up his hand for attention. "It's the Embassy in Athens, Marty," he said. "They want to break in with a relay from Jerusalem."

Kurtz hesitated. "Tell them to go ahead," he said grudgingly.

"It's for your eyes only," David said and, getting up, walked across the room.

The teleprinter gave a shudder. Flinging his towel round his neck, Kurtz sat himself in David's chair, inserted a disc, and watched the message turn to clear text. The printing ceased; Kurtz read it, then ripped the tearsheet from the roller and read it again. Then he let out an angry laugh. "A message from the very highest twig," he announced bitterly. "The great Rook says we are to pose as Americans. Isn't that nice? 'On no account will you admit to her you are Israeli subjects acting in official or near-official capacity.' I love it.

It's constructive, it's helpful, it's timely and it's Misha Gavron at his unmatchable best. I never in my life worked for anyone so totally dependable. Cable back 'Yes repeat no,' " he snapped at the astonished boy, handing him the tearsheet, and the three men trooped back on stage.

7

To resume his little chat with Charlie, Kurtz had selected a tone of benevolent finality, as if he wished to check a few last fiddly points before moving to other things.

"Charlie, regarding your parents once more," he was saying. Litvak had pulled a file from his briefcase, and was holding it out of Charlie's line of sight.

"Regarding them," she said, and reached bravely for a cigarette.

Kurtz took a little break while he studied certain documents that Litvak had slipped into his hand. "Looking at the final phase of your father's life now, his crash, financial disgrace, death, and so forth. Can we just confirm with you the exact sequence of those events? You were at English boarding school. The terrible news came. Take it from there, please."

She didn't quite follow him. "From where?"

"The news comes. Go on from there."

She shrugged. "The school threw me out, I went home, the bailiffs were swarming over the house like rats. We've been there, Mart. What else is there?"

"The headmistress sent for you, you said," Kurtz reminded her after a pause. "Great. So what did she say? Precisely, please?"

" 'Sorry but I've asked Matron to pack your things. Goodbye and good luck.' Far as I remember."

"Oh, you'd remember *that*," said Kurtz with quiet good humour, leaning across to take another look at Litvak's papers. "No homily from her on the big wicked world out there?" he asked, still reading. " 'Don't give yourself away too easy' type of thing? No? No explanation of why, exactly, you were being asked to leave?"

"The fees hadn't been paid for two terms already—isn't that enough? They're in business, Mart. They've got their bank account to think of. This was a private school, remember?" She made a show of weariness. "Don't you think we'd better call it a day? I can't think why but I seem to be a trifle flaked."

"Oh, I don't think so. You are rested and you have resources. So you went home. By rail?"

"All the way by rail. On my own. With my little suitcase. Homeward bound." She stretched, and smiled around the room, but Joseph's head was turned away from her. He seemed to be listening to other music.

"And you came home to *what* precisely?"

"To chaos. I told you."

"Just specify the chaos a little, will you?"

"Furniture van in the drive. Men in aprons. Mother weeping. Half my room already emptied."

"Where was Heidi?"

"Not there. Absent. Not counted among those present."

"Nobody sent for her? Your elder sister, the apple of your father's eye? Living ten miles up the road? Safely married? Why didn't Heidi come over and help?"

"Pregnant, I expect," said Charlie carelessly, looking at her hands. "She usually is."

But Kurtz was looking at Charlie, and he took a good long time to say anything at all. "Who did you say was pregnant, please?" he asked, as if he hadn't quite heard.

"Heidi."

"Charlie, Heidi was not pregnant. Heidi's first pregnancy occurred the following year."

"All right, she wasn't pregnant for once."

"So why didn't she come along, lend some family help?"

"Maybe she didn't want to know. She stayed away, that's all I remember. Mart, for Christ's sake, it's ten years ago. I was a kid, a different person."

"It was the disgrace, huh? Heidi couldn't take the disgrace. Of your father's bankruptcy, I mean."

"What other disgrace was there?" she snapped.

Kurtz treated her question rhetorically. He was back at his papers, watching Litvak's long finger point things out to him. "In any case, Heidi stayed away and the entire responsibility of coping with the family crisis fell upon your young shoulders, okay? Charlie, aged a mere sixteen, to the rescue. Her 'crash course in the fragility of the capitalist system,' as you put it so nicely a while back. 'An object lesson you never

forgot.' All the toys of consumerism—pretty furniture—
pretty dresses—all the attributes of bourgeois respectability—you saw them physically dismantled and removed before
your very eyes. You alone. Managing. Disposing. In undisputed mastery over your pathetic bourgeois parents who
should have been working class but carelessly were not. Consoling them. Easing them in their disgrace. Almost a kind of
absolution you gave them, I guess. Tough," he added sadly.
"Very, very tough," and stopped dead, waiting for her to
speak.

But she didn't. She stared him out. She had to. His
slashed features had undergone a mysterious hardening, particularly around the eyes. But she stared him out all the
same; she had a special way of doing it left over from her
childhood, of freezing her face into an ice-picture, and thinking other thoughts behind it. And she won, she knew she did,
because Kurtz spoke first, which was the proof.

"Charlie, we recognise that this is very painful for you,
but we ask you to continue in your own words. We have the
van. We see your possessions leaving the house. What else do
we see?"

"My pony."

"They took that too?"

"I told you already."

"With the furniture? In the same van?"

"No, a separate one. Don't be bloody silly."

"So there were two vans. Both at the same time? Or one
after the other?"

"I don't remember."

"Where was your father physically located all this time?
Was he in the study? Looking through the window, say,
watching it all go? How does a man like him bear up—in his
disgrace?"

"He was in the garden."

"Doing what?"

"Looking at the roses. Staring at them. He kept saying
they mustn't take the roses. Whatever happened. He kept saying it, on and on. 'If they take my roses, I'll kill myself.' "

"And your mother?"

"Mums was in the kitchen. Cooking. It was the only
thing she could think of to do."

"Gas or electricity?"

"Electricity."

"But did I mishear you or did you say the company switched the power off?"

"They reconnected it."

"And they didn't take away the cooker?"

"They have to leave it by law. The cooker, a table, a chair for everyone in the house."

"Knives and forks?"

"One set for each person."

"Why didn't they just sequester the house? Throw you all out?"

"It was in Mother's name. She'd insisted on it years before."

"Wise woman. However, it was in your father's. And where, did you say, did the headmistress read about your father's bankruptcy?"

She had almost lost it. For a second, the images inside her head had wavered, but now they hardened again, providing her with the words she needed: her mother, in her mauve headscarf, bowed over the cooker, frantically making bread-and-butter pudding, a family favourite. Her father, grey-faced and mute in his blue double-breasted blazer, staring at the roses. The headmistress, hands behind her back, warming her tweed rump before the unlit fire in her imposing drawing-room.

"In the London *Gazette*," she replied stolidly. "Where everybody's bankruptcies are reported."

"The headmistress was a subscriber to this journal?"

"Presumably."

Kurtz gave a long slow nod, then picked up a pencil and wrote the one word *presumably* on a pad before him, in a way that made it visible to Charlie. "So. And after the bankruptcy came the fraud charges. That right? Want to describe the trial?"

"I told you. Father wouldn't let us be there. At first he was going to defend himself—be a hero. We were to sit in the front seats and cheer him on. When they showed him the evidence, he changed his mind."

"What was the charge?"

"Stealing clients' money."

"How long did he get?"

"Eighteen months, less remission. I told you, Mart. I said it all to you before. What is this?"

"Ever visit him in prison?"

"He wouldn't let us. He didn't want us to see his shame."

"His shame," Kurtz echoed thoughtfully. "His disgrace. The Fall. It really got to you, didn't it?"

"Would you like me better if it hadn't?"

"No, Charlie, I don't suppose I would." He took another small break. "Well, there we are. So you stayed home. Gave up school, forsook the proper instruction of your excellent developing mind, looked after your mother, waited for your father's release. Right?"

"Right."

"Never went near the prison once?"

"Jesus," she muttered hopelessly. "Why do you keep twisting the knife like this?"

"Not even near it?"

"No!"

She was holding back her tears with a courage they must surely admire. How could she take it? they must be wondering—either then or now? Why did he persist in tapping away so remorselessly at her secret scars? The silence was like a pause between screams. The only sound was from Litvak's ballpoint pen as it flew across the pages of his notebook.

"Any of that any use to you, Mike?" Kurtz asked of Litvak, without turning his gaze from her.

"Great," Litvak breathed as his pen continued racing. "It's gritty, it adds up, we can use it. I just wonder whether she might have a catchy anecdote for that prison stuff somewhere. Or maybe when he came out is better—the final months—why not?"

"Charlie?" said Kurtz shortly, passing on Litvak's enquiry.

Charlie made a show of pondering for them till inspiration came to her. "Well, there was the thing about the *doors*," she said doubtfully.

"Doors?" said Litvak. "What doors?"

"Tell it to us," Kurtz suggested.

A beat while Charlie lifted one hand and delicately pinched the bridge of her nose between her forefinger and thumb, indicating deepest grief and a slight migraine. She had told the story often, but never as well as this. "We weren't expecting him for another month—he didn't phone, how could he? We'd moved house. We were on National Assistance. He just showed up. Looked slimmer, younger. Hair cut. 'Hullo, Chas, I'm out.' Gave me a hug. Wept. Mums upstairs, too scared to come down to him. He was completely unchanged. Except for the doors. He couldn't open them. He'd go up to them, stop, stand at attention with his feet together and his head down, and wait for the warder to come and unlock them."

"And the warder was *her*," said Litvak softly from Kurtz's side. "His own daughter. *Wow!*"

"The first time it happened, I couldn't believe it. I screamed at him, 'Open the bloody door!' His hand literally refused."

Litvak was writing like a man possessed. But Kurtz was less enthusiastic. Kurtz was at the file again, and his expression suggested serious reservations. "Charlie, in this one interview you gave—the Ipswich *Gazette*, is this?—you tell some story how you and your mother used to climb a hill outside the prison together and wave so as your father could see you from his cell window. Yet, ah, according to what you told *us*, just now, you never went near that prison once."

Charlie actually managed to laugh—a rich, convincing laugh, even if it was not echoed from the shadows. "Mart, that was an *interview* I gave," she said, humouring him because he looked so grave.

"So?"

"So in interviews one tends to sauce up one's past to make it interesting."

"You been doing that here at all?"

"Of course not."

"Your agent Quilley recently told someone of our acquaintance that your father died in prison. Not at home at all. *More* saucing it up?"

"That's Ned talking, not me."

"Quite so. So it is. Agreed."

He closed the file, still unconvinced.

She couldn't help herself. Turning right round in her chair, she addressed Joseph, indirectly begging him to get her off the hook.

"How's it going, Jose—all right?"

"Very effectively, I would say," he replied, and continued as before with his own affairs.

"Better than *Saint Joan*?"

"But, my dear Charlie, your lines are a lot better than Shaw's!"

He's not congratulating me, he's consoling me, she thought sadly. Yet why was he so harsh to her? So brittle? So abstaining after he had brought her here?

South African Rose had a tray of sandwiches. Rachel was following her with cakes and a thermos of sweet coffee.

"Doesn't anybody sleep around here?" Charlie complained as she helped herself. But her question went unheard. Or, rather, since they had all heard it clearly, unanswered.

The sweet time was over and now it was the long-awaited dangerous time, the middle hour of watchfulness before the dawn, when her head was clearest and her anger sharpest; the time, in other words, to transfer Charlie's politics—which Kurtz had assured her they all deeply respected—from the back burner to a more conspicuous heat. Once again, in Kurtz's hands, everything had its chronology and its arithmetic. Early influences, Charlie. Date, place, and people, Charlie: name us your five guiding principles, your first ten encounters with the militant alternative. But Charlie was in no mood for objectivity any more. Her fit of drowsiness was past, and in place of it a sense of rebellion was beginning to turn restlessly inside her, as the crispness of her voice and her darting, suspicious glances should have told them. She was sick of them. Sick of being helpful in this shotgun alliance, of being led blindfold from room to room without knowing what these trained, manipulating hands were doing on her elbow and what these clever voices were whispering in her ear. The victim in her was spoiling for a fight.

"Charlie, dear, this is strictly but strictly for the record," Kurtz declared. "Once we have it for the record, we shall be able to shed a couple of veils for you," he assured her. But he still insisted on dragging her through a wearying catalogue of demos and sit-ins and marches and squats and Saturday-afternoon revolutions, asking in each case for what he called "the argumentation" behind her action.

"For Christ's sake, stop trying to evaluate us, will you?"

she threw back at him. "We're not logical, we're not informed, we're not organised—"

"So what are we, dear?" said Kurtz with saintly kindness.

"We're not *dear* either. We're *people*! Adult human beings, get it? So stop riding me!"

"Charlie, we are surely not riding you. Nobody here is riding you."

"Oh, screw you all."

She hated herself in this mood. She hated the harshness that came over her when she was cornered. She had a picture of herself beating her puny, girl's fists uselessly against a huge wood door, while her strident voice battled with dangerously unconsidered slogans. At the same time, she loved the bright colours that came with anger, the glorious release, the smashed glass.

"Why do you have to *believe* before you reject?" she demanded, remembering a grand phrase Long Al had fed to her—or was it someone else? "Maybe rejecting *is* believing. Has that occurred to you? We're fighting a different war, Mart—the real one. It's not power against power, East against West. It's the hungry against the pigs. Slaves against oppressors. You think you're free, don't you? That's because someone else is in chains. You eat, someone starves. You run, someone has to stand still. We have to change that whole thing."

She had believed it once; she really had. Perhaps she still did. She had seen it and had it clear before her in her mind. She had knocked on strangers' doors with it and watched the hostility lift from their faces as she made her pitch. She had felt it and marched for it: for the people's right to free the people's minds, to unclog one another from the engulfing morass of capitalist and racist conditioning, and turn towards each other in unforced companionship. Out there, on a clear day, the vision even now could fill her heart and stir her to feats of courage that, cold, she would have shrunk from. But inside these walls, with all these clever faces, she had no space to spread her wings.

She tried again, more strident: "You know, Mart, one of the differences between being your age and mine is we're actually a bit *fussy* about who we give up our existence for. We're not keen, for some reason, on laying down our lives for a multi-national corporation registered in Liechtenstein and banking in the bloody Dutch Antilles." That bit was Al's for certain. She had even borrowed his sarcastic rasp to wash it down. "We don't think it's a very good idea to have people we've never met or heard of or voted for going round ruining the world for us. We're not in love with dictators, funnily enough, whether they're groups of people or countries or institutions, and we're not in love with the arms race, or chemical warfare, or any part of the whole catastrophe game. We don't think that the Jewish state has to be an imperialist American garrison and we don't think Arabs are either flea-ridden savages or decadent oil-sheikhs. So we reject. In favour of not having certain hang-ups—certain prejudices and alignments. So rejection is positive, right? Because *not having them* is positive, got it?"

"*How* ruining the world, exactly, Charlie?" Kurtz asked while Litvak patiently jotted.

"Poisoning it. Burning it. Fouling it up with trash and colonialism and the total, calculated mindbending of the workers, and"—and the other lines I'll remember in a minute, she thought. "So just don't come asking me for the names and addresses of my five main gurus—right, Mart?—because they're in *here*"—she thumped her chest—"and don't go sneering at me when I can't recite Che Guevara to you all bloody night; just ask me whether I want the world to survive and my babies to—"

"*Can* you recite Che Guevara?" Kurtz asked, interested.

"Hold it," said Litvak, and lifted one flimsy hand for pause while he wrote furiously with the other. "This is *great*. Just hold it for *one* minute, Charlie, will you?"

"Why don't you dash out and buy yourself a bloody tape-recorder?" Charlie snapped. Her cheeks were hot. "Or steal one, since that's what you're into?"

"Because we don't have a week set aside for reading transcripts," Kurtz replied while Litvak continued writing. "The ear selects, you see, dear. Machines don't. Machines are uneconomical. *Can* you recite Che Guevara, Charlie?" he repeated while they waited.

"No, of course I bloody well can't."

From behind her—it seemed a mile away—Joseph's disembodied voice gently modified her answer.

"But she could if she *learnt* him. She has excellent recall," he assured them, with a touch of the creator's pride. "She has only to hear something and it belongs to her. She could learn his entire writings in a week, if she put her mind to it."

Why had he spoken? Was he trying to mitigate? Warn? Or impose himself between Charlie and her imminent destruction? But Charlie was in no mood to heed his subtleties, and Kurtz and Litvak were conferring again, this time in Hebrew.

"Do you mind speaking English in front of me, you two?" she demanded.

"In just one moment, dear," said Kurtz pleasantly. And went on talking in Hebrew.

In the same clinical fashion—strictly for the record, Charlie—Kurtz led her painstakingly through the remaining disparate articles of her uncertain faith. Charlie flailed and rallied and flailed again with the growing desperation of the half-taught; Kurtz, seldom criticising, always courteous, glanced at the file, paused for a word with Litvak, or, for his own oblique purposes, jotted himself a note on the pad before him. In her mind, as she floundered fiercely on, she saw herself in one of those improvised happenings at drama school, working her way into a part that increasingly lacked meaning for her as she advanced. She watched her own gestures and they no longer belonged to her words. She was protesting, therefore she was free. She was shouting, therefore she was protesting. She listened to her voice and it belonged to nobody at all. From the pillow-talk of a forgotten lover she snatched a line of Rousseau, from somewhere else a phrase from Marcuse. She saw Kurtz sit back and, lowering his eyes, nod to himself and put down his pencil, so she supposed that she had finished, or he had. She decided that, given the superiority of her audience and the poverty of her lines, she had managed quite decently after all. Kurtz seemed to think so too. She felt better, and a lot safer. Kurtz too, apparently.

"Charlie, I surely congratulate you," he declared. "You have articulated with great honesty and frankness and we thank you."

"Sure do," murmured Litvak the scribe.

"Be my guest," she retorted, feeling ugly and over-heated.

"Mind if I attempt to structure it a little for you?" Kurtz enquired.

"Yes, I do."

"Why's that?" said Kurtz, unsurprised.

"We're an alternative, that's why. We're not a party, we're not organised, we're not a manifesto. And we're not for bloody-well structuring."

She wished she could get out of the bloodies somehow. Or else that her swearing would come more easily to her in their austere company.

Kurtz did his structuring all the same, and made a point of being ponderous while he was about it.

"On the one hand, Charlie, we seem to have what is the basic premise of classic anarchism as preached from the eighteenth century down to the present day."

"Oh balls!"

"Namely, a revulsion against regimentation. Namely, a conviction that government is evil, *ergo* the nation-state is evil, an awareness that the two together contradict the natural growth and freedom of the individual. You add to this certain modern postures. Such as a revulsion against boredom, against prosperity, against what I believe is known as the air-conditioned misery of Western capitalism. And you remind yourself of the genuine misery of three-quarters of the earth's population. Yes, Charlie? You want to quarrel with that? Or shall we take the 'Oh balls' for granted this time?"

She ignored him, preferring to smirk at her fingernails. For Christ's sake—what did theories *matter* any more? she wanted to say. The rats have taken over the ship, it's often as simple as that; the rest is narcissistic crap. It must be.

"In today's world," Kurtz continued, unperturbed, "in today's world I would say you have more sound reasons for that view than ever your forebears had, because today the nation-states are more powerful than ever; so are the corporations, so are the opportunities for regimentation."

She realised he was leading her, yet she had no way left to stop him. He was pausing for her comments, but all she could do was turn her face away from him and hide her growing insecurity behind a mask of furious negation.

"You oppose technology gone mad," he continued equably. "Well, Huxley did that for you already. You aim to release human motives that are for once neither competitive nor aggressive. But in order to do this, you have first to remove exploitation. But how?"

Yet again he paused, and his pauses were becoming more threatening to her than his words; they were the pauses between footsteps to the scaffold.

"Stop patronising me, will you, Mart? Just stop!"

"It is on this issue of exploitation, so far as I read you, Charlie," Kurtz continued, with implacable good humour, "that we spill over from anarchism *observed*, as we might call it, to anarchism *practised*." He turned to Litvak, playing him off against her. "You had a point here, Mike?"

"I would say exploitation was the crunch issue, Marty," Litvak breathed. "For exploitation read *property* and you have the whole bit. First the exploiter hits the wage-slave over the head with his superior wealth; then he brainwashes him into believing that the pursuit of property is a valid motive for breaking him at the grindstone. That way he has him hooked twice over."

"Great," said Kurtz comfortably. "The pursuit of property is evil, *ergo* property itself is evil, *ergo* those who protect property are evil, *ergo*—since you avowedly have no patience with the evolutionary democratic process—blow up property and murder the rich. You go along with that, Charlie?"

"Don't be bloody silly! I'm not into that stuff!"

Kurtz seemed disappointed. "You mean you decline to dispossess the robber state, Charlie? What's the matter? Shy, suddenly?" To Litvak again: "Yes, Mike?"

"The state is tyrannous," Litvak put in helpfully. "Charlie's words exactly. She also referred to the *violence* of the state, the *terrorism* of the state, the *dictatorship* of the state—just about everything bad a state can be," Litvak added, in a rather surprised voice.

"That doesn't mean I go round murdering people and robbing bloody banks! Christ! What is this?"

Kurtz was not impressed by her alarm. "Charlie, you have indicated to us that the forces of law-and-order are no more than the satraps of a false authority."

Litvak offered a footnote: "Also that true justice is not available to the masses through the law courts," he reminded Kurtz.

"It isn't! The whole system is crap! It's fixed, it's corrupt, it's paternalistic, it's—"

"Then why don't you destroy it?" Kurtz enquired perfectly pleasantly. "Why don't you blow it up and shoot every policeman who tries to stop you, and for that matter every policeman who doesn't? Why don't you blow up colonialists and imperialists wherever you find them? Where's your vaunted integrity suddenly? What's gone wrong?"

"I don't want to blow anything up! I want peace! I want people to be free!" she insisted, scurrying desperately for her one safe tenet.

But Kurtz seemed not to hear her: "You disappoint me, Charlie. All of a sudden you lack consistency. You've made the perceptions. Why don't you go out and do something about them? Why do you appear here one minute as an intellectual who has the eye and brain to see what is not visible to the deluded masses, the next you have not the courage to go out and perform a small service—like *theft*—like *murder*—like *blowing something up*—say, a police station—for the benefit of those whose hearts and minds are enslaved by the capitalist overlords? Come on, Charlie, where's the action? You're the free soul around here. Don't give us the words, give us the deeds."

The infectious jolliness in Kurtz had reached new heights. His eyes were so creased at the corners that they were black curves cut into his battered skin. But Charlie could fight too, and she was talking straight at him, using words the way he did, clubbing him with them, trying to beat a last desperate exit past him to freedom.

"Look, I'm superficial, got it, Mart? I'm unread, illiterate, I can't add or reason or analyse, I went to tenth-rate expensive schools, and I wish to God—more than anything on earth I do—I wish I'd been born in a Midland back-street and my father had worked with his hands instead of ripping off old ladies' life savings! I'm sick of being brainwashed and I'm sick of being told fifteen thousand reasons every day why I shouldn't love my neighbour on equal terms, and I want to go to bloody bed!"

"You telling me you're recanting on your stated position, Charlie?"

"I haven't *got* a stated position!"

"You haven't."

"No!"

"No stated position, no commitment to activism, except that you are unaligned."

"Yes!"

"*Peaceably* unaligned," Kurtz added contentedly. "You belong to the extreme centre."

Slowly unbuttoning a pocket of his jacket, he fished in it with his thick fingers, producing, from among a lot of junk, a folded press cutting, quite a long one, which, judging by its exclusive position, differed in some way from those contained in the folder.

"Charlie, you mentioned in passing a while back that you and Al attended a certain residential forum down in Dorset some place," said Kurtz as he laboriously unfolded the cutting. " 'A weekend course in radical thinking' was how you described it, I believe. We didn't enter very deeply into what transpired there; it is my memory that for some reason we kind of glossed over that part of our discussion. Mind if we dig a little deeper?"

Like a man refreshing his memory, Kurtz silently read the press cutting to himself, occasionally shaking his head as if to say "Well, well."

"Seems quite a place," he remarked genially as he read. "Weapon training with dummy guns. The techniques of sabotage—using plasticine instead of the real stuff, naturally. How to live in hiding. Survival. The philosophy of the urban guerrilla. Even how to look after an unwilling guest, I see: 'Restraint of unruly elements in a domestic situation.' I like that. That's a fine euphemism." He glanced over the top of his cutting. "This correct, this report, more or less, or are we dealing with the typical exaggerations of the capitalist-Zionist press here?"

She no longer believed in his goodwill, nor did he want her to. Kurtz's one aim now was to alarm her with the extremity of her opinions, and force her into flight from positions she did not realise she had taken. Some interrogations are conducted in order to elicit truth, others to elicit lies. Kurtz wanted lies. His grating voice had therefore discernibly hardened, and the fun was fading quickly from his face.

"Want to give us a more objective picture, Charlie, maybe?" Kurtz enquired.

"It was Al's scene, not mine," she said defiantly, making her first withdrawal.

"But you went together."

"It was a cheap weekend in the country at a time when we were broke. That's all."

"That's all," Kurtz murmured, leaving her with a vast and guilty silence too heavy for her to shift single-handed.

"It wasn't just me and him," she protested. "It was— God—twenty of us. Kids, acting people. Some of them were still at drama school. They'd hire a bus, take some hash, play musical beds till morning. What's wrong with that?"

Kurtz had no opinion, just then, of what was wrong with anything.

"*They*," he said. "What were *you* doing? Driving the bus?—the great driver we hear you are?"

"I was with Al. I told you. It was his scene, not mine."

She had lost her hold and was falling. She scarcely knew how she had slipped, or who had stamped on her fingers. Perhaps she had just grown tired and let go. Perhaps she had wanted to all along.

"And how often would you say you indulged yourself in this fashion, Charlie? Talking hot air. Smoking hash. Participating in free love innocently while others engaged in terrorist training? You speak as if it was a habitual thing. Correct? Habitual?"

"No, it is *not* habitual! It's over, and I did not *indulge* myself!"

"Want to say how frequent?"

"It wasn't frequent either!"

"How often?"

"A couple of times. That's all. Then I got cold feet."

Falling and spinning, and the dark getting darker. The air all round her but not touching her.

Joseph, get me out of this! But Joseph had got her into it. She listened for him, sent messages to him with the back of her head. But she received nothing in return.

Kurtz looked straight at her and she looked straight back. She'd have looked clean through him if she could; she'd have blinded him with her defiant glower.

"A couple of times," he repeated thoughtfully. "Right, Mike?"

Litvak glanced up from his notes. "A couple," he echoed.

"Want to say *why* you got cold feet?" Kurtz asked.

Without allowing his gaze to leave her face, he reached for Litvak's folder.

"It was a rough scene," she said, dropping her voice for effect.

"It sounds it," said Kurtz, opening the folder.

"I don't mean politically. I mean the sex. It was more than I wanted to handle. Don't be so obtuse."

Kurtz licked his thumb and turned a page; he licked his thumb and turned another page; he muttered something to Litvak, who breathed a couple of words in return, and they were not in English. He closed the buff folder and slipped it into the briefcase. " 'A couple of times. That's all. Then I got cold feet,' " he intoned thoughtfully. "Want to revise that statement at all?"

"Why should I?"

" 'A couple of times.' That correct?"

"Why shouldn't it be?"

"A couple is two. Right?"

Above her, the light wavered, or was it her mind? She turned deliberately in her chair. Joseph was bowed over his desk lamp, too busy even to look up. She turned back and found Kurtz still waiting.

"Two or three," she said. "What the hell?"

"Four? Is a couple four as well?"

"Oh, get lost!"

"I guess it's a matter of linguistics. 'I visited my aunt a couple of times last year.' Well, that could be three, couldn't it? Four is possible. Five, I guess five is around the limit. With five it's 'half a dozen.' " He continued slowly shuffling through his papers. "Want to revise 'couple,' make it 'half a dozen,' Charlie?"

"I said a couple and I mean a couple."

"Two?"

"Yes, two!"

"Two then. 'Yes, I have been to this forum on two occasions only. Others may have engaged in warlike practices but

my interests were sexual, recreational, and social. Amen.'
Signed Charlie. Want to put a date on the two visits?"

She gave a date last year, soon after she and Al had got
together.

"And the other one?"

"I forget. What does it matter?"

"She forgets." His voice had slowed almost to a halt, yet
lost none of its power. She had an image of it lumbering
towards her like an ungainly animal. "Did the second time
come soon after the first time, or was there a gap between the
two occasions?"

"I don't know."

"She doesn't know. Your first weekend was an introduc-
tory course for novices. Correct?"

"Yes."

"What were you introduced to?"

"I told you—group sex."

"No discussions, no seminars, no instruction?"

"We had discussions, yes."

"On what subjects, please?"

"Basic principles."

"Of what?"

"Of radicalism, what do you think?"

"Remember who addressed you?"

"A spotty lesbian on Women's Lib. A Scotsman on
Cuba, someone Al admired."

"And the next occasion—date forgotten, the second and
last—who addressed you that time?"

No answer.

"Forgotten that as well?"

"Yes!"

"That's unusual, isn't it? That you remember the first occasion intimately—the sex, the topics of discussion, the tu-
tors. And the second not at all?"

"After staying up all night answering your crazy questions—no, it's not!"

"Where are you going?" Kurtz asked. "You want the
bathroom? Rachel, take Charlie to the bathroom. Rose."

She was standing. From the shadows she heard soft feet
approaching her.

"I'm leaving. Exercising my options. I want out. Now."

"Your options will be exercised at specific stages, and

only when we invite you. If you forget who addressed you at this second seminar you attended, then perhaps you will tell me at least the nature of the course."

She was still standing, and somehow being upright made her smaller. She glanced round and saw Joseph, head in hand, his face turned away from the lamplight. To her frightened eye, he seemed to be suspended in a kind of middle city, between her world and his. But wherever she looked, Kurtz's voice kept filling her head and deafening the people inside it. She put her hands on the table, she leaned forward; she was in a strange church without friends to advise her, not knowing whether to stand or kneel. But Kurtz's voice was everywhere and it wouldn't have mattered whether she had lain on the ground or flown out through the stained-glass window and a hundred miles away, nowhere was safe from its dinning intrusion. She took her hands off the table and put them behind her back, holding them tight because she was losing control of her gestures. Hands matter, hands speak. Hands act. She felt them comfort each other like terrified children. Kurtz was asking her about a resolution.

"Did you not *sign* it, Charlie?"

"I don't know!"

"But, Charlie, there is always a resolution passed at the termination of a session. There is discussion. There is a resolution. What was the resolution? You trying seriously to tell me you don't *know* what it was, you don't *know* whether you signed it even? Might you have *refused* to sign it?"

"No."

"Charlie, be reasonable. How can a person of your much underrated intelligence forget such a thing as a formal resolution at the end of a three-day seminar? A thing which you draft and redraft—and vote about—and pass and don't pass—sign and don't sign? How do you do that? A resolution, that's a whole laborious series of incidents, for goodness' sake. Why are you so vague suddenly, when you are capable of such fine precision on other matters?"

She didn't care. She cared so damn little she couldn't be bothered to *tell* him she didn't care. She was tired to death. She wanted to sit again but she was stuck standing. She wanted an interval and a pee and time to fix her make-up, and five years' sleep. Nothing but a leftover sense of theatrical proprieties told her she must stand and see it through.

Below her, Kurtz had dug himself out a fresh piece of paper from the briefcase. Having worried over it, he decided to address himself to Litvak. "She said two occasions, right?"

"Two was maximum," Litvak agreed. "You gave her every chance to raise the bidding but she stuck at two."

"And what do *we* make it?"

"Five."

"So where does she get two from?"

"She's understating," Litvak explained, contriving to look even more disappointed than his companion. "She's understating by like two hundred per cent."

"Then she's lying," said Kurtz, slow to accept the inference.

"She sure is," said Litvak.

"I didn't lie! I forgot! It was Al! I went for Al's sake, *that's all!*"

Among the gunmetal pens in the top pocket of his bushjacket, Kurtz kept a khaki handkerchief. Taking it out, he now passed it in an odd dusting motion over his face, ending with his mouth. Then he put it back in his pocket. Then he moved his watch again, from left to right in a private piece of ritual.

"You want to sit down?"

"No."

Her refusal only saddened him. "Charlie, I have ceased to understand you. My confidence in you is ebbing."

"Then it can bloody well ebb! Find someone else to kick around! Why should I play parlour games with a bunch of Israeli thugs? Go and car-bomb some more Arabs. Get out of my hair. I hate you! All of you!"

Saying this, Charlie had a most curious intimation. She decided that they were only half listening to her words, and with the other half of their attention studying her technique. If somebody had called out "Let's take that one again, Charlie, maybe a little slower," she would not have been a bit surprised. But Kurtz meanwhile had his point to make, and nothing on his Jewish God's earth—as she by now well knew—was going to stop him.

"Charlie, I do *not* understand your evasion," he insisted. His voice was recovering its pace. Its power was undiminished. "I do not understand the discrepancies between the Charlie you are giving us and the Charlie we have on record.

Your first visit to this revolutionary school took place on July fifteenth last year, a two-day course for novices on the general subject of colonialism and revolution, and yes, you all went by bus, a group of acting people, Alastair included. Your second visit took place a month later, also with Alastair, on which occasion you and your fellow students were addressed by a so-called Bolivian exile who declined to give his name, also by a similarly anonymous gentleman claiming to speak for the provisional wing of the Irish Republican Army. You generously signed both of those organisations a personal cheque for five pounds, and we have photocopies of the cheques right here."

"It was for Al! He was broke!"

"The third time you went was a month later, when you took part in a very pathetic discussion on the work of the American thinker Thoreau. The group's verdict on that occasion, to which you subscribed, was that when it came to militancy, Thoreau was an irrelevant idealist with little practical understanding of activism—in short, a bum. You not only supported that verdict but initiated a supplementary resolution calling for greater radicalism on the part of all comrades."

"It was for Al! I wanted them to accept me! I wanted to please Al! I'd forgotten it next day!"

"Come October, you and Alastair were back there, this time for a particularly apposite session on the subject of bourgeois Fascism in Western capitalist societies, at which you played a leading rôle in group discussions, regaling your comrades with many mythical anecdotes regarding your criminal father, your inane mother, and your repressive upbringing generally."

She had stopped protesting. She had stopped thinking or seeing. She had blurred her gaze and taken a piece of the inside flesh of her mouth between her teeth and she was softly biting it as a punishment. But she couldn't stop listening, because Marty's voice didn't allow that.

"And the very last occasion occurred, as Mike here reminded us, in February this year, when you and Alastair graced a session whose theme you have obstinately dismissed from your memory, except just a moment previously when you lapsed into abuse of the State of Israel. This time the discussion was devoted exclusively to the lamentable expansion of world Zionism and its links with American imperialism. The leading performer was a gentleman purportedly representing the Palestinian revolution, though he declined to say which wing of that great movement he belonged to. He also refused in the most literal sense to reveal himself, since his features were hidden behind a black balaclava helmet, which gave him a becomingly sinister air. Do you still not recall this speaker?" He left her no time to answer. "His theme was his own heroic life as a great warrior and killer of Zionists. 'The gun is my passport to my homeland,' he declared. 'We are no longer refugees! We are a revolutionary people!' He caused a certain alarm around him and one or two voices, not your own, felt he had gone a little far." He paused, but still she did not speak. He moved his watch closer to him and smiled at her a little wanly. "Why don't you tell us these things, Charlie? Why do you flop from place to place not knowing which lie to tell us next? Did I not assure you that we need your past? That we like it very much?"

Again he waited patiently for her answer, but in vain. "We know your father never went to prison. You never had the bailiffs in, nobody took your pony from you. The poor gentleman suffered a small, incompetent bankruptcy, injuring nobody except a couple of local bank managers. He was discharged with honour, if that is the expression, long before his death; a few friends raised a little money between them, and your mother remained a proud and devoted wife to him. It was never your father's fault that you left school prematurely, it was your own. You had made yourself, let us say, a little too available to several boys in the local town, and word of this had duly gotten back to the school staff. You were accordingly expelled from the school in haste as a corrupting and potentially scandalous element, and returned to your grossly over-indulgent parents, who as usual forgave you your transgressions, to your great frustration, and did their best to believe everything you told them. Over the years you have spun an ingenious fiction around the incident in order to make it bearable, and you have come to believe in it yourself, though secretly the memory still turns you inside out and drives you in many strange directions." Yet again, he transferred his watch to a safer spot on the table. "We're your friends, Charlie. Do you think we would ever blame you for such a thing? Do you think we do not understand that your politics are the externalisation of a search for dimensions and responses not supplied to you when you most needed them? We're your *friends*, Charlie. We're not mediocre, bored, apathetic, suburban, conformist. We want to share with you, to make use of you. Why do you sit there deceiving us when all we wish to hear from you, from start to end, is the unadorned objective truth? Why do you hinder your *friends*, instead of giving us your full-hearted trust?"

Her anger swept over her like a red-hot sea. It lifted her, it cleansed her; she felt it swell and she embraced it like her one true ally. With the calculation of her trade, she let it take command of her entirely, while she herself, that tiny gyroscopic creature deep inside that always managed to stay upright, tiptoed gratefully to the wings to watch. Anger suspended her bewilderment and dulled the pain of her disgrace; anger cleared her mind and made her vision brilliant. Taking a step forward, she lifted her fist to swipe at him, but he was too senior, too daunting, he had been hit too much before. Besides, she had unfinished business just behind her.

True, it was Kurtz who by his deliberate enticement of her had struck the match that kindled her explosion. But it was Joseph's cunning, Joseph's courtship, and Joseph's cryptic silence that had brought about her real humiliation. She swung round, she took two strides to him, waiting for someone to stop her, but someone didn't. She swung her foot up and kicked away the table and watched the desk lamp curve gracefully to God knew where before it reached the limit of its flex and went out with a surprised pop. She drew back her fist, waiting for him to defend himself. He didn't, so she lunged at him where he sat, catching him across the cheekbone with all her strength. She was screaming all her filthy epithets at him, the ones she used on Long Al and the whole blank, painful nothingness of her tangled, too-small life, but she wished he would put up an arm or hit her back. She hit him a second time with her other hand, wanting to mark and hurt the whole of him. Again she waited for him to defend himself, but his familiar brown eyes continued to watch her as steadily as shore lights in a storm. She hit him again with her half-closed fist and felt her knuckles wrench, but she saw the blood running down his chin. She was screaming "Fascist bastard!" and she went on repeating it, feeling her strength wasting with her breath. She saw Raoul, the flaxen hippy boy, standing in the doorway, and one of the girls—South African Rose—position herself before the French windows and spread her arms in case Charlie made a leap for the verandah, and she wished terribly that she could go mad so that everyone would be sorry for her; she wished she was just a raving lunatic waiting to be let off, not a stupid little fool of a radical actress, who made up feeble versions of herself as she went along, who had denied her father and mother and embraced a half-cock faith she hadn't the courage to renounce, and anyway, what was there till now to replace it? She heard Kurtz's voice in English ordering everyone to stay still. She saw Joseph turn away; she saw him draw a handkerchief from his pocket and dab his lip, as indifferent to her as he might have been to a rude child of five. She screamed "Bastard!" at him again, she hit him on the side of the head, a big open-fisted clattering blow that bent her wrist and momentarily numbed her hand, but by now she was exhausted and alone and all she wanted was for Joseph to hit her back.

"Help yourself, Charlie," Kurtz advised quietly, from his chair. "You've read Frantz Fanon. Violence is a cleansing force, remember? It frees us from our inferiority complexes, it makes us fearless and restores our self-respect."

There was only one way out for her, so she took it. Hunching her shoulders, she dropped her face dramatically into her hands and wept inconsolably until, on a nod from Kurtz, Rachel came forward from the window and put her arm round her shoulder, which Charlie resisted and then let be.

"She gets three minutes, not more," Kurtz called as the two of them headed for the doorway. "She does not change her dress or put on some new identity, she comes straight back in here. I want the engine kept running. Charlie, stop where you are a minute. Wait. I said *stop*."

Charlie stopped, but did not turn round. She stood motionless, acting with her back and wondering wretchedly whether Joseph was doing something about that cut face.

"You did well, Charlie," Kurtz said, without condescension, down the room to her. "Congratulations. You took a dive but you recovered. You lied, you lost your way, but you hung in there and when the line broke you threw a tantrum and blamed your troubles on the whole world. We were proud of you. Next time we'll think you up a better story to tell. Hurry back, okay? Time is very, very short right now."

In the bathroom, Charlie stood with her head against the wall, sobbing, while Rachel ran a basin of water for her and Rose stood outside in case.

"I don't know how you can put up with England for one minute," said Rachel while she set the soap and towel ready. "I had fifteen years of it before we left. I thought I'd die. Do you know Macclesfield? It's death. It is if you're a Jew, anyway. All that class and coldness and hypocrisy. I think it's the unhappiest place on earth, Macclesfield is, for a Jew, I do really. I used to scrub my skin with lemon juice in the bath because they told me I was greasy. Don't go near that door without me, will you, love, or I'll have to stop you."

It was dawn and therefore bedtime and she was back with them, where she wanted more than anything to be. They had told her a little, they had brushed across the story as a headlight brushes across a dark doorway, giving a passing glimpse of whatever lies hidden in it. Imagine, they said—and told her of a perfect lover whom she'd never met.

She hardly cared. They wanted her. They knew her through and through; they knew her fragility and her plurality. And they still wanted her. They had stolen her in order to rescue her. After all her drifting, their straight line. After all her guilt and concealment, their acceptance. After all her words, their action, their abstemiousness, their clear-eyed zeal, their authenticity, their true allegiance, to fill the emptiness that had yawned and screamed inside her like a bored demon ever since she could remember. She was a feather-weight, caught in a swirling storm, but suddenly, to her amazed relief, theirs was the commanding wind.

She lay back and let them carry her, assume her, have her. Thank God, she thought: a homeland at last. You will play yourself, but more so, they said—and when had she ever not? Yourself, with all your bluffs called, they said—put it that way. Put it any way you like, she thought.

Yes, I'm listening. Yes, I follow.

They had given Joseph the seat of authority at the centre of the table. Litvak and Kurtz sat still as moons to either side of him. Joseph's face was raw where she had hit him, a chain of small bruises ran along the bone-line of his left cheek. Through the slatted shutters, ladders of early light shone on to the floorboards and across the trestle table. They stopped talking.

"Have I decided yet?" she asked him.

Joseph shook his head. A dark stubble emphasised the hollows of his face. The downlight showed a web of fine lines round his eyes.

"Tell me about the usefulness again," she suggested.

She felt their interest tighten like a cord. Litvak, his white hands folded before him, dead-eyed yet strangely angry in his contemplation of her; Kurtz, ageless and prophetic, his cracked face sprinkled with a silver dust. And round the walls still, the kids, devout and motionless, as if they were queuing for their first communion.

"They say you will save lives, Charlie," Joseph explained, in a detached tone from which all hint of theatre had been rigorously expunged. Did she hear reluctance in his voice? If so, it only emphasised the gravity of his words. "That you will give mothers back their children and help to bring peace to peaceful people. They say that innocent men and women will live. Because of you."

"What do *you* say?"

His answer sounded deliberately dull. "Why else would I be here? For one of *us*, we would call the work a sacrifice, an atonement for life. For you—well, maybe it's not so different after all."

"Where will you be?"

"We shall stay as close to you as we can."

"I said you. You singular. Joseph."

"I shall be close, naturally. That will be my job."

And only my job, he was saying; not even Charlie could have mistaken the message.

"Joseph will be right with you all along the line, Charlie," Kurtz put in softly. "Joseph is a fine, fine professional. Joseph, tell her about the time factor, please."

"We have very little," Joseph said. "Every hour counts."

Kurtz was still smiling, seeming to wait for him to go on. But Joseph had finished.

She had said yes. She must have done. Or yes to the next phase at least, because she felt a slight movement of relief around her, and then, to her disappointment, nothing more. In her hyperbolic state of mind she had imagined her whole audience bursting into applause: exhausted Mike sinking his head into his spidery white hands and weeping unashamedly; Marty, like the old man he had turned out to be, grasping her shoulders in his thick hands—my child, my daughter—pressing his prickly face against her cheek; the kids, her soft-footed fans, breaking ranks to gather round and touch her. And Joseph folding her to his breast. But in the theatre of deeds, it seemed, people didn't do that. Kurtz and Litvak were busy tidying papers, closing briefcases. Joseph was conferring with Dimitri and the South African Rose. Raoul was clearing away the débris of tea and sugary biscuits. Rachel alone seemed concerned with what became of their recruit. Touching Charlie's arm, she led her towards the landing for what she called a nice lie down. They had not reached the door before Joseph softly spoke her name. He was staring at her with pensive curiosity.

"So good night then," he repeated, as if the words were a puzzle to him.

"So good night to you, too," Charlie retorted, with a battered grin that should have signified the final curtain. But it didn't. As Charlie followed Rachel down the corridor, she was surprised to discover herself in her father's London club, on her way towards the ladies' annexe for lunch. Stopping, she gazed round her trying to identify the source of this hallucination. Then she heard it: the restless ticking of an unseen teleprinter, pushing out the latest market prices. She guessed it came from behind a half-closed door. But Rachel hurried her past before she had a chance to find out.

The three men were back in the resting room, where the chattering of the code machine had summoned them like a bugle. While Becker and Litvak looked on, Kurtz crouched at the desk deciphering with an air of utter disbelief the newest, unexpected, urgent, and strictly private telegram from Jerusalem. From behind him they could watch the dark sweat patch spread across his shirt like a leaking wound. The radio operator was gone, packed off by Kurtz as soon as Jerusalem's coded text began to print itself. The silence in the house was otherwise very deep. If birds sang or traffic passed, they did not hear it. They heard only the stop and start of the printer.

"I never saw you better, Gadi," declared Kurtz, for whom no one activity was ever quite enough. He was speaking English, the language of Gavron's text. "Masterful, high-minded, incisive." He tore off a sheet and waited for the next to print itself. "All that a girl adrift could wish for in her saviour. That right, Shimon?" The machine resumed.

"Some of our colleagues in Jerusalem—Mr. Gavron, to name but one—they questioned my selection of you. Mr. Litvak here for another. Not me. I had the confidence." Muttering a mild curse, he tore off the second sheet. "That Gadi, he's the best I ever had, I told them," he resumed. "A lion's heart, a poet's head: my very words. A life of violence has not coarsened him, I said. How does she handle, Gadi?"

And he actually turned his head and tilted it, watching for Becker's answer.

"Didn't you notice?" Becker said.

If Kurtz had noticed, he was not at present saying so. The message completed, he swung right round on his swivel chair, holding the sheets strictly upright before him to catch the desk light that came over his shoulder. But it was Litvak, oddly, who spoke first—Litvak who gave vent to a clenched and strident outburst of impatience that took his two colleagues by surprise. "They've planted another bomb!" he blurted. "Tell us! Where was it? How many of us have they killed this time?"

Kurtz slowly shook his head, and smiled for the first time since the message had come in.

"A bomb, maybe, Shimon. But nobody died from it. Not yet."

"Just let him read it," Becker said. "Don't let him play you."

But Kurtz preferred to extrapolate. "Misha Gavron greets us and sends us three further messages," he said. "Message one, certain installations in the Lebanon will be hit tomorrow, but those concerned will be sure to avoid our target houses. Message two"—he tossed aside his pieces of paper—"message two is an order, akin in quality and perception to the order we received earlier tonight. We are to drop the gallant Dr. Alexis by yesterday. No further contact. Misha Gavron has turned over his case file to certain wise psychologists who have ruled him as crazy as a bedbug."

Litvak again began to protest. Perhaps extreme tiredness affected him that way. Perhaps the heat did, for the night had turned very hot. Kurtz, still with his smile, talked him gently down to earth.

"Calm yourself, Shimon. Our gallant leader is being a little bit political, that is all. If Alexis jumps the wall and there is a scandal affecting our country's relationship with a sorely needed ally, Marty Kurtz here takes the rap. If Alexis stays our side, keeps his mouth shut, and does what we tell him, Misha Gavron takes the glory. You know how Misha treats me. I'm his Jew."

"And the third message?" Becker said.

"Our leader advises us that there is very little time. The hounds are baying at his heels, he says. He means *our* heels, naturally."

At Kurtz's suggestion, Litvak went off to pack his toothbrush. Left alone with Becker, Kurtz gave a grateful sigh of relief, and, much easier in his manner, wandered over to the truckle bed and picked up a French passport, opened it, and studied the personal particulars, committing them to memory. "You are the deliverer of our success, Gadi," he observed as he read. "Any gaps, special needs, you let me know. Hear me?"

Becker heard him.

"The kids say you made a fine couple up there on the Acropolis. Like a pair of movie stars, they tell me."

"Thank them for me."

Armed with an old, clogged hairbrush, Kurtz stood himself before the mirror and set to work to give himself a parting.

"A case like this, a girl involved, a concept, I leave it to the case officer's discretion," he remarked reflectively as he laboured. "Sometimes it pays to keep a distance, sometimes—" He tossed the hairbrush into an open case.

"This one's distance," Becker said.

The door opened. Litvak, dressed for the city and carrying a briefcase, was impatient for his master's company.

"We're late," he said, with an unfriendly glance at Becker.

And yet Charlie, for all their manipulation of her, was not coerced—not by Kurtz's standards, anyway. It was a point on which he placed stress from the outset. A durable basis of morality, he ruled, was essential to their plan. In the early stages, yes, there had been fancy talk of pressure, domination, even sexual enslavement to some less scrupulous Apollo than Becker; of confining Charlie in fragmenting circumstances for a few nights before offering her the hand of friendship. Gavron's wise psychologists, having read her dossier, put forward all sorts of fatuous suggestions, including some that were on the brutal side. But it was the tested operational mind of Kurtz that won the day against Jerusalem's swelling army of experts. Volunteers fight harder and longer, he had argued. Volunteers find their own ways to persuade themselves. And besides, if you are proposing marriage to a lady, it is wiser not to rape her first.

Others, of whom Litvak had been one, had voted loudly for an Israeli girl who could be fitted out with Charlie's kind of background. Litvak was viscerally opposed, as others were, to the idea of counting on the loyalty of a Gentile, least of all an English one, for anything. Kurtz had disagreed with equal vehemence. He loved the naturalness in Charlie and coveted the original, not the imitation. Her ideological drift did not dismay him in the least; the nearer she was to drowning, he said, the greater would be her pleasure at coming aboard.

Yet another school of thought—for the team was nothing if not democratic, if you ignored Kurtz's natural tyranny—had advocated a longer and more gradual courtship in advance of Yanuka's kidnapping, ending with a straight, sober offer along the classically defined lines of intelligence recruitment. Once again, Kurtz strangled the suggestion at birth. A girl of Charlie's temperament did not make up her mind by idle hours of reflection, he shouted—and neither, as a matter of fact, did Kurtz. Better to compress! Better to research and prepare down to the last detail, and take her by storm in one tremendous push! Becker, when he had taken a look at her himself, agreed: impulse recruitment was best.

But what if she says no, for God's sake? they had cried,

Gavron the Rook among them. To have prepared so much, only to be jilted at the altar!

In that case, Misha my friend, said Kurtz, we will have wasted a little time, and a little money, and a few prayers. He held that view through thick and thin; even if, in his most private circle—which comprised his wife and occasionally Becker—he confessed that he was taking one devil of a gamble. But there again, perhaps he was playing the cocotte. Kurtz had had his eye on Charlie ever since she had first surfaced at the weekend sessions of the forum. He had marked her down, enquired about her, twisted her around in his mind. You assemble tools, you look for the tasks, you improvise, he would say. You match the operation to the resources.

But why drag her to Greece, Marty? And all the others with her? Are we a charity, suddenly, lavishing our precious secret funds on rootless left-wing English actors?

But Kurtz was unbudgeable. He demanded scale from the start, knowing he would only be whittled down thereafter. Since Charlie's odyssey must begin in Greece, he insisted, let her be brought to Greece ahead of time, where the foreignness and magic of her situation would detach her more easily from domestic ties. Let the sun soften her. And since Alastair would never let her go alone, let him come also—and be removed at the psychological moment, thus further depriving her of support. And since all actors collect families—and do not feel secure unless they have the protection of the flock—and since no other natural method presented itself by which to lure the couple aboard— So it went on, one argument predicating another, until the only logic was the fiction, and the fiction was a web that enmeshed everyone who tried to sweep it away.

As to the removal of Alastair, it provided on that very day in London an amusing postscript to all their planning up till now. The scene occurred, of all places, in the domain of poor Ned Quilley, while Charlie was still deeply sleeping, and Ned was treating himself to a small refreshment in the privacy of his room in order to fortify himself for the rigours of lunch. He was in the act of unstopping his decanter when he was startled by a stream of obscenities, delivered in a male Celtic brogue, from the direction of Mrs. Longmore's cubby-hole downstairs, and ending with the demand that she "call the old goat out of his shed before I personally go up and drag him out." Wondering who of his more erratic clients had elected to have his nervous breakdown in Scottish, and before lunch, Quilley tiptoed gingerly to the door and put his ear to the panel. But he failed to recognise the voice. A moment later there was a thunder of footsteps, the door was flung open, and there before him stood the swaying figure of Long Al, known to him from occasional sorties to Charlie's dressing-room, where Alastair was in the habit of sitting out her performances with the aid of a bottle during his own protracted spells of idleness. He was filthy, he had three days' growth, he was blind drunk. Quilley attempted, in his best Pickwickian style, to demand the meaning of this outrage, but he might as well have spared his breath. Besides, he had been through a number of such scenes in his day, and experience had taught him that one does one's best to say as little as possible.

"You contemptible old faggot," Alastair began pleasantly, holding a shaking index finger directly beneath Quilley's nose. "You mean, scheming old queen. I'm going to break your stupid neck."

"My dear chap," said Quilley. "Whatever for?"

"I'm phoning for the police, Mr. Ned!" cried Mrs. Longmore from downstairs. "I'm dialling nine-nine-nine *now*!"

"Either sit down and explain your business at once," Quilley said sternly, "or Mrs. Longmore will phone for the police."

"I'm dialling!" called Mrs. Longmore, who had done this occasionally before.

Alastair sat down.

"Now then," said Quilley, with all the fierceness at his command. "What about a little black coffee while you tell me what I have done to offend you?"

The list was long: played him a fool's trick, Quilley had. For Charlie's sake. Pretended to be a non-existent film company. Persuaded his agent to send telegrams to Mykonos. Made a conspiracy with clever friends in Hollywood. Prepaid air tickets, all to make a ninny out of him in front of the gang. And to get him out of Charlie's hair.

Gradually, Quilley unravelled the story. A Hollywood film production company calling itself Pan Talent Celestial had telephoned his agent from California saying that their leading man had fallen sick and they required Alastair for immediate screen tests in London. They would pay whatever was necessary to obtain his attendance, and when they heard he was in Greece they arranged for a certified cheque for a thousand dollars to be delivered to the agent's office. Alastair returned from holiday hot-foot, then sat on his thumbs for a week while no screen test materialised. "STAND BY," said the telegrams. Everything by telegram, note well. "ARRANGE-MENTS PENDING." On the ninth day, Alastair, in a state of near dementia, was instructed to present himself at Shepperton Studios. Ask for one Pete Vyschinsky, Studio D.

No Vyschinsky, not anywhere. No Pete.

Alastair's agent rang the number in Hollywood. The telephone operator advised him that Pan Talent Celestial had closed its account. Alastair's agent rang other agents; nobody had heard of Pan Talent Celestial. Doom. Alastair's judgment was as good as anyone's, and in the course of a two-day drunk, on the balance of his thousand dollars' expenses, Alastair had concluded that the only person with the motive and ability to play such a trick was Ned Quilley, known in the trade as "Desperately Quilley," who had never concealed his dislike for Alastair, or his conviction that Alastair was the evil influence behind Charlie's zany politics. He had therefore come round in person to wring Quilley's neck. After a few cups of coffee, however, he began protesting his undying admiration for his host, and Quilley told Mrs. Longmore to get him a cab.

The same evening, while the Quilleys sat in the garden enjoying a sundowner before dinner—they had recently invested in some rather decent outdoor furniture, cast-iron but done in the original Victorian moulds—Marjory listened gravely to his story, then to his great annoyance burst out laughing.

"What a very naughty girl," she said. "She must have found some rich lover to buy the boy off!"

Then she saw Quilley's face. Rootless American production companies. Telephone numbers that no longer answer. Film-makers who cannot be found. And all of it happening around Charlie. And her Ned.

"It's even worse," said Quilley miserably.

"What is, darling?"

"They've stolen all her letters."

"They've *what!*"

All her handwritten letters, Quilley said. Going back over the last five years or more. All her chatty, intimate *billets-doux* scribbled when she was on tour or lonely. Marvellous things. Pen-portraits of producers and members of the cast. The dear little drawings she liked to do when she was feeling happy. Gone. Whipped from the file. By those awful Americans who wouldn't drink—Karman and his frightful chum. Mrs. Longmore was having a fit about it. Mrs. Ellis had gone sick.

Write them a filthy letter, Marjory advised.

But to what effect? Quilley wondered miserably. And to what address?

Talk to Brian, she suggested.

All right, Brian was his solicitor; so what the hell was Brian supposed to do?

Wandering back into the house, Quilley poured himself a stiff one and turned on the television, only to get the early-evening news with film of the latest beastly bombing somewhere. Ambulances, foreign policemen carting off the injured. But Quilley was in no mood for such frivolous distractions. They actually *ransacked* Charlie's file, he kept repeating to himself. A *client's*, dammit. In *my* office. And son of old Quilley sits by and sleeps his lunch off while they do it! He hadn't been so put out for years.

8

If she dreamed, she had no knowledge of it when she woke. Or perhaps, like Adam, she woke and found the dream true, because the first thing she saw was a glass of fresh orange juice by her bed, and the second, Joseph striding purposefully about the room, pulling open cupboards, drawing back the curtains to let in the sunshine. Pretending to be still asleep, Charlie watched him through half-closed eyes, as she had watched him on the beach. The line of his wounded back. The first light frost of age touching the sides of his black hair. The silk shirt again, with its gold furnishings.

"What's the time?" she asked.

"Three o'clock." He gave a tug of the curtain. "In the afternoon. You have slept enough. We must get on our way."

And a gold neckchain, she thought; with the medallion tucked inside the shirt.

"How's the mouth?" she asked.

"Alas, it appears that I shall never sing again." He crossed to an old painted wardrobe and extracted a blue kaftan, which he laid on the chair. She saw no marks on his face, only heavy rings of tiredness beneath his eyes. He stayed up, she thought, recalling his absorption with the papers on his desk; he's been finishing his homework.

"You remember our conversation before you went to bed this morning, Charlie? When you get up, I would like you please to put on this dress, also the new underclothes you will find in the box here. I prefer you best in blue today and your hair brushed long. No knots."

"Plaits."

He ignored the correction. "These clothes are my gift to you and it is my pleasure to advise you what to wear and how to look. Sit up, please. Take a thorough look at the room."

She was naked. Clutching the sheet to her throat, she

cautiously sat up. A week ago, on the beach, he could have studied her body to his heart's content. That was a week ago.

"Memorise everything around you. We are secret lovers and this room is where we spent the night. It happened as it happened. We were reunited in Athens, we came to this house and found it empty. No Marty, no Mike, nobody but ourselves."

"So who are you?"

"We parked the car where we parked it. The porch light was burning as we arrived. I unlocked the front door, we ran together hand in hand up the broad staircase."

"What about luggage?"

"Two pieces. My briefcase, your shoulder bag. I carried both."

"Then how did you hold my hand?"

She thought she was outguessing him, but he was pleased by her precision.

"The shoulder bag with its broken strap was under my right arm. My grip was in the right hand. I ran on your right side, my left hand was free. We found the room exactly as it is now, everything prepared. We were scarcely through the door before we embraced each other. We could not contain our desire a second longer."

With two steps he was at the bed, rummaging among the tumbled bedclothes on the floor until he found her blouse, which he held out for her to see. It was ripped at every button-hole and two buttons were missing.

"Frenzy," he explained as flatly as if frenzy were the day of the week. "Is that the word?"

"It's one of them."

"Frenzy then."

He tossed aside the blouse and allowed himself a strict smile. "You want coffee?"

"Coffee would be great."

"Bread? Yoghurt? Olives?"

"Coffee will do fine." He had reached the door as she called after him, in a louder voice: "Sorry I swiped you, Jose. You should have launched one of those Israeli counterstrikes and felled me before I thought of it."

The door closed, she heard him stride away down the passage. She wondered whether he would ever come back. Feeling utterly unreal, she stepped gingerly from the bed. It's pantomime, she thought—Goldilocks in the bears' house. The evidence of their imagined revelry lay all round her: a vodka bottle, two-thirds full, floating in an ice bucket. Two glasses, used. A bowl of fruit, two plates complete with apple peel and grape pips. The red blazer draped over a chair. The smart black leather grip with side pockets, part of every budding executive's virility kit. Hanging from the door, a karate-style kimono, Hermès of Paris—his again, heavy black silk. In the bathroom, her own schoolgirl's sponge-bag cuddled up beside his calf-skin holdall. Two towels were offered; she used the dry one. Her blue kaftan, when she examined it, turned out to be rather pretty, in a heavy cotton with a high, demure neckline and the shop's own tissue paper still inside it: Zelide, Rome and London. The underclothes were high-class tart's stuff, black and her size. On the floor, a brand-new leather shoulder bag and a pair of smart flat-soled sandals. She tried one on. It fitted. She dressed and was brushing out her hair when Joseph marched back into the room bearing a tray with coffee. He could be heavy, and he could be so light you'd think they'd lost the soundtrack. He was somebody with a wide range of stealth.

"You look excellent, I would say," he remarked, placing the tray on the table.

"Excellent?"

"Beautiful. Enchanting. Radiant. You have seen the orchids?"

She hadn't, but she saw them now and her stomach turned over the way it had on the Acropolis: a sprig of gold and russet with a small white envelope propped against the vase. Deliberately, she finished her hair, then picked the little envelope from its perch and took it to the chaise longue, where she sat down. Joseph remained standing. Lifting the flap, she drew out a plain card with the words "I love you" written in a sloping, un-English hand, and the familiar signature, "M."

"Well? What does it remind you of?"

"You know damn well what it reminds me of," she snapped as, far too late, she made the connection in her memory, as well.

"So tell me."

"Nottingham, the Barrie Theatre. York, the Phoenix.

Stratford East, the Cockpit. You, crouching in the front row making cow eyes at me."

"The same handwriting?"

"The same hand, the same message, the same flowers."

"You know me as Michel. 'M' for Michel." Opening the smart black grip, he began swiftly packing his clothes into it. "I am all you ever desired," he said, without even looking at her. "To do the job, you don't just have to remember it; you have to believe it and feel it and dream it. We are building a new reality, a better one."

She put aside the card and poured herself some coffee, playing deliberately slow against his haste.

"Who says it's a better one?" she said.

"You passed your holiday in Mykonos with Alastair, but in your secret heart you were waiting desperately for me, Michel." He darted into the bathroom and returned with his holdall. "Not Joseph—Michel. As soon as the holiday was over, you hurried to Athens. On the boat you told your friends you wanted to be alone for a few days. A lie. You had an assignation with Michel. Not Joseph—Michel." He tossed the holdall into the grip. "You took a taxi to the restaurant, you met me there. Michel. In my silk shirt. My gold watch. Lobsters ordered. Everything you saw. I brought brochures to show you. We ate what we ate, we talked excited sweet nothings in the manner of secret lovers reunited." He unhooked the black kimono from the door. "I tipped lavishly and kept the bill, as you noticed; then I took you up the Acropolis, a forbidden journey, unique. A special taxi, my own, was waiting. I addressed the driver as Dimitri—"

She interrupted him. "So that was the only reason you took me up the Acropolis," she said flatly.

"It was not I who took you. It was Michel. Michel is proud of his languages, of his abilities as a fixer. He loves flourish, romantic gestures, sudden leaps. He is your magician."

"I don't like magicians."

"He also has a genuine if superficial interest in archaeology, as you observed."

"So who kissed me?"

Carefully folding the kimono, he laid it in the grip. He was the first man she had met who knew how to pack.

"His more practical reason for taking you up the Acropolis was to enable him to take discreet delivery of the Mercedes, which for his own reasons he did not wish to bring into the city centre during the rush hour. You do not question the Mercedes; you accept it as part of the magic of being with me, just as you accept a clandestine flavour in whatever we do. You accept everything. Hurry, please. We have much driving to do, much talking."

"What about you?" she said. "Are you in love with me too, or is it all a game?"

Waiting for him to answer, she had a vision of him physically stepping aside to allow the shaft to speed harmlessly past him towards the shadowy figure of Michel.

"You love Michel, you believe Michel loves you."

"But am I right?"

"He says he loves you, he gives you proof of it. What more can a man do to convince you, since you cannot live inside his head?"

He had set off round the room again, poking at things. Now he stopped before the card that had accompanied the orchids.

"Whose house is this?" she said.

"I never reply to such questions. My life is an enigma to you. It has been so since we met and that is how I like it to remain." He picked up the card and handed it to her. "Keep this in your new handbag. From now on I expect you to cherish these small mementoes of me. See this?"

He had lifted the vodka bottle halfway out of its bucket.

"As a man, I naturally drink more than you. I don't drink well; alcohol gives me a headache, occasionally it makes me sick. But vodka is what I like." He dropped the bottle back into the bucket. "As for you, you get one small glass because I am emancipated, but basically I do not approve of women drinking." He picked up a dirty plate and showed it to her. "I have a sweet tooth, I like chocolates, cakes, and fruit. Particularly fruit. Grapes, but they must be green like the grapes of my home village. So what did Charlie eat last night?"

"I don't. Not when it's like that. I just smoke my postcoital fag."

"I'm afraid I do not allow smoking in the bedroom. In the Athens restaurant, I tolerated it because I am liberated. Even in the Mercedes, for you I occasionally allow it. But never in the bedroom. If you were thirsty in the night, you drank water from the tap." He began pulling on the red blazer. "You noticed how the tap gurgled?"

"No."

"Then it didn't gurgle. Sometimes it does, sometimes it doesn't."

"He's an Arab, isn't he?" she said, still watching him. "He's your archetypal Arab chauvinist. It's his car you've nicked."

He was closing the grip. Straightening, he gazed at her a second, partly in calculation and partly, she could not help feeling, in rejection.

"Oh, he is more than just Arab, I would say. He is more than just chauvinist. There is nothing *ordinary* about him at all, least of all in your eyes. Go over to the bed, please." He waited while she did so, watching her intently. "Feel under my pillow. Slowly—take care! I sleep on the right-hand side. So."

Cautiously, as he commanded, she slid her hand under the cold pillow, imagining the weight of Joseph's sleeping head pressing down on it.

"You have found it? I said take care."

Yes, Jose, she had found it.

"Lift it carefully. The safety catch is off. Michel is not in the habit of giving warnings before he shoots. The gun is a child to us. It shares every bed we sleep in. We call it 'our child.' Even when we are making passionate love, we never disturb that pillow and we never forget what is underneath it. That is how we live. Do you see now that I am not ordinary?"

She contemplated it, how it lay so neatly in her palm. Small. Brown and prettily proportioned.

"Have you ever handled such a gun?" Joseph asked.

"Frequently."

"Where? Who against?"

"On stage. Night after night after night." ·

She handed it to him and watched him slip it inside his blazer as easily as if he were putting away his wallet. She followed him downstairs. The house was empty and unexpectedly cold. The Mercedes stood waiting in the forecourt. At first she just wanted to leave: go anywhere, get out, the open road and us. The pistol had scared her and she needed movement. But as he started down the drive something made her turn and gaze back at the crumbling yellow plaster, the red flowers, the shuttered windows and old red tiles. And she realised too late how beautiful it all was, how welcoming just as she was leaving. It's the house of my youth, she decided: one of the many youths I never had. It's the house I never got married from; Charlie not in blue but white, my bloody mother in tears, and goodbye to all that.

"Do *we* exist as well?" she asked him as they joined the evening traffic. "Or is it just the other two?"

The three minute warning again before he answered. "Of course we exist. Why not?" Then the lovely smile, the one she would have tied herself to the railings for. "We are Berkeleyans, you see. If we do not exist, how can they?"

What's a Berkeleyan? she wondered. But she was too proud to ask.

For twenty minutes by the quartz clock on the dashboard, Joseph had barely spoken. Yet she had sensed no relaxation in him; rather, a methodical preparation before the attack.

"So, Charlie," he said suddenly, "you are ready?"

Jose, I am ready.

"On the twenty-sixth of June, a Friday, you are playing Saint Joan at the Barrie Theatre, Nottingham. You are not with your regular company; you have stepped in at the last minute to replace an actress who defaulted on her contract. The scenery is late arriving, the lighting is still on its way, you have been rehearsing all day long, two of the staff have gone sick with influenza. The occasion is so far clear in your memory?"

"Vivid."

Mistrusting her levity, he threw a questioning glance at her, but apparently could find nothing to object to. It was early evening. The dusk was falling fast, but Joseph's concentration had the immediacy of sunlight. This is his element, she thought; this is what he does best in his life; this remorseless momentum is the explanation that was missing till now.

"Minutes before curtain-up, a sprig of gold-brown orchids is delivered for you at the stage door with a note addressed to Joan. 'Joan, I love you infinitely.' "

"No stage door."

"There is a back entrance for stage deliveries. Your admirer, whoever he was, rang the bell and put the orchids into the arms of the janitor, a Mr. Lemon, together with a five-pound note. Mr. Lemon was suitably impressed by the large tip and promised to take them to you instantly—did he?"

"Barging into ladies' dressing-rooms unannounced is Lemon's best thing."

"So then. Tell me what you did when you received the orchids."

She hesitated. "The signature was 'M.' "

"M is correct. What did you do?"

"Nothing."

"Nonsense."

She was stung: "What was I supposed to do? I had about ten seconds before I was on."

A dust-laden lorry was careering towards them on the wrong side of the road. With majestic unconcern Joseph guided the Mercedes on to the soft shoulder and accelerated out of the slide. "So you threw thirty pounds' worth of orchids into your waste-paper basket, shrugged your shoulders, and went on stage. Perfect. I congratulate you."

"I put them in water."

"And what did you put the water in?"

The unexpected question sharpened her recollection. "A paint jar. The Barrie doubles as an art school in the mornings."

"You found a jar, you filled it with water, you put the orchids in the water. So. And what were your feelings while you did this? You were impressed? Excited?"

His question somehow caught her on the wrong foot. "I just got on with the show," she said, and giggled without meaning to. "Waited to see who turned up."

They had stopped for traffic lights. The stillness made a new intimacy.

"And the 'I love you'?" he asked.

"That's theatre, isn't it? Everybody loves everybody, some of the time. I liked the 'infinitely,' though. That was class."

The lights changed and they were driving again.

"You did not consider looking at the audience in case you saw anyone you recognised?"

"There wasn't time."

"And in the interval?"

"In the interval, I peeked, but I didn't see anyone I knew."

"And after the show, what did you do?"

"Returned to my dressing-room, changed, hung around a bit. Thought, sod it; went home."

"Home being the Astral Commercial Hotel, near the railway station."

She had long ago lost her capacity to be surprised by him. "The Astral Commercial and Private Hotel," she agreed. "Near the railway station."

"And the orchids?"

"Went with me to the hotel."

"You did not, however, ask Mr. Lemon the caretaker for a description of the person who had brought them?"

"Next day I did. Not the same night, no."

"And what answer did you obtain from Lemon when you did ask him?"

"He said a foreign gent but respectable. I asked what age; he leered and said just right. I tried to think of a foreign M but couldn't."

"Not in your whole private menagerie, one single foreign M? You disappoint me."

"Not a one."

Briefly, they both smiled, though not at each other.

"So, Charlie. We now have day two, a Saturday matinée followed by the evening performance, as usual—"

"And you were there, weren't you, bless you? Out there in the middle of the front row in your nice red blazer, surrounded by sticky school kids all coughing and wanting the loo."

Irritated by her levity, he devoted his attention to the road for a while, and then he resumed his line of questioning, it had a pointed earnestness that made his eyebrows come together in a schoolmasterly frown. "I wish you please to describe to me your feelings exactly, Charlie. It is mid-afternoon, the hall is in a half daylight owing to the poor curtains; we are sitting less in a theatre, I would say, than in a large classroom. I am in the front row; I have a decidedly foreign look, a foreign manner somehow, foreign clothes; I am extremely conspicuous among the children. You have

Lemon's description of me and, furthermore, I do not take my eyes off you. Do you not suspect at any point that I am the giver of the orchids, the strange man signed M who claims to love you infinitely?"

"Of course I did. I knew."

"How? Did you check with Lemon?"

"I didn't need to. I just knew. I saw you there, mooning at me, and I thought, hullo, it's you. Whoever *you* are. Then when the curtain went down for the end of the matinée, and you stayed put in your seat and produced your ticket for the next performance—"

"How did you know I did that? Who told you?"

And you're *that* sort too, she thought, adding one more hard-earned recognition of him to her album: when you get what you want, you turn all male and suspicious.

"You said it yourself. It's a small company in a one-horse theatre. We don't get many orchids—about one bunch per decade is average—and we don't get many punters staying to see the show round a second time." She could not resist the question: "Was it a bore, Jose? The show—actually? Twice running like that? Or did you quite enjoy it now and then?"

"It was the most monotonous day of my life," he replied without a second's hesitation. Then his rigid face broke and re-formed itself into the best smile ever, so that for a moment he really did look as if he had slipped through the bars of whatever confined him. "As a matter of fact, I thought you quite excellent," he said.

This time she did not object to his choice of adjective. "Will you crash the car now, please, Jose? This will do me fine. I'll die here."

And before he could stop her, she had grabbed his hand and kissed him hard on the knuckle of his thumb.

The road was straight but pot-holed; hills and trees to either side were powdered with moondust from a cement works. They were in their own capsule, where the nearness of other moving things only made their world more private. She was coming to him all over again, in her mind and in his story. She was a soldier's girl, learning to be a soldier.

"So tell me, please. Apart from the orchids, did you receive any other gifts while you were playing at the Barrie Theatre?"

"The box," she said with a shudder, before she had even made a show of pondering.

"What box, please?"

She had expected the question and already she was acting out her distaste for him, believing it was what he wanted. "It was some kind of trick. Some creep sent me a box to the theatre. Registered, special delivery."

"When was this?"

"Saturday. The same day you came to the matinée and stayed."

"And what was in the box?"

"Nothing. It was an empty jeweller's box. Registered and empty."

"How very strange. And the label—the label on the parcel? Did you examine it?"

"It was written in blue ballpoint. Capitals."

"But if it was registered, there must have been a sender also."

"Illegible. Looked like Marden. Could have been Hordern. Some local hotel."

"Where did you open it?"

"In my dressing-room between performances."

"Alone?"

"Yes."

"And what did you make of it?"

"I thought it was someone having a go at me because of my politics. It's happened before. Filthy letters. Nigger-lover. Commie pacifist. A stink-bomb through my dressing-room window. I thought it was them."

"Did you not associate the empty box with the orchids in some way?"

"Jose, I *liked* the orchids! I liked *you*."

He had stopped the car. Some layby in the middle of an industrial estate. Lorries were thundering past. For a moment she thought he might turn the world upside down and grab her, so paradoxical and erratic was the tension in her. But he didn't. Instead, reaching into the door pocket beside him, he handed her a reinforced registered envelope, with sealing wax on the flap and a hard square shape inside it, a replica of the one she had received that day. Postmark Nottingham, the twenty-fifth of June. On the front, her name and the address of the Barrie Theatre done in blue ballpoint. On the back, the sender's scrawl as before.

"Now we make the fiction," Joseph announced quietly while she slowly turned the envelope over. "On the old reality we impose the new fiction."

Too close to him to trust herself, she did not answer.

"The day has been hectic, as the day was. You are in your dressing-room, between performances. The parcel, still unopened, is awaiting you. You have how long before you are due on stage again?"

"Ten minutes. Maybe less."

"Very well. Now open the parcel."

She stole a glance at him but he was staring hard ahead at the enemy horizon. She looked down at the envelope, glanced at him again, shoved a finger into the flap, and wrenched it open. The same red jeweller's box, but heavier. Small white envelope, unsealed, plain white card within. *To Joan, spirit of my freedom,* she read. *You are fantastic. I love you!* The handwriting unmistakable. But instead of "M," the signature "Michel," written large, with the final "l" turned backward in a tail to underline the importance of the name. She shook the box and felt a soft, exhilarating thud from inside.

"My teeth," she said facetiously, but she did not succeed in destroying the tension inside herself, or him. "Do I open it? What is it?"

"How should I know? Do as you would do."

She lifted the lid. A thick gold bracelet, mounted with blue stones, nestled in the satin lining.

"Jesus," she said softly, and closed the box with a snap. "What do I have to do to earn *that*?"

"Very well, that is your first reaction," said Joseph immediately. "You take a look, you mutter a blasphemy, you shut the lid. Remember that. Exactly that. That was your response, from now on, always."

Opening the box again, she cautiously took out the bracelet and weighed it in her palm. But she had no experience of jewellery apart from the paste she sometimes wore on stage.

"Is it real?" she asked.

"Unfortunately you do not have experts present who can advise you. Make your own decisions."

"It's old," she pronounced finally.

"Very well, you decide it is old."

"And heavy."

"Old and heavy. Not out of a Christmas cracker, not some piece of child's nonsense, but a serious item of jewellery. What do you do?"

His impatience distanced them from one another: she so thoughtful and disturbed, he so practical. She studied the fittings, the hallmarks, but she understood nothing of hallmarks either. She scratched at the metal lightly with her fingernail. It felt oily and soft.

"You have very little time, Charlie. You are due on stage in one minute and thirty seconds. What do you do? Do you leave it in your dressing-room?"

"God, no."

"They are calling you. You must move, Charlie. You must decide."

"Stop pressuring me! I give it to Millie to look after for me. Millie's my understudy. She prompts."

The suggestion did not suit him at all.

"You do not trust her."

She was nearly in despair. "I put it in the loo," she said. "Behind the cistern—"

"Too obvious."

"In the waste-paper basket. Cover it over."

"Someone could walk in and empty it. Think."

"Jose, get off my— I put it behind the paint stuff! That's right. Up on one of the shelves. Nobody's dusted there for years."

"Excellent. You put it at the back of the shelf, you hurry to take up your position. Late. Charlie, Charlie, where have you been? The curtain rises. Yes?"

"Okay," she said, and puffed out about a gallon of air.

"What are your feelings? *Now*. About the bracelet—about its giver?"

"Well, I'm—I'm appalled—aren't I?"

"Why should you be appalled?"

"Well, I can't accept it—I mean it's money—it's valuable."

"But you *have* accepted it. You've signed for it and now you've hidden it."

"Only till after the show."

"And then?"

"Well, I'll give it back. Won't I?"

Relaxing a little, he too gave a sigh of relief, as if she had at long last proved his thesis. "And in the meantime, how do you feel?"

"Amazed. Shattered. What do you want me to feel?"

"He is a few feet away from you, Charlie. His eyes are fixed on you passionately. He is attending his third consecutive performance of your play. He has sent you orchids and jewellery and he has told you twice that he loves you. Once normally, once infinitely. He is beautiful. Much more beautiful than I am."

In her irritation, she ignored, for the time being, the steady intensification of his authority as he described her suitor.

"So I act my heart out then," she said, feeling trapped as well as foolish. "And that doesn't mean he's won set and match, either," she snapped.

Carefully, as if trying not to disturb her, Joseph restarted the car. The light had died, the traffic had thinned to an intermittent line of stragglers. They were skirting the Gulf of Corinth. Across the leaden water, a chain of shabby tankers pulled westward as if drawn magnetically by the glow of the vanished sun. Above them a ridge of hills was forming darkly in the twilight. The road forked, they began the long climb, turn after turn towards the emptying sky.

"You remember how I clapped for you?" said Joseph. "You remember I stood for you, curtain call after curtain call?"

Yes, Jose, I remember. But she didn't trust herself to say it out loud.

"Well then—now remember the bracelet too."

She did. An act of imagination all for him—a gift in return to her unknown, beautiful benefactor. The Epilogue over, she took her curtain calls, and the moment she was free she hurried to her dressing-room, recovered the bracelet from its hiding place, cleaned off her make-up at record speed, and flung on her day clothes in order to go to him fast.

But having connived at Joseph's version of events this far, Charlie backed sharply away as a belated sense of the proprieties came to her protection. "Just a minute—hang on—hold it—why doesn't *he* come to *me*? He's making the running. Why don't I just stay put in my dressing-room and wait for him to show up, instead of going out into the bushes to look for him?"

"Perhaps he hasn't the courage. He is too much in awe of you, why not? You have bowled him off his feet."

"Well, why don't I sit tight and *see*? Just for a bit."

"Charlie, what is your intention? You are saying to him *what*, in your mind, please?"

"I'm saying: 'Take this back—I can't accept it,' " she replied virtuously.

"Very well. Then will you seriously risk the chance he will slip away into the night—never to appear again—leaving you with this valuable gift which you so sincerely do not want to accept?"

With an ill grace she agreed to go and seek him out.

"But how—where will you find him? Where do you look first?" said Joseph.

The road was empty, but he was driving slowly in order that the present should intrude as little as possible upon the reconstructed past.

"I'd run round the back," she said before she had seriously thought. "Out of the back entrance, into the street, round the corner to the theatre foyer. Catch him on the pavement coming out."

"Why not through the theatre?"

"I'd have to fight my way through the milling throng, that's why. He'd be gone long before I ever got to him."

He thought about this. "Then you will need your mackintosh," he said.

Once again, he was right. She had forgotten the Nottingham rain that night, one cloudburst after another, all through the show. She began again. Having changed at lightning speed, she put on her new mackintosh—her long French one from the Liberty's sale—knotted the belt, and charged out into the teeming rain, down the street, round the corner to the front of the theatre—

"Only to find half the audience crammed under the canopy waiting for it to clear," Joseph interrupted. "Why are you smiling?"

"I need my yellow foulard round my head. You remember—the Jaeger one I got from my television commercial."

"We note also, then, that even in your haste to be rid of him, you do not forget your yellow headscarf. So. Wearing her mackintosh and yellow headscarf, Charlie dashes through the rain in search of her over-ardent lover. She arrives at the crowded foyer—calling 'Michel! Michel!' perhaps? Yes? Beautiful. Her cries are in vain, however. Michel is not there. So what do you do?"

"Did you *write* this, Jose?"

"Never mind."

"Go back to my dressing-room?"

"Does it not occur to you to look in the auditorium?"

"All right, damn it—yes, it does."

"You take which entrance?"

"The stalls. That's where you were sitting."

"Where Michel was. You take the stalls entrance, you push the bar to the door. Hooray, it yields. Mr. Lemon has not yet locked up. You enter the empty auditorium, you walk slowly down the aisle."

"And there he is," she said softly. "Jesus, that's corny."

"But it plays."

"Oh, it *plays*."

"Because there he is, still in his same seat, in the middle of the front row. Staring at the curtain as if by staring at it he could make it rise again upon the apparition of his Joan, the spirit of his freedom, whom he loves infinitely."

"I mean this is *awful*," Charlie murmured. But he ignored her.

"The same seat he has been sitting in for the last seven hours."

I want to go home, she thought. A long sleep all on my own at the Astral Commercial and Private. How many destinies can a girl meet in one day? For she could no longer miss the extra note of assurance in him, the drawing near, as he described her new admirer.

"You hesitate, then you call his name. 'Michel!' The only name you know. He turns to look at you but does not move. He does not smile, or greet you, or in any way demonstrate his considerable charm."

"So what does he do, the creep?"

"Nothing. He stares at you with his deep and passionate eyes, challenging you to speak. You may think him arrogant, you may think him romantic, but he is not ordinary and he is certainly not apologetic or bashful. He has come to claim you. He is young, cosmopolitan, well dressed. A man of movement and money, and lacking any sign of self-consciousness. So." He switched to the first person: "You walk towards me down the aisle, realising already that the scene is not unfolding in the way you expected. It is you, not I, apparently, who must provide the explanations. You take the bracelet from your pocket. You offer it to me. I make no move. The rain is dripping from you becomingly."

The road was leading them up a winding hill. His commanding voice, coupled to the mesmeric rhythm of successive bends, forced her mind further and further into the labyrinth of his story.

"You say something. What do you say?" Obtaining no answer from her, he supplied his own. " 'I do not know you. Thank you, Michel, I am flattered. But I do not know you and I cannot accept this gift.' Would you say that? Yes, you would. But better, perhaps."

She barely heard him. She was standing before him in the auditorium, holding the box to him, gazing into his dark eyes. And my new boots, she thought; the long brown ones I bought myself for Christmas. Ruined by the rain, but who cares?

Joseph was continuing his fairy tale. "Still I speak not one word. You will know from your theatrical experience that there is nothing like silence to establish communication. If the wretched fellow won't speak, what can you do? You are obliged to speak again yourself. Tell me what you say to me this time."

An unwonted shyness struggled with her burgeoning imagination. "I ask him who he is."

"My name is Michel."

"I know that part. Michel who?"

"No answer."

"I ask you what you are doing in Nottingham."

"Falling in love with you. Go on."

"Christ—Jose—"

"Go on!"

"He can't say that to me!"

"Then tell him!"

"I reason with him. Appeal to him."

"Then let's hear you do it—he's waiting for you, Charlie! Speak to him!"

"I'd say . . ."

"Yes?"

" 'Look, Michel . . . it's nice of you . . . I'm very flattered. But sorry—it's too much.' "

He was disappointed. "Charlie, you must do better than that," he reproved her austerely. "He's an Arab—even if you don't know that yet, you may suspect it—you are refusing his gift. You must try harder."

" 'It's not fair to you, Michel. People often get fixations about actresses . . . and actors . . . happens every day. That's no reason to go ruining yourself . . . just for a kind of . . . illusion.' "

"Good. Continue."

It was coming more easily to her. She hated his browbeating of her, as she hated any producer's, but she could not deny its effect. " 'That's what acting's all about, Michel. Illusion. The audience sits down here hoping to be enchanted. The actors stand up there hoping to enchant you. We succeeded. But I can't accept this. It's beautiful.' " She meant the bracelet. " 'Too beautiful. I can't accept anything. We've fooled you. That's all that's happened. Theatre's a con trick, Michel. Do you know what that means? Con trick? You've been deceived.' "

"I still don't speak."

"Well, make him!"

"Why? Are you running out of conviction already? Don't you feel responsible for me? A young boy like this—so handsome—throwing away my money on orchids and expensive jewels?"

"Of course I do! I've told you!"

"Then protect me," he insisted, in an impatient tone. "Save me from my infatuation."

"I'm trying!"

"That bracelet cost me hundreds of pounds—even you can guess that. For all you know, thousands. I might have stolen it for you. Killed. Pawned my inheritance. All for you. I am besotted, Charlie! Be charitable! Exercise your power!"

In her imagination's eye, Charlie had sat herself beside Michel in the next seat. Her hands clasped on her lap, she was leaning forward earnestly to reason with him. She was a nurse to him, a mother. A friend.

"I tell him he would be disappointed if he knew me in reality."

"The exact words, please."

She took a deep breath and plunged: " 'Listen, Michel, I'm just an ordinary girl. I've got torn tights, and an over-draft, and I'm certainly no Joan of Arc, believe me. I'm no virgin, and no soldier, and God and I haven't exchanged a word since I was chucked out of school for'—I'm not going to say that bit—'I'm Charlie, a feckless Western slut.' "

"Excellent. Go on."

" 'Michel, you've got to snap out of this. I mean I'm do-ing what I can to help, okay? So here, take this back, keep your money and your illusions—and thanks. Thanks, truly. Really thanks. Over and out.' "

"But you don't *want* him to keep his illusions," Joseph objected aridly. "Or do you?"

"All right, give up his bloody illusions!"

"So how does it end?"

"It just did. I put the bracelet on the seat beside him and walked out. Thanks, world, and bye-bye. If I hurry to the bus-stop, I'll be just in time for rubber chicken at the Astral."

Joseph was appalled. His face said so, and his hand left the wheel in a rare, if limited, gesture of supplication.

"But, Charlie, how can you do this? Do you not know you are leaving me to commit suicide perhaps? To roam the rain-swept streets of Nottingham all night? Alone? While you lie beside my orchids and my note in the warmth of your ele-gant hotel."

"Elegant! Christ, the bloody fleas are damp!"

"Do you have no sense of responsibility? You of all people, champion of the underdog—for a boy you have en-snared with your beauty and your talents and your revolu-tionary passion?"

She tried to bridle but he gave her no opportunity.

"You have a warm heart, Charlie. Others might think of Michel at that moment as some kind of refined seducer. Not you. You believe in people. And that is how you are tonight, with Michel. Without thought for yourself, you are sincerely affected by him."

On the skyline ahead of them a crumbling village marked a small peak in their ascent. She saw the lights of a taverna strung along the roadside.

"Anyway, your response at this moment is irrelevant because Michel finally decides to speak to you," Joseph resumed, with a swift, measuring glance at her. "In a soft and appealing foreign accent, part French, part something else, he addresses you without shyness or inhibition. He is not interested in arguments, he says, you are everything he has ever dreamed of, he wishes to become your lover, preferably tonight, and he calls you Joan although you tell him you are Charlie. If you will go out with him to dinner, and after dinner you still do not want him any more, he will consider taking back the bracelet. No, you say, he must take it back now; you already have a lover, and besides, don't be ridiculous, where is dinner in Nottingham at half past ten on a pouring wet Saturday night? . . . You would say this? Is it true?"

"It's a dump," she admitted, refusing to look at him.

"And dinner—you would say specifically that dinner is an impossible dream?"

"It's Chinese or fish and chips."

"Nevertheless, you have made a dangerous concession to him."

"How?" she demanded, stung.

"You have made a practical objection. 'We cannot dine together because there is no restaurant.' You might as well say you cannot sleep together because you have no bed. Michel senses this. He brushes your hesitations aside. He knows a place, he has made arrangements. So. We can eat. Why not?"

Swinging off the road, he had brought the car to a halt in the gravel layby in front of the taverna. Dazed by his wilful leap from past fiction to present time, perversely elated by his harassment of her, and relieved that, after all, Michel had not let her go, Charlie remained in her seat. So did Joseph. She turned to him and her eyes made out, by the coloured fairy lights outside, the direction of his own. He was gazing at her hands, still linked on her lap, the right hand uppermost. His face, as far as she could read it by the fairy lights, was rigid and expressionless. Reaching out, he clasped her right wrist with a swift, surgical confidence and, lifting it, revealed the wrist below, and round it the gold bracelet, twinkling in the dark.

"Well, well, I must congratulate you," he remarked impassively. "You English girls don't waste much time!"

Angrily she snatched back her hand. "What's the matter?" she snapped. "Jealous, are we?"

But she could not hurt him. He had the face that did not mark. Who are you? she wondered hopelessly as she followed him in. Him? Or you? Or nobody?

9

Yet, much as Charlie might have supposed the contrary, she was not the only centre of Joseph's universe that night; not of Kurtz's; and certainly not of Michel's.

Well before Charlie and her putative lover had said a last goodbye to the Athens villa—while they still, in the fiction, lay in each other's arms, sleeping off their frenzy—Kurtz and Litvak were chastely seated in different rows of a Lufthansa plane bound for Munich, and travelling under the protection of different countries: for Kurtz, France, and for Litvak, Canada. On landing, Kurtz repaired immediately to the Olympic Village, where the so-called Argentinian photographers eagerly awaited him, and Litvak to the Hotel Bayerischer Hof, where he was greeted by a munitions expert known to him only as Jacob, a sighing, other-worldish fellow in a stained suède jacket, who carried with him a wad of large-scale maps in a pop-down plastic folder. Posing as a surveyor, Jacob had spent the last three days taking laborious measurements along the Munich-to-Salzburg autobahn. His brief was to calculate the likely effect, in a variety of weathers and traffic conditions, of a very big explosive charge detonated at the roadside in the early hours of a weekday morning. Over several pots of excellent coffee in the lounge, the two men discussed Jacob's tentative suggestions, then, in a hired car, slowly toured the entire hundred-and-forty-kilometre stretch together, annoying the faster traffic and stopping at almost every point where they were allowed, and some where they were not.

From Salzburg, Litvak continued alone to Vienna, where a new team of outriders was awaiting him with fresh transport and fresh faces. Litvak briefed them in a soundproofed conference room at the Israeli Embassy and, having attended to other small matters there, including reading the latest bulletins from Munich, led them southward in a ragged trippers' convoy to the area of the Yugoslav border, where with the frankness of summer sightseers they made a reconnaissance of urban car parks, railway stations, and picturesque market squares, before distributing themselves over several humble *pensions* in the region of Villach. His net thus spread, he hurried back to Munich in order to contemplate the crucial preparation of the bait.

The interrogation of Yanuka was entering its fourth day when Kurtz arrived to take up the reins, and had proceeded till then with unnerving smoothness.

"You have six days with him maximum," Kurtz had warned his two interrogators in Jerusalem. "After six days your errors will be permanent, and so will his."

It was a job after Kurtz's heart. If he could have been in three places at once rather than merely two, he would have kept it to himself, but he couldn't, so he chose as his proxies these two heavy-bodied specialists in the soft approach, famous for their muted histrionic talents and a joint air of lugubrious good nature. They were not related, nor, so far as anybody knew, were they lovers, but they had worked in unison for so long that their befriending features gave a sense of duplication, and when Kurtz first summoned them to the house in Disraeli Street, their four hands rested on the table-edge like the paws of two big dogs. At first he had treated them harshly, because he envied them, and was of a mood to regard delegation as defeat. He had given them only an inkling of the operation, then ordered them to study Yanuka's file and not report to him again until they knew it inside out. When they had returned too quickly for his liking, he had grilled them like an interrogator himself, snapping questions at them about Yanuka's childhood, his life-style, behaviour patterns, anything to ruffle them. They were word perfect. So grudgingly he had called in his Literacy Committee, consisting of Miss Bach, the writer Leon, and old Schwili, who in the intervening weeks had pooled their eccentricities and turned themselves into a neatly interlocking team. Kurtz's briefing on that occasion was a classic of the art of unclarity.

"Miss Bach here has the supervision, holds all the strings," he had begun, by way of introducing the new boys. After thirty-five years of it, his Hebrew was still famously awful. "Miss Bach monitors the raw material as it comes down to her. She makes up the bulletins for transmission to the field. She supplies Leon here with his guidelines. She checks out his compositions, makes sure they fit the overall game-plan for the correspondence." If the interrogators had known a little before, they knew less now. But they had kept their mouths shut. "Once Miss Bach has approved a composition, she calls a conference with Leon here and Mr. Schwili jointly." It had been a hundred years since anyone had called Schwili "Mister." "At this conference are agreed the stationery, are agreed the inks, pens, the emotional and physical condition of the writer inside the terms of the fiction. Is he or she high or low? Is he or she angry? With each projected item, the team considers the entire fiction in all its aspects." Gradually, despite their new chief's determination to imply his information rather than impart it, the interrogators had begun to discern the outlines of the plan they were now part of. "Maybe Miss Bach will also have on record an original sample of handwriting—letter, postcard, diary—that can serve as a model. Maybe she won't." Kurtz's right forearm had batted either possibility across the desk at them. "When all these procedures have been observed, and only then, Mr. Schwili forges. Beautifully. Mr. Schwili is not merely a forger, he is an *artist*," he had warned—and they had better remember it. "His work complete, Mr. Schwili hands it straight back to Miss Bach. For further checking, for fingerprinting, for docketing, for storage. Questions?"

Smiling their meek smile, the interrogators had assured him they had none.

"Start at the end," Kurtz barked after them as they trooped out. "You can go back to the beginning later if there's time."

Other meetings had been taken up with the more tricky issue of how best to persuade Yanuka to fall in with their plans at such short notice. Once again, Misha Gavron's beloved psychologists were called in, peremptorily listened to, and shown the door. A lecture on hallucinatory and disintegrating drugs fared better, and there was a hasty hunt around for other interrogators who had used them with success. Thus to the long-term planning was added, as ever, an atmosphere of last-minute improvisation that Kurtz and all of them loved. Their orders agreed, Kurtz dispatched the interrogators to Munich ahead of time to set up their lighting and sound effects and rehearse the guards in their rôle. They arrived looking like a two-piece band, with heavy luggage clad in dimpled metal, and suits like Satchmo's. Schwili's committee followed a couple of days later and settled themselves discreetly into the lower apartment, giving themselves out as professional stamp dealers here for the big auction in the city. The neighbours found no fault with this story. Jews, they told each other, but who cares these days? Jews had been normalised long ago. And of course they would be dealers, what else did one expect? For company, apart from Miss Bach's portable memory-storage system, they had tape-recorders, earphones, crates of tinned food, and a thin boy called "Samuel the pianist" to man the little teleprinter that was linked to Kurtz's own command set. Samuel wore a very large Colt revolver in a special pocket of his quilted kapok waistcoat, and when he transmitted they heard it knocking against the desk, but he never took it off. He was of the same quiet cast as David of the Athens house; in manner, he could have been his twin.

The allocation of rooms was Miss Bach's responsibility. To Leon, on account of its quietness, she assigned the child's room. On its walls, dew-eyed deer peacefully cropped giant daisies. To Samuel went the kitchen with its natural access to the rear courtyard, where he rigged up his aerial and hung babies' socks from it. But when Schwili caught sight of the bedroom set aside for his own use—office and sleep space combined—he let out a spontaneous wail of woe.

"My light! Dear God, look at my light! A man could not forge a letter to his own grandmother in such a light!"

With Leon, full of nervous creativity, reeling before this unexpected storm, the practical Miss Bach spotted the problem immediately: Schwili needed more daylight for his work—but also, after his long incarceration, for his soul. In a trice she had phoned upstairs, the Argentinian boys appeared, furniture was whisked around like playblocks under her direction, and Schwili's desk was repositioned in the living-room window bay, with a view of green leaves and sky. Miss Bach herself tacked up an extra thickness of net curtain for his privacy and ordered Leon to make an extension for his posh Italian lamp. Then, on Miss Bach's nod, they quietly left him, though Leon watched him covertly from his door.

Seated before the dying evening sunlight, Schwili laid

out his precious inks and pens and stationery, everything to
its appointed place, as if tomorrow were his big exam. Then
he took off his cuff-links and slowly rubbed his palms together to warm them, though it was warm enough even for
an old prisoner. Then he removed his hat. Then he pulled at
each finger one by one, loosening the joints with a salvo of
little snapping noises. Then he settled to wait, as he had
waited all his adult life.

The star they were all poised to receive flew into Munich
punctually the same evening by way of Cyprus. No flashing
cameras celebrated his arrival, for he was got up as a
stretcher case attended by an orderly and a private doctor.
The doctor was genuine, if his passport was not; as to
Yanuka, he was a British businessman from Nicosia being
rushed to Munich for heart surgery. A file of impressive medical papers bore this out, but the German airport authorities
paid them not a glance. One uncomfortable sight of the patient's lifeless face told them all they needed to know. An
ambulance rushed the party in the direction of the city hospital, but in a side street turned off and, as if the worst had
happened, slipped into the covered courtyard of a friendly
undertaker. At the Olympic Village, the two Argentinian photographers and their friends were seen to manhandle a wicker
laundry basket marked "GLASS DELICATE" from their battered
minibus to the service lift, and no doubt, said the neighbours,
they were adding one more extravagance to their already in-
flated stock of equipment. There was amused speculation
about whether the stamp dealers downstairs would complain
about their tastes in music: Jews complained of everything.
Upstairs, meanwhile, they unpacked their prize and, with
the doctor's help, established that nothing was broken from
the voyage. Minutes later, they had laid him carefully on the
floor of the padded priesthole where he could be expected to
come round in about half an hour, though it was always possible that the light-proof hood which they had tied over his
head would retard the waking process. Soon after that, the
doctor departed. He was a conscientious man and, fearing for
Yanuka's future, had sought assurances from Kurtz that he
would not be asked to compromise his medical principles.

Sure enough, in less than forty minutes they saw Yanuka

pull against his chains, first the wrists and then the knees, and
then all four together, like a chrysalis trying to burst its skin,
till presumably he realised that he was trussed face downward; for he paused, and seemed to take stock, then let out a
tentative groan. After which, with no further warning, all hell
broke loose as Yanuka gave vent to one anguished, sobbing
roar after another, writhed, bucked, and generally threw himself about with a vigour that made them doubly grateful for
his chains. Having observed this performance for a while, the
interrogators withdrew and left the field to the guards until
the storm raged itself out. Probably Yanuka's head had been
crammed with hair-raising stories about the brutality of Israeli
methods. Probably in his bewilderment he actually wanted
them to live up to their reputation and make his terrors come
true. But the guards declined to oblige him. Their orders were
to play the sullen jailers, to keep their distance and inflict no
injury, and they obeyed them to the letter, even if to do so
cost them dear—Oded the baby, in particular. From the moment of Yanuka's ignominious arrival in the apartment,
Oded's young eyes had darkened with hatred. Each day that
passed, he looked more ill and grey, and by the sixth his
shoulders had gone rigid, just from the tension of having
Yanuka under their roof alive.

At last, Yanuka seemed to drop off to sleep again and
the interrogators decided it was time to make a start, so they
played sounds of morning traffic, switched on a lot of white
light, and together brought him breakfast—though it was not
yet midnight—loudly ordering the guards to unbind him and
let him eat like a human being, not a dog. Then they themselves solicitously untied his hood, for they wanted his first
knowledge of them to be their kind, un-Jewish faces gazing at
him with fatherly concern.

"Don't you ever put these things on him again," one of
them said quietly to the guards, in English, and with an angry
heave symbolically tossed both hood and chains into a corner.

The guards withdrew—Oded in particular with theatrical
reluctance—and Yanuka consented to drink a little coffee
while his two new friends looked on. They knew he had a
raging thirst because they had asked the doctor to induce one
before he left, so the coffee must have been tasting wonderful
to him, whatever else was mixed into it. They knew also that
his mind was in a state of dreamlike fragmentation and there-

fore undefended in certain important areas—for instance, when compassion was on offer. After several more visits conducted in this way, some with only minutes between them, the interrogators decided it was time to take the plunge and introduce themselves. In outline, their plan was the oldest in the game, but it contained ingenious variations.

They were Red Cross observers, they said in English. They were Swiss subjects, but resident here in the prison. What prison, where, they were not at liberty to reveal, though they gave clear hints it might be Israel. They produced impressive prison passes in well-thumbed plastic cases, with stamped photographs of themselves and red crosses done in wavy lines like banknotes to prevent easy forgery. They explained that their job was to make sure that the Israelis observed the rules for prisoners of war laid down by the Geneva Convention—though, God knew, they said, that wasn't easy—and to provide Yanuka's link with the outside world, in so far as prison regulations allowed this. They were pressing to get him out of solitary and into the Arab block, they said, but they understood that "rigorous interrogation" was to start any day, and that until then the Israelis intended willy-nilly to keep him in isolation. Sometimes, they explained, the Israelis simply lost themselves in their own obsessions, and forgot about their image completely. They pronounced "interrogation" with distaste, as if they wished they knew a better word. At this point Oded came back in, as instructed, and pretended to busy himself with the sanitation. The interrogators at once stopped speaking until he left.

Next they produced a big printed form and helped Yanuka to complete it in his own hand: name here, old fellow, address, date of birth, next of kin, that's the way, occupation—well, that would be student, wouldn't it?—qualifications, religion, and sorry about all this but it's regulations. Yanuka complied accurately enough, despite an initial reluctance, and this first sign of collaboration was noted by the Literacy Committee downstairs with quiet satisfaction—even if his handwriting was puerile on account of the drugs.

Taking their leave, the interrogators handed Yanuka a printed booklet setting out his rights in English and, with a wink and a pat on the shoulder, a couple of bars of Swiss chocolate. And they called him by his first name, Salim. For an hour, from the adjoining room, they watched him by infra-red light as he lay in the pitch dark, weeping and tossing his head. Then they raised the lighting and barged in cheer-fully, calling out, "Look what we've got for you; come on, wake up, Salim, it's morning." It was a letter, addressed to him by name. Postmark Beirut, sent care of the Red Cross, and stamped "Prison Censor Approved." From his beloved sister Fatmeh, who had given him the gilded charm to wear round his neck. Schwili had forged it, Miss Bach had com-piled it, Leon's chameleon talent had supplied the authentic pulse of Fatmeh's censorious affection. Their models were the letters Yanuka had received from her while he was under sur-veillance. Fatmeh sent her love and hoped Salim would show courage when his time came. By "time" she seemed to mean the dreaded interrogation. She had decided to give up her boyfriend and her office job, she said, and resume her relief work in Sidon because she could no longer bear to be so far from the border of her beloved Palestine while Yanuka was in such desperate straits. She admired him; she always would; Leon swore it. To the grave and beyond, Fatmeh would love her gallant, heroic brother; Leon had seen to it. Yanuka ac-cepted the letter with pretended indifference, but when they left him alone again, he fell into a pious crouch, with his head turned nobly sideways and upward like a martyr waiting for the sword, while he clutched Fatmeh's words to his cheek.

"I demand paper," he told the guards, with panache, when they returned to sweep out his cell an hour later.

He might as well not have spoken. Oded even yawned.

"I demand paper! I demand the representatives of the Red Cross! I demand to write a letter under the Geneva Con-vention to my sister Fatmeh! Yes!"

These words also were favourably greeted downstairs, since they proved that the Literacy Committee's first offering had gained Yanuka's acceptance. A special bulletin was im-mediately transmitted to Athens. The guards slunk off, osten-sibly to take advice, and reappeared bearing a small stack of Red Cross stationery. They also handed Yanuka a printed "Advice to Prisoners," explaining that only letters in English would be forwarded, "and only those containing no hidden message." But no pen. Yanuka demanded a pen, begged for one, screamed at them, wept, all in slow motion, but the boys retorted loudly and distinctly that the Geneva Convention said nothing about pens. Half an hour later, the two interrogators bustled in full of righteous anger, bringing a pen of their own, stamped "For Humanity."

Scene by scene, this charade continued over several more hours while Yanuka in his weakened state struggled vainly to reject the offered hand of friendship. His written reply to Fatmeh was a classic: a rambling three-page letter of advice, self-pity, and bold postures, providing Schwili with his first "clean" sample of Yanuka's handwriting under emotional stress, and Leon with an excellent foretaste of his English prose-style.

"My darling sister, in one week now I face the fateful testing of my life at which your great spirit will accompany me," he wrote. That news too was the subject of a special bulletin: "Send me everything," Kurtz had told Miss Bach. "No silences. If nothing's happening, then signal to me that nothing is happening." And to Leon, more fiercely, "See she signals me every two hours at least. Best is every hour."

Yanuka's letter to Fatmeh was the first of several. Sometimes their letters crossed; sometimes Fatmeh answered his questions almost as soon as he had put them; and asked him her own questions in return.

Start at the end, Kurtz had told them. The end, in this case, was miles of seemingly irrelevant small talk. For hour upon hour the two interrogators chatted to Yanuka with unflagging geniality, fortifying him, as he must have thought, with their stolid Swiss sincerity, building up his resistance against the day when the Israeli henchmen dragged him off to his inquisition. First, they sought his opinions on almost everything he cared to discuss, flattering him with their respectful curiosity and responsiveness. Politics, they shyly confessed, had never really been their field: their inclination had always been to place man above ideas. One of them quoted from the poetry of Robert Burns, who turned out quite by chance to be a favourite with Yanuka also. Sometimes it almost seemed they were asking him to convert them to his own way of thinking, so receptive were they to his arguments. They asked him for his reactions to the Western world now that he had been there for a year or more, first generally, then country by country, and listened entranced to his unoriginal generalisations: the self-interest of the French; the greed of the Germans; the decadence of the Italians.

And England? they enquired innocently.

Oh, England was the worst of all! he replied decisively. England was decadent, bankrupt, and directionless; England was the agent of American imperialism; England was everything bad, and her greatest crime was to have given his country to the Zionists. He wandered away into yet another diatribe against Israel, and they let him. They did not wish at this early stage to kindle the least suspicion in him that his travels in England were of special interest. They asked him instead about his childhood—his parents, his home in Palestine—and it was observed with silent satisfaction that he never once mentioned his elder brother; that even now, big brother was written out of Yanuka's life entirely. With so much going for them, they noted, Yanuka would still talk only of matters he considered harmless to his cause.

They listened with unflinching sympathy to his stories of Zionist atrocities, and to his reminiscences about his days as goalkeeper with his camp's victorious football team in Sidon. "Tell us about your best match," they urged. "Tell us about your best save ever. Tell us about that cup you won, and who was there when the great Abu Ammar himself pressed it into your hand!" Haltingly, shyly, Yanuka obliged them. Downstairs the tape-recorders turned and Miss Bach entered one nugget after another into her machine, only pausing to pass interim bulletins to Samuel the pianist for dispatch to Jerusalem, and to his counterpart, David, in Athens. Leon meanwhile was in his private heaven. Eyes half closed, he was immersing himself in Yanuka's idiosyncratic spoken English: in his impulsive, rushing style of delivery; his spurts of literary flourish; his cadence and vocabulary; his unheralded changes of theme, which occurred practically in mid-sentence. Across the passage from him, Schwili penned and muttered to himself and chortled. But sometimes, Leon noticed, he broke off and lapsed into despair. A few seconds later, Leon would see him padding softly round his room, pacing out its dimensions with an old prisoner's empathy for the luckless boy above.

To talk about the diary, they had a different bluff, and a far more hazardous one. They put it off until the third real day, by which time they had picked him as clean as they knew how by the simple conversational methods. Even then, they insisted on Kurtz's say-so before they went ahead, so nervous were they of breaking the eggshell of Yanuka's trust in them at a point where they had no time left to resort to other methods. The watchers had found it on the day after Yanuka's kidnapping. They had marched into his flat, three of them, wearing canary overalls with badges describing them as members of a commercial cleaning firm. A house key and an almost genuine letter of instruction from Yanuka's landlord gave them all the authority they needed. From their canary van they fetched vacuum cleaners, mops, and a stepladder. Then they closed the door and drew the curtains and for eight full hours went through that flat like locusts, till there seemed to be nothing left they had not probed, photographed, and put back in its rightful place before laying dust over it from a puffer. And among their finds, wedged behind a bookcase in a spot handy for the telephone, was this brown leather-clad pocket diary, a handout from Middle East Airlines that Yanuka must somehow have come by. They knew he kept one; they had missed it among his effects when they grabbed him. Now, to their joy, they had found it. Some entries were in Arabic, some in French, some in English. Some were indecipherable in any language, others in a none too private word-code. Mostly, the jottings related to forward appointments, but a few had been added retrospectively: "Met J, phoned P." In addition to the diary, they discovered another prize they had been looking out for: a plump manila envelope containing a wad of receipts, kept against the day when Yanuka got round to making up his operational accounts. On instruction, the team purloined that also.

But how to interpret the crucial entries in the diary? How to decipher them without Yanuka's help?

How therefore to obtain Yanuka's help?

They considered an increase in his drug intake, but decided against it. They feared he might unhinge completely. To resort to violence was to throw all their hard-earned goodwill out of the window. Besides, as professionals they genuinely deplored the very thought. They preferred to build on what they had already established—on fear, on dependence, and on the imminence of the fearful Israeli interrogation still to come. So first they brought him an urgent letter from Fatmeh, one of Leon's briefest and best: "I have heard that the

hour is very near. I beg you, I pray you, to have courage."
They switched on the lights for him to read it, switched them
off again, and stayed away longer than was customary. In the
pitch darkness, they played muffled screams to him, the clang-
ing of distant cell doors, and the sounds of a slumped body
being dragged in chains along a stone corridor. Then they
played the funeral bagpipes of a Palestinian military band
and perhaps he thought he was dead. Certainly he lay still
enough. They sent him the guards, who stripped him, chained
his hands behind his back, and put irons on his ankles. And
left him again. As if for ever. They heard him whispering "oh
no," on and on.

They dressed Samuel the pianist in a white tunic and
gave him a stethoscope, and had him listen, without interest,
to Yanuka's heart rate. All in the dark still, but perhaps the
white coat was just visible to him as it flitted round his body.
Again they left him. By the infra-red light they watched him
sweating and shuddering, and at one point he appeared to
contemplate killing himself by butting his head against the
wall, which in his chained state was about the only uninhib-
ited movement he could make. But the wall was deep in kapok, and if he had beaten himself against it all year, he
would have had no satisfaction from it. They played more
screams to him, then made an absolute silence. They fired
one pistol shot in the darkness. It was so sudden and clear
that he bucked at the sound of it. Then he began howling,
but quietly, as if he couldn't get the volume to rise.

That was when they decided to move.

First the guards walked into his cell, purposefully, and
lifted him to his feet, one arm each. They had dressed themselves very lightly, like people prepared for strenuous activity.
By the time they had dragged his shaking body as far as the
cell door, Yanuka's two Swiss saviours appeared and blocked
their way, their kindly faces the very picture of concern and
outrage. Then a long-delayed, passionate argument broke out
between the guards and the Swiss. It was waged in Hebrew
and therefore only partly comprehensible to Yanuka, but it
had the ring of a last appeal. Yanuka's interrogation had still
to be approved by the governor, said the two Swiss: Regula-
tion 6, para 9 of the Convention laid down emphatically that
no intensive duress could be applied without the authority of
the governor and the presence of a doctor. But the guards

could not give a fig for the Convention, and said so. They had had the Convention till it was coming out of their noses, they said, indicating where their noses were. There was nearly a scuffle. Only Swiss forbearance prevented it. It was agreed instead that they would all four go to the governor *now* for an immediate ruling. So they stormed off together, leaving Yanuka in the dark yet again, and quite soon he was seen to hunch up to the wall and pray, though he could have had no earthly idea, by then, where the East was.

Next time, the two Swiss returned without the guards but looking very grave indeed, and bringing with them Yanuka's diary as if, small though it might be, it somehow changed things completely. They also had with them his two spare passports, one French, one Cypriot, which had been found hidden under the floorboards in his flat, and the Cypriot passport on which he had been travelling at the time of his kidnapping.

Then they explained their problem. Laboriously. But with an ominous manner that was new to them—not threatening but warning. At the request of the Israelis, the West German authorities had made a search of his apartment in central Munich, they said. They had found this diary and these passports and a quantity of other clues to his movements over the last few months, which they were now determined to investigate "with full vigour." In their representations to the governor, the Swiss had insisted that such a proposal was neither legal nor necessary. Let the Red Cross place the documents before the prisoner, they suggested, and obtain his explanation for the entries. Let the Red Cross, in decency, invite him, rather than force him, as a first step, to prepare a statement—if the governor wished, a written one, in the prisoner's own hand—of his whereabouts during the last six months, with dates, places, whom he had met, where he had stayed, and on what papers he had travelled. If military honour dictated reticence, they said, then let the prisoner honestly indicate this at the appropriate points. Where it did not—well, at least it would buy time while their representations continued.

Here they ventured to offer Yanuka—or Salim as they now called him—some private advice of their own. Above all, be *accurate*, they implored him as they set up a folding table for him, gave him a blanket, and unchained his hands.

Tell them nothing you wish to keep secret, but make absolutely certain that what you do tell them is the truth. Remember that we have our reputation to maintain. Think of those like yourself who may come after you. For their sakes, if not for ours, do your best. The way they said this suggested somehow that Yanuka was already halfway to martyrdom. Quite why seemed not to matter; the only truth he knew by then was the terror in his own soul.

It was thin, as they had always known it would be. And there was a moment, a rather long one, in which they feared they had lost him. It took the form of a straight, unclouded stare at each of them as Yanuka seemed to shake aside the curtains of delusion and look out clearly at his oppressors. But clarity had never been the basis of their relationship and it wasn't now. As Yanuka accepted the proffered pen, they read in his eyes the unmistakeable supplication that they should continue to deceive him.

It was on the day following these dramas—around lunchtime in the normal scheme of things—that Kurtz arrived directly from Athens, in order to inspect Schwili's handiwork, and to give his own personal approval for the diary, passports, and receipts, with certain ingenious embellishments, to be put back where they legally belonged.

To Kurtz himself went also the task of going back to the beginning. But first, seated comfortably in the downstairs apartment, he called in everyone except the guards and let them brief him, in their own style and at their own pace, on the progress so far. Wearing white cotton gloves, and looking none the worse for his all-night interrogation of Charlie, he examined their exhibits, listened appreciatively to tape-recordings of crucial moments, and watched with admiration as Miss Bach's desk computer printed out one day after another of Yanuka's recent life in green type on its television screen: dates, flight numbers, arrival times, hotels. Then he watched again while the screen cleared and Miss Bach superimposed the fiction: "Writes Charlie from City Hotel, Zürich, letter posted on arrival de Gaulle Airport eighteen-twenty hours . . . meets Charlie Excelsior Hotel, Heathrow . . . phones Charlie from Munich railway station . . ." And with each insertion, the collateral: which receipts and diary entries referred to which encounter; where deliberate gaps and obscurities had been introduced, because in the reconstruction nothing should ever be too easy or too clear.

When Kurtz had done all this—it was by then evening—he took off the gloves, changed into a plain Israeli Army uniform with a colonel's badges and a few grimy campaign ribbons above the left pocket, and generally reduced his external self until he was the epitome of any military remittance man turned prison officer. Then he went upstairs and tiptoed spryly to the observation window, where for some time he watched Yanuka very closely. Then he sent Oded and his companion downstairs with orders that he and Yanuka should be left with their privacy. Speaking Arabic in a grey, bureaucratic voice, Kurtz began asking Yanuka a few simple, dull questions, tiny things: where a certain fuse came from, or explosive, or a car; or the exact spot, say, where Yanuka and the girl had met up before she planted the Godesberg bomb. Kurtz's detailed knowledge, so casually displayed, was terrifying to Yanuka, whose reaction was to shout at him and order him to keep quiet for reasons of security. Kurtz was puzzled by this.

"But why should I keep quiet?" he protested, with the glazed stupidity which comes over people who have spent too long in prison, whether as guards or inmates. "If your great brother won't keep quiet, what secrets are there left for me to preserve?"

He asked this question not as a revelation at all, but as the logical outcome to a piece of common knowledge. While Yanuka was still staring wildly at him, Kurtz told him a few more things about himself that only his big brother could have known. There was nothing magical about this. After weeks of sifting through the boy's daily life, monitoring his phone calls and his correspondence—not to mention his dossier in Jerusalem from two years back—it was no wonder if Kurtz and his team were as familiar as Yanuka himself was with such minutiae as the safe addresses where his letters went to earth; the ingenious one-way system by which his orders were handed to him; and the point at which Yanuka, like themselves, was cut off from his own command structure. What distinguished Kurtz from his predecessors was the evident indifference with which he referred to these items, and his indifference also to Yanuka's reaction.

"Where is he?" Yanuka began screaming. "What have you done with him? My brother does not talk! He would never talk! How did you capture him?"

The deal was done in moments. Downstairs, as they crowded round the loudspeaker, a kind of awe settled over the whole room as they heard Kurtz, within three hours of his arrival, sweep away Yanuka's last defences. As governor, my job is limited to matters of administration, he explained. Your brother is in a hospital cell downstairs, he is a little tired; naturally one hopes he will live but it will be some months before he can walk. When you have answered the following questions, I shall sign an order permitting you to share his accommodation and nurse him to recovery. If you refuse, you stay where you are. Then, to avoid any mistaken notions of chicanery, Kurtz produced for Yanuka the Polaroid colour photograph they had rigged, showing the barely recognisable face of Yanuka's brother peering out of a bloodstained prison blanket as the two guards carried him away from his interrogation.

But there again the genius of Kurtz was never static. When Yanuka really started talking, Kurtz immediately grew a heart to match the poor boy's passion; suddenly the old jailer needed to hear everything that the great fighter had ever said to his apprentice. By the time Kurtz returned downstairs, therefore, the team had really obtained pretty well everything from Yanuka that was obtainable—which amounted to nothing at all, as Kurtz was quick to point out, when it came to establishing his big brother's whereabouts. In the margin, it was further noted that the old interrogator's adage was borne out once again: namely, that physical violence is contrary to the ethics and spirit of the profession. Kurtz stressed this vehemently to Oded in particular. He made really heavy weather of it. If you have to use violence, and sometimes you couldn't do much else, always be sure to use it against the mind, not the body, he said. Kurtz believed there were lessons everywhere if the young would only have the eyes to see them.

He made the same point to Gavron also, but to less effect.

Yet even then Kurtz would not, perhaps could not, rest. By early next morning, with the matter of Yanuka now dispatched in all but its final resolution, Kurtz was back in the city centre, consoling the surveillance team, whose spirits had recently plummeted with Yanuka's disappearance. What had become of him? cried old Lenny—such a future the boy had, such promise in so many fields! From there again, his mission of mercy accomplished, Kurtz set off northward for yet another tryst with Alexis, quite undaunted by the fact that the good doctor's allegedly erratic nature had caused Misha Gavron to place him out of bounds.

"I'll tell him I'm American," he promised Litvak, with a broad smile, recalling Gavron's fatuous telegram to the Athens house.

His mood nevertheless was one of guarded optimism. We are moving, he told Litvak; and Misha only hits me when I'm sitting still.

10

The taverna was rougher than those on Mykonos, with a black-and-white television fluttering like a flag nobody saluted, and old hillsmen too proud to take an interest in tourists, even pretty red-headed English girls in blue kaftans and gold bracelets. But in the story Joseph now related, it was Charlie and Michel who were dining alone in the grill-room of a roadhouse outside Nottingham that Michel had bribed to stay open. Charlie's own pathetic car, as usual, was off the road at her latest pet garage in Camden. But Michel had a Mercedes saloon, he liked no other make so well; he had it waiting at the back entrance of the theatre and whisked her off in it immediately, ten minutes through the eternal Nottingham rain. And no passing tantrum of Charlie's, whether here or there, no momentary doubts, could arrest the pull of Joseph's narrative.

"He wears driving gloves," Joseph said. "They are a fad with him. You notice it but do not remark on it."

With holes in the back, she thought. "How does he drive?"

"He is not a natural driver but you do not hold this against him. You ask him where he lives and he replies that he has driven up from London in order to see you. You ask him what his occupation is and he says 'Student.' You ask him where he studies; he replies 'Europe,' implying somehow that Europe is a bad word. When you press him, not too hard, he says he takes semesters in different cities, depending on his mood and who is lecturing. The English, he says, do not understand the system. When he speaks the word 'English,' it sounds hostile to you, you don't know why, but hostile. Your next question?"

"Where's he living now?"

"He is evasive. Like me. Sometimes Rome, he says vaguely, sometimes Munich, Paris a little, wherever he decides. Vienna. He does not say he lives in a box, but he makes it clear that he is unmarried, which does not totally dismay you." He smiled and took back his hand. "You ask which city he likes best, he dismisses the question as irrelevant; you ask what subject he is studying, he replies 'Freedom'; you ask him where home is, and he replies that his home is presently under enemy occupation. Your response to this?"

"Confusion."

"However, with your customary persistence you again press him and he speaks the name *Palestine*. With passion. You hear it at once in his voice—*Palestine*, like a challenge. Like a war-cry—*Palestine*." His eyes were so fixedly upon her that she had to give a nervous smile and look away. "I may remind you, Charlie, that though you are heavily involved with Alastair at this period, he is presently safely in Argyll making a commercial for some totally valueless consumer product, and you happen to know he is keeping company with his leading lady. Correct?"

"Correct," she said, and to her astonishment found that she was blushing.

"So now you must tell me, please, what *Palestine*, spoken in this way by this eager boy, means to you in a roadhouse in Nottingham on a rainy night. Let us say he asks you this himself. Yes. He asks you. Why not?"

Oh glory, she thought, how many sides to a threepenny bit? "I admire them," she said.

"Call me Michel, please."

"I admire them, Michel."

"What for?"

"Their suffering." She felt a bit of a fool. "For hanging on."

"Nonsense. We Palestinians are a bunch of uneducated terrorists, who should have reconciled ourselves long ago to the loss of our homeland. We are nothing but former shoeshine boys and street vendors, delinquent children with machine guns in our hands, and old men who refuse to forget. So who are we then, please? Tell me your opinion. I shall value it. I am still calling you Joan, remember."

She took a deep breath. Not for nothing, after all, my weekend sessions at the forum. "All right. Here it is. The Palestinians—you—are gentle, decent farming people of great tradition, unfairly driven from your land, from 1948 onwards, in order to appease Zionism—and make way for a Western foothold in Arabia."

"Your words do not displease me. Kindly continue."

It was wonderful to discover how much came back to her under his perverse prompting. Snatches of forgotten pamphlets, lovers' lectures, the harangues of freedom fighters, bits of half-read books—all rallied to her like faithful allies in her need. "You're the invention of a European guilt complex about the Jews . . . you've been forced to pay the penalty for a Holocaust you had no part in . . . you're the victims of a racist, anti-Arab imperialist policy of dispossession and banishment—"

"And murder," Joseph suggested quietly.

"And murder." Faltering again, she caught the stranger's gaze fixed steadily upon her and, as at Mykonos, she had suddenly no idea what she read there. "Anyway, that's who Palestinians are," she said lightly. "Since you enquire. Since you do," she added when he still said nothing.

She went on looking at him, waiting for the lead that would tell her what to be. Under the compulsion of his presence, she had consigned her convictions to the dross of an earlier existence. She wanted none of them, unless he did.

"Notice he has no small talk," Joseph ordered, as if they had never smiled at each other in their lives. "How quickly he has appealed to the serious side of you. He is also in certain ways meticulous. For example, tonight he has prepared everything—the food, the wine, the candles, even his conversation. We may say that with Israeli-style efficiency, he has mounted a complete campaign to capture his Joan single-handed."

"Disgraceful," she said gravely, studying her bracelet.

"Meanwhile he tells you that you are the most brilliant actress on earth, which once again, I take it, does not incurably dismay you. He persists in confusing you with Saint Joan, but by now you are no longer quite so upset that life and theatre are inseparable for him. Saint Joan, he tells you, has been his heroine ever since he first read about her. She was a woman, yet she successfully aroused the class awareness of the French peasantry and led them in battle against the British imperialist oppressors. She was a true revolutionary, who lit the flame of freedom for the exploited peoples of the world. She turned slaves into heroes. That is the sum of his critical analysis. The voice of God addressing her is no more than her own revolutionary conscience urging her to resist the colonialist. It cannot be the actual voice of God, because Michel has decided God is dead. Perhaps you were not aware of all these implications when you played the part?"

She was still fiddling with the bracelet. "Well, I might have missed out on *some* of them," she admitted carelessly—only to look up and meet head on with his granite disapproval. "Oh Christ," she said.

"Charlie, I warn you most sincerely never to tease Michel with your Western wit. His sense of humour is capricious, and stops well short of jokes against himself, particularly when made by women." A pause for the admonition to sink in. "Very well. The food is dreadful, but you are totally indifferent to it. He has ordered steak and does not know that you are going through one of your vegetarian phases. You chew some in order not to offend him. In a later letter you tell him it was the worst steak you ever ate, but also the best. All you can think of while he is talking is his animated, passionate voice and his beautiful Arab face across the candle. Yes?"

She hesitated, then smiled. "Yes."

"He loves you, he loves your talent, he loves Saint Joan. 'For the British colonialists she was a criminal,' he tells you. 'So were all freedom fighters. So was George Washington, so was Mahatma Gandhi, so was Robin Hood. So are the secret soldiers of the Irish freedom struggle.' These are not exactly new ideas he is expressing, as you appreciate, but in his fervent Oriental voice, so full of—what shall we say, animal naturalness?—they have a hypnotic effect upon you; they give new life to the old clichés, they are like a rediscovery of love. 'For the British,' he tells you, 'whoever fights the terror of the colonialist is himself a terrorist. The British are my enemies, all but you. The British gave away my country to the Zionists, they shipped the Jews of Europe to us with orders to turn the East into the West. *Go and tame the Orient for us*, they said. *The Palestinians are trash, but they will make good coolies for you!* The old British colonisers were tired and defeated, so they handed us over to the new colonisers who had the zeal and the ruthlessness to cut the knot. *Don't worry about the Arabs*, the British said to them. *We promise to look the other way while you deal with them.* Listen. Are you listening?"

Jose, when was I not?

"Michel is a prophet to you tonight. Nobody has ever before concentrated the full force of his fanaticism on you alone. His conviction, his commitment, his devotion—they all shine out of him as he speaks. In theory, of course, he is already preaching to the converted, but in reality he is planting the human heart into the ragbag of your vague left-wing principles. That too you tell him in a later letter, whether or not it is logical that a ragbag should acquire a human heart. You want him to lecture you: he does. You want him to play upon your British guilt: he does that too. Your protective cynicism is swept aside completely. You are renewed. How apart he is from your middle-class prejudices, still not eradicated! From your lazily formed Western sympathies! Yes?" he enquired softly, as if she had asked a question. She shook her head and he was away again, filled with the borrowed fervour of his Arab surrogate.

"He ignores entirely that you are already in theory on his side; he demands your total obsession with his cause, a new conversion. He throws statistics at you as if you had caused them yourself. Over two million Christian and Muslim Arabs driven from their homeland and disenfranchised since 1948. Their houses and villages bulldozed—he tells you how many—their land stolen under laws they had no part in making—he recites the number of dunams—one dunam is a thousand square metres. You ask him and he tells you. And when they reach exile, their brother Arabs slaughter them and treat them like scum and the Israelis bomb their camps and shell them because they continue to resist. Because to resist being dispossessed is to be a terrorist, whereas to colonise, and to bomb refugees, to decimate a population—these are unfortunate political necessities. Because ten thousand dead Arabs are not worth one dead Jew. Listen." He leaned forward and grasped her wrist. "There is not a Western liberal who will hesitate to speak out against the injustices of Chile, South Africa, Poland, Argentina, Cambodia, Iran, Northern Ireland, and other fashionable trouble spots." His grasp tightened. "Yet who has the simple courage to tell out loud the cruellest joke in history: that thirty years of Israel have turned the Palestinians into the new Jews of the earth?

You know how the Zionists described my country before they seized it? 'A land without a people for a people without land.' *We did not exist!* In their minds, the Zionists had already committed genocide; all that remained for them was the fact. And you, the British, were the architects of this great vision. You know how Israel was born? A European power made a present of an Arab territory to a Jewish lobby. And did not consult a single inhabitant of the territory concerned. And that power was Britain. Shall I *describe* to you how Israel was born? . . . Is it late? You are tired? Must you go home to your hotel?"

As she gave him the answers he wanted, she still found time to marvel inside herself at the paradoxes of a man who could dance with so many of his own conflicting shadows, and still stand up. A candle burned between them. It was jammed in a greasy black bottle and under constant attack by an old drunk moth that Charlie occasionally pushed away with the back of her hand, making the bracelet sparkle. By its glow, as Joseph spun his story round her, she watched his strong, disciplined face alternate with Michel's like two images overlaid upon a single photographic plate.

"Listen. Are you listening?"

Jose, I am listening. Michel, I am listening.

"I was born of a patriarchal family in a village not far from the town of El Khalil, which the Jews call Hebron." He paused, his dark eyes vigorously upon her. "*El Khalil,*" he repeated. "Remember the name, it is of great importance to me for many reasons. You remember Khalil? Say it!"

She said it. El Khalil.

"El Khalil is a great centre for the pure faith of Islam. In Arabic the word means a friend of God. The people of El Khalil or Hebron are the élite of Palestine. And I will tell you a small joke that will make you laugh very much. There is a belief that the only place from which the Jews were never exiled is the Hebron mountain south of the city. It is therefore possible that Jewish blood flows in my veins. Yet I am not ashamed. I am not anti-Semitic, only anti-Zionist. You believe me?"

He did not wait to be assured; he did not need to.

"I was the youngest of four brothers and two sisters. Everyone worked on the land, my father was the *mukhtar*, or chief, selected by the wise elders. Our village was famous for its figs and grapes, for its fighters, and for its women, as beautiful and obedient as you are. Most villages are famous for one thing only. Ours was famous for many."

"Naturally," she murmured. But he was a long, long way from being teased.

"It was most famous of all, however, for the wise counsels of my father, who believed that Muslims should make a common society with Christians and Jews, exactly as their prophets lived harmoniously together in Heaven under one God. I talk to you a great deal about my father, my family, and my village. Now and later. My father admired the Jews. He had studied their Zionism and he liked to summon them to our village and speak with them. He obliged my elder brothers to learn Hebrew. As a boy, I listened at night to the menfolk singing songs of ancient wars. By day, I took my grandfather's horse to the water and heard the tales of travellers and pedlars. When I describe to you this paradise, I sound as if I am speaking real poetry to you. I can do that. I have the gift. How in our village square we danced the *dabke* and listened to the *oud,* while the old men played backgammon and smoked their *narjeels.*"

The words meant nothing to her but she was wise enough not to interrupt him.

"In reality, as I freely admit to you, I remember little of such things. In reality, I am handing on the reminiscences of my elders, for that is how our traditions survive in the exile of the camps. As the generations pass, we must live our homeland more and more through the memory of our elders. The Zionists will tell you we had no culture, that we did not exist. They will tell you we were degenerate and lived in mud huts and went about in stinking rags. They will tell you word for word the things that were formerly said of the Jews by the anti-Semites of Europe. The truth, in both cases, is the same: we were a noble people."

A nod of the dark head suggested that his two identities had agreed upon this point of fact.

"I describe our peasant life to you, and the many intricate systems by which the communality of our village was maintained. The wine harvest, how the whole village went out together to the grapefields on the orders of the *mukhtar,* my father. How my elder brothers began their education in a school which you British founded in the Mandate. You will laugh, but my father believed in the British also. How the coffee in our village guest house was kept hot all hours of the day in order that nobody could ever say of us, 'This village is too poor, these people are inhospitable to strangers.' You want to know what happened to my grandfather's horse? He sold it for a gun, so that he could shoot the Zionists when they attacked our village. The Zionists shot my grandfather instead. They made my father stand beside them while they did it. My father, who had believed in them."

"Is that true too?"

"Of course."

But she could not tell whether Joseph or Michel was replying, and she knew he did not mean her to.

"I refer to the war of '48 as 'the Catastrophe.' Never the war—the Catastrophe. In the Catastrophe of '48, I tell you, the fatal weaknesses of a peaceable society were revealed. We had no organisation, we could not defend ourselves against the armed aggressor. Our culture was tended in small communities, each one complete in itself, our economy also. But like the Jews of Europe before their Holocaust we lacked political unity, and this was our downfall, and too often our communities fought each other, which is the curse of Arabs everywhere and perhaps of Jews. Do you know what they did to my village, those Zionists? Because we would not flee like our neighbours?"

She knew, she did not know. It did not matter because he paid her no heed.

"They made barrel bombs filled with petrol and explosives, and rolled them down the hill, setting fire to our women and children. I could talk to you for a week, just of the tortures of my people. Hands cut off. Women raped and burned. Children blinded."

Once again she tested him, trying to discover whether he believed himself; but he would give her no clue beyond an intense solemnity of expression, which could have suited any of his natures.

"I whisper the words 'Deir Yasseen' to you. Have you ever heard them before? You know what they mean?"

No, Michel, I have not heard them before.

He seemed pleased. "Then ask me now, 'What is Deir Yasseen?' "

She did. Please, sir, what is Deir Yasseen?

"Once more I answer as if I saw it happen yesterday with my own eyes. In the small Arab village of Deir Yasseen on April 9, 1948, two hundred and fifty-four villagers—old men, women, and children—were butchered by Zionist terror squads while the young men were working in the fields. Pregnant women had their unborn children killed in their bellies. Most of the bodies were thrown down a well. Within days, nearly half a million Palestinians had fled their country. My father's village was an exception. 'We will stay,' he said. 'If we go into exile, the Zionists will never let us come back.' He even believed you British would return to save us. He did not understand that your imperialist ambitions required an obedient Western ally to be implanted in the heart of the Middle East."

She felt his glance and wondered whether he was aware of her inner withdrawal, or whether he was determined to ignore it. Only afterwards did it occur to her that he was deliberately encouraging her away from himself, and into the opposing camp.

"For almost twenty years after the Catastrophe, my father clung to what was left of our village. Some called him stubborn, some foolish. Outside Palestine, his compatriots called him a collaborator. They knew nothing. They had not felt the Zionist boot on their necks. All round us in the neighbouring regions, the people were driven away, beaten, arrested. The Zionists confiscated their land, flattened their houses with bulldozers, and built new settlements on top of them in which no Arab was allowed to live. But my father was a man of peace and wisdom, and for a time he kept the Zionists from our doors."

Again she wanted to ask him, Is this true? But again she was too late.

"But in the war of '67, as the tanks approached our village, we too fled across the Jordan. With tears in his eyes, my father called us together and told us to assemble our possessions. 'The pogroms are about to begin,' he said. I asked him—I, the smallest, who knew nothing—'Father, what is pogrom?' He replied, 'What the Westerners did to the Jews, so the Zionists now do to us. They have won a great victory and they could afford to be generous. But their virtue is not to be found in their politics.' Until my death I shall never forget watching my proud father enter the miserable hut that was now our home. For a long time he stood at the threshold, waiting for the strength to cross. He did not weep, but for days he sat on a box full of his books and ate nothing. I think he grew twenty years older in those days. 'I have entered my grave,' he said. 'This hut is my tomb.' From the moment of our arrival in Jordan we had become stateless citizens, without papers, rights, future, or work. My school? It is a tin shed crammed to the roof with fat flies and undernourished children. The Fatah teaches me. There is much to learn. How to shoot. How to fight the Zionist aggressor."

He paused, and at first she thought he was smiling at her, but there was no mirth in his expression.

" 'I fight, therefore I exist,' " he announced quietly. "You know who said these words, Charlie? A Zionist. A peace-loving, patriotic, idealistic Zionist, who has killed many British and many Palestinians by terrorist methods, but because he is a Zionist he is not a terrorist but a hero and a patriot. You know who he was when he spoke these words, this peace-loving, civilised Zionist? He was the Prime Minister of a country they call Israel. You know where he comes from, this terrorist Zionist Prime Minister? From Poland. Can you tell me, please—you an educated Englishwoman, me a simple stateless peasant—can you tell me how it happened, please, that a Pole came to be the ruler of my country, Palestine, a Pole who exists only because he fights? Can you explain to me, please, by what principle of English justice, of English impartiality and fair play, this man rules over *my* country? And calls *us* terrorists?"

The question slipped from her before she had time to censor it. She had not meant it as a challenge. It emerged by itself, from the chaos he was sowing in her: "Well, can *you*?"

He did not answer, yet he did not avoid her question. He received it. She had a momentary impression he was expecting it. Then he laughed, not very nicely, reached for his glass, and raised it to her.

"Make a toast to me," he ordered. "Come. Lift your glass. History belongs to the winners. Have you forgotten that simple fact? Drink with me!"

Doubtfully she raised her own glass to him.

"To tiny, gallant Israel," he said. "To her amazing survival, thanks to an American subsidy of seven million dollars a day, and the entire might of the Pentagon dancing to her tune." Without drinking, he put his glass down again. She did the same. With the gesture, to her relief, the melodrama seemed temporarily over. "And you, Charlie, you listen. Overawed. Amazed. By his romanticism, his beauty, his fanaticism. He has no reticence. No Western inhibitions. Does it play—or does the tissue of your imagination reject the disturbing transplant?"

Taking his hand, she began exploring the palm with the tip of her finger. "And his English is up to all this, is it?" she asked, buying time.

"He has a jargon-ridden vocabulary and an impressive store of rhetorical phrases, questionable statistics, and tortuous quotations. Despite this, he communicates the excitement of a young and passionate mind, and an expanding one."

"And what's Charlie doing all this time? I'm just stuck there, am I, with egg on my face, hanging on his every word? Do I encourage him? What am I doing?"

"According to the script, your performance is practically irrelevant. Michel is half hypnotising you across the candle. That is how you describe it to him later in one of your letters. 'As long as I live, I will never forget your lovely face across the candlelight on that first night we were together.' Is that too lurid for you, too kitschy?"

She gave him back his hand. "What letters? Where are we getting letters from all the time?"

"For the moment, let us agree only that you will later write to him. Let me ask you again, does it play? Or shall we shoot the writer and go home?"

She took a drink of wine. Then another. "It plays. So far it plays."

"And the letter—not too much—you can live with it?"

"If you can't let it all hang out in a love-letter, where can you?"

"Excellent. Then that is how you write to him, and that is how the fiction runs so far. Except for one small point. This is not your first meeting with Michel."

Not stagily at all, she put down her glass with a snap.

A new excitement had taken hold of him: "Listen to me," he said, leaning forward, and the candlelight struck his bronzed temple like sunlight on a helmet. "Listen to me," he repeated. "You are listening?"

Again, he did not bother to wait for her answer.

"A quotation. A French philosopher. *'The greatest crime is to do nothing because we fear we can only do a little.'* Does it ring a bell with you?"

"Oh Jesus," said Charlie softly, and on an impulse folded her arms across her breast in self-protection.

"Shall I go on?" He went on anyway. "Does this not remind you of someone? *'There is only one class war and it is between the colonialists and the colonised, the capitalists and the exploited. Our task is to bring the war home to those who make it. To the racist millionaires, who see the Third World as their private farm. To the corrupt oil-rich sheikhs who have sold the Arab birthright.'* " He paused, observing how her head had slipped between her hands.

"Jose, stop," she muttered. "It's too much. Go home."

" *'To the imperialist warmongers, who arm the Zionist aggressors. To the mindless Western bourgeoisie who are themselves the unconscious slaves and perpetuators of their own system.'* " He was barely whispering, yet his voice was all the more penetrating on account of it. " *'The world tells us we should not attack innocent women and children. But I tell you there is no such thing as innocence any more. For every child who dies of hunger in the Third World, there is a child in the West who has stolen his food—'* "

"Stop it," she repeated through her fingers, now all too certain of her ground. "I've had enough. I surrender."

But he continued his recitation. " *'When I was six, I was driven from our land. When I was eight, I joined the Ashbal.'* *'What is Ashbal, please?'* Come, Charlie. That was *your* question. Was it not you who asked me—you who put up your hand—'What is Ashbal, please?' How did I reply?"

"Children's militia," she said, her head between her hands. "I'm going to be sick, Jose. Now."

" *'When I was ten, I crouched in a homemade shelter while the Syrians poured rockets into our camp. When I was fifteen, my mother and my sister were killed in a Zionist air raid.'* Go on, please, Charlie. Complete my life story for me."

She had grasped his hand again, this time with both of hers, and was gently beating it against the table in reproof.

" *'If children can be bombed, they can also fight,'* " he reminded her. "And if they colonise? What then? Go on!"

"They must be killed," she muttered unwillingly.

"And if their mothers feed them, and teach them to steal our homes and bomb our people in their exile?"

"Then their mothers are in the front line with their husbands. Jose—"

"So what do we do about them?"

"They must be killed also. But I didn't believe him then, and I don't now."

He ignored her protests. He was making his protestations of eternal love. "Listen. Through the eyeholes of my black balaclava helmet, while I was inspiring you with my message at the forum, I observed your enraptured face upon me. Your red hair. Your strong, revolutionary features. Is it not ironic that on the first occasion that we met, it was I who was on stage, and you who were among the audience?"

"I was not enraptured! I thought you were way over the top, and I had a damn good mind to tell you so!"

He was unrepentant. "Whatever you felt at the time, here in the Nottingham motel, under my hypnotic influence, you instantly revise your memory. Though you could not see my face, you tell me, my words have remained seared in your memory ever since. Why not? . . . Come, Charlie! It is in your letter to me!"

She was not to be drawn. Not yet. Suddenly, for the first time since Joseph's story had begun, Michel had become a separate, living creature for her. Till this moment, she realised, she had unconsciously used Joseph's features to describe her imaginary lover, and Joseph's voice to characterise his declamations. Now, like a cell dividing itself, the two men were independent and conflicting beings, and Michel had acquired his own dimension in reality. She saw again the unswept lecture-room with its curling photograph of Mao and its scratched school benches. She saw the rows of unequal heads, from Afro to Jesus and back again, and Long Al slumped at her side in a state of alcoholic boredom. And on the podium she saw the isolated, unreadable figure of our gallant representative from Palestine—shorter than Joseph, maybe a fraction stockier as well, though it was hard to tell, for he was muffled in his black mask and his shapeless khaki blouse, and his black-and-white *kaffiyeh*. But younger—that for certain—and more fanatical. She remembered his fish-like lips, expressionless within the ragged cage. She remembered the red handkerchief tied defiantly round his neck, and the gloved hands gesticulating to his words. Most of all, she remembered his voice: not guttural, as she had expected, but literary and considerate, in macabre contrast to his bloodthirsty message. But not Joseph's either. She remembered how it paused, un-Joseph-like, to rephrase an awkward sentence, hunted for grammatical aptness: *"The gun and the Return are one for us . . . an imperialist is whoever does not aid us in our revolution . . . to do nothing is to endorse injustice . . ."*

"I loved you immediately," Joseph was explaining, in the same pretended tone of retrospection. "Or so I tell you now. As soon as the lecture was over, I enquired who you were, but I did not feel able to approach you before so many people. I was also aware that I was unable to show you my face, which is one of my greatest assets. I therefore decided to seek you out at the theatre. I made enquiries, tracked you to Nottingham. Here I am. I love you infinitely, signed Michel!"

As if making amends, Joseph put on a show of fussing over her welfare, refilling her glass, ordering coffee—medium sweet, the way you like it—did she want to wash? No thanks, I'm fine. The television was showing news footage of a grinning politician descending the gangway of an aeroplane. He made the bottom step without mishap.

His ministrations complete, Joseph glanced significantly round the taverna, then at Charlie, and his voice became the essence of practicality.

"So then, Charlie. You are his Joan. His love. His obsession. The staff have gone home, the two of us are alone in the dining-room. Your unmasked admirer, and you. It is after midnight and I have been talking far too long, though I have scarcely begun to tell you what is in my heart, or ask you about yourself, whom I love beyond comparison, such an experience is entirely new to me, etcetera. Tomorrow is Sunday, you have no commitments, I have rented a room in the motel. I make no attempt to persuade you. That is not my way. Perhaps I am also too respectful of your dignity. Or perhaps I am too proud to think you need persuading. Either you will come to me as a comrade-in-arms, a true, free lover, soldier to soldier—or you will not. How do you respond? Are you suddenly impatient to return to the Astral Commercial and Private Hotel, near the railway station?"

She stared at him, and then away from him. She had

half a dozen facetious answers ready but suppressed them. The hooded, totally separate figure at the forum was once more an abstraction. It was Joseph, not the stranger, who had put the question. And what was there to say when, in her imagination, they were already lying in bed together, Joseph's cropped head resting on her shoulder, Joseph's strong wounded body stretched along her own, while she willed his true nature out of him?

"After all, Charlie—as you told us yourself—you have been to bed with many men for less, I would say."

"Oh, much less," she agreed, developing a sudden interest in the plastic salt-pourer.

"You are wearing his expensive jewellery. You are alone in a dismal city. It's raining. He has enchanted you—flattered the actress, inspired the revolutionary. How can you possibly refuse him?"

"Fed me too," she reminded him. "Even if I was off meat."

"He is everything a bored Western girl ever dreamed of, I would say."

"Jose, for Christ's sake," she muttered, not even able to look at him.

"So then," he said briskly, signalling for the bill. "Congratulations. You have met your soulmate at last."

A mysterious brutality had entered his manner. She had the ridiculous feeling that her acquiescence had angered him. She watched him pay the bill, she saw him pocket the receipt. She stepped after him into the night air. I'm the twice-promised girl, she thought. If you love Joseph, take Michel. He's pimped me for his phantom in the theatre of the real.

"In bed, he tells you that his real name is Salim, but that is a great secret," said Joseph casually as they got into the car. "He prefers Michel. Partly for security, partly because he is already slightly in love with European decadence."

"I like Salim better."

"But you use Michel."

Just whatever you all say, she thought. But her passivity was a deception, even to herself. She could feel her anger on the move, still far down but rising, rising.

*   *   *

The motel was like a low factory block. At first there was no space to park; then a white Volkswagen minibus lumbered forward to make room for them, and she glimpsed the figure of Dimitri at the wheel. Clutching the orchids as Joseph had instructed her, she waited while he pulled on his red blazer, then followed him across the tarmac to the front porch; but reluctantly, keeping her distance. Joseph was carrying her shoulder bag as well as his smart black grip. Give that back, it's mine. In the foyer, out of the corner of her eye, she saw Raoul and Rachel standing under the vile strip-lighting, reading notices about tomorrow's tours. She glowered at them. Joseph went to the desk and she drew close to watch him sign the register, though he had specifically told her not to. Arab name, nationality Lebanese, address an apartment number in Beirut. His manner disdainful: a man of position, ready at any time to take offence. You're good, she thought ruefully, while she tried to hate him. No wasted gestures but plenty of style, and you make the part your own. The bored night manager cast her a lustful glance, but showed none of the disrespect she was accustomed to. The porter was loading their luggage onto an enormous hospital trolley. I'm wearing a blue kaftan and a gold bracelet and un-derwear from Persephone of Munich and I'll bite the first peasant who calls me a tart. Joseph took her arm and his hand burned her skin. She pulled free of him. Sod off. To the strains of canned Gregorian plainsong, they followed their luggage down a grey tunnel of pastel-painted doors. Their bedroom was double-bedded, *grande luxe* and sterile as an operating theatre.

"Christ!" she exploded, staring round her in black hostility.

The porter turned to her in surprise but she ignored him. She spotted a bowl of fruit, a bucket of ice, two glasses, and a vodka bottle waiting beside the bed. A vase for the orchids. She dumped them into it. Joseph tipped the porter, the trolley gave a departing shriek, and suddenly they were alone, with a bed the size of a football field, two framed Minoan bulls in charcoal providing the tastefully erotic atmosphere, and a balcony with an unspoilt view of the car park. Taking the vodka bottle from the bucket, Charlie poured herself a stiff one and flopped onto the edge of the bed.

"Cheers, old man," she said.

Joseph was still standing, watching her without expression. "Cheers, Charlie," he replied, though he had no glass.

"So what do we do now? Play Monopoly? Or is this the big scene we bought our tickets for?" Her voice rose. "I mean, who the hell are we in this? Just for information. *Who?* Right? Just who?"

"You know very well who we are, Charlie. We are two lovers enjoying our Greek honeymoon."

"I thought we were in a Nottingham motel."

"We are playing both parts at once. I thought you understood that. We are establishing the past and the present."

"Because we are so short of time."

"Let us say, because human lives are at risk."

She took another pull of vodka, and her hand was as steady as a rock because that was how her hand went when the black mood got into her. "Jewish lives," she corrected him.

"Are they different from other lives?"

"I'll say they bloody are! Jesus Christ! I mean Kissinger can bomb the poor bloody Cambodians till the cows come home. Nobody lifts a finger. The Israelis can hack the Palestinians to pieces any time. But a couple of rabbis knocked off in Frankfurt or whatever—I mean that's a real grade-one prime-beef international disaster, isn't it?"

She was staring straight past him at some imaginary enemy, but out of the corner of her eye she saw him take a firm step in her direction, and for a brilliant moment she really thought he was going to remove her choices for good. But instead he walked past her to the window and unlocked the door, perhaps because he needed the drumming of the traffic to drown her voice.

"They are all disasters," he replied unemotionally, looking out. "Ask me what the inhabitants of Kiryat Shmonah feel when the Palestinian shells come down. Ask them in the kibbutzim to tell you about the whining of the Katyusha rockets, forty at a time, while they hide their children in the shelters pretending it is all a game." He paused and gave a kind of bored sigh, as if he had listened too often to his own arguments. "However," he added, in a more practical tone, "on the next occasion you use that argument, I suggest you please remember that Kissinger is a Jew. That also has a place in Michel's somewhat elementary political vocabulary."

She put her knuckles in her mouth and discovered she was weeping. He came and sat beside her on the bed, and she waited for him to put his arm round her or offer more wise arguments or simply take her, which was what she would have liked best, but he did nothing of the kind. He was content to let her mourn, until gradually she had the illusion that he had somehow caught her up, and they were mourning together. More than any words could have done, his silence seemed to mitigate what they had to do. For an age, they stayed that way, side by side, till she allowed her choking to give way to a deep, exhausted sigh. But he still did not move—not towards her, not away from her.

"Jose," she whispered hopelessly, taking his hand once more. "Who the hell are you? What do you *feel* inside all those barbed-wire entanglements?"

Raising her head, she began to listen to the sounds of other lives in adjoining rooms. The querulous burbling of a sleepless child. A strident marital argument. She heard a footfall from the balcony and glanced round in time to see Rachel in a towelling tracksuit, armed with a sponge-bag and a thermos flask, stepping over the threshold into the room.

She lay awake, too exhausted to sleep. Nottingham was never like this. From next door came the muffled sound of telephoning and she thought she recognised his voice. She lay in Michel's arms. She lay in Joseph's. She longed for Al. She was in Nottingham with the love of her life, she was safe in her own bed back in Camden, she was in the room her bloody mother still called the nursery. She lay as she had lain as a child after her horse had thrown her, watching the picture-show of her life and exploring her mind as she had tentatively explored her body, feeling out each bit in turn, testing it for damage. A mile away on the other side of the bed, Rachel lay reading Thomas Hardy in paperback by the light of a tiny lamp.

"Who's he got, Rache?" she said. "Who darns his socks and cleans out his pipes for him?"

"Better ask him, hadn't you, dear?"

"Is it you?"

"Wouldn't work, would it? Not in the long run."

Charlie dozed, still trying to figure him out. "He was a fighter," she said.

"The best," said Rachel contentedly. "Still is."

"How did he pick his quarrels then?"

"They were picked for him, weren't they?" Rachel said, still deep in her book.

Charlie tried a dare: "He had a wife once. What happened to her?"

"Sorry, dear," said Rachel.

" 'Did she jump or was she pushed?' one asks oneself," Charlie mused, ignoring the rebuff. "I'll say one bloody does. Poor bitch, she'd have to be about six chameleons just to ride on a bus with him."

She lay still a while.

"How did *you* get into this lot, Rache?" she asked, and, to her surprise, Rachel laid her book on its stomach and told her. Her parents were Orthodox Jews from Pomerania, she said. They had settled in Macclesfield after the war and become wealthy in the weaving industry. "Branches in Europe and a penthouse in Jerusalem," she said, unimpressed. They had wanted Rachel to go to Oxford and into the family firm, but she had preferred to study Bible and Jewish history at the Hebrew University.

"It just happened," she replied when Charlie pressed her about the next step.

But how? Charlie persisted. Why? "Who picked you, Rache, what do they say?"

Rachel was not telling how or who, but she was telling why. She knew Europe and she knew anti-Semitism, she said. And she had wanted to show those stuck-up little sabra war heroes at the university that she could fight for Israel as well as any boy.

"So what's Rose then?" said Charlie, forcing her luck.

Rose was complicated, Rachel replied, as if she herself were not. Rose had done Zionist Youth in South Africa, and come to Israel not knowing whether she should have stayed put and fought apartheid.

"She sort of tries harder because she doesn't know which she should be doing," Rachel explained, and, with a firmness that ended further discussion, went back to her *Mayor of Casterbridge*.

A surfeit of ideals, thought Charlie. Two days ago I had none. She wondered whether she had any now. Ask me in the morning. For a while she indulged drowsily in headlines. "FAMOUS FEMALE FANTASIST MEETS REALITY." "JOAN OF ARC BURNS PALESTINIAN ACTIVIST." Well, Charlie, yes, good night.

Becker's room lay a few yards down the corridor and it had twin beds, which was the nearest the hotel came to acknowledging that anyone was single. He lay on one and stared at the other, with the telephone on the table between them. In ten minutes it would be one-thirty, and one-thirty was the time. The night porter had his tip, and had promised to put through the call. He was very wakeful, as often at this hour. To think too brightly and come down too slowly. To get everything to the front of your head and forget what is behind. Or what is not. The phone rang on time and Kurtz's voice greeted him immediately. Where is he? Becker wondered. He heard canned music in the background and rightly guessed a hotel. Germany, he remembered. A hotel in Germany talks to a hotel in Delphi. Kurtz spoke English because it was less conspicuous, and he spoke with an overlay of casualness that should not alarm the unlikely eavesdropper. Yes, everything was fine, Becker assured him; the deal was going through nicely, and he foresaw no immediate snags. What about the latest product? he asked.

"We are getting a lot of first-rate cooperation," Kurtz assured him, in the fulsome tone he used for rallying his far-flung troops. "You go right down to the warehouse as soon as you like, you will surely not be disappointed in the product. And another thing."

Becker seldom completed his telephone conversations with Kurtz as a rule, nor Kurtz with him. It was an odd thing between them that each vied to be the first to get out of the other's company. This time, however, Kurtz listened all the way to the end, and so did Becker. But as he put down the receiver, Becker caught sight of his attractive features in the mirror, and stared at them with sharp distaste. For a moment, they were like a wrecker's light to him, and he had a morbid and overwhelming wish to extinguish them for good: *Who the hell are you? . . . What do you feel?* He drew closer to the mirror. I *feel* as if I am looking at a dead

friend, hoping he will come alive. I *feel* as if I am searching
for my old hopes in someone else, without success. I *feel* that
I am an actor, as you are, surrounding myself with versions
of my identity because the original somehow went missing
along the road. But in truth I feel nothing, because real
feeling is subversive and contrary to military discipline.
Therefore I do not feel, but I fight and therefore I exist.

In the town he walked impatiently, striding wide and
looking hard ahead of him, as if walking bored him, and the
distance, as ever, were too short. It was a town waiting for
attack, and over twenty years or more he had known too
many towns in that condition. The people had fled the streets,
there was not a child to be heard. Knock down the houses.
Shoot whatever moves. The parked charabancs and cars lay
abandoned by their owners, and God alone knew when they
would see them next. Occasionally, his quick glance slipped
to an open doorway or the entrance to an unlit alley, but observation was habitual to him and his stride did not relent.
Reaching a side street, he lifted his head to read the name
but again swept past, before turning swiftly in to a building
site. A gaudy minibus was parked among tall stacks of bricks.
The masts of a washing-line drooped beside it, disguising
thirty feet of thread aerial. Faint music issued from inside.
The door opened, the barrel of a pistol pointed at his face
like one eye scanning him, then vanished. A respectful voice
said, "Shalom." He stepped inside and closed the door behind
him. The music did not quite drown the unsteady chatter of
the little teleprinter. David, the operator from the Athens
house, was crouched over it; two of Litvak's boys kept him
company. With no more than a nod, Becker sat down on the
padded bench and began to read the fat bundle of tearsheets
set aside for his arrival.

The boys eyed him respectfully. He felt them counting
his medal ribbons in their hungry minds, and probably they
knew his feats of heroism better than he did himself.

"She's looking good, Gadi," said the bolder of the two.

Becker ignored him. Sometimes he sidelined a paragraph,
sometimes he underlined a date. When he had finished, he
handed the papers to the boys, and made them test him until
he was satisfied that he knew his lines.

Outside the minibus again, he paused at the window

despite himself and heard their cheerful voices discussing him.

"The Rook got him a whole directorship to himself, running some great new textile factory near Haifa," said the bold one.

"Great," said the other. "So let's retire and let Gavron make us millionaires."

11

For his forbidden but vital reunion with the good Dr. Alexis that same night, Kurtz had donned an attitude of collegial affinity between professionals, coloured by ancient friendship. They met, at Kurtz's suggestion, not in Wiesbaden but down the road in Frankfurt, where the crowds are thicker and more itinerant, at a large and dowdy conference hotel which was that week playing host to disciples of the soft-toy industry. Alexis had proposed his house, but Kurtz had declined with an innuendo Alexis was not slow to sense. It was ten at night when they met and most of the delegates were already out on the town in search of other varieties of soft toy. The bar was three-quarters empty and, to look at, they were just two more traders solving the world's problems over a bowl of plastic flowers. Which, in a manner of speaking, they were. Canned music played, but the barman was listening to a Bach recital on his transistor.

In the time since they had first met, the imp in Alexis seemed finally to have gone to sleep. The first faint shadows of failure lay on him like the advance notice of an illness, and his television smile had a new and unbecoming modesty. Kurtz, who was preparing himself for the kill, confirmed this gratefully at a glance—Alexis, less gratefully, each morning, when in the privacy of his bathroom he pushed back the skin around his eyes and briefly restored the last of his ebbing youthfulness. Kurtz brought greetings from Jerusalem and, as a token, a small bottle of clouded water certified by the label to have been taken from the true Jordan. He had heard that the new Mrs. Alexis was expecting a baby, and suggested the water might eventually come in handy. This gesture touched Alexis, and amused him somewhat more than the occasion of it.

"But you knew about it before I did," he protested when he had gazed at the bottle in polite marvel. "I haven't even

234

told my office yet." Which was true: his silence had been a kind of last-ditch effort at preventing the conception.

"Tell them when it's over and apologise," Kurtz suggested, not without meaning. Quietly, as became people who make no ceremony, they drank to life, and to a better future for the Doctor's unborn child.

"They tell me you are a coordinator these days," said Kurtz, with a twinkle in his eye.

"To all coordinators," Alexis replied gravely, and once again each took a token sip. They agreed to call each other by their first names, but Kurtz nevertheless retained the formal style of *Sie*, rather than *du*. He did not want his ascendancy over Alexis undermined.

"May I ask what you coordinate, Paul?" asked Kurtz.

"Herr Schulmann, I must advise you that liaison with friendly services is no longer included among my official duties," Alexis intoned in deliberate parody of the Bonn syntax: and waited for Kurtz to press him further.

But instead Kurtz ventured a guess, which was not a guess at all. "A coordinator has administrative responsibility for such vital matters as transport, training, recruitment, and the financial accountability of operational sections. Also for the exchange of intelligence between federal and state agencies."

"You have left out official leave," Alexis objected, as much amused as he was horrified, once more, by the quality of Kurtz's information. "You want more leave, come to Wiesbaden, I give you some. We've got a very high-powered committee just for official leave."

Kurtz promised that he would do this—it really was high time he gave himself a break, he confessed. The hint of overwork reminded Alexis of his own days in the field, and he digressed in order to relate a case in which he had not slept—but literally, Marty, not even lain down—for three successive nights. Kurtz heard him out with respectful sympathy. Kurtz was an excellent listener, a breed Alexis met with all too rarely in Wiesbaden.

"You know something, Paul," Kurtz said when they had batted back and forth a while in this agreeable way. "I was a coordinator once myself. My supervisor decided I had been a naughty boy"—Kurtz pulled an accomplice's rueful grin—"so he made me a coordinator. I got so bored that after one month I wrote to General Gavron and I told him officially he was a bum. 'General, this is official. Marty Schulmann says you are a bum.' He sent for me. You have met this Gavron? No? He's small and shrivelled with a big mop of black hair. No peace in him. No rest. 'Schulmann,' he yells at me. 'What the hell is this, one month and calling me a bum? How did you find out my dark secret?' A cracked voice, like someone dropped him when he was a kid. 'General,' I say. 'If you had one ounce of self-respect, you would reduce me to the ranks and throw me back into my old unit where I cannot insult you to your face.' You know what Misha did? He threw me out, then he promoted me. That's how I got my unit back."

This story was the more amusing since it reminded Alexis of his own vanished days as a well-publicised maverick among the stuffed shirts of the Bonn hierarchy. So that it was the most natural thing on earth that the conversation should pass to the matter of the Bad Godesberg outrage, which after all had been the occasion of their getting to know each other.

"I heard they're making a little progress at last," Kurtz remarked. "Tracing the girl back to Paris Orly, that's quite a breakthrough, even if they still don't know who she is."

Alexis was not a little irritated to hear this careless praise from the lips of someone he so admired and respected. "You call that a breakthrough? Yesterday I got their most up-to-date analysis. Some girl flies Orly–Cologne on the day of the bombing. They think. She's wearing jeans. They think. Headscarf, good figure, maybe she's a blonde, so what? The French can't even trace her embarkation. Or say they can't."

"Maybe that's because she didn't embark for Cologne, Paul," Kurtz suggested.

"How does she fly to Cologne when she doesn't embark for Cologne?" Alexis objected, slightly missing the point. "Those cretins couldn't trace an elephant through a heap of cocoa."

The neighbouring tables were still empty, and what with Bach on the transistor and *Oklahoma* over the loudspeakers, there was enough music to drown several heresies at once.

"Suppose she takes a ticket for somewhere else," said Kurtz patiently. "Say, Madrid. She embarks at Orly but takes a ticket to Madrid."

Alexis accepted the hypothesis.

"She takes a ticket Orly–Madrid, and when she gets to

Orly she checks in for Madrid. She goes to the departure lounge with her Madrid boarding-card, picks a certain place to wait; waits. Like close to a certain departure gate, why not? Say, departure gate eighteen, which is where she waited. Somebody comes up to her, a girl, speaks the agreed words, they go to the ladies' room, switch tickets. Nicely organised. A really nice arrangement. They switch passports too. With girls, that's no problem. Make-up—wigs—Paul, when you dig down, all pretty girls are the same."

The truth of this aphorism pleased Alexis very much, for he had recently come to the same gloomy conclusion regarding his second marriage. But he did not dwell on it, for he sensed already the imminence of serious information, and the policeman in him was alive again. "And when she gets to Bonn?" he asked, lighting himself a cigarette.

"She arrives on a Belgian passport. A nice fake, one of a batch made in East Germany. She's met at the airport by a bearded boy on a stolen motorbike with false plates. Tall, young, bearded: that's all the girl knows, it's all anyone knows, because these are good people in the matter of security. A beard? What's a beard? Also he never removed his helmet. In security, these people are way above the average. Outstanding, even. I would say outstanding."

Alex said he had noticed this already.

"The boy's job in this operation is to play cut-out," Kurtz continued. "That's all he does. He breaks the circuit. He meets the girl, he makes sure she isn't being followed, he drives her around a little, takes her to the safe house for briefing." He paused. "There's a stockbroker farm near Mehlem, calls itself the Haus Sommer. A converted barn sits at the end of the south drive. This drive feeds straight on to a slip-road to the autobahn. Under the sleeping accommodation is a garage and in the garage waits an Opel, Siegburg registration, driver already aboard."

This time, to his bemused delight, Alexis was able to join in. "Achmann," he said, below his breath. "The publicist Achmann from Düsseldorf! Are we mad? Why did nobody think of this man?"

"Achmann is correct," said Kurtz approvingly to his pupil. "Haus Sommer is the property of Dr. Achmann of Düsseldorf, whose distinguished family owns a flourishing timber business, some magazines, and a fine string of pornography shops. As a sideline, he also publishes romantic calendars of the German landscape. The converted barn belongs to Dr. Achmann's daughter Inge, and has been the scene of many fringe conferences attended mostly by wealthy and disenchanted explorers of the human soul. At the time in question, Inge had lent the house to a friend in need, a boyfriend who had a girlfriend . . ."

"*Ad infinitum*," Alexis completed for him admiringly.

"Clear away the smoke, you find more smoke. The fire is always down the road a little. That is the way these people work. That is how they always worked."

From caves in the Jordan Valley, thought Alexis excitedly. With a skein of surplus wire wound into a dummy. With bikini bombs you can make in your own back yard.

As Kurtz spoke, the face and figure of Alexis underwent a mysterious easing, which had not escaped his notice. The lines of worry and human weakness that so distressed him had been brushed away. He sat well back; he had folded his small arms comfortably across his chest, a rejuvenating smile had settled on his face, and his sandy head had tilted forward in harmonious submission to the great performance of his mentor.

"May I ask what basis you have for these interesting theories?" Alexis enquired, with an unconvincing stab at scepticism.

Kurtz made a show of pondering, though Yanuka's information was as fresh in his mind as if he were still sitting with him back in Munich in his padded cell, holding his head while he coughed and wept. "Well now, Paul, we have both licence numbers of the Opel, and we have a photocopy of the car-hire contract, and we have a signed deposition from one of the participants," he confessed, and—in the modest hope that these meagre clues might decently pass as a basis for the time being—proceeded with his tale.

"The bearded boy, he leaves her at the barn, departs, never to be seen again. The girl, she changes into her neat blue dress, puts on her wig, gets herself up really nicely, in a manner calculated to please the somewhat gullible and over-affectionate Labour Attaché. She gets into the Opel and is driven to the target house by a second young man. On the way, they pause to prime the bomb. Please?"

"This boy," Alexis asked eagerly. "Does she know him, or is he a mystery to her?"

Declining absolutely to elaborate further upon Yanuka's rôle, Kurtz left the question unanswered and merely smiled, yet his evasion was not offensive; for Alexis was by now straining for every detail, and could not expect to have his plate filled every time. Nor was it desirable that he should.

"The mission accomplished, the same driver changes over the number plates and papers and takes the girl to the handsome little Rhineland spa of Bad Neuenahr, where he drops her," Kurtz resumed.

"And then?"

Kurtz became very slow spoken, as if each word were now a danger to his complex plan; as indeed it was. "And there—at a guess—I would say that the girl is introduced to a certain secret admirer of hers—someone who maybe coached her a little in her part that day. Say, in how to arm the bomb. How to set the timer. Rig the booby trap. At a guess, I would say that this same admirer had already rented a hotel room somewhere, and that under the stimulus of their shared achievement, the couple engaged in much passionate love-making. Next morning, while they're sleeping off their pleasures, the bomb goes off—later than intended, but who cares?"

Alexis leaned swiftly forward, almost accusing in his excitement. "And the *brother*, Marty? The great fighter who has killed so many Israelis already? Where was he all this while? In Bad Neuenahr, I think, having a bit of fun with his little bomber girl. Yes?"

But Kurtz's features had set into a rigid impassivity, which the good Doctor's enthusiasm seemed only to intensify.

"Wherever he is, he runs an efficient operation, nicely compartmented, nicely delegated, everything well researched," Kurtz replied, with seeming contentment. "The bearded boy, he had the girl's description, nothing more. Not even the target. The girl knew the number of his motorbike. The driver, he knew the target but not the bearded boy. There's a brain at work."

After which Kurtz appeared to be afflicted by a seraphic deafness; so that Alexis, after further fruitless questioning, felt the need to order up fresh whiskies. The truth was the good Doctor was experiencing a shortage of oxygen. It was as if his life till now had been spent at a lower level of existence, and latterly at a very low level indeed. Now suddenly the great Schulmann was wafting him to heights he had not dreamed of.

"And you are here in Germany to pass this information to your official German colleagues, I suppose," Alexis remarked provocatively.

But Kurtz replied only with a long and speculative silence, during which he seemed to be testing Alexis with his eyes and thoughts. Then he made that gesture which Alexis so admired, of pushing back his sleeve and raising his wrist to contemplate his watch. And it reminded Alexis yet again that while his own time was ebbing wearily away before his eyes, for Kurtz there was never enough of it.

"Cologne will be very grateful to you, you may be sure," Alexis pressed. "My excellent successor—you remember him, Marty?—he will score an immense personal triumph. With the assistance of the media, he will become the most brilliant and popular policeman in West Germany. Quite rightly, yes? And all thanks to you."

Kurtz's broad smile conceded that this was so. He took a tiny sip of his whisky, and wiped his lips with an old khaki handkerchief. Then he put his chin into the cup of his hand and sighed, implying that he hadn't really meant to say this, but since Alexis had brought it up, he would.

"Well now, Jerusalem gave quite a lot of thought to this question, Paul," he confessed, "and we're not quite as sure as you seem to be that your successor is the type of gentleman whose progress in life we are over-enthusiastic to advance." So what could one do about *that*? his frown seemed to ask. "It occurred to us, however, that there was an alternative available to us, and maybe we should explore that a little with you and test your response to it. Maybe, we said to ourselves, there are ways in which the good Dr. Alexis could pass our information to Cologne on our behalf? Privately. Unofficially yet officially, if you take my meaning. On a basis of his own personal enterprise and wise stewardship. This is a question we have been putting to ourselves. Maybe we could go to Paul, and we could say to him: 'Paul, you are a friend of Israel. Take this. Use it. Profit from it. Have it as our gift and keep us out of it.' Why always promote a wrong man in these cases? we asked ourselves. Why not the right one, for once? Why not deal with friends, which is our principle? Advance them? Reward them for their loyalty to us?"

Alexis affected not to understand. He had gone rather red, and there was a slightly hysterical note to his denials. "But, Marty, listen to me, I have no sources! I am not operational, I am a bureaucrat! Shall I pick up the telephone— 'Cologne, here is Alexis, I advise you, go immediately to Haus Sommer, arrest the Achmann daughter, pull in all her friends for questioning'? Am I a conjurer—an alchemist— that I make such wonderful pieces of information out of stones? What are they thinking about in Jerusalem—that a *coordinator* is suddenly a magic man?" His self-ridicule became cumbersome, and increasingly unreal. "Shall I demand the arrest of all bearded motorcyclists who are possibly Italian? They will laugh at me!"

He had dried up, so Kurtz helped him out, which was what Alexis wanted, for he was in the mood of a child who is criticising authority only in order to be reassured of its embrace.

"Nobody is looking for arrests, Paul. Not yet. Not on our side of the house. Nobody is looking for anything overt at all, least of all in Jerusalem."

"Then what are you looking for?" Alexis demanded, with sudden snappishness.

"Justice," said Kurtz kindly. But his straight, unflinching smile was transmitting another kind of message. "Justice, a little patience, a little nerve, a lot of creativity, a lot of inventiveness from whoever plays our game for us. Let me ask you something, Paul." His big head drew suddenly much closer. His powerful hand settled on the Doctor's forearm. "Suppose, now. Suppose a very anonymous and exceptionally secret informant—I see a high Arab here, Paul, an Arab of the moderate centre, who likes Germany, admires her, and possesses information regarding certain terror operations which he disapproves of—suppose such a man had seen the great Alexis on television a while back. Suppose, for instance, that he was sitting in his hotel room one night in Bonn, say—Düsseldorf, wherever he was sitting—and he happened to turn the switch of his television set for a distraction, and there was the fine Dr. Alexis, a lawyer, a policeman, sure; but a man of humour also, flexible, pragmatic, a humanist to his fingertips— in short, a lot of man—yes?"

"Suppose," Alexis said, half deafened in his mind by the volume of Kurtz's words.

"And this Arab, Paul, he was moved to approach you," Kurtz resumed. "Would speak to no one else. Trusted you on impulse, declined to have dealings with any other German representative. Bypassed the ministries, the police, the intelligence people. Looked you up in the telephone directory, say—called you at your home. Or at your office. How you like—the story's yours. And met you here in this hotel. Tonight. And drank a couple of whiskies with you. Let you pay. And over those whiskies he presented you with certain facts. The great Alexis—no one else will do for him. Do you see a line of advantage here, for a man unjustly deprived of the proper flowering of his career?"

Reliving this scene later, a thing that Alexis did repeatedly in the light of many conflicting moods of amazement, pride, and total, anarchic horror, he came to regard the speech that followed as Kurtz's oblique justification in advance for what he had in mind.

"Terror people get better and better these days," he complained gloomily. " 'Put in an agent, Schulmann,' Misha Gavron shrieks at me from halfway inside his desk. 'Sure, General,' I tell him. 'I'll find you an agent. I'll train him, help him trail his coat, gain attention in the right places, feed him to the opposition. I'll do whatever you ask. And you know the first thing they'll do?' I say to him. 'They'll invite him to authenticate himself. To go shoot a bank guard or an American soldier. Or bomb a restaurant. Or deliver a nice suitcase to someone. Blow him up. Is that what you want? Is that what you are inviting me to do, General—put in an agent, then sit back and watch him kill our people for the enemy?' " Once again, he cast Alexis the unhappy smile of someone who was also at the mercy of unreasonable superiors. "Terrorist organisations don't carry passengers, Paul. I told Misha this. They don't have secretaries, typists, coding clerks, or any of the people who would normally make natural agents without being in the front line. They require a special kind of penetration. 'You want to crack the terror target these days,' I told him, 'you practically have to build yourself your own terrorist first.' Does he listen to me?"

Alexis could no longer withhold his fascination. He leaned right forward, his eyes bright with the dangerous glamour of his question. "And have you done that, Marty?" he whispered. "Here in *Germany*?"

Kurtz, as so often, did not answer directly, and his Slav eyes seemed already to look beyond Alexis to the next goal along his devious and lonely road.

"Suppose I were to report an accident to you, Paul," he suggested, in the tone of one selecting a remote option from the many that had presented themselves to his resourceful mind. "One that was going to happen, say, in around four days' time."

The barman's concert had ended and he was noisily shutting down the bar as a prelude to going off to bed. At Kurtz's suggestion, they took themselves to the hotel lounge and huddled there head to head like passengers on a wind-swept deck. Twice during their discussions, Kurtz glanced at his old steel watch and hurriedly excused himself to make a telephone call; and later, when Alexis out of idle curiosity investigated them, he established that he had spoken to a hotel in Delphi, Greece, for twelve minutes, and paid cash, and to a number in Jerusalem, untraceable. At three o'clock or more, several Oriental-looking guestworkers appeared in frayed overalls, wheeling a great green vacuum cleaner that resembled a Krupp cannon. But Kurtz and Alexis kept talking over the din. Indeed, it was well after dawn before the two men walked out and shook hands on their bargain. But Kurtz was careful not to thank his latest recruit too lavishly, for Alexis, as Kurtz well knew, was of a type to be alienated by too much gratitude.

The re-born Alexis hurried home, and, having shaved and changed and tarried long enough to impress his bride with the high secrecy of his mission, arrived at his glass-and-concrete office wearing an expression of mysterious contentment such as had not been seen on his face for a long while. Among his staff it was remarked that he joked a lot, and ventured some risqué comment about his colleagues. Quite the old Alexis, they said; he's even showing signs of humour, though humour was never his strong point. He called for blank writing paper and, excluding even his private secretary, set to work penning a long and deliberately obscure report to his masters on an approach he had received from a "highly placed Oriental source known to me in my previous capacity," and including a mass of brand-new information on the Godesberg outrage—though none of it sufficient, as yet, to do more than authenticate the bona fides of the informant and, by extension, of the good Doctor as his controller. He requested certain powers and facilities, and also a nonaccountable operational fund to be opened in Switzerland and dispensed at his sole discretion. He was not a grasping man, though it was true his remarriage had been expensive and his divorce ruinous. But he did recognise that, in these materialistic days, people valued most highly what cost them most.

And lastly he made a tantalising prediction, which Kurtz had dictated to him word by word, and had him read back while he listened to it. It was imprecise enough to be virtually useless, precise enough to impress greatly once it was fulfilled. Unconfirmed reports claimed that a large consignment of explosive had recently been supplied by Islamic Turkish extremists in Istanbul for the purpose of anti-Zionist actions in Western Europe. A fresh outrage should be expected in the next few days. Rumours suggested a target in southern Germany. All frontier posts and local police forces to be alerted. No further details available. The same afternoon, Alexis was summoned by his superiors, and the same night he conducted a very long clandestine telephone call with his great friend Schulmann, in order to receive his congratulations and encouragement, as well as fresh instructions.

"They are biting, Marty!" he cried excitedly, in English. "They are sheep. They are completely in our hands!"

Alexis has bitten, Kurtz told Litvak back in Munich, but he's going to need one hell of a lot of shepherding. "Why can't Gadi hurry that girl up?" he muttered, staring moodily at his watch.

"Because he doesn't like the killing any more!" Litvak cried with a jubilation he could not hold back. "You think I can't feel it? You think you can't?"

Kurtz told him to be quiet.

12

The hilltop smelt of thyme and was a special place for Joseph. He had looked for it on the map and led Charlie to it with an air of moment, first by car and now on foot, climbing purposefully past rows of wattle beehives, through glades of cypress trees and stony fields of yellow flowers. The sun was still not at its height. Inland lay range after range of brown mountains. Eastward she glimpsed the silver plains of the Aegean until the haze turned them into sky. The air smelt of resin and honey and rang to the din of goat bells. A fresh breeze burned one side of her face and clamped her light dress against her body. She held his arm, but Joseph, deep in concentration, seemed not to notice. Once she thought she saw Dimitri sitting on a gate, but when she exclaimed, he warned her sharply not to greet him. Once she could have sworn she saw the silhouette of Rose, up above them on the skyline, but when she looked again she saw nothing.

Their day till then had had its own choreography and she had let him steer her through it with his customary restlessness. She had woken early to find Rachel standing over her, telling her that she was please to wear the other blue, dear, the one with the long sleeves. She showered quickly and marched back into the bedroom stark naked, but Rachel was gone and it was Joseph who sat perched before a breakfast tray for two, listening to a Greek news bulletin on his little radio, for all the world her companion of the night. She shot back into the bathroom, he handed the dress round the door to her; they ate hurriedly and in near silence. In the foyer he paid cash and pocketed the receipt. At the Mercedes, when they took their luggage to it, she found Raoul the hippy boy lying not six feet from the rear bumper, fiddling with the engine of an overladen motorbike, and Rose reclining on the grass with her hip cocked while she munched a bread roll. Charlie wondered how long they'd been there and why they had to guard the car. Joseph drove the mile down the road to the ancient sites, parked once more, and long before other mortals had started to queue and swelter, he had spirited her through a side gate and treated her to another privately conducted tour of the centre of the universe. He showed her the Temple of Apollo and the Doric wall inscribed with hymns of praise, and the stone that had marked the world's navel. He showed her the Treasuries and the running track and treated her to a commentary on the many wars that had been fought to obtain possession of the Oracle. But there was no lightness to his manner, as there had been on the Acropolis. She had a picture of him with a checklist in his mind, ticking each heading as he hurried her through.

Returning to the car, he handed her the key.

"Me?" she said.

"Why not? I thought fine cars were your weakness."

They headed north over winding empty roads and at first he did little but assess her driving technique, much as if she were taking her Advanced Test again, but he could not make her nervous, nor she him apparently, for quite soon he spread the map over his knees and ignored her. The car handled like a dream, the road changed from tarmac to gravel. With each sharp turn a cloud of dust shot up and, lit by the fresh sunlight, drifted away into the stupendous landscape. Abruptly he folded up the map and returned it to the pocket at his side.

"So, Charlie? You are ready?" he enquired, as brusquely as if she had been keeping him waiting. And resumed his narrative.

At first, they were still in Nottingham, their frenzy at its height. They had spent two nights and one day in the motel, he said, and the register bore this out.

"The staff, if pressed, will recall a loving couple answering our description. Our bedroom was at the western end of the complex, looking on to its own piece of garden. In due course, you will be taken there and see for yourself what it looked like."

Most of their time they had spent in bed, he said, talking politics, exchanging lives, making love. The only interruptions, it seemed, were a couple of flips into the Nottingham countryside, but the lovers' desire soon got the better of them and they hurried back to the motel.

"Why didn't we just have it off in the car?" she

enquired, in an effort to draw him from his dark mood. "I like those unscheduled ones."

"I respect your taste, but unfortunately Michel is shy in these matters and prefers the privacy of the bedroom."

She tried again: "So how does he rate in the charts?"

He had the answer to that too. "According to the best-informed reports, he is a little unimaginative, but his enthusiasm is boundless and his virility impressive."

"Thank you," she said gravely.

Early on the Monday morning, he resumed, Michel returned to London, but Charlie, who had no rehearsal till afternoon, remained behind, heartbroken, in the motel. He briskly described her grief.

"The day is dark as a funeral. The rain is still falling. Remember the weather. At first you are crying so much you cannot even stand. You lie in the bed that is still warm from his body, weeping your heart out. He has told you he will try to come to York next week, but you are convinced you will never see him again in your life. So what do you do?" He gave her no chance to answer. "You sit yourself at the cramped dressing-table in front of the mirror, you stare at the marks of his hands on your body, at your own tears as they continue falling. You open a drawer. Take out the motel folder. And, from the folder, motel stationery and a courtesy ballpoint pen. And you write to him as you sit there. Describing yourself. Your inmost thoughts. Five pages. The first of many, many letters which you send to him. You would do this? In your despair? You are an impulsive letter-writer, after all."

"If I had his address, I would."

"He has given you an address in Paris." He gave it to her himself, now. Care of a tobacconist's in Montparnasse. To Michel, please forward, no surname needed or supplied.

"The same night, from the misery of the Astral Commercial and Private Hotel, you write to him again. In the morning as soon as you wake, you once more write to him. On all sorts and scraps of stationery. At rehearsals, in the intervals, at all odd times, henceforth you write to him passionately, unthinkingly, with total frankness." He glanced at her. "You would do that?" he insisted again. "You would really write such letters?"

How much reassurance does a man need? she wondered.

But he was already away again. For, joy of joys—despite her pessimistic forecasts—Michel came not only to York, he came to Bristol and, better still, to London, where he spent a whole miraculous night in Charlie's flat in Camden, frenzy all the way. And it was there, said Joseph—as gratefully as if rounding off a complicated mathematical premise—"in your own bed, in your own flat, between protestations of eternal love, that we planned this very Greek holiday which we are here and now enjoying."

A long silence while she drove and thought. We are here at last. From Nottingham to Greece in one hour's driving.

"To join up with Michel after Mykonos," she said sceptically.

"Why not?"

"Mykonos with Al and the family, jump ship, meet Michel in the Athens restaurant, away we go?"

"Correct."

"No Al," she pronounced finally. "If I'd had you, I wouldn't have taken Al to Mykonos. I'd have chucked him. He wasn't invited by the sponsors. He tagged on. One at a time, that's me."

He dismissed her objection out of hand. "Michel does not ask for that type of loyalty; he does not give it and he does not receive it. He is a soldier and an enemy of your society, liable to be arrested at any time. It may be a week before you see him or six months. You think he wants you to live like a nun suddenly? Sit around pining, having tantrums, confiding your secret to your girlfriends? Nonsense. You would sleep with a whole army if he told you to." They passed a wayside chapel. "Slow down," he ordered, and again studied the map.

Slow down. Park here. March.

He had quickened his step. Their path led to a cluster of derelict sheds and past it to a disused stone quarry hacked like a volcanic crater into the summit of the hill. At the foot of the hewn face stood an old oil can. Without a word, Joseph weighted it with small pebbles while Charlie looked on mystified. Removing the red blazer, he folded it and laid it carefully on the ground. The gun was at his waist, dropped into a leather loop fastened to his belt, the butt tipped slightly forward on a line below his right armpit. He wore a second holster over his left shoulder but it was empty. Grasping her wrist, he drew her to the ground to squat, Arab-style, beside him.

"So then. Nottingham is in the past, so is York, so is Bristol, so is London. Today is today, the third of our great Greek honeymoon; we are where we are, we made love all night in our hotel in Delphi, rose early, and Michel supplied you with another memorable insight into the cradle of your civilisation. You drove the car and I confirmed what I had heard from you already, that you like to drive and for a woman you drive well. And now I have brought you here, to this hilltop, you do not know why. My mood, as you have noticed, is withdrawn. I am brooding—perhaps wrestling with a great decision. Your efforts to break in upon my thoughts only annoy me. What is happening? you wonder. Is our love advancing? Or have you done something which displeases me? And if advancing, how? I sit you here—beside me— so—and I draw the gun."

She watched in fascination how he slipped it nimbly from its holster and made it the natural extension of his hand.

"As a great and unique privilege, I am going to initiate you into the history of this gun, and for the first time"—his voice slowed down to make the emphasis—"I am going to mention to you my great brother, whose very existence is a military secret which only the most loyal few may share. I do this because I love you, and because—" He hesitated.

And because Michel likes telling secrets, she thought; but nothing on earth would have prompted her to spoil his act.

"Because today I intend to take the first step towards initiating you as a fighting comrade in our secret army. How often—in your many letters, in our lovemaking—have you begged for a chance to prove your loyalty in action? Today we are taking the first step along that path."

Once again, she was aware of his seemingly effortless ability to put on Arab clothes. As last night in the taverna, when at times she barely knew which of his conflicting spirits was speaking out of him, so now she listened entranced to his adoption of the ornate Arab style of narrative.

"All through my nomadic life as a victim of the Zionist

usurpers, my great elder brother shone before me like a star. In the Jordan, in our first camp, when school was a tin hut filled with fleas. In Syria, where we fled after the Jordanian troops had driven us out with tanks. In the Lebanon, where the Zionists shelled us from the sea and bombed us from the air, and the Shiites helped them to do it. Still, in the midst of these deprivations, I unfailingly remind myself of the great absent hero, my brother, whose feats, reported to me in whispers by my beloved sister Fatmeh, I long more than anything to rival."

He no longer asked her whether she was listening.

"I see him seldom, and only in great secrecy. Now in Damascus. Now in Amman. A summons—come! Then, for a night, I am at his side, drinking in his words, his nobility of heart, his clear commander's mind, his courage. One night he orders me to Beirut. He has just returned from a mission of great daring of which I may know nothing except that it was a total victory over the Fascists. I am to go with him to hear a great political speaker, a Libyan, a man of wonderful rhetoric and persuasiveness. The most beautiful speech I ever heard in my life. To this day I can quote it to you. The oppressed peoples of the entire earth should have heard this great Libyan." The gun lay flat in his palm. He was holding it out for her, willing her to covet it. "With our hearts beating with excitement, we depart from the secret lecture place and walk back through the Beirut dawn. Arm in arm, after the Arab fashion. There are tears in my eyes. On an impulse, my brother stops and embraces me as we stand there on the pavement. I can feel now his wise face pressed against my own. He takes this gun from his pocket and presses it into my hand. So." Grasping Charlie's hand, he transferred the gun to it, but kept his own hand over hers while he pointed the barrel towards the quarry wall. " 'A gift,' he says. 'To avenge. To set our people free. A gift from one fighter to another. With this gun I declared my oath upon the grave of my father.' I am speechless."

His cool hand was still on hers, clasping the gun to her, and she could feel her own hand trembling inside it like a separate creature.

"Charlie, this gun is a holy thing to me. I tell you this because I love my brother and I loved my father and I love you. In a minute I shall teach you to shoot with it, but first of all I ask you, kiss the gun."

She stared at him, then at the gun. But his excited expression offered no respite. Placing his other hand round her arm, he lifted her to her feet.

"We are lovers, do you not remember? We are comrades, servants of the revolution. We live in the closest companionship of mind and body. I am a passionate Arab and I like words and gestures. Kiss the gun."

"Jose, I can't do that."

She had addressed him as Joseph, and as Joseph he replied.

"You think this is an English tea-party, Charlie? You think that because Michel is a pretty boy he must be playing games? Where should he have learnt to play games when the gun was the only thing that gave him value as a man?" he asked perfectly reasonably.

She shook her head, still staring at the gun. But her resistance did not anger him. "Listen, Charlie. Last night, as we were making love, you asked me: 'Michel, where is the battlefield?' You know what I did? I put my hand over your heart and I told you: 'We are fighting a *jehad* and the battlefield is here.' You are my disciple. Your sense of mission has never been so exalted. Do you know what that is—a *jehad*?"

She shook her head.

"A *jehad* is what you were looking for until you met me. A *jehad* is a holy war. You are about to fire your first shot in our *jehad*. Kiss the gun."

She hesitated, then pressed her lips to the blue metal of the barrel.

"So," he said, breaking briskly away from her. "From now on, this gun is part of both of us. This gun is our honour and our flag. You believe this?"

"Yes, Jose, I believe it. Yes, Michel, I believe it. Don't ever make me do that again." She wiped her wrist involuntarily across her lips as if there were blood on them. She hated both herself and him, and she was feeling a little mad.

"Type Walther PPK," Joseph was explaining when she next heard him. "Not heavy, but remember that every handgun is a compromise between concealment, portability, and efficiency. This is how Michel speaks to you about guns.

Strictly, the way he has been spoken to himself by his brother."

Standing behind her, he turned her hips till she was square to the target, her feet apart. Then he placed his fist round hers, mingling his fingers with her own, keeping her arm at full stretch and the barrel pointing to the ground midway between her feet.

"The left arm free and comfortable. So." He loosened it for her. "Both eyes open, you raise the gun slowly till it is in a natural line with the target. Keeping the gun-arm straight. So. When I say fire, shoot twice, come down again, wait."

Obediently she lowered the gun till it was aiming at the ground again. He gave the order; she raised her arm, stiffly as he had instructed her; she pulled the trigger and nothing happened.

"This time," he said, and slipped the safety catch.

She repeated the action, pulled the trigger again, and the gun bucked in her hand as if it had itself been hit by a bullet. She fired a second time and her heart filled with the same perilous excitement she had felt when she had first jumped a horse or swum naked in the sea. She lowered the gun, Joseph gave a fresh order, she swung it up much faster and fired again twice in quick succession, then three times for luck. Then repeated the movement without an order, firing at will as the mounting clatter of shots filled the air on every side of her and the ricochets whined into the valley and away over the sea. She went on firing till the magazine was empty, then stood with the gun at her side, her heart thumping while she breathed the smells of thyme, and cordite.

"How did I do?" she asked, turning to him.

"Look for yourself."

Leaving him where he was, she ran forward to the oil can. Then stared at it in disbelief because it was unmarked.

"But what went wrong?" she cried indignantly.

"You missed," Joseph replied, taking the gun from her.

"They were blanks!"

"They were nothing of the kind."

"I did everything you told me!"

"For a start, you should not be shooting with one hand. For a girl weighing a hundred and ten pounds, wrists like asparagus, it's ridiculous."

"Then why the hell did you tell me that was how to shoot?"

He was heading for the car, guiding her by the arm. "If you're taught by Michel, then you must shoot like Michel's pupil. He knows nothing of two-handed grips. He had modelled himself on his brother. You want me to print 'Made in Israel' all over you?"

"Why doesn't he?" she insisted angrily, and seized his arm. "*Why* doesn't he know how to shoot properly? Why hasn't he been taught?"

"I told you. He was taught by his brother."

"Then why didn't his brother teach him right?"

She really wanted an answer. She was humiliated and prepared to make a scene, and he seemed to recognise this, for he smiled and, in his own way, capitulated.

" 'It is God's will that Khalil shoots with one hand,' he says."

"Why?"

With a shake of his head, he dismissed her question. They returned to the car.

"Is Khalil his brother's name?"

"Yes."

"You said it was the Arab name for Hebron."

He was pleased, if strangely distracted. "It is both." He started the engine. "Khalil for our town. Khalil for my brother. Khalil for the friend of God and of the Hebrew prophet Abraham, whom Islam respects, and who rests in our ancient mosque."

"Khalil then," she said.

"Khalil," he agreed shortly. "Remember it. Also the circumstances in which he told it to you. Because he loves you. Because he loves his brother. Because you have kissed his brother's gun and become of his blood."

They set off down the hillside, Joseph driving. She no longer knew herself, if she ever had. The sound of her own shooting was still ringing in her ears. The taste of the gun barrel was on her lips, and when he pointed out Olympus to her, all she saw was black and white rainstacks like atomic cloud. Joseph's preoccupation was as great as her own, but his aim lay once more ahead of them, and while he drove he pressed forward ceaselessly with his narrative, heaping detail upon detail. Khalil again. The times they had together before he went off to fight. Nottingham, the great meeting of their souls. His sister Fatmeh and his great love for her. About his other brothers, dead. They hit the coast road. The traffic was thunderous and much too fast; the sullied beaches were strewn with broken huts, the factory towers like prisons looking in on her.

She tried to keep herself awake for him, but eventually the effort was too much. She put her head on his shoulder and for a while escaped.

The hotel in Thessalonika was an antique Edwardian pile with floodlit domes and an air of circumstance. Their suite was on the top floor, with a children's alcove, a twenty-foot bathroom, and scratched twenties furniture like home. She had put on the light but he ordered her to switch it off. He had had food sent up, but neither of them had touched it. There was a bay window and he stood in it with his back to her, gazing down into the green square and the moonlit waterfront beyond it. Charlie sat on the bed. The room was filled with stray Greek music from the street.

"So, Charlie."

"So, Charlie," she echoed quietly, waiting for the explanation that was owed to her.

"You have pledged yourself to my battle. But what battle? How is it fought? Where? I have talked of the cause, I have talked of action: we believe, therefore we do. I have told you that terror is theatre, and that sometimes the world has to be lifted up by its ears before it will listen to justice."

She shifted restlessly.

"Repeatedly, in my letters, in our long discussions, I have promised to bring you to the point of action. But I have prevaricated. I have delayed. Until tonight. Perhaps I do not trust you. Or perhaps I have learned to love you too much and do not wish to put you in the front line. You do not know which of these is true, but sometimes you have felt hurt by my secrecy. As your letters reveal."

The letters, she thought again; always the letters.

"So how, in practical terms, do you become my little soldier? That is what we are discussing tonight. Here. In that bed you are sitting on. On the last night of our Greek honeymoon. Maybe our last night ever, for you can never be sure that you will see me again."

He turned to face her, nothing rushed. It was as if he had bound his body in the same careful bonds that held his voice. "You weep a lot," he remarked. "I think you are weeping tonight. As you hold me. Pledging yourself to me for all eternity. Yes? You weep, and while you weep, I tell you: 'It is time.' Tomorrow you shall have your chance. Tomorrow, in the morning, you shall fulfil the vow you swore to me by the great Khalil's gun. I am ordering you—asking you"—carefully, almost majestically, he went back to the window—"to drive that Mercedes car across the Yugoslav border, northward and into Austria. Where it will be collected from you. Alone. Will you do that? What do you say?"

On the surface, she felt nothing beyond a concern to match his apparent barrenness of feeling. No fear, no sense of danger, no surprise: she shut them all out with a bang. It's now, she thought. Charlie, you're on. A driving job. Away you go. She was staring straight at him, hard-jawed, the way she stared at people when she lied.

"Well—how do you respond to him?" he enquired, jollying her slightly. "Alone," he reminded her. "It's some distance, you know. Eight hundred miles through Yugoslavia—that's quite something, for a first mission. What do you say?"

"What's in it?" she asked.

Whether deliberately or not she could not tell, but he chose to misunderstand her: "Money. Your début in the theatre of the real. Everything Marty promised you." His mind seemed as closed to her as it was perhaps to himself. His tone was clipped and deprecating.

"I meant what's in the car?"

The three minute warning before his voice became hectoring. "What does it matter what's in the car? A military message perhaps. Papers. Do you think you can know every secret of our great movement on your first day?" A break, but she did not answer. "Will you drive the car or not? That is all that matters."

She did not want Michel's reply. She wanted his.

"Why doesn't he drive it himself?"

"Charlie, it is not your task, as a new recruit, to question orders. Naturally, if you are shocked—" Who was he? She felt his mask slipping, but did not know which mask it was.

"If suddenly you suspect—within the fiction—that you have been manipulated by this man—that all his adoration of you, his glamour, his protestations of eternal love—" Yet again he seemed to lose his footing. Was it her own wishful thinking, or dared she suppose that, in the half darkness, some sentiment had crept up on him unnoticed, which he would have preferred to hold at bay?

"I mean only that if, at this stage"—his voice recovered its strength—"if the scales should somehow fall from your eyes, or your courage fail you, then naturally you must say no."

"I was asking you a question. Why don't you drive it yourself—you, Michel?"

He swung swiftly back to the window and it seemed to Charlie that he had much to quell in himself before replying. "Michel tells you this and no more," he began, with strained forbearance. "Whatever is in that car"—he could look down on it from where he stood, parked in the square and guarded by a Volkswagen bus—"it is vital to our great struggle, but it is also very dangerous. Whoever was caught driving that car at any point in those eight hundred miles—whether the car contains subversive literature or some other kind of material, messages perhaps—to be caught with it would be extremely incriminating. Not all the influence—the diplomatic pressures, good lawyers—could prevent that person from having a very bad time indeed. If you are considering your own skin, that is what you have to consider." And he added, in a voice quite unlike Michel's: "You have your own life, after all. You are not one of us."

But his faltering, however slight, had given her an assurance she had not felt in his company before. "I asked why he wasn't driving it himself. I'm still waiting for his answer."

Once more, he rallied, too strongly. "Charlie! I am a Palestinian activist. I am known as a fighter for the cause. I am travelling on a false passport which may at any time be compromised. But you—an attractive English girl of good appearance—no record, quick-witted, charming—naturally for you there is no danger. Now surely that is enough!"

"You just said there *was* a danger."

"Nonsense. Michel assures you there is none. For himself, maybe. But for you—none. 'Do it for me,' I say. 'Do it and be proud. Do it for our love and for the revolution. Do it for all we have sworn to each other. Do it for my great brother. Are your vows meaningless? Were you merely mouthing Western hypocrisies when you professed yourself a revolutionary?' " He paused once more. "Do it because if you don't, your life will be even emptier than it was before I picked you up at the beach."

"You mean at the theatre," she corrected him.

He barely bothered with her. He remained standing with his back to her, his gaze still upon the Mercedes. He was Joseph again, Joseph of the pressed-out vowels and careful sentences and the mission that would save innocent lives.

"So there you are. This is your Rubicon. You know what that is? The Rubicon? Cut off now—go home—you can take some money, forget the revolution, Palestine, Michel, everything."

"Or?"

"Drive the car. Your first blow for the cause. Alone. Eight hundred miles. Which is it to be?"

"Where will you be?"

His calm was once more unassailable, and once more he took refuge in Michel: "In spirit, close to you, but I cannot help you. Nobody can help you. You will be on your own, performing a criminal act in the interests of what the world will call a gang of terrorists." He started again, but this time he was Joseph. "Some of the kids will make an escort for you, but there is nothing they can do if things go wrong, except report the fact to Marty and myself. Yugoslavia is no great friend of Israel."

Charlie hung on. All her instincts of survival told her to. She saw that he had once more turned round to look at her, and she met his black stare knowing that her own face was visible where his was not. Who are you fighting? she thought; yourself or me? Why are you the enemy in both camps?

"We haven't finished the scene," she reminded him. "I'm asking you—both of you—what's in the car? You want me to drive the car—whoever does—however many of you there are in there—I need to know what's in it. Now."

She thought she would have to wait. She had expected another three minute warning while his mind whirred through the options before it printed out its deliberately desiccated answers. She was wrong.

"Explosives," he retorted, in his most detached voice.

"Two hundred pounds of Russian plastic explosive divided into half-pound sticks. Good new stuff, well cared for, capable of standing extremes of heat and cold, and reasonably plastic at all temperatures."

"Oh, well, I'm glad it's well cared for," Charlie said cheerfully, fighting off the tidal wave. "Where's it hidden?"

"In the valance, cross members, roof-lining, and seats. As an older make of car, it has the advantage of box sections and girders."

"What's it going to be used for?"

"Our struggle."

"But why does he have to schlep all the way down to Greece for the stuff—why not get it in Europe?"

"My brother has certain rules of secrecy and he obliges me to obey them scrupulously. The circle he trusts is extremely small, and he will not enlarge it. In essence he trusts neither Arab nor European. What we do alone, we alone can betray."

"And what form exactly—in this case—does our struggle take, would you say?" Charlie enquired, in the same blithe, over-relaxed voice.

Again he did not hesitate. "Killing the Jews of the diaspora. As they have dispersed the people of Palestine, so we punish them in their diaspora and declare our agony to the ears and eyes of the world. By this means we also arouse the sleeping consciousness of the proletariat," he added, as a less assured afterthought.

"Well, that seems reasonable enough."

"Thank you."

"And you and Marty—you just thought it would be nice if I ran it up to Austria for them as a favour." With a small intake of breath, she rose and very deliberately went to the window. "Will you put your arms round me, please, Jose? I'm not being fast. It's just, for a minute there, I felt a trifle lonely."

One arm went round her shoulder and she shivered violently against it. Leaning her body along his, she turned in to him and reached her arms round him, and hugged him to her, and to her joy she felt him soften, and return her clasp. Her mind was working everywhere at once, like an eye turned upon a vast and unexpected panorama. But clearest of all, beyond the immediate danger of the drive, she began to see at last the larger journey that was stretching ahead of her and, along the route, the faceless comrades of the other army she was about to join. Is he sending me or holding me back? she wondered. He doesn't know. He's waking up and putting himself to sleep at the same time. His arms, still locked around her, gave her a new courage. Till now, under the spell of his determined chastity, she had believed in some dark way that her promiscuous body was unfit for him. Now, for reasons she had yet to understand, that self-distaste had left her.

"Keep convincing me," she said, still holding him. "Do your job."

"Is it not enough that Michel sends you, yet does not want you to go?"

She didn't answer.

"Should I quote Shelley to you—'the tempestuous loveliness of terror'? Must I remind you of our many promises to each other—that we are ready to kill because we are ready to die?"

"I don't think words do it any more. I think I've had all the words I can eat." She had buried her face in his chest. "You promised to stay close to me," she reminded him, and felt his grasp slacken as his voice hardened.

"I shall be waiting for you in Austria," he said, in a tone calculated more to repel than persuade her. "That is Michel's promise to you. It is also mine."

She stood back from him and held his head between her hands the way she had held it on the Acropolis, studying it critically by the lights from the square. And she had the feeling that it had locked against her like a door that would let her neither in nor out. Cold and aroused at the same time, she walked back to the bed and sat down again. Her voice too had a new confidence that impressed her. Her eyes were on her bracelet, which she was turning thoughtfully in the half dark.

"So which way do *you* want it to be?" she asked. "You, Joseph? Does Charlie stay and do the job, or does Charlie take the money and bolt? What's your *personal* scenario?"

"You know the dangers. Decide."

"So do you. Better than I do. You knew them from the start."

"You have heard all the arguments, from Marty and from me."

Unclasping the bracelet, she let it slip into her hand. "We save innocent life. Assuming I deliver the explosive, that is. There *are* those, of course—simpletons—who might suppose one would save more lives by *not* delivering the explosive. But they would be wrong, I take it?"

"In the long run, if all goes well, they will be wrong."

He had his back to her once more, and to all appearances had resumed his examination of the view from the window.

"If you're Michel talking to me, it's easy," she continued reasonably, fastening the bracelet on her other wrist. "You've bowled me off my feet; I've kissed the gun, and I can't wait to get to the barricades. If we don't believe that, your best endeavours over the last few days have failed. Which they haven't. That's how you cast me, and that's how you've got me. End of argument. I'll go."

She saw his head nod slightly in acceptance. "And if you're Joseph talking, what's the difference? If I said no, I'd never see you again. It would be back to Nowheresville with my golden handshake."

She noticed to her surprise that he had lost interest in her. His shoulders lifted, he let out a long breath; his head remained turned to the window, his gaze fixed on the horizon. He resumed speaking, and she thought at first that he was again evading the thrust of what she had been saying. But as she continued to listen, she realised he was explaining why, so far as he was concerned, there had never been any real choice for either of them.

"Michel would be pleased with this town, I think. Until the Germans began their occupation here, sixty thousand Jews lived fairly happily up on that hillside. Postworkers, merchants, bankers. Sephardim. They came here from Spain, through the Balkans. By the time the Germans left, there were none. Those who were not exterminated found their way to Israel."

She lay in bed. Joseph was still at the window, watching the street fires die. She wondered whether he would come to her, knowing he would not. She heard a creak as he stretched himself on the divan, his body parallel to hers and only the length of Yugoslavia between them. She wanted him more than she had ever wanted anyone. Her fear of tomorrow intensified her desire.

"Got any brothers and sisters, Jose?" she asked.

"One brother."

"What's he do?"

"He died in the war of '67."

"The war that drove Michel across the Jordan," she said. She had never expected him to give a truthful answer, but she knew that he had. "Did you fight in that war too?"

"I expect so."

"And in the war before? The one I can't remember the date of?"

" '56."

"Yes?"

"Yes."

"And in the war after? '73?"

"Probably."

"What did you fight for?"

Wait again.

"In '56 because I wanted to be a hero, in '67 for peace. And in '73"—he seemed to find it harder to remember—"for Israel," he said.

"And now? What are you fighting for this time?"

Because it is there, she thought. To save lives. Because they asked me to. So that my villagers can dance the *dabke*, and listen to the tales of travellers at the well.

"Jose?"

"Yes, Charlie."

"How did you pick up those dishy scars?"

In the darkness, his long pauses had acquired a campfire excitement.

"The burn marks, I would say, I got them sitting in a tank. The bullet-holes from getting out of it."

"How old were you?"

"Twenty. Twenty-one."

At the age of eight I joined the Ashbal, she thought. At the age of fifteen—

"So who's Daddy?" she asked, determined to keep up the momentum.

"He was a pioneer. An early settler."

"Where from?"

"Poland."

"When?"

"In the twenties. In the third *aliyah*, if you know what that means."

She didn't, but for the moment it didn't matter.

"What was his trade?"

"A construction worker. Worked with his hands. Turned a sand dune into a city. Called it Tel Aviv. A Socialist—the practical kind. Didn't think much of God. Never drank. Never owned anything worth more than a few dollars."

"Is that what you would have liked to be too?" she asked.

He'll never answer, she thought. He's asleep. Don't be impertinent.

"I chose the higher calling," he replied drily.

Or it chose you, she thought, which is what choice is called when you are born into captivity. And somehow, quite quickly, she fell asleep.

But Gadi Becker, the seasoned warrior, lay patiently awake, staring at the darkness and listening to the uneven breathing of his young recruit. Why had he spoken to her like that? Why had he declared himself to her at the very moment when he was dispatching her on her first mission? Sometimes he no longer trusted himself. He would flex his muscles only to find that the cords of discipline did not tighten against him as they used to. He would set a straight course, only to look back and marvel at his degree of error. What am I dreaming of, he wondered, the fighting or the peace? He was too old for both. Too old to go on, too old to stop. Too old to give himself, yet unable to withhold. Too old not to know the smell of death before he killed.

He listened again as her breathing settled to the calmer rhythm of sleep. Holding his wrist Kurtz-style before him in the darkness, he looked at the luminous dial of his watch. Then, so quietly that even wide awake she would have been hard-pressed to hear him, he put on his red blazer and stole from the room.

The night concierge was an alert man, and had only to see the well-dressed gentleman approach him to sense at once the proximity of a large tip.

"You have telegram forms?" Becker demanded, in a peremptory tone.

The night concierge dived below his counter.

Becker began writing. Large, careful letters in a black ink. He had the address in his head—care of a lawyer in Geneva; Kurtz had signalled it to him from Munich after confirming with Yanuka, for safety's sake, that it was still in use. He had the text in his head too. It began "Kindly advise your client" and referred to the maturing of bonds in accordance with our standard contract. It ran to forty-five words, and when he had checked them over he added the stiff self-conscious signature in which Schwili had patiently instructed him. Then he handed the form across the counter, and gave the concierge five hundred drachmas for himself.

"I wish you to send it twice, you understand? The same message, twice. Once now by telephone, again in the morning from the post office. Don't give the job to a boy, do it yourself. Afterwards, you send me a confirmatory copy to my room."

The concierge would do everything exactly as the gentleman ordered. He had heard of Arab tips, he had dreamed of them. Tonight, out of the blue, he had finally landed one. There were many other services he would have wished to perform for the gentleman, but the gentleman, alas, was unreceptive to his suggestions. Forlornly, the concierge watched his prey stride into the street, then cut away towards the waterfront. The communications van stood in a car park. It was time for the great Gadi Becker to file his report and make sure all was clear for the big launch.

13

The monastery lay two kilometres from the border, in a hollow of boulders and yellow sedge. It was a sad, desecrated place of caved-in roofs and a courtyard of broken cells with psychedelic hula girls painted on the stone walls. Some post-Christian had started a discothéque here, but, like the monks, had fled. On the concrete pad intended as a dance floor stood the red Mercedes, like a warhorse being tended for the battle; beside it, the champion who would ride it, with Joseph the administrator supervising at her elbow. This is where Michel brought you to change the number plates and see you off, Charlie; this is where he handed you the false papers and the keys. Rose, wipe down that door panel again, please. Rachel, what's that scrap of paper on the floor? He was Joseph the perfectionist once more, ordering every tiny detail. The communications van stood against the outer wall, its aerial gently nodding in the hot breeze.

The Munich number plates were already bolted in position. A dusty German "D" had replaced the diplomatic sticker. Unwanted rubbish had been removed. With meticulous care, Becker now began introducing eloquent souvenirs to replace it: a thumbed guidebook to the Acropolis shoved into a door pocket and forgotten; grape pips for the ashtray, fragments of orange-peel for the floor; Greek ice-cream sticks, scraps of chocolate paper. Next, two cancelled tickets to the ancient sites of Delphi, followed by an Esso road map of Greece with the route between Delphi and Thessalonika marked in fibre-tip pen, with a couple of Michel's scribbled marginal annotations in Arabic close to the point in the hills where Charlie had fired the gun one-handed, and missed. A comb with a few black hairs in it, the teeth smeared with Michel's pungent German hair lotion. A pair of leather driving gloves, lightly sprayed with Michel's body-mist. A spectacles case by Frey of Munich, the one that went with the sunglasses which had been inadvertently smashed when their owner tried to pick up Rachel at the border.

And lastly he submitted Charlie herself to an equally searching scrutiny, covering the whole surface of her clothed body, from her shoes to her head and down again by way of her bracelet before he turned—reluctantly, as it seemed to her—to a small trestle table on which were laid out the revised contents of her handbag.

"So now put them in, please," he said finally, when he had made another check; and watched her pack everything in her own way—handkerchief, lipsticks, driver's licence, coins, wallet, keepsakes, keys, and all the meticulously calculated junk that, on examination, would testify to the complex fictions of her several lives.

"What about his letters?" she said. A Joseph pause. "If he wrote me all those hot-breath letters, I'd cart them round with me everywhere, wouldn't I?"

"Michel does not permit that. You have strict instructions to keep his letters in a safe place in your flat and above all never to cross a frontier with them in your possession. However—" From the side pocket of his jacket, he had drawn a small diary wrapped in protective cellophane. It was clothbound, with a little pencil in the spine. "Since you do not keep a diary, we decided to keep one for you," he explained. Gingerly, she accepted it and pulled away the cellophane. She took out the pencil. It was lightly dented with teethmarks, which was what she still did with pencils: chewed them. She leafed through half a dozen pages. Schwili's entries were sparse but, with Leon's flair and Miss Bach's electronic memory, all her own. Over the Nottingham period, nothing: Michel had descended on her without warning. For York, a big "M," with a question mark and a ring round it. In the corner of the same day, a long, contemplative doodle, the sort she did when she was daydreaming. Her car was featured: *Fiat to Eustace, 9 a.m.* Her mother also: *1 week to Mum's birthday. Buy present now.* So also was Alastair: *A to Isle of Wight—Kellogg's commercial?* He hadn't gone, she remembered; Kellogg's found a better and more sober star. For her monthly periods, wavy lines, and once or twice the facetious entry *off games.* Turning forward to the Greek holiday, she found the name Mykonos, printed in large pensive capitals, and beside it the departure and arrival times of the

charter. But when she came to the day of her arrival in
Athens, the whole double page was illuminated with a flock
of soaring birds, in blue and red ballpoint like a sailor's tattoo. She dropped the diary into the handbag and closed the
catch with a snap. It was too much. She felt dirty and in-
vaded. She wanted new people she could still surprise—
people who could not fake her feelings and her handwriting
so that she could no longer distinguish them from the originals. Perhaps Joseph knew that. Perhaps he read it in her
brusque manner. She hoped so. With his gloved hand he was
holding open the car door for her. She got in quickly.

"Look at the papers once more," he ordered.

"I don't need to," she said, looking straight ahead of her.

"Number of the car?"

She gave it.

"Date of registration?"

She gave it all: story within the story within the story.
The car was the private property of a fashionable Munich
doctor, name supplied, her current lover. Insured and registered in his name, see the false papers.

"Why is he not with you, this active doctor? It is Michel
asking you this, you understand?"

She understood. "He had to fly back from Thessalonika
this morning for an urgent case. I agreed to drive the car for
him. He was in Athens to deliver a lecture. We've been touring together."

"How did you meet him in the first place?"

"In England. He's a buddy of my parents—he cures
their hangovers. My parents are mountainously rich, hint,
hint."

"For the extreme case, you have Michel's one thousand
dollars in your handbag, which he has lent to you for the
trip. Conceivably, for their overtime, for the inconvenience
you have caused these people, they may graciously consider a
small subsidy. What is the name of his wife?"

"Renate, and I hate the bitch."

"The children?"

"Christoph and Dorothea. I'd make a marvellous mother
to them if only Renate would stand aside. I want to go now.
Anything else?"

"Yes."

Like you love me, she suggested to him in her mind.

Like you're a bit apologetic about launching me halfway across Europe with a carful of high-quality Russian plastic explosive.

"Don't be overconfident," he advised her, with no more feeling than if he were examining her driver's licence. "Not every frontier guard is a fool or a sex maniac."

She had promised herself no farewells and perhaps Joseph had done the same.

"So, Charlie," she said. And started the engine.

He neither waved nor smiled. Perhaps he said "So, Charlie" back, but if he did she didn't hear. She reached the main road; the monastery and its temporary inhabitants vanished from her mirror. She drove a couple of kilometres fast and came to an old painted arrow saying "JUGOSLAWIEN." She drove on slowly, following the traffic. The road spread and became a car park. She saw a line of charabancs and a line of cars and the flags of all nations cooked to pale pastel by the sun. I'm English, German, Israeli, and Arab. She took her place behind an open sports car. Two boys sat in the front, two girls in the back. She wondered whether they were Joseph's. Or Michel's. Or police of some kind. She was learning to see the world that way: everyone belongs to someone. A grey-uniformed official waved her impatiently forward. She had everything ready. False papers, false explanations. Nobody wanted them. She was over.

Standing on the hilltop high above the monastery, Joseph lowered his binoculars and returned to the waiting van.

"Package posted," he said curtly to the boy David, who typed the words obediently into his machine. For Becker he would have typed anything—risked anything, shot anybody. Becker was a living legend for him, complete in all his abilities, somebody he should aspire ceaselessly to copy.

"Marty replies congratulations," the boy said reverently.

But the great Becker seemed not to hear.

She drove for ever. She drove with her arms aching from grasping the wheel too tight, and her neck aching from keeping her legs too rigid. She drove with her belly feeling sick from too much slackness. Then sick again from too much fear. Then sicker still when the engine stalled and she thought: Oh hooray, we're having a breakdown. *If you do, then dump it,* Joseph had said; *run it into a side turning, hitch a lift, lose the papers, catch a train. Above all, get as far away from it as you can.* But now that she had started, she didn't think she could do that: it would be like running out on a performance. She went deaf from too much music; she turned off the radio and went deaf again from the din of the lorries. She was in a sauna, she was freezing to death, she was singing. There was no progress, only movement. She chatted brightly with her dead father and her bloody mother: "Well, I met this simply *charming* Arab, Mother, *marvellously* well educated and *frightfully* rich and cultural, and it was just one long screw from dawn till dusk and back again. . . ."

She drove with her mind whited out and her thoughts deliberately foreshortened. She forced herself to remain on the outer surface of experience: Oh look, a village; oh look, a lake, she would think, never allowing herself to break through to the chaos below. I'm free and relaxed and having a simply marvellous time. For lunch she ate fruit and bread, which she bought from a garage kiosk. And ice-cream—she had a sudden passion for it, like an appetite in pregnancy. Yellow, watery Yugoslav ice-cream, with a girl with big tits on the wrapper. Once she saw a boy hitchhiker and had an overwhelming urge to ignore Joseph's orders and give him a lift. Her loneliness was suddenly so awful she would have done anything to keep him with her: married him in one of the little chapels scattered on the treeless hilltops, raped him in the yellow grass beside the road. But she never once admitted to herself, in all the years and miles of driving, that she was ferrying two hundred pounds of prime-quality Russian plastic explosive divided into half-pound sticks, concealed in the valance, cross members, roof-lining, and seats. Or that an older make of car had the advantage of box sections and girders. Or that it was good new stuff, well cared for, capable of withstanding heat and cold, and reasonably plastic in all temperatures.

Keep going, girl, she repeated to herself determinedly, sometimes aloud. *It's a sunny day and you're a rich whore driving your lover's Mercedes.* She recited her lines from *As*

You Like It, and lines from her first part ever. She recited lines from *Saint Joan.* But of Joseph she thought not at all; she had never met an Israeli in her life, never longed for him, never changed her spots and her religion for him, or become his creature while pretending to be the creature of his enemy; never marvelled and fretted at the secret wars that were going on inside him.

At six in the evening, though she would have preferred to keep driving all night, she saw the painted sign that nobody had told her to watch out for, and she said, "Oh well, *that* looks a nice place, I'll try it." Just like that. She said it aloud, bright as brass, probably to her bloody mother. She drove a mile into the hills and there it was, exactly as he-who-did-not-exist had described it, a hotel built inside a ruin, with a pool and miniature golf course. And as she entered the foyer, whom should she walk straight into but her old pals Dimitri and Rose, whom she'd met on Mykonos. Gosh, look, darling, it's Charlie, *what* a coincidence, why don't we all have dinner together? They ate a barbecue by the pool and swam, and when the pool shut and Charlie couldn't sleep they played Scrabble with her in the bedroom, like warders on the eve of her execution. She dozed for a few hours, but at six in the morning she was back on the road, and by mid-afternoon she had hit the queue for the Austrian border, at which point her appearance suddenly became desperately important to her.

She was wearing a sleeveless blouse from Michel's trousseau; she had brushed out her hair and looked great in each of her three mirrors. Most cars were being waved straight through, but she wasn't counting on that, not again. The rest were showing papers and a few were being fished out for a thorough search. She wondered whether it was random, or whether they had advance warning, or whether they went by certain illegible indications. Two men in uniform were coming slowly down the line, pausing at each car window. One wore green, the other blue, and the blue one had bent his peaked cap to make himself look like an air ace. They glanced at her, then walked slowly round the car. She heard one of them kick her rear tyre and she had a good mind to yell "Ouch, that hurt," but restrained herself because Joseph, whom she dared not think of, had said, don't go to them, keep your distance, decide what you think is necessary and

halve it. The man in green asked her something in German
and she said "Sorry?" in English. She was holding up her
British passport to him, profession actress. He took it, compared her with her photograph, handed it to his colleague.
They were goodlooking boys; she hadn't realised they were so
young. Blond, full of sap, straight-eyed, with the permanent
tan of mountaineers. It's prime quality, she wanted to tell
them, in a dreadful lurch towards self-extinction: I'm Charlie,
weigh me.

Their four eyes stayed on her while they asked their
questions—your turn, my turn. No, she said—well, just a
hundred Greek cigarettes and a bottle of ouzo. No, she said,
no gifts, honest. She looked away from them, resisting the
temptation to flirt. Well, a piece of junk for her mother, but
no value. Say, ten dollars. Copybook stuff: give them something to think about. They opened her door and asked to see
the bottle of ouzo, but she had a shrewd suspicion that, having had a good look down the front of her blouse, they were
keen to see her legs and match everything up. The ouzo was
in a basket on the floor beside her. Leaning across the passenger seat, she drew it out and as she did so her skirt opened,
which was ninety per cent accidental but for a moment her
left thigh was exposed all the way north to the hip. She lifted
the bottle to show it to them and in the same moment felt
something damp and cold strike her bare flesh. *Jesus, they've
stabbed me!* She let out an exclamation, clapped her hand
over the spot, and was astonished to see, printed on her thigh,
an inky blue entry stamp recording her arrival in the Republic of Austria. She was so angry she nearly flew at them; she
was so grateful she nearly burst into uncontrollable laughter.
Without Joseph's words of caution to stop her, she would
have embraced them both then and there for their incredible,
lovable, innocent generosity. She was through, she was bloody
marvellous. She looked in the mirror and saw the darlings
shyly waving goodbye to her for about thirty-five minutes on
end, oblivious to all other comers.

She had never loved authority so well.

The long watch of Shimon Litvak began in early morning, eight hours before Charlie had been reported safely
across the border, and two nights and one day since Joseph,

acting on behalf of Michel, had sent the duplicated telegrams to the lawyer in Geneva, for onward transmission to his client. It was now mid-afternoon and Litvak had changed the guard three times, but nobody was bored, nobody was less than very vigilant; his problem was not to keep the team alert but to persuade them to rest properly in their off-hours.

From his commanding position at the window of the bridal suite of an old hotel, Litvak looked down upon a pretty Carinthian market square of which the main features were a couple of traditional inns with outdoor tables, a small car park, and an agreeably antique railway station with an onion dome on the stationmaster's office. The inn nearer to him was called the Black Swan, and boasted an accordion player, a pale, introspective boy who played too well for his comfort and glowered when cars went by, which was quite often. The second inn was called the Carpenter's Arms, and possessed a fine golden sign made up of hand tools. The Carpenter's had class: white tablecloths and trout, which you could choose from an outside tank. There were few pedestrians at this time of day; a heavy, dusty heat cast a pleasant somnolence over the scene. Outside the Swan, two girls drank tea and giggled over a letter they were jointly writing, and their job was to keep a list of vehicle numbers of whoever entered or left the square. Outside the Carpenter's Arms, an earnest young priest sipped wine and read his breviary, and in southern Austria nobody asks a priest to go away. The priest's real name was Udi, short for Ehud, the left-handed killer of the King of Moab. Like his namesake, he was armed to the teeth and left-handed and he was there in case there was fighting to be done. He was backed by a middle-aged English couple seated in the car park in their Rover, to all the world sleeping off the effects of a good luncheon. All the same, they had firearms wedged between their feet and a variety of other hardware within handy reach. Their radio was tuned to the communications van parked two hundred metres up the road towards Salzburg.

Litvak had, in all, nine men and four girls. He could have done with sixteen but he was not complaining. He liked a good stake-out, and the tension always filled him with a sense of well-being. This is what I was born for, he thought: in the run-up to action he thought it always. He was becalmed, his body and his intellect were in a deep sleep, his crew was lying on the deck daydreaming about boyfriends, girlfriends, summer rambles in the Galilee. Yet the lightest whisper of a breeze and every one of them would be at his post before the sails had caught the first strain of it.

Litvak muttered a routine checkword over his headset and had one in reply. They were speaking German in order to attract less attention. Their cover was now a radio-taxi firm in Graz, now a helicopter rescue service based on Innsbruck. They changed wavebands frequently, and used a variety of confusing call signs.

At four o'clock, Charlie pottered into the square with the Mercedes, and one of the watchers in the car park cheekily trumpeted three notes of a fanfare over his headset. She had problems finding a space, but Litvak had ruled she should not be helped in this. Let her play it as it plays, no featherbedding. A space became vacant; she took it, got out, stretched, rubbed her backside, fished her shoulder bag and guitar from the boot. She's good, thought Litvak, watching her through his glasses. A natural. Now lock the car. She did, leaving the boot till last. Now slip the key into the exhaust pipe. She did that too, a really deft movement as she stooped to her luggage; then set course wearily for the railway station, looking neither left nor right. Litvak settled down to wait again. The goat is tethered, he thought, recalling a favourite phrase of Kurtz's. Now all we need is a lion. He spoke a word into his headset and heard his order confirmed. He imagined Kurtz in the Munich flat, crouching over the little teleprinter as the communications van tapped the signal through. He imagined the fraught, unconscious wiping gesture of his stubby fingers pulling nervously at his constant smile; the lifting of his thick forearm as he sightlessly consulted his watch. We're stepping into the dark at last, Litvak thought as he watched the early dusk gather. The dark is what we have been looking forward to all these months.

An hour passed, the good priest Udi paid his modest bill and disappeared at a pious pace down a side street for a rest and a change of profile in the safe flat. The two girls had finished their letter at last and wanted a stamp. When they had one, they departed for the same reason. Litvak watched with satisfaction as their replacements took up their positions: a battered laundry van; two male hikers needing a late lunch; an Italian guestworker for a coffee and the Milan newspapers. A police car entered the square and made three slow laps of honour, but neither the driver nor his colleague showed any interest in a parked red Mercedes with its ignition key hidden in the exhaust pipe. At seven-forty, amid a resurgence of excitement among the watchers, a fat woman marched straight up to the driving door, forced a key into the lock, then did a comedy double-take and drove off in a red Audi instead. She had got her make wrong. At eight, a powerful motorbike made one swift pass before anyone could get the number and roared out again. Pillion passenger, long hair, could be female, looked like two kids on a spree.

"Contact?" Litvak asked over his headset.

Opinions were divided. Too careless, said one voice. Too fast, said another—why run the risk of being stopped by the police? Litvak's own view differed. It was a first reconnaissance, he was sure of it, but he didn't say so for fear of influencing their judgment. He settled down to wait again. The lion has taken a sniff, he thought. Will he come back?

It was ten o'clock. The restaurants were beginning to empty. A deep country quiet was descending over the town. But the red Mercedes sat untouched, and the motorcycle had not returned.

If you have ever watched one, you know that an empty car is a truly stupid thing to stare at, and Litvak had watched a lot of them. With time, just by holding it in focus, you find yourself remembering what a fatuous thing a car really is without man to give it meaning. And what a fatuous thing man is to have invented cars in the first place. After a couple of hours it is the worst piece of junk you have ever seen in your life. You start to dream of horses or a world of pedestrians. Of getting away from the scrap metal of life, and returning to the flesh. Of your kibbutz and its orange groves. Of the day when the whole world finally learns the risks of spilling Jewish blood.

You want to blow all the enemy cars in the world to pieces and set Israel free for ever.

Or you remember it is the Sabbath; and that the Law says it is better to save a soul by working than to observe the Sabbath and not save the soul.

Or that you are expected to marry a plain and very pious girl you do not particularly care for, and settle down in Herzlia with a mortgage and enter the baby-trap without a word of protest.

Or you reflect on the Jewish God, and on certain Biblical parallels to your present situation.

But whatever you think or don't think, and whatever you do, if you are as well trained as Litvak was, and if you are in command, and if you are one of those to whom the prospect of action against the tormentors of Jewry is a drug that will never let you go, you do not for one second take your eyes off that car.

The motorbike had returned.

It had been in the station square for five and a half eternal minutes by Shimon Litvak's luminous wristwatch. From his place at the window of the darkened hotel room, not twenty yards away as the bullet flies, he had been watching it all that time. It was a motorbike from the upper end of the range—Japanese, Vienna registration, and the high handlebars were custom built. It had coasted into the square on no engine, like a runaway, bearing one leather-clad, helmeted driver, gender still to be determined, and one male, broad-shouldered pillion passenger, instantaneous alias Longhair, in jeans and sneakers and a heroic neckscarf knotted at the nape. It had parked close to the Mercedes, but not so close as to suggest they had designs on it. Litvak would have done that too.

"Party collected," he said softly over the headset, and received four acknowledgments immediately. Litvak was so sure of his ground that if the couple had caught fright and run for it at that moment, he would have given the order without a second thought, though it would have meant the end of the operation. Aaron, from the cab of the laundry van, would have stood up and shot them to pieces in the square; then Litvak would have gone down and rolled a charge into the mess to make sure. But they didn't run for it, which was much, much better. They stayed on their bike, they fidgeted with their chinstraps and buckles and sat tight seemingly for hours, in the way motorcyclists can, though it was actually about two minutes. They continued to take the scent of the place, checking side turnings and parked cars, and upper windows such as Litvak's, though the team had made sure long ago that absolutely nothing showed.

Their period of meditation over, Longhair languidly dismounted from his pillion, then ambled past the Mercedes, his head innocently tilted while he presumably marked down the fishtail of the ignition key protruding from the exhaust. But he didn't make a lunge for it, which Litvak as a fellow performer appreciated. He strolled past the car and headed for the station concourse to the public lavatory, from which he emerged again immediately, hoping to wrong-foot anybody unwise enough to be following him. Nobody was. The girls couldn't anyway, and the boys were far too canny. Longhair passed the car a second time, and Litvak besought him very hard to stoop and help himself to the key, because he wanted a conclusive gesture. But Longhair declined to oblige. He returned instead to the motorbike and his companion, who had stayed in the saddle, doubtless in order to be able to make a smooth getaway if one were needed. Longhair said something to his companion, then pulled off his helmet, and, with a flick of the head, turned his face carelessly into the light.

"*Luigi*," said Litvak into his headset, giving the agreed covername.

As he did so, he experienced the rare and timeless blessing of pure satisfaction. It's you, he thought calmly. Rossino, the apostle of the peaceful solution. Litvak knew him really well. He knew the names and addresses of his girlfriends and boyfriends, of his right-wing parents in Rome and of his left-wing mentor at the musical academy in Milan. He knew the upmarket Neapolitan journal that still published his preachy articles insisting that non-violence was the only acceptable path. He knew Jerusalem's long-nurtured suspicions about him, and the whole history of their repeated fruitless efforts to obtain the proof. He knew the smell of him and his shoe size; he was beginning to guess the part he had played in Bad Godesberg and in several other places, and he had very clear ideas, as they all had, about what could best be done with him. But not yet. Not for a long time. Not till the whole tortuous journey was behind them could that score be settled.

She's paid her way, he thought joyously. With this one identification, she has paid her whole long trip till here. She was a righteous Gentile, and in Litvak's estimation one of a rare breed.

Now at last the driver himself was dismounting. He was dismounting, and stretching, and unbuttoning his chinstrap, and Rossino was replacing him at the custom-built handlebars.

Except that the driver was a girl.

A slim blonde girl, according to Litvak's light-intensifying glasses, with delicate bony features and an altogether ethereal air to her, despite her mastery of the motorbike. And Litvak at this critical stage refused point-blank to bother himself about whether her travels might ever have taken her from Paris Orly apparently to Madrid, and whether she made a practice of delivering suitcases of gramophone records to Swedish girlfriends. Because if he had gone that route, the cumulative hatred among the team might have overridden their sense of discipline; most of them had shot people in their time, and in cases like this were quite without compunction. So he said nothing at all over his headset; he let them make their own tentative identifications, and that was all.

It was the girl's turn to visit the lavatory. Fishing a small bag from the luggage grid and handing Rossino her helmet to look after, she walked bareheaded across the square and straight into the concourse, where, unlike her companion, she remained. Once more, Litvak waited for her to make a dive for the ignition key but she didn't. Her walk, like Rossino's, was lithe and effortless, and it didn't falter. She was undeniably a most attractive girl—no wonder that wretched Labour Attaché had fallen for her. His glasses went back to Rossino. Rising slightly in the front saddle, he had cocked his head as if listening for something. Of course, thought Litvak, as he strained his own ears to catch the same faint rumble: the ten-twenty-four from Klagenfurt, due any minute. With a long slow shudder, the train pulled up at the platform. The first bleary-eyed arrivals emerged in the concourse. A couple of taxis shuffled forward and stopped again. A couple of private cars drove away. A tired excursion group appeared, a carriage-load of them, everyone with the same luggage labels.

Do it now, Litvak pleaded. *Grab the car and get out with the traffic. Make sense of what you are here for.*

He was still not prepared for what they actually did. An elderly couple was standing at the cab rank and, behind them, a demure young girl like a nanny or companion. She wore a brown double-breasted suit and a strict little brown hat with the brim down. Litvak noticed her as he noticed a lot of other people in the concourse—with a trained, clear eye made clearer by the tension. A pretty girl, carrying a small travel bag. The elderly couple hailed a taxi, both together, and the girl stayed close behind them, watching it arrive. The elderly couple clambered in; the girl helped them, handing in their bits and pieces—obviously their daughter. Litvak returned his gaze to the Mercedes, then to the motorbike. If he thought anything about the girl in brown, he assumed she had got into the taxi and driven away with her parents. Naturally. It was not till he gave his attention to the tired group of trippers who were filing along the pavement towards two waiting coaches that, with a leap of sheer pleasure, he realised it was *his* girl, *our* girl, the girl from the motorbike: she had done a quick change in the lavatory and fooled him. And, having done so, tagged herself on to the coach party in order to get herself across the square. He was still rejoicing as she unlocked the car door with her own key, tossed in her travel bag, settled herself into the driving seat as chastely as if she were leaving for church, and drove away with the fishtail still glinting inside the exhaust pipe. This touch too delighted him. How obvious! How sensible! Duplicate telegrams, duplicate keys: our leader believes in doubling his chances.

He gave the one-word order and watched the followers discreetly peel away: the two girls in their Porsche; Udi in his big Opel with the Euroflag on the back, stuck there by himself; then Udi's partner on a much less flashy motorbike than Rossino's. He stayed at his window and watched the square slowly empty, like the end of a show. The cars departed, the charabancs departed, the pedestrians departed, the lights went down around the station concourse, and he heard a clang as someone closed an iron gate and locked it for the night. Only the two inns had stayed awake.

Finally the codeword he was waiting for crackled over his headset. *"Ossian"*: the car is heading north.

"So where's Luigi heading?" he asked.

"For Vienna."

"Wait," Litvak said, and actually took off his headset so that he could think more clearly.

He had an immediate choice to make, and immediate choices were what training was about. To follow both Rossino and the girl was impossible. He lacked the resources. In theory he should follow the explosives, and therefore the girl—yet he still hesitated, for Rossino was elusive and by far the greater catch, whereas the Mercedes was by definition conspicuous, and its destination a near certainty. For a moment longer, Litvak hesitated. The headset crackled but he ignored it while he went on running the logic of the fiction through his mind. The idea of letting Rossino out of his grasp was nearly unbearable to him. Yet Rossino was for certain an important link in the opposition's chain: and, as Kurtz had repeatedly argued, if the chain did not hold, how could it draw Charlie into its toils? Rossino would return to Vienna satisfied that thus far nothing had been compromised: he was a crucial link, but also a crucial witness. Whereas the girl— the girl was a functionary, a driver of cars, a placer of bombs, the expendable infantry of their great movement. Moreover, Kurtz had vital plans for her future, whereas Rossino's future could wait.

Litvak replaced the headset. "Stay with the car. Let Luigi go."

His decision taken, Litvak allowed himself a contented smile. He knew the formation exactly. First, Udi riding point on his motorbike, then the blonde girl in the red Mercedes, and, after her, the Opel. And after the Opel again, lying well back from everyone, the two girls in the reserve Porsche, ready to change places with anyone as soon as they were ordered. He rehearsed to himself the static posts that would monitor the Mercedes to the German border. He imagined the kind of cock-and-bull story Alexis would have spun in order to make certain she was let through without complications.

"Speed?" Litvak asked, with a glance at his watch.

Udi reports her speed very moderate, came the reply. This lady wants no trouble with the law. She is nervous of her cargo.

And so she should be, thought Litvak approvingly as he removed his headset. If I were that girl, the cargo would scare me stiff.

He walked downstairs, briefcase in hand. He had already paid his bill, but if they had asked him he would have paid it again; he was in love with the whole world. His command car was waiting for him in the hotel car park. With a self-control bred of long experience, Litvak set off in calm pursuit of the convoy. How much would she know? How much time would they have to find out? Take it easy, he thought; first tether the goat. His mind went back to Kurtz and with an ache of pleasure he imagined his ramming, inexhaustible voice heaping praise on him in awful Hebrew. It pleased Litvak very much to think he was bringing Kurtz so plump a sacrifice.

Salzburg had still to hear of summer. A fresh spring air was blowing off the mountains and the Salzach River smelt of the sea. How they arrived there was still half a mystery to her, because she slept so often along the journey. From Graz they had flown to Vienna, but the trip had taken about five seconds, so she must have slept on the plane. In Vienna he had a hire car waiting, a smart BMW. She slept again, and as they entered the city she thought for a moment the car must be on fire, but it was only the evening sun catching the crimson paintwork as she opened her eyes.

"Anyway, why Salzburg?" she had asked him.

Because it is one of Michel's cities, he had replied. Because it is on the way.

"On the way where to?" she asked, but once more struck his reserve.

Their hotel had a roofed interior courtyard, with old gilded banisters and potted plants in marble urns. Their suite looked straight down on to the fast brown river, and across it at more domes than are in Heaven. Behind the domes rose a castle with a cable car that switched up and down the hillside.

"I need to walk," she said.

She took a bath and fell asleep in it, and he had to bang on the door to wake her. She dressed and once more he knew the places to show her and the things that would please her most.

"It's our last night, isn't it?" she said, and this time he didn't hide behind Michel.

"Yes, it's our last night, Charlie; tomorrow we have a visit to make and then you return to London."

Clutching his arm in both her hands, she wandered with him through narrow streets, and squares that ran into each other like drawing-rooms. They stood outside the house where Mozart was born, and the trippers were like a matinée audience to her, cheerful and unaware.

"I did well, didn't I, Jose? I did really well. Say it."

"You did excellently," he said—but somehow his reservations meant more to her than his praise.

The doll's-house churches were more beautiful than anything she had imagined, with scrolled golden altars and voluptuous angels and tombs where the dead seemed still to be dreaming of pleasure. A Jew pretending to be a Muslim shows me my Christian heritage, she thought. But when she demanded information of him, the most he would do was buy a glossy guidebook and put the receipt in his wallet.

"I fear that Michel has not yet had the time to launch himself upon the Baroque period," he explained, in his dry way; and yet again she sensed in him the shadows of some unexplained obstruction.

"Shall we go back now?" he asked.

She shook her head. Make it last. The evening darkened, the crowds disappeared, choirboy singing issued from unexpected doorways. They sat by the river and listened to the deaf old bells chiming at each other in stubborn competition. They started to walk again and suddenly she was so floppy she needed his arm round her waist just to keep her upright.

"Food," she ordered as he guided her into the lift. "Champagne. Music."

But by the time he had rung room service she was fast asleep on the bed, and nothing on God's earth, not even Joseph, was going to wake her.

She lay as she had lain in the sand on Mykonos, her left arm crooked and her face pressed into it; and Becker sat in the armchair watching her. The first weak glow of dawn was appearing through the curtains. He could smell fresh leaves and timber. There had been a rainstorm in the night, so loud and sudden it was like an express train crashing up the valley. From the window he had watched the city rock under the long slow onslaughts of its lightning, and the rain dancing on the glistening domes. But Charlie had lain so still he had actually stooped over her and put his ear to her mouth to make sure she was breathing.

He glanced at his watch. Plan, he thought. Move. Let action kill the doubt. The dinner-table with its uneaten food stood in the window bay, the ice bucket with its unopened bottle of champagne. Taking each fork in turn, he began scooping the lobster meat from its shell, dirtying plates, mixing up the salad, spoiling the strawberries, adding one last fiction to the many they had already lived: their gala banquet in Salzburg; Charlie and Michel celebrate the successful completion of her first mission for the revolution. He took the champagne bottle to the bathroom, and closed the door in case the pop of the cork should wake her. He poured the champagne down the basin and ran water after it; he flushed the lobster meat and strawberries and salad down the lavatory and had to wait and flush again because they wouldn't disappear the first time. He left enough champagne to pour a little into his own glass, and for Charlie's glass he took lipstick from her bag and drew traces round the brim before adding the dregs from the bottle. Then he went to the window again, where he had spent much of the night, and gazed at the rain-soaked blue hills. I am a climber weary of the mountains, he thought.

He shaved, he put on his red blazer. He went to the bed, stretched out his hand to wake her, and drew it back. A reluctance, like a heavy tiredness, descended over him. He sat down in the armchair again, his eyes closed, he forced them open; he woke with a jolt, feeling the weight of the desert dew clinging to his battledress, smelling the scent of damp sand before the sun had burned it dry.

"Charlie?" He again reached out, this time to touch her cheek, then touched her arm instead. Charlie, it's a triumph; Marty says you are a star, and that you have presented him with a whole new cast of characters. He called his Gadi in the night but you didn't wake. Better than Garbo, he says. There is nothing we can't achieve together, he says. Charlie, wake up. We have work to do. Charlie.

But aloud he merely said her name again, then went downstairs, paid the bill, and obtained the last receipt. He walked out the back of the hotel to collect the hired BMW, and the dawn was the way the dusk had been, fresh and not yet summer.

"You're to wave me off, then appear to take a walk," he told her. "Dimitri will bring you separately to Munich."

14

She entered the lift without speaking. It smelt of disinfectant and the graffiti were scratched deep into the grey vinyl. She had shoved the toughness in her to the front, the way she did at demos and talk-ins and all the other junkets. She was excited and she felt a sense of impending completion. Dimitri pressed the bell, Kurtz himself opened the door. Behind him stood Joseph, and behind Joseph hung a brass shield with a beaten image of Saint Christopher dandling a child.

"Charlie, this is truly great, and *you* are great," said Kurtz, with a soft, heartfelt urgency, and clutched her intensely to his chest. "Charlie, incredible."

"Where is he?" she said, looking past Joseph at the closed door. Dimitri had not come in. Having delivered her, he had taken the lift down again.

Still speaking as if they were in church together, Kurtz chose to treat her question as a general one. "Charlie, he is just fine," he assured her as he released her. "A little tired from his travels, which is natural, but fine. Dark glasses, Joseph," he added. "Give her dark glasses. Do you have dark glasses, dear? Here's a headscarf to hide that lovely hair. Keep it." It was of green silk, a rather nice one. Kurtz had it ready for her in his pocket. Crammed close together, the two men looked on while she made a nurse's head-dress for herself in the mirror.

"Just a precaution," Kurtz explained. "In this business, we can never be too careful. That correct, Joseph?"

From her handbag, Charlie had taken out her new powder compact and was straightening her make-up.

"Charlie, this could be a little emotional," Kurtz warned.

She put away the compact and took out her lipstick.

"If you get seasick, just remember he killed a lot of innocent human beings," Kurtz advised her. "Everybody has a human face and this boy is no exception. A lot of good looks,

lot of talent, a lot of unused capacity—all wasted. That's
never very nice at all to see. Once we get in there, I don't
want you speaking. Remember that. Leave all the speaking to
me." He opened the door for them. "You'll find him docile.
We had to have him docile while we shipped him and we
have to keep him that way while he's here with us. Otherwise
he's in good shape. No problems. Just don't speak to him."

Trendy split-level duplex gone to seed, she recorded automatically, noting the tasteful open-tread staircase, the rustic
minstrel gallery and the handcrafted iron balustrade. One English-style fireplace with mock coals in painted canvas. Photographic lamps in evidence, supported by impressive cameras
on tripods. One family-size tape-recorder on its own legs, one
gracious Marbella-style curved sofa, foam rubber and harder
than iron. She sat on it and Joseph sat beside her. We should
hold hands, she thought. Kurtz had picked up a grey telephone and was pressing the extension button. He said something in Hebrew, looking up at the gallery as he spoke. He
put the phone down, smiled at her reassuringly. She smelt
male bodies, dust, coffee, and liver sausage. And about a million dead cigarettes. She recognised another smell but
couldn't identify it because there were too many possibilities
in her mind, from the harness of her first pony to the sweat
of her first lover.

Her mind changed pace and she nearly fell asleep. I'm
ill, she thought. I'm waiting for the results of the tests. Doctor, Doctor, give it to me straight. She noticed a stack of
waiting-room magazines and wished she could have one on
her lap as a prop. Now Joseph was looking up at the gallery
too. Charlie followed his gaze, but not till a little afterwards,
because she wanted to give herself the impression that she
had done this so often she barely needed to look at all, she
was a buyer at a fashion show. The door on the balcony
opened on a bearded boy, backing into the room with a
stage-hand's lopsided waddle, and contriving to convey anger,
even from behind.

For a moment came nothing, then a kind of low scarlet
bundle appeared, and after it a clean-shaven boy followed,
looking not so much angry as resolutely pious.

Finally she got it straight. It was three boys, not two, but
the middle one was sagging between them in his red blazer:

the slender Arab boy, her lover, her collapsed puppet from the theatre of the real.

Yes, she thought, from deep inside her sunglasses, perfectly reasonably. Yes—well, not a bad likeness at all given the few years' age difference, and Joseph's indefinable maturity. Sometimes, in her fantasies, she had used Joseph's features, letting him understudy for the lover of her dreams. At other times a different figure had evolved, built upon her imperfect memory of the masked Palestinian at the forum, and she was impressed by how close he now came to the reality. You don't think the mouth a *touch* too long at the corners? she asked herself. Not overdoing the sensuality a *mite*? The nostrils too flared? Too much nip at the waist? She thought of getting up and rushing to protect him, but on stage one doesn't, not unless it's in the script. And besides, she'd never have broken free of Joseph.

For a second, all the same, she nearly lost her hold on herself. For that second, she was everything that Joseph said she was—she was Michel's saviour and liberator, his Saint Joan, his body-slave, his star. She had acted her heart out for him, she had dined with him in a lousy candlelit motel, she had shared his bed and joined his revolution and worn his bracelet and drunk his vodka and torn his body to pieces and had him tear her own to pieces in return. She had driven his Merc for him and kissed his gun and carried his best-quality Russian TNT to the beleaguered armies of freedom. She had celebrated the victory with him in a riverside hotel in Salzburg. She had danced with him on the Acropolis by night and had the whole world revived for her; and she was filled with an insane guilt that she had ever contemplated any other love.

He was so beautiful—as beautiful as Joseph had promised. He was more beautiful. He had the absolute attraction that Charlie and her kind acknowledge with rueful inevitability: he was of that monarchy and knew it. He was slight but perfect, with well-formed shoulders and very slender hips. He had a pugilist's brow and a Pan-child's face, crowned with a cap of flat black hair. Nothing they had done to tame him could conceal from her the rich passion of his nature, or extinguish the light of rebellion in his coal-dark eyes.

He was so trivial—a little peasant boy fallen out of an olive tree, with a repertoire of learned phrases and a magpie eye for pretty toys, pretty ladies, and pretty cars. And a peasant's indignation against those who drove him from his farm. Come into my bed, you little baby, and let Mummy teach you some of life's long words.

They were supporting him under the arms, and as he flopped down the wood stairs his Gucci shoes kept missing their mark, which seemed to embarrass him, for a flickering smile came over him and he gazed shamefully at his errant feet.

They were bringing him towards her and she wasn't sure she could stand it. She turned to Joseph to tell him so, and saw his eyes looking straight at her and heard him say something, but in the same moment the family-size tape-recorder started speaking very loud and as she swung round, there was dear Marty in his cardigan stooped over the deck, twiddling the knobs to get the volume down.

The voice was soft and heavily accented exactly as she remembered it from the forum. The words were slogans of defiance read with uncertain zest.

"We are the colonised! We speak for the native against the settled! . . . We speak for the mute, we feed the blind mouths and encourage the mute ears! . . . We, the animals with patient hooves, have finally lost our patience! . . . We live by the law that is born each day under fire! . . . The entire world except us has something to lose! . . . We will fight anyone who appoints himself the caretaker of our land!"

The boys had arranged him on the sofa, across the horseshoe from her. His balance was not at all good. He was leaning forward with a heavy list, using his forearms to shore himself up. His hands lay on top of each other as if chained, but only by the gold bangle they had put on him to get his costume right for the show. The bearded boy stood sulking behind him, his clean-shaven companion sat devoutly at his side, and as his recorded voice continued triumphant in the background, she saw Michel's lips slowly moving, trying to catch up with the words. But the voice was too fast for its owner, too strong. Gradually he gave up trying and instead pulled a silly grin of apology, reminding her of her father after his stroke.

"Acts of violence are not criminal . . . when carried out

in opposition to force used by a state . . . deemed criminal by the terrorist." A rustle of paper as he turned to a new page. The voice grew puzzled and unwilling. *"I love you . . . you are my freedom. . . . Now you are one of us. . . . Our bodies and our blood are mixed . . . you are mine . . . my soldier . . . please, why do I say this? Together we shall put the match to the fuse."* A puzzled silence. *"Please, sir. What is this, please? I ask you."*

"Show her his hands," Kurtz ordered when he had switched off the machine.

Picking up one of Michel's hands, the clean-shaven boy swiftly unfolded it, offering it to her like a trade sample.

"As long as he was in the camps, his hands were hard from manual work," Kurtz explained, coming down the room to join them. "Now he's a great intellectual. Lot of money, lot of girls, good food, an easy time. That right, little fellow?" Approaching the sofa from behind, he laid the flat of his thick hand on Michel's head and turned it round to face him. "You're a great intellectual, that right?" His voice was neither cruel nor teasing. He might have been talking to his own erring son—he had the same sad fondness in his face. "You get your girls to do the work for you, don't you, little fellow? One girl, he actually used her as a bomb," he explained to Charlie. "Put her on a plane with some nice-looking luggage, the plane blew up. I guess she never even knew she'd done it. That was bad manners, wasn't it, little fellow? Very bad manners towards a lady."

She recognised the smell that she had not been able to place: it was the aftershave lotion that Joseph had laid out in every bathroom they had never shared. They must have smeared some on him for the occasion.

"Don't you want to speak to this lady?" Kurtz was asking. "Don't you want to welcome her to our villa here? I'm beginning to wonder why you don't cooperate with us any more!" Gradually, under his persistence, Michel's eyes woke, and his body straightened slightly in obedience. "You want to greet this pretty lady politely? You want to wish her good day? Good day? You want to tell her good day, little fellow?"

Of course he did: "Good day," said Michel, in a listless version of the voice in the tapes.

"Don't answer," Joseph warned her softly from her side.

"Good day, *madame*," Kurtz insisted, still without the least rancour.

"Madame," said Michel.

"Have him write something," Kurtz ordered, and let him go.

They sat him at a table and put a pen and a sheet of paper before him, but he couldn't manage much. Kurtz didn't care about that. See how he holds his pen, he was saying. See the way his fingers shape naturally for the Arab script.

"Maybe in the middle of the night you woke up once and found him doing his accounts. Okay? So this is how he looked."

She was talking to Joseph but only in her mind. *Get me out. I think I'm dying.* She heard the bump of Michel's feet as they took him up the stairs and out of hearing, but Kurtz allowed her no respite, just as he allowed none to himself. "Charlie, we have one further stage of this thing. I think we should go through with it now, even if it costs a little effort. Some things have to be done."

The drawing-room was very quiet, just an apartment somewhere. Holding Joseph's arm, she followed Kurtz upstairs. She didn't know why, but she found it helpful to limp a little, like Michel.

The wooden handrail was still sticky from sweat. The steps had strips of stuff like emery paper on them, but when she trod on them the expected rasping sound did not result. She picked out these details with accuracy because there are times when details can supply the only link with reality. A lavatory door stood open, but when she took a second look she realised that there was no door, only a doorway, and no chain hanging from the cistern; and she supposed that if you were dragging a prisoner around all day, even one who was doped out of his mind, you had to think of these things, you had to get your house in order. Not till she had pondered earnestly on each of these important issues did she allow herself to admit that she had entered a padded room with a single bed shoved against the far wall. And on the bed Michel again, naked except for his gold medallion, his hands clutched over his crotch and hardly a crease where his belly folded. The muscles of his shoulders were full and round, the muscles of his chest were flat and broad, the shadows beneath them crisp as lines of India ink. On an order from Kurtz, the two boys stood him up and pulled away his hands. Circumcised, well grown, beautiful. Silently, with scowling disapproval, the bearded boy pointed to the white birthmark like a milkstain on the left flank, and the smeared scar of a knife-wound on the right shoulder; and the endearing rivulet of black hair that ran downward from the navel. Silently they turned him round, and she remembered Lucy and her favourite kind of back: a spine recessed in muscle. But no bullet-holes, nothing at all to spoil the sheerness of his beauty.

They stood him up again, but by then Joseph had apparently decided that Charlie might have had enough of a good thing, for he was leading her down the stairs, fast, one arm locked around her waist and the other grasping her wrist so tight it hurt. In the lavatory off the hall she paused long enough to vomit, but all she wanted after that was to get out. Out of the apartment, out of sight of them, out of her own mind and skin.

She was running. It was sports day. She was running as fast as she could; the concrete teeth of the surrounding sky-line were bobbing past her from the other direction. The roof gardens were linked for her by dinky brick paths, toy-town signposts pointed her to places she could not read, overhead pipes of blue and yellow plastic made streaks of colour above her head. She was running as far as she could, upstairs and downstairs, taking a keen horticultural interest in the variety of vegetation on her way, the tasteful geraniums and stunted flowered shrubs and cigarette ends and the patches of raw earth like unmarked graves. Joseph was at her side and she was yelling at him to go, go away; an elderly couple sat on a bench grinning nostalgically at this lovers' tiff. She ran the whole length of two platforms this way, till she reached a fence and a sheer drop into a car park, but she didn't commit suicide because she'd decided already that she wasn't the type, and besides she wanted to live with Joseph and not die with Michel. She stopped and she was scarcely panting. The run had done her good; she should run more often. She asked him for a cigarette but he hadn't one. He drew her to a bench; she sat on it, then stood up in order to assert herself. She had learned that emotional scenes did not play effectively between people who were walking, so she stood still.

"I advise you to keep your sympathy for the innocent," Joseph warned her, calmly cutting in upon her invective.

"He *was* innocent till you invented him!"

Mistaking his silence for disarray, and his disarray for weakness, she paused and affected to contemplate the monstrous skyline. " 'It's *necessary*,' " she said scathingly. " 'I wouldn't be here if it wasn't *necessary*.' Quote. 'No sane court on earth would condemn us for what we are asking you to do.' Quote again. Your words, I think. Care to take them back?"

"No, I don't think so."

"*I don't think so.* Well, you'd better be awfully sure, hadn't you? Because if there *are* any doubts around here, I'd rather they were mine."

Still standing, her attention shifted to a point immediately ahead of her, somewhere in the belly of the opposite building, which she now studied with the earnestness of a potential buyer. But Joseph had remained seated, which somehow made the scene all wrong. They should have been face to face in close-up. Or he behind her, looking at the same distant chalkmark.

"Mind if we add up a few things?" she enquired.

"Please do."

"He has killed Jews."

"He has killed Jews and he has killed innocent bystanders who were not Jews and did not have any position in the conflict."

"I'd like to do a book, actually, on the guilt of all these innocent bystanders you go on about. I'd start with your Lebanese bombings and fan out from there."

Seated or not, he came back faster and harder than she had bargained for. "That book has been done, Charlie, and it is called the Holocaust."

With her thumb and forefinger she made a little spyhole, and squinted through it at a distant balcony. "On the other hand, you personally have killed Arabs, I take it."

"Of course."

"Lots?"

"Enough."

"But only in self-defence. Israelis only ever kill in self-defence." No reply. " '*I have killed enough Arabs*,' signed 'Joseph.' " Still she got no rise from him. "Well that's a turn-up for the book, I will say. An Israeli who's killed enough Arabs."

Her tartan skirt was from Michel's trousseau. It had pockets either side, which she had only recently discovered. Thrusting her hands into them, she made the skirt swing while she pretended to study the effect.

"You *are* bastards, aren't you?" she asked carelessly. "You are definitely bastards. Wouldn't you say so?" She was still looking at her skirt, really interested in the way it filled and turned. "And *you* are the biggest bastard of them all actually, aren't you? Because *you* get it both ways. One minute our bleeding heart, the next our red-toothed warrior. Whereas all you really are—when it comes down to it—is a blood-thirsty, landgrabbing little Jew."

Not only did he stand up, but he hit her. Twice. Having first removed her sunglasses. Harder and faster than she had ever been hit before, and on the same side of the face. The first blow was so heavy that a cussed triumph made her thrust her face against the direction of it. Quits, she thought, remembering the Athens house. The second was a fresh explosion in the same crater, and when it was over he pushed her down onto the bench, where she could cry her heart out, but she was too proud to shed another tear. Did he hit me for his sake or for mine? she wondered. She hoped desperately it was for his own; that at the twelfth hour of their mad marriage she had finally penetrated his reserve. But one glance at his closed face and sparse, unbothered stare told her that she, not Joseph, was the patient. He was holding out a handkerchief to her but she waved it vaguely away.

"Forget it," she muttered.

She took his arm and he walked her slowly back along the concrete walkway. The same old couple smiled at them as they passed. Children, they told each other—as we were once. One minute quarrelling like murderers; the next back to bed to make it even better than before.

The lower apartment was much like the upper one except that it possessed no balcony and no prisoner, and sometimes while she read or listened she managed to convince herself that she had never been upstairs at all—upstairs was a chamber of horrors in the dark attics of her mind. Then she would hear the bump of a packing case through the ceiling as the boys cleared up their photographic equipment and generally prepared for the end of term, and she had to admit that upstairs was as real as downstairs after all: more real, since the letters were fabrications, whereas Michel was flesh.

They sat in a ring, the three of them, and Kurtz began with one of his preambles. But his style was a lot crisper and less roundabout than usual, perhaps because she was a proven soldier now, a veteran "with a whole basket of exciting new intelligence already to her credit," as he put it. The letters were in a briefcase on the table, and before opening it he reminded her once more of the "fiction," a word he had in common with Joseph. The fiction was that she was not only a passionate lover, but a passionate correspondent who in Michel's long absences was deprived of all other outlets. Explaining this, he pulled on a pair of cheap cotton gloves. The letters were therefore not a mere sideshow in the relationship; they were "the only place you could live aloud, dear." They recorded her increasingly obsessive love for Michel—often with disarming frankness—but also her political reawakening and her transition to a "global activism" that took for granted the "linkage" of anti-repressive struggles anywhere in the world. Put together, they comprised the diary of "an emotionally and sexually aroused person" as she advanced from vaguely focussed protest to wholesale activism, with its implicit acceptance of violence.

"And since we could not rely on you, in the circumstances, to provide us with the full variety of your literary style," he ended as he unlocked the briefcase, "we decided to compose the letters for you."

Naturally, she thought. She glanced at Joseph, who was sitting straight-backed and uncommonly innocent, with his palms pressed virtuously together between his knees, like a man who had never hit anyone in his life.

They were in two brown wrapped packages, one much larger than the other. Selecting the smaller first, Kurtz clumsily opened it with his gloved fingertips and spread the papers flat. She recognised the black, schoolboy writing of Michel. He unwrapped the second and, like a dream come true, she recognised the handwriting as her own. Michel's to you are in photostat, dear, Kurtz was saying; we have the originals waiting for you in England. Your own letters, now, they're the originals, so they belong to Michel, don't they, dear?

"Naturally," she said, this time aloud, and on an instinct glanced in Joseph's direction, but this time quite specifically at his locked-up hands so intent upon disowning authorship.

She read Michel's letters first because she felt she owed him the attention. There were a dozen, and they varied from the frankly sensual and passionate to the brief and authoritarian. "Kindly in your letters be sure to number. If you do not number, do not write. I cannot enjoy your letters if I do not know I receive them all. This for my personal safety." Between passages of ecstatic praise for her acting came arid exhortations to perform only "rôles of social significance which can awaken awareness." At the same time she was to "avoid public acts that reveal your true politics." She was to go to no more radical forums, attend no more demonstrations or rallies. She was to conduct herself "in the bourgeois manner," appearing to accept capitalist standards. She should let it be thought she had "renounced to the revolution" while secretly "continuing, by all means, with your radical reading." There were many confusions of logic, many lapses of syntax, many misspellings. There was talk of "our soon reunion," meaning presumably in Athens, and there were a couple of coy references to white grapes, vodka, and taking "plenty of sleep before we are together again."

As she read on, she began to form a new and humbler picture of Michel, one that came suddenly much closer to their prisoner upstairs. "He's a baby," she muttered. She glanced accusingly at Joseph. "You built him up so much. He's a kid."

Receiving no answer, she turned to her own letters to Michel, picking them up gingerly, as if they solved a great mystery. "Schoolbooks," she said aloud, with a stupid smile, as she took a first nervous look at them, and this was because, thanks to poor Ned Quilley's archives, the old Georgian had been able to reproduce not merely Charlie's exotic taste in stationery—the backs of menus, bills, the headed notepaper of hotels and theatres and boarding houses along her route—but had caught, to her mounting awe, the spontaneous variations in her writing, from the infantile scrawls of early sadness to the passionate woman in love; to the goodnight scribble of the bone-weary actress holed out in the

sticks and longing for a little light relief to the would-be eru-
dite copperplate of the revolutionary who troubled to write
out a lengthy passage of Trotsky, but missed the second "r"
in "occurred."

Thanks to Leon, her prose was given no less exactly;
Charlie actually blushed to see how perfectly they had imi-
tated her lurid hyperbole, her lapses into awkward, incom-
plete philosophising, her rampant, violent fury against the
ruling Tory government. Unlike Michel's, her references to
their lovemaking were graphic and explicit; to her parents
abusive; to her childhood wrathful and unavenged. She met
Charlie the romancer, Charlie the penitent, and Charlie the
hardnosed bitch. She met what Joseph called the Arab in
her—the Charlie who was in love with her own rhetoric,
whose notions of truth were inspired less by what had happened than by what should have happened. And when she
had read them all through, she put the two piles together and,
head in hands, read them again as a complete correspondence—her five letters to his every one, her answers in reply
to his questions, his evasions in reply to hers.

"Thanks, Jose," she said finally, without lifting her head.
"Thanks a hell of a lot. If you'd lend me our nice gun a moment, I'll just pop out and shoot myself."

Kurtz was already laughing, though he was alone in his
mirth: "Now, Charlie, I don't think that's quite fair to our
friend Joseph here at all. This was a committee thing. We
had a lot of heads at work here."

Kurtz had a final request: the envelopes that contain
your letters, dear. He had them right here with him, look,
they weren't franked or cancelled, and he hadn't yet put the
letters inside for Michel to take them out again at the cere-
monial opening. Would Charlie oblige? It was mainly for the
fingerprints, he said; yours first, dear, afterwards the post office sorters', finally Michel's. But there was also the little
point about it being her saliva on the flap and underneath the
stamps; her blood group, lest anybody clever should ever
think of checking, because don't ever forget they have some
very clever people, as your fine, fine work has even last night
confirmed to us.

* * *

She remembered the long fatherly hug from Kurtz, because at the time it seemed as inevitable and necessary as parenthood. Of her farewell from Joseph, however, her last of the series, she afterwards had no recollection at all—not the manner of it, not the place. The briefing, yes; the covert return to Salzburg, yes: an hour and a half in the back of Dimitri's clapped-out van, and no talking after lights out. And she remembered the landing in London, more alone than she had ever been in her life; and the smell of English sadness that had greeted her even on the runway, reminding her of what it was that had turned her towards radical solutions in the first place: the malign sloth of authority, the caged despair of the losers. There was a luggage handlers' go-slow and a rail strike; the women's lavatory was like a taste of prison. She went through green and, as usual, the bored Customs officer stopped and questioned her. With the difference that this time she wondered whether he had a reason beyond wanting to chat her up.

Coming home is like going abroad, she thought as she joined the despondent queue for the bus. Let's blow the whole lot up and start again.

15

The motor lodge was called Romanz and was set among pine trees on a rise beside the autobahn. It had been built twelve months ago for mediaevally minded lovers, with cement-stippled cloisters, plastic muskets, and tinted neon lighting, and Kurtz had the last chalet of the row, with a leaded jalousie window that looked over the westbound lane. It was two in the morning, an hour of day he was on cheerful terms with. He had showered and shaved, he had made himself coffee on the clever coffee machine and drunk Coca-Cola from the teak-lined refrigerator, and for the rest of the time he had done what he was doing now: he had sat in his shirt-sleeves at the little writing-table, with all the lights out and a pair of binoculars at his elbow, watching the headlamps as they switched through the tree trunks on their way to Munich. Traffic was light at that hour, on average five vehicles a minute; in the rain, they had a tendency to bunch.

It had been a long day and a long night, too, if you counted nights, but Kurtz believed that lassitude clouded the head. Five hours' sleep was enough for anyone, and for himself too much. It had been a long day all the same, not really starting until Charlie had left the city. There had been the Olympic Village apartments to clear, and Kurtz had supervised that operation personally, because he knew it gave the kids an extra edge when they were reminded of his determination to handle detail. There had been the letters to place in Yanuka's apartment, and Kurtz had seen to that as well. From the surveillance post across the street, he had been able to observe the watchers let themselves in, and he had remained there to flatter them on their return, and assure them that their long, heroic vigil would soon be rewarded.

"What's happening to him?" Lenny had asked querulously. "Marty, that boy has a future, now. Just you remember it."

Kurtz's reply had struck a Delphic note: "Lenny, that boy has a future, just not with us."

Shimon Litvak sat behind Kurtz on the edge of the double bed. He had taken off his dripping raincoat and dumped it on the floor at his feet. He looked cheated and angry. Becker sat apart from both of them on a dainty bedroom chair, with his own small ring of light around him, much as he had sat in the Athens house. The same aloneness; yet sharing the same close atmosphere of vigilance before the battle.

"The girl knows nothing," Litvak reported indignantly to Kurtz's still back. "She's a half-wit." His voice had risen slightly and had a quaver. "She's Dutch, her name is Larsen, she thinks Yanuka picked her up while she was squatting with a commune in Frankfurt, but she can't be sure because she's had so many men and she forgets. Yanuka took her on a few trips, taught her to shoot his gun all wrong, and lent her to big brother for his rest and recreation. That part she remembers. Even for Khalil's sex-life they used cut-outs, never the same place twice. She found that groovy. Between times she drove cars for them, placed a couple of bombs for them, stole a few passports for them. For friendly. Because she's an anarchist. Because she's a half-wit."

"A comfort girl," said Kurtz thoughtfully, speaking less to Litvak than to his own reflection in the window.

"She admits Godesberg, she half admits Zürich. If we had the time, she'd admit Zürich totally. Antwerp no."

"Leyden?" asked Kurtz. And now there was a knot in Kurtz's voice as well, so that from where Becker sat, it might have sounded as if the two men were suffering from the same minor throat affliction, a clenching of the cords.

"Leyden a solid no," Litvak replied. "No, no, no again. Then still no. She was on holiday with her parents at the time. On Sylt. Where's Sylt?"

"Off the coast of northern Germany," said Becker, but Litvak glared at him as if suspecting an insult.

"She's so damn slow," Litvak complained, talking to Kurtz once more. "She started talking around midday, but by mid-afternoon she was backing away from everything she'd said. 'No, I never said that. You're lying.' We find the place on the tape, play it to her, still she says it's a forgery, and starts spitting at us. She's stubborn Dutch and she's nuts."

"I understand," said Kurtz.

But Litvak wanted more than understanding: "Hurt her, we raise her anger so she gets more stubborn. Stop hurting her, we give her the strength back, she gets even more stubborn, starts to call us names."

Kurtz turned half the distance, till, if he had been looking at anyone, he would have been looking straight at Becker.

"She bargains," Litvak continued, in the same note of strident complaint. "We're Jews so she bargains. 'I tell you this much, you keep me alive. *Yes?* I tell you that much, you let me go. *Yes?*'" He swung suddenly on Becker. "So what's the hero's way?" he demanded. "I should enchant her maybe? Have her fall in love with me?"

Kurtz was looking at his watch, and beyond it. "Whatever she knows, it's already history," he remarked. "Important is only what we do with her. And when." But he spoke as the man who must give the final answer himself. "How does the fiction play, Gadi?" he asked of Becker.

"It fits," said Becker. He let them wait a moment. "Rossino had the use of her in Vienna for a couple of days, drove her south, delivered her to the car. All true. She drove the car to Munich, met Yanuka. Untrue, but they're the only two people who know it."

Litvak greedily took up the story: "They met in Ottobrunn. That's a village south-east of town. From there they went somewhere and made love. Who cares where? Not everything has to fit a reconstruction. Maybe in the car. She likes it all the time, she says so. But best she likes it with the fighters, as she calls them. Maybe they rented a room somewhere and the proprietor is too scared even to come forward. Gaps like that are normal. The opposition will expect them."

"And tonight?" said Kurtz, with a glance towards the window. "Now?"

Litvak did not like to be so closely questioned. "So now they're in the car and on their way into town. To make love. To pull a job and hide the rest of the explosive. Who will ever know? Why should we explain so much?"

"So where is she at this moment?" Kurtz asked, gathering in the details while he continued to deliberate. "In reality?"

"In the van," said Litvak.

"And where's the van?"

"Beside the Mercedes. In the layby. You give the word, we transfer her."

"And Yanuka?"

"Also in the van. Their last night together. We sedated both of them, just like we agreed."

Taking up his binoculars again, Kurtz held them halfway to his eyes, then returned them to the table. Then he put his hands together and frowned into them.

"Tell me a different method," he suggested, addressing himself by the pose of his head to Becker. "We fly her home, stick her in the Negev Desert, lock her up. Then what? What has become of her? they will ask. From the moment she disappears, they will think the worst. They will think she has defected. That Alexis has got her. That the Zionists have. In any case, that their operation is at risk. That is what they will say, no question: 'Disband the team, send everybody home.'" He summarised: "They have to have the evidence that nobody has got her except God and Yanuka. They have to know she's as dead as Yanuka is. You disagree with me, Gadi? Or do I perceive from your expression that you know better?"

Kurtz merely waited, but Litvak's gaze, trained upon Becker, remained hostile and accusing. Perhaps he suspected him of innocence at a moment when he needed him to share the guilt.

"No," said Becker, after an age. But his face, as Kurtz had noticed, had the hardness of a willed allegiance.

Then suddenly Litvak was on him—so tense and jerky in his voice that his words were like a leap from where he sat. "*No?*" he repeated. "No what? No operation? What is *no?*"

"*No* is: we have no alternative," Becker replied again, taking his time. "Spare the Dutch girl, they'll never accept Charlie. Alive, Miss Larsen is as dangerous as Yanuka. If we are going on, this is where we do it."

"*If,*" Litvak echoed with contempt.

Kurtz restored order with another question.

"Does she have no useful names at all?" he asked Litvak, seeming to want the answer yes. "Nothing that we should maybe pursue with her? A reason to hold her back?"

Litvak pulled a high shrug. "She knows of a big north German called Edda. She only met her once. Beyond Edda there's another girl, who's a voice from Paris on the telephone. Beyond the voice is Khalil, but Khalil doesn't hand out visiting cards. She's a half-wit," he repeated. "She drugs so hard you get stoned just standing over her."

"So she's a dead end," said Kurtz.

Litvak was already buttoning his dark raincoat. "A dead end is what she is," he agreed, with a mirthless grin. But he didn't move towards the door. He was still awaiting the specific order.

Kurtz had a last question. "How old is she?"

"Twenty-one next week. Is that a reason?"

Slowly, self-consciously, Kurtz too stood up, and faced Litvak formally across the cramped little room, with its carved, hunting-lodge furniture and wrought-iron fittings.

"Ask each kid individually, Shimon," he ordered. "Does he or she wish to stand down? No explanations needed, no mark against anyone's name who does. A free vote, right across the board."

"I asked them already," Litvak said.

"Ask them again." Kurtz raised his left wrist and looked at his watch. "One hour from now exactly, telephone me. Not earlier. Do nothing until you have spoken to me."

When the traffic is at its thinnest, Kurtz meant. When I have made my dispositions.

Litvak departed. Becker stayed.

Kurtz's first call was to his wife, Elli, and he reversed the charges because he was punctilious about expenses.

"Stay right where you are, please, Gadi," he said quietly as Becker rose to leave, for Kurtz prided himself on living a very open life. So for ten minutes Becker listened to such urgent trivia as how Elli was getting along with her Bible study group, or coping with her shopping problems while the car was off the road. He did not need to ask why Kurtz had chosen such a moment to discuss these matters. In his day, he had done the same thing exactly. Kurtz wanted to touch base before the killing. He wanted to hear Israel talking to him live.

"Elli's just fine," Kurtz assured Becker enthusiastically as he rang off. "She sends love, she says 'Gadi, hurry on back home.' She bumped into Frankie a couple of days back. Frankie was fine too. A little lonely for you, but fine."

Kurtz's second phone call was to Alexis, and at first

Becker might have supposed, if he hadn't known Kurtz better, that it was all part of the same affable round-up of good friends. Kurtz listened to his agent's family news; he asked about the coming baby—yes, mother and child in excellent health. But once these preliminaries were over, Kurtz braced himself and went straight and hard to the nub, for in his last few conversations with Alexis he had sensed a distinct easing in the Doctor's devotion.

"Paul, it appears that a certain accident we recently spoke of is about to occur at any moment and there is nothing you or I can do to prevent it, so get yourself a pen and paper," he announced jovially. Then, changing tone, he poured out his instructions in a brisk Germanic stream: "For the first twenty-four hours after you receive the official word, you will confine your enquiries to the student quarters of Frankfurt and Munich. You will let it be known that the principal suspects are a left-wing group of activists known to have connections with a cell in Paris. You have that?" He paused, allowing Alexis time to write things down.

"On day two, after midday, you present yourself at the Munich main post office and you collect a *poste restante* letter addressed to you in your own name," Kurtz continued when he had apparently obtained the required reassurance. "This will provide you with the identity of your first culprit, a Dutch girl, together with certain background data regarding her involvement in previous incidents."

Kurtz's orders now proceeded at dictation speed, and with great force: no searches to be made in Munich city centre until day fourteen; the results of all forensic tests to be sent to Alexis alone in the first instance, and not put into distribution until cleared by Kurtz; public comparison with other incidents made only with Kurtz's approval. Hearing his agent bridle, Kurtz held the receiver a distance from his ear so that Becker could hear it too. "But, Marty, listen—my friend—I must ask something, actually—"

"Ask it."

"What are we *looking* at here? An *accident* is not a picnic, after all, Marty. We are a civilised democracy, you know what I mean?"

If Kurtz did, he refrained from saying so.

"Listen. I must demand something. Marty, I demand it,

I insist on it. No damage, no loss of life. This is a condition.
We are friends. You follow?"

Kurtz followed, as his terse answers testified. "Paul,
there will surely be no damage to German property. A little
bruising maybe. No damage."

"And life? For God's sake, Marty, we are not *primitive*
here!" cried Alexis, with a resurgence of alarm.

A massive calm entered Kurtz's voice. "No innocent
blood will be shed, Paul. You have my word. No German citizen will suffer so much as a scratch."

"I can rely on this?"

"You'll have to," said Kurtz, and rang off without leaving his number.

In normal circumstances, Kurtz would not have used the
telephones so freely, but since Alexis now had the responsibility for the tapping of them, he felt entitled to take the risk.

Litvak rang ten minufes later. Go, said Kurtz; the green
light; do it.

They waited, Kurtz at the window, Becker in his chair
again, looking past him at the uneasy night sky. Grabbing the
central catch, Kurtz unfastened it and shoved the two case-
ments as wide as they would go, admitting the boom of the
traffic from the autobahn.

"Why take needless risks?" he muttered, as if he had
caught himself in an act of negligence.

Becker began counting at the soldier's speed. So long to
arrange the two of them in position. So long for the last
check-up. So long to get clear. So long before a break in the
traffic was signalled from both directions. So long to wonder
how much human life is worth, even to those who dishonour
the human bond completely. And to those who do not.

It was as usual the loudest bang anyone had ever heard.
Louder than Godesberg, louder than Hiroshima, louder than
all the battles he had fought. Still sitting in his chair, looking
past Kurtz's silhouette, Becker saw one orange ball of flame
burst out of the ground, then vanish, taking the late stars and
early daylight with it. It was followed at once by a wave of
oily black smoke that rushed to fill the space left behind by
the expanding gases. He saw débris fly into the air and a spray
of black fragments spin away from the rear—a wheel, a
chunk of tarmac, something human, who would ever tell? He
saw the curtain brush itself affectionately against Kurtz's bare

arm, and felt the warm puff of a hairdryer. He heard the insect-like buzz of hard objects trembling against each other and, well before that had stopped, the first cries of indignation, the yapping of dogs, and the slopping of scared feet as people in bedroom slippers collected in the covered gangway that linked the chalets, and said the nonsense sentences to each other that people say in films of sinking ships: "Mother! Where's Mother! I've lost my jewels." He heard a woman in hysterics insist that the Russians were coming, and an equally frightened voice assure her that it was only a petrol tanker going up. Someone said it was military—the things they move at night are a disgrace! There was a radio by the bed. While Kurtz stayed at the window, Becker switched it to a local chat programme for insomniacs and kept it running in case they cut into it with a bulletin. To the wail of a siren, a police car hurtled down the autobahn, blue light flashing. Then nothing, then a fire engine, followed by an ambulance. The music stopped and gave way to the first announcement. Unexplained explosion west of Munich, cause unknown, no further details. Closure of autobahn in both directions, traffic advised to take alternative route.

Becker switched off the radio and put on the lights. Kurtz closed the window and drew the curtains, then sat on the bed and pulled off his shoes without untying the laces.

"I, ah, had a word from our people in the Embassy in Bonn the other day, Gadi," said Kurtz, as if something had just refreshed his memory. "I asked them to make a couple of enquiries about those Poles you are working with in Berlin. Check their finances."

Becker said nothing.

"The news is not too good, it seems. Looks as though we'll have to find you some more money or some more Poles."

Still receiving no answer, Kurtz slowly lifted his head, and saw Becker staring at him from the doorway, and something in the taller man's posture fired his anger quite remarkably.

"You wish to tell me something, Mr. Becker? You have a moral point to make that will ease you into a nice frame of mind?"

Becker apparently had none. Softly closing the door behind him, he was gone.

Kurtz had one last call to make: to Gavron, on the direct line to his home. He reached for the phone, hesitated, then drew back his hand. Let the little Rook wait, he thought as the anger lit in him again. He rang him nevertheless. Beginning gently, everything controlled and sensible. The way they began always. Speaking English. And using the cover-names designated for the week. "Nathan, here is Harry. Hi. How is your wife? Great, and give her mine. Nathan, two little goats of our acquaintance just caught a bad cold. That will surely please those people who from time to time require satisfaction."

Listening to Gavron's scratched, non-committal response, Kurtz felt himself begin to shake. But still he contrived to keep his voice on a tight rein. "Nathan, I think that now begins your big moment. It is owed to me that you hold off certain pressures and let this thing mature. Promises have been made and kept, a degree of trust is now in order, a little patience." Of all the men and women of his acquaintance, Gavron alone tempted him to say things he afterwards regretted. Still he kept himself in check. "Like nobody expects a chess game to be won before breakfast, Nathan. I need air, hear me? Air—a little freedom—some territory of my own." His anger welled over: "So tie those crazies down, will you? Go out into the marketplace and buy me some support for a change!"

The line was dead. Whether the explosion was responsible, or Misha Gavron, Kurtz never knew, for he did not try to ring back.

PART TWO

THE PRIZE

16

For three interminable weeks, while London slipped from summer to autumn, Charlie lived in a state of half-reality, vacillating from disbelief to impatience, from excited preparation to spasmodic terror.

Sooner or later they will come for you, he kept saying. They must. And he set about preparing her mind for her accordingly.

Yet why must they come? She did not know and he did not tell her, but used his remoteness as a protection. Would Mike and Marty somehow make Michel their man, as they had made Charlie their girl? She had days of imagining that Michel would one day catch up with the fiction they had built for him, and appear before her, ardent for his lover's due. And Joseph gently encouraged her in her schizophrenia, guiding her ever closer to his absent proxy. Michel, my darling own Michel; come to me. Love Joseph, but dream of Michel. At first she hardly dared look at herself in the mirror, she was so convinced her secret showed. Her face was stretched tight by the outrageous information hidden just behind it; her voice and movements had an underwater deliberation that set her miles apart from the rest of humanity: I'm a one-girl show right round the clock; it's all the world, then me.

Then slowly, as the time dragged by, her fear of exposure gave way to an affectionate disrespect for the innocents around her who failed to see what was shoved under their noses every day. They are where I came from, she thought. They are me before I walked through the looking-glass.

Towards Joseph himself, she used the technique she had perfected on her drive through Yugoslavia. He was the familiar to whom she referred her every action and decision; he was the lover she cracked her jokes and put on her make-up for. He was her anchor, her best friend, her best thing altogether. He was the sprite who popped up at all odd places, with quite impossible prescience about her movements—now at a bus-stop, now at the library, now at the launderette, sitting under the neon lights among the dowdy mums, watching his shirts go round. But she never admitted his existence. He was outside her life completely, out of time and touch—except for their furtive assignations, which sustained her. Except for his proxy, Michel.

For rehearsing *As You Like It*, the company had rented an old Territorial Army drill hall near Victoria Station and she went there each morning, and each evening she washed the smell of stale military beer from her hair.

She allowed Quilley to lunch her at Bianchi's and found him odd. He seemed to be trying to warn her of something, but when she asked him outright what it was, he clammed up and said that politics were people's own affair, which was what he'd fought the war for, in the Green jackets. But he got awfully drunk. Having helped him sign the bill, she rejoined the crowds in the street and had the feeling of riding out ahead of herself; of following her own elusive shape as it slipped away from her, through the bobbing people. I am separated from life. I'll never find my way back. But even while she thought this, she felt the brush of a hand against her elbow as Joseph drew momentarily alongside before peeling away into Marks & Sparks. The effect of these sightings upon her was soon extraordinary. They kept her in a constant state of vigilance and, if she was honest with herself, desire. A day without him was a nothing day; one glimpse, and her heart and body thrilled to him like a sixteen-year-old's.

She read the respectable Sunday newspapers and studied the latest amazing revelations about Sackville-West—or was it Sitwell?—and marvelled at the self-regarding irrelevance of the ruling English mind. She looked at the London she had forgotten, and found everywhere support for her identity as the radical committed to the violent path. Society as she knew it was a dead plant; her job was to clear it away and use the soil for something better. The hopeless faces of the shoppers shuffling like manacled slaves through the neon-lit supermarket told her so; so did the despairing old, and the venomous-eyed policemen. So did the lounging black kids watching the Rolls-Royces sweep by, and the shiny banks with their air of secular worship and their righteous martinets of managers. The building societies luring the deluded into their property traps; the booze shops, the betting shops, the vomit—with little effort on Charlie's part, the entire London scene presented an unemptied dustbin of discarded hopes and disappointed souls. Thanks to the inspiration of Michel, she constructed her mental bridges between capitalist exploitation in the Third World and here on her doorstep in Camden Town.

Lived so brightly, life even sent her a heavy symbol of man adrift. Taking an early Sunday-morning walk along the Regent's Canal towpath—in reality, for one of her few scheduled meetings with Joseph—she heard the sound of a deep-throated string instrument warbling a Negro spiritual. The canal opened up and she saw, in the centre of a harbour of discarded warehouses, an old black man straight out of *Uncle Tom's Cabin*, sitting on a tethered raft and playing his cello to a group of spellbound children. It was a scene from Fellini; it was kitsch; it was a mirage; it was an inspired vision risen from her subconscious.

Whatever it was, for several days it became a private term of reference for everything she saw around her, too private to confide even to Joseph, for fear he would laugh at her—or, worse still, offer a rational explanation.

She went to bed with Al a few times because she wanted no crisis with him and because, after the long drought with Joseph, her body needed him; and, besides, Michel had ordered her to. She wouldn't let him visit her flat because he was homeless again and she was afraid he would try and stay, which was what he had done before, until she had flung his clothes and razor into the street. Anyway, her flat possessed new secrets that nothing on God's earth would have persuaded her to share with him: her bed was Michel's, his gun had lain beneath the pillow, and there was nothing Al or anyone else could do to force her to desecrate it. She also trod wary with Al because Joseph had warned her that his movie deal had fallen through, and she knew of old how bad he could get when his pride was hurt.

Their first impassioned reunion took place in his usual pub, where she found the great philosopher ensconced with a couple of female disciples. As she walked across to join him, she thought: He'll smell Michel; he's in my clothes, my skin,

my smile. But Al was too busy demonstrating his indifference
to smell anything. He pushed back a chair for her with his
foot, and as she sat down she thought: God help me, not one
month ago this midget was my top adviser on what makes the
world tick. When the pub closed and they went to a friend's
flat and commandeered his spare room, she was appalled to
find herself imagining it was Michel inside her, and Michel's
face gazing down at her, and Michel's olive body bearing in
on her in the half dark—Michel, her own little killer boy,
driving her to the brink. But beyond Michel there was another figure still, Joseph, hers at last; his burning, locked-in
sexuality finally burst loose; his scarred body and his scarred
mind hers.

Apart from the Sundays, she read capitalist newspapers
sporadically, listened to consumer-orientated radio bulletins,
but heard nothing of a red-headed English girl sought in connection with the smuggling of high-grade Russian plastic explosive into Austria. It never happened. It was two other
girls, one of my little fantasies. In most other respects, the
state of the wider world had ceased to interest her. She read
of a Palestinian bombing in Aachen, and of an Israeli reprisal
raid on some camp in the Lebanon claiming large numbers
of civilian dead. She read of mounting popular fury in Israel,
and was duly chilled by an interview with an Israeli general
who promised to solve the Palestinian problem "from the
roots up." But after her crash course in conspiracy, she had
no faith in the official description of events and never would
have again. The only news items she followed with any loyalty concerned a female giant panda at London Zoo who was
declining to mate, though feminists insisted it was the male's
fault. Also, the zoo was one of Joseph's places. They would
meet on a bench there, if only to squeeze hands like lovers
before going their separate ways.

Soon, he would say. Soon.

Floating this way, acting all the time for an unseen audience, guarding her every word and gesture against a momentary carelessness, Charlie found herself relying heavily on
ritual. At weekends she usually went to her kids' club in
Peckham and, in a great arched hall big enough for Brecht,

whipped her kids' drama group back into action, which she loved. They were planning a rock pantomime for Christmas, a piece of sheer anarchy.

On Fridays she sometimes went to Al's pub, and on Wednesdays she took two quart bottles of brown ale to Miss Dubber, who lived round the corner, a retired tart from the chorus line. Miss Dubber had arthritis and rickets and woodworm and several serious ailments as well, and cursed her body with a zeal she had once reserved for ungenerous lovers. Charlie in return filled Miss Dubber's ear with marvellous made-up stories about the scandalous goings-on in the world of showbusiness, and they laughed so raucously together that the people next door turned up their television set to drown the din.

Otherwise Charlie could not manage company, though her acting career had provided her with half a dozen families she could have called on if she'd had a mind to.

She chatted to Lucy on the phone; they agreed to meet but left it open. She tracked down Robert in Battersea, but the Mykonos crowd were like schoolfriends from ten years ago; there was no life left to share with them. She had a curry with Willy and Pauly, but they were thinking about breaking up and it was a flop. She tried a few other bosom friends from previous existences but with no better success, and after that she became an old maid. She watered the young trees in her street when the weather went dry and hung fresh nut-bunches in steel pouches from her window-sill for the sparrows, because that was one of her signs to him, like the World Disarmament sticker on her car and the brass "C" she wore on a leather label strapped to her shoulder bag. He called them her safety signals and rehearsed her repeatedly in their uses. The disappearance of any one of them meant a cry for help. And in her handbag lived a brand-new white silk scarf, not for surrender but to say "They've come," if they ever did. She maintained her pocket diary, taking over where the Literacy Committee had left off; she completed the repair of an embroidery picture she had bought before she went on holiday, showing Lotte in Weimar pining to death over Werther's tomb. Me again, gone classic. She wrote endless letters to her missing man, but little by little ceased to post them.

Michel, darling, oh Michel, for mercy's sake, come to me.

But she steered clear of the squats and the alternative bookshops in Islington where she used to drop in for torpid coffee sessions; and very clear indeed of the angry bunch down in St. Pancras whose occasional cocaine-based pamphlets she used to distribute because no one else would. She got her car back from Eustace, the repair man, at last, a souped-up Fiat that Al had smashed for her, and, on her birthday, gave it a first airing by driving it to Rickmansworth to visit her bloody mother and take her the tablecloth that she had bought for her in Mykonos. She dreaded these visits as a rule: the Sunday-lunch mealtrap, with three vegetables and a rhubarb pie, followed by her mother's detailed summary of what the world had done wrong to her since they had last met. But this time, to her surprise, she found herself on delightful terms with her. She stayed the night, and the next morning put on a dark headscarf, never the white one, and drove her to church, careful not to think of the last time she had worn a headscarf. Kneeling, she found herself stirred by an unexpected residual sense of piety, and fervently laid her several identities at God's service. Listening to the organ music, she began weeping, which made her wonder how much, after all, she had her mind under control.

It's because I can't face going back to my flat, she thought.

What disconcerted her was the ghostly way that her flat had been altered to meet the new personality into which she was so carefully easing herself: a scene-change of which the scale only gradually declared itself. Of her entire new life, the insidious reconstruction of her flat during her absence was the most disturbing. Till now she had regarded it as the safest place ever, a kind of architectural Ned Quilley. She had inherited it from an out-of-work actor who, having taken to burglary, had retired and removed himself and his boyfriend to Spain. It was situated on the northern edge of Camden Town over a Goanese Indian transport café, which warmed up at two in the morning and stayed awake to serve *samosas* and fried breakfasts till seven. To reach her staircase, you had to squeeze between the lavatory and the kitchen and cross a courtyard, by which time you were an object of scrutiny by the patron, the chef, and the chef's cheeky boyfriend, not to mention anyone who happened to be in the loo. And when you reached the top of the staircase there was a second front door to get through before you entered the sacred domain, which consisted of an attic room with the best bed in the world, and a bathroom and kitchen, all separate and rent-controlled.

Now suddenly she had lost that consolation of security. They had stolen it away from her. She felt as if she had lent the flat to someone during her absence and he had done all sorts of wrong things to it as a favour. Yet how had they got in unnoticed? When she asked in the café, they knew nothing. There was her writing drawer, for instance, with Michel's letters to her jammed into the back—all the originals, of which she had seen the photostats in Munich. There was her fighting fund, three hundred quids' worth in old fivers stowed behind the cracked panel of the bath, where she used to keep her grass in the days when she smoked. She moved them to a space under the floorboards, then back to the bath, then back to the floorboards again. There were the mementoes, the hoarded fragments of her love-affair from day one in Nottingham onwards: book-matches from the motel; the cheap ballpoint with which she had written her first letters to Paris; the very first russet orchids pressed and weighted between the pages of her *Mrs. Beeton* cookbook; the first dress he had ever bought for her—in York that was, they had gone to the store together; the hideous earrings he had given her in London, which she really couldn't wear except to please him. Such things she had half expected; Joseph had as good as warned her of them. What disturbed her was that these tiny touches, as she began to live with them, became more herself than she was: in her bookcase, the well-thumbed copies of glossy works of information on Palestine, signed with cautious dedications from Michel; on the wall, the pro-Palestinian poster with the frog-like features of the Israeli Prime Minister unflatteringly displayed above the silhouettes of Arab refugees; pinned next to it, the set of coloured maps tracing the course of Israeli expansion since 1967, with her own hand-drawn question mark over Tyre and Sidon, derived from her readings of Ben-Gurion's claims to them; the stack of ill-printed English-language magazines of anti-Israeli propaganda.

That's me all over, she thought as she picked her way slowly through the collection; once I'm hooked, I go out and buy the shop.

Except that I never did. It was them.

But saying so didn't help her, nor with time did she quite retain the distinction in her mind.

Michel, for Christ's sake, have they caught you?

Soon after her return to London, as instructed, she visited the post office in Maida Vale, presented her credentials, and collected one letter only, postmark Istanbul, which had evidently arrived after she had left London for Mykonos. *Darling. Not long now till Athens. I love you.* Signed "M." A scribbled note to keep her going. But the sight of this live communication disturbed her deeply. A horde of buried images leapt out to haunt her. Michel's feet slopping down the staircase in his Gucci shoes. His slack, lovely body supported by his jailers. His fawn's face, too young for conscription. His voice, too rich, too innocent. The gold medallion gently slapping his naked olive breast. *Joseph, I love you.*

After that she went every day to the post office and sometimes twice, becoming a feature of the place, if only because she always left empty-handed looking more and more distraught; a delicate, well-directed piece of acting, which she worked upon with care, and which Joseph, in his capacity of secret coach, more than once personally witnessed while he bought stamps at the next-door counter.

In the same period, hoping to prompt life from him, she posted three letters to Michel in Paris, begging him to write, loving him, and forgiving him in advance for his silence. These were the first letters she had composed and written for herself. Mysteriously, she found relief in sending them; they gave an authenticity to their predecessors, and to her professed feelings. Each time she wrote one, she took it to a postbox chosen for her, and she supposed there were people covering it, but she had learned not to stare around and not to think about it. Once she spotted Rachel in the window of a Wimpy Bar looking very dowdy and English. Once Raoul and Dimitri rode past her on a motorbike. The last of her letters to Michel she sent express, from the same post office where she asked in vain for mail, and she scrawled "darling please please please oh please write" along the back of the envelope after she had franked it, while Joseph waited patiently behind her.

Gradually she came to think of her life over these weeks as possessing a large print and a small print. The large print was the world she lived in. The small was the world she slipped in and out of when the large world wasn't watching. No love-affair, even with very married men, had ever been so secret for her.

Their trip to Nottingham came on her fifth day. Joseph took exceptional precautions. He picked her up in a Rover from a remote tube station on a Saturday evening and drove her back on the Sunday afternoon. He had brought a blonde wig for her, a really good one, and a change of clothes, including a fur coat, in a suitcase. He had arranged a late dinner and it was as awful as the original; in the middle of it, Charlie confessed to an absurd panic lest the staff might recognise her despite her wig and fur coat and demand to know what had become of her one true lover.

Then they went to their bedroom, two chaste twin beds, which in the fiction they had remade by pulling them together and laying the mattresses the other way. For a moment, she really thought it was going to happen. She came out of the bathroom and Joseph was lying full length on the bed, looking at her, and she lay beside him and put her head on his chest, then lifted her face to him and began kissing him, light selective kisses on favourite places around the temples, cheeks, and finally the lips. His hand held her back, then lifted to her face, and he kissed her in return, keeping his hand along her cheek and his eyes open. Then very gently he pushed her away from him, and sat up. And kissed her once more: goodbye.

"Listen," he said as he picked up his coat.

He was smiling. His beautiful, kind smile, his very best. She listened, and heard the Nottinghamshire rain clattering against their window—the same rain that had kept them in bed for two nights and one long day.

Next morning they retraced nostalgically the little excursions that she and Michel had made together into the surrounding countryside until their desire swept them back to the motel; all for the visual memories, Joseph assured her earnestly, and for the added confidence of having seen. Between such lessons, like a light relief, he taught her other things. Silent signals, as he called them; and a method of secret writing on the inside of Marlboro cigarette packets, which somehow she could not take seriously.

Several times, they met in a theatrical costumier's behind the Strand, usually after rehearsals.

"You'll have come for the fitting, won't you, dear?" said a mountainous blonde lady of sixty in flowing robes, each time Charlie stepped through the doorway. "That's the way then, dear," and showed her into a back bedroom where Joseph sat waiting for her like a whore's client. Autumn becomes you, she thought, noticing the frost on his hair again, and the pink nip of his frugal cheeks; it always will.

Her greatest worry was not knowing how to reach him. "Where are you staying? How can I get in touch with you?"

Through Cathy, he would say. You have the safety signals and you have Cathy.

Cathy was her lifeline, and Joseph's front office, the preserver of his exclusiveness. Each evening between six and eight Charlie would enter a phone box, always a different one, and ring a West End number so that Cathy could take her through her day: how the rehearsals had gone, what news of Al and the gang, how was Quilley and had they discussed future parts, had she auditioned for the movie yet, and was there anything she needed?—often for half an hour or more. At first Charlie resented Cathy as a diminution of her relationship with Joseph, but gradually she came to look forward to their chats because Cathy turned out to possess a nice line in senior wit and a great deal of earthy wisdom. Charlie had a picture of somebody warm-hearted and detached and possibly Canadian: one of those unshockable lady-shrinks she used to visit at the Tavistock Clinic after she was expelled from school and thought she might be going bananas. And this was clever of Charlie, for though Miss Bach was American and not Canadian, her family had been doctors for generations.

The house in Hampstead that Kurtz had rented for the watchers was very large, set in a quiet backwater favoured by the Finchley driving schools. Its owners, at the suggestion of their good friend Marty from Jerusalem, had tiptoed off to Marlow, but their house remained a garrison of hushed and intellectual elegance. There were pictures by Nolde in the drawing-room and a signed photograph of Thomas Mann in the conservatory, and a cage-bird that sang when you wound it up, and a library with cracking leather chairs, and a music room with a Bechstein grand. There was ping-pong in the basement and at the back a tangled garden with a crumbling grey tennis court too far gone, so the kids invented a new game for it, a kind of tennis-golf to accommodate its bunkers. At the front was a tiny gatehouse, and that was where they put their notices saying "Hebraic and Humanist Study Group, Students and Staff Only," which in Hampstead did not raise an eyebrow.

There were fourteen of them in all, including Litvak, but they spread themselves over the four floors with such a discreet and catlike orderliness you could hardly have told there was anyone there at all. Their morale had never been a problem, and the Hampstead house raised it even higher. They loved the dark furniture and the feeling that every object around them seemed to know more than they did. They loved working all day and often half the night, and coming back to this temple of gracious Jewish living; and living out that heritage as well. When Litvak played Brahms, which he did very well, even Rachel, who was pop-mad, put aside her prejudices and came downstairs to hear him, though—as they were not slow to remind her—she had at first kicked against the very idea of coming back to England at all, and had made an ostentatious point of not travelling on a British passport.

With such a fine team spirit, they settled to the wait like clockwork. They avoided, without even being told, the local pubs and restaurants and unnecessary contact with local people. On the other hand, they took care to send themselves mail and buy milk and newspapers and do the things that the inquisitive otherwise notice by omission. They bicycled a lot and were hugely tickled to discover what distinguished and sometimes questionable Jews had been here ahead of them, and there was not one who did not pay his wry respects to the house of Friedrich Engels, or to the tomb of Karl Marx in Highgate Cemetery. Their transport stable was a smart little pink-painted garage off Haverstock Hill, with an old silver Rolls-Royce in the window marked "Not for Sale" and a proprietor called Bernie. Bernie was a big, growling man, with a dark face and a blue suit and a half-smoked cigarette and a blue Homburg hat like Schwili's that he wore while he did his own typing. He had vans and cars and motorbikes and number plates galore, and on the day they arrived he put up a big sign saying "CONTRACT BUSINESS ONLY. NO CALLERS." "A bunch of bleeding poofters," he told his business friends coarsely. "Called themselves a film company. Hired everything in my bleeding shop, paid me in bleeding used-oncers—well, how can you bleeding resist?"

All of which, to a point, was true, for that was the fiction they had agreed with him. But Bernie knew a whole lot better. Bernie too, in his day, had done a thing or two.

Meanwhile, almost daily, tidbits of news came in by way of the London Embassy, like the word of a distant battle. Rossino had called again at Yanuka's flat in Munich, this time accompanied by a blonde woman who satisfied their theories about the girl known as Edda. So-and-so had visited so-and-so in Paris, or Beirut, or Damascus, or Marseilles. With the identification of Rossino, new avenues had opened in a dozen different directions. As often as three times a week, Litvak held a briefing and a free discussion. Where photographs had been taken, he held a magic-lantern show as well, with short lectures on known aliases, behaviour patterns, personal appetites, and habits of tradecraft. Periodically he mounted quiz competitions with amusing prizes for the winners.

Occasionally, though not often, the great Gadi Becker slipped in to hear the latest word, seating himself at the back of the room apart from everyone and leaving as soon as the meeting ended. Of his life away from them they knew nothing at all, nor did they expect to: he was the agent runner, a breed apart; he was Becker, unsung hero of more secret missions than most of them had had birthdays. They called him affectionately "the Steppenwolf," and told each other impressive half-true stories about his feats.

The call came on day eighteen. A telex from Geneva put them on standby, a cable from Paris gave the confirmation. Within an hour, two-thirds of the team was on the road, headed westward through black rain.

17

The company was called the Heretics and its tour had opened in Exeter before a congregation straight from the Cathedral: women in the mauve of half mourning, old priests permanently on the brink of tears. When there was no matinée, the cast drifted round the city and yawned, and in the evenings after the show they took wine and cheese with earnest disciples of the Arts, because it was part of the deal that you exchanged beads with the natives.

From Exeter, they had gone to Plymouth and played in the naval base before mystified young officers who agonised about whether stagehands should be awarded the temporary condition of gentlemen and admitted to their mess.

But both Exeter and Plymouth had been cities of devilment and wild living by comparison with the dripping, granite mining-town far down the Cornish peninsula, with cramped alleys steaming with sea-mist, and stunted trees made hunchback by the gales. The cast was spread round half a dozen guest houses, and Charlie's luck was a slate-gabled island entirely surrounded by hydrangeas, where the drumming of the London-bound trains as she lay in bed made her feel like a castaway taunted by the glimpse of distant ships. Their theatre was a rig inside a sports hall, and from its creaking stage she could smell the chlorine from the swimming pool and hear the sluggish thud of squash-balls through the wall. Their audience was the headscarf-and-lentils brigade, whose drugged, envious eyes told you they would do it better than you if they ever sank so low as to try. And their dressing-room, finally, was a women's locker-room, and that was where they brought her the orchids—while she was putting on her make-up ten minutes before curtain-up.

She saw them first in the long mirror over the hand-basins, floating through the door, wrapped to the neck in damp white paper. She saw them hesitate, then advance uncertainly towards her. But she went on with her make-up as if she had never seen an orchid in her life. One spray, carried like a paper-wrapped baby across the arms of a fifty-year-old Cornish Vestal named Val, with black plaits and a vapid, disregarded smile. Russet.

"I hereby declare you to be fair Rosalind," said Val skittishly.

A hostile silence fell, in which the entire female cast savoured Val's irrelevance. It was the hour when actors are at their most nervous, and their quietest.

"I'm Rosalind," Charlie agreed unhelpfully. "Why?" And went to work with an eyeliner to show she didn't care very much what the answer was.

Making a brave ceremony of it, Val laid the orchids in the handbasin and scurried out, while Charlie picked up the envelope in full view of everyone who cared to look. *For Miss Rosalind.* Continental hand, blue ballpoint instead of black ink. Inside, one continental visiting card, high gloss. The name not printed but raised in spiky, colourless capitals on the slant. *ANTON MESTERBEIN, GENEVA.* Below it, the one word *Justice.* No message added, and no "Joan, spirit of my freedom."

She transferred her attention to her other eyebrow, very carefully, as if her eyebrow were the most important thing on earth.

"Who is he, Chas?" said a Rural Shepherdess at the next-door basin. She was just out of college, mental age fifteen.

Frowning into the mirror in her concentration, Charlie critically studied her handiwork.

"Must have cost a bomb, mustn't they, Chas?" said the Shepherdess.

"Mustn't they, Chas?" Charlie echoed.

It's him!

It's word of him!

Then why isn't he here? Why is the note not written in his hand?

Trust no one, Michel had warned her. *But especially mistrust those who claim to know me.*

It's a trap. It's the pigs. They've found out about my drive through Yugoslavia. They're setting me up to snare my lover.

Michel, Michel! Lover, life—tell me what to do!

She heard her name being called: "Rosalind—where the hell's Charlie? Charlie, for Christ's sake."

In the corridor, a group of swimmers with towels round their necks stared without expression at the sight of a red-headed lady in threadbare Elizabethan drag emerging from the women's locker-room.

Somehow she performed. Perhaps she even acted too. During the interval, the director, a monkish soul whom they called Brother Mycroft, asked her with a strange look whether she would mind "taking it down a bit" and she meekly promised him she would. But she barely heard him: she was too busy scanning the half-empty rows in the hope of glimpsing a red blazer.

In vain.

She saw other faces—Rachel's, Dimitri's, for example— but did not recognise them. He's not there, she thought in despair. It's a trick. It's the police.

In the locker-room, she changed quickly, put on her white headscarf, and dawdled there till the janitor threw her out. In the foyer, standing like a white-headed ghost among the departing athletes, she waited again, the orchids clutched to her breast. An old lady asked whether she had grown them. A schoolboy wanted her autograph. The Shepherdess plucked at her sleeve: "Chas—the party, for God's sake—Val is looking for you *everywhere!*"

The front doors of the sports hall slammed behind her, she stepped into the night air and nearly fell flat before the bluff gale whipping over the tarmac. Staggering to her car, she unlocked it, laid the orchids on the passenger seat, and heaved the door shut after her. The ignition wouldn't catch at first, and when it did the engine raced like a horse straining to get home. As she roared down the drive into the main road, she saw in her mirror the headlamps of another car pull out after her, then follow her at an even distance to her guest house.

She parked and heard the same wind tearing into the hydrangeas. She wrapped her coat round her and, with the orchids inside it, made a dash for the front door. There were four steps and she counted them twice: once as she bounded up them, and the second time while she was standing panting at the reception desk, as someone tripped after her with a light and purposeful tattoo. There were no residents about, not in the lounge, not in the hall. The sole survivor was Humphrey, a Dickensian fat-boy who played night porter.

"Not *six*, Humph," she said gaily as he groped for her key. "*Sixteen*. Come on, sweetheart. Up on the top row. There's a love-letter in there too, before you give it to someone else."

She took the folded piece of paper from him, hoping it might be from Michel, then let her features register suppressed disappointment when she discovered it was only from her sister, saying "Good luck for the show tonight," which was Joseph's way of whispering "We're with you," but so low she barely heard.

The hall door opened and closed behind her. A man's feet were approaching across the hall carpet. She allowed herself one swift glance at him in case he was Michel. But he wasn't, as her expression of disappointment showed. He was someone from the rest of the world, and of no use to her at all. A slender, dangerously peaceful boy, with dark, mother-loving eyes. Wearing a long brown gabardine trench coat with a military yoke to give breadth to the civilian shoulders. And a brown tie to match the eyes which matched the coat. And brown helpless shoes with stubby toecaps, double stitched. Not a man of justice at all, she decided—but of justice denied. A forty-year-old gabardine boy, robbed of his justice at an early age.

"Miss Charlie?"

And a small overfed mouth in a pale field of chin.

"I bring you greetings from our mutual acquaintance Michel, Miss Charlie."

Charlie had hardened her face like someone preparing to take punishment. "Michel who?" she said—and saw how nothing in him stirred, which in turn made her very still herself, in the way we stand still for paintings, and statues, and motionless policemen.

"Michel from Nottingham, Miss Charlie." The Swiss accent aggrieved and faintly accusing. The voice furry, as if justice were a secret matter. "Michel asked me to bring you gold orchids and take you to dinner for him. He was insistent that you come. Please. I am the good friend of Michel. Come."

You? she thought. Friend? Michel wouldn't have a friend like you to save his bloody life. But she let her glower say it for her.

"I am also charged with the responsibility to represent Michel legally, Miss Charlie. Michel is entitled to the full protection of the law. Come, please. Now."

The gesture took a large effort but she meant it to. The orchids were awfully heavy and it was a long way through the air to lift them from her arms to his. But she managed it; she found her courage and her strength, and his arms came up to receive them. And she found the right brassy tone for the words she had decided to say.

"You've got the wrong show," she said. "I don't know Michel from Nottingham, I don't know Michel from anywhere. And we didn't meet in Monte last season either. Nice try, but I'm tired. Of all of you."

Turning to the counter to pick up her key, she realised as she did so that Humphrey the porter was addressing her on a matter of great moment. His glazed face was shaking, and he held a pencil poised over a great ledger.

"I *said*," he puffed indignantly, in his steep, North Country drawl, "what *time* was it you was wanting morning tea, miss?"

"Nine o'clock, dear, and not a second earlier." She moved wearily towards the stairs.

"Paper, miss?" said Humphrey.

She turned and glanced heavily back at him. "Jesus," she whispered.

Humphrey was suddenly very excited. He seemed to think that only animation would wake her up. "Morning paper! For reading in! What's your fancy?"

"*Times*, dear," she said.

Humphrey sank back into contented apathy. "*Telegraph*," he wrote, aloud. "*Times* is orders only," by which time she had started to haul herself up the big staircase towards the historic darkness of the landing.

"Miss Charlie!"

You call at me like that again, she thought, and I just may come down a few steps and smack you very hard on your smooth Swiss mountain pass. She took two more steps before he spoke again. She had not anticipated such force in him.

"Michel will be very glad to know that Rosalind was wearing his bracelet tonight! And is actually wearing it still, I think! Or is that a gift from some other gentleman?"

Her head, then her whole body faced him down the stairs. He had transferred the orchids to his left arm. His right hung at his side like an empty sleeve.

"I said go away. Get out. *Please*—okay?"

But she was arguing against her own conviction, as her faltering voice betrayed.

"Michel orders me to buy you fresh lobster, and a bottle of Boutaris wine. White and cold, he says. I have other messages from him also. He will be very angry when I tell him you refused his hospitality, also insulted."

It was too much. He was her own dark angel, claiming the soul she had carelessly pledged. Whether he was lying, whether he was the police or a common blackmailer, she would follow him to the centre of the underworld if he could lead her to Michel. Jolting on her heels, she bumped slowly down the stairs to the reception counter.

"Humphrey." Tossing her key to the counter, she took the pencil from his unresisting hand and wrote the name CATHY on the block of paper before him. "American lady. Got it? Mate of mine. If she rings, tell her I've gone out with six lovers. Tell her maybe I'll drive over for lunch tomorrow. Got it?" she repeated.

Tearing the sheet of paper from the block, she tucked it into his handkerchief pocket, then gave him a distracted kiss while Mesterbein looked on with the masked resentment of a lover waiting to claim her for the night. At the porch, he produced a neat Swiss torch. By its light she saw the yellow Hertz sticker on the windscreen of his car. He opened the passenger door for her and said "Please," but she walked straight past it to her Fiat, got in, started the engine, and waited. To drive, she noticed as he went ahead of her, he wore a black beret, the brim quite level like a bathing hat, except that it made his ears stick out.

They drove in slow convoy because of the fog patches. Or perhaps Mesterbein drove that way always, for he had the aggressive poker-back of the habitually cautious driver. They climbed a hill and made north over empty moorland. The fog broke, the telegraph poles stuck up like threaded needles against the night sky. A torn Greek moon peered briefly from the clouds before they dragged it back inside. At a crossroads Mesterbein stopped to consult a map. Finally he indicated left, first with his light, then with a white hand, which he rotated. Yes, Anton, I get the message. She followed him down a hill and through a village; she lowered her window and filled the car with the salt smell of the sea. The rushing air opened her mouth for her in a scream. She followed him under a tattered banner that read "East West Timesharer Chalets Ltd.," then up a narrow new road through dunes towards a ruined tin-mine perched on the skyline, an advertisement for "Come to Cornwall." Left and right of her, clapboard bungalows, unlit. Mesterbein parked, she parked behind him, leaving her car in gear because of the gradient. New groan in the handbrake, she thought; take it back to Eustace. He climbed out; she did the same and locked her car. The wind had dropped; they were on the lee side of the peninsula. Gulls were wheeling low and squalling, as if they had lost something valuable on the ground. Torch in hand, Mesterbein reached for her elbow to guide her forward.

"Leave me alone," she said. He pushed a gate and it creaked. A light went on ahead of them. Short concrete path, blue door called Sea-Wrack. Mesterbein had a key ready. The door opened; he stepped ahead of her and stood back to let her by, an estate agent showing the place to a potential client. There was no porch and somehow no warning. She followed him in, he closed the door behind her, she was in a drawing-room. She smelt damp laundry and saw black fungus spots spattered on the ceiling. A tall blonde woman in a blue corduroy suit was jamming a coin into the electric meter. Seeing them enter, she peered quickly round with a bright smile, then leapt to her feet, punching away a strand of long gold hair as she did so.

"Anton! Oh this is *too* nice! You have brought me Charlie! Charlie, welcome. And you will be twice welcome if you will please show me how to work this impossible machine." Grabbing Charlie's shoulders, she embraced her excitedly on each cheek. "I mean, Charlie, listen, you were completely fantastic tonight in that Shakespeare, yes? Wasn't she, Anton? I mean superb. I am *Helga*, okay?" Names are a game to me, she meant. "*Helga.* Yes? As you are Charlie, I am Helga."

Her eyes were grey and lucid and, like Mesterbein's, dangerously innocent. A militant simplicity gazed out from them upon a complicated world. To be true is to be untamed, thought Charlie, quoting to herself from one of Michel's letters. I feel, therefore I do.

From a corner of the room, Mesterbein offered a belated answer to Helga's question. He was threading a coat-hanger into his gabardine trench coat. "Oh, she was *very* impressive, naturally."

Helga's hands still rested on Charlie's shoulders, her strong thumbs lightly grazing her neck. "Is it difficult to learn so many words, Charlie?" she asked, staring brightly into Charlie's face.

"I don't have that problem," she said, and broke away from her.

"You learn easily then?" Grasping Charlie's hand, she pressed a fifty-pence piece into her palm. "Come. Show me. Show me how to work this fantastic English invention called *fire*."

Charlie crouched to the meter, turned the lever one way, slipped in the coin, turned it the other, and let the coin fall with a clunk. There was a protesting whine as the fire came on.

"Incredible! Oh, Charlie! But you see that is typical of me. I am completely untechnical," Helga explained immediately, as if this were an important thing about her that a new friend should know. "I am completely anti-possessions, so if I don't own anything, how can I know how to work it? Anton will please translate for me. I believe in *Sein, nicht Haben*." It was an order, issued by a nursery autocrat. Her English was quite good enough without his help. "You have read Erich Fromm, Charlie?"

"She means being, not possession," said Mesterbein gloomily while he regarded the two women. "It is the essence of Fräulein Helga's moral. She believes in fundamental goodness, also Nature over Science. We both do," he added, as if wishing to interpose himself between them.

"You have read Erich Fromm?" Helga repeated, sweeping back her blonde hair again and already thinking of something quite different. "I am completely in love with him." She crouched before the fire, hands outstretched. "When I admire a philosopher, I love him. That also is typical of me." There was a surface grace to her movements, and a teenager's lumpiness. She wore flat shoes to help her with her height.

"Where's Michel?" Charlie asked.

"Fräulein Helga does not know where Michel is," Mesterbein objected sharply from his corner. "She is not a lawyer, she came only for the journey and for justice. Fräulein Helga has no knowledge of Michel's activities or whereabouts. Sit down, please."

Charlie remained standing. But Mesterbein sat himself on a dining-chair and folded his clean white hands on his lap. The trench coat discarded, he displayed a new brown suit. It could have been a birthday present from his mother.

"You said you had news of him," Charlie said. A tremor had entered her voice and her lips felt stiff.

Still crouching, Helga had turned to face her. She had pressed her thumbnail thoughtfully against her strong front teeth.

"When did you see him last, please?" Mesterbein asked.

She no longer knew which of them to look at. "In Salzburg," she said.

"Salzburg, that's not a date, I think," Helga objected from the floor.

"Five weeks ago. Six. Where is he?"

"And you heard from him last when?" asked Mesterbein.

"Just tell me where he is! What's happened to him?" She swung back to Helga. "Where is he?"

"Nobody came to you?" Mesterbein asked. "No friends of his? Police?"

"Maybe you are not so good at memory as you say, Charlie," Helga suggested.

"Tell us who you have been in touch with, please, Miss Charlie," Mesterbein said. "Immediately. It is most necessary. We are here for urgent matters."

"Actually she could lie easily, such an actress," Helga said, while her wide eyes gazed up at Charlie in a questing, unshadowed stare. "A woman so trained to pretend, how can one believe anything, actually?"

"We must be very careful," Mesterbein agreed, as a private note to himself for the future.

Their double-act had a ring of sadism; they were playing

upon a pain she had yet to feel. She stared at Helga, then at Mesterbein. Her words slipped from her. She could no longer keep them in.

"He's dead, isn't he?" she whispered.

Helga seemed not to hear. She was entirely taken up with watching.

"Oh yes. Michel is dead," said Mesterbein glumly. "I'm sorry, naturally. Fräulein Helga is also sorry. We are both very sorry. From the letters you wrote to him, we assume you will be sorry also."

"But maybe the letters are also pretending, Anton," Helga reminded him.

It had happened to her once before in her life, at school. Three hundred girls lining the gymnasium wall, the headmistress in the middle, everybody waiting for the culprit to confess. Charlie had been peering around with the best of them, looking for the guilty one—is it *her*? I'll bet it's *her*— she wasn't blushing, she was looking grave and innocent, and she hadn't—it was really true and later positively proved— she hadn't stolen anything at all. Yet suddenly her knees sagged and she fell straight over her feet, feeling perfectly all right from the waist up, but paralysed below. She did it now, not a studied thing at all; she did it before she was herself aware of it, before she had even halfway considered the enormity of the information, and before Helga could put out a hand to catch her. She keeled over and hit the floor with a thud that made the ceiling light hop on its flex. Helga knelt quickly beside her, muttered something in German, and laid a comforting woman's hand on her shoulder—a gentle, unaffected act. Mesterbein stooped to gaze at her but didn't touch her. His interest was directed more towards examining the way she wept.

She had her head sideways and she was resting her cheek on her clenched fist, so that the stream of her tears ran across her face instead of down it. Gradually, as he went on watching, her tears seemed to cheer him up. He gave a mousy nod that might have been approval; he stayed close while Helga manhandled her to the sofa, where she lay again, her face buried in the prickly cushions and her hands locked over her face, weeping as only the bereaved and children can. Turmoil, anger, guilt, remorse, terror: she perceived each one of them like the phases of a controlled, yet deeply felt performance. I knew; I didn't know; I didn't dare allow myself to think. You cheats, you murdering Fascist cheats, you bastards who killed my darling lover in the theatre of the real.

She must have said some of this aloud. Indeed she knew she had. She had monitored and selected her strangled phrases even while the grief tore at her: *You Fascist bastards, swine, oh Jesus, Michel.*

A pause, then she heard Mesterbein's unaltered voice inviting her to enlarge on this, but she ignored him and continued to roll her head from side to side behind her hands. She choked and retched and her words clogged in her throat and stumbled on her lips. The tears, the agony, the repeated sobs were no problem to her—she was on excellent terms with the sources of her grief and outrage. She did not need to think of her late father, hastened to his grave by the disgrace of her expulsion from school, nor paint herself as a tragic child in the wilderness of adult life, which was what she usually did. She had only to remember the half-tamed Arab boy who had restored her capacity for love, who had given her life the direction it had always craved, and who now was dead for the tears to come running on command.

"She says it was the Zionists," Mesterbein objected to Helga, in English. "Why does she say it was the Zionists when it was an accident? The police have assured us it was an accident. Why does she contradict the police? It is very dangerous to contradict police."

But Helga had either heard it already for herself or didn't care. She had put a coffee pot on the electric stove. Kneeling at Charlie's head, she pensively smoothed her red hair away from her face with her strong hand, waiting for her weeping to stop and her explanations to begin.

The coffee pot suddenly bubbled; Helga rose and tended it. Charlie sat on the sofa cradling her mug in both hands, bowed over it as if inhaling its vapour, while the tears ran steadily down her cheeks. Helga had her arm round Charlie's shoulder and Mesterbein sat opposite, peering out at the two women from the shades of his own dark world.

"It was an explosion accident," he said. "On the autobahn Salzburg–Munich. According to police, his car was full of explosive. Hundreds of pounds. Why? Why should explosive detonate suddenly, on a flat autobahn?"

"Your letters are safe," Helga whispered, drawing back another hank of Charlie's hair and tucking it lovingly behind her ear.

"The car was a Mercedes," Mesterbein said. "It had Munich licences, but the police say they are false. Also the papers. Forgeries. Why should my client drive a car with false papers and full of explosive? He was a student. He was not a bomber. It is a conspiracy, actually. I think so."

"Do you know this car, Charlie?" Helga murmured into her ear, and pressed her more fondly against her in an effort to coax an answer out of her. But all Charlie could see in her mind was her lover blown to pieces by two hundred pounds of Russian plastic explosive hidden in the valance, cross members, roof-lining, and seats: an inferno, tearing apart the body she adored. And all she could hear was the voice of her other nameless mentor saying: *Distrust them, lie to them, deny everything; reject, refuse.*

"She spoke something," said Mesterbein accusingly.

"She said 'Michel,' " said Helga, wiping away a fresh onslaught of tears with a sensible handkerchief from her handbag.

"A *girl* died also," Mesterbein said. "She was with him in the car, they say."

"A Dutch," Helga said softly, so close that Charlie could feel her breath upon her ear. "A real beauty. Blonde."

"They died together, apparently," Mesterbein continued, raising his voice.

"You were not the only one, Charlie," Helga explained confidingly. "You did not have the exclusive use of our little Palestinian, you know."

For the first time since they had broken the news to her, Charlie spoke a coherent sentence.

"I never asked for it," she whispered.

"The police say the Dutch was a terrorist," Mesterbein complained.

"They say also that *Michel* was a terrorist," said Helga.

"They say that the Dutch planted bombs for Michel several times already," said Mesterbein. "They say Michel and the girl were planning another action, and that in the car they found a city map of Munich with the Israeli Trade Centre marked in Michel's handwriting. On the River Isar," he added. "An upper floor—really a difficult target, actually. Did he speak to you of this action, Miss Charlie?"

Shivering, Charlie sipped a little coffee, which seemed to please Helga quite as well as a reply. "There! She is waking up at last. You want more coffee, Charlie? Shall I heat some? Food? We have cheese up here, eggs, sausage, we have everything."

Shaking her head, Charlie let Helga lead her to the lavatory, where she stayed a long time, throwing water in her face, retching, and between whiles wishing to Heaven that she knew enough German to follow the uneasy, staccato conversation that was reaching her through the paper-thin door.

She returned to find Mesterbein standing at the front door dressed in his gabardine trench coat.

"Miss Charlie, I remind you that Fräulein Helga is entitled to the full protection of the law," he said, and stalked out of the front door.

Alone at last. Girls together.

"Anton is a genius," Helga announced, with a laugh. "He is our guardian angel, he hates the law, but naturally he falls in love with what he hates. Do you agree? . . . Charlie, you must always agree with me. I am otherwise too disappointed." She drew nearer. "Violence is not the issue," she said, resuming a conversation they had not yet had. "Never. We make a violent action, we make a peaceful one, it is indifferent. The issue with us is to be logical, not to stand aside while the world runs itself, but to turn opinion into conviction and conviction into action." She paused, examining the effect of her statements upon her pupil. Their heads were very close. "Action is self-realisation, it is also objective. Yes?" Another pause, but still no answer. "You know something else that will surprise you completely? I have an excellent relationship with my parents. You, you are different. One sees it in your letters. Anton also. Naturally, my mother is the more intelligent, but my father—" She broke off again, but this time she was angered by Charlie's silence, and her renewed weeping.

"Charlie, stop now. *Stop,* okay? We are not old women finally. You loved him, we accept that as logical, but he is dead." Her voice had hardened surprisingly. "He is dead, but we are not individualists for private experience, we are fighters and workers. Stop weeping."

Grasping Charlie's elbow, Helga lifted her bodily to her feet and marched her slowly down the length of the room.

"Listen to me. Immediately. Once I had a very rich boyfriend. Kurt. Very fascistic, completely primitive. I used him for sex, like I use Anton, but also I tried to educate him. One day the German Ambassador in Bolivia, a Graf somebody, was executed by the freedom fighters. You remember this action? Kurt, who did not even know him, was immediately enraged: 'The swine! These terrorists! It's disgraceful!' I said to him, 'Kurt'—this was his name—'who do you mourn for? People starve to death every day in Bolivia. Why should we bother about one dead Graf?' You agree with this evaluation, Charlie? Yes?"

Charlie gave a faint shrug. Turning her round, Helga started the return journey.

"Now I take a harder argument. Michel is a martyr, but the dead cannot fight and there are many other martyrs also. One soldier is dead. The revolution continues. Yes?"

"Yes," Charlie whispered.

They had reached the sofa. Taking up her sensible handbag, Helga pulled out a flat half-bottle of whisky on which Charlie noticed a duty-free label. She unscrewed the cap and handed her the bottle.

"To Michel!" she declared. "We drink to him. To Michel. Say it."

Charlie took a small sip, pulled a face. Helga took back the bottle.

"Sit down, please. Charlie, I wish you to sit down. Immediately."

She sat listlessly on the sofa. Helga once more stood over her.

"You listen to me and you answer, okay? I do not come here for fun, you understand? Nor for discussions. I like to discuss but not now. Say 'Yes.'"

"Yes," said Charlie wearily.

"He was attracted to you. This is a scientific fact. Even infatuated, actually. There was an unfinished letter to you on the desk in his apartment, full of fantastic statements concerning love and sex. All for you. Also politics."

Slowly, as if the sense of this had only gradually got through to her, Charlie's blotched and twisted face became eager. "Where is it?" she said. "Give it to me!"

"It is being processed. In operations, everything must be evaluated, everything must be processed objectively."

Charlie started to her feet. "It's mine! Give it to me!"

"It is the property of the revolution. Possibly you shall have it later. One shall see." Not very gently, Helga pushed her back to the sofa. "This car. The Mercedes which is now an ash box. You drove it over the border into Germany? For Michel? A mission? Answer me."

"Austria," she muttered.

"Where from?"

"Through Yugoslavia."

"Charlie, I think you are seriously quite bad at accuracy: *where from?*"

"Thessalonika."

"And Michel accompanied you on the journey, of course he did. This was normal with him, I think."

"No."

"What no? You drove alone? So far? Ridiculous! He would never entrust you such a responsibility. I do not believe you one word. The whole story is lies."

"Who cares?" said Charlie, with a return to apathy.

Helga did. She was already furious. "Of course you don't care! If you are a spy, why should you care? It is already clear to me what happened. I need ask no more questions, they are pure formality. Michel recruited you, he made you his secret love, and as soon as you were able, you took your story to the police in order to protect yourself and make a fortune of money. You are a police spy. I shall report this to certain quite effective people we are in touch with and you will be taken care of, even if it is twenty years from now. Executed."

"Great," said Charlie. "Terrific." She stubbed out her

cigarette. "You do that, Helg. That's just exactly what I need. Send them round, will you? Room sixteen, up the hotel."

Helga had gone to the window and torn back the curtain, apparently intending to summon Mesterbein. Looking past her, Charlie saw his little hire car with the interior light on, and Mesterbein's hatted outline seated impassively in the driving seat.

Helga tapped on the window. "Anton? Anton, come here at once, we have a complete spy among us!" But her voice was too low for him, as she intended. "Why did Michel not tell us about you?" she demanded, closing the curtain again and turning round to face her. "Why did he not share you with us? You—his dark horse for so many months. It's too ridiculous!"

"He loved me."

"*Quatsch!* He was using you. You have his letters still—to you?"

"He ordered me to destroy them."

"But you didn't. Of course you didn't. How could you? You are a sentimental idiot, which may be seen immediately from your own letters to him. You exploited him, he spent money on you, clothes, jewels, hotels, and you sell him to the police. Of course you do!"

Finding herself close to Charlie's handbag, Helga picked it up and, on an impulse, tipped its contents over the dining-table. But the clues that were planted in it—the diary, the ballpoint pen from Nottingham, the matches from the Diogenes in Athens—were in her present mood too fine for her, she was looking for evidence of Charlie's treachery, not her devotion.

"This radio."

Her little Japanese job with an alarm clock on it for rehearsals.

"What is it? It is a spy device. Where does it come from? Why does a woman like you carry a radio in her handbag?"

Leaving her to her own preoccupations, Charlie turned away from her and stared sightlessly at the fire. Helga fiddled with the dials of the radio and picked up some music. She switched it off and put it irritably aside.

"In Michel's last letter that he did not post to you, he says you have kissed the gun. What does this mean?"

"It means I kissed his gun." She corrected herself. "His brother's gun."

Helga's voice rose abruptly. "His brother? What brother?"

"He had an elder brother. His hero. A great fighter. The brother gave him the gun, Michel made me kiss it as a pledge."

Helga was staring at her in disbelief. "Michel told you this?"

"I read it in the papers, didn't I?"

"*When* did he tell it to you?"

"On a hilltop in Greece."

"What else of this brother—quickly!" She almost screamed.

"Michel worshipped him. I told you."

"Give facts. Only facts. What else did he tell you about his brother?"

But Charlie's secret voice was telling her she had already gone far enough. "He's a military secret," she said, and helped herself to a fresh cigarette.

"Did he tell you where he is? What he is doing? Charlie, I order you to tell me!" She drew nearer. "Police, intelligence, maybe even the Zionists—everybody is looking for you. We have excellent relations with certain elements of the German police. They know already it was not the Dutch girl who drove the car through Yugoslavia. They have descriptions. They have many informations to incriminate you. If we wish, we can help you. But not until you have told everything that Michel has revealed to you about his brother." She leaned forward until her big pale eyes were not a hand's width from Charlie's own. "He had no right to talk to you about him. You have no right to this information. Give it to me."

Charlie considered Helga's application but after due reflection rejected it.

"No," she said.

She was intending to go on: I promised and that's it—I don't trust you—get off my back—but when she had listened to plain "no" for a time, she decided she liked it best alone.

Your job is to make them need you, Joseph had said.

Think of it as courtship. They will treasure most what they cannot have.

Helga had developed an unearthly composure. The histrionics were over. She had entered a period of ice-cold disconnection, which Charlie understood instinctively because it was something she could do herself.

"So. You drove the car to Austria. And then?"

"I dumped it where he told me, we met up and went to Salzburg."

"How?"

"Plane and car."

"And? In Salzburg?"

"We went to a hotel."

"The name of the hotel, please?"

"I don't remember. I didn't notice."

"Then describe it."

"It was old and big and near a river. And beautiful," she added.

"And you had sex. He was very virile, he had many orgasms, as usual."

"We went for a walk."

"And after the walk you had sex. Don't be silly, please."

Once more, Charlie let her wait. "We meant to, but I fell asleep as soon as we'd had dinner. I was exhausted from the drive. He tried to wake me a couple of times, then gave up. In the morning he was dressed by the time I woke."

"And then you went with him to Munich—yes?"

"No."

"So what did you do?"

"Caught an afternoon plane to London."

"What car did he have?"

"A hire car."

"What make?"

She pretended not to remember.

"Why did you not go with him to Munich?"

"He didn't want us crossing the border together. He said he had work to do."

"He *told* you this? Work to do? Nonsense! What work? No wonder you were able to betray him!"

"He said he had orders to pick up the Mercedes and deliver it somewhere for his brother."

This time Helga showed no astonishment, not even indignation, at the scale of Michel's abysmal indiscretion. Her mind was upon action, and action was what she believed in. Striding to the door, she flung it open and waved imperiously for Mesterbein to return. She swung round, hands on hips, and stared at Charlie, and her big pale eyes were a dangerous and alarming void.

"You are suddenly like Rome, Charlie," she remarked. "All roads lead to you. It is too perverse. You are his secret love, you drive his car, you spend his last night on earth with him. You knew what was in that car when you drove it?"

"Explosives."

"Nonsense. Of what sort?"

"Russian plastic, two hundred pounds of it."

"The police told you this. It is their lie. The police lie always."

"Michel told me."

Helga let out a false, angry laugh. "Oh, Charlie! Now I don't believe you one word. You are lying to me completely." With a soundless tread, Mesterbein loomed up behind her. "Anton, everything is known. Our little widow is a complete liar, I am sure of it. We shall do nothing to help her at all. We leave at once."

Mesterbein stared at her, Helga stared at her. Neither seemed half as certain as Helga's words suggested. Not that Charlie cared either way. She sat like a slumped doll, indifferent once more to anything except her own bereavement.

Sitting beside her again, Helga put her arm round Charlie's unresponsive shoulders. "What was the brother's name?" she said. "Come." She kissed her lightly on the cheekbone. "We shall be your friends perhaps. We must be careful, we must bluff a little. This is natural. All right, tell me first Michel's name."

"Salim, but I swore never to use it."

"And the brother's name?"

"Khalil," she muttered. She began weeping again. "Michel worshipped him," she said.

"And his workname?"

She didn't understand, she didn't care. "It was a military secret," she said.

She had decided to keep driving till she dropped—a Yugoslavia all over again. I'll walk out of the show, I'll go to Nottingham and kill myself in our motel bed.

She was on the moor again, alone and touching eighty before she nearly went off the road. She stopped the car and took her hands sharply from the wheel. The muscles in the back of her neck were twisting like hot wires and she felt sick.

She was sitting on the verge, putting her head forward between her knees. A couple of wild ponies had come over to stare at her. The grass was long and full of the dawn's dew. Trailing her hands, she moistened them and pressed them to her face to cool it. A motorcycle went slowly by and she saw a boy looking at her as if uncertain whether to stop and help. Between her fingers she watched him disappear below the skyline. One of ours, one of theirs? She returned to the car and wrote down the number; just for once, she didn't trust her memory. Michel's orchids lay on the seat beside her; she had claimed them when she took her leave.

"But, Charlie, don't be too utterly ridiculous!" Helga had protested. "You are too sentimental altogether."

And screw you too, Helg. They're mine.

She was on a high, treeless plateau of pink and brown and grey. Sunrise was in her driving mirror. Her car radio gave nothing but French. It sounded like question and answer about girlish problems, but she couldn't understand the words.

She was passing a sleeping blue caravan parked in a field. An empty Landrover stood beside it, and beside the Landrover baby linen hung from a telescopic clothesline. Where had she seen a clothesline like that before? Nowhere. Nowhere ever.

She lay on her bed at the guest house, watching the day lighten on the ceiling, listening to the clatter of the doves on her window-sill. *Most dangerous is when you come down from the mountain,* Joseph had warned. She heard a surreptitious footfall in the corridor. It's them. But which them? Always the same question. Red? No, Officer, I have never driven a red Mercedes in my life so get out of my bedroom. A drop of cold sweat ran over her naked stomach. In her mind, she traced its course across her navel to her ribs, then onto the sheet. A creak of floorboards, a suppressed puff of exertion: he's looking through the keyhole. A corner of white paper appeared beneath her door. And wriggled. And grew. Humphrey the fat-boy was delivering her *Daily Telegraph*.

She had bathed and dressed. She drove slowly, taking lesser roads, stopping at a couple of shops along the way, as he had taught her. She had dressed herself dowdily, her hair was anyhow. Nobody observing her numb manner and neglected appearance could have doubted her distress. The road darkened; diseased elm trees closed over her, an old Cornish church crouched among them. Stopping the car again, she pushed open the iron gate. The graves were very old. Few were marked. She found one that lay apart from the others. A suicide? A murderer? Wrong: a revolutionary. Kneeling, she reverently laid the orchids at the end where she had decided his head was. Impulse mourning, she thought, stepping into the bottled, ice-cold air of the church. Something Charlie would have done in the circumstances, in the theatre of the real.

For another hour she continued aimlessly in this way, pulling up for no reason at all, except perhaps to lean on a gate and stare at a field. Or to lean on a gate and stare at nothing. It wasn't till after twelve that she was certain the motorcyclist had finally stopped tailing her. Even then, she made several vague detours and sat in two more churches before joining the main road to Falmouth.

The hotel was a pantiled ranch on the Helford Estuary, with an indoor pool and a sauna and a nine-hole golf course and guests who looked like hoteliers themselves. She had been to the other hotels, but not, till now, to this one. He had signed in as a German publisher, bringing a stack of unreadable books with him to prove it. He had tipped the switchboard ladies lavishly, explaining that he had international correspondents who were no respecters of his sleep. The waiters and porters knew him as a good touch who sat up all hours of the night. He had lived that way under different names and pretexts for the last two weeks, as he stalked

Charlie's progress down the peninsula on his solitary safari. He had lain on beds and stared at ceilings as Charlie had. He had talked to Kurtz on the telephone, and kept himself abreast of Litvak's field operations hour by hour. He had talked to Charlie sparingly, fed her little meals, and taught her more tricks of secret writing and communications. He had been as much a prisoner to her as she to him.

He opened the door to her and she walked past him with a distracted frown, not knowing what to feel. Murderer. Bully. Cheat. But she had no appetite for the obligatory scenes; she had played them all, she was a burnt-out mourner. He was already standing as she entered, and she expected him to come forward and embrace her, but he stood his ground. She had never seen him so grave, so held back. Deep shadows of worry ringed his eyes. He was wearing a white shirt, sleeves rolled to the elbows—cotton, not silk. She stared at it, aware after all of what she felt. No cuff-links. No medallion at the neck. No Gucci shoes.

"You're on your own then," she said.

He did not follow her meaning.

"You can forget the red blazer, can't you? You're you and no one else. You've killed your own bodyguard. No one left to hide behind."

Opening her handbag, she handed him her little clock radio. From the table, he picked up her original model and dropped it into the handbag for her. "Oh indeed," he said with a laugh, closing her bag. "Our relationship is henceforth unmediated, I would say."

"How did I sound?" said Charlie. She sat down. "I thought I was the best thing since Bernhardt."

"Better. In Marty's view, the best thing since Moses came down the mountain. Maybe before he went up. If you wished, you could stop now with honour. They owe you enough. More than enough."

They, she thought. Never *we.* "And in Joseph's view?"

"Those are big people, Charlie. Big little people from the centre. The real thing."

"Did I fool them?"

He came and sat beside her. To be near but not to touch.

"Since you are still alive, we must assume that so far you fooled them," he said.

"Let's go," she said. A smart little tape-recorder lay ready on the table. Reaching past him, she switched it on. With no more preamble, they passed to the debriefing, like the old married couple they had become. For though Litvak's audio van had listened to every word of last night's conversation as it was transmitted by the cunningly adapted little radio in Charlie's handbag, the pure gold of her own perceptions had still to be mined and sifted.

18

The swift young man who called at the Israeli Embassy in London wore a long leather coat and granny glasses, and said his name was Meadows. The car was a spotless green Rover with extra pace. Kurtz sat in the front in order to keep Meadows company. Litvak smouldered in the back. Kurtz's manner was diffident and a little shabby, as became him in the presence of colonial superiors.

"Just flown in, have we, sir?" Meadows asked airily.

"Yesterday as ever is," said Kurtz, who had been in London a week.

"Pity you didn't let us know, sir. The Commander could have smoothed things over for you at the airport."

"Oh now, we didn't have *that* much to declare, Mr. Meadows!" Kurtz protested, and they both laughed because liaison was so good. From the back, Litvak laughed too, but without conviction.

They drove fast to Aylesbury, then fast through pretty lanes. They reached a sandstone gateway mastered by stone cockerels. A blue-and-red sign proclaimed "No. 3 TLSU," a white boom blocked their path. Meadows left Kurtz and Litvak to themselves while he went into the gatehouse. Dark eyes surveyed them from its windows. No cars passed, no distant tractor chattered. There seemed little around that was alive.

"Looks like a fine place," said Kurtz, in Hebrew, while they waited.

"Beautiful," Litvak agreed for the microphone, if there was one. "Nice people, too."

"First rate," said Kurtz. "Top of the profession, no question."

Meadows returned, the boom lifted, and for a surprisingly long time they wove through the uneasy parkland of paramilitary England. In place of sweetly grazing thoroughbreds, blue-uniformed sentries in Wellington boots. Low-backed brick buildings with no windows lay half buried in the earth. They passed an assault course and a private landing strip laid out with orange cones. Rope bridges were strung across a troutstream.

"A dream," said Kurtz politely. "Just beautiful, Mr. Meadows. We should have all this at home, but how can we?"

"Well, thanks," said Meadows.

The house had once been old but its façade was vandalised with ministerial paint of battleship blue, and the red flowers in the window-boxes were dressed strictly by the left. A second young man was waiting at the entrance and led them quickly up a glistening staircase of polished pine.

"I'm Lawson," he explained breathlessly, as if they were already late; and rapped bravely with his knuckles on a double door. A voice inside barked "Come!"

"Mr. Raphael, sir," Lawson announced. "From Jerusalem. Bit of bother with the traffic, I'm afraid, sir."

For as long as it takes to be rude, Deputy Commander Picton stayed seated at his desk. He took up a pen and, with a frown, signed his name on a letter. He looked up, and fixed Kurtz with a yellow-eyed stare. Then he leaned his head right forward as though he were about to butt someone, and lifted himself slowly to his feet, all the way, until he was standing to attention.

"And good day to you, Mr. Raphael," he said. And he smiled sparsely, as if smiles were out of season.

He was big and Aryan, with waved fair hair parted like a razor slash. He was broad and thick-faced and violent, with pressed-together lips and a bully's straight gaze. He had the senior policeman's fastidious bad grammar and the borrowed good manners of a gentleman, and both were returnable without notice any time he damn well felt like it. He had a spotted handkerchief stuffed in his left sleeve and a tie with flat gold crowns to tell you he played his games in better company than you. He was a self-made counter-terrorist, "part soldier, part copper, part villain," as he liked to say, and he belonged to the fabled generation of his trade. He had hunted Communists in Malaya and Mau Mau in Kenya, Jews in Palestine, Arabs in Aden, and the Irish everywhere. He had blown people up with the Trucial Oman Scouts; in Cyprus he had missed Grivas by a whisker and when he was drunk he talked of it with regret—but let anybody dare to pity him! He had been second man in several places, first man rarely, for there were other shadows too.

"Misha Gavron in good shape?" he enquired, selecting a button on his telephone and pushing it so hard it might never come up again.

"Commander, Misha is just fine!" said Kurtz enthusiastically, and started to ask after Picton's superior in return, but Picton was not interested in what Kurtz might have to say, least of all about his Chief.

A highly polished silver cigarette box lay prominently on his desk with the signatures of brother officers engraved on the lid. Picton opened it and held it out, if only for Kurtz to admire its shine. Kurtz said he did not smoke. Picton returned the box to its correct position, an exhibit disposed of. There was a knock at the door and two men were admitted, one grey, one tweed. The grey was a forty-year-old Welsh bantamweight with claw marks on the lower jaw. Picton described him as "my Chief Inspector."

"Never ever been to Jerusalem, I'm afraid, sir," the Chief Inspector announced, rising on his toes and pulling down the skirts of his jacket at the same time, as if he were trying to stretch himself an inch or two. "The wife's all for spending Christmas in Bethlehem, but Cardiff was always good enough for me, oh yes!"

The tweeded one was Captain Malcolm, who possessed the class that Picton sometimes longed for and always hated. Malcolm had a soft-toned courtesy that was its own aggression.

"Honour, sir, actually," he confided to Kurtz very sincerely, and gave his hand before Kurtz needed it.

But when Litvak's turn came, Captain Malcolm appeared not quite to grasp his name: "Say again, old boy?" he said.

"Levene," Litvak repeated, not quite so softly. "I have the good fortune to work with Mr. Raphael here."

A long table was laid for a conference. There were no pictures—no framed photograph of a wife, not even of the Queen in Kodachrome. The sash windows gave on to an empty yard. The one surprise was the lingering smell of warm oil, as if a submarine had just passed by.

"Well, why don't you simply shoot straight off then,

Mr."—the pause was really much too long—"Raphael, isn't it?" said Picton.

The phrase at least had a curious aptness. As Kurtz unlocked his briefcase and started handing round the dossiers, the room was shaken by the long thud of an explosive charge detonated in controlled circumstances.

"I *knew* a Raphael once," said Picton as he lifted the top cover of his dossier and peered inside, like a first peek at a menu. "We made him mayor for a while. Young chap. Forget the town. Wasn't you, was it?"

With a sad smile, Kurtz regretted that he was not that lucky person.

"No relation? Raphael—like the painter chap?" Picton turned a couple of pages. "Still, you never know, do you?"

The forbearance in Kurtz was unearthly. Not even Litvak, who had seen him through a hundred different shades of his identity, could have predicted such a saintly muzzling of his demons. His roistering energy had disappeared entirely, to be replaced by the servile smile of the underdog. Even his voice, at least to start with, had a diffident, apologetic ring.

" 'Mesterbine,' " the Chief Inspector read out. "Is that the way we pronounce it?"

Captain Malcolm, anxious to show his languages, intercepted the question. " 'Mesterbein' it is, Jack."

"Personal particulars in the left pocket, gentlemen," Kurtz said indulgently, and paused to let them plunder their dossiers for a little longer. "Commander, we have to have your formal undertaking regarding use and distribution."

Picton slowly lifted his fair head. "In writing?" he asked.

Kurtz gave a deprecating grin. "A British officer's word will surely be enough for Misha Gavron," he said, still waiting.

"Agreed then," said Picton, with an unmistakable flush of anger; and Kurtz passed quickly to the less contentious person of Anton Mesterbein.

"The father a conservative Swiss gentleman with a nice villa on the lakeside, Commander, no known interests beyond making money. The mother a free-thinking lady of the radical left, spends half the year in Paris, keeps a salon there, very popular among the Arab community—"

"Ring a bell, Malcolm?" Picton interrupted.

"A faint tinkle, sir."

"Young Anton, the son, is a lawyer of substance," Kurtz continued. "Studied political science in Paris, philosophy in Berlin. Attended Berkeley for a year, law and politics. Rome a semester, four years in Zürich, graduated *magna cum laude*."

"An intellectual," said Picton. He might as well have said "leper."

Kurtz acknowledged the description. "Politically, we would say that Mr. Mesterbein leans the mother's way—financially, he favours the father."

Picton let out the huge laugh of a humourless man. Kurtz paused long enough to share the joke with him.

"The photograph before you was taken in Paris, but Mr. Mesterbein's legal practice is in Geneva, effectively a down-town law shop for radical students, Third Worlders, and guestworkers. A variety of progressive organisations short of money are also clients." He turned a page, inviting his audience to keep pace with him. He was wearing heavy spectacles on the tip of his nose and they gave him the mousiness of a bank clerk.

"Got him, Jack?" Picton asked of the Chief Inspector.

"Not a tremor, sir."

"Who's the blonde lady drinking with him, sir?" asked Captain Malcolm.

But Kurtz had his own march route and, for all his docile manners, Malcolm was not going to deflect him.

"Last November," Kurtz continued, "Mr. Mesterbein attended a conference of so-called Lawyers for Justice in East Berlin, at which the Palestine delegation got a somewhat over-lengthy hearing. However, that may be a partial view," he added, with meek joviality, but no one laughed. "In April, responding to an invitation extended to him on that occasion, Mr. Mesterbein made his first recorded visit to Beirut. Paid his respects to a couple of the more militant rejectionist organisations there."

"Touting for business, was he?" Picton enquired.

As Picton said this, he clenched his right fist and punched the air. Having thus freed his hand, he scribbled something on the pad before him. Then he tore off the sheet and passed it to the suave Malcolm, who, with a smile to everybody, quietly left the room.

"Returning from that same visit to Beirut," Kurtz continued, "Mr. Mesterbein stopped over in Istanbul, in which city he held dialogues with certain underground Turkish activists committed, among other goals, to the elimination of Zionism."

"Ambitious chaps, then," said Picton.

And this time, because it was Picton's joke, everybody laughed loudly, except for Litvak.

With surprising speed, Malcolm had returned from his errand. "Not a *lot* of joy, I'm afraid," he murmured silkily and, having passed the slip of paper back to Picton, smiled at Litvak and resumed his seat. But Litvak seemed to have gone to sleep. He had rested his chin in his long hands and tipped his head forward over his unopened dossier. His expression, thanks to his hands, was not defined.

"Told the Swiss any of this, have you?" Picton enquired, tossing Malcolm's bit of paper aside.

"Commander, we have not yet informed the Swiss," Kurtz confessed, in a tone that suggested that this raised a problem.

"I thought you chaps were pretty close to the Swiss," Picton objected.

"We surely are close to the Swiss. However, Mr. Mesterbein has a number of clients who are wholly or partly domiciled in the Federal Republic of Germany, a fact which places us in a fairly embarrassing position."

"Don't follow you," said Picton stubbornly. "Thought you and the Huns had kissed and made up long ago."

Kurtz's smile might have been starched into his skin, but his answer was a model of bland evasion. "Commander, that is so, but nevertheless Jerusalem still feels—given the sensitivity of our sources and the complexity of German political sympathy at this present time—that we cannot advise our Swiss friends without also advising their German counterparts. To do so would be to impose an unfair burden of silence upon the Swiss in their dealings with Wiesbaden."

Picton had a good way with silence himself. In its day, his liverish stare of disbelief had done wonders with men of lesser breed who were worrying about what might happen to them next.

"I suppose you heard they put that twerp Alexis back in the hot seat, did you?" Picton asked, out of the blue. Something about Kurtz was beginning to hold him: a recognition, if not of the person, then of the species.

Kurtz had heard the news, naturally, he said. But it did not appear to have affected him, for he moved firmly to the next exhibit.

"Hang on," said Picton quietly. He was staring into his dossier, exhibit 2. "I know that beauty. He's the genius who scored an own goal on the Munich autobahn a month back. Took his piece of Dutch crumpet with him too, didn't he?"

Neglecting his mantle of assumed humility for a moment, Kurtz stepped in fast. "Commander, that is so, and it is our information that both the vehicle and the explosives in that unfortunate accident were supplied by Mr. Mesterbein's contacts in Istanbul and ferried northward through Yugoslavia into Austria."

Picking up the scrap of paper that Malcolm had restored to him, Picton began moving it back and forth in front of him as if he were short-sighted, which he was not. "I am advised that our magic box downstairs contains not a single Mesterbein," he announced with feigned carelessness. "Not white-listed, not black-listed, not bugger all."

Kurtz seemed pleased rather than the reverse: "Commander, this reflects no inefficiency on the part of your fine records department. Until a matter of days ago, I would say, Mr. Mesterbein has also been regarded by Jerusalem as innocuous. The same goes for his accomplices."

"Including Blondie?" Captain Malcolm asked, harking back to Mesterbein's lady companion.

But Kurtz only smiled, and tugged a little at his spectacles as a way of calling the attention of his audience to the next photograph. It was one of many that the Munich surveillance team had taken from across the street, and it showed Yanuka by night about to enter the street door to his own apartment. It was fuzzed, as infra-red pictures on slow speed tend to be, but it showed him clearly enough for identification purposes. He was in the company of a tall blonde woman in quarter profile. She was standing back while he put a house key into the front door, and she was the same woman who had already caught Captain Malcolm's fancy from the earlier photograph.

"Where are we now?" said Picton. "Not Paris any more. Buildings are wrong."

"Munich," said Kurtz, and gave the address.

"And the *when*?" Picton demanded, so brusquely that one might have imagined he had momentarily mistaken Kurtz for one of his own staff.

But Kurtz again chose to mishear the question. "The name of the lady is Astrid Berger," he said, and once again Picton's yellowed gaze settled on him with an air of informed suspicion.

Deprived for too long of major speeches, meanwhile, the Welsh policeman had chosen to read Miss Berger's particulars aloud from the dossier: " 'Berger, Astrid, alias Edda alias Helga'—alias you name it . . . 'born Bremen '54, daughter of a wealthy shipping owner.' You do move in fine circles, I will say, Mr. Raphael. 'Educated universities of Bremen and Frankfurt, graduated politics and philosophy 1978. Sometime contributor West German radical and satirical journals, last known address 1979, Paris, frequent visitor Middle East—' "

Picton cut him short. "Another bloody intellectual. Get her, Malcolm."

As Malcolm again slipped from the room, Kurtz deftly took back the initiative.

"If you will kindly compare the dates there a little, Commander, you will find that Miss Berger's most recent visit to Beirut occurred in April this year, thus coinciding with Mr. Mesterbein's own tour. She was also in Istanbul during Mr. Mesterbein's stopover there. They flew different flights but stayed in the same hotel. Yes, Mike. Please."

Litvak's offering was a couple of photocopied hotel registration forms for Mr. Anton Mesterbein and Miss Astrid Berger, dated April 18th. Beside them, much reduced by reproduction, was a receipted bill, paid by Mesterbein. The hotel was the Hilton, Istanbul. While Picton and the Chief Inspector studied them, the door once more opened and closed.

"NRA on Astrid Berger too, sir. Can you *believe* it?" said Malcolm, with the most forlorn of smiles.

"Is that Nothing Recorded Against, please?" Kurtz enquired swiftly.

Taking up his silver propelling pencil with the tips of both hands, Picton revolved it before his dyspeptic gaze.

"It is," he said thoughtfully. "It is. Go to the top of the class, Mr. Raphael."

Kurtz's third photograph—or, as Litvak later irreverently called it, his third card in the trick—had been so beautifully forged that even the best guess of Tel Aviv's aerial reconnaissance experts had failed to pick it out from the bunch that they had been invited to inspect. It showed Charlie and Becker approaching the Mercedes in the forecourt of the Delphi hotel on the morning of their departure. Becker was carrying Charlie's shoulder bag and his own black grip. Charlie was in her Greek finery and carrying her guitar. Becker was wearing the red blazer, silk shirt, and Gucci shoes. He had his gloved hand stretched towards the driving door of the Mercedes. He was also wearing Michel's head.

"Commander, this picture was taken by a lucky chance just two weeks before the bomb incident outside Munich, in which, as you rightly say, a certain pair of terrorists had the misfortune to destroy themselves with their own explosives. The red-headed girl in the foreground is a British subject. Her escort addressed her as 'Joan.' She called him in return 'Michel,' which was not, however, the name on his passport."

The change in atmosphere was like a sudden drop in temperature. The Chief Inspector smirked at Malcolm, Malcolm seemed to smile in return; but then Malcolm's smile, it was becoming slowly clear, had little to do with what commonly passes for humour. But it was Picton's massive immobility that held the centre stage—his refusal, as it seemed, to take his information from anywhere but the photograph before him. For Kurtz, by his reference to a British subject, had ventured as if unawares upon Picton's holy territory, and men did that at their peril.

"*A lucky chance,*" Picton echoed through tight lips while he went on staring at the photograph. "A *good friend* who just happened to have his camera ready, I suppose—that sort of lucky bloody chance."

Kurtz grinned shyly but said nothing.

"Banged off a couple of frames—sent 'em to Jerusalem on the off-chance. Terrorist he happened to spot on holiday—thought he'd be helpful."

Kurtz's grin broadened; and to his surprise, he saw Picton grinning in return, if not very nicely.

"Yes, well, I think I *do* remember friends like that. You

people have friends everywhere, now I come to think of it. High places, low places, rich places—" For an unfortunate moment, it appeared that certain old frustrations of Picton's days in Palestine had unexpectedly revived themselves and were threatening to spill out of him in a gush of temper. But he contained himself. He tamed his features, he brought his voice down. He relaxed his smile until it could have passed for friendly. But Kurtz's smile was an all-weather thing, and Litvak's face was so twisted by his hand that for all anybody knew he could as well have been laughing his head off or nursing a raging toothache.

Clearing his throat, the grey Chief Inspector, with Welsh bonhomie, ventured another timely intervention. "Well now, even given she *was* English, sir, which seems to me on the face of it something of a hypothetical longshot, there's still no *law*, is there, not in this country, against sleeping with Palestinians? We can't mount a nationwide hunt for a lady, just on account of *that*! My goodness, if we—"

"He's got more," said Picton, returning his gaze to Kurtz. "*Much* more."

But his tone went further. *They always do have,* he was saying.

His courteous good humour undimmed, Kurtz invited his audience to study the Mercedes to the right of the photograph. Forgive him for not knowing too much about cars, but his people assured him this was a saloon model, wine red, with the radio aerial forward on the offside wing, two wing mirrors, central locking, and seat belts in the front only. In all of these details, and many others not visible, he said, the Mercedes in the picture corresponded to the Mercedes that had been accidentally blown up outside Munich, and of which most of the front had miraculously survived.

Malcolm had a sudden solution. "But surely, sir—all this about her being English—isn't she the *Dutch* girl? Red hair, blonde hair—that doesn't mean a thing. *English* in this case just means their common language."

"Quiet," Picton ordered, and lit himself a cigarette without offering them to anyone. "Let him go on," he said. And drank in a huge amount of smoke without expelling it.

Kurtz's voice meanwhile had thickened, and so, for a moment at least, had his shoulders. He had placed both fists on the table either side of the dossier.

"It is also our information by a different source, Commander," Kurtz announced, with greater force, "that on its northward journey from Greece through Yugoslavia, the same Mercedes was driven by a young woman with a British passport. Her lover did not accompany her, but flew ahead to Salzburg with Austrian Airlines. The same airline was privileged to reserve prestige accommodation for him in Salzburg, at the hotel Österreichischer Hof, where our enquiries show that the couple called themselves Monsieur and Madame Laserre, though the lady in question spoke no French, only English. This lady is remembered for her striking looks, her red hair, the absence of a wedding ring, for her guitar, which caused a certain merriment, also for the fact that though she left the hotel early in the morning with her husband, she returned later in the day to make use of its facilities. The head porter recalls summoning a taxi for Madame Laserre to take her to Salzburg Airport and he remembers the time of day he ordered it—2 p.m., just before he went off duty. He offered to confirm her flight reservation and establish that her plane's departure was not delayed, but Madame Laserre would not permit him to do this, presumably because she was not travelling under that name. Three flights out of Salzburg fit the timing, one of them Austrian to London. The lady at the Austrian Airlines sales desk distinctly recalls a red-headed English girl who had an unused charter ticket Thessalonika to London, and wished to have it rewritten, which was not possible. In the event, she was obliged to buy a full-fare one-way ticket, which she paid for in U.S. dollars, mostly twenty bills."

"Don't be so damn coy," Picton growled. "What's her name?" And he stubbed out his cigarette very violently, holding it down long after it had ceased to struggle.

In answer to his question, Litvak was already passing round photocopies of a passenger list. He looked pale and might have been in pain. When he had gone all the way round the table, he helped himself to a little water from the carafe, though he had barely breathed a word all morning.

"To our initial consternation, Commander, there was no Joan," Kurtz confessed as they all settled to the passenger list. "The best we could come up with was a Charmian. Her surname you have before you. The Austrian Airlines lady confirms our identification—number thirty-eight on the list.

The lady even remembers her guitar. By a happy chance, she is herself a devotee of the great Manitas de Plata; the guitar therefore left a deep impression on her memory."

"Another bloody friend," said Picton coarsely, and Litvak coughed.

Kurtz's last exhibit also came from Litvak's briefcase. Kurtz held out both hands for it, Litvak placed it into them: a wad of photographs still tacky from the printing pan. He dealt them out summarily. They showed Mesterbein and Helga in an airport departure lounge, Mesterbein staring despondently into the middle air. Helga, behind him, was buying a half-litre bottle of duty-free whisky. Mesterbein was carrying a bunch of orchids wrapped in tissue paper.

"Charles de Gaulle Airport, Paris, thirty-six hours ago," Kurtz said cryptically. "Berger and Mesterbein, about to fly Paris–Exeter via Gatwick. Mesterbein ordered a self-drive Hertz car to be available to him on arrival at Exeter Airport. They returned to Paris yesterday, minus the orchids, by the same route. Berger was travelling under the name of Maria Brinkhausen, Swiss, a new alias we may add to her many others. Her passport, one of a bunch prepared by the East Germans for Palestinian use."

Malcolm had not waited for the order. He was already through the door.

"Pity you haven't got a shot of them arriving in Exeter too," said Picton with innuendo, while they waited.

"Commander, as you well know, we could not do that," said Kurtz piously.

"Do I?" said Picton. "Oh."

"Our masters have a reciprocal trading deal, sir. No fishing in one another's waters without prior consent in writing."

"Oh *that*," said Picton.

The Welsh policeman once more applied his diplomatic unction. "Exeter her home town, is it, sir?" he asked Kurtz. "Devon girl? You wouldn't think a country girl would take to terror, not in the normal way of things, I suppose?"

But Kurtz's information seemed to have stopped dead at the English coast. They heard footsteps mounting the big staircase, and the squeak of Malcolm's suède boots. The Welshman, never daunted, tried again.

"I never think of red-heads as *Devon*, somehow, I will say," he lamented. "Nor *Charmian*, truthfully, to be honest.

Bess, Rose, I suppose—I can see a Rose. But not Charmian, not Devon. Up country, I'd say *Charmian* was. London, more likely."

Malcolm came in warily, one soft tread following cautiously upon the other. He was carrying a heap of files: the fruit of Charlie's forays into the militant left. Those at the bottom were tattered with age and use. Press cuttings and cyclostyled pamphlets poked from the edges.

"Well I must say, sir," said Malcolm, with a grunt of relief as he set his burden on the table, "if she's *not* our girl, she jolly well ought to be!"

"Lunch," Picton snapped, and, having muttered a quite furious stream of orders to his two subordinates, marched his guests to a vast dining-room smelling of cabbage and furniture polish.

A pineapple chandelier hung over the thirty-foot table, two candles burned, two stewards in shining white coats attended their every need. Picton ate woodenly; Litvak, deathly pale, picked at his food like an invalid. But Kurtz was oblivious to everybody's tantrums. He chatted, though nothing in the way of business, naturally: he doubted whether the Commander would recognise Jerusalem, if ever he had the fortune to go back there; he really appreciated his first meal in an English officers' mess. Even then, Picton did not stay the meal through. Twice, Captain Malcolm summoned him to the door for a murmured conversation; once he was required on the telephone by his superior. And when the pudding came, he suddenly stood up as if he had been stung, handed his damask napkin to the servant, and strode off, ostensibly to make some phone calls of his own, but perhaps also to consult the locked cupboard in his office where he kept a private store.

The park, apart from the ever-present sentries, was as empty as a school playing field on the first day of holidays, and Picton strolled in it with the faddish restlessness of a landowner, grumpily eyeing the fences, stabbing with his walking stick at anything he didn't like the look of. Nine inches below him, Kurtz bobbed cheerfully at his side. From a distance, they might have resembled a prisoner and his captor, though it would not have been quite certain which was

which. Behind them trailed Shimon Litvak holding both
briefcases, and, behind Litvak, Mrs. O'Flaherty, Picton's
fabled Alsatian bitch.

"Mr. Levene likes to listen, does he?" Picton burst out,
quite loud enough for Litvak to hear. "Good listener, good
memory? I like that."

"Mike is close, Commander," Kurtz replied with a dutiful smile. "Mike comes everywhere."

"Sulky chap, he strikes me as. My Chief said a one-to-
one, if it's all the same to you."

Kurtz turned and said something to Litvak in Hebrew.
Litvak dropped back until he was out of earshot. And it was
a strange thing, which neither Kurtz nor Picton could quite
have explained, even if they had admitted to it, that an indefinable sense of comradeship settled over them as soon as
they were left alone.

The afternoon was grey and blustery. Picton had lent
Kurtz a duffle coat, which gave him a sea-dog look. Picton
himself wore a British Warm, and his face had darkened instantly with the fresh air.

"Decent of you to come all this way really, just to tell us
about her," said Picton, like a challenge. "My Chief's going to
drop old Misha a line, the devil."

"Misha will surely appreciate that," said Kurtz without
enquiring which devil Picton was referring to.

"Funny, really, all the same. You chaps tipping us off
about our own terrorists. In my day the traffic tended to go
the other way."

Kurtz said something soothing about the wheel of history, but Picton was no poet.

"Your operation, of course," said Picton. "Your sources,
your shout. My Chief is adamant about it. Our job is to sit
tight and do what we're bloody told," he added, with a sideways glance.

Kurtz said cooperation was what it was all about these
days, and for a second Picton looked as though he might
blow up. His yellowed eyes widened, and his chin shot into
his neck and stuck there. But instead, perhaps to calm himself, he lit a cigarette, turning his back on the wind and cup-
ping his huge catcher's hands to shield the flame.

"Meanwhile, you'll be amazed to hear your information
is confirmed," Picton said, with the heaviest sarcasm, as he

flicked away the match. "Berger and Mesterbein flew Paris–Exeter return, took a Hertz car on arrival Exeter Airport, notched up four hundred and twenty miles. Mesterbein paid by American Express credit card in his own name. Don't know where they spent the night, but no doubt you'll advise us in due course."

Kurtz preserved a virtuous silence.

"As to the lady in the case," Picton went on, with the same forced levity, "you will be equally astonished to hear that she is currently doing a spot of acting in deepest Cornwall. She's with a classical drama group, name of the Heretics, which I like, but you wouldn't know that either, would you? Her hotel says a man answering Mesterbein's description picked her up after the show and she didn't get home till morning. Proper little bedhopper by the sound of her, your lady." He allowed a monumental pause, which Kurtz affected to ignore. "Meanwhile, I am to advise you that my Chief is an officer and a gentleman and will provide you with every assistance. He's grateful, my Chief is. Grateful and touched. He's soft on Jews and he thinks it's very handsome of you to take the trouble to come over here and put us on to her." He shot Kurtz a malevolent glance. "My Chief is young, you see. He's a great fan of your fine new country, barring accidents, and not disposed to listen to any nasty suspicions *I* might have."

Stopping before a big green shed, Picton thumped his stick on the iron door. A boy in running shoes and a blue tracksuit admitted them to an empty gymnasium. "Saturday," Picton said, presumably to explain the atmosphere of desertion, and launched himself upon an angry tour of the premises, now eyeing the state of the changing-rooms, now running an enormous finger along the parallel bars to check for dust.

"I hear you've been bombing those camps again," Picton said accusingly. "That Misha's idea, is it? Misha never did like a rapier when a blunderbuss would do."

Kurtz began to confess quite truthfully that the processes of decision-taking in the upper levels of Israeli society had always been something of a mystery to him; but Picton had no time for that type of answer.

"Well, he won't get away with it. You tell him that from

me. Those Pallies will come back to haunt you lot for the rest of time."

This time Kurtz only smiled and shook his head in wonder at the world's ways.

"Misha Gavron was Irgun, wasn't he?" Picton said, in merest curiosity.

"Haganah," Kurtz corrected him.

"Which was your lot then?" said Picton.

Kurtz affected the loser's shy regret. "Fortunately or not, Commander, we Raphaels arrived in Israel too late to be of any inconvenience to the British," he said.

"Don't bullshit me," said Picton. "*I* know where Misha gets his friends from. I gave him his bloody job."

"So he told me, Commander," Kurtz said, with his waterproof smile.

The athletic boy was holding open a door. They passed through. In a long glass case lay a display of homemade weapons for silent killing: a knobkerrie with nails driven into the head, a hat-pin, very rusty, with a wooden handle added, homemade syringes, an improvised garrotte.

"Labels fading," Picton snapped at the boy when he had regarded these instruments nostalgically for a moment. "New labels by ten hundred hours Monday, hear me, or I'll have you."

He stepped back into the fresh air, Kurtz plodding agreeably at his side. Mrs. O'Flaherty, who had waited for them, fell in at her master's heels.

"All right, what do you want?" said Picton, like a man driven against his will to settle. "Don't tell me you came here to bring me a love-letter from my old mate Misha the Rook, because I won't believe you. I doubt whether I'll believe you anyway, as a matter of fact. I'm hard to convince, where your lot's concerned."

Kurtz smiled and shook his head in appreciation of Picton's English wit.

"Well, sir, Misha the Rook feels that a simple arrest in this case is just out of the question. Owing to the delicacy of our sources, naturally," he explained, in the tone of a mere messenger.

"I thought your sources were all just good friends," Picton put in nastily.

"And even if Misha were to consent to a formal arrest,"

Kurtz continued, still smiling, "he asks himself what charges could be filed against the lady and in what court. Who is to prove the explosive was aboard that car when she drove it? The explosive was put aboard afterwards, she will say. Which leaves us, I believe, with the somewhat minor infringement of driving a car through Yugoslavia on false papers. And where *are* those papers? Who is to prove they ever existed? It's very flimsy."

"Very," Picton agreed. "Misha become a lawyer, has he, in his old age?" he enquired, with a sideways look. "Christ, that would be a case of poacher turned gamekeeper if ever I heard one."

"There is also—Misha argues—the matter of her value. Her value to us, and to yourselves, as she stands at present. In what we might call her state of near innocence. What does she *know* finally? What can she *reveal*? Take the case of Miss Larsen."

"Larsen?"

"The Dutch lady who was involved in the unfortunate accident outside of Munich."

"What of her?" Stopping in his tracks, Picton turned to Kurtz and glowered down on him with growing suspicion.

"Miss Larsen also drove cars and ran errands for her Palestinian boyfriend. The same boyfriend, as a matter of fact. Miss Larsen even placed bombs for him. Two. Maybe three. On paper, Miss Larsen was a very implicated lady." Kurtz shook his head. "But in terms of usable intelligence, Commander, she was an empty vessel." Unaffected by Picton's menacing proximity, Kurtz lifted his hands and opened them to show how empty the vessel was. "Just a little groupie kid who liked the scene, who liked the danger and the boys, and liked to please. And they told her nothing. No addresses, no names, no plans."

"How do you know that?" said Picton accusingly.

"We had a little talk with her."

"When?"

"A while ago. Quite some while. A little sell-and-tell deal, before we threw her back into the pool. You know the way it goes."

"Like five minutes before you blew her up, I suppose," Picton suggested, as his yellowed eyes continued to hold Kurtz in their stare.

But Kurtz's smile was wonderfully unruffled. "If it were only so easy, Commander," he said, with a sigh.

"I asked what you wanted, Mr. Raphael."

"We'd like her set in motion, Commander."

"I thought you might."

"We'd like her smoked out a little, but not arrested. We'd like her running scared—so scared maybe that she is obliged to make further contact with her people, or they with her. We'd like to take her all the way through. What we call an unconscious agent. Naturally, we would share the product with you, and when the operation is over, you are welcome to both the lady and the credit."

"She's made contact already," Picton objected. "They came and saw her in Cornwall, brought her a bunch of bloody flowers, didn't they?"

"Commander, our reading of that meeting suggests to us that it was a somewhat exploratory exercise. Left to itself, we fear that the meeting is unlikely to bear further fruit."

"How the hell do you know *that*?" Picton's voice filled with a marvelling wrath. "*I'll* tell you how you know. You had your ear pressed up to the bloody keyhole! What do you think I am, Mr. Raphael? Some kind of jungle nignog? That girl belongs to you, Mr. Raphael, I know she does! I know you Izzies, I know that poison dwarf Misha, and I'm beginning to know *you*!" His voice had risen alarmingly. Striding out ahead of Kurtz, he waited until he had brought it under control. Then waited again till Kurtz fell in beside him. "I have a very nice scenario in my mind at this moment, Mr. Raphael, and I'd like to share it with you. May I do that?"

"It will be a privilege, Commander," said Kurtz pleasantly.

"Thank you. The trick is normally done with dead meat. You find a nice corpse, you dress him up and leave him somewhere where the enemy will stumble on him. 'Hullo,' says the enemy, 'what's this? A dead body carrying a briefcase? Let's look inside.' They look, and they find a little message. 'Hullo,' they say, 'he must have been a courier! Let's read the message and fall into the trap.' So they do. And we all get medals. 'Disinformation,' we used to call it, designed to misguide the enemy's eye, and very nice too." Picton's sarcasm was as awesome as his wrath. "But that's too simple for you and Misha. Being a bunch of over-educated fanatics, you've gone one further. 'No dead meat for us, *oh no!* We'll use *live* meat. Arab meat. Dutch meat.' So you did. And you blew it up in a nice Mercedes motorcar. Theirs. What I don't know, of course—and I never will, because you and Misha will deny the whole thing on your deathbeds, won't you?—is where you've planted that disinformation. But planted it you have, and now they've bitten. Or they'd never have brought her those nice flowers, would they?"

Ruefully shaking his head in admiration of Picton's amusing fantasy, Kurtz started to move away from him, but Picton with a policeman's unerring touch lightly held him where he was.

"You tell this to Master bloody Gavron. If I'm right and you lot have recruited one of our nationals without our consent, I'll personally come over to his nasty little country and take his balls off. Got it?" But suddenly, as if against his wish, Picton's face relaxed into an almost tender smile of recollection. "What was it the old devil used to say?" he asked. "Tigers, was it? *You'd* know."

Kurtz said it too. Often. Grinning his pirate's grin, he said it now. "You want to catch the lion, first you tether the goat."

The moment of adversarial kinship past, Picton's features once more set to stone. "And at the formal level, Mr. Raphael, compliments of my Chief, your service has got itself a deal," he snapped. Swinging on his heel, he marched briskly back towards the house, leaving Kurtz and Mrs. O'Flaherty to plod after him. "And tell him this too," Picton added, pointing his stick at Kurtz in a final assertion of his colonial authority. "He will please to stop using our bloody passports. If other people can manage without them, so can the Rook, damn him."

For the return journey to London, Kurtz sat Litvak in the front seat of the car to teach him English manners. Meadows, who had grown a voice, wanted to discuss the problem of the West Bank: how could one solve the thing, actually, sir, while giving the Arabs a fair deal, of course, do you think? Cutting himself off from their futile conversation, Kurtz abandoned himself to memories he had held at bay till now.

There is a working gallows in Jerusalem where nobody is hanged any more. Kurtz knew it well: close to the old Russian compound, on the left-hand side as you drive down a half-made road and stop before a pair of aged gates that lead to what was once Jerusalem's central prison. The signs say "TO THE MUSEUM" but also "HALL OF HEROISM" and there is a rather cracked old man who loiters outside and bows you in, sweeping his shallow black hat in the dust. The entrance fee is fifteen shekels but rising. It is where the British hanged the Jews during the Mandate time, from a noose with a leather lining to it. Only a handful, actually, and they hanged Arabs galore; but this was where they hanged two of Kurtz's friends, in the years when he was in the Haganah with Misha Gavron. Kurtz might well have joined them. They had imprisoned him twice and interrogated him four times, and the occasional troubles he had with his teeth were still ascribed by his dentist to the beatings he had received at the hand of an amiable young field security officer, now dead, whose manner, though not his looks, reminded him a little of Picton's.

But a nice man, that Picton, all the same, thought Kurtz, with an inward smile, as he contemplated yet another successful step along the road. A little rough maybe; a little heavy with the mouth and hand; and sad about his taste for alcohol—a waste as always. But in the end as fair as most men. A fine practitioner too. A fine mind inside the violence. Misha Gavron always said he'd learned a lot from him.

19

It was back to London and the waiting. For two wet autumn weeks, ever since Helga had broken the terrible news to her, the Charlie of her imagination had entered a morbid, vengeful hell, and burned in it alone. I am in shock; I am an obsessive, solitary mourner without a friend to turn to. I am a soldier robbed of my general, a revolutionary cut off from the revolution. Even Cathy had deserted her. "From now on, you manage without a nanny," Joseph told her, with a drawn smile. "We cannot have you going into phone boxes any more." Their meetings during this period were sparse and businesslike, usually elaborately planned car pickups. Sometimes he took her to out-of-the-way restaurants on the edge of London; once to Burnham Beeches for a walk; once to the zoo in Regent's Park. But wherever they were, he talked to her about her state of mind and briefed her constantly for various contingencies, without ever quite describing what they were.

What will they do next? she asked.

They are checking. They are observing you; thinking about you.

Sometimes she alarmed herself with unscripted outbreaks of hostility towards him, but, like a good doctor, he hastened to assure her that the symptoms were normal to her condition. "I am the archetypal enemy, good heavens! I killed Michel and if I had half a chance I would kill you. You should regard me with the most serious misgivings, why not?"

Thanks for the absolution, she thought in secret wonder at the seemingly endless facets of their shared schizophrenia: to understand is to forgive.

Until the day came when he announced they must temporarily abandon meetings of any kind, unless an extreme emergency occurred. He seemed to know something was about to happen, but refused to tell her what it was for fear she might respond out of character. Or not respond at all. He would be close, he said, reminding her of his promise in the Athens house: close—but not present—from day to day. And having thus, perhaps deliberately, stretched her sense of insecurity almost to breaking point, he sent her back again to the life of isolation that he had invented for her; but this time with her lover's death as its theme.

Her once-loved flat, under her diligent neglect of it, now became the unkempt shrine to Michel's memory, a place of grimy, chapel-like quiet. Books and pamphlets he had given her were spread face downward over the floor and table, opened at marked passages. At night, when she could not sleep, she would sit at her desk with an exercise book jammed among the clutter, while she copied out quotations from his letters. Her aim was to compile a secret memoir of him that would reveal him to a better world as the Arab Che Guevara. She contemplated approaching a fringe publisher she knew: "Night Letters from a Murdered Palestinian," done on bad paper with a lot of misprints. There was a certain madness to these preparations, as Charlie, when she stood back from them, well knew. But in another sense she knew that without the madness there was no sanity; there was the rôle, or there was nothing.

Her excursions into the outside world were few, but one night, as further evidence to herself of her determination to carry Michel's flag into battle for him, if she could only find the battlefield, she attended a comrades' get-together in the upper room of a St. Pancras pub. She sat with the Very Crazies, most of whom were stoned into oblivion by the time they got there. But she saw it through, and she scared both herself and them with a really furious peroration against Zionism in all its Fascist and genocidal manifestations, which, to the secret amusement of another part of her, brought forth nervous complaints from representatives of the radical Jewish left.

At other times she made a show of pestering Quilley about future parts—what had happened about the screen test? For Christ's sake, Ned, I need work! But the truth was that her zest for the artificial stage was waning. She was committed—for as long as it lasted, and despite its mounting hazards—to the theatre of the real.

Then the warnings began, like the advance creakings of a sea-storm in the rigging.

The first came from poor Ned Quilley, a phone call much earlier in the day than was his custom, ostensibly to return one she had made to him the day before. But she knew at once it was something Marjory had ordered him to do the moment he got into the office—before he forgot, or lost heart, or treated himself to a sharpener. No, he had nothing for her, but he wanted to cancel their lunch that day, said Quilley. No problem, she replied, trying gallantly to hide her disappointment, for lunch was the big one they had planned to celebrate her end of tour, and talk about what she might do next. She had been really looking forward to it as a treat she might decently allow herself.

"It's absolutely fine," she insisted, and waited for him to come out with his excuse. Instead of which, he lurched the other way and made a stupid stab at being rude.

"I just don't think it would be appropriate at this time," he said loftily.

"Ned, what's up? It's not Lent. What's come over you?"

Her false frivolity, intended to make things easier for him, only spurred him to greater feats of pomposity.

"Charlie, I don't know *what* you've been up to," he began, from his High Altar. "I was young once myself and not as hidebound as you may think, but if one half of what is being implied is true, then I can't help feeling that you and I may do better, a lot better for *both* parties—" But, being her lovely Ned, he couldn't bring himself to deliver the final blow, so he said, "To put off our date until you have come to your senses." At which point, in Marjory's scenario, he was clearly supposed to ring off, and indeed, after several false curtains and a lot of help from Charlie, he managed it. She rang back immediately and got Mrs. Ellis, which was what she wanted.

"What's up, Pheeb? Why have I got bad breath suddenly?"

"Oh, Charlie, what *have* you been up to?" Mrs. Ellis said, speaking very low because she feared the phone might be tapped. "The police came for a whole morning about you, three of them, and none of us are allowed to say."

"Well, screw them," she said bravely.

One of their seasonal checkups, she told herself. The Discreet Enquiry brigade, barging in with hobnailed boots to top up her dossier for Christmas. They had done it periodically ever since she had started going to the forum. Except that somehow this didn't sound like routine. Not a whole morning and three of them. That was V.I.P. stuff.

Next came the hairdresser.

She had fixed her hair appointment for eleven, and she kept it, lunch or no. The proprietress was a generous Italian lady called Bibi. She frowned when she saw Charlie come in, and said she would do Charlie herself today.

"You been going with a married fellow again?" she yelled as she worked shampoo into Charlie's hair. "You don't look good, you know that? You been a bad girl, stole someone's husband? What you do, Charlie?"

Three men, said Bibi, when Charlie made her tell. Yesterday.

Said they were tax inspectors, wanted to check Bibi's appointments book and her accounts for the Value Added.

But all they really wanted to hear about was Charlie.

" 'Who's this Charlie, here?' they say me. 'Know her well then, Bibi?' 'Sure,' I say to them; 'Charlie's a good girl, regular.' 'Oh, a regular, is she? Talk to you about her boyfriends, does she? Who's she got? Where she sleep these days?' All about you been on holiday—who you go with, where you go after Greece. Me, I say them nothing. Trust Bibi." But at the door, when Charlie had safely paid, Bibi turned a little bit nasty, the first time ever. "Don't come again a little while, okay? I don't like trouble. I don't like police."

Nor do I, Beeb. Believe me, nor do I. And these three beauties least of all. *The quicker the authorities know about you, the quicker we force the opposition's hand,* Joseph had promised her. But he hadn't said it was going to be like this.

Next came the pretty boy, not two hours later.

She had eaten a hamburger somewhere, then started walking although it was raining, because she had a silly idea that while she was moving she was safe, and safer in the rain. She headed west, thinking vaguely of Primrose Hill, then changed her mind and hopped on a bus. It was probably coincidence, but as she glanced back from the departing platform she saw a man get into a taxi fifty yards behind her. And the way she replayed it in her mind, the flag had been down before he hailed it.

Stay with the logic of the fiction, Joseph had told her, again and again. *Weaken, and you ruin the operation. Stay with the fiction, and when it's over we'll repair the damage.*

Halfway to panic, she had a mind to hightail it to the dressmaker's and demand Joseph immediately. But her loyalty to him held her back. She loved him without shame and without hope. In the world he had turned upside down for her, he was her one remaining constant, in both the fiction and the fact.

So she went to the cinema instead and that was where the pretty man tried to pick her up; and where she very nearly let him.

He was tall and puckish, with a long new leather coat and granny glasses, and as he edged along the row towards her during the interval, she stupidly assumed that she knew him and in her turmoil couldn't put a name or place to him. So she returned his smile.

"Hullo, how are *you?*" he cried, sitting down beside her. "Charmian, isn't it? Gosh, you were good in *Alpha Beta* last year! Weren't you absolutely wonderful? Have some popcorn."

Suddenly nothing fitted: the carefree smile didn't fit the skull-like jaw, the granny glasses didn't fit the rat's eyes, the popcorn didn't fit the polished shoes, and the dry leather coat didn't fit the weather. He had arrived here from the moon with nothing else in mind but to pull her.

"You want me to call the manager or are you going quietly?" she said.

He kept up his pitch, protesting, smirking, asking whether she was a dyke, but when she stormed to the foyer to find someone, the staff had disappeared like summer snow, all but one little black girl in the ticket box, who pretended she was too busy counting change.

Going home took more courage than she possessed, more than Joseph had any right to expect of her, and all the way there she prayed that she would break her ankle or be run over by a bus or have another of her fainting fits. It was seven in the evening and the café was having a lull. The chef grinned at her brilliantly and his cheeky boyfriend, as usual, waved as if she were daft. Inside her flat, instead of putting on the light, she sat on the bed and left the curtains open, and watched in the mirror how the two men on the opposite pavement loitered and never talked to each other and never looked in her direction. Michel's letters were still under their floorboard; so was her passport and what was left of her fighting fund. *Your passport is now a dangerous document,* Joseph had warned her, in his sermon on her new status since Michel's death; *he should not have let you use it for the drive. Your passport must be guarded with your other secrets.*

Cindy, Charlie thought.

Cindy was a Geordie waif who worked an evening shift downstairs. Her West Indian lover was in prison for grievous bodily harm, and Charlie occasionally gave her free guitar lessons to help her pass the time.

"Cind," she wrote. "Here's a birthday present for you, for whenever your birthday is. Take it home and practise till you're half dead. You've got the touch so don't give up. Take the music case too, but like an idiot I've left the key at Mum's. I'll bring it when I next call. Anyway the music's not right for you yet. Love you, Chas."

Her music case was her father's, a sturdy Edwardian job with serious locks and stitching. She put Michel's letters into it, together with her money and passport and plenty of music. She took it downstairs with the guitar.

"This lot's for Cindy," she told the chef, and the chef burst into a fit of giggles and put them in the Ladies with the Hoover and the empties.

She returned upstairs, switched on the light, pulled the curtains, and dressed herself in her full warpaint because it was Peckham night and not all the coppers on earth, and not all her dead lovers, were going to stop her rehearsing her kids for their pantomime. She got home soon after eleven; the pavement was clear; Cindy had taken her music case and guitar. She rang Al because suddenly she wanted a man desperately. No answer. Bastard's out screwing again. She tried a couple of other old stand-bys without success. Her phone sounded funny to her, but the way she was feeling, it could have been her ears. About to go to bed, she took a last look out of the window and there were her two guardians back in position on the pavement.

The next day nothing happened, except that when she

called on Lucy, half expecting to find Al there, Lucy said Al had vanished from the earth, she'd phoned the police and the hospitals and everyone.

"Try Battersea Dogs' Home," Charlie advised her. But when she got back to her own flat, there was her old awful Al on the phone in a state of alcoholic hysteria.

"Come round *now,* woman. Don't talk, just bloody well come *now.*"

She went, knowing it was more of the same. Knowing there was no corner of her life any more that was not occupied by danger.

Al had parked himself on Willy and Pauly, who weren't breaking up after all. She arrived there to find that he had convened a whole supporters' club. Robert had brought a new girlfriend, an idiot in white lipstick and mauve hair called Samantha. But it was Al, as usual, who held the stage.

"And you can tell me what you like, you can!" he was yelling as she entered. "This is *it!* This is war! Oh yes, it *is,* and total war at *that!*"

He raged on till Charlie screamed at him: just shut up and tell her what had happened.

"Happened, girl? *Happened?* What has happened is that the counter-revolution has fired its first salvo is what's happened, and the target was Joe Soap here!"

"Let's have it in bleeding English!" Charlie screamed back, but she still went nearly mad before she dragged the plain facts out of him.

Al was coming out of this pub when these three gorillas just fell on him, he said. One, even two, he could have managed, but they were three and hard as bloody Brighton Rock, and they worked him over as a team. But it wasn't till they'd got him in the police car, half castrated, that he realized they were pigs pulling him in on a trumped-up indecency charge.

"And you know what they wanted to talk about *really,* don't you?" He struck out an arm at her. "*You,* girl! *You* and *me* and our bloody politics, oh yes! And did we count any friendly Palestinian activists among our acquaintance, by any chance? Meanwhile they're telling me I flashed my dick at some fetching copper-boy in the Gents at the Rising Sun and made movements of the right hand of a masturbatory

nature. And when they're not telling me *that*, they're telling
me they'll pull out my fingernails one by one and get me ten
years in Sing Sing for hatching anarchist plots with my faggy
little radical friends on Greek islands, such as Willy and
Pauly here. I mean this is *it*, girl! This is day one and we, in
this room, are the front line."

They had smacked his ear so hard he couldn't hear himself speak, he said; his balls were like ostrich eggs, and look
at the bloody bruise on his arm. They'd kept him twenty-four
hours in the can, questioned him for six. They'd offered him
the phone but no small change, and when he wanted a phone
book they'd lost it so he couldn't even ring his agent. Then
unaccountably they had dropped the indecency charge and let
him go with a caution.

There was a boy called Matthew among the party, a
tubby-chinned articled accountant looking for life's alterna-
tives; and he had a flat. To his surprise, Charlie went back
there and slept with him. Next day there was no rehearsal
and she had been meaning to visit her mother, but at
lunchtime when she woke in Matthew's bed she hadn't the
stomach, so she rang and cancelled, which was probably what
threw the police, because when she arrived outside the
Goanese café that evening she found a squad car parked on
the kerb, and a uniformed Sergeant standing in the open
doorway, and the chef beside him, grinning at her with Asian
embarrassment.

It's happened, she thought calmly. High time too.
They've come out of the woodwork at last.

The Sergeant was the angry-eyed, close-cropped type
who hates the whole world, but Indians and pretty women
most. Perhaps it was this hatred which blinded him to who
Charlie might be at that crucial moment in the drama.

"Café's temporarily closed," he snapped at her. "Find
somewhere else."

Bereavement engenders its own responses. "Has someone
died?" she asked fearfully.

"If they have, they haven't told me. There's a suspected
burglar been seen on the premises. Our officers are investigating. Now hop it."

Perhaps he had been on duty too long and was sleepy.
Perhaps he did not know how fast an impulsive girl can think
and duck. In any case she was under his guard and into the

café in a second, slamming the doors behind her as she ran
The café was empty and the machines switched off. Her own
front door was closed but she could hear men's voices mur-
muring through it. Downstairs the Sergeant was yelling and
hammering on the door. She heard: "*You*. Stop that. Come
out." But only faintly. She thought, Key, and opened her
handbag. She saw the white headscarf and put it on instead, a
lightning change between scenes. Then she pressed the bell,
two quick, confident rings. Then pushed the flap of her letter
box.

"Chas? Are you in? It's me, Sandy."

The voices stopped dead, she heard a footstep and a
whispered "Harry, quick!" The door lurched open and she
found herself staring straight into the eyes of a grey-haired,
savage little man in a grey suit. Behind him, she could see
her treasured relics of Michel scattered everywhere, her bed
upended, her posters down, her carpet rolled back, and the
floorboards open. She saw a downward-faced camera on a
stand, and a second man peering through the eyepiece, and
several of her mother's letters spread beneath it. She saw chis-
els, pliers, and her would-be lover-boy from the cinema in his
granny glasses kneeling among a heap of her expensive new
clothes and she knew with one glance that she was not interrupting the investigation, but the break-in itself.

"I'm looking for my sister Charmian," she said. "Who
the hell are you?"

"She's not here," the grey-haired man replied, and she
caught a whiff of the Welsh on his voice, and noticed claw
marks on his jaw.

Still looking at her, he raised his voice to a bellow. "Sergeant Mallis! Sergeant Mallis, get this lady out of here and
take her particulars!"

The door slammed in her face. From below she could
hear the luckless Sergeant still yelling. She went softly down
the stairs but only as far as the half-landing, where she
squeezed between heaps of cardboard boxes to the courtyard
door. It was bolted but not locked. The courtyard gave on to
a mews and the mews on to the street where Miss Dubber
lived. Passing her window, Charlie tapped on it and gave her
a cheery wave hullo. How she did that, where she got the wit
from, she would never know. She kept going, but no footsteps
or furious voices came after her, no car screeched alongside.

She reached the main road, and somewhere along the way she pulled on one leather glove, which was what Joseph had told her to do if and when they flushed her. She saw a free cab and hailed it. Well then, she thought cheerfully, here we all are. It was only much, much later in her many lives that it crossed her mind they had let her go deliberately.

Joseph had ruled her Fiat out of bounds, and reluctantly she knew he was right. So she moved by stages, nothing hasty. She was talking herself down. After the taxi, we take a bus ride, she told herself, walk a bit, then a stretch by tube. Her mind was sharp as a flint, but she had to get her thoughts straight; her gaiety had not subsided; she knew she had to grab a firm hold on her responses before she made her next move, because if she fluffed this, she fluffed the whole show. Joseph had told her so and she believed him.

I'm on the run. They're after me. Christ, Helg, what do I do?

You may call this number only in extreme emergency, Charlie. If you call unnecessarily, we shall be most angry, do you hear me?

Yes, Helg, I hear you.

She sat in a pub and drank one of Michel's vodkas, remembering the rest of the gratuitous advice Helga had given her while Mesterbein was skulking in the car. Make sure you are not followed. Don't use the telephones of friends or family. Don't use the box on the corner or the box across the road or down the street or up the street from your flat.

Never, do you hear? They are all extremely dangerous. The pigs can tap a phone in one second, you may be certain. And never use the same telephone twice. Do you hear me, Charlie?

Helg, I hear you perfectly.

She stepped into the street and saw one man staring into an unlit shop window and a second sauntering away from him towards a parked car with an aerial. Now the terror had her, and it was so bad she wanted to lie down whimpering on the pavement and confess to everything and beg the world to take her back. The people ahead of her were as frightening as the people behind her, the ghostly lines of the kerb led to some dreadful vanishing point which was her own extinction. Helga, she prayed; oh, Helg, get me out of this. She caught a bus in the wrong direction, waited, caught another and walked again, but funked the tube because the thought of being below ground scared her. So she weakened and caught another cab and watched out of the back window. Nothing was following her. The street was empty. To hell with walking, to hell with tubes and buses.

"Peckham," she said to the driver, and went right to the gates in style.

The hall they used for rehearsals was at the back of the church, a barn-like place next to an adventure playground, which the kids had smashed to pieces long ago. To reach it she had to walk down a line of yew trees. No lights burned, but she pressed the bell because of Lofty, a retired boxer. Lofty was the nightwatchman, but since the cuts he came three nights a week at most, and the bell, to her relief, produced no answering tread. She unlocked the door and stepped inside, and the cold institutional air reminded her of the Cornish church she had gone into after laying her wreath to the unknown revolutionary. She closed the door behind her and lit a match. Its flame flickered on the glossy green tiles and the high vault of the Victorian pine roof. She called out "Loftee" humorously to keep her spirits up. The match went out, but she found the door-chain and slipped it into its housing before lighting another. Her voice, her footsteps, the rattle of the chain in the pitch darkness echoed crazily for hours.

She thought of bats and other aversions; of seaweed dragged across her face. A staircase with an iron handrail led upward to a pine gallery, known euphemistically as "the common room," and, ever since her clandestine visit to the Munich duplex, reminiscent of Michel. Grabbing the rail, she followed it upstairs, then stood motionless on the gallery staring into the gloom of the hall and listening while her eyes grew accustomed to the dark. She made out the stage, then the billowing psychedelic clouds of her backdrop, then the trusses and the roof. She picked out the silver glow of their one spotlight, a headlamp converted by a Bahamian kid called Gums, who'd nicked it from a car dump. There was an old sofa on the gallery and beside it a pale plastic-topped table that caught the city's glow from the window. On the table stood the black telephone for staff only, and the exercise book where you were supposed to enter private calls, which sparked off about six major rows a month.

Sitting on the sofa, Charlie waited till her stomach had untied itself and her pulse rate dropped below the three hundred mark. Then she lifted phone and cradle together and laid them on the floor beneath the table. There used to be a couple of household candles in the table drawer for when the wiring failed, which it often did, but somebody had nicked them too. So she twisted a page of an old parish magazine into a spill and, having propped it in a dirty teacup, lit one end to make a tallow. With the table above and the balcony to one side, the flame was as contained as it could be, but as soon as she had dialled she blew it out all the same. She had fifteen numerals to dial altogether and the first time the phone just howled at her. The second time she mis-dialled and got some mad Italian yelling at her, and the third her fingertip slipped. But on the fourth she got a pensive silence followed by the peep of a continental ringing tone. Followed a lot later by the strident voice of Helga speaking German.

"It's Joan," said Charlie. "Remember me?" and got another pensive silence.

"Where are you, Joan?"

"Mind your own bloody business."

"You have a problem, Joan?"

"Not really. I just wanted to thank you for bringing the pigs to my fucking doorstep."

Then, to her glory, the old luxurious fury took command of her, and she let rip with an abandon she had not managed since the time she was not allowed to remember, when Joseph had taken her to see her little lover-boy before cutting him up for bait.

Helga heard her out in silence. "Where are you?" she said when Charlie seemed to have finished. She spoke reluctantly, as if she were breaking her own rules.

"Forget it," Charlie said.

"Can you be reached anywhere? Tell me where you will be for the next forty-eight hours."

"No."

"Will you phone me again in one hour, please."

"I can't."

A long silence. "Where are the letters?"

"Safe."

Another silence. "Get paper and a pencil."

"I don't need one."

"Get one all the same. You are not in a condition for accurate remembering. You are ready?"

Not an address, not a telephone number either. But street directions, a time, and the route by which she should approach. "Do exactly as I am telling you. If you cannot make it, if you have more problems, telephone to the number on Anton's card and say you wish to contact Petra. Bring the letters. Do you hear me? Petra, and bring the letters. If you don't bring the letters, we shall be extremely angry with you."

Ringing off, Charlie heard the sound of one pair of hands softly clapping from the auditorium downstairs. She went to the edge of the balcony and looked over, and to her immeasurable joy saw Joseph sitting all alone in the centre of the front row. She turned and ran down the stairs to him. She reached the bottom step to find him waiting with his arms out for her. He was afraid she might lose her footing in the darkness. He kissed her, and went on kissing her; then he led her back to the gallery keeping his arm round her even on the narrowest bit of the staircase, and carrying a basket in the other hand.

He had brought smoked salmon and a bottle of wine. He had put them on the table without unwrapping them. He knew where the plates lived under the sink, and how you plugged the electric fire into the spare socket on the cooker. He had brought a thermos of coffee and a couple of rather ripe blankets from Lofty's lair downstairs. He put the thermos down with the plates, then went round checking the big Victorian doors, putting them on the bolt from the inside. And she knew, even in the gloomy light—she could tell by the line of his back and the private deliberation of his gestures—that he was doing something outside the script, he was closing the doors on every world but their own. He sat beside her on the sofa and put a blanket over her because the cold in the hall was something that really had to be dealt with; and so was her shivering, she couldn't stop. The phone call to Helga had frightened her stiff, so had the executioner's eyes of the policeman in her flat, so had the accumulated days of waiting and half knowing, which was far, far worse than knowing nothing.

The only light came from the electric fire and it shone

upwards on his face like a pale footlight from the days when
theatres used them. She remembered him in Greece, telling
her that the floodlighting of ancient sites was an act of modern vandalism, because the temples were built to be seen with
the sun above them, not below. He had his arm round her
shoulder under the blanket and it occurred to her how thin
she was against him.

"I've lost weight," she said, as a kind of warning to him.

He didn't answer, but held her tighter to keep her trembling in check, to absorb it and make it his. It occurred to
her that she had always known, despite his evasions and dis-
guises, that he was in essence a kind man, of instinctive sympathy for everyone; in battle and in peace, a troubled man
who hated causing pain. She put her hand to his face and she
was pleased to find he hadn't shaved, because tonight she
didn't want to think he had calculated anything, though it
was not their first night, nor yet their fiftieth—they were old
frenzied lovers with half the motels in England behind them,
with Greece and Salzburg and God knew how many other
lives as well; because suddenly it was clear to her that their
whole shared fiction was nothing but foreplay for this night
of fact.

He took her hand away and drew her into him and
kissed her mouth and she responded chastely, waiting for him
to light the passions they had so often spoken of. She loved
his wrists, his hands. No hands had been so wise. He was
touching her face, her neck, her breasts, and she held back
from kissing him because she wanted her flavours separate:
now he is kissing me, now he is touching me, undressing me,
he is lying in my arms, we are naked, we are on the beach
again, on the scratchy sand of Mykonos, we are vandalised
buildings with the sun burning us from below. He laughed
and, rolling away from her, moved back the electric fire. And
in all her loving she had never seen anything as beautiful as
his body stooped over the red glow, the fire brightest where
his own body burned. He returned to her and, kneeling
beside her, started again from the beginning in case she had
forgotten the story this far, kissing and touching everything
with a light possessiveness that slowly lost its diffidence, but
always returning to her face because they needed to see and
taste each other repeatedly and reassure themselves that they
were who they said they were. He was the best, long before

he entered her, the one incomparable lover she had never had, the distant star she had been following through all that rotten country. If she had been blind, she would have known it by his touch; if she had been dying, by his sad victorious smile that conquered terror and unbelief by being there ahead of her; by his instinctive power to know her, and to make her own knowledge more.

She woke and found him sitting over her, waiting for her to come round. He had packed everything away.

"It's a boy," he said, and smiled.

"It's twins," she replied, and pulled his head down until it was against her shoulder. He started to speak, but she stopped him with a stern warning. "I don't want a squeak out of you," she said. "No cover stories, no apologies, no lies. If it's part of the service, don't tell me. What's the time?"

"Midnight."

"Then come back to bed."

"Marty wants to talk to you," he said.

But there was something in his voice and manner that told her it was an occasion not of Marty's making but his own.

It was Joseph's place.

She knew as soon as she entered: a bookish, rectangular little room at street level somewhere in Bloomsbury, with lace curtains and space for one small tenant. On this wall hung maps of inner London; along that one, there was a sideboard with two telephones. A bunk bed, unslept in, made a third side; the fourth was a deal desk with an old lamp on it. A pot of coffee was bubbling beside the telephones, and a fire was burning in the grate. Marty did not get up as she entered, but turned his head towards her and gave her the warmest, best smile she had ever had from him, but perhaps that was because she saw the world so kindly herself. He held out his arms for her and she bent down and entered his long fatherly embrace: my daughter, back from her travels. She sat opposite him and Joseph crouched on the floor, Arabstyle, the way he had crouched on the hilltop when he drew her down to him and lectured her about the gun.

"You want to listen to yourself?" Kurtz invited her, indicating a tape-recorder at his side. She shook her head. "Charlie, you were terrific. Not the third best, not the second best, just the best ever."

"He's flattering you," Joseph warned her, but he wasn't joking.

A little lady in brown came in without knocking, and there was business about who took sugar.

"Charlie, you are free to pull out," said Kurtz when she had gone. "Joseph here insists that I remind you of this, loudly and plainly. Go now, you go with honour. Right, Joseph? A lot of money, a lot of honour. All we promised you and more."

"I told her already," Joseph said.

She saw Kurtz's smile broaden to conceal his irritation. "Sure you told her, Joseph, and now *I'm* telling her. Isn't that what you want me to do? Charlie, you have lifted the lid for us on a whole box of worms we've been looking for since a long time. You have thrown up more names and places and connections than you can know about, and there'll be more to come. With you or without you. Near enough you're still clean, and where there are dirty areas, give us a few months and we'll have them cleaned up. A period of quarantine somewhere, a cooling-off period, take a friend with you—you want it that way, that's the way you're entitled to have it."

"He means it," Joseph said. "Don't just say you'll go on. Think about it."

Once again, she noticed the edge of annoyance in Marty's voice as he came back at his subordinate: "I surely do mean it, and if I did not mean it, this would be about the last moment on earth to *flirt* with meaning it," he said, contriving by the end to turn his retort into a joke.

"So where are we?" Charlie said. "What is this moment?"

Joseph started to speak, but Marty cut in first like a piece of bad driving. "Charlie, there is an above the line in this thing, and a below the line. Until now, you've been above the line, but you've managed all the same to show us what's going on lower down. But from here on in—well, it just may get a little different. That's how we read it. We may be wrong, but that's how we read the signs."

"What he means is, until now you have been on friendly territory. We can be close to you, we can pull you out if we need to. But from now on, all that's over. You'll be one of them. Sharing their lives. Their mentality. Their morals. You could spend weeks, months out of touch with us."

"Not out of touch, perhaps, but out of reach, that is mainly true," Marty conceded; he was smiling, but not at Joseph. "But we'll be around you, you can count on us."

"What's the end?" Charlie asked.

Marty appeared momentarily confused. "What kind of end, dear—the end that justifies these means? I don't think I have you quite."

"What am I looking for? When will you be satisfied?"

"Charlie, we are more than satisfied now," said Marty handsomely, and she knew that he was prevaricating.

"The end is a man," said Joseph abruptly, and she saw Marty's head swing round to him till his face was lost to her. But Joseph's was not, and his stare, as he returned Marty's, had a defiant straightness she had not seen in him before.

"Charlie, the end is a man," Marty finally agreed, coming back to her once more. "If you are going ahead, these are things you will have to know."

"Khalil," she said.

"Khalil is right," said Marty. "Khalil heads up their whole European thing. He's the man we have to have."

"He's dangerous," Joseph said. "He's as good as Michel was bad."

Perhaps to outmanoeuvre him, Kurtz took up the same refrain. "Khalil has nobody he relies on, no regular girlfriend. Never sleeps in the same bed two nights running. He's cut himself off from people. Reduced his basic needs to the point where he is almost self-sufficient. A smart operator," Kurtz ended, smiling his most indulgent smile at her. But as he lit himself another cigar, she could tell by the shake of the match that he was very angry indeed.

Why did she not waver?

An extraordinary calm had descended over her, a lucidity of feeling beyond anything she had known till now. Joseph had not slept with her in order to send her away, but to hold her back. He was suffering on her behalf all the fears and hesitations that should have been her own. Yet she knew also that in this secret microcosm of existence they had made for her, to turn back now was to turn back for ever; that a love that did not advance could never renew itself; it could only slump into the pit of mediocrity to which her other loves had consigned themselves since her life with Joseph had begun. The fact that he wanted her to stop did not deter her; to the contrary, it fortified her resolve. They were partners. They were lovers. They were married to a common destiny, a common forward march.

She was asking Kurtz how she would recognise the quarry. Did he look like Michel? Marty was shaking his head and laughing. "Alas, dear, he never posed for our photographers!"

Then, while Joseph deliberately stared away from him towards the soot-smeared window, Kurtz quickly got up and, from an old black briefcase that stood beside the armchair where he had been sitting, fished out what resembled a fat ballpoint refill, crimped at one end, with a pair of thin red wires, like lobster whiskers, protruding from it.

"This is what we call a detonator, dear," he explained as his stubby finger gingerly tapped the refill. "At the end here, this is the bung, and fed into the bung you see the wires here. A little of the wire, he needs. The rest, what is spare, he packages it like this." Producing a pair of wiresnippers, also from the briefcase, he cut each strand separately, leaving about eighteen inches still attached. Then, with a deft and practised gesture, he wound the spare wires into a neat dummy, complete with belt. Then he passed it to her to hold. "The little doll is what we call his signature. Sooner or later, everybody has a signature. That's his."

She let him take it from her hand.

Joseph had an address for her to go to. The little lady in brown showed her to the door. She stepped into the street and found a taxi ready waiting for her. It was early dawn and the sparrows were starting to sing.

20

She started earlier than Helga had told her, partly because in some ways she was a worrier, and partly because she had clothed herself deliberately in a coarse scepticism about the whole plan. What if it's out of order? she had objected—this is England, Helg, not super-efficient Germany—what if it's occupied when you ring? But Helga had refused to entertain these arguments: do exactly as you are ordered, leave everything else to me. So she started from Gloucester Road all right, and she sat upstairs; but instead of catching the first bus after seven-thirty, she caught the one that came at twenty past. At Tottenham Court Road tube station she was lucky; a train pulled up just as she reached the southbound platform, with the result that she had to sit like a wallflower at Embankment Cross until she made her last connection. It was Sunday morning, and apart from a few insomniacs and churchgoers she was the only person awake in the whole of London. The City, when she reached it, had been abandoned totally, and she had only to find the street to see the phone box a hundred yards ahead of her, exactly as Helga had described it, winking at her like a lighthouse. It was empty.

"You walk first to the end of the road, you turn round, and you come back again," Helga had said, so she dutifully made a first pass and established that the phone did not look too smashed up; though by then she had decided that it was an absurdly obvious place to hang around waiting for phone calls from international terrorists. She made the turn and started back again; and, to her great annoyance, as she did so, a man got into the box ahead of her and closed the door. She glanced at her watch and there were twelve minutes still to go, so, not unduly worried, she parked herself a few feet away and waited. He was wearing a bobble hat like a fisherman's and a leather flying-coat with a fur collar, too much for such a sticky day. He had his back to her and was talking Italian non-stop. That's why he needs the fur-lined, she thought; his Latin blood doesn't fancy our climate. Charlie herself was wearing the clothes she had worn since she picked up the boy Matthew at Al's party: old jeans and her Tibetan jacket. She had combed her hair but not brushed it; she felt fraught and haunted, and hoped she looked it.

Seven minutes to go, and the man in the box had launched himself upon one of those passionate Italian monologues that could as well have been about unrequited love as the state of the Milan stock market. Nervous now, she licked her lips and looked up and down the street, but not a soul stirred—no sinister black sedans or men in doorways; no red Mercedes either. The only car in sight was a grotty little van, with corrugated sides and the driver's door still open, standing directly in front of her. All the same, she was beginning to feel very naked. Eight o'clock arrived, announced by an amazing variety of secular and religious chimes. Helga had said five past. The man had stopped speaking, but she heard the chink of coin in his pockets as he fumbled for more; then she heard a tapping as he tried to attract her attention. She turned round and saw him holding a fifty-pence piece at her and looking appealing.

"Can't you let me go first?" she said. "I'm in a hurry."

But English was not his language.

To hell with it, she thought; Helga will just have to keep dialling. It's exactly what I warned her of. Slipping the shoulder strap of her handbag, she unpopped it and delved in the sump for tens and fives till she made up fifty. Christ, look at the sweat on my fingers. She stuck her closed fist towards him, damp fingers downward, ready to drop the stuff into his grateful Latin palm, and saw that he was pointing a small pistol at her from within the folds of his flying-jacket, straight at the point where her stomach met her rib cage, as neat a piece of conjuring as she was likely to find. Not a big gun, though guns do look a lot bigger when they're pointed at you, she noticed. About the size of Michel's. But as Michel himself had told her, every handgun is a compromise between concealment, portability, and efficiency. He was still holding the telephone in his other hand and she supposed that someone was still listening at the other end, because although he was addressing Charlie now, he kept his face close to the mouthpiece.

"What you do, you walk beside me to the car, Charlie," he explained, in good English. "You keep to my right side, you walk on my right side a little ahead of me, hands behind your back where I can see them. Joined behind your back, you follow me? If you try to get away or make a signal to someone, if you call out, then I shall shoot you through the left side—here—and kill you. If the police show up, if anyone shoots, if I'm suspicious, it's the same. I shoot you."

He indicated to her the same point on his own body, so that she understood. He added something Italian into the telephone and rang off. Then he stepped out onto the pavement and cracked a big confiding smile at her just at the moment when his face was closest to hers. It was a real Italian face, not a single lazy line to it. A real Italian voice too, rich and musical. She could imagine it echoing round ancient marketplaces and chatting up the women at their balconies.

"Let's go," he said. One hand had stayed in the pocket of his flying-jacket. "Not too fast, okay? Nice and easy."

A moment earlier she had desperately needed a pee, but with walking the urge left her and she developed instead a cramp in the nape of the neck and a wailing in her right ear like a mosquito in the dark.

"As you get into the passenger seat, transfer your hands to the dashboard in front of you," he advised as he walked behind her. "The girl in the back has a gun too and she is *very* quick to shoot people. Much quicker than me."

Charlie opened the passenger door, sat down, and placed her fingertips on the dashboard like a good girl at table.

"Relax, Charlie," said Helga cheerfully from behind her. "Lower your shoulders, my dear, you are looking like an old woman already!" Charlie kept her shoulders where they were. "Now smile. Hoorah. Keep smiling. Everybody's happy today. Whoever is not happy must be shot."

"Start with me," said Charlie.

The Italian got into the driving seat and switched the radio to the God slot.

"Turn it off," Helga ordered. She was wedged against the rear doors with her knees up, and holding her gun with both hands, and she didn't look like somebody who would miss an oil can at fifteen paces. With a shrug, the Italian turned off the radio and, in the restored quiet, once more addressed her.

"Okay, so put on your seat belt, then link your hands together and put them on your lap," he said. "Hang on, I do it for you." Picking up her handbag, he tossed it to Helga, then grabbed the seat belt and buckled it, carelessly brushing her breasts. Thirtyish. Handsome as a movie star. A spoilt Garibaldi in a red neckscarf going for the hero kick. Very calmly, with all the time in the world to kill, he fished a pair of large sunglasses from his pocket and fitted them over her eyes. At first she thought she had gone blind with funk, because she could see nothing through them at all. Then she thought, they're the self-adjusting kind; I'm supposed to sit tight and wait for them to clear. Then she realised that seeing nothing was what was intended.

"If you take them off, she'll shoot you through the back of the head for sure," the Italian boy warned her as he started the car.

"Oh, she *will*," said jolly old Helga.

They set off, first bumping over a bit of cobble, then settling into calmer water. She listened for the sound of another car but heard only their own engine ticking and rattling through the streets. She tried to work out which way they were heading but she was already lost. Without warning, they stopped. She had no sensation of slowing down, nor of the driver shaping up to park. She had counted three hundred of her own pulsebeats, and two previous stops, which she assumed were traffic lights. She had memorised such trivia as the new rubber mat under her feet and the red devil with a trident in his hand dangling from the car keyring. The Italian was helping her out of the car; a stick was put into her hand, she supposed a white one. With plenty of help from her friends, she was negotiating the six paces and four rising steps to somebody's front door. The lift mechanism had a warble in it that was an exact reproduction of the water-whistle she had blown in her prep-school orchestra to make the bird noises in the Toy Symphony. *They are good performers,* Joseph had warned her. *There is no apprenticeship. You will go from drama school straight to the West End.* She was sitting on some kind of leather saddle with no back. They had made her link her hands and keep them on her lap again. They had kept her handbag and she heard them tip its contents onto a glass table, which chimed when her keys and small change landed. And thudded to the weight of Michel's letters, which she had collected that morning on Helga's orders. There was a smell of body lotion in the air, sweeter than Michel's, and sleepier. The carpet at her feet was thick nylon and russet-coloured, like Michel's orchids; she guessed the curtains must be heavy and drawn tight, because the light at the edges of her spectacles was electric yellow, not a hint of day. They had been in the room some minutes with no word spoken.

"I need Comrade Mesterbein," Charlie pronounced suddenly. "I need the full protection of the law."

Helga laughed rapturously. "Oh, Charlie! This is too completely crazy. She is wonderful. Don't you think so?" This to the Italian, presumably, for she was aware of no one else in the room. Yet the question received no answer, and Helga seemed to expect none. Charlie sent out another probe.

"A gun suits you, Helg, I'll give you that. From now on, I'll never think of you dressed in anything else."

And this time Charlie distinctly heard the note of nervous pride in Helga's laughter; she was showing Charlie off to someone—someone she respected a great deal more than she respected the Italian boy. She heard a footstep and saw, at the very bottom of her vision, laid out on the russet carpet for her inspection, the black and highly polished toecap of one very expensive male shoe. She heard breathing, and the suck of a tongue placed against the upper teeth. The foot disappeared and she felt a disturbance of air as the warm-scented body passed very close to her. Instinctively, she leaned away from it but Helga ordered her to be still. She heard a match struck and smelled one of her father's Christmas cigars. Yet again Helga was warning her to keep still—"exactly still, otherwise you will be punished, there will be no hesitation." But Helga's threats were a mere intrusion into Charlie's thoughts as she tried by every means known to her to define the unseen visitor. She imagined herself as a kind of bat, sending out signals and listening to how they bounced back to her. She remembered the blindfold games she used to play at children's parties at Hallowe'en. Smell this, feel that, guess who is kissing you on your thirteen-year-old lips.

The darkness was making her dizzy. I'm going to fall over. Lucky I'm sitting down. He was at the glass table, inspecting the contents of her handbag, much as Helga had done in Cornwall. She heard a snatch of music as he fiddled with her little clock radio, and a clunk as he set it aside. *This time we play no tricks*, Joseph had said. *You take your very own model, no substitutes.* She heard him flipping through her diary while he puffed. He's going to ask me what "off games" means, she thought. See M . . . meet M . . . love M . . . ATHENS!! . . . He asked her nothing. She heard a grunt as he sat himself gratefully on the sofa; she heard the crackle of his trouser seat on stiffened chintz. A tubby man wearing expensive body oil and handmade shoes and smoking a Havana cigar sits himself gratefully on a tart's sofa. The darkness was hypnotic. Her hands were still linked on her lap but they were someone else's. She heard the snap of an elastic band. The letters. We shall be very cross with you if you do not bring the letters. Cindy, you have just paid for your music lessons. If only you knew where I was going when I called on you. If only I did.

The darkness was making her a little mad. If they imprison me, I've had it—claustrophobia's my worst thing. She was reciting T. S. Eliot to herself, something she had learnt at school the term they sacked her: about time present and time past all being contained in time future. About all time being eternally present. She hadn't understood it then and she didn't now. Thank God I didn't take in Whisper, she thought. Whisper was a scurrilous black lurcher who lived across the road from her, and his owners were going abroad. She imagined Whisper sitting beside her now, wearing dark glasses too.

"You tell us the truth, we don't kill you," said a man's voice softly.

It was Michel! Almost. Michel is almost alive again! It was Michel's accent, Michel's beauty of cadence, Michel's rich and drowsy tone, produced from the back of the throat.

"You tell us everything you told to them, what you did for them already, how much they pay you, that's okay. We understand. We let you go."

"Keep your head still," Helga snapped from behind her.

"We don't think you betrayed him like betray, okay? You were frightened, you got in too deep, so now you play along with them. Okay, that's natural. We are not inhuman people. We take you out of here, we drop you at the edge of town, you tell them everything that happened to you here. We still don't mind. So long as you come clean."

He sighed, as if life were becoming a burden to him.

"Maybe you develop a dependence on some nice police-man guy, yes? You do him a favour. We understand those things. We're committed people but we are not psychopaths. Yes?"

Helga was annoyed. "Do you understand him, Charlie? Answer or you will be punished!"

She made a point of not answering.

"When did you first go to them? Tell me. After Nottingham? York? It doesn't matter. You went to them. We agree. You got frightened, you ran to the police. 'This crazy Arab boy is trying to recruit me as a terrorist. Save me, I do whatever you tell me.' That how it happened? Listen, when you go back to them, it's still no problem. You tell them what a heroine you are. We'll give you some information you can take to them, make you feel good. We're nice people. Reasonable. Okay, let's get to business. Let's not fool around. You're a nice lady but out of your depth. Let's go."

She was at peace. A profound lassitude had come over her, brought on by isolation and blindness. She was safe, she was in the womb, to begin again or to die peacefully, however nature disposed. She was sleeping the sleep of infancy or old age. Her silence enchanted her. It was the silence of perfect freedom. They were waiting for her—she could feel their impatience but had no sense of sharing it. Several times she went so far as to think of what she might say, but her voice was a long way from her and there seemed no point in going to fetch it. Helga spoke some German, and though Charlie couldn't understand a word of it, she recognised as clearly as if it were her own language the note of bewildered resignation. The fat man answered and he sounded quite as perplexed, but not hostile. Maybe—maybe not, he seemed to be saying. She had an impression of the two of them disclaiming responsibility for her as they passed her back and forth between them: a bureaucratic hassle. The Italian joined in, but Helga told him to shut up. The discussion between the fat man and Helga resumed and she caught the word *"logisch."* Helga is being logical. Or Charlie isn't. Or the fat man is being told he should be.

Then the fat man said, "Where did you spend the night after you telephoned Helga?"

"With a lover."

"And last night?"

"With a lover."

"A different one?"

"Yes, but they were both policemen."

She reckoned that if she hadn't had the glasses on, Helga would have hit her. She stormed up to her and her voice rasped with anger as she flung a volley of orders at her—not to be impertinent, not to lie, to answer everything immediately and without sarcasm. The questions began again and she answered wearily, letting them drag the answers out of her, sentence by sentence, because ultimately it was none of their damn business. In Nottingham what room number? In Thessalonika what hotel? Did they swim? What time did they arrive, eat; what drinks did they have sent up to their room? But gradually, as she listened first to herself and then to them, she knew that, this far at least, she had won—even though they made her wear the sunglasses when she left, and keep them on her till they had driven her a decent distance from the house.

21

It was raining as they landed in Beirut and she knew it was a hot rain, because the heat of it came into the cabin while they were still circling and made her scalp itch again from the dye that Helga had made her put on her hair. They flew in over cloud like rock that burned red hot under the plane's lights. The cloud stopped and they were low over the sea, skimming to destruction in the approaching mountains. She had a recurring nightmare that went the same way, except that her plane was flying down a crowded street with skyscrapers either side. Nothing could stop it, because the pilot was making love to her. Nothing could stop it now. They made a perfect landing, the doors opened, she smelled the Middle East for the first time, greeting her like a homecomer. The hour was seven in the evening, but it could have been three in the morning, for she knew at once that this was not a world that went to bed. The uproar in the reception hall reminded her of Derby Day before the "off"; there were enough armed men in different uniforms to begin their own war. Clutching her shoulder bag to her chest, she shoved her way towards the immigration queue and discovered to her surprise that she was smiling. Her East German passport, her false appearance, which five hours ago at London Airport had been matters of life and death to her, were trivial in this atmosphere of restless, dangerous urgency.

"Take the left queue, and when you show your passport ask to speak to Mr. Mercedes," Helga had commanded as they sat in the Citroën in the car park at Heathrow.

"What happens if he looses off at me in German?"

The question was beneath her. "If you get lost, take a taxi to the Commodore Hotel, sit in the foyer, and wait. That is an order. Mercedes like the car."

"Then what?"

"Charlie, I think actually you are being a bit stubborn and a bit stupid. Please stop this now."

"Or you'll shoot me," Charlie suggested.

389

"Miss Palme! Passport. *Pass.* Yes, please!"

Palme was her German name. Pronounced "Pal-mer," Helga had said. It was spoken by a small, happy Arab with a day's growth of beard and curly hair and immaculate, threadbare clothes. "Please," he repeated, and plucked at her sleeve. His jacket was open and he had a big silver automatic shoved into his waistband. There were twenty people between herself and the immigration officer, and Helga hadn't said it would be like this at all.

"I am Mr. Danny. Please. Miss Palme. Come."

She gave him her passport and he dived away with it into the crowd holding his arms wide for her to follow in his wake. So much for Helga. So much for Mercedes. Danny had vanished, but a moment later he reappeared looking very proud, clutching a white landing-card in one hand and in the other a big official-looking man in a black leather coat.

"Friends," Danny explained, with a patriot's grand smile. "Everybody friends of Palestine."

Somehow she doubted it, but faced with his enthusiasm she was too polite to say so. The big man looked her over gravely, then studied the passport, which he handed to Danny. Lastly, he studied the white card, which he posted into his top pocket.

"*Willkommen,*" he said, with a swift diagonal nod, but it was an invitation to hurry.

They were at the doors as the fight broke out. It began small, as something that a uniformed official had apparently said to a prosperous-looking traveller. Suddenly both were shouting and passing their hands very close to each other's faces. Within seconds, each man had acquired champions, and as Danny guided her to the car park, a group of soldiers in green berets were hobbling towards the scene, unslinging their machine guns on the way.

"Syrians," Danny explained, and smiled philosophically at her as if to say that every country had its Syrians.

The car was an old blue Peugeot full of stale cigarette smoke, and it was parked beside a coffee stall. Danny opened the back door and dusted the cushions with his hand. As she got in, a boy slipped in beside her from the other side. As Danny started the engine, another boy appeared and sat himself in the passenger seat. It was too dark for her to see their features, but she could see their machine guns clearly. They were so young that for a moment she had difficulty in believing that their guns were real. The boy beside her offered her a cigarette and was sad when Charlie declined.

"You speak Spanish?" he enquired with the greatest courtesy, by way of an alternative. Charlie did not. "Then you forgive my English language. If you would speak Spanish, I would speak perfectly."

"But your English is wonderful."

"This is not true," he replied reprovingly, as if he had already identified a Western perfidy, and lapsed into a troubled silence.

A couple of shots rang out behind them, but nobody remarked on them. They were approaching a sandbagged emplacement. Danny stopped the car. A uniformed sentry stared at her, then waved them through with his machine gun.

"Was he Syrian too?" she asked.

"Lebanese," said Danny, and sighed.

But she could feel his excitement all the same. She could feel it in all of them—a keening, a quickness of eye and mind. The street was part battlefield, part building site; the passing street lamps, those that worked, revealed it in hasty patches. Stubs of charred tree recalled a gracious avenue; new bougainvillaea had begun to cover the ruins. Burnt-out cars, peppered with bullet-holes, lay around the pavements. They passed lighted shanties, with garish shops inside, and high silhouettes of bombed buildings broken into mountain crags. They passed a house so pierced with shellholes that it resembled a gigantic cheese-grater balanced against the pale sky. A bit of moon, slipping from one hole to the next, kept pace with them. Occasionally, a brand-new building would appear, half built, half lit, half lived in, a speculator's gamble of red girders and black glass.

"Prague I was two years. Havana, Cuba, three. You have been to Cuba?"

The boy next to her seemed to have recovered from his disappointment.

"I have not been to Cuba," she confessed.

"Now I am official interpreter, Spanish Arabic."

"Fantastic," said Charlie. "Congratulations."

"I interpret for you, Miss Palme?"

"Any time," said Charlie, and there was much laughter. Western woman was reinstated after all.

Danny was braking the car to a walking pace and lowering his window. Dead ahead of them in the centre of the road a brazier glowed, and round it sat a group of men and boys in white *kaffiyehs* and bits of khaki battledress. Several brown dogs had made their own encampment close to them. She remembered Michel in his home village, listening to the tales of travellers, and thought, Now they have made a village in the street. As Danny dipped his lights, an old, beautiful man stood up, rubbed his back, shuffled over to them, machine gun in hand, and leaned his lined face into Danny's window until they could embrace. Their conversation flowed timelessly back and forth. Ignored, Charlie listened to every word, imagining that she could somehow understand. But, looking past him, she had a less comfortable vision: standing in a motionless half circle, four of the old man's audience had their machine guns trained upon the car, and not one of them was above fifteen years old.

"Our people," said Charlie's neighbour, with reverence, as they continued on their way. "Palestinian commandos. Our part of town."

Michel's part too, she thought proudly.

You will find them an easy people to love, Joseph had told her.

Charlie spent four nights and four days with the boys, and loved them singly and collectively. They were the first of her several families. They moved her constantly, like a treasure, always by dark, always with the greatest courtesy. She had arrived so suddenly, they explained, with charming regret; it was necessary for our Captain to make certain preparations. They called her "Miss Palme" and perhaps they really thought it was her name. They returned her love for them, yet they asked her nothing personal and nothing obtrusive; they maintained in every sense a shy and disciplined reticence, which made her curious about the nature of the authority that governed them. Her first bedroom was at the top of an old shell-torn house empty of all other life except for the absent proprietor's parrot, which had a smoker's cough and produced it every time someone lit a cigarette. Its other trick was to squawk like a telephone, which it did in the dead hours, causing her to steal to the door and wait for it to be answered. The boys slept on the landing outside, one at a time, while the other two smoked, drank tiny glasses of sweet tea, and kept up a campfire murmur over their card games.

The nights were eternal, yet no two minutes were the same. The very sounds were at war with one another, first lying off at a safe distance, then advancing, then grouping, then falling upon each other in a skirmish of conflicting dins—a burst of music, the scream of car tyres and sirens—followed by the deep silence of a forest. In that orchestra, gunfire was a minor instrument: a drumbeat here, a tattoo there, sometimes the slow whistle of a shell. Once she heard peals of laughter, but human voices were few. And once, in early morning after an urgent tapping at her door, Danny and the two boys tiptoed together to her window. Going after them, she saw a car parked a hundred yards along the street. Smoke poured out of it; it lifted and rolled itself onto its side like someone turning over in bed. A puff of warm air pushed her back into the room. Something fell off a shelf. She heard a thud inside her head.

"Peace," said Mahmoud, the prettiest, with a wink; and they all retired, bright-eyed and confiding.

Only the dawn was predictable, when from crackling loudspeakers wailed the *muezzin,* summoning the faithful to prayer.

Yet Charlie accepted everything, and gave herself entirely in return. In the unreason around her, in this unlooked-for truce for meditation, she found at last a cradle for her own irrationality. And since no paradox was too great to bear amid such chaos, she found a place in it for Joseph too. Her love for him, in this world of unexplained devotions, was in everything she heard and looked at. And when the boys, over tea and cigarettes, regaled her with brave stories of their families' sufferings at the hands of the Zionists—just as Michel had done, and with the same romantic relish—it was her love for Joseph once more, her memory of his soft voice and rare smile, that opened her heart to their tragedy.

Her second bedroom was high up in a glittering apartment house. From her window, she could stare into the black façade of a new international bank, and past it to the unmoving sea. The empty beach with its deserted beach-huts was like a holiday resort permanently out of season. A single beachcomber had the eccentricity of a Christmas Day bather at the

Serpentine. But the strangest thing in that place was the curtains. When the boys drew them for her at night, she noticed nothing odd. But when the dawn came, she saw a line of bullet-holes running in a wavy snake across the window. That was the day she cooked the boys omelettes for breakfast, then taught them gin rummy for matches.

On the third night, she slept above some sort of military headquarters. There were bars over the windows and shell-holes on the staircase. Posters showed children waving machine guns or bunches of flowers. Dark-eyed guards lounged at every landing, and the whole building had a rackety, Foreign Legion air.

"Our Captain will see you soon," Danny assured her tenderly, from time to time. "He is making preparations. He is a great man."

She was beginning to learn the Arab smile that explained delay. To console her in her waiting, Danny told her the story of his father. After twenty years in the camps, it seemed the old man had grown light-headed with despair. So one morning before sunrise he packed his few belongings into a bag, together with the deeds of his land, and without telling his family, set off across the Zionist lines with the aim of reclaiming his farm in person. Hastening after him, Danny and his brothers arrived in time to see his little crooked figure advance farther and farther into the valley until a landmine blew him up. Danny related all this with a puzzled exactness, while the other two patrolled his English, interrupting to rephrase a sentence when its syntax or cadence displeased them, nodding like old men to approve a phrase. When he had finished, they asked her a number of grave questions about the chastity of Western women, of which they had heard disgraceful but not wholly uninteresting things.

So she loved them more and more, a four-day miracle. She loved their shyness, their virginity, their discipline, and their authority over her. She loved them as captors and as friends. But for all her love, they never gave her back her passport, and if she came too near to their machine guns they drew back from her with dangerous and unbending glances.

"Come, please," said Danny, tapping softly on her door to wake her. "Our Captain is prepared."

It was three in the morning and still dark.

*   *   *

She remembered afterwards about twenty cars, but it could have been only five, because it all happened very fast, a zigzag of increasingly alarming journeys across town, in sand-coloured saloons with aerials front and back and body-guards who didn't speak. The first car was waiting at the foot of the building, but on the courtyard side where she hadn't been before. It wasn't till they were out of the courtyard and racing down the street that she realised that she had left the boys behind. At the bottom of the street, the driver seemed to see something he didn't like, for he threw the car into a screeching U-turn that nearly tipped it, and as they raced back up the road she heard a rattle and a shout from close to her, and felt a heavy hand shove her head down, so she supposed that the gunfire was meant for them.

They went over a crossroads on red and missed a lorry by a prayer; they mounted a pavement to the right, then made a wide arc left into a sloped car park overlooking a deserted lido. She saw Joseph's half moon again, hanging over the sea, and for a second she imagined she was on the drive to Delphi. They pulled up beside a big Fiat and almost tossed her into it; she was away again, the property of two new bodyguards, heading down a pitted motorway with riddled buildings either side and a pair of lights following very close. The mountains straight ahead of her were black, but those to her left were grey because a glow from the valley lit their flanks, and beyond the valley lay the sea again. The needle was on 140, but suddenly it was on nothing at all because the driver had turned his lights out and the pursuit car had done the same.

To their right ran a line of palms, to their left the central reservation that divided the two carriageways, a pavement six feet across, sometimes gravel, sometimes vegetation. With a great bump they mounted it and with another landed on the opposing carriageway. Traffic was hooting at them and Charlie was shouting "Jesus!" but the driver was not receptive to blasphemy. Putting his lights on full, he drove straight at the oncoming traffic before wrenching the car left again under a small bridge, and suddenly they were careering to a halt in an empty mud road and changing to a third car, this time a Landrover with no windows. It was raining. She hadn't noticed it till now, but as they bundled her into the back of the Landrover, a downpour soaked her to the skin and she saw a shellburst of white lightning smash against the mountains. Or perhaps it was a shell.

They were climbing steeply, a winding road. Through the back of the Landrover she could see the valley fall away; through the windscreen, between the heads of the bodyguard and driver, she could watch the rain leaping out of the tarmac like shoals of dancing minnows. There was a car in front of them, and Charlie knew from the way they followed it that it was theirs; there was a car behind them, and from the way they didn't bother with it, it was theirs as well. They made another change and perhaps another; they approached what seemed to be a deserted schoolhouse, but this time the driver cut the engine while he and the bodyguard sat with their machine guns at the windows, waiting to see who else came up the hill. There were road checks where they stopped and others where they drove through with no more than a slow lift of the hand at the passive sentries. There was a road check where the bodyguard in the front seat lowered his window and fired a burst of machine-gun fire into the darkness, but the only response was a panicky whining of sheep. And there was a last terrifying leap into blackness between two sets of headlamps that were turned full on to them, but by then she was past being terrified; she was shaken and punch-drunk and she didn't give a damn.

The car pulled up; she was in the forecourt of an old villa with boy sentries with machine guns posing in silhouette on the roof like heroes in a Russian movie. The air was cold and clean and full of all the Greek smells that the rain had left behind—cypress and honey and every wild flower in the world. The sky was full of storms and smoking cloud; the valley lay stretched below them in receding squares of light. They led her through a porch and into the hall, and there, by the dimmest of overhead lamps, she had her first sight of Our Captain: a brown, lopsided figure with a hank of straight black schoolboy hair, and an English-looking walking stick of natural ash to support his limping legs, and a wry smile of welcome brightening his pitted face. To shake hands with her, he hung the walking stick over his left forearm, letting it dangle, so that she had the feeling of holding him up for a second before he set himself straight again.

"Miss Charlie, I am Captain Tayeh and I greet you in the name of the revolution."

His voice was brisk and businesslike. It was also, like Joseph's, beautiful.

Fear will be a matter of selection, Joseph had warned her. *Unfortunately, no one can be frightened all the time. But with Captain Tayeh, as he calls himself, you must do your best, because Captain Tayeh is a very clever man.*

"Forgive me," Tayeh said, with cheerful insincerity.

The house was not his, for he could find nothing he wanted. Even for an ashtray he had to stomp around in the gloom, humorously questioning objects, whether they were too valuable to use. Nevertheless the house belonged to somebody he liked, for she observed a friendliness about his manner that said *That's typical of them—yes, that's exactly where they would keep their drink.* The light was still sparse, but as her eyes grew accustomed to it she decided she was in a professor's house; or a politician's; or a lawyer's. The walls were lined with real books that had been read and flagged and shoved back none too tidily; a painting that hung over the fireplace could have been Jerusalem. All else was a masculine disorder of different tastes: leather chairs and patchwork cushions and a jarring hotchpotch of Oriental carpets. And pieces of Arab silver, very white and ornate, glinting like treasure chests out of dark recesses. And a separate study down two steps into an alcove, with an English-style desk and a panoramic view of the valley she had just emerged from, and of the sea coast in the moonlight.

She was sitting where he had told her to sit, on the leather sofa, but Tayeh himself was still bumping relentlessly about the room on his stick, doing everything singly while he shot her glances from different angles, getting the measure of her; now the glasses; now a smile; now, with another smile, vodka; and lastly Scotch, apparently his favourite brand, for he studied the label approvingly. A boy sat either end of the room, each with a machine gun across his knees. A pile of letters lay strewn over the table, and she knew without looking that they were her own letters to Michel.

Do not mistake seeming confusion for incompetence,

Joseph had warned her; *no racist thoughts, please, about Arab inferiority.*

The lights went out completely but they often did; even in the valley. He stood over her, framed against the huge window, a vigilant smiling shadow leaning on a stick.

"Do you know what it's like for us when we go home?" he asked, still gazing at her. But his stick was pointed to the big picture window. "Can you imagine what it is like to be in your own country, under your own stars, standing on your own land, with a gun in your hand, looking for the oppressor? Ask the boys."

His voice, like other voices she knew, was even more beautiful in the dark.

"They liked you," he said. "Did you like them?"

"Yes."

"Which one you liked best?"

"All equally," she said, and he laughed again.

"They say you are much in love with your dead Palestinian. Is that true?"

"Yes."

His stick was still pointing at the window. "In the old days, if you had the courage, we would take you with us. Over the border. Attack. Avenge. Come back. Celebrate. We would go together. Helga says you want to fight. You want to fight?"

"Yes."

"Anybody, or just Zionists?" He didn't wait for an answer. He was drinking. "Some of the scum we get, they want to blow the whole world up. Are you like that?"

"No."

"They are scum, those people. Helga—Mr. Mesterbein—necessary scum. Yes?"

"I haven't had time to find out," she said.

"Are *you* scum?"

"No."

The lights came on. "No," he agreed, continuing to examine her. "No, I don't think you are. Maybe you change. Ever killed anybody?"

"No."

"You're lucky. You've got police. Your own land. Parliament. Rights. Passports. Where do you live?"

"In London."

"Which part?"

She had a feeling that his injuries made him impatient of her answers; that they drove his mind beyond them all the time, to other questions. He had found a tall chair and was dragging it carelessly towards her, but neither of the boys got up to help him, and she guessed they didn't dare. When he had the chair where he wanted, he pulled a second up to it, then sat on the one and with a grunt swung his leg onto the other. And when he had done all that, he dragged a loose cigarette from the pocket of his tunic and lit it.

"You're our first English, know that? Dutch, Italian, French, German. Swedes. Couple of Americans. Irish. They all come to fight for us. No English. Not till now. The English come too late as usual."

A wave of recognition passed over her. Like Joseph, he spoke from pains she had not experienced, from a viewpoint she had yet to learn. He was not old, but he had a wisdom that had been acquired too early. Her face was close to the little lamp. Perhaps that was why he had put her there. Captain Tayeh is a very clever man.

"If you want to change the world, forget it," he remarked. "The English did that already. Stay home. Act your little parts. Improve your mind in a vacuum. It's safer."

"Not now it isn't," she said.

"Oh, you could go back." He drank some whisky. "Confess. Reform. A year in prison. Everyone should spend a year in prison. Why kill yourself fighting for us?"

"For him," she said.

With his cigarette, Tayeh irritably waved away her romanticism. "Tell me what's for him? He's dead. In a year or two, we shall all be dead. What's for him?"

"Everything. He taught me."

"Did he tell you what we do—bomb?—shoot?—kill? . . . Never mind."

For a time the only thing he cared about was his cigarette. He watched it burn, he inhaled from it and scowled at it, then stubbed it out and lit another. She guessed he did not really like to smoke.

"*What* could he teach you?" he objected. "A woman like you? He was a little boy. He couldn't teach anybody. He was nothing."

"He was everything," she repeated woodenly, and once

again felt him lose interest, like someone bored by callow conversation. Then she realised he had heard something ahead of everybody else. He gave a swift order. One of the boys leapt to the door. We run faster for crippled men, she thought. She heard soft voices from outside.

"Did he teach you to hate?" Tayeh suggested, as if nothing had happened.

"He said hate was for Zionists. He said that to fight we must love. He said anti-Semitism was a Christian invention."

She broke off, hearing what Tayeh had heard so long before: a car coming up the hill. He hears like the blind, she thought. It's because of his body.

"You like America?" he enquired.

"No."

"Ever been?"

"No."

"How can you tell you don't like it if you haven't been?" he asked.

But once again the question was rhetorical, a point he was making to himself in the dialogue he was conducting around her. The car was pulling into the forecourt. She heard footsteps and subdued voices, and saw the beams of its head-lamps cross the room before they were put out.

"Stay where you are," he ordered.

Two other boys appeared, one carrying a plastic bag, the other a machine gun. They stood still, waiting respectfully for Tayeh to address them. The letters lay between them on the table and, when she remembered how important they had been, their disorder was majestic.

"You are not followed and you are going south," Tayeh said to her. "Finish your vodka and go with the boys. Maybe I believe you, maybe I don't. Maybe it won't matter too much. They have clothes for you."

It was not a car but a grimy white ambulance with green crescents painted on the sides and a lot of red dust over the bonnet, and a tousled boy in dark glasses at the wheel. Two more boys crouched on the torn bunk beds in the back with their machine guns jammed uncomfortably into the narrow space, but Charlie sat up boldly beside the driver, wearing a grey hospital tunic and headscarf. It was not night any more but a cheerful dawn, with a heavy red sun to their left that kept hiding as they wound carefully down the hill. She tried

English small talk on the driver but he became angry. She gave a happy "Hi there" to the boys behind, but one was sullen and the other ferocious, so she thought, Fight your own damn revolution, and studied the view. South, he had said. For how long? For what? But there was an ethic about not asking questions, and her pride and her instinct of survival required she conform to it.

The first checkpoint came as they entered the city; there were four more before they left it on the coast road south, and at the fourth a dead boy was being loaded into a taxi by two men, while women screamed and beat on the roof. He was on his side with an empty hand pointing downwards, still grasping for something. *After the first death there is no other,* Charlie recited to herself, thinking of the murdered Michel. The blue sea opened to their right, and once more the landscape became ridiculous. It was as if civil war had broken out along the English seaside. Wrecks of cars and bullet-spattered villas lined the road; in a playing field, two children kicked a football to each other across a shell crater. The little yachting jetties lay smashed and half submerged; even the northbound fruit lorries that nearly ran them off the road had a fugitive desperation.

Again they stopped for a road check. Syrians. But German nurses in Palestinian ambulances were of no interest to anyone. She heard the revving of a motorcycle and glanced incuriously towards it. A dusty Honda, its carrier bags crammed with green bananas. A live chicken dangling by its legs from the handlebar. And, in the saddle, Dimitri listening earnestly to the engine. He wore the half uniform of a Palestinian soldier, and a red *kaffiyeh* round his neck. Shoved through the khaki epaulette of his shirt, like a girl's favour, was a bold sprig of white heather to say "We're with you," because white heather was the sign she had been looking out for these last four days.

From now on, only the horse knows the way, Joseph had told her; *your job is stay in the saddle.*

Once again, they made a family and waited.

Their home this time was a small house near Sidon with a concrete verandah that had been split in two by a shell from an Israeli warship, leaving rusted iron rods sticking out like the antennae of a giant insect. The back garden was a tangerine orchard where an old goose pecked at the fallen fruit; the front was a tip of mud and scrap metal that had been a famous emplacement during the last invasion, or the last but five. In the adjacent paddock a wrecked armoured car was shared between a family of yellow chickens and a refugee spaniel with four fat puppies. Beyond the armoured car lay the blue Christian sea of Sidon, with its Crusader fortress stuck out on the waterfront like a perfect sandcastle. From Tayeh's seemingly endless stock of boys, Charlie had acquired two more: Kareem and Yasir. Kareem was plump and clownish, and made a show of regarding his machine gun as a dead weight, puffing and grimacing whenever he was obliged to shoulder it. But when she smiled at him in sympathy he became flustered and hurried away to join Yasir. His ambition was to become an engineer. He was nineteen and had been fighting six years. He spoke English in a whisper, and put "use to" with almost every verb.

"When Palestine will use to be free, I study in Jerusalem," said Kareem. "Meantime"—he tilted his hand and sighed at the awful prospect—"maybe Leningrad, maybe Detroit."

Yes, Kareem agreed politely, he use to have a brother and a sister, but his sister had died in a Zionist air attack on the camp at Nabatiyeh. His brother was moved to Rashidiyeh camp and died in a naval bombardment three days later. He described these losses modestly, as if they ranked low in the general tragedy.

"Palestine is use to be a little cat," he told Charlie mysteriously one morning, as she was standing patiently at her bedroom window in a billowing white nightdress while he held his machine gun at the ready. "She needs much stroking or she use to go wild."

He had seen a bad-looking man in the street, he explained, and had come up to see whether he should kill him.

But Yasir, with his boxer's lowered brow and scorching, furious gaze, could not speak to her at all. He wore a red check shirt and a black lanyard looped over his shoulder to denote Military Intelligence, and when darkness fell, he stood in the garden, watching the sea for Zionist raiders. He was a big Communist, Kareem explained sympathetically, and he was going to destroy colonialism everywhere in the world.

Yasir hated Westerners even when they claimed to love Palestine, said Kareem. His mother and all his family had died at Tal al-Zataar.

Of what? Charlie asked.

Of thirst, said Kareem, and explained a small piece of modern history to her: Tal al-Zataar, the hill of thyme, was a refugee camp in Beirut. Tin-roofed huts, often eleven to a room. Thirty thousand Palestinians and poor Lebanese held out there for seventeen months against persistent shelling.

By whom? Charlie asked.

Kareem was puzzled by her question. By the Kata'ib, he said, as if it were obvious. By Fascist Maronite irregulars, assisted by the Syrians and doubtless by the Zionists also. Thousands died, but no one knew how many, he said, because so few remained to miss them. When the attackers came in, they shot most of the survivors. The nurses and doctors were lined up and shot dead too, which was logical, since they had no medicine left, and no water, and no patients.

"Were you there?" Charlie asked Kareem.

No, he replied; but Yasir was.

"In the future, do not sunbathe," Tayeh told her when he arrived to collect her the next evening. "This is not the Riviera."

She never saw the boys again. She was entering by degrees exactly that condition which Joseph had predicted. She was being educated to tragedy, and the tragedy absolved her of the need to explain herself. She was a blinkered rider, being conveyed through events and emotions too great for her to encompass, into a land where merely to be present was to be part of a monstrous injustice. She had joined the victims and was finally reconciled to her deceit. As each day passed, the fiction of her pretended allegiance to Michel became more firmly based in fact, while her allegiance to Joseph, if not a fiction, survived only as a secret mark upon her soul.

"Soon we shall all use to be dead,'" Kareem told her, echoing Tayeh. "The Zionists will genocide us to death, you will use to see."

The old prison was in the centre of town, and it was the place, Tayeh had said cryptically, where the innocent served their life sentences. To reach it, they had to park in the main square and enter a maze of ancient passages open to the sky but hung with plastic-covered slogans, which she at first mistook for washing. It was the evening hour of trading; shops and stalls were full. The street lamps shone deeply into the old marble of the walls, seeming to light them from inside. The noise in the alleys was piecemeal, and sometimes when they turned a corner it stopped, except for their own footsteps clipping and shuffling on the polished Roman paving stones. A hostile man in bowlegged trousers led the way.

"I have explained to the Administrator that you are a Western journalist," Tayeh told her as he hobbled at her side. "His manners towards you are not good, because he does not love those who come here to improve their knowledge of zoology."

The torn moon kept pace with them; the night was very hot. They entered another square and a burst of Arab music greeted them, relayed from improvised loudspeakers on poles. The high gates stood open and gave on to a bright-lit courtyard from which a stone staircase lifted to successive balconies. The music was louder.

"So who are they?" Charlie whispered, still mystified. "What have they done?"

"Nothing. That is their crime. They are the refugees who have taken refuge from the refugee camps," Tayeh replied. "The prison has thick walls and was empty, so we took possession of it to protect them. Greet people solemnly," he added. "Do not smile too readily or they will think you are laughing at their misery."

An old man on a kitchen chair stared blankly at them. Tayeh and the Administrator went forward to greet him. Charlie gazed around. *I see this every day. I am a hardnosed Western journalist describing deprivation to those who have everything and are miserable.* She was in the centre of a vast stone silo whose ancient walls were lined to the sky with cage doors and wooden balconies. Fresh white paint, covering everything, gave an illusion of hygiene. The cells on the ground floor were arched. Their doors stood open as if for hospitality; the figures inside them appeared at first motionless. Even the children moved with great economy. Clotheslines hung before every cell, and their symmetry suggested the competitive pride of village life. Charlie smelt coffee, open drains, and wash-day. Tayeh and the Administrator returned.

"Allow them to speak to you first," Tayeh advised her, yet again. "Do not be forward to these people, they will not understand. You are observing a species already half extinct."

They climbed a marble staircase. The cells on this floor had solid doors, with peepholes for the jailers. The noise seemed to rise with the heat. A woman passed wearing full peasant costume. The Administrator addressed her and she pointed along the balcony to a hand-drawn sign in Arabic, shaped like a crude arrow. Looking downward into the well, Charlie saw the old man back on his chair, staring into nothing. He has done his day's work, she thought; he has told us "Go upstairs." They reached the arrow, followed its direction, came upon another, and were soon advancing into the very centre of the prison. I'll need string to find my way back, she thought. She glanced at Tayeh, but he did not want to look at her. In future don't sunbathe. They entered a former staff-room or canteen. At the centre stood a plastic-covered examination table and, on a new trolley, medicines, swab buckets, and syringes. A man and a woman were ministering; the woman, dressed in black, was swabbing a baby's eyes with cotton wool. The waiting mothers sat patiently along the wall while their babies dozed or fretted.

"Stand here," Tayeh ordered, and this time went forward himself, leaving Charlie with the Administrator. But the woman had already seen him enter; her eyes lifted to him, then to Charlie, and remained on her, full of meaning and question. She said something to the child's mother and handed back the baby. She went to the handbasin and methodically washed her hands while she studied Charlie in the mirror.

"Follow us," Tayeh said.

Every prison has one: a small bright room with plastic flowers and a photograph of Switzerland, where blameless people can be entertained. The Administrator had departed. Tayeh and the girl sat either side of Charlie, the girl as straight as a nun, and Tayeh on the slope, with one leg stuck stiffly to one side of him and the stick like a tentpole down the centre of him, and the sweat running over his cratered face while he smoked and fidgeted and frowned. The sounds from the prison had not ceased, but had joined together in a single jangle, partly of music, partly of human voices. Sometimes, amazingly, Charlie heard laughter. The girl was beautiful and stern, and a little awesome in her blackness, with straight strong features and a dark, direct gaze that had no interest in dissembling. She had cut her hair short. The door stood open. The usual two boys guarded it.

"You know who she is?" Tayeh enquired, already stubbing out his first cigarette. "You recognise something familiar in the face? Look hard."

Charlie did not need to. "Fatmeh," she said.

"She has returned to Sidon to be among her people. She speaks no English, but she knows who you are. She has read your letters to Michel, also his letters to you. Translated. She is interested in you, naturally."

Shifting painfully in his chair, Tayeh fished out a sweat-smeared cigarette and lit it.

"She is in grief, but so are we all. When you speak to her, please do not sentimentalise. She has lost three brothers and a sister already. She knows how it is done."

Very calmly, Fatmeh began speaking. When she stopped, Tayeh interpreted—with contempt, which was his manner tonight.

"She wishes first to thank you for the great comfort you gave to her brother Salim while he was fighting Zionism, also that you yourself have joined the struggle for justice." He waited as Fatmeh resumed. "She says, now you are sisters. Both loved Michel, both are proud of his heroic death. She asks you—" Again he paused to let her speak. "She asks you, will you also accept death rather than become the slave of imperialism? She is very political. Tell her yes."

"Yes."

"She wishes to hear about how Michel spoke of his family and of Palestine. Don't fabricate. She has a good instinct."

Tayeh's manner was no longer careless. Clambering to his feet, he began a slow tour of the room, now interpreting, now throwing in his own subsidiary questions.

Charlie spoke directly ahead of her, from the heart, from her wounded memory. She was an impostor to nobody, not even to herself. At first, she said, Michel would not speak of his brothers at all; and only once, in passing, of his beloved

Fatmeh. Then one day—it was in Greece—he started with great love to reminisce about them, remarking that since his mother's death, his sister Fatmeh had made herself the mother of all the family.

Tayeh brusquely translated. The girl made no response, but her eyes were all the time on Charlie's face, watching it, listening to it, questioning it.

"What did he say about them—the brothers," Tayeh ordered impatiently. "Repeat it to her."

"He said that all through his childhood, his elder brothers were his shining inspiration. In Jordan, in their first camp, when he was still too young to fight, the brothers would slip away without saying where they were going. Then Fatmeh would come to his bed and whisper to him that they had made another attack against the Zionists—"

Tayeh interrupted with a swift translation.

Fatmeh's questions lost their nostalgic note and acquired the harshness of examination. What had her brothers studied? What were their skills and aptitudes, how had they died? Charlie answered where she could, piecemeal: Salim—Michel —had not told her everything. Fawaz was a great lawyer, or had meant to be. He had been in love with a student in Amman—she was his childhood sweetheart from their village in Palestine. The Zionists shot him down as he came out of her house early one morning. "According to Fatmeh—" she began.

"What according to Fatmeh?" Tayeh demanded.

"According to Fatmeh, the Jordanians had betrayed her address to the Zionists."

Fatmeh was putting a question. Angrily. Tayeh again translated:

"In one of his letters, Michel mentions his pride at sharing torture with his great brother," Tayeh said. "He writes regarding this incident that his sister Fatmeh is the only woman on earth, other than you, whom he can love completely. Explain this to Fatmeh, please. Which brother does he mean?"

"Khalil," said Charlie.

"Describe the whole incident," Tayeh ordered.

"It was in Jordan."

"Where? How? Describe exactly."

"It was evening. A convoy of Jordanian jeeps came into the camp, six of them. They grabbed Khalil and Michel—

Salim—and ordered Michel to go and cut some branches from a pomegranate tree"—she held out her hands, just as Michel had done that night in Delphi—"six young branches, one metre each. They made Khalil take his shoes off and Salim kneel down and hold Khalil's feet while they beat them with the pomegranate branches. Then they had to change over. Khalil holds Salim. Their feet aren't feet any more, they're unrecognisable. But the Jordanians make them run all the same, by shooting behind them into the ground."

"So?" said Tayeh impatiently.

"So what?"

"So why is Fatmeh so important in this matter?"

"She nursed them. Day and night, bathing their feet. She gave them courage. Read to them from the great Arab writers. Made them plan new attacks. 'Fatmeh is our heart,' he said. 'She is our Palestine. I must learn from her courage and her strength.' He said that."

"He even wrote it, the fool," said Tayeh, hanging his walking stick over the back of a chair with an angry clank. He lit himself another cigarette.

Staring stiffly towards the blank wall as if there were a mirror on it, leaning backward on his ash stick, Tayeh was drying off his face with a handkerchief. Fatmeh rose and went silently to the basin and fetched a glass of water for him. From his pocket, Tayeh pulled a flat half-bottle of Scotch and poured some in. Not for the first time it occurred to Charlie that they knew each other very well, in the manner of close colleagues, even lovers. They talked together a moment; then Fatmeh turned and faced her again, while Tayeh put her last question.

"What is this in his letter: 'The plan we agreed over the grave of my father'—explain this also. What plan?"

She started to describe the manner of his death, but Tayeh impatiently cut her short.

"We know how he died. He died of despair. Tell us about the funeral."

"He asked to be buried in Hebron—in El Khalil—so they took him to the Allenby Bridge. The Zionists wouldn't let him cross. So Michel and Fatmeh and two friends carried the coffin up a high hill, and when evening came they dug a grave at a place where he could look down into the land the Zionists stole from him."

"Where is Khalil while they are doing this?"

"Absent. He's been away for years. Out of touch. Fighting. But that night, while they were filling in the grave, he suddenly showed up."

"And?"

"He helped fill in the grave. Then he told Michel to come and fight."

"*Come* and fight?" Tayeh repeated.

"He said it was time to attack the Jewish entity. Everywhere. There was to be no distinction any more between Jew and Israeli. He said the whole Jewish race was a Zionist power base and that the Zionists would never rest until they had destroyed our people. Our only chance was to lift the world up by the ears and make it listen. Again and again. If innocent life was to be wasted, why should it always be Palestinian? The Palestinians were not going to imitate the Jews and wait two thousand years to get back their homeland."

"So what was the plan?" Tayeh insisted, unimpressed.

"Michel should come to Europe. Khalil would arrange it. Become a student, but also a fighter."

Fatmeh spoke. Not for very long.

"She says her small brother had a big mouth, and that God was wise to close it when he did," said Tayeh and, beckoning to the boys, he limped quickly ahead of her down the stairs. But Fatmeh put a hand on Charlie's arm and held her back, then yet again stared at her with a frank but friendly curiosity. Side by side, the two women returned along the corridor. At the door to the clinic, Fatmeh again stared at her, this time with undisguised bewilderment. Then she kissed Charlie on the cheek. The last Charlie saw of her, she had recovered the baby and was once more swabbing its eyes, and if Tayeh hadn't been calling to her to make haste, she would have stayed and helped Fatmeh for the rest of her life.

"You must wait," Tayeh told her as he drove her up to the camp. "We were not expecting you, after all. We did not invite you."

She thought at first sight that he had brought her to a

village, for the terraces of white huts that clambered down the hillside looked quite attractive enough in the headlights. But as the drive continued, the scale of the place began to reveal itself, and by the time they had reached the hilltop, she was in a makeshift town built for thousands, not hundreds. A grizzled, dignified man received them, but it was Tayeh on whom he lavished his warmth. He wore polished black shoes and a khaki uniform pressed into razor-sharp creases, and she guessed he had put on his best clothes for Tayeh's coming.

"He is our headman here," Tayeh said simply, introducing him. "He knows you are English, otherwise nothing. He will not ask."

They followed him to a sparse room lined with sporting cups in glass cases. On a coffee table at the centre lay a plate piled high with packets of cigarettes of different brands. A very tall young woman brought sweet tea and cakes, but no one spoke to her. She wore a headscarf, a traditional full skirt, and flat shoes. Wife? Sister? Charlie could not make her out. She had bruises of grief beneath her eyes and seemed to move in a realm of private sadness. When she had gone, the headman fixed Charlie with a ferocious stare and delivered a sombre speech with a distinct Scottish accent. He explained without smiling that during the Mandate years he had served in the Palestine police, and still drew a British pension. The spirit of his people, he said, had been greatly strengthened by its suffering. He supplied statistics. In the last twelve years, the camp had been bombed seven hundred times. He gave the casualty figures and dwelt upon the proportion of dead women and children. The most effective weapons were American-built cluster bombs; the Zionists also dropped booby traps disguised as children's toys. He gave an order and a boy disappeared and returned with a battered toy racing-car. He lifted off the casing and revealed wiring and explosive inside. Maybe, thought Charlie. Maybe not. He referred to the variety of political theory among Palestinians, but earnestly assured her that, in the fight against Zionism, such distinctions disappeared.

"They bomb us all," he said.

He addressed her as "Comrade Leila," which was how Tayeh had announced her, and when he had finished, he declared her welcome and handed her gratefully to the tall sad woman.

"For justice," he said, by way of good night.

"For justice," Charlie replied.

Tayeh watched her go.

The narrow streets had a candlelit darkness. Open drains ran down the centre; a three-quarter moon drifted above the hills. The tall girl led the way; the boys followed with machine guns and Charlie's shoulder bag. They passed a mud playing-field and low huts that could have been a school. Charlie remembered Michel's football, and wondered too late whether he had won any silver cups for the headman's shelves. Pale blue lights burned over the rusted doors of the air-raid shelters. The noise was the night noise of exiles. Rock and patriotic music mingled with the timeless murmur of old men. Somewhere a young couple was feuding. Their voices welled into an explosion of pent-up fury.

"My father apologises for the sparseness of the accommodation. It is a rule of the camp that buildings should not be permanent, lest we forget where our true home is. If there is an air raid, please do not wait for the sirens, but follow the direction in which everybody is running. After a raid, please be sure to touch nothing that is lying on the ground. Pens, bottles, radios—nothing."

Her name was Salma, she said with her sad smile, and her father was the headman.

Charlie allowed herself to be ushered forward. The hut was tiny, and clean as a hospital ward. It had a handbasin and a lavatory and a rear courtyard the size of a pocket handkerchief.

"What do you do here, Salma?"

The question seemed momentarily to puzzle her. To be here was already an occupation.

"So where did you learn your English?" Charlie said.

In America, Salma replied; she was a graduate in biochemistry from the University of Minnesota.

There is a terrible, yet pastoral peace that comes from living for a long time among the world's real victims. In the camp, Charlie experienced at last the sympathy that life till now had denied her. Waiting, she joined the ranks of those who had waited all their lives. Sharing their captivity, she dreamed that she had extricated herself from her own. Lov-

ing them, she imagined that she was receiving their for-
giveness for the many duplicities that had brought her here.
No sentries were assigned to her, and on her first morning, as
soon as she woke, she set to work cautiously probing the lim-
its of her freedom. There seemed to be none. She walked the
perimeter of the playing fields and watched small boys with
hunched shoulders straining bitterly to achieve the physique
of manhood. She found the clinic and the schools and the
tiny shops that sold everything from oranges to family-size
bottles of Head and Shoulders shampoo. In the clinic, an old
Swedish woman talked to her contentedly about God's will.

"The poor Jews cannot rest while they have us on their
consciences," she explained dreamily. "God has been so *hard*
on them. Why can't he teach them how to love?"

At midday Salma brought her a flat cheese pie and a pot
of tea, and when they had lunched in her hut they climbed
together through an orange grove to a hilltop very like the
spot where Michel had taught her to shoot his brother's gun.
A range of brown mountains stretched along the western and
southern horizons.

"Those to the east are Syria," said Salma, pointing
across the valley. "But those"—she moved her arm southward
then let it fall in a sudden gesture of despair—"those are
ours, and that is where the Zionists will come from to kill
us."

On the way down, Charlie glimpsed army trucks parked
under camouflage netting and, in a coppice of cedar trees, the
dull glint of gun barrels pointed south. Her father came from
Haifa, all of forty miles away, Salma said. Her mother was
dead, machine-gunned by an Israeli fighter plane as she left
the shelter. She had a brother who was a successful banker in
Kuwait. No, she said with a smile, in answer to the obvious
question; men found her too tall, and too intelligent.

In the evening Salma took Charlie to a children's
concert. Afterwards they went to a schoolroom and, with
twenty other women, glued lurid patches to children's tee-
shirts for the great demonstration, using a machine like a big
green waffle-iron that kept fusing. Some of the patches were
slogans in Arabic, promising the total victory; some were
photographs of Yasir Arafat, whom the women called Abu
Ammar. Charlie stayed up most of the night with them and

became their champion. Two thousand shirts, the right sizes, ali done in time, thanks to Comrade Leila.

Soon her hut was full of children from dawn to dusk, some to speak English with her, some to teach her to dance and sing their songs. And some to hold her hand and march up and down the street with her, for the prestige of being in her company. As to their mothers, they brought her so many sugar biscuits and cheese pies that she could have held out here for ever, which was what she wanted to do.

So who is she? Charlie wondered, addressing her imagination to yet another unfinished short story, as she watched Salma make her sad and private way among her people. It was only gradually that an explanation began to suggest itself. Salma had been out in the world. She knew how Western people talked of Palestine. And she had seen more clearly than her father just how far away were the brown mountains of their homeland.

The great demonstration took place three days later, starting on the playing field in the middle of the morning heat and progressing slowly round the camp, through streets overflowing with crowds and emblazoned with hand-embroidered banners that would have been the pride of any English Women's Institute. Charlie was standing on the doorstep of her hut holding up a little girl who was too young to march, and the air attack began a couple of minutes after the model of Jerusalem had been carried past her shoulder-high by half a dozen kids. First came Jerusalem, represented— Salma explained—by the Mosque of Omar done in gold paper and sea shells. Then came the children of the martyrs, each holding an olive branch and wearing an all-night teeshirt. Then, like a continuation of the festivities, came the jolly little tattoo of cannon fire from the hillside. But no one screamed or started to move away. Not yet. Salma, who was standing beside her, did not even lift her head.

Until then, Charlie had not really thought about aircraft at all. She had noticed a couple, high up, and admired their white plumes as they lazily circled the blue sky. But it had not occurred to her, in her ignorance, that the Palestinians might possess no planes, or that the Israeli Air Force might take exception to fervent claims to their territory made within walking distance of their border. She had been more interested in the uniformed girls dancing to each other on the tractor-drawn floats, tossing their machine guns back and forth to the rhythm of the crowd's handclap; in the fighting boys with strips of red *kaffiyeh* bound Apache-style round their foreheads, posing on the backs of lorries with their machine guns; in the unflagging ululation of so many voices from one end of the camp to the other—did they never get hoarse?

Also, at the precise moment, her eye had been drawn to a small sideshow directly in front of where she and Salma stood—a child being chastened by a guard. The guard had taken off his belt and folded it, and was slapping the child across the face with the loop, and for a second, while she was still considering whether to intervene, Charlie had the illusion, amid so much conflicting din around her, that the belt was causing the explosions.

Then came the whine of aircraft turning under strain, and a lot more fire from the ground, though surely it was too light and small to impress something so fast and high up. The first bomb, when it struck, was almost an anti-climax: if you hear it, you're still alive. She saw its flash a quarter of a mile away on the hillside, then a black onion of smoke as the noise and blast swept over her at the same time. She turned to Salma and shouted something at her, raising her voice as if a storm were blowing, though everything by then was surprisingly quiet; but Salma's face was fixed in a stare of hatred as she looked into the sky.

"When they want to hit us, they hit us," she said. "Today they are playing with us. You must have brought us luck."

The significance of this suggestion was too much for Charlie, and she rejected it outright.

The second bomb fell and it seemed farther away, or perhaps she was less impressionable: it could fall anywhere it liked except in these packed alleys, with their columns of patient children waiting like tiny, doomed sentries for the lava to roll down the mountain. The band struck up, much louder than before; the procession started, twice as brilliant. The band was playing a marching song and the crowd was clapping to it. Unfreezing her hands, Charlie set down her little girl and started to clap too. Her hands stung and her shoul-

ders ached, but she went on clapping. The procession drew to
the side; a jeep raced by, lights flashing, followed by ambulances and a fire engine. A pall of yellow dust hung behind
them like battle smoke. The breeze dispersed it, the band
resumed, and now it was the turn of the fishermen's union,
represented by a sedate yellow van decked in pictures of Arafat, with a giant paper fish, painted red, white, and black, on
its roof. After it, led by a band of pipers, came yet another
river of children with wooden guns, singing the words to the
march. The singing swelled, the whole crowd was taking part
in it, and Charlie, words or none, was singing her heart out.

The planes disappeared. Palestine had won another victory.

"They are taking you to another place tomorrow,"
Salma said that evening as they walked on the hillside.

"I'm not going," said Charlie.

The planes returned two hours later, just before dark,
when she was back in her hut. The siren started too late and
she was still running for the shelters as the first wave came
in—two of them, straight out of an air display, deafening the
crowd with their engines—will they ever pull out of the dive?
They did, and the blast of their first bomb threw her against
the steel door, though the noise was not as bad as the earth-
quake that accompanied it, and the hysterical swimming-pool
screams that filled the black, rank smoke on the other side of
the playing field. The thud of her body alerted someone inside, the door opened, and strong women's hands pulled her
into the darkness and forced her onto a wooden bench. At
first she was stone deaf, but gradually she heard the whimpering of terrified children, and the steadier but fervent voices of
their mothers. Someone lit an oil lamp and fixed it to a hook
at the centre of the ceiling, and for a while it seemed to
Charlie in her giddiness that she was living inside a Hogarth
print that had been hung the wrong way up. Then she realised Salma was beside her, and she remembered she had been
with her ever since the alarm had sounded. Another pair of
planes followed—or was it the first pair making a second
run?—the oil lamp swung, and her vision righted itself as a
stick of bombs approached in careful crescendo. She felt the
first two like blows on her body—no, not again, not again, oh
please. The third was the loudest and killed her outright, the
fourth and fifth told her she was alive after all.

"America!" a woman shouted suddenly, in hysteria and pain, straight at Charlie. "America, America, America!" She tried to get the other women to accuse her also, but Salma told her gently to be quiet.

Charlie waited an hour, but it was probably two minutes, and when still nothing happened she looked at Salma to say "Let's go," because she had decided that the shelter was worse than anywhere. Salma shook her head.

"They are waiting for us to come out," she explained quietly, perhaps thinking of her mother. "We cannot come out before dark."

The dark came and Charlie returned alone to her hut. She lit a candle because the electricity was off, and the last thing she saw in the whole room was the sprig of white heather in the tooth mug above her handbasin. She studied the kitschy little painting of the Palestinian child; she stepped into the courtyard where her clothes still hung on the line— hooray, they're dry. She had no means of ironing, so she opened a drawer of her tiny clapboard chest and folded the clothes into it with a camp dweller's concentration upon neatness. One of my kids put it there, she told herself gaily when the white heather once more forced itself upon her vision. The jolly one with gold teeth I call Aladdin. It's a present from Salma on my last night. How sweet of her. Of him.

"We are a love-affair," Salma had said as they parted. *"You'll go, and when you've gone, we'll be a dream."*

You bastards, she thought. You rotten, killing Zionist bastards. If I hadn't been here, you'd have bombed them to Kingdom Come.

"The only loyalty is to be here," Salma had said.

22

Charlie was not alone in watching the time pass and her life unfold before her eyes. From the moment she had crossed the line, Litvak, Kurtz, and Becker—her whole former family, in fact—had been forced, in one way and another, to harness their impatience to the alien and desultory tempo of their adversaries. "There is nothing so hard in war," Kurtz liked to quote to his subordinates—and assuredly to himself as well—"as the heroic feat of holding back."

Kurtz was holding back as never before in his career. The very act of withdrawing his ragged army from its English shadows appeared—to its foot soldiers, at least—more like a defeat than the victories they had so far scored but scarcely celebrated. Within hours of Charlie's departure, the Hamstead house was given back to the diaspora, the radio van stripped, its electronic equipment shipped as diplomatic baggage to Tel Aviv, somehow in disgrace. The van itself, its false plates removed, its engine numbers sheared from their casings, became yet another burnt-out roadside wreck somewhere between Bodmin moor and civilisation. But Kurtz did not linger for these obsequies. He returned hot-foot to Disraeli Street, chained himself reluctantly to the desk he hated, and became that same coordinator whose functions he had derided to Alexis. Jerusalem was enjoying a balmy spell of winter sunshine, and as he hastened from one secret office building to another, fighting off attacks, begging resources, the gold stone of the Walled City mirrored itself in the shimmering blue sky. For once, Kurtz drew little solace from the sight. His war machine, he said later, had become a horse-drawn carriage with the horses pulling different ways. In the field, despite all Gavron's effort to prevent him, he was his own man; at home, where every second-class politician and third-class soldier saw himself as some kind of genius at intelligence, he had more critics than Elijah and more enemies than the Samaritans. His first battle was for Charlie's continued existence and perhaps for his own too, a kind of obligatory scene that started the moment Kurtz set foot in Gavron's office.

Gavron the Rook was already standing, his arms lifted, shaping for the brawl. His shaggy black hair was more disorderly than ever.

"Had a nice time?" he squawked. "Eaten some good meals? You have put on some weight out there, I see."

Then bang and they were off, their raised voices echoing everywhere while they screamed and shouted at each other and hammered the table with clenched fists like a married couple having a cathartic quarrel. What had become of Kurtz's promises of progress? the Rook demanded. Where was this great reckoning he had spoken of? What was this he heard about Alexis, when he had specifically instructed Marty not to proceed with this man?

"Do you wonder that I lose faith in you—so much invention and money, so many orders disobeyed, so few results?"

As a punishment, Gavron obliged him to attend a meeting of his guidance committee, which by now could talk of nothing but the ultimate recourse. Kurtz had to lobby his heart away, even to obtain a modification of their plans.

"But what have you got going, Marty?" his friends begged him in low urgent voices in the corridors. "Give us a hint at least, so that we know why we are helping you."

His silence offended them, and they left him feeling more like a shabby appeaser.

There were the other fronts to fight on too. To monitor Charlie's progress through enemy territory, he was obliged to go cap in hand to the department that specialised in the maintenance of grass-roots courier lines and listening posts along the north-east seaboard. Its director, a Sephardi from Aleppo, hated everyone but hated Kurtz particularly. A trail like that could take him anywhere! he objected. What about his own operations? As to providing field support for three of Litvak's watchers merely to give the girl a sense of hominess in her new surroundings, such featherbedding was unknown to him, it could not be done. It cost Kurtz blood, and all sorts of underhand concessions, to obtain the scale of collaboration he required. From these and similar deals, Misha Gavron remained callously aloof, preferring to allow the market forces to find their natural solution. If Kurtz believed enough, he would get his way, he told his people secretly; a little curbing, added to a little of the whip, did such a man no harm said Gavron.

Reluctant to leave Jerusalem even for a night while these intrigues continued, Kurtz consigned Litvak to the European shuttle as his emissary charged with strengthening and recasting the surveillance team, and to prepare by all possible means for what they all prayed would be the final phase. The carefree days of Munich, when a couple of boys on double shift could meet their needs, were over for good. To maintain a full-time watch on the heavenly trio of Mesterbein, Helga, and Rossino, whole platoons of fieldmen had to be levied— all German-speakers and many of them rusty from disuse. Litvak's suspicion of non-Israeli Jews only added to the headache, but he would not yield: they were too soft in action, he said; too divided in their loyalties. On Kurtz's orders, Litvak also flew to Frankfurt for a clandestine meeting with Alexis at the airport, partly in order to obtain his help in the surveillance operation, and partly—as Kurtz had it—"to test his spine, a notably uncertain article." In the event, the renewal of their acquaintance was a disaster, for the two men loathed each other on sight. Worse still, Litvak's opinion confirmed the earlier prediction of Gavron's psychiatrists: that Alexis should not be trusted with a used bus-ticket.

"The decision is taken," Alexis announced to Litvak, even before they had sat down, in a furious, half-whispered, half-coherent monologue that kept slipping into falsetto. "I never go back on a decision; it is known of me. I shall present myself to my Minister as soon as this meeting is over, and make a clean breast of everything. For a man of honour there is no alternative." Alexis, it quickly developed, had suffered not merely a change of heart but a full-blown political realignment:

"Nothing against Jews, naturally—as a German, one has one's conscience—but from recent experiences—a certain bomb incident—certain measures one has been forced— blackmailed—into undertaking—one begins also to see reasons why historically the Jews have attracted persecution. Forgive me."

Litvak, with his locked-in glower, forgave him nothing.

"Your friend Schulmann—an able man, impressive— persuasive also—your friend is without all moderation. He has performed unlicensed acts of violence on German soil; he is showing a degree of excess which has too long been attributed to us Germans."

Litvak had had enough. His expression white and sickly, he had turned his eyes away, perhaps to conceal their fire. "Why don't you call him up and tell him all that yourself?" he suggested. So Alexis did. From the airport telephone office, using the special number Kurtz had given him, while Litvak stood at his side, holding the spare earpiece to his head.

"Well now, you do that, Paul," Kurtz advised heartily when Alexis had finished. Then his voice changed: "And while you're talking to the Minister, Paul, just you make sure you tell him all about that Swiss bank account of yours as well. Because if you don't, I may be so impressed by your fine example of candour that I'll have to go down there and tell him about it myself."

After which Kurtz ordered his switchboard to receive no more calls from Alexis for the next forty-eight hours. But Kurtz bore no grudges. Not with agents. The cooling-off period over, he squeezed himself a free day and made his own pilgrimage to Frankfurt, where he found the good Doctor much recovered. The reference to the Swiss bank account, though Alexis ruefully called it "unsporting," had sobered him, but the factor most conducive to his recovery was the joyous sight of his own features in the middle pages of a mass-circulation German tabloid—resolute, dedicated, but always that underlying Alexis wit—which convinced him he was who they said he was. Kurtz left him with this happy fiction and, as a prize, brought back one tantalising clue for his overworked analysts that Alexis in his dudgeon had been holding back: the photocopy of a picture postcard addressed to Astrid Berger under one of her many other aliases.

Handwriting unfamiliar, postmark the seventh district of Paris. Intercepted by the German post office, on orders from Cologne.

The text, in English, ran: "Poor Uncle Frei will be operated next month as planned. But at least that is convenient because you can use V's house. See you there. Love K."

Three days later, the same dragnet pulled in a second in the same hand, sent to another of Berger's safe addresses, the postmark this time Stockholm. Alexis, fully collaborating once more, had it flown to Kurtz by special delivery. The text was brief: "Frei appendectomy room 251 at 1800 hours 24th." And the signature was "M," which told the analysts there was a missing communication in between; or such, at least, had been the pattern by which Michel had also from time to time received his orders. Postcard L, despite everyone's efforts, was never found. Instead, two of Litvak's girls picked up a letter posted by the quarry herself, in this case Berger, to none other than Anton Mesterbein in Geneva. The thing was finely done. Berger was visiting Hamburg at the time, staying with one of her many lovers in an upper-class commune in Blankenese. Following her into town one day, the girls saw her drop a letter surreptitiously into a postbox. The moment she had gone, they posted an envelope of their own, a big yellow one, franked and ready for just such a contingency, to lie on top of it. Then the prettier of the girls stood guard over the box. When the postman came to empty it, she pitched him such a story about love and anger, and made such explicit promises to him, that he stood by grinning sheepishly while she fished her letter out of the bunch before it ruined her life for ever. Except that it was not her letter but Astrid Berger's, nestling just beneath the big yellow envelope. Having steamed it open and photographed it, they got it back in the same box in time for the next collection.

The prize was an eight-page scrawl of gushing schoolgirl passion. She must have been high when she wrote it, but perhaps on nothing more than her own adrenaline. It was frank, it praised Mesterbein's sexual powers. It shot away on wild ideological detours arbitrarily linking El Salvador with the West German defence budget, and the elections in Spain with some recent scandal in South Africa. It raged about the Zionist bombings of Lebanon and spoke of the Israelis' "Final Solution" for the Palestinians. It delighted in life, but saw everything wrong everywhere; and on the clear assumption that Mesterbein's mail was being read by the authorities, it referred virtuously to the need to remain "within the legal borders at all times." But it had a postscript, one line, scribbled off like a parting conceit, heavily underscored, and backed with exclamation marks. A strutting, teasing pun, personal to both of them, yet, like other parting words, containing perhaps the purpose of the whole discourse up to this point. And it was in French: *Attention! On va épater les 'Bourgeois!*

The analysts froze at the sight of it. Why the capital "B"? Why the underlining? Was Helga's education so poor that she applied her native German usage to French nouns? The idea was ridiculous. And why the apostrophe, so carefully added above and to the left of it? While the cryptologists and analysts sweated blood to break the code, while the computers shuddered and creaked and sobbed out impossible permutations, it was the uncomplicated Rachel, none other, with her English North Country directness, who sailed straight for the obvious conclusion. Rachel did crosswords in her spare time and dreamed of winning a free car. "Uncle Frei" was one half, she declared simply, and "Bourgeois" was the other. The "Freibourgeois" were the people of Freiburg, and they were to be shocked by an "operation" that would take place at six in the evening of the twenty-fourth. Room 251? "Well, we'd have to enquire, wouldn't we?" she told the bemused experts.

Yes, they agreed. We would.

The computers were switched off, but still, for a day or two, scepticism lingered. The supposition was absurd. Too easy. Frankly childish.

Yet, as they had learned already, Helga and her kind eschewed almost as a matter of philosophy any systematic method of communication. Comrades should speak to each other from one revolutionary heart to another, in looped allusions beyond the grasp of pigs.

Put it to the test, they said.

There were half a dozen Freiburgs at least, but their first thought was the little town of Freiburg in Mesterbein's native Switzerland, where French and German were spoken side by side, and where the bourgeoisie, even among the Swiss themselves, is famed for its stolidity. With no further delay, Kurtz dispatched a pair of very soft-footed researchers with orders to ferret out any conceivable target attractive to anti-Jewish attack, with a special eye to business houses with Israeli defence contracts; to check, as best they could without official help, all rooms 251, whether in hospitals, hotels, or office buildings; and the names of all patients scheduled for appendectomies on the twenty-fourth of the month; or for operations of any sort at 1800 hours on that day.

From the Jewish Agency in Jerusalem Kurtz obtained an up-to-date list of prominent Jews known to be resident in the town, together with their places of worship and association. Was there a Jewish hospital? If not, a hospital that catered to Orthodox Jewish needs? And so on.

Yet Kurtz was arguing against his own convictions, as they all were. Such targets lacked all the dramatic effect that had distinguished their predecessors; they would *épater* nobody; they made no point that anyone could think of.

Till one afternoon in the middle of all this—almost as if their energies, applied at one spot, had forced the truth into the open at another—Rossino, the murderous Italian, took a plane from Vienna to Basel, where he rented a motorbike. Crossing the border into Germany, he drove forty minutes to the ancient cathedral city of Freiburg-im-Breisgau, once the capital of the state of Baden. There, having first enjoyed a lavish luncheon, he presented himself to the university's *Rektorat* and enquired courteously about a course of lectures on humanist subjects that was available, on a limited basis, to members of the general public. And more covertly, where room 251 was situated on the university's diagram of its premises.

It was a dart of light through the fog. Rachel was right; Kurtz was right; God was just, and so was Misha Gavron. The market forces had found their natural solution.

Only Gadi Becker did not share the general elation.

Where was he?

There were times when others seemed to know the answer better than he himself. One day he was pacing about the house in Disraeli Street, focussing his restless stare on the cipher machines, which, far too rarely for his taste, reported sightings of his agent, Charlie. The same night—or, more accurately, on the early morning of the next day—he was pressing the doorbell of Kurtz's house, waking Elli and the dogs, and demanding reassurances that there would be no strike against Tayeh or whomever until Charlie was laid off; he had heard rumours, he said: "Misha Gavron is not famous for his patience," he said drily.

If anyone came back from the field—the boy known as Dimitri, for instance, or his companion Raoul, exfiltrated by

rubber boat—Becker insisted on being present at his debriefing, and firing questions at him regarding her condition.

After a few days of this, Kurtz got sick of the sight of
him—"haunting me like my own bad conscience"—and
threatened openly to forbid him the house, until wiser counsels got the better of him. "An agent-runner without his agent
is a conductor without an orchestra," he explained to Elli
profoundly, while he wrestled to quell his own anger. "More
appropriate is to humour him, help him to pass the time."

Secretly, with no one's connivance but Elli's, Kurtz rang
Frankie, telling her that her former husband was in town,
and giving her the number to reach him; for Kurtz, with
Churchillian magnanimity, expected everyone to have a marriage like his own.

Frankie duly phoned; Becker listened to her voice for a
time—if indeed it was he who answered—and softly replaced
the receiver on its cradle without replying, which enraged
her.

Kurtz's ploy had some effect, however, for the next day
Becker set out on what was later regarded as a kind of journey of self-appraisal regarding the basic assumptions of his
life. Hiring a car, he drove first to Tel Aviv, where, having
transacted some pessimistic business with his bank manager,
he visited the old cemetery where his father was buried. He
put flowers on the grave, cleaned meticulously around it with
a trowel that he borrowed, and said *Kaddish* aloud, though
neither he nor his father had ever had much time for religion.
From Tel Aviv he headed south-east to Hebron or, as Michel
would have called it, El Khalil. He visited the mosque of
Abraham, which since the war of '67 doubles uneasily as a
synagogue; he chatted to the reservist soldiers, in their sloppy
bush hats and shirts unbuttoned to the belly, who lounged at
the entrance and patrolled the battlements.

Becker, they told each other when he had gone—except
that they used his Hebrew name—the legendary Gadi himself—the man who fought the battle for the Golan from behind the Syrian lines—what the hell was *he* doing in this
Arab hellhole, looking so uneasy?

Under their admiring gaze, he wandered through the ancient covered market, apparently unheeding of the explosive
quiet and of the smouldering dark glances of the occupied.
And sometimes, seemingly with other thoughts in mind, he

paused and spoke to a shopkeeper in Arabic, asking after a spice or the price of a pair of shoes, while small boys gathered round to listen to him, and once, for a dare, to touch his hand. Returning to his car, he nodded farewell to the troops and headed into the small roads that thread themselves among the rich red grape terraces, until he came by stages to the hilltop Arab villages on the eastern side, with their squat stone houses and Eiffel Tower aerials on the roofs. A light snow lay on the upper slopes; stacks of dark cloud gave the earth a cruel and unappeasing glow. Across the valley, a huge new Israeli settlement stood like the emissary of some conquering planet.

And in one of the villages, Becker got out and took the air. It was where Michel's family had lived until '67 when his father had seen fit to flee.

"So did he go visit his own tomb as well?" Kurtz demanded sourly when he heard all this. "First his father's, now his own—did he?"

A moment's puzzlement preceded the general laughter as they recalled the Islamic belief that Joseph son of Isaac had also been buried at Hebron, which every Jew knows to be untrue.

From Hebron, it seems, Becker drove northward up the Jordan Valley to Beit She'an, an Arab town resettled by the Jews when it was left empty in the war of '48. Having dawdled there long enough to admire the Roman amphitheatre, he continued at a slow pace to Tiberias, which is fast becoming the modern spa-city of the north, with giant new American-style hotels along the waterfront, a lido, many cranes, and an excellent Chinese restaurant. But his interest there seemed to be slight, for he did not stop, but merely drove slowly, peering out of the window at the skyscrapers as if counting them. He surfaced next at Metulla, at the very northern border with Lebanon. A ploughed strip with several depths of wire marked the frontier, named in better days The Good Fence. On one side, Israeli citizens stood on an observation platform, gazing with bewildered expressions through the barbed wire into badland. On the other, the Lebanese Christian militia drove up and down in all manner of transport, receiving their Israeli supplies for the interminable blood feud against the Palestinian usurper.

But Metulla in those days was also the natural terminus

for courier lines running up to Beirut, and Gavron's service maintained a discreet section there to administer its agents in transit. The great Becker presented himself in the early evening, leafed through the section's logbook, asked some desultory questions about the location of United Nations forces, left again. Looking troubled, the section Commander said. Maybe sick. Sick in his eyes and his complexion.

"So what the devil was he looking for?" Kurtz asked of the Commander when he heard this. But the Commander, a prosaic man and dulled by secrecy, could offer no further theories. Troubled, he repeated. The way agents look sometimes when they come in from a long run.

And still Becker kept driving, till he reached a twisting mountain road ripped by tank tracks, and continued by way of it to the kibbutz where, if anywhere, he kept his heart: an eagle's-nest perched high above the Lebanon on three sides. The place first became a Jewish habitation in '48, when it was established as a military strongpoint to control the only east-west road south of the Litani. In '52, the first young sabra settlers arrived there to live the hard, secular life that was once the Zionist ideal. Since then, the kibbutz had endured occasional shellings, apparent affluence, and a worrying depletion in its membership. Sprinklers were playing on the lawns as Becker arrived; the air was sweet with the scent of red and pink roses. His hosts received him shyly, and with great excitement.

"You have come to join us finally, Gadi? Your fighting days are over? Listen, there is a house waiting for you. You can move in tonight!"

He laughed, but did not say yes or no. He asked for a couple of days' work, but there was little they could give him; it was the slack season, they explained. The fruit and cotton were all picked, the trees pruned, the fields ploughed in readiness for the spring. Then, because he insisted, they promised he might dole out the food in the communal dining-room. But what they really wanted of him was his opinion on the way the country was going—from Gadi, who, if anyone, can tell us. Which meant, of course, that they wished him most of all to hear their own opinions—of this rackety government, of the decadence of Tel Aviv politics.

"We came here to work, to fight for our identity, to turn Jews into Israelis, Gadi! Are we to be a country finally—or are we to be a showcase for international Jewry? What is our future, Gadi? Tell us!"

They addressed these questions to him with a trusting liveliness, as if he were some kind of prophet among them, come to give fresh inwardness to their outdoor lives; they could not know—not at first, anyway—that they were speaking into the void of his own soul. And whatever happened to all our fine talk of coming to terms with the Palestinians, Gadi? The great mistake was in '67, they decided, answering their own questions as usual: in '67 we should have been generous; we should have offered them a proper deal. Who can be generous if not the victors: "We are so powerful, Gadi, and they so weak!"

But after a while, these insoluble issues became too familiar to Becker, and in keeping with his introverted mood he took to sauntering about the camp alone. His favourite spot was a smashed watchtower that looked straight down into a little Shiite town, and north-eastward to the Crusader bastion of Beaufort, at that time still in Palestinian hands. They saw him there on his last evening with them, standing clear of any cover, as close to the electronic border fence as he could get without actually setting off the alarms. He had a light side and a dark side because of the setting sun, and he seemed, by his erect posture, to be inviting the whole Litani basin to know that he was there.

Next morning, he had returned to Jerusalem and, having presented himself at Disraeli Street, spent the day wandering the city's streets where he had fought so many battles and seen the shedding of so much blood, his own included. And still he seemed to question everything he saw. He stared in dazed bewilderment at the sterile arches of the re-created Jewish quarter; he sat himself in the lobbies of the tower hotels that now wreck the Jerusalem skyline, and brooded over the parties of decent American citizens from Oshkosh, Dallas, and Denver who had come in their jumbo-loads, in good faith and middle age, to keep in touch with their heritage. He peered into the little boutiques that sold hand-embroidered Arab kaftans and Arab artefacts guaranteed by the proprietor; he listened to the innocent chatter of the tourists, inhaled their costly scents, and heard them complain, but with comradely politeness, about the quality of the New York–style cuts of prime beef, which were not somehow just the way they tasted back home. And he spent a whole afternoon in the Holocaust Museum, worrying over the photographs of children who would have been his age if they had lived.

Having heard all this, Kurtz cut short Becker's leave and put him back to work. Find out about Freiburg, he told him. Comb the libraries, the records. Find out who we know there, get the layout of the university. Get architects' drawings and town plans. Work out everything we need and double it. By yesterday.

A good fighting man is never normal, Kurtz told Elli, to console himself. If he's not plain stupid, he thinks too much.

But to himself Kurtz marvelled to discover how deeply his unrecovered ewe-lamb could still anger him.

23

It was the end of the line. It was the worst place of all her lives this far, a place to forget even while she was there, her bloody boarding school with rapists added, a forum stuck out in the desert and played with live ammunition. The battered dream of Palestine lay five hours' back-breaking drive behind the hills, and in place of it they had this tatty little fort, like a film set for a *Beau Geste* remake, with yellow stone battlements and a stone staircase and half its side bombed out, and a sandbagged main gate with a flagpole on it that slapped its frayed ropes in the scalding wind and never flew a flag. No one slept in the fort that she knew of. The fort was for administration and interviews; and lamb and rice three times a day; and the turgid group discussions till after midnight at which the East Germans harangued the West Germans and the Cubans harangued everybody, and an American zombie who called himself Abdul read a twenty-page paper on the immediate achievement of world peace.

Their other social centre was the small-arms range, which was not a disused quarry on a hilltop, but an old barrack hut with the windows blocked and a line of electric light-bulbs rigged from the steel beams, and leaking sandbags round the walls. The targets were not oil cans either, but brutish man-sized effigies of American marines, with painted grimaces and fixed bayonets and rolls of sticky brown paper at their feet to patch up their bullet-holes after you had shot them. It was a place constantly in demand, often at dead of night, full of boisterous laughter and groans of competitive disappointment. One day a great fighter came, some kind of terrorist V.I.P. in a chauffeur-driven Volvo, and the place was cleared while he shot in it. Another day a bunch of very wild blacks burst in on Charlie's class, and loosed off magazine after magazine without paying the smallest attention to the young East German in command.

"That satisfy you, whitey?" one of them bellowed over his shoulder, in a rich South African accent.

"Please—oh yes—very good," said the East German, very thrown by their discrimination.

They swaggered away, laughing their heads off, leaving the marines holed like colanders, with the result that the girls' first hour of that day was spent patching them from head to toe.

For living quarters, they had the three long huts, one with cubicles for women; one without cubicles for men; and a third with a so-called library for the training staff—and if they invite you to the library, said a tall Swedish girl called Fatima, don't expect too much in the way of reading. To wake them in the morning, they had a belch of martial music over a loudspeaker they couldn't turn off, followed by physical exercises on a sand flat smeared with lines of sticky dew like gigantic snail tracks. But Fatima said the other places were worse. Fatima, to believe her version of herself, was a training freak. She had been trained in the Yemen, and in Libya, and in Kiev. She was playing the circuit like a tennis pro until somebody decided what to do with her. She had a three-year-old son, called Knut, who ran around naked and looked lonely, but when Charlie talked to him he cried.

Their guards were a new kind of Arab she hadn't met till now and didn't need to meet again: strutting, near-silent cowboys whose game was humiliating Westerners. They postured on the perimeters of the fort and rode six up in jeeps at breakneck speed. Fatima said they were a special militia raised on the Syrian border. Some were so young Charlie wondered their feet could reach the pedals. At night, till Charlie and a Japanese girl raised hell, the same kids arrived in raiding parties of twos and threes and tried to persuade the girls to take a ride into the desert. Fatima usually went, so did an East German, and they came back looking impressed. But the rest of the girls, if they bothered, played safe with Western instructors, which made the Arab boys even crazier.

All the trainers were men, and for morning prayers they ranged themselves before the comrade students like a rabble army while one of them read an aggressive condemnation of the day's arch-enemy: Zionism, Egyptian treachery, European capitalist exploitation, Zionism again, and a new one to Charlie called Christian expansionism—but perhaps that was because it was Christmas Day, a feast celebrated by determined official neglect. The East Germans were cropped and sullen and pretended that women bored them; the Cubans were by turns flamboyant, homesick, and arrogant, and most of them stank and had rotting teeth, except for gentle Fidel, who was everybody's favourite. The Arabs were the most volatile and acted toughest, screaming at the stragglers and, more than once, spraying bullets at the feet of the supposedly inattentive, so that one of the Irish boys bit clean through his finger in a panic, to the great amusement of Abdul the American, who was watching from a distance, which he often did, smirking and slopping after them like a stills man on a film set, taking notes on a pad for his great revolutionary novel.

But the star of the place during those first insane days was a bomb-crazed Czech called Bubi, who on their first morning shot his own combat hat along the sand, first with a Kalashnikov, then with a massive .45 target pistol, and lastly, to finish the brute off, with a Russian grenade, which blew it fifty feet in the air.

Lingua franca for political discussion was O-level English with a bit of French here and there, and if Charlie ever got home alive she swore in her secret heart that she would dine out on those cretinous midnight exchanges concerning the "Dawn of the Revolution" for the rest of her unnatural life. Meanwhile, she laughed at nothing. She had not laughed since the bastards blew up her lover on the road to Munich; and her recent vision of the agony of his people had only intensified her bitter need for retribution.

You will treat everything with a great and lonely seriousness, Joseph had told her, himself as lonely and serious as he could wish her. *You will be aloof, maybe a little crazy, they are used to that. You will ask no questions, you will be private to yourself, day and night.*

Their numbers vacillated from the first day. When their lorry left Tyre, their party was five boys and three girls and conversation was forbidden by order of two guards with cordite smears on their faces who rode with them in the back while their lorry bucked and slithered over the stony hill trail. A girl who turned out to be Basque managed to whisper to her that they were in Aden; two Turkish boys said they were in Cyprus. They arrived to find ten other students waiting, but by the second day the two Turks and the Basque had vanished, presumably at night when lorries could be heard arriving and leaving without lights.

For their inauguration they were required to swear an oath of loyalty to the Anti-Imperialist Revolution and to study the "Rules for This Camp," which were set out like the Ten Commandments on a flat space of white wall in the Comrades' Reception Centre. All comrades to use their Arab names at all times, no drugs, no nudity, no swearing by God, no private conversations, no alcohol, no cohabitation, no masturbation. While Charlie was still wondering which of these injunctions to break first, a recorded address of welcome, no credits, was played over the loudspeaker.

"My comrades. Who are we? We are the ones with no name, no uniform. We are the escaped rats from the capitalist occupation. From the pain-ridden camps of the Lebanon—we come! And shall fight the genocide! From the concrete tombs of Western cities—we come! And find each other! And together we shall light the torch on behalf of eight hundred million starving mouths across the world!"

But when it was over, she felt a cold sweat on her back and a pounding anger in her breast. *We shall,* she thought. *We shall, we shall.* Glancing at an Arab girl beside her, she saw the same fervour in her eye.

Day and night, Joseph had said.

Day and night, therefore, she strove—for Michel, for her own mad sanity, for Palestine, for Fatmeh and for Salma and the bombed children in the Sidon prison; driving herself outward in order to escape the chaos inside; gathering together the elements of her assumed character as never before, welding them into a single combative identity.

I am a grieving, outraged widow and I have come here to take up my dead lover's fight.

I am the awakened militant who has wasted too long on half measures and now stands before you sword in hand.

I have put my hand on the Palestinian heart; I am pledged to lift the world up by its ears to make it listen.

I am on fire but I am cunning and resourceful. I am the sleepy wasp that can wait all winter long to sting.

I'm Comrade Leila, a citizen of the world revolution.

Day and night.

She played this part to its limit, from the angry snap with which she performed her unarmed combat to the unyielding glower with which she regarded her own face in the mirror as she savagely brushed out her long black hair with its red roots already showing. Until what had begun as an effort of will became a habit of mind and body, a sickly, permanent, solitary anger that quickly communicated itself to her audience, whether staff or students. Almost from the first, they accepted the certain strangeness in her, which gave her distance. Perhaps they had seen it in others before her; Joseph said they had. The cold-eyed passion she brought to the weapon training sessions—which extended from hand-held Russian rocket launchers through bomb-making with red circuit wire and detonators to the inevitable Kalashnikov—impressed even the ebullient Bubi. She was dedicated, but she was apart. Gradually she felt them defer to her. The men, even the Syrian militia, ceased to proposition her indiscriminately; the women gave up their suspicion of her striking looks; the weaker comrades started timidly to gather to her, and the strong to acknowledge her as an equal.

There were three beds in her dormitory but to begin with she had only one companion—a tiny Japanese girl who spent much time kneeling in prayer, but to fellow mortals spoke no word of any language but her own. Asleep, she ground her teeth so loudly that one night Charlie woke her up, then sat beside her, holding her hand while she wept silent Asian tears till the music belched and it was time to get her up. Soon afterwards, without explanation, she too vanished, to be replaced by two Algerian sisters, who smoked rancid cigarettes and seemed to know as much about guns and bombs as Bubi did. They were plain girls to Charlie's eye, but the training staff held them in veneration for some unexplained feat of arms against the oppressor. In the mornings they were to be seen wandering sleepily out of the training staff's quarters in their woollen jump-suits as the less favoured were finishing their unarmed combat. Thus Charlie for a while had the dormitory to herself, and though Fidel, the gentle Cuban appeared one night, scrubbed and brushed like a chorister, to press his revolutionary love for her, she maintained her pose of stiff-jawed self-denial and granted him not so much as a kiss before sending him on his way.

The next to apply for her favours after Fidel was Abdul the American. He called on her late one night, knocking so softly that she expected to see one of the Algerian girls, since both regularly forgot their keys. By now, Charlie had decided that Abdul was a permanency of the camp. He was too close to the staff, he had too much licence, and no function but to read his dreary papers and quote Marighella in a rambling Deep South accent, which Charlie suspected was put on. Fidel, who admired him, said he was a Vietnam deserter who hated imperialism and had come here by way of Havana.

"Hi," said Abdul, and slipped past her, grinning, before she had a chance to slam the door on him. He sat on her bed and started to roll himself a cigarette.

"Blow," she said, "Scram."

"Sure," he agreed, and went on rolling his cigarette. He was tall and balding and, seen at close quarters, very thin. He wore Cuban fatigues and a silky brown beard that seemed to have run out of hair.

"What's your *real* name, Leila?" he asked.

"Smith."

"I like it. *Smith.*" He repeated the name several times in different keys. "You Irish, Smith?" He lit the cigarette and offered her a pull. She ignored it. "I hear you are the personal property of Mr. Tayeh. I admire your taste. Tayeh's a very picky guy. What d'you do for a living, Smith?"

She strode to the door and pulled it open, but he stayed on the bed, grinning at her in a weakly, knowing way through his cigarette smoke.

"You don't want to screw?" he enquired. "Pity. These Fräuleins are like Barnum's baby elephants. Thought we might raise the standard a little. Demonstrate the Special Relationship."

Languidly he got up, dropped his cigarette at her bedside, and ground it with his boot.

"You don't have a little hash for a poor man, do you, Smith?"

"Out," she said.

Passively acceding to her judgment, he shuffled towards her, then stopped and lifted his head, and stayed still; and to her embarrassment she saw that his exhausted, characterless eyes were filled with tears, and there were lumps of childish supplication round his jaw.

"Tayeh won't let me jump off the merry-go-round," he complained. His Deep South had given way to East Coast ordinary. "He fears my ideological batteries have run low. And rightly, I'm afraid. I kind of forgot the reasoning about how every dead baby is a step towards world peace. Which is a drag, when you happen to have killed a few. Tayeh is being very sporting about it. Tayeh's a sporting man. 'If you want to go, go,' he says. Then he points at the desert. Sportingly."

Like a puzzled beggar, he took her right hand in both of his and stared into the empty palm. "My name is Halloran," he explained, as if he himself had trouble remembering it. "For Abdul, read Arthur J. Halloran. And if you are ever passing a U.S. Embassy someplace, Smith, I'd be *awfully* grateful if you'd drop a note in to say that Arthur Halloran, formerly of Boston and the Vietnam show, latterly of less official armies, would like to hurry home and pay his debt to society before those crazy Maccabees come over the hill and zap the lot of us. Will you do that for me, Smith, old girl? I mean when the chips are down, us Anglos *are* a cut above the field, don't you think?"

She could barely move. An irresistible drowsiness had come over her like the first feelings of cold in a very wounded body. She wanted only to sleep. With Halloran. To give him the comfort he asked and extract it in return. Never mind if in the morning he would inform on her. Let him. All she knew was she could not face, for one more night, this hellish empty cell.

He was still holding her hand. She let him, hovering like a suicide on the window-ledge who stares longingly into the street far below. Then, with a huge effort, she freed herself, and with both hands together shoved his unresisting, emaciated body into the corridor.

She sat on her bed. It was the same night, definitely. She could smell his cigarette. See the stub of it at her feet.

If you want to go, go, said Tayeh. Then he pointed at the desert. Tayeh is a very sporting man.

There is no fear like it, Joseph had said. *Your courage will be like money. You will spend and spend, and one night you will look in your pockets and you'll be bankrupt and that is when the real courage begins.*

There is only one logic, Joseph had said: *you. There can be only one survivor: you. One person you can trust: you.*

She stood at the window, worrying about the sand. She had not realised sand could climb so high. By day, tamed by the scalding sun, it lay docile, but when the moon shone, as

now, it swelled into restive cones that dodged from one horizon to another, so that she knew it was only a matter of time
before she heard it spilling through the windows, stifling her
in her sleep.

Her interrogation began next morning and lasted, she
reckoned afterwards, one day and two half nights. It was a
wild, unreasoning process, depending on whose turn it was to
scream at her and whether they were challenging her revolutionary commitment or accusing her of being a British or
Zionist or American informer. For as long as it lasted, she
was excused all tuition and, between sessions, ordered to remain in her hut under house arrest, though no one seemed to
bother when she took to wandering around the camp. The
shifts were divided between four Arab boys of great fervour
working in pairs and barking their prepared questions from
pages of handwritten notes, and they got angriest when she
failed to understand their English. She was not beaten,
though it might have been easier if she had been, for at least
she would have known when she was pleasing them and when
not. But their rages were quite frightening enough and sometimes they would take turns shouting at her, keeping their
faces close to hers, covering her with spit, and leaving her
with a sickening migraine. Another trick was to offer her a
glass of water, then throw it in her face as she was about to
take it. But the next time they met, the boy who had insti-
gated this scene read out a written apology in front of his
three colleagues, then left the room in deep humiliation.
    Another time they threatened to shoot her for her
known attachment to Zionism and the British Queen. But
when she still refused to confess to these sins, they seemed to
lose interest, and told her instead proud stories about their
home villages, which they had never seen, and how they had
the most beautiful women, and the best olive oil and the
best wine in the world. And that was when she knew she had
come home to sanity again; and to Michel.

An electric punkah turned on the ceiling; on the walls
hung grey curtains partly concealing maps. Through the open
window, Charlie could hear the intermittent thud of bombing

practice from Bubi's range. Tayeh had taken the sofa, and laid one leg along it. His wounded face looked white and ill. Charlie stood in front of him like a naughty girl, her eyes lowered and her jaw clamped with rage. She had tried to speak once, but Tayeh had upstaged her by fishing his whisky bottle from his pocket and taking a swig from it. With the back of his hand he wiped his mouth each way as if he had a moustache, which he had not. He was more contained than she had known him, and somehow less at ease with her.

"Abdul the American," she said.

"So?"

She had prepared it. In her mind, she had practised it repeatedly: Comrade Leila's high sense of revolutionary duty overcomes her natural reluctance to rat on a fellow soldier. She knew the lines by heart. She knew the bitches at the forum who had spoken them. To deliver them, she kept her face turned away from his and spoke with a harsh, mannish fury.

"His real name is Halloran. Arthur J. Halloran. He's a traitor. He asked me, when I leave, to tell the Americans that he wants to go home and face trial. He frankly admits to harbouring counter-revolutionary beliefs. He could betray us all."

Tayeh's dark gaze had not left her face. He held his ash walking stick in both hands, and was tapping the end of it lightly on the toe of his bad leg, as if to keep it awake.

"Is this why you asked to see me?"

"Yes."

"Halloran came to you three nights ago," he remarked, looking away from her. "Why did you not tell me earlier? Why wait three days?"

"You weren't here."

"Others were. Why did you not ask for me?"

"I was afraid you would punish him."

But Tayeh did not seem to think that Halloran was on trial. "Afraid," he repeated, as if that were a grave admission. "*Afraid?* Why should you be *afraid* for Halloran? For three whole days? Do you secretly sympathise with his position?"

"You know I don't."

"Is this why he spoke to you so frankly? Because you gave him reason to trust you? I think so."

"No."

"Did you sleep with him?"

"*No.*"

"So why should you wish to protect Halloran? Why should you fear for the life of a traitor when you are learning to kill for the revolution? Why are you not true to us? You disappoint me."

"I am not experienced. I was sorry for him and I did not wish him harmed. Then I remembered my duty."

Tayeh seemed increasingly confused by the whole conversation. He took another pull of whisky.

"Sit down."

"I don't need to."

"Sit down."

She did as he ordered. She was looking fiercely to one side of him, at some hated spot on her own private horizon. In her mind she had passed the point where he had any right to know her. I have learnt what you sent me here to learn. Blame yourself if you do not understand me.

"In a letter you wrote to Michel, you speak of a child. You have a child? His?"

"I was talking about the gun. We slept with it."

"What type of gun?"

"A Walther. Khalil gave it to him."

Tayeh sighed. "If you were me," he said at last, turning his head away from her, "and you had to deal with Halloran—who asks to go home, but who knows too much—what would you do with him?"

"Neutralise him."

"Shoot him?"

"That's your business."

"Yes. It is." He was considering his bad leg once more, holding his walking stick above it and parallel to it. "But why execute a man who is already dead? Why not let him work for us?"

"Because he's a traitor."

Once again, Tayeh seemed wilfully to misunderstand the logic of her position.

"Halloran approaches many people in this camp. Always with a reason. He is our vulture, showing us where there is weakness and disease. Pointing the way to potential traitors. Don't you think we would be silly to get rid of such a useful creature? Did you go to bed with Fidel?"

"No."

"Because he is a dago?"

"Because I didn't want to go to bed with him."

"With the Arab boys?"

"No."

"You are too fastidious, I think."

"I wasn't fastidious with Michel."

With a sigh of perplexity, Tayeh took a third pull of whisky. "Who is *Joseph*?" he asked, in a mildly querulous tone. "Joseph. Who, please?"

Was the actress in her dead at last? Or was she so reconciled with the theatre of the real that the difference between life and art had disappeared? None of her repertoire occurred to her; she had no sense of selecting her performance. She did not consider falling over her feet and lying still on the stone floor. She was not tempted to embark on a wallowing confession, trading her own life for everything she knew, which she had been told was her final, permissible option. She was angry. She was sick to death of having her integrity dragged out and dusted down and subjected to fresh scrutiny every time she reached another milestone in her march towards Michel's revolution. So she flung straight back at him without thinking—a card flipped off the top of the pack—take it or leave it, and to hell with you.

"I don't know a Joseph."

"Come. Think. On Mykonos. Before you went to Athens. One of your friends, in casual conversation with an acquaintance of ours, was heard to make a reference to *Joseph,* who joined your group. He said Charlie was quite captivated by him."

There were no barriers left, no twists. She had cleared them all, and was running free.

"Joseph? Ah, *that* Joseph!" She let her face register the belated recollection: and as it did so, to cloud in disgust.

"I remember him. He was a greasy little Jew who tagged on to our group."

"Don't talk about Jews like that. We are not anti-Semitic, we are merely anti-Zionist."

"Tell me another," she snapped.

Tayeh was interested. "You are describing me as a liar, Charlie?"

"Whether he was a Zionist or not, he was a creep. He reminded me of my father."

"Was your father a Jew?"

"No. But he was a thief."

Tayeh thought about this for a long time, using first her face, then her whole body as a term of reference for whatever doubts still lingered in his mind. He offered her a cigarette but she didn't take it: her instinct told her to make no step towards him. Once more he tapped his dead foot with his stick. "That night you spent with Michel in Thessalonika —in the old hotel—you remember?"

"What of it?"

"The staff heard raised voices from your room late at night."

"So what's your question?"

"Don't hurry me, please. Who was shouting that night?"

"No one. They were snooping at the wrong bloody door."

"Who was shouting?"

"We weren't shouting. Michel didn't want me to go. That's all. He was afraid for me."

"And you?"

It was a story she had worked up with Joseph: her moment of being stronger than Michel.

"I offered him his bracelet back," she said.

Tayeh nodded. "Which accounts for the postscript in your letter: 'I am so glad I kept the bracelet.' And of course—there was no shouting. You are right. Forgive my simple Arab trick." He took a last searching look at her, trying once more, in vain, to resolve the enigma; then pursed his lips, soldier-like, as Joseph sometimes did, as a prelude to issuing an order.

"We have a mission for you. Get your possessions and return here immediately. Your training is complete."

Leaving was the most unexpected madness of all. It was worse than end of term; worse than dumping the gang at Piraeus harbour. Fidel and Bubi clutched her to their breasts, their tears mixing with her own. One of the Algerian girls gave her a wooden Christ-child as a pendant.

*　　*　　*

Professor Minkel lived on the saddle that joins Mount Scopus to French Hill, on the eighth floor of a new tower close to the Hebrew University, one of a great cluster on the skyline which have caused pain to Jerusalem's luckless conservationists. Every apartment looked down on the Old City, but the trouble was, the Old City looked up at every apartment too. Like its neighbours, it was a fortress as well as a skyscraper, and the positioning of its windows was determined by the most favourable arcs of fire if an attack were to be riposted. Kurtz made three wrong tries before he found the place. He lost himself first in a shopping centre built in concrete five feet deep; then again in a British cemetery devoted to the fallen of the First World War: "A Free Gift from the People of Palestine," read the engraving. He explored other buildings, mostly the gifts of millionaires from America, and came finally upon this tower of hewn stone. The name signs had been vandalised and so he pressed a bell at random and unearthed an old Pole from Galicia who spoke only Yiddish. The Pole knew which building all right—this one as you see me!—he knew Dr. Minkel and admired him for his stand; he himself had attended the venerated Kraków University. But he also had a lot of questions on his own account, which Kurtz was obliged to answer as best he could: like where did Kurtz come from originally? Well, my heaven, did he know so-and-so? And what was Kurtz's business here, a grown man, eleven in the morning when Dr. Minkel should be instructing future fine philosophers of our people?

The lift engineers were on strike, so Kurtz was obliged to take the staircase, but nothing could have dampened his good spirits. For one thing, his niece had just announced her engagement to a young boy in his own service—though not before time. For another, Elli's Bible conference had passed off happily; she had given a coffee party at the end of it and, to her great contentment, he had managed to be present. But best of all, the Freiburg breakthrough had been followed by several reassuring pointers, of which the most satisfactory was obtained but yesterday, by one of Shimon Litvak's listeners, testing a new-fangled directional microphone on a rooftop in Beirut: Freiburg, Freiburg, three times in five pages, a real delight. Sometimes luck treated you that way, Kurtz reflected as he climbed. And luck, as Napoleon and everybody in Jerusalem knew, was what made good generals.

Reaching a small landing, he paused to collect his breath a little, and his thoughts. The staircase was lit like an air-raid shelter, with wire cages over the light-bulbs, but today it was the sounds of his own childhood in the ghettos that Kurtz heard bouncing up and down the gloomy well. I was right not to bring Shimon, he thought. Sometimes Shimon puts a chilly note on things; a surface lightness would improve him.

The door of number 18D had a steel-plated eyehole and locks all down one side of it, and Mrs. Minkel undid them one by one like boot buttons, calling "Just one moment, please" while she got lower and lower. He stepped inside and waited while she patiently replaced them. She was tall and fine-looking, with blue eyes very bright, and grey hair pinned in an academic bun.

"You are Mr. Spielberg from the Ministry of the Interior," she informed him with a certain guardedness as she gave him her hand. "Hansi is expecting you. Welcome. Please."

She opened the door to a tiny study and there her Hansi sat, as weathered and patrician as a Buddenbrook. His desk was too small for him, and had been so for many years; his books and papers lay stacked about him on the floor with an order that could not have been haphazard. The desk stood askew to a window bay, and the bay was half a hexagon, with thin smoked windows like arrow slits, and a bench seat built in. Rising carefully, Minkel picked his way with unworldly dignity across the room until he had reached the one small island that was not claimed by his erudition. His welcome was uneasy, and as they sat themselves in the window bay, Mrs. Minkel drew up a stool and sat herself firmly between them, as if intent upon seeing fair play.

An awkward silence followed. Kurtz pulled the regretful smile of a man obliged by his duty. "Mrs. Minkel, I fear there are a couple of things on the security side which my office insists I am to discuss with your husband alone in the first instance," he said. And waited again, still smiling, until the Professor suggested she make a coffee; how did Mr. Spielberg like it?

With a warning glance at her husband from the doorway, Mrs. Minkel reluctantly withdrew. In reality there could have been little difference between the two men's ages; yet Kurtz was careful to speak up to Minkel because that was what the Professor was accustomed to.

"Professor, I understand that our mutual friend, Ruthie Zadir, spoke to you only yesterday," Kurtz began, with a bedside respectfulness. He could understand this very well, for he had stood over Ruthie while she made the call, and listened to both sides of the conversation in order to get the feel of his man.

"Ruth was one of my best students," the Professor observed, with an air of loss.

"She is surely one of ours too," said Kurtz, more expansively. "Professor, are you aware, please, of the nature of the work in which Ruthie is now engaged?"

Minkel was not really used to answering questions outside his subject, and he required a moment's puzzled thought before replying.

"I feel I should say something," he said, with awkward resolution.

Kurtz smiled hospitably.

"If your visit here concerns the political leanings—sympathies—of present or former students under my charge, I regret that I am unable to collaborate with you. These are not criteria which I can accept as legitimate. We have had this discussion before. I am sorry." He seemed suddenly embarrassed, both by his thoughts and by his Hebrew. "I stand for something here. When we stand for something, we must speak out, but most important is to act. That is what I stand for."

Kurtz, who had read Minkel's file, knew exactly what he stood for. He was a disciple of Martin Buber, and a member of a largely forgotten idealistic group that between the wars of '67 and '73 had championed a real peace with the Palestinians. The rightists called him a traitor; sometimes, when they remembered him these days, so did the leftists. He was an oracle on Jewish philosophy, on early Christianity, on the humanist movements in his native Germany, and on about thirty other subjects as well; he had written a three-volume tome on the theory and practice of Zionism, with an index as long as a telephone directory.

"Professor," said Kurtz, "I am well aware of your pos-

ture in these matters and it is surely no intention of mine to
seek to interfere in any way with your fine moral stand." He
paused, allowing time for his assurance to sink in. "May I
take it, by the way, that your forthcoming lecture at the University of Freiburg also touches upon this same issue of individual rights? The Arabs—their basic liberties—isn't that
your subject on the twenty-fourth?"

The Professor could not go along with this. He did not
deal in careless definitions.

"My subject on that occasion is different. It concerns the
self-realisation of Judaism, not by conquest, but by the exem-
plification of Jewish culture and morality."

"So how does that argument run exactly?" Kurtz asked
benignly.

Minkel's wife returned with a tray of homemade cakes.
"Is he asking you to inform again?" she demanded. "If he's
asking, tell him no. Then when you've said no, say no again,
until he hears. What do you think he'll do? Beat you with a
rubber truncheon?"

"Mrs. Minkel, I surely am asking your husband no such
thing," said Kurtz, quite unperturbed.

With a look of patent disbelief, Mrs. Minkel once more
withdrew.

But Minkel barely paused. If he had noticed the inter-
ruption at all, he ignored it. Kurtz had asked a question;
Minkel, who renounced all barriers to knowledge as unaccept-
able, proposed to answer it.

"I will tell you exactly how the arguments run, Mr.
Spielberg," he replied solemnly. "As long as we have a small
Jewish state, we may advance democratically, as Jews,
towards our Jewish self-realisation. But once we have a larger
state, incorporating many Arabs, we have to choose." With
his old mottled hands, he showed Kurtz the choice. "On this
side, democracy without Jewish self-realisation. On that side,
Jewish self-realisation without democracy."

"And the solution, therefore, Professor?" Kurtz
enquired.

Minkel's hands flew in the air in a dismissive gesture of
academic impatience. He seemed to have forgotten that
Kurtz was not his pupil.

"Simple! Move out of the Gaza and the West Bank before we lose our values! What other solution is there?"

"And how do the Palestinians themselves respond to this proposal, Professor?"

A sadness replaced the Professor's earlier assurance. "They call me a cynic," he said.

"They do?"

"According to them, I want both the Jewish state and world sympathy, so they say I am subversive of their cause." The door opened again, and Mrs. Minkel entered with the coffee pot and cups. "But I am *not* subversive," the Professor said hopelessly—though he got no further, owing to his wife.

"*Subversive?*" Mrs. Minkel echoed, slamming down the crockery and colouring purple. "You are calling *Hansi* subversive? Because we speak our hearts about what is happening to this country?"

Kurtz would not have been able to stop her if he had tried, but in the event he made no effort to. He was content to let her run her course.

"In the Golan, the beatings and the torture? On the West Bank, how they treat them, worse than the S.S.? In the Lebanon, in Gaza? Here in Jerusalem, even, slapping the Arab kids around because they are Arabs! And we should be *subversive* because we dare to talk about oppression, merely because no one is oppressing *us*—Jews from Germany, *subversive* in Israel?"

"*Aber, Liebchen*—" the Professor said, with an embarrassed fluster.

But Mrs. Minkel was clearly a lady who was used to making her point. "We couldn't stop the Nazis, now we can't stop ourselves. We get our own country, what do we do? Forty years later, we invent a new lost tribe. Idiocy! And if *we* don't say it, the world will. The world says it already. Read the newspapers, Mr. Spielberg!" As if warding off a blow, Kurtz had lifted his forearm until it was between her face and his. But she had not nearly finished. "That *Ruthie*," she said, with a sneer. "A good brain, studies three years under Hansi here. And what does she do? She joins the apparatus."

Lowering his hand, Kurtz revealed that he was smiling. Not in derision, not in anger, but with the confused pride of a man who truly loved the astonishing diversity of his people. He was calling "Please," he was appealing to the Professor, but Mrs. Minkel still had a wealth to say.

Finally, however, she stopped, and when she had done so, Kurtz asked her whether she too would not sit down and listen to what he had come to talk about. So she perched herself on the stool once more, waiting to be appeased.

Kurtz picked his words very carefully, very kindly. What he had to say was about as secret as a secret could be, he said. Not even Ruthie Zadir—a fine officer, handling many secrets every day—not even Ruthie was aware of it, he said; which was not true, but never mind. He had come not about the Professor's pupils, he said, and least of all to accuse him of being subversive or to quarrel with his fine ideals. He had come solely about the Professor's forthcoming address in Freiburg, which had caught the attention of certain extremely negative elements. Finally he came clean.

"So here's the sad fact," he said, and drew a long breath. "If some of those Palestinians, whose rights you have both been so bravely defending, have their way, you will make no speech at all on the twenty-fourth of this month in Freiburg. In fact, Professor, you will never make a speech again." He paused, but his audience showed no sign of interrupting. "According to information now available to us, it is evident that one of their less academic groups has singled you out as a dangerous moderate, capable of watering the pure wine of their cause. Just as you described to me, sir, but worse. A protagonist of the Bantustan solution for Palestinians. As a false light, leading the weak-brained into one more fatal concession to the Zionist jackboot."

But it took far, far more than the mere threat of death to persuade the Professor to accept an untested version of events.

"Excuse me," he said sharply. "That is the very description of myself which appeared in the Palestinian press after my speech at Beer Sheva."

"Professor, that is precisely where we got it from," said Kurtz.

24

She flew into Zürich in early evening. Storm flares lined the runway and blazed before her like the path of her own purpose. Her mind, as she had desperately prepared it, was an assembly of her old frustrations, matured and turned upon the rotten world. Now she *knew* there was not a shred of good in it; now she had *seen* the agony that was the price of Western affluence. She was who she had always been: an angry reject, getting her own back; with the difference that the Kalashnikov had replaced her useless tantrums. The flares sped past her window like burning wreckage. The plane touched down. But her ticket said Amsterdam, and theoretically she had still to land. *Single girls returning from the Middle East are suspect*, Tayeh had said, at her final briefing in Beirut. *Our first task is to give you a more respectable provenance.* Fatmeh, who had come to see her off, was more specific: *Khalil has ordered that you acquire a fresh identity when you arrive.*

Entering the deserted transit lounge, she had the feeling of being the first pioneer ever to set foot there. Canned music played but there was nobody to hear it. A smart shop sold chocolate bars and cheese, but it was empty. She went to the lavatory and considered her appearance at leisure. Her hair bobbed, and dyed a vague brown. Tayeh himself had hobbled round the Beirut flat while Fatmeh butchered it. No make-up, no sex appeal, he had ordered. She wore a heavy brown suit and a pair of vaguely astigmatic spectacles to scowl through. All I need is a boater and crested blazer, she thought. She had come a long way from Michel's revolutionary *poule de luxe*.

Give my love to Khalil, Fatmeh had told her as she kissed her goodbye.

Rachel was standing beside her at the next basin, but Charlie saw straight through her. She didn't like her, didn't know her, and it was sheer coincidence that Charlie put her open handbag between them, her packet of Marlboros on top, in the way that Joseph had instructed her. And she didn't see Rachel's hand either, swapping the Marlboros with a packet of her own, or her quick, reassuring wink in the mirror.

I have no life but this one. I have no love but Michel and no loyalty except to the great Khalil.

Sit as close to the departures board as you can get, Tayeh had ordered. She did so, and from her little case took a book on Alpine plants, broad and slim like a schoolgirls' annual. Opening it, she perched it on her lap at an angle that allowed the title to be seen. She was sporting a round badge saying "Save the Whale" and that was the other sign, said Tayeh, because from now on Khalil requires that there always be two things: two plans, two signs, in everything a second system in case the first fails; a second bullet in case the world is still alive.

Khalil trusts nothing the first time, Joseph had said. But Joseph was dead and buried long ago, a discarded prophet from her adolescence. She was Michel's widow and Tayeh's soldier and she had come to enlist in the army of her dead lover's brother.

A Swiss soldier was eyeing her, an older man carrying a Heckler & Koch machine pistol. Charlie turned a page. Hecklers were her favourite. At her last weapon-training session she had put eighty-four shots out of a hundred into the storm-trooper target. It was the top score, men or women. Out of the corner of her eye she saw that he was still looking at her. An angry idea struck her. I'll do to you what Bubi once did in Venezuela, she thought. Bubi had been ordered to shoot a certain Fascist policeman as he came out of his house in the morning, a very favourable hour. Bubi hid in a doorway and waited. His target carried a gun under his arm, but he was also a family man, forever romping with his kids. As he stepped into the road, Bubi took a ball from his pocket and sent it bouncing down the street towards him. A kid's rubber ball—what family man would not instinctively bend down to catch it? As soon as he did, Bubi stepped out of his doorway and shot him dead. For who can fire a weapon while he is catching a rubber ball?

Someone was trying to pick her up. Pipe smoker, pigskin shoes, grey flannels. She felt him hover, and advance.

"I say, do excuse me, but do you speak English?"

Standard issue, middle-class English rapist, fair-haired, fifty, and tubby. Falsely apologetic. *No, I don't*, she wanted to reply to him; *I just look at the pictures.* She hated his type so much she was nearly sick on the spot. She glowered at him, but he was a stayer, like all his kind.

"It's simply that this place is so *awfully* desolate," he explained. "I wondered if you'd care to have a drink with me? No strings. Do you good."

She said no thank you, she nearly said, "Daddy says I mustn't speak to strangers," and after a while he strode away indignantly, looking for a policeman to report her to. She returned to her study of the common edelweiss, listening to the place fill up, one pair of feet at a time. Past her to the cheese shop. Past her to the bar. Towards her. And stop.

"Imogen? You remember me. Sabine!"

Look up. Pause for recognition.

A jolly Swiss headscarf to hide the bobbed hair dyed a vague brown. No spectacles, but if Sabine were to put on a pair like mine, any bad photographer could make twins of us. A large carrier bag by Franz Carl Weber of Zürich dangled from her hand, which was the second sign.

"Gosh. Sabine. It's you."

Get up. Formal peck on cheek. How amazing. Where are you going?"

Alas, Sabine's flight is just leaving. What a pity we can't have a girlish talk, but that's life, isn't it? Sabine dumps carrier bag at Charlie's feet. Keep an eye for me, darling. Sure, Sabs, no problem. Sabine vanishes into Ladies. Nosing inside bag, boldly, as if it were her own, Charlie draws out gaily covered envelope with ribbon round it, detects outline of a passport and air ticket within. Smoothly replaces it with own Irish passport, air ticket, and transit card. Sabine returns, grabs bag—must dash, exit right. Charlie counts twenty and returns to loo, roosts. Baastrup, Imogen, South African, she reads. Born Johannesburg three years and one month later than me. Destination Stuttgart in one hour and twenty minutes' time. Goodbye Irish colleen, welcome to our tight-arsed little Christian racist from the outback, claiming her white-girl's heritage.

Coming out of the Ladies, she found the soldier once

more looking at her. He saw it all. He's on the verge of ar-
resting me. He thinks I've got the runs, and doesn't know
how right he nearly is. She stared at him until he walked
away. He just wanted something to look at, she thought as
she once more dug out her book on Alpine flowers.

The flight seemed to take five minutes. An out-of-date
Christmas tree stood in Stuttgart's arrivals hall and there was
an air of family bustle and everybody going home. Queuing
with her South African passport, Charlie studied the photographs of wanted women terrorists and had a premonition
that she was about to see her own. She passed through immigration without a blink; she passed through green. Approaching the exit, she saw Rose, her fellow South African,
lounging on a rucksack, half asleep, but Rose was as dead as
Joseph or anyone else for her and as invisible as Rachel. The
electric doors opened, a swirl of snow hit her face. Pulling up
her coat collar, she hurried across the broad pavement
towards the car park. Fourth floor, Tayeh had said; far left
corner and look for a foxtail on the radio aerial. She had pic-
tured an extended aerial with a bold red fox's brush waving
from the top of it. But this foxtail was a scruffy nylon imitation on a ring, and it lay dead as a mouse on the little
Volkswagen bonnet.

"I'm Saul. What's your name, honey?" said a man's
voice close to her, in soft American. For a dreadful moment
she thought Arthur J. Halloran alias Abdul had come back to
haunt her, so that when she peered round the pillar she was
relieved to find a fairly normal-looking boy propped against
the wall. Long hair, Bean boots, and a fresh, lazy smile. And
a "Save the Whale" badge like hers pinned to his windcheater.

"Imogen," she replied, because Saul was the name Tayeh
had told her to expect.

"Lift the hood, Imogen. Put your suitcase right inside.
Now look around, see who you see. Anybody bothering
you?"

She gave the parking hall a leisurely inspection. In the
cab of a Bedford van plastered with crazy daisies, Raoul and
a girl she could not see properly were halfway to consumma-
tion.

Nobody, she said.

Saul opened the passenger door for her.

"And fix your seat belt, honey," he said as he got in beside her. "They got laws in this country, okay? Where you been, Imogen? Where'd you get your suntan?"

But little widows bent on murder do not engage strangers in small talk. With a shrug, Saul switched on the radio and listened to the news in German.

The snow made everything beautiful, and the traffic cautious. They drove down the helter-skelter and joined a ribbon-built dual carriageway. Fat flakes raced into their headlights. The news ended and a woman announced a concert.

"Care for this, Imogen? It's classical."

He let it play anyway. Mozart from Salzburg, where Charlie had been too tired to make love to Michel on the night before he died.

They skirted the high glow of the city, and the snowflakes wandered into it like black ash. They mounted a clover-leaf and below them, in an enclosed playground, children in red anoraks were playing snowballs by arc-light. She remembered her kids' group back in England, ten million miles ago. I'm doing it for them, she thought. Somehow Michel had believed that. Somehow we all do. All of us except Halloran, who had ceased to see the point. Why was he so much on her mind? she wondered. Because he doubted, and doubt was what she had learned to fear the most. *To doubt is to betray,* Tayeh had warned her.

Joseph had said much the same.

They had entered another country and their road became a black river through canyons of white field and laden forest. Her sense of time slipped, then her sense of scale. She saw dream castles and train-set villages in silhouette against the pale sky. The toy churches with their onion domes made her want to pray, but she was too grown-up for them, and besides religion was for weaklings. She saw shivering ponies cropping bales of hay, and remembered the ponies of her childhood one by one. As each beautiful thing went by, she cast her heart after it, trying to attach to it and slow it down. But nothing stayed, nothing left an imprint on her mind; they were breath on polished glass. Occasionally a car overtook them; once a motorbike raced by and she thought she recognised Dimitri's retreating back, but he was beyond the range of their headlights before she could be certain.

They mounted a hilltop and Saul began to put on speed. He swung left and crossed a road, then right, bumping down a track. Felled trees lay either side, like frozen soldiers in a Russian newsreel. Far ahead, Charlie began to make out a blackened old house with high chimney stacks, and for a second it reminded her of the house in Athens. *Frenzy, is that the word?* Stopping the car, Saul dipped his headlights twice. From what seemed to be the centre of the house, a handtorch winked in return. Saul was looking at his wristwatch, softly counting the seconds aloud. "Nine—ten—got to be *now,*" he said, and the distant light winked once more. Leaning across her, he pushed her door open.

"Far as we go, honey," he said. "It was a great conversation. Peace, okay?"

Suitcase in hand, she selected a rut in the snow and started walking towards the house with only the snow's pallor and the strips of moonlight through the trees to show her the way. As the house drew nearer, she made out an old clock tower with no clock, and a frozen pond with no statue on the plinth. A motorcycle glinted under a wooden canopy.

Suddenly she heard a familiar voice addressing her with conspiratorial restraint: "Imogen, take care from the roof. If a piece of roof hits you, it will kill you immediately. Imogen—oh, Charlie—this is *too* absurd!" The next moment, a soft strong body had emerged from the darkness of the porch to enfold her own, only slightly hampered by a torch and an automatic pistol.

Seized by a flood of ridiculous gratitude, Charlie returned Helga's embrace. "Helg—Christ—it's you—great!"

By the light of her torch, Helga guided her across a marble-floored hall of which half the stones had already been removed; then cautiously up a sagging wooden staircase with no banister. The house was dying, but someone had been hastening its death. The weeping walls were smeared with slogans in red paint; door handles and light fittings had been plundered. Recovering her hostility, Charlie tried to withdraw her hand, but Helga grasped it as of right. They passed through a succession of empty rooms, each big enough to hold a banquet. In the first, a smashed porcelain stove, stuffed with newspaper. In the second, a hand printing-press, thick with dust, and the floor around it ankle-deep with the yellowed newsprint of yesterday's revolutions. They entered a third room and Helga trained her torch on a mass of files and papers flung into an alcove.

"You know what my friend and I do here, Imogen?" she demanded, suddenly raising her voice. "My friend is too fantastic. She is Verona and her father was a complete Nazi. A landlord, an industrialist, everything." Her hand relaxed, only to close again round Charlie's wrist. "He died, so we are selling him for revenge. The trees to the tree destroyers. The land to the land destroyers. The statues and furniture to the flea market. If it is worth five thousand, we sell for five. Here was her father's desk. We chopped it with our own hands and burnt it in a fire. For a symbol. It was the headquarters of his Fascist campaign—he signed his cheques from it, made all his repressive actions. We broke it up and burnt it. Now Verona is free. She is poor, she is free, she has joined the masses. Is she not fantastic? Perhaps you should have done this too."

A servants' staircase climbed crookedly to a long corridor. Helga went quietly ahead. From above them, Charlie heard folk music and smelled the fumes of burning paraffin. They reached a landing, passed a row of servants' bedrooms, and stopped before the last door. A light shone beneath it. Helga knocked and spoke something softly in German. A lock was turned and the door opened. Helga went in ahead, beckoning Charlie after her. "Imogen, this is Comrade Verona." A note of command had entered her voice. "Vero!"

A plump, distraught girl waited to receive them. She wore an apron over wide black trousers and her hair was cut like a boy's. A Smith & Wesson automatic in a holster dangled over her fat hip. Verona wiped her palm on her apron and they exchanged a bourgeois handshake.

"One year ago, Vero was completely Fascistic like her father," Helga remarked with proprietorial authority. "A slave and a Fascist together. Now she fights. Yes, Vero?"

Dismissed, Verona relocked the door, then took herself

to a corner where she was cooking something on a camping stove. Charlie wondered whether she was secretly dreaming of her father's desk.

"Come. Look who is here," said Helga, and swept her away down the room. Charlie looked swiftly round her. She was in a large attic, the very one she had played in countless times on holidays in Devon. The feeble lighting came from an oil lamp dangling from a rafter. Thicknesses of velvet curtain had been nailed across the dormer windows. A jolly rocking-horse strutted along one wall; beside it stood a governess's blackboard on an easel. A street plan was drawn on it; coloured arrows pointed to a large rectangular building at its centre. On an old ping-pong table lay remnants of salami, black bread, cheese. Clothes of both sexes hung drying before an oil fire. They had reached a short wooden stair and Helga was marching her up it. On the raised floor two waterbeds were laid side by side. On one, naked to the waist and lower, reclined the dark Italian who had had Charlie at gunpoint that Sunday morning in the City. He had spread a tattered coverlet across his thighs, and she noticed the broken-down parts of a Walther automatic lay around him while he cleaned them. A transistor radio was playing Brahms at his elbow.

"And here we have the energetic Mario," Helga announced with sarcastic pride, prodding his genitals with her toe. "Mario, you are completely shameless, you know that? Cover yourself immediately and greet our guest. I order you!"

But Mario's only response was to roll himself playfully to the edge of the bed, inviting whoever wished to join him.

"How's Comrade Tayeh, Charlie?" he asked. "Tell us all the family news."

Like a scream in church, a phone rang: the more alarming because it had never crossed Charlie's mind they might possess one. Seeking to raise her spirits, Helga was proposing they drink Charlie's health, and making a palaver of it. She had balanced glasses and a bottle on a bread board and was in the act of bearing them ceremoniously across the room. Hearing the ring, she froze where she stood, then in slow motion set down the bread board on the ping-pong table, which happened to be close. Rossino switched off his radio. The phone stood alone on a small marquetry table that Verona and Helga had not yet burnt; it was of the old hanging type, with the earpiece separate. Helga stood over it but made no effort to lift the earpiece. Charlie counted eight long peals before it stopped. Helga remained where she was, staring at it. Stark naked, Rossino walked nonchalantly down the room and helped himself to a shirt from the clothesline.

"He said he would call tomorrow," he complained as he pulled it over his head. "What goes on suddenly?"

"Be quiet," Helga snapped.

Verona continued stirring whatever she was cooking, but more slowly, as if speed were dangerous. She was one of those women whose every movement seems to come from their elbows.

The phone rang again, two rings, and this time Helga lifted the earpiece and at once replaced it. But the next time it rang, she answered it with a curt "Yes" and then listened, without a nod or a smile, for perhaps two minutes, before ringing off.

"The Minkels have changed their plans," she announced. "They are spending tonight in Tübingen, where they have friends in the faculty. They have four large suitcases, many small pieces, and a *briefcase*." With a fine instinct for effect, she took a damp cloth from Verona's handbasin and wiped the blackboard clean. "The briefcase is black, it has simple hinges. The location of the lecture is also changed. The police are not suspicious but they are nervous. They are taking what they call sensible precautions."

"What's with the bulls?" said Rossino.

"The police wish to increase the guards, but Minkel is refusing this completely. He is a so-called man of principle. If he is to preach about law and justice, he insists that he cannot himself be seen surrounded by secret police. For Imogen, nothing is changed. Her orders are the same. It is her first action. She will be the complete star. No, Charlie?"

Suddenly they were all looking at her—Verona with a mindless fixity, Rossino with an appraising grin, and Helga with a frank straight stare to which self-doubt, as ever, was a stranger.

* * *

She lay flat, using her forearm as a pillow. Her bedroom was not a gallery in a church hall but a garret without light or curtains. Her bed was an old horsehair mattress and a yellowed blanket that smelt of camphor. Helga sat beside her, smoothing Charlie's dyed hair with her strong hand. Moonlight came through the high window; the snow made its own deep silence. Somebody should write a fairy story here. My lover should put on the electric fire and take me by its red glow. She was in a log cabin, safe from everything except tomorrow.

"What is the matter, Charlie? Open your eyes. Don't you like me any more?"

She opened her eyes and stared ahead of her, seeing and thinking nothing.

"Are you dreaming of your little Palestinian still? Are you worried what we do here? Do you want to give up and run away while you have time?"

"I'm tired."

"So why don't you come and sleep with us? We can have sex. Then we can sleep. Mario is an excellent lover."

Bending over her, Helga kissed her on the neck.

"You want Mario to come to you alone? You are shy? Even that I allow you." She kissed her again. But Charlie lay cold and rigid, her body like iron.

"Tomorrow night you will be more affectionate perhaps. With Khalil there can be no rejections. He is most fascinated to meet you already. He has asked for you personally. You know what he told a friend of ours once? 'Without women I would lose my human warmth and fail as a soldier. To be a good soldier, it is essential to have humanity.' Now you may imagine what a great man he is. You loved Michel, therefore he will love you. There is no question. So."

Bestowing a last, lingering kiss on her, Helga left the room and Charlie lay on her back, wide-eyed, watching the half night slowly lighten in the window. She heard a woman's wail rising to a clenched, beseeching sob; then a man's urgent shout. Helga and Mario were advancing the revolution without her assistance.

Follow them wherever they lead you, Joseph had said. *If they tell you to kill, then kill. It will be our responsibility, not yours.*

Where will you be?

Close.

Close to the edge of the world.

In her handbag she had a Mickey Mouse hand-torch with a pinlight, the kind of thing she would have played with under the blankets at her boarding school. She took it out, together with Rachel's packet of Marlboros. There were three cigarettes left and she put them back loose. Carefully, as Joseph had taught her, she removed the wrapping paper, tore open the cardboard of the box, and spread it flat, the inside surface upward. Licking her finger, she began gently rubbing saliva onto the blank cardboard. The letters came up in brown, drawn fine as if with a mapping pen. She read the message, then poked the flattened packet through a crack in the floorboards until it dropped out of sight.

Courage. We're with you. The whole of the Lord's Prayer on the head of a pin.

Their operations room in Freiburg city centre was a hastily rented ground-floor office in a busy main street, their cover the Walker & Frosch Investment Company, GmbH, one of dozens that Gavron's secretariat kept permanently registered. Their communications equipment had more or less the appearance of commercial software; in addition they had three ordinary telephones, courtesy of Alexis, and one of them, the least official, was the Doctor's own hot line to Kurtz. It was early morning after a busy night taken up first with the delicate business of tracking and housing Charlie; and afterwards with a tense argument about demarcation between Litvak and his West German counterpart, for Litvak was by now arguing with everyone. Kurtz and Alexis had kept aloof from such bickering between subordinates. The broad agreement held, and Kurtz had no interest yet in breaking it. Alexis and his men should have the credit; Litvak and his the satisfaction.

As to Gadi Becker, he was finally back at war. With the imminence of action, his manner had acquired a settled and determined swiftness. The introspections that had haunted him in Jerusalem had lifted; the gnawing idleness of waiting was past. While Kurtz dozed under an army blanket and

Litvak, nervous and depleted, paced the office or spoke cryptically into one or another telephone, building himself into some kind of unclear temper, Becker stood sentry at the Venetian blinds of the wide window, gazing patiently upward into the snowclad hills across the olive Dreisam River. For Freiburg, like Salzburg, is a city ringed with heights, and every street seems to lead upward to its own Jerusalem.

"She's panicked," Litvak announced suddenly to Becker's back.

Puzzled, Becker turned and glanced at him.

"She's gone over to them," Litvak insisted. His voice had a throaty instability.

Becker returned to the window. "Part of her has gone over, part has stayed," he replied. "That is what we asked of her."

"She's gone over!" Litvak repeated, rising on the swell of his own provocation. "It's happened with agents before. It's happened now. I saw her at the airport, you didn't. She looks like a ghost, I tell you!"

"If she looks like a ghost, that's how she wants to look," said Becker, majestically unruffled. "She's an actress. She'll see it through, don't worry."

"So what's her motivation? She's not Jewish. She's not anything. She's theirs. Forget her!"

Hearing Kurtz stir beneath his blanket, Litvak lifted his voice higher to include him.

"If she's ours still, why did she give Rachel a blank cigarette packet at the airport, tell me that? Weeks on end among that rabble and she doesn't even write us a note when she comes out again? What kind of agent is that, who is so loyal to us?"

Becker seemed to be looking for his answer in the far mountains. "Maybe she has nothing to say," he said. "She's voting with her actions. Not her words."

From the shallows of his sparse camp bed, Kurtz offered drowsy consolation. "Germany makes you jumpy, Shimon. Ease off. What does it matter who she belongs to, so long as she keeps showing us the way?"

But the effect of Kurtz's words was the opposite of their intention. In his self-tormenting mood, Litvak sensed an unfair alliance against him, and it made him wilder still.

"And if she breaks down, confesses? If she tells them

the whole story, Mykonos till here? Does she still show us the way?"

He seemed set upon collision; nothing else would satisfy him.

Lifting himself on one elbow, Kurtz took a harsher tone. "So what do we do, Shimon? Give us the team solution. Suppose she has gone over. Suppose she has blown the entire operation from breakfast to dinner. You want me to call Misha Gavron, say we're finished?"

Becker had not abandoned the window, but he had turned himself round once more and was watching Litvak thoughtfully down the room. Staring from one to the other of them, Litvak flung out his arms, a very wild gesture to make before two such static men.

"He's somewhere out there!" Litvak cried. "In a hotel. An apartment. In a doss house. He must be. Seal off the town. Roads, the railway. Buses. Have Alexis put a cordon round. Search every house till we find him!"

Kurtz tried a little kindly humour: "Shimon, Freiburg is not the West Bank."

But Becker, interested at last, seemed anxious to pursue the argument. "And when we have found him?" he said, as if he hadn't quite got his mind around Litvak's plan. "What do we do then, Shimon?"

"Then we find him! Kill him! The operation's over!"

"And who kills Charlie?" Becker asked, in the same perfectly reasonable way. "Us or them?"

Suddenly there was more going on in Litvak than he could handle on his own. Under the tensions of the past night and of the day to come, the whole knotted mass of his frustrations, male and female, swam suddenly to the surface of his being. His face coloured, his eyes blazed, as one thin arm struck out towards Becker in accusation. "She's a whore and she's a Communist and she's an Arab-lover!" he shouted, loud enough to be heard through the partition wall. "Dump her. Who cares?"

If Litvak was expecting Becker to make a fight of it, then he was disappointed, for the most Becker offered was one quiet nod of confirmation, as if everything that he had been thinking about Litvak for some time had now been demonstrated. Kurtz had pushed away his blanket. He was sitting on the bed in his underpants, head forward while he rubbed the tips of his fingers in his short grey hair.

"Go take a bath, Shimon," he ordered quietly. "A bath, a nice rest, some coffee. Come back around midday. Not before." A phone was ringing. "Don't answer that," he added, and lifted the receiver himself while Litvak, in mute self-horror, watched him from the doorway. "He's busy," Kurtz said, in German. "Yes, this is Helmuth, who's speaking?"

He said yes; then yes again; and well done. He rang off. Then he smiled his ageless, mirthless smile. First to Litvak, to console him, then to Becker also, because at that moment their differences were unimportant. "Charlie arrived at the Minkels' hotel five minutes ago," he said. "Rossino's with her. They're having a nice breakfast together, well ahead of time, just the way our friend likes it."

"And the bracelet?" said Becker.

Kurtz liked this part best. "On her right wrist," he said proudly. "She has a message for us. She's a fine girl, Gadi, and I congratulate you."

The hotel had been built in the sixties when the catering industry still believed in large, milling lobbies with soothing illuminated fountains and gold watches under glass. A wide double staircase rose to a mezzanine, and from the balcony table where they sat, Charlie and Rossino had a view of both the main door and the reception. Rossino was wearing a middle-management blue suit, Charlie her South African girl guide's uniform and her wooden Christ-child from the training camp. The lenses of her spectacles, which Tayeh had insisted should be real, made her eyes ache when it was her turn to watch. They had eaten eggs and bacon because she was ravenous, and now they were drinking fresh coffee while Rossino read the Stuttgarter *Zeitung* and periodically regaled her with facetious news items. They had driven into town early and she had almost frozen to death riding pillion. They had parked at the railway station, where Rossino had made enquiries, and they had come on to the hotel by taxi. In the hour they had been here, Charlie had watched police outriders deliver a Catholic bishop, and return with a delegation of West Africans in tribal costume. She had watched a busload of Americans arrive and a busload of Japanese depart; she knew the check-in procedure by heart, right down to the name of the chasseur who grabbed the suitcases from the new arrivals as they came through the sliding doors, loaded them on their little trolleys, and hovered at a yard's distance while the guests filled in their registration forms.

"And His Holiness the Pope plans a tour of all Fascist South American States," Rossino announced from behind his newspaper as she stood up. "Maybe this time they finish him off. Where are you going, Imogen?"

"To piss."

"What's the matter? Nervous?"

The women's room had fluttering pink lights over the handbasins and soft music to drown the whirr of the ventilators. Rachel was putting on her eye shadow. Two other women were washing. One door was closed. Brushing past her, Charlie pressed the scribbled message into Rachel's waiting hand. She cleaned up and returned to the table.

"Let's get out of here," she said, as if the relief had changed her mind. "It's ridiculous."

Rossino lit a thick Dutch cigar and deliberately blew the smoke into her face.

An official-looking Mercedes drew up and disgorged a bunch of dark-suited men with name badges on their lapels. Rossino had started to make an obscene joke about them when he was interrupted by a bellboy calling him to the telephone: Signor Verdi, who had left his name and five marks with the concierge, was required in cabin 3. She sipped her coffee, feeling the heat of it all the way down her chest. Rachel was sitting with a boyfriend under an aluminum palm tree, reading *Cosmopolitan*. The boyfriend was new to her and looked German. He was clutching a document in a plastic folder. There were twenty-odd people sitting around, but Rachel was the only one she recognised. Rossino had returned.

"The Minkels arrived at the station two minutes ago. Grabbed themselves a blue Peugeot cab. Should be here any moment."

He called for the bill and paid it, then took up his newspaper once more.

I shall do everything once, she had promised herself as she lay waiting for the morning; everything will be a last time. She repeated it to herself. If I sit here now, I shall never have to sit here again. When I go downstairs, I shall never have to come up again. When I leave the hotel, I shall never return.

"Why don't we just shoot the bastard and be done with it?" Charlie whispered, with a sudden welling up of fear and hatred as she once more fixed her gaze upon the entrance.

"Because we want to stay alive to shoot other bastards," Rossino explained patiently, and turned a page. "Manchester United lost again," he added complacently. "Poor old Empire."

"Action," said Charlie.

A blue Peugeot taxi had pulled up on the other side of the glass doors. A grey-haired woman was scrambling out. She was followed by a tall, distinguished-looking man with a slow and ceremonious walk.

"Watch the small pieces, I'll watch the big ones," Rossino told her as he relit his cigar.

The driver was unlocking the boot; Franz, the chasseur, was standing behind him with his trolley. First came two matching suitcases in brown nylon, neither new nor old. Belts round the centre for extra support. Red tie-on labels. Now an old leather suitcase, much bigger, with a pair of wheels at one corner. Followed by yet another suitcase.

Rossino let out a soft Italian oath. "So how long are they staying?" he complained.

The small pieces were stacked on the front passenger seat. Having locked the boot, the driver began unloading them, but Franz's trolley wasn't going to take all of them at once. One shabby carrier bag in patchwork leather, and two umbrellas, his and hers. A paper carrier bag with a black cat on it. Two large boxes in festive wrapping, presumably belated Christmas presents. Then she saw it: a black briefcase. Hard sides, steel frame, leather name-tag. Good old Helg, thought Charlie; spot on. Minkel was paying off the cab. Like someone else Charlie had once known, he kept his coins in a purse, and spilt them into his palm before parting with the unfamiliar currency. Mrs. Minkel picked up the briefcase.

"Shit," said Charlie.

"Wait," said Rossino.

Laden with parcels, Minkel followed his wife through the sliding doors.

"Around now you tell me you think you recognise him," Rossino said quietly. "I tell you, why don't you go down and take a closer look? You hesitate, you're a shy little virgin." He was holding her by the sleeve of her dress. "Don't force it. If it doesn't work, there's lots of other ways. Frown. Adjust your spectacles. Go."

Minkel was approaching the reception desk with small, slightly silly steps, as if he had never done this before. His wife, holding the briefcase, was at his side. There was only one receptionist on duty and she was occupied with two other guests. Waiting, Minkel gazed round in confusion. His wife, unimpressed, sized the place up. Across the lobby from them, behind a smoked-glass partition, a group of well-dressed Germans was assembling for some kind of function. She studied the guests disapprovingly, muttered something to her husband. The reception desk became vacant and Minkel took the briefcase from her hand: a tacit, instinctive transaction between partners. The receptionist was a blonde in a black dress. She checked the card index with her red fingernails before passing Minkel a form to fill in. The stairs were hitting Charlie's heels, her damp hand was sticking on the wide banister, Minkel was a misted abstraction through her astigmatic spectacles. The floor lifted to her and she started her hesitant journey towards the reception desk. Minkel was stooped over the counter, filling in his form. He had put his Israeli passport at his elbow and was copying out its number. The briefcase stood on the floor beside his left foot; Mrs. Minkel was out of shot. Placing herself on Minkel's right, Charlie peered crookedly over his shoulder as he wrote. Mrs. Minkel entered left, and was looking at Charlie in puzzlement. She nudged her husband. Aware finally that he was being studied at close quarters, Minkel slowly raised his venerable head and turned to her. Charlie cleared her throat, acting shy, which was no hardship. *Now*.

"Professor Minkel?" she said.

He had grey troubled eyes and looked even more embarrassed than Charlie was. It was suddenly like supporting a bad actor.

"I am Professor Minkel," he conceded, as if he were not quite sure. "Yes. I am he. Why?"

The sheer badness of his performance gave her strength. She took a deep breath.

"Professor, my name is Imogen Baastrup from Johannesburg and I'm a graduate in social studies from Witwatersrand University," she said, all of a rush. Her accent was less South African than vaguely Antipodean; her manner mawkish but determined. "I had the great good fortune to hear your centenary lecture last year on minority rights in racially determined societies. That was a fine lecture. It changed my life, in fact. I meant to write to you but never got around to it. Do you mind, please, if I shake your hand?"

She practically had to take it from him. He stared foolishly at his wife, but she had the better talent and was at least giving Charlie a smile. Taking his cue from her, Minkel smiled too, if wanly. If Charlie was sweating, she was nothing to Minkel: it was like dipping her hand in an oil pot.

"Are you staying here long, Professor? What are you doing here? Don't say you're lecturing again?"

In the background, out of focus, Rossino was asking the receptionist in English whether a Mr. Boccaccio had checked in from Milan yet.

Again Mrs. Minkel came to the rescue: "My husband is making a European tour," she explained. "We are having a holiday, lecturing a little, visiting friends. We are really looking forward."

Thus encouraged, Minkel himself managed finally to speak: "And what brings you to Freiburg—Miss Baastrup?" he asked, in the thickest German accent she had ever heard off stage.

"Oh, I just thought I'd better see a little of the world before I decided what to do with my life," said Charlie.

Get me out. Christ get me out. The receptionist was regretting that no reservation could be found for Mr. Boccaccio, and alas the hotel was full; with the other half of herself, she was handing Mrs. Minkel a room key. Somehow Charlie was thanking the Professor again for a really stimulating and instructive lecture, Minkel was thanking her for her kind words; Rossino, having thanked the receptionist, was heading briskly for the main entrance, Minkel's briefcase mostly hidden by the smart black raincoat over his arm. With a last bashful effusion of thanks and apologies, Charlie went out after him, careful to show no sign of haste. As she reached the glass doors, she was in time to see the reflected image of the

Minkels peering helplessly round them, trying to remember who had it last and where.

Stepping between the parked taxis, Charlie reached the hotel car park, where Helga, wearing a loden cape with horn buttons, sat waiting in a green Citroën. Charlie got in beside her; Helga drove sedately to the car park exit, put in her ticket and money. As the boom lifted, Charlie began laughing, as if the boom had triggered off her laughter. She gulped, she put her knuckles in her mouth and her head on Helga's shoulder, and broke into helpless, glorious mirth.

"I was incredible, Helg! You should have seen me—Jesus!"

At the junction, a young traffic policeman stared in puzzlement at the sight of two grown women weeping and laughing their heads off. Lowering her window, Helga blew him a kiss.

In the operations room, Litvak sat over the radio, Becker and Kurtz stood behind him. Litvak seemed frightened of himself, muted and pale. He wore a headset with one earpiece, and a throat-pad microphone.

"Rossino has taken a cab to the station," Litvak said. "He has the briefcase with him. He's going to collect his bike."

"I don't want him followed," Becker said across Litvak's back to Kurtz.

Litvak pulled off his throat pad and acted as though he couldn't believe his ears. "Not followed? We've got six men round that bike. Alexis has like fifty. We've put a homer on it and we've got cars standing by all over town. Follow the bike, we follow the briefcase. The briefcase takes us to our man!" He swung to Kurtz, appealing for his support.

"Gadi?" said Kurtz.

"He'll use cut-outs," Becker said. "He always has done. Rossino will take it so far, hand it over, somebody else will take it on the next stage. By this afternoon, they'll have dragged us through small streets, open country, and empty restaurants. There's not a surveillance team in the world that could survive that without being recognised."

"And your special interest, Gadi?" Kurtz enquired.

"Berger will stay on Charlie all day long. Khalil will

phone her at agreed intervals and places. If Khalil smells a rat, he'll order Berger to kill her. If he doesn't call for two hours, three hours, whatever their arrangement is, Berger will kill her anyway."

Seemingly undecided, Kurtz turned his back to both of them and wandered down the room. Then up again. Then down again, while Litvak watched him like a madman. Finally Kurtz picked up the hot line to Alexis and they heard him say "Paul" in a consultative, do-me-a-favour sort of tone. He spoke quietly for a while, listened, spoke again, and rang off.

"We have about nine seconds before he reaches the station," Litvak said wildly, listening to his headset. "Six."

Kurtz ignored him. "I am advised that Berger and Charlie have just entered a fashionable hairdresser's," he said, coming back down the room again. "Looks like they're going to have themselves prettied up for the great event." He drew to a halt before them.

"Rossino's cab just reached the station concourse," Litvak reported in despair. "He's paying him off *now*."

Kurtz was looking at Becker. His regard was respectful, even tender. He was an old coach whose favourite athlete had finally found his form.

"Gadi has won the day, Shimon," he said, his gaze still upon Becker. "Call off your kids. Tell them to rest up till evening."

A phone rang and again Kurtz took the call. It was Professor Minkel, having his fourth nervous breakdown of the operation. Kurtz heard him out, then spoke long and soothingly to his wife.

"It's a really nice day," he said, in suppressed exasperation as he rang off. "Everyone's having a great time." Putting on his blue beret, he went off to meet Alexis for their joint inspection of the lecture hall.

It was her most fraught wait ever, and her longest; a first night to end first nights. Worse still, she could do nothing alone, for Helga had appointed Charlie her ward and favoured niece, and would not let her out of her sight. From the hairdresser, where Helga, under the hairdryer, had received her first phone call, they went to a clothes store where

Helga bought Charlie a pair of fur-lined boots, and silk gloves against what she called "fingers marks." From there to the Cathedral, where Helga imperiously treated Charlie to a history lesson, and from there again, with much giggling and insinuation, to a small square where she was determined to introduce her to one Berthold Schwarz, "the most sexy person ever—Charlie, you are certain to fall completely in love with him!" Berthold Schwarz turned out to be a statue.

"Is he not fantastic, Charlie? Do you not wish we could lift his skirts once? You know what he did, our Berthold? He was a Franciscan, a famous alchemist, and he invented gunpowder. He loved God so much he taught all His creatures to blow each other up. So the good citizens build him a statue. Naturally." Grasping Charlie's arm, she cuddled her excitedly against her. "You know what we do after tonight?" she whispered. "We come back, we bring some flowers for Berthold, we put them at his feet. Yes? Yes, Charlie?"

The Cathedral spire was beginning to get on Charlie's nerves: a fretted, jagged beacon, always black, stalking out ahead of her every time she turned a corner or entered a new street.

For lunch they went to a smart restaurant where Helga treated Charlie to Baden wine, which had been grown, she said, in the volcanic soil of the Kaiserstuhl—a volcano, Charlie, think!—and now everything they ate or drank or saw had to be the subject of wearying and facetious innuendo. Over the Black Forest pie—"We must have everything bourgeois today"—Helga was again summoned to the telephone, and returned saying they must leave for the university or they would never get everything done. So they entered a pedestrian underpass lined with prosperous little shops, and emerged before a portentous building of strawberry sandstone, with pillars and a curved front with gold lettering above it, which Helga was quick to translate.

"So here is a fine message to you, Charlie. Listen. 'The truth will make you free.' They are quoting Karl Marx for you, is that not beautiful and thoughtful?"

"I thought it was Noel Coward," Charlie said and saw a flash of anger pass across Helga's over-excited face.

A stone concourse surrounded the building. An elderly policeman patrolled it, eyeing the girls incuriously as they gawped and pointed, tourists to their fingertips. Four steps led to the front entrance. Inside it, the lights of a large hall glinted through darkened glass doors. The side entrance was guarded by statues of Homer and Aristotle, and it was here that Helga and Charlie lingered longest, admiring the sculptures and the pompous architecture while they secretly measured distances and approaches. A yellow poster announced Minkel's lecture for that evening.

"You are scared, Charlie," Helga whispered, without waiting for an answer. "Listen, after this morning you will triumph totally, you are perfect. You will show what is truth and what is lies, you will show them also what freedom is. For great lies, we need a great action, it is logical. A great action, a great audience, a great cause. Come."

A modern pedestrian bridge led across the dual carriageway. Macabre stone totem-poles presided at either end. From the bridge they passed through the university library to a student café slung like a concrete cradle over the carriageway. Through its glass walls, while they drank their coffee, they could watch staff and students leave and enter the lecture hall. Helga was once again waiting for a phone call. It came, and as she returned from it, she saw something in Charlie's expression that angered her.

"What is the matter with you?" she hissed. "You are filled with compassion for Minkel's charming Zionist opinions suddenly? So noble, so fine? Listen, he is worse than Hitler, a complete tyrant in disguise. I buy you a schnapps to give you courage."

The heat of the schnapps was still burning her as they reached the empty park. The pond was frozen over; early darkness was gathering; the evening air prickled with specks of freezing water. Very loudly, an old bell chimed the hour. A second bell, smaller and higher-pitched, tinkled after it. Her green cape pulled tight around her, Helga at once let out a cry of pleasure.

"Oh, Charlie, listen! You hear that little bell? It is silver. You know why? I tell you. A traveller on his horse lost his way one night. There were robbers, it was bad weather, he was so glad to see Freiburg that he gave a silver bell to the Cathedral. Every evening now, it rings. Is that not beautiful?"

Charlie nodded, trying to smile, but without success. Throwing a strong arm round her, Helga gathered her into the folds of her cape. "Charlie—listen—you want I give you another sermon?"

She shook her head.

Still holding Charlie to her breast, Helga glanced at her watch, then down the path into the half darkness.

"You know something else about this park, Charlie?"

I know that it is the second most awful place in the world. And I never award first prizes.

"Then I tell you another story about it. Yes? In the war there was a he-goose here. You say he-goose?"

"Gander."

"This gander was an air-raid siren. When the bombers came, he was the first who heard them, and when he screamed the citizens went at once to their cellars, not waiting for the official warning. The gander died, but after the war the citizens were so grateful they built him a monument. So there is Freiburg for you. One statue to their bomber monk, another to their air-raid warning. Are they not crazy, these little Freibourgeois?" Stiffening, Helga glanced at her watch again and then into the misty darkness. "He is here," she said very quietly, and turned to say goodbye.

No, thought Charlie. Helg, I love you, you can have me for breakfast every day, just don't make me go to Khalil.

Laying her hands flat on Charlie's cheeks, Helga kissed her softly on the lips.

"For Michel, yes?" She kissed her again, more fiercely. "For the revolution and peace and for Michel. Walk straight down the path, you come to a gate. A green Ford is waiting there. You sit in the back, directly behind the driver." One more kiss. "Oh, Charlie, listen, you are too fantastic. We shall be friends always."

Charlie started down the path, paused, looked back. Stiff and oddly dutiful in the twilight, Helga stood watching her, her green loden cape hanging round her like a policeman's.

Helga waved, a royal side-to-side flap of her big hand. Charlie waved back, watched by the Cathedral spire.

The driver wore a fur hat that hid half his face, and he had pulled up the fur collar of his coat. He did not turn to greet her, and from where she sat she had no picture of him, except that by the line of his cheekbone he was young, and she had a suspicion he was Arab. He drove slowly, first through the evening traffic, then into countryside, down straight, narrow lanes where the snow still lay. They passed a small railway station, approached a level crossing, and stopped. Charlie heard a warning bell ring and saw the high painted boom waver and start its descent. Her driver slammed the car into second gear and raced over the crossing, which closed neatly behind them just as they reached safety.

"Thanks," she said, and heard him laugh—one guttural peal; he was Arab, for sure. He drove up a hill and once more stopped the car, this time at a bus-stop. He handed her a coin.

"Take a two-mark ticket, the next bus that way," he said.

It's our annual school treasure hunt on Foundation Day, she thought; the next clue takes you to the next clue; the last clue takes you to the prize.

It was pitch dark and the first stars were appearing. A biting country wind was blowing off the hills. Away down the road she saw the lights of a petrol station, but no houses anywhere. She waited five minutes, a bus pulled up with a sigh. It was three-quarters empty. She bought her ticket and sat down near the door, knees together, eyes nowhere. For the next two stops no one boarded; at the third, a boy in a leather jacket leapt in and sat himself cheerfully beside her. He was her American chauffeur of last night.

"Two stops from now is a new church," he said conversationally. "You get out, you walk past the church, down the road, keeping on the right sidewalk. You come to a parked red vehicle with a little devil hanging from the driver's mirror. Open the passenger door, sit down, wait. That's all you do."

The bus drew up, she got out and started walking. The boy remained on the bus. The road was straight and the night extremely dark. Ahead of her, perhaps five hundred yards, she saw a crooked splash of red under a street lamp. No sidelights. The snow squeaked under her new boots, and the noise added to her feeling of being detached from her body. Hullo, feet, what are you doing down there? March, girl, march. The van came nearer and she saw it was a little Coca-Cola van driven high on the kerb. Fifty yards beyond it under the next lamp was a tiny café, and beyond the café again nothing but the bare snow plateau and the straight, pointless road to nowhere. What had possessed anybody to put a café in such a godless spot was a riddle for another life.

She opened the van door and got in. The interior was strangely bright from the street lamp overhead. She smelt onions and saw a cardboard box full of them among the crates of empty bottles that filled the back. A plastic devil with a trident dangled from the driver's mirror. She remembered a similar mascot in the van in London, when Mario had hijacked her. A heap of grimy cassettes lay at her feet. It was the quietest place in the world. A single light approached her slowly down the road. It came level and she saw a young priest on a bicycle. His face turned to her as he ticked past, and he looked offended, as if she had challenged his chastity. She waited again. A tall man in a peaked cap stepped out of the café, sniffed the air, then peered up and down the street, uncertain what time of day it was. He returned to the café, came out again, walked slowly towards her until he came alongside. He tapped on Charlie's window with the fingertips of one gloved hand. A leather glove, hard and shiny. A bright torch shone on her, blacking him off from her completely. Its beam held her, travelled slowly round the van, returned to her, dazzling her in one eye. She lifted a hand to shield herself, and as she lowered it, the beam followed it to her lap. The torch went out, her door opened, one hand closed on her wrist and hauled her out of the car. She was standing face to face with him, and he was taller than she was by a foot, broad and square to her. But his face was in black shadow under the peak of his cap, and he had turned his collar up against the cold.

"Stand very still," he said.

Unslinging her shoulder bag, he first felt the weight of it, then opened it and looked inside. For the third time in its recent life, her little clock radio received careful attention. He switched it on. It played. He switched it off, fiddled with it, and slipped something into his pocket. For a second, she thought he had decided to keep the radio for himself. But he hadn't after all, for she saw him drop it back into the bag, and the bag into the van. Then, like a deportment instructor correcting her posture, he put the tips of a gloved hand on each of her shoulders, straightening her up. His dark gaze was on her face all the time. Letting his right arm dangle, he began lightly touching her body with the flat of his left hand, first her neck and shoulders, now her collarbone and shoulder blades, testing the spots where the straps of her bra would have been if she had worn one. Now her armpits and down her sides to her hips; her breasts and belly.

"This morning in the hotel you wear your bracelet on your right wrist. Tonight you wear it on your left wrist. Why?"

His English was foreign and educated and courteous; his accent, so far as she could judge, Arab. A soft voice but powerful; a speaker's voice.

"I like to change it around," she said.

"Why?" he repeated.

"To make it feel new."

Dropping into a crouch, he explored her hips and legs and the inside of her thighs with the same minute attention as the rest of her; then, still only with his left hand, carefully prodded her new fur boots.

"You know how much it is worth, that bracelet?" he asked as he stood up again.

"No."

"Stay still."

He was standing behind her, tracing her back, her buttocks, her legs again, down to the boots.

"You didn't insure it?"

"No."

"Why not?"

"Michel gave it to me for love. Not money."

"Get in the car."

She did so; he walked round the front and climbed in beside her.

"Okay, I take you to Khalil." He started the engine. "Door-to-door delivery. Okay?"

The van had an automatic gearbox, but she noticed he steered mainly with his left hand while the right rested on his lap. The jangle of the empties took her by surprise. He reached a crossroads and turned left into a road as straight as the first, but without lamps. His face, as much as she could see of it, reminded her of Joseph's, not in its features but in its intentness, in the drawn-back corners of his fighter's eyes, which kept a constant watch on the van's three mirrors, as well as on herself.

"You like onions?" he called above the clatter of the bottles.

"Quite."

"You like to cook? What you cook? Spaghetti? Wiener-schnitzel?"

"Things like that."

"What did you cook for Michel?"

"Steak."

"When?"

"In London. The night he stayed in my flat."

"No onions?" he shouted.

"In the salad," she said.

They were heading back towards the city. Its glow made a pink wall under the heavy evening cloud. They descended a hill and arrived in a flat, sprawling valley suddenly without form. She saw half-built factories and huge lorry parks, unoccupied. She saw a rubbish tip that was being shaped into a mountain. She saw no shops, no pub, no lights in any window. They entered a concrete forecourt. He stopped the van but did not switch off the engine. "HOTEL GARNI EDEN," she read, in red neon letters, and above the garish doorway: *"Willkommen! Bienvenu! Well-come!"*

As he handed her the shoulder bag, an idea struck him. "Here—give him these. He likes them too," he said, fishing for the box of onions from among the crates. As he dumped it in her lap, she noticed again the stillness of his gloved right hand. "Room five, fourth floor. The stairs. Not the elevator. Go well."

With the van's engine still running, he watched her across the forecourt to the lighted entrance. The box was heavier than she had expected and claimed both her arms. The lobby was empty, the lift stood waiting, but she didn't take it. The staircase was narrow and twisting, the carpet worn to the thread. The canned music had a panting insinuation, the fuggy air reeked of cheap scent and stale tobacco smoke. At the first landing, an old woman called *"Grüss Gott"* to her from inside her glass cubicle but did not raise her head. It seemed to be a place where unexplained ladies came and went a good deal.

At the second landing, she heard music and female

laughter; at the third she was overtaken by the lift and wondered why he had made her take the stairs, but she had no will any more, no resistance; her words and actions had all been written for her. The box was making her arms ache, and by the time she entered the fourth-floor corridor the ache was her greatest concern. The first door was a fire exit and the second, right beside it, was marked 5. The lift, the fire exit, the stairs, she thought automatically; he always has at least two things.

She knocked on the door, it opened, and her first thought was: Oh Christ, typical, I've mucked it up: because the man who stood before her was the man who had just driven her here in the Coca-Cola van, minus his hat and left glove. He took the box from her and laid it on the luggage stand. He took off her spectacles, folded them, and handed them back to her. When he had done that, he again unslung her shoulder bag and emptied its contents onto the cheap pink eiderdown, much as they had done to her in London when they put the black glasses on her. About the only other thing in the room apart from the bed was the briefcase. It was lying on the washstand, empty, its black mouth turned towards her like an open jaw. It was the one she had helped to steal from Professor Minkel, back in that big hotel with the mezzanine, when she was too young to know any better.

An utter calm had descended over the three men in their operations room. No phone calls, even from Minkel and Alexis; no desperate recantations over the cipher link with the Embassy in Bonn. In their collective imagination the whole tortuous conspiracy seemed to be holding its breath. Litvak sat slumped despondently in an office chair; Kurtz was in some kind of sunny dream, his eyes half closed, smiling like an old alligator. And Gadi Becker, as before, was the stillest of them, staring self-critically into the gathering dark, like a man examining all the promises of his past life—which had he kept? Which broken?

"We should have given her the homer this time round," Litvak said. "They trust her by now. Why didn't we give her the homer?—wire her up?"

"Because he'll search her," Becker said. "He'll search her for weapons and wires and he'll search her for a homer."

Litvak roused himself enough to argue. "So why do they use her? You're crazy. Why use a girl you don't trust—for a job like this?"

"Because she hasn't killed," said Becker. "Because she's clean. That's why they use her, and that's why they don't trust her. For the same reason."

Kurtz's smile became almost human. "When she's made her first kill, Shimon. When she's no longer a novice. When she's the wrong side of the law forever, an illegal unto death—*then* they'll trust her. Then everybody will trust her," he assured Litvak contentedly. "By nine o'clock tonight, she'll be one of them—no problem, Shimon, no problem."

Litvak remained unconsoled.

25

Once more, he was beautiful. He was Michel full-grown, with Joseph's abstinence and grace and Tayeh's unbothered absolutism. He was everything she had imagined when she was trying to turn him into somebody she was looking forward to. He was broad-shouldered and sculptured, with the rarity of a precious object kept from sight. He could not have walked into a restaurant without the talk dying round him, or walked out of it without leaving a kind of relief in his wake. He was a man of the outdoors condemned to hiding in small rooms, with the pallor of the dungeon in his complexion.

He had drawn the curtains and put on the bedside light. There was no chair for her and he was using the bed as a carpenter's bench. He had tossed the pillows on the floor beside the box and sat her in their place while he went to work, and he was talking all the time that he worked, half to himself and half to her. His voice knew only attack: a thrusting, forward march of thoughts and words.

"They say Minkel's a nice person. Maybe he is. When I read about him, I too said to myself—this old fellow Minkel, maybe he's got some courage to say those things. Maybe I would respect him. I can respect my enemy. I can honour him. I have no problem concerning this."

Having dumped the onions in a corner, he was fishing out a succession of small packages from the box with his left hand and unwrapping them one by one while he used his right to hold them down. Desperate to concentrate on something, Charlie tried to commit the whole lot to memory, then gave up: two new supermarket torch batteries in a single pack, one detonator of the type she had used at the fort for training, with red wires sprouting from the crimped end. Penknife. Pliers. Screwdriver. Soldering iron. A coil of fine red wire, steel staples, copper thread. Insulating tape, a torch bulb, assorted lengths of wooden dowelling. And a rectangular piece of softwood as a base for the device. Taking the soldering iron to the handbasin, Khalil plugged it into a nearby power point, causing a smell of burning dust.

"Do the Zionists think of all the nice people when they bomb us? I don't think so. When they napalm our villages, kill our women? This I doubt very much. I do not think the terrorist Israeli pilot, sitting up there, says to himself, 'Those poor civilians, those innocent victims.'" He talks like this when he is alone, she thought. And he is alone a lot. He talks to keep his faith alive; and his conscience quiet. "I have killed many people whom I would no doubt respect," he said, back at the bed. "The Zionists have killed many more. But I kill only for love. I kill for Palestine and for her children. Try to think like this also," he advised her piously, interrupting himself as he glanced at her. "You are nervous?"

"Yes."

"It's natural. I too am nervous. Are you nervous in the theatre?"

"Yes."

"It is the same. Terror is theatre. We inspire, we frighten, we awaken indignation, anger, love. We enlighten. The theatre also. The guerrilla is the great actor of the world."

"Michel wrote me that too. It's in his letters."

"But I told it to him. It was my idea."

The next parcel was wrapped in oil paper. He opened it with respect. Three half-pound sticks of Russian plastic. He laid them in pride of place at the centre of the eiderdown.

"The Zionists kill for fear and for hate," he announced. "Palestinians for love and justice. Remember this difference. It is important." The glance again, swift and commanding. "You will remember this when you are afraid? You will say to yourself 'for justice'? If you do, you will no longer be afraid."

"And for Michel," she said.

He was not entirely satisfied. "And for him also, naturally," he conceded, and from a brown paper bag shook two household clothespegs onto the bed, then brought them to the bedside light to compare their simple mechanisms. Observing him from so near, she noticed a patch of creased white skin where the cheek and lower ear seemed to have been melted together and cooled again.

"Why do you put your hands over your face, please?"

Khalil enquired, out of curiosity, when he had selected the better peg.

"I was tired for a moment," she said.

"Then wake up. Be alert for your mission. Also for the revolution. You know this type of bomb? Did Tayeh teach it to you?"

"I don't know. Maybe Bubi did."

"Then pay attention." Sitting beside her on the bed, he picked up the wood base and with a ballpoint pen briskly drew some lines on it for the circuit. "What we make is a bomb for all occasions. It works as a timer—here—also as a booby trap—here. Trust nothing. That is our philosophy." Handing her a clothespeg and two drawing-pins, he watched while she pushed the pins into either side of the peg's mouth. "I am not anti-Semitic, you know that?"

"Yes."

She gave him back the clothespeg; he took it to the handbasin and set to work soldering wires to the heads of the two drawing-pins.

"*How* do you know?" he demanded, puzzled.

"Tayeh told me the same. So did Michel." And so did about two hundred other people, she thought.

"Anti-Semitism, this is a strictly Christian invention." He again returned to the bed, this time bringing Minkel's open briefcase with him. "You Europeans, you are anti-everybody. Anti-Jew, anti-Arab, anti-black. We have many friends in Germany. But not because they love Palestine. Only because they hate Jews. That Helga—you like her?"

"No."

"Me neither. She is very decadent, I think. You like animals?"

"Yes."

He sat next to her, the briefcase on the bed beside him. "Did Michel?"

Choose, never hesitate, Joseph had said. *It is better to be inconsistent than to be uncertain.*

"We never talked about them."

"Not even about horses?"

And never, never correct yourself.

"No."

From his pocket, Khalil had pulled a folded handkerchief, and from the centre of the handkerchief a cheap pocket watch with the glass and hour hand removed. Setting it beside the explosive, he took up the red circuit wire and unwound it. She had the base-board on her lap. He took it from her, then grasped her hand and placed it so that she could hold the staples while he lightly tapped them home, fixing the red wire to the board according to the pattern he had drawn. Next, returning to the basin, he soldered the wires to the battery while she cut up lengths of insulating tape for him with the scissors.

"See," he said proudly as he added the watch.

He was very near her. She felt his nearness like a heat. He was stooped like a cobbler to his last, engrossed by his work.

"Was my brother religious with you?" he asked, taking up a light-bulb and twisting a pared end of wire to it.

"He was an atheist."

"Sometimes he was an atheist, sometimes he was religious. Other times he was a silly little boy, too much with women and ideas and cars. Tayeh says you were modest at the camp. No Cuban boys, no Germans, nobody."

"I wanted Michel. That's all I wanted. Michel," she said, too emphatically to her own ear. But when she glanced at him, she could not help wondering whether their brotherly love had been quite as infallible as Michel had proclaimed, for his face had set into a scowl of doubt.

"Tayeh is a great man," he said, implying perhaps that Michel was not. The bulb lit. "The circuit is good," he announced and, reaching gently past her, picked up the three sticks of explosive. "Tayeh and myself—we died together. Did Tayeh describe to you this incident?" he asked, as with Charlie's help he began taping the explosive tightly together.

"No."

"The Syrians caught us—cut here. First they beat us. This is normal. Stand up, please." From the box he had extracted an old brown blanket, which he made her stretch across her chest for him while he deftly sliced it into strips. Their faces across the blanket were very close. She could smell the warm sweetness of his Arab body.

"In the course of beating us they make themselves very angry, so they decide to break all our bones. First fingers, then arms, then legs. Then they break our ribs with rifles."

The knife point through the blanket was inches from her

body. He cut swiftly and cleanly, as if the blanket were something he had hunted and killed. "When they finish with us,
they leave us in the desert. I am glad. At least we die in the
desert! But we don't die. A patrol of our commandos finds
us. For three months Tayeh and Khalil lie side by side in
hospital. Snowmen. Covered in plaster. We have some nice
conversations, we become good friends, we read some good
books together."

Folding the strips into neat military piles, Khalil
addressed himself to Minkel's cheap black briefcase, which
she noticed for the first time was opened from the back, by
way of the hinges, while the fastenings at the front were still
firmly closed. One by one he laid the folded strips inside, until he had built up a soft platform for the bomb to lie on.

"You know what Tayeh said to me one night?" he
enquired as he did this. "'Khalil,' he said, 'for how much
longer do we play the nice guys? Nobody helps us, nobody
thanks us. We make great speeches, we send fine orators to
the United Nations, and if we wait another fifty years, maybe
our grandchildren, if they're alive, they get a little piece of
justice.'" Interrupting himself, he showed her how much with
the fingers of his good hand. "'Meanwhile our brother Arabs
kill us, the Zionists kill us, the Falangists kill us, and those of
us who remain alive go into their diaspora. Like the Armeni-
ans. Like the Jews themselves.'" He became cunning. "'But
if we make a few bombs—kill a few people—make a slaugh-
terhouse, just for two minutes of history—'"

Without finishing the sentence, he took up the device
and solemnly, with great precision, laid it inside the case.

"I need spectacles," he explained with a smile, and
shook his head like an old man. "But where should I go for
them—a man like me?"

"If you were tortured like Tayeh, why don't you limp
like Tayeh?" she demanded, growing suddenly loud in her
nervousness.

Delicately, he removed the light-bulb from the wires,
leaving the pared ends free for the detonator.

"The reason I do not limp is because I prayed to God
for strength, and God gave it me so that I could fight the real
enemy and not my brother Arabs."

Handing her the detonator, he looked on approvingly
while she attached it to the circuit. When she had finished, he

took what wire remained and, with a deft, almost unconscious movement, wound it like wool round the tips of his dead fingers, until he had made a little dummy. Then wound two strands horizontally for a belt.

"You know what Michel wrote to me before he died? In his last letter?".

No, Khalil, I do not know, she replied as she watched him toss the dummy into the briefcase.

"Please?"

"No. I said *no,* I don't know."

"Posted only hours before his death? 'I love her. She is not like the others. It is true that when I first met her she had the paralysed conscience of a European'—here, wind the watch, please—'also she was a whore. But now she is an Arab in her soul and one day I shall show her to our people and to you.' "

There remained the booby trap, and for this they had to work in still closer intimacy, for he required her to loop a length of steel wire through the fabric of the lid, then he himself held the lid as low as possible while her small hands led the wire to the dowelling in the clothespeg. Gingerly now, he took the whole contraption to the basin once more, and, with his back to her, refitted the hinge-pins with a blob of solder for each side. They had passed the point of no return.

"You know what I told to Tayeh once?"

"No."

" 'Tayeh, my friend, we Palestinians are very lazy people in our exile. Why do we have no Palestinians in the Pentagon? In the State Department? Why are we not yet running the New York *Times,* Wall Street, the CIA? Why are we not making Hollywood movies about our great struggle, getting ourselves elected Mayor of New York, head of the Supreme Court? What is wrong with us, Tayeh? Why are we without enterprise? It is not enough that our people become doctors, scientists, schoolmasters. Why do we not run America as well? Is it because of this that we have to use bombs and machine guns?' "

He was standing strictly before her, holding the briefcase by its handle like a good commuter.

"You know what we should do?"

She didn't.

"March. All of us. Before they destroy us for ever." Offering her his forearm, he lifted her to her feet. "From the United States, from Australia, Paris, Jordan, Saudi Arabia, Lebanon—from everywhere in the world where there are Palestinians. We take ships to the borders. Planes. Millions of us. Like a great tide which nobody can turn back." He handed her the briefcase, then began swiftly gathering up his tools and packing them in the box. "Then all together, we march into our homeland, we claim our houses and our farms and our villages, even if we have to knock down their towns and settlements and kibbutzim in order to find them. It wouldn't work. You know why not? They would never come." He dropped to a crouch, examining the threadbare carpet for tell-tale traces. "Our rich would not be able to sustain their *social-economic drop in life-style,*" he explained, ironically emphasising the jargon. "Our merchants would not leave their banks and shops and offices. Our doctors would not give up their smart clinics, the lawyers their corrupt practices, our academics their comfortable universities." He was standing before her, and his smile was a triumph over all his pain. "So the rich make the money and the poor do the fighting. When was it any different?"

She walked ahead of him down the stairs. Exit one tart, carrying her little box of tricks. The Coca-Cola van stood in the forecourt still, but he strode past it as if he had never seen it in his life and climbed into a farmer's Ford, a diesel with bales of straw strapped to the roof. She got in beside him. Hills again. Pine trees laden on one side with fresh wet snow. Instructions, Joseph-style: Charlie, do you understand? Yes, Khalil, I understand. Then repeat it to me. She did. It is for peace, remember that. I will, Khalil, I will: for peace, for Michel, for Palestine; for Joseph and Khalil; for Marty and the revolution and for Israel, and for the theatre of the real.

He had stopped beside a barn and put out the headlights. He was looking at his watch. From down the road a torch flashed twice. He reached across her and pushed open her door.

"His name is Franz and you will tell him you are Margaret. Good luck."

The evening was moist and quiet, the street lamps of the old city centre hung over her like caged white moons in their iron brackets. She had made Franz drop her at the corner because she wanted the short walk across the bridge before she made her entrance. She wanted the puffed look of someone stepping in from outdoors, and the nip of cold on her face, and the hatred back in her mind. She was in an alley among low scaffolding, which closed round her like a spindly tunnel. She passed an art gallery full of self-portraits of a blond, unpleasing boy in spectacles, and another next to it with idealised landscapes that the boy would never enter. Graffiti screamed at her but she could not understand a word until she suddenly read "Fuck America." Thanks for the translation, she thought. She was in the open air again, climbing concrete steps strewn with sand to beat the snow, but they were still slippery underfoot. She reached the top and saw the glass doors of the university library to her left. The lights were still burning in the students' café. Rachel and a boy were sitting tensely at the window. She passed the first marble totem-pole, she was on the treewalk high above the carriageway, crossing to the farther side. Already the lecture hall rose ahead of her, its strawberry stone turned to blazing crimson by the floodlighting. Cars were pulling up; the first members of the audience were arriving, climbing the four steps to the front entrance, pausing to shake hands and congratulate one another on their immense prominence. A couple of security men perfunctorily checked ladies' handbags. She kept walking. The truth will make you free. She passed the second totem-pole, heading for the down staircase.

The briefcase was dangling in her right hand and she felt it brushing her thigh. A whining police siren made her shoulder muscles convulse in terror, but she kept going. Two police motorcycles with whirling blue lights pulled up, cosseting a shiny black Mercedes with a pennant. Usually when grand cars passed, she turned her head away in order not to give the occupants the satisfaction of being looked at, but tonight was different. Tonight she could walk tall; she had the answer in her hand. So she stared at them and was rewarded by a glimpse of a florid, overfed man in a black suit and silver tie; and a sullen wife with three chins and a mink rug. *For great lies we need naturally a great audience*, she remembered. A camera flashed and the eminent couple ascended to the glass doors, admired by at least three passers-by. *Soon, you bastards*, she thought, *soon*.

At the bottom of the steps turn right. She did so and kept going till she reached the corner. Be sure you do not fall into the stream, Helga had said for extra humour; Khalil's bombs are not waterproof, Charlie, and nor are you. She turned left and began skirting the building, following a pebble pavement on which the snow had failed to settle. The pavement widened and became a courtyard, and in its centre, beside a group of concrete flower tubs, stood a police caravan. In front of it, two uniformed policemen were preening at each other, lifting their boots and laughing, then scowling round at anyone who dared watch. She was not fifty feet from the side door, and she began to feel the calm that she was waiting for—the sensation, almost of levitation, that came over her when she stepped on stage and left her other identities behind her in the dressing-room. She was Imogen from South Africa, long on courage, short on grace, hastening to assist a great liberal hero. She was embarrassed—dammit, she was embarrassed to death—but she was going to do the right thing or bust. She had reached the side entrance. It was closed. She tried the door handle but it didn't turn. Dither. She put the flat of her hand on the panel and pushed but it wouldn't budge. She stood back and stared at it, then looked round for someone to help her, and by then the two policemen had stopped flirting with each other and were eyeing her suspiciously, but neither came forward.

Curtain up. Go.

"I say, excuse me," she called to them. "Do you speak English?"

Still they did not move. If there was a distance to be covered, then let her do the walking herself. She was only a citizen, after all, and a woman at that.

"I said do you speak English? *Englisch—sprechen Sie?* Someone needs to give this to the Professor. Immediately. Will you come over here, please?"

Both scowled, but only one of them came over to her. Slowly, as befitted his dignity.

"*Toilette nicht hier,*" he snapped, and tipped his head up the road where she had come from.

"I don't want the toilet. I want you to find somebody who will give this briefcase to Professor Minkel. *Minkel,*" she repeated, and held up the briefcase.

The policeman was young and did not care for youth.

He did not take the briefcase from her, but he made her hold it while he pressed the catch and ascertained that it was locked.

Oh boy, she thought: *you just committed suicide and you're still scowling at me.*

"*Öffnen*," he ordered.

"I can't open it. It's *locked*." She let a note of desperation enter her voice. "It's the Professor's, don't you understand? For all I know, it's got his lecture notes in it. He needs it for tonight." Turning from him, she beat loudly on the door. "Professor Minkel? It's me, Imogen Baastrup from Wits. Oh *God*."

The second policeman had joined them. He was older and dark-jawed. Charlie appealed to his greater wisdom. "Well, do *you* speak English?" she said. At the same moment, the door opened a few inches and a goatish male face peered at her with deep suspicion. He spoke something in German to the nearer policeman, and Charlie caught the word "*Amerikanerin*" in his reply.

"I am *not* American," she retorted, now nearly in tears. "My name is Imogen Baastrup, I'm from South Africa, and I'm bringing Professor Minkel's briefcase to him. He lost it. Would you kindly give him this immediately, because I'm sure he's desperate for it. *Please!*"

The door opened wide enough to reveal the rest of him: a pudgy, mayoral-looking man of sixty or more in a black suit. He was very pale, and to Charlie's secret eye he was very frightened too.

"Sir. Do you speak English, please? Do you?"

Not only did he speak it, he had sworn oaths in it. For he said "I do" so solemnly that there would be no going back on it for the rest of his life.

"Then will you please give this to Professor Minkel with Imogen Baastrup's compliments and tell him she's *sorry*, the hotel made a *stupid* muddle, and I'm greatly looking forward to hearing him tonight—"

She held out the briefcase but the mayoral man refused to take it. He looked at the policeman behind her, and seemed to receive some faint reassurance from him; he looked at the briefcase again, and then at Charlie.

"Come this way," he said, like a stage butler earning his ten quid a night, and stood aside to admit her.

She was appalled. This wasn't in the script. Not in Khalil's or Helga's or anybody else's. What happened if Minkel unlocked it under her very eyes?

"Oh, I can't do that. I have to take my place in the *auditorium*. I haven't got my *ticket* yet! *Please!*"

But the mayoral man had his orders too, and he had his fears, for as she shoved the briefcase at him he leapt away from it as if it were on fire.

The door closed, they were in a corridor with lagged pipes running along the ceiling. Briefly they reminded her of the overhead pipes at the Olympic Village. Her reluctant escort walked ahead of her. She smelled oil and heard the repressed thunder of a furnace; she felt a wave of heat across her face and considered fainting or being sick. The handle of the briefcase was drawing blood, she could feel the warm slime of it trickling between her fingers.

They had reached a door marked *"Vorstand."* The mayoral man tapped and called, *"Oberhauser! Schnell!"* As he did so, she looked desperately back and saw two fair boys in leather jackets in the corridor behind her. They carried machine guns. *Christ Almighty, what is this?* The door opened, Oberhauser stepped in first and stood quickly aside as if disowning her. She was in a movie set for *Journey's End*. Wings and rear stage were sandbagged; great bales of wadding lined the ceiling, held in place by chicken wire. Sandbag barriers made a zigzag walkway from the door. Centre stage stood a low coffee table with a tray of drinks. Beside it, in a low armchair, sat Minkel like a waxwork, staring straight towards her. Opposite him his wife, and next to him a tubby German woman with a fur stole whom Charlie took to be Oberhauser's wife.

So much for the talent, and crammed into the wings among the sandbags was the rest of the unit, in two distinct groups, their spokesmen shoulder to shoulder at the centre. The home side was led by Kurtz; to his left stood a randy, middle-aged man with a weak face, which was Charlie's swift dismissal of Alexis. Next to Alexis stood his wolf-boys, their hostile faces turned towards her. Facing them stood bits of the family she already knew, with strangers added, and the darkness of their Jewish features in contrast to their German counterparts was one of those images that would remain a tableau in her memory for as long as she lived. Kurtz the ringmaster had his finger to his lips, and his left wrist lifted for him to study his watch.

She started to say "Where is he?" and then, with a rush of joy and anger, she saw him, apart from everyone as usual, the fraught and lonely producer on his first night. Coming swiftly to her, he placed himself a little to one side, leaving her a path to Minkel.

"Say your piece to him, Charlie," he instructed her quietly. "Say what you would say and ignore everyone who is not at the table"—and all she needed was the *clack* of the clapperboard in her face.

His hand came near to her own, she could feel the hairs touching her skin. She wanted to say "I love you—how are you?" But there were other lines to say, so she took a deep breath and said them instead, because that was, after all, the name of their relationship.

"Professor, a most terrible thing has happened," she began in a rush. "The stupid hotel people sent your briefcase to my room with my luggage, they saw me talking to you, I suppose, and there was *my* luggage and there was *your* luggage and somehow that *crazy* boy just took it into his *dumb* head that it was my case—" She turned to Joseph to tell him she'd run dry.

"Give the briefcase to the Professor," he ordered.

Minkel was standing up, looking wooden and far away in his mind, like a man receiving a long prison sentence. Mrs. Minkel was making a show of smiling. Charlie's knees were paralysed, but with Joseph's hand on her elbow, she managed to topple forward, holding the case out to him while she said some more lines.

"Only I didn't *see* it till half an hour ago, they'd shoved it in the cupboard there and my dresses were all hanging down over it, then when I *did* see it and I read the label, I nearly had a blue fit—"

Minkel would have accepted the briefcase, but no sooner did she offer it than other hands spirited it to a large black box lying on the floor with heavy cables snaking from it. Suddenly everyone seemed scared of her and was cowering behind the sandbags. Joseph's strong arms gathered her after them; his hand shoved her head down until she was looking at her own waist. But not before she had seen a deep-sea diver muffled in a heavy bomb suit wade towards the box. He wore a helmet with a thick glass visor, and under it a surgical mask to stop it fogging from inside. A muffled order commanded silence; Joseph had drawn her to him and was half smothering her with his own body. Another order signalled a general relief; heads rose again, but still he held her down. She heard the sounds of feet departing in orderly haste, and when at last he released her, she saw Litvak hastening forward with what was evidently a bomb of his own, a more obvious affair than Khalil's, with trailing wires not yet connected. Joseph meanwhile was leading her firmly back to the centre of the room.

"Continue your explanations," he ordered in her ear. "You were describing how you read the label. Go on from there. What did you do?"

Take a deep breath. Speech continues.

"Then when I asked at reception they said you were out for the evening, you had this lecture down at the university, so I just hopped a cab and—I mean I don't know how you can forgive me. Look, I must fly. Good luck, Professor, have a great speech."

On a nod from Kurtz, Minkel had taken a key chain from his pocket and was pretending to select a key, even though he had no briefcase to play with. But Charlie, under Joseph's urgent guidance, was already making for the door, half walking, half carried by his arm round her waist.

I won't do it, Jose, I can't, I've spent my courage like you said. Don't let me go, Jose, don't. Behind her she heard muffled orders and the sounds of hasty footsteps as everyone seemed to beat a retreat.

"Two minutes," Kurtz called after them in warning.

They were back in the corridor with the two fair boys and their machine guns.

"Where did you meet him?" Joseph asked, in a low fast voice.

"A Hotel Eden. A sort of brothel on the edge of town. Next to a chemist. He's got a red Coke van. FR stroke BT something something 5. And a clapped-out Ford saloon. I didn't get the number."

"Open your bag."

She did so. Fast, the way he talked. Taking out her little clock radio, he replaced it with a similar one from his own pocket.

"It is not the same device that we used before," he warned swiftly. "It will receive on one station only. It will still tell the time, but it has no alarm. But it transmits, and it tells us where you are."

"When?" she said stupidly.

"What are Khalil's orders to you now?"

"I'm to walk down the road and keep walking—Jose, *when* will you come?—for Christ's sake!"

His face had a haggard and desperate seriousness, but there was no concession in it.

"Listen, Charlie. Are you listening?"

"Yes, Jose, I am listening."

"If you press the volume button on your clock radio— not turn it, but *press* it—we shall know he is asleep. Do you understand?"

"He won't sleep like that."

"What do you mean? How do you know how he sleeps?"

"He's like you, he's not the kind, he's awake all day and night. He's—Jose, I can't go back. Don't make me."

She was staring pleadingly at his face, still waiting for it to yield, but it had set rigidly against her.

"He wants me to sleep with him, for God's sake! He wants a wedding night, Jose. Doesn't that stir you slightly? He's taking me over where Michel left off. He didn't like him. He's going to even the score. Do I still go?"

She held him so fiercely that he had difficulty breaking her grasp. She stood against him with her head down, against his chest, wanting him to take her back into his protection. But instead he put his hands under her arms and straightened her, and she saw his face again, locked and bolted, telling her that love was not their province: not his, not hers, and least of all Khalil's. He started her on her journey, she shook him off and went alone; he took a step after her and stopped. She looked back and hated him; she closed her eyes and opened them, she let out a deep breath.

I'm dead.

She stepped into the street, straightened herself and, crisp as a soldier and quite as blind, marched briskly up a narrow street, passing a seedy nightclub displaying illuminated photographs of girls of thirty-something baring unimpressive breasts. That's what I should be doing, she thought. She reached a main road, remembered her pedestrian drill, looked left and saw a mediaeval gate tower with a sign for McDonald's hamburgers written tastefully across it. The lights turned green for her; she kept going and saw high black hills blocking the end of the road and a pale, clouded sky twisting restively behind them. She glanced round and saw the Cathedral spire following her. She turned to her right and walked more slowly than she had ever walked in her life, down a leafy avenue of patrician houses. Now she was counting to herself. Numbers. Now she was saying rhymes. Jose Goes Down Town. Now she was remembering what had happened in the lecture hall, but without Kurtz, without Joseph, and without the murderous technicians of the two unreconciled sides. Ahead of her, Rossino was pushing his motorbike silently out of a gateway. She walked up to him, he handed her a helmet and a leather jacket, and as she started to put them on, something made her look back in the direction she had come from, and she saw a lazy orange flash stretch towards her down the damp cobble like the path of the setting sun, and she noticed how long it stayed on the eye after it had disappeared. Then at last she heard the sound she had been dully expecting: a distant yet intimate thud, like a breaking of something unmendable deep inside herself; the precise and permanent end to love. Well, Joseph, yes. Goodbye.

At the same second exactly, Rossino's engine burst into life, ripping the damp night apart with its roar of triumphant laughter. Me too, she thought. It's the funniest day of my life.

Rossino drove slowly, keeping to small roads and following a carefully thought-out route.

You drive, I'll follow. Maybe it's time I became Italian.

A warm drizzle had cleared away much of the snow, but he drove with respect for the bad surface, and for his important passenger. He was yelling joyful things at her and seemed to be having a great time, but she wasn't interested in sharing his mood. They passed through a big gateway and she shouted "Is this the place?" without knowing or caring from Adam what place she was talking about, but the gateway gave on to an unmade road over hills and valleys of private forest, and they crossed them alone, under a bobbing moon

that used to be Joseph's private property. She looked down
and saw a sleeping village draped in a white shroud; she
smelt Greek pine trees and felt her warm tears being dashed
away by the wind. She held Rossino's trembling, unfamiliar
body tucked into her own, and told him: Help yourself,
there's nothing left.

They descended a last hill, came out of another gateway,
and entered a road lined with bare larches like the trees in
France on family holidays. The track climbed again, and as
they reached the crest, Rossino cut the engine and coasted
down a footpath into a forest. He opened a saddle bag and
pulled out a bundle of clothes and a handbag, and tossed
them to her. He held a torch, and while she changed he
watched her by the light of it, and there was a moment when
she stood half naked in front of him.

You want me, take me; I'm available and unattached.

She was without love and without value to herself. She
was where she had started, and the whole rotten world could
screw her.

She poured her junk from one handbag to the other,
powder compact, tampons, bits of money, her packet of
Marlboros. And her cheap little radio alarm clock for rehearsals—*press the volume, Charlie, are you listening?* Rossino took her old passport and handed her a new one, but she
didn't bother to find out what nationality she had become.

Citizen of Nowheresville, born yesterday.

He gathered up her old clothes and dumped them into
the saddle bag, together with her old shoulder bag and spectacles. Wait here but look towards the road, he said. He'll
shine a red light twice. He had been gone barely five minutes
before she saw it winking through the trees. Hooray, a friend
at last.

26

Khalil took her arm and almost carried her to the shiny new car because she was weeping and trembling so much she wasn't very good at walking. After the humble clothes of a van driver, he seemed to have put on the full disguise of the unimpeachable German manager: soft black overcoat, shirt and tie, groomed and swept-back hair. Opening her door, he took off the overcoat and tucked it solicitously round her as if she were a sick animal. She had no idea how he expected her to be, but he seemed less shocked by her condition than respectful of it. The engine was already running. He turned the heating on full.

"Michel would be proud of you," he said kindly, and considered her a moment by the interior light. She started to answer, but broke out weeping again instead. He gave her a handkerchief; she held it in both hands, twisting it round her fingers while the tears fell and fell. They set off down the wooded hillside.

"What happened?" she whispered.

"You have won a great victory for us. Minkel died as he was opening the briefcase. Other friends of Zionism are reported to be severely wounded. They are still counting." He spoke in savage satisfaction. "They speak of outrage. Shock. Cold-blooded murder. They should visit Rashidiyeh one day. I invite the whole university. They should sit in the shelters and be machine-gunned as they come out. They should have their bones broken and watch their children being put to torture. Tomorrow the whole world will read that Palestinians will not become the poor blacks of Zion."

The heating was powerful, but it was still not enough. She pulled his coat more tightly round her. Its lapels were of velvet and she could smell its newness.

"You want to tell me how it went?" he enquired.

She shook her head. The seats were plush and soft, the engine quiet. She listened for cars but heard none. She looked in the mirror. Nothing behind, nothing in front. When was there ever? She caught Khalil's dark eye staring at her.

"Don't worry. We look after you. I promise. I am glad you are in grief. Others when they kill, they laugh and triumph. Got drunk, tore off their clothes like animals. All this I have seen. But you—you weep. This is very good."

The house was beside a lake and the lake was in a steep valley. Khalil drove past it twice before he turned into the drive, and his eyes as he scanned the roadside were Joseph's eyes, dark and purposeful and all-seeing. It was a modern bungalow, a rich man's second home. It had white walls and Moorish windows and a sloping red roof where the snow had not managed to lie. The garage was joined to it. He drove in and the doors closed. He switched off the engine and drew a long-barrelled automatic pistol from inside his jacket. Khalil, the one-handed shooter. She stayed in the car, staring at the toboggans and the firewood stored along the back wall. He opened her door.

"Walk after me. Three metres, no closer."

A steel side door led to an interior corridor. She waited, then went after him. The drawing-room lights were already lit, a wood fire was burning in the grate. Pony-skin sofa. Suburban rustic furniture. A log table laid for two. In an ice bucket on its wrought-iron stand, one bottle of vodka.

"Stay here," he said.

She stood at the centre of the floor, clutching her handbag in both hands, while he moved from room to room, so silently that the only sound she heard was the opening and closing of cupboards. She began to shiver again, violently. He returned to the drawing-room, put away his gun, dropped into a crouch before the fire, and set to work to build it into a blaze. To keep away the animals, she thought, watching him. And the sheep safe. The fire roared and she sat before it on the sofa. He switched on the television. It showed an old black-and-white movie from the taverna on the hilltop. He did not turn up the sound. He placed himself before her.

"Would you like some vodka?" he asked politely. "I do not drink, but you must please yourself."

She would, so he poured some for her, far too much.

"You want to smoke?"

He handed her a leather box and lit her cigarette for her.

The lighting in the room brightened; her glance went swiftly to the television and she found herself staring straight into the excited, over-expressive features of the weaselly little German she had seen not an hour earlier at Marty's side. He was posed beside the police van. Behind him she could see her bit of pavement and the side door of the lecture hall, fenced off with fluorescent tape. Police cars, fire engines and ambulances bustled in and out of the cordoned area. Terror is theatre, she thought. The background changed to a shot of green tarpaulins, erected to keep the weather out while the search continued. Khalil turned up the sound and she heard the wailing of ambulances behind the sleek, well-modulated voice of Alexis.

"What's he saying?" she asked.

"He's leading the investigation. Wait. I tell you."

Alexis vanished, and was replaced with a studio shot of Oberhauser unscathed.

"That's the idiot who opened the door to me," she said.

Khalil held up his hand to her to be quiet. She listened and realised, with a detached curiosity, that Oberhauser was giving a description of herself. She caught *"Süd Afrika"* and a reference to brown hair; she saw his hand lift to describe her spectacles; the camera switched to a trembling finger pointing to a pair similar to those which Tayeh had given to her.

After Oberhauser came our artist's first impression of the suspect, which looked like nobody on earth, except possibly an old advertisement for a liquid laxative that had featured large at railway stations ten years earlier. After that came one of the two policemen who had spoken to her, adding his own shamefaced description.

Switching off the set, Khalil again came and stood before her.

"You allow?" he asked shyly.

She picked up her handbag and put it the other side of her so that he could sit down. Did it hum? Bleep? Was it a microphone? What the hell did it do?

Khalil spoke precisely—a seasoned practitioner offers his diagnosis.

"You are a little bit at risk," he said. "Mr. Oberhauser remembers you, so does his wife, so do the policemen, and so do several people in the hotel. Your height, your figure, your spoken English, your acting talent. Also unfortunately there was an Englishwoman who overheard part of your conversation with Minkel and believes you are not South African at all, but English. Your description has gone to London, and we know that the English already have bad thoughts about you. The region here is on full alert, road blocks, spot checks, everybody is falling over his feet. But you will not worry." He took her hand and held it firmly. "I shall protect you with my life. Tonight we shall be safe. Tomorrow we shall smuggle you to Berlin and send you home."

"Home," she said.

"You are one of us. You are our sister. Fatmeh says you are our sister. You have no home, but you are part of a great family. We can make you a new identity, or you can go to Fatmeh, live with her as long as you wish. Though you never fight again, we shall take care of you. For Michel. For what you have done for us."

His loyalty was appalling. Her hand was still in his, his touch powerful and reassuring. His eyes shone with a possessive pride. She got up and walked from the room, taking her handbag with her.

A double bed, the electric fire lit, both bars regardless of expense. A bookshelf of Nowheresville bestsellers: *I'm OK— You're OK, The Joy of Sex*. The corners of the bed turned down. The bathroom lay beyond it, pine-clad, sauna adjoining. She took out the radio and looked at it, and it was her old one, down to the last scratch: just a little heavier, stronger in the hand. Wait until he sleeps. Until I do. She stared at herself. That artist's impression wasn't so bad after all. A land for no people, for a people with no land. First she scrubbed her hands and fingernails; then on an impulse she stripped and treated herself to a long shower, if only to stay away from the warmth of his trust for a little longer. She doused herself with body lotion, helping herself from the cabinet above the basin. Her eyes interested her; they reminded her of Fatima the Swedish girl at the training school— they had the same furious blankness of a mind that had learned to renounce the perils of compassion. The same self-hate exactly. She returned to find him laying food on the table. Cold meats, cheese, a bottle of wine. Candles, already lit. He pulled back a chair for her in the best European style. She sat down; he sat opposite her and began eating at once, with the natural absorption he gave to everything. He had killed and now he was eating: what could be more right? My maddest meal, she thought. My worst and maddest. If a violinist comes to our table, I'll ask him to play "Moon River."

"You still regret what you have done?" he asked, as a matter of interest, like "Has your headache gone?"

"They're pigs," she said and meant it. "Ruthless, murderous—" She started to weep again but caught herself in time. Her knife and fork were shaking so much she had to put them down. She heard a car pass; or was it an aeroplane? My handbag, she thought chaotically—where did I leave it? In the bathroom, away from his prying fingers. She picked up her fork again and saw Khalil's beautiful, untamed face studying her across the guttering candlelight exactly as Joseph's had done on the hilltop outside Delphi.

"Maybe you are trying too hard to hate them," he suggested, as a cure.

It was the worst play she had ever been in, and the worst dinner party. Her urge to smash the tension was the same as the urge to smash herself. She stood up and heard her knife and fork clatter to the floor. She could just see him through the tears of her despair. She started to unbutton her dress, but her hands were in such disorder that she couldn't make them work for her. She went round the table to him and he was already getting up as she hauled him to his feet. His arms came round her; he kissed her, then lifted her across his body, and bore her like his wounded comrade to the bedroom. He laid her on the bed and suddenly, by God knew what desperate chemistry of her mind and body, she was taking him. She was upon him and undressing him; she was drawing him into her as if he were the last man on earth, on the earth's last day; for her own destruction and for his. She was devouring him, suckling him, cramming him into the screaming empty spaces of her guilt and loneliness. She was weeping, she was shouting to him, filling her own deceiving mouth with him, turning him over and obliterating herself and Joseph's memory beneath his fierce body's weight. She felt his surge but clasped him defiantly inside her long after his movement had ceased, her arms locked round him as she hid herself from the advancing storm.

*   *   *

He was not asleep, but he was already dozing. He lay with his tousled dark head on her shoulder, his good arm thrown carelessly across her breast.

"Salim was a lucky boy," he murmured, with a smile in his voice. "A girl like you, that's a cause to die for."

"Who says he died for me?"

"Tayeh said this was possible."

"Salim died for the revolution. The Zionists blew up his car."

"He blew himself up. We read many German police reports of this incident. I told him never to make bombs, but he disobeyed me. He had no talent for the task. He was not a natural fighter."

"What's that noise?" she said, pulling away from him.

It was a patter, like paper crackling, a row of dotted sounds, then nothing. She imagined a car rolling softly over gravel with its engine off.

"Someone is fishing on the lake," Khalil said.

"At this time of night?"

"You never fished at night?" He laughed drowsily. "You never took a little boat on the sea, with a lamp, and caught fishes with your hands?"

"Wake up. Talk to me."

"Better to sleep."

"I can't. I'm afraid."

He began to tell her a story of a night mission he had made into the Galilee long ago, he and two others. How they were crossing the sea in a rowing boat, and it was so beautiful that they lost all sense of what they had come for, and fished instead. She interrupted him.

"It wasn't a boat," she insisted. "It was a car. I heard it again. Listen."

"It was a boat," he said sleepily.

The moon had found a space between the curtains, and shone towards them across the floor. Getting up, she went to the window and without touching the curtains stared out. Pine woods lay all around, the moonpath on the lake was a white staircase reaching downward to the centre of the world. But there was no boat anywhere and no light to lure the fish. She returned to the bed and his right arm slipped across her body, drawing her to him, but when he sensed her resistance he gently drew away from her and turned languidly onto his back.

"Talk to me," she said again. "Khalil. Wake up." She shook him fiercely, then kissed him on the lips. "Wake up," she said again.

So he roused himself for her, because he was a kind man, and had appointed her his sister.

"You know what was strange about your letters to Michel?" he asked. "The gun. 'From now on, I shall dream of your head on my pillow, and your gun beneath it'—lovers' talk. Beautiful lovers' talk."

"Why was it strange? Tell me."

"I had exactly such a conversation with him once. Precisely on this very matter. 'Listen, Salim,' I told him. 'Only cowboys sleep with their guns under the pillow. If you remember nothing else I teach you, remember this. When you are in bed, keep your gun at your side where you can hide it better, and where your hand is. Learn to sleep that way. Even when you have a woman.' He said he would. Always he promised me. Then he forgot. Or found a new woman. Or a new car."

"Broke the rules then, didn't he?" she said and, seizing his gloved hand, considered it in the half darkness, pinching each dead finger in turn. They were of wadding, all but the smallest and the thumb.

"So what did this lot?" she demanded brightly. "Mice? What did this lot, Khalil? Wake up."

He took a long time to answer. "One day in Beirut, I am a little stupid like Salim. I am in the office, the post comes, I am in a hurry, I am expecting a certain parcel, I open it! This was an error."

"So? What happened? You opened it and there was a bang, was there? Bang go your fingers. That how you did your face too?"

"When I woke up in hospital, there was Salim. You know something? He was very pleased I had been stupid. 'Next time, before you open a parcel, show it to me or read the postmark first,' he says. 'If it comes from Tel Aviv, better you return it to the sender.'"

"Why do you make your own bombs then? If you've only got one hand?"

The answer was in his silence. In the twilit stillness of

his face as it lay turned to her, with its straight, unsmiling fighter's stare. The answer was in everything she had seen since the night she had signed on with the theatre of the real. For Palestine, it ran. For Israel. For God. For my sacred destiny. To do back to the bastards what the bastards did to me. To redress injustice. With injustice. Until all the just are blown to smithereens, and justice is finally free to pick herself out of the rubble and walk the unpopulated streets.

Suddenly he was demanding her, and no longer to be resisted.

"Darling," she whispered. "Khalil. Oh Christ. Oh, darling. Please."

And whatever else whores say.

It was dawn, but still she would not let him sleep. With the pale daylight, a wakeful light-headedness possessed her. With kisses, with caresses, she used every wile she knew to keep him present with her, and his passion burning. You're my best, she whispered to him, and I never award first prizes. My strongest, my bravest, my most clever lover of all time. Oh, Khalil, Khalil, Christ, oh please. Better than Salim? he asked. More patient than Salim, more cherishing, more grateful. Better than Joseph, who sent me to you on a plate.

"What's the matter?" she said as he suddenly disengaged from her. "Did I hurt you?"

Instead of answering, he reached out his good hand and with a commanding gesture lightly pinched her lips together. Then lifted himself stealthily on his elbow. She listened with him. The clatter of a waterbird lifting from the lake. The shriek of geese. The crowing of a cockerel, the chiming of a bell. Foreshortened by the snowbound countryside. She felt the mattress lift beside her.

"No cows," he said softly, from the window.

He was standing at the side of the window, still naked, but with his gun looped by its belt over his shoulder. And for a second, in the extremity of her tension, she imagined the mirror image of Joseph standing facing him, red-lit by the electric fire, separated from him only by the thin curtain.

"What do you see?" she whispered at last, unable to bear the tension any more.

"No cows. And no fishermen. And no bicycles. I see much too little."

His voice was tense with action. His clothes lay beside the bed where she had thrown them in their frenzy. He pulled on his dark trousers and white shirt, and buckled the gun into place beneath his armpit.

"No cars, no passing lights," he said evenly. "Not one labourer on his way to work. And no cows."

"They've gone to milking."

He shook his head. "Not for two hours do they go for milking."

"It's the snow. They're keeping them indoors."

Something in her voice caught his ear; the quickening in him had sharpened his awareness of her. "Why do you apologise for them?"

"I don't. I'm just trying—"

"Why do you apologise for the absence of all life around this house?"

"To quell your fears. Comfort you."

An idea was growing in him—a terrible idea. He could read it in her face, and in her nakedness; and she in turn could feel his suspicions form. "Why do you wish to quell my fears? Why are you more frightened for me than for yourself?"

"I'm not."

"You are a wanted woman. Why are you so able to love me? Why do you speak of my comfort, and not of your own safety? What guilt is in your mind?"

"None. I didn't like killing Minkel. I want to get out of this whole thing. Khalil?"

"Is Tayeh right? Did my brother die for you after all? Answer me, please," he insisted, very, very quietly. "I wish for an answer."

Her whole body begged for his reprieve. The heat in her face was terrible. It would burn for ever.

"Khalil—come back to bed," she whispered. "Love me. Come back."

Why was he so leisurely if they were all around the house? How could he stare at her like this while the ring tightened round him every second?

"What is the time, please?" he asked, still staring at her. "Charlie?"

"Five. Half past. What does it matter?"

"Where is your *clock*? Your little *clock*. I require to know the time, please."

"I don't know. In the bathroom."

"Stay where you are, please. Otherwise I shall perhaps kill you. We shall see."

He fetched it, and handed it to her on the bed.

"Kindly open it for me," he said, and watched her while she wrestled with the clasp.

"So what is the time, please, Charlie?" he asked again, with a terrible lightness. "Kindly advise me, from your clock, what hour of the day it is."

"Ten to six. Later than I thought."

He snatched it from her and read the dial. Digital, twenty-four-hour. He switched on the radio and it gave a wail of music before he switched it off again. He held it to his ear, then weighed it appreciatively in his hand.

"Since last night when you left me, you have not had much time to yourself, I think. Is that so? None, in fact."

"None."

"Then how did you buy new batteries for this clock?"

"I didn't."

"Then why is it working?"

"I didn't need to—they hadn't run out—it goes for years, just on one set—you buy special ones—long life—"

She had reached the end of her invention. All of it, for all time, here and for ever after, because by now she had remembered the moment on the hilltop when he had stood her outside the Coca-Cola van to search her; and the moment when he dropped the batteries into his pocket before returning the clock to her shoulder bag and tossing the bag into the van.

He had lost interest in her. The clock had all his attention. "Bring me that imposing radio beside the bed, please, Charlie. We make a little experiment. An interesting technological experiment relating to high-frequency radio."

She whispered, "Can I put something on?" She pulled on her dress and took the bedside radio to him, a modern thing in black plastic, with a speaker like a telephone dial. Placing the clock and the radio together, Khalil switched on the radio and worked through the channels until suddenly it let out a wounded wail, up and down like an air-raid warning. Then he picked up the clock, pushed back the hinged flap of the battery chamber with his thumb, and shook the batteries onto the floor, much as he must have done last night. The wailing stopped dead. Like a child who has performed a successful experiment, Khalil lifted his head to her and pretended to smile. She tried not to look at him, but could not help herself.

"Who do you work for, Charlie? For the Germans?"

She shook her head.

"For the Zionists?"

He took her silence for yes.

"Are you Jewish?"

"No."

"Do you believe in *Israel*? What are you?"

"Nothing," she said.

"Are you Christian? Do you see them as the founders of your great religion?"

Again she shook her head.

"Is it for money? Did they bribe you? Blackmail you?"

She wanted to scream. She clenched her fists and filled her lungs, but the chaos choked her, and she sobbed instead. "It was to save life. It was to take part. To be something. I loved him."

"Did you betray my brother?"

The obstructions in her throat disappeared, to be replaced by a mortal flatness of tone. "I never knew him. I never spoke to him in my life. They showed him to me before they killed him, the rest was invented. Our love-affair, my conversion—everything. I didn't even write the letters, they did. They wrote his letter to you too. The one about me. I fell in love with the man who looked after me. That's all there is."

Slowly, without aggression, he reached out his left hand and touched the side of her face, apparently to make sure that she was real. Then looked at the tips of his fingers, and back at her again, somehow comparing them in his mind.

"And you are the same English who gave away my country," he remarked quietly, as if he could hardly believe the evidence of his eyes.

He lifted his head and as he did so, she saw his face snatch away in disapproval and then, under the force of whatever Joseph had shot him with, catch fire. Charlie had been taught to stand still when she pulled the trigger, but Joseph didn't do that. He didn't trust his bullets to do their work, but ran after them, trying to beat them to the target. He rushed through the door like an ordinary intruder, but instead of pausing, hurled himself straight forward as he fired. And he fired with his arms at full stretch, to reduce the distance still more. She saw Khalil's face burst, she saw him spin round and spread his arms to the wall, appealing for its help. So the bullets went into his back, ruining his white shirt. His hands flattened against the wall—one leather, one real—and his wrecked body slipped to a rugger player's crouch as he tried desperately to shove a way through it. But by that time, Joseph was close enough to kick his feet away from under him, hastening him on his last journey to the ground. After Joseph came Litvak, whom she knew as Mike, and had always, as she now realised, suspected of an unhealthy nature. As Joseph stood back, Mike knelt down and put a last precise shot into the back of Khalil's neck, which must have been unnecessary. After Mike came about half the world's executioners, in black frogmen's clothes, followed by Marty and the German weasel and two thousand stretcher bearers and ambulance drivers and doctors and unsmiling women, holding her, cleaning the vomit off her, guiding her down the corridor and into God's fresh air, though the sticky warm smell of blood clogged her nose and throat.

An ambulance was being backed to the front door. There were bottles of blood inside and the blankets were red too, so at first she refused to get in. In fact, she resisted quite hard and must have lashed out, because one of the women holding her suddenly let her go and swung away with her hand to her face. She had gone deaf, so she could only vaguely hear her own screaming, but her main concern was to get her dress off, partly because she was a whore, partly because there was so much of Khalil's blood on it. But the dress was still more unfamiliar to her than it had been last night, and she couldn't fathom whether it had buttons or a zip, so she decided not to bother with it after all. Then Rachel and Rose appeared either side of her, and each grabbed an arm exactly as they had done in the Athens house when she first arrived there for her audition for the theatre of the real; the experience told her that further resistance was futile. They led her up the steps to the ambulance and sat either side of her on one of the beds. She looked down and saw all the silly faces staring at her—the tough little boys with their heroes' scowls, Marty and Mike, Dimitri and Raoul, and other friends as well, some of them not yet introduced. Then the crowd parted, and Joseph emerged, considerately having got rid of the gun with which he had shot Khalil, but still unfortunately with quite a lot of blood over his jeans and running shoes, she noticed. He came to the foot of the steps and looked up at her, and at first it was like staring into her own face, because she could see exactly the same things in him that she hated in herself. So a sort of exchange of character occurred, where she assumed his rôle of killer and pimp, and he, presumably, hers of decoy, whore, and traitor.

Till suddenly, as she continued to stare at him, a surviving spark of outrage kindled in her, and gave her back the identity that he had stolen from her. She stood up, and neither Rose nor Rachel was in time to hold her down; she drew an enormous breath, and she shouted "*Go*" at him—or so at least it sounded to herself. Perhaps it was "*No*." It hardly mattered.

27

Of the immediate and less immediate aftermath of the operation, the world knew a lot more than it realised; and certainly a lot more than Charlie. It knew, for instance—or could have done if it had studied the smaller news items of the foreign pages of the Anglo-Saxon press—that a suspected Palestinian terrorist had died in a shoot-out with members of a crack West German unit, and that his woman hostage, not named, had been removed to hospital in a state of shock, but was otherwise unhurt. The German newspapers carried more lurid versions of the story—"THE WILD WEST COMES TO THE BLACK FOREST"—but the stories were so remarkably assured, yet contradictory, that it was hard to make anything of them. A link with the abortive Freiburg bomb attack against Professor Minkel—originally reported dead, but later discovered to have made a miraculous escape—was so wittily denied by the urbane Dr. Alexis that everyone took it for granted. But it was only proper, said the wiser leader-writers, that we should not be told too much.

A succession of other minor incidents around the Western hemisphere raised occasional speculation about the doings of one or another Arab terrorist organisation, but really with so many rival groups these days, it was a toss-up where one should point the finger. The senseless gunning-down in broad daylight of Dr. Anton Mesterbein, for instance, the Swiss humanist lawyer, campaigner for minority rights, and son of the eminent financier, was laid squarely at the door of an extremist Falangist organisation that had recently "declared war" against Europeans overtly sympathetic to the Palestinian "occupation" of the Lebanon. The outrage occurred as the victim was leaving his villa for work—unprotected, as usual—and the world was deeply shocked for at least the first part of a morning. When a letter claiming responsibility and signed "Free Lebanon" was received by the editor of a Zürich newspaper, and declared authentic, a junior Lebanese diplomat was asked to leave the country, and did so philosophically.

The car-bombing of a Rejectionist Front diplomat outside the newly completed mosque in St. John's Wood rated hardly a notice anywhere; it was the fourth such killing in as many months.

On the other hand, the bloodthirsty knifing of the Italian musician and newspaper columnist Albert Rossino, and of his German lady companion, whose naked and barely recognisable bodies were discovered weeks later beside a Tyrolean lake, was declared by the Austrian authorities to have no political significance at all, despite the fact that both victims had radical connections. On the evidence available, they preferred to treat the case as a crime of passion. The lady, one Astrid Berger, was well known for her bizarre appetites, and it was held probable, if grotesque, that no third party was involved. A succession of other, less interesting deaths passed virtually unnoticed, as did the Israeli bombing of an ancient desert fortress on the Syrian border, which Jerusalem sources claimed was being used as a Palestinian training base for foreign terrorists. As to the four-hundred-pound bomb that exploded on a hilltop outside Beirut, destroying a luxurious summer villa and killing its occupants—which included both Tayeh and Fatmeh—it was about as impenetrable as any other act of terror in that tragic region.

But Charlie, in her seaside fastness, knew none of this; or, more accurately, she knew it all in general, and was either too bored or too frightened to receive the details. At first, she would only swim or take slow, aimless walks to the end of the beach and back, clutching her bathrobe to her throat while her bodyguards followed her at a respectful distance. In the sea, she was inclined to sit herself at the shallow, waveless edge, and make washing movements with the sea water, first her face and then her arms and hands. The other girls, on instruction, bathed naked; but when Charlie declined to follow this liberating example, the psychiatrist ordered them to cover themselves again, and wait.

Kurtz came to see her once a week, sometimes twice. He was extremely gentle with her; patient and faithful, even when she screamed at him. His information was practical, and all to her advantage.

A godfather had been invented for her, he said, an old

friend of her father's who had struck it rich and recently died in Switzerland, leaving her a large sum of money which, since it came from foreign sources, would be free of capital transfer tax in the United Kingdom.

The British authorities had been spoken to, and had accepted—for reasons Charlie could not be party to—that no useful purpose would be served by digging further into her relationship with certain European and Palestinian extremists, he said. Kurtz was also able to reassure her of Quilley's good opinion of her: the police, he said, had actually made a point of calling on him to explain that their suspicions about Charlie had been misdirected.

Kurtz also discussed with Charlie methods of explaining her abrupt disappearance from London, and Charlie passively agreed to a concoction involving fear of police harassment, a mild nervous breakdown, and a mystery lover whom she had picked up after her stay in Mykonos, a married man who had led her a dance and finally dumped her. It was not till he started to school her in this, and presume to test her on small points, that she became pale and started to tremble. A similar manifestation occurred when Kurtz announced to her, somewhat unwisely, that "the highest level" had ruled she could claim Israeli citizenship any time she wished for the rest of her life.

"Give it to Fatmeh," she snapped, and Kurtz, who by then had a number of new cases going, had to consult the file in order to remind himself who Fatmeh was; or had been.

As to her career, said Kurtz, there were some exciting things waiting for her as soon as she felt ready to handle them. A couple of fine Hollywood producers had developed a sincere interest in Charlie during her absence, and were anxious to have her come right out to the Coast and do some screen tests. One actually had a small part up his sleeve that he thought might be just right for her; Kurtz didn't know the details. And there were some nice things happening in the London theatre scene as well.

"I just want to go back to where I was," Charlie said.

Kurtz said that could be arranged, dear, no problem.

The psychiatrist was a bright young fellow with a twinkle in his eye and a military background, and he was not at all given to self-analysis or any other kind of gloomy introspection. Indeed, his concern seemed to be less to make her

talk than to convince her that she shouldn't; in his profession,
he must have been a most divided man. He took her for
drives, first along the coast roads, then into Tel Aviv. But
when he injudiciously pointed out some of the few fine old
Arab houses that had survived development, Charlie became
incoherent with anger. He took her to out-of-the-way restaurants, swam with her, and even lay beside her on the
beach and chatted her up a little, until she told him, with a
strange twist in her voice, that she would prefer to talk to
him in his office. When he heard that she liked to ride, he ordered horses, and they had a grand day's riding during which
she seemed to forget herself completely. But the next day she
was too quiet again for his taste, and he told Kurtz to wait
another week at least. And sure enough the same evening she
began a prolonged and unexplained fit of vomiting, which
was all the more strange considering how little she was
eating.

Rachel came, having resumed her studies at university,
and she was frank and sweet and relaxed, quite different
from the harder version Charlie had first met in Athens.
Dimitri was also back at school, she said; Raoul was thinking
of reading medicine and maybe becoming an army doctor; on
the other hand, he just might take up archaeology. Charlie
smiled politely at these items of family news—Rachel told
Kurtz it was like talking to her grandmother. But in the longer run, neither her North Country origins nor her jolly
middle-class English ways made their desired impact on
Charlie, and after a while, still politely, Charlie asked
whether she might please be left alone again.

Meanwhile within Kurtz's service a number of valuable
lessons had been added to the great sum of technical and human knowledge that formed the treasury of its many operations. Non-Jews, despite the inherent prejudice against them,
were not only usable, but sometimes essential. A Jewish girl
might never have held the middle ground so well. The technicians were also fascinated by the business of the batteries in
the clock radio; it's never too late to learn. An expurgated case
history was duly assembled for training use, to great effect. In
a perfect world, it was argued, the case officer should have
noticed when he made the swap that the batteries were missing from the agent's model. But at least he put two and two
together when the homing signal stopped, and went in

straight away. Becker's name, of course, appeared in none of this; quite apart from the question of security, Kurtz had heard no recent good of him and was not disposed to see him canonised.

And in the late spring at last, as soon as the Litani basin was dry enough for tanks, Kurtz's worst fears and Gavron's worst threats were fulfilled: the long-awaited Israeli push into Lebanon occurred, ending that present phase of hostilities or, according to where you stood, heralding the next one. The refugee camps that had played host to Charlie were sanitised, which meant roughly that bulldozers were brought in to bury the bodies and complete what the tanks and artillery bombing raids had started; a pitiful trail of refugees set off northward, leaving their hundreds, then their thousands, of dead behind. Special groups eradicated the secret places in Beirut where Charlie had stayed; of the house in Sidon only the chickens and the tangerine orchard remained. The house was destroyed by a team of Sayaret, who also put an end to the two boys Kareem and Yasir. They came in at night, from the sea, exactly as Yasir, the great intelligence officer, had always predicted, and they used a special kind of American explosive bullet, still on the secret list, that has only to touch the body to kill. Of all this—of the effective destruction of her brief love-affair with Palestine—Charlie was wisely spared all knowledge. It could unhinge her, the psychiatrist said; with her imagination and self-absorption, she could perfectly easily hold herself responsible for the entire invasion. Better to keep it from her, therefore; let her find out in her own good time. As to Kurtz, for a month or more he was hardly seen, or, if seen, hardly recognised. His body seemed to shrink to half its size, his Slav eyes lost all their sparkle, he looked his age, whatever that was, at last. Then one day, like a man who has shaken off a long and wasting illness, he returned, and within hours, it seemed, had vigorously resumed his strange running feud with Misha Gavron.

In Berlin, Gadi Becker at first floated in a vacuum comparable to Charlie's; but he had floated there before, and was in certain ways less sensitive to its causes and effects. He returned to his flat, and to his failing business prospects: insolvency was once more round the corner. Though he spent days arguing on the telephone with wholesalers, or else hauling boxes from one side of the storeroom to the other, the world slump seemed to have hit the Berlin garment industry harder and further than any other. There was a girl he sometimes slept with, a rather stately creature straight out of the thirties, warm-hearted to a fault and even, to appease his inherited standards, vaguely Jewish. After several days' futile reflection, he phoned her and said he was temporarily in town. Just for a few days, he said; maybe only one. He listened to her joy at his being back, and to her light-hearted remonstrations at his disappearance; but he listened also to the unclear voices of his own inner mind.

"So come round," she said when she had finished scolding him.

But he didn't. He could not approve of the pleasure she might give him.

Scared of himself, he hastened to a fashionable Greek nightclub he knew of, run by a woman of cosmopolitan wisdom and, having at last succeeded in getting drunk, watched the guests smash the plates too eagerly, in the best German-Greek tradition. Next day, without too much planning, he began a novel about a Berlin-Jewish family that had fled to Israel and then uprooted itself again, unable to come to terms with what was being done in the name of Zion. But when he looked at what he had written, he consigned his notes first to the waste-paper basket and then, for security reasons, to the grate. A new man from the Bonn Embassy flew up to visit him, and said he was the replacement for the last man: if you need to communicate with Jerusalem or anything, ask for me. Without seeming to be able to prevent himself, Becker embarked on a provocative discussion with him about the State of Israel. And he ended with a most offensive question, something he claimed to have culled from the writings of Arthur Koestler, and evidently adapted to his own preoccupation: "What are we to become, I wonder?" he said. "A Jewish homeland or an ugly little Spartan state?"

The new man was hard-eyed and unimaginative and the question clearly annoyed him without his understanding the meaning of it. He left some money and his card: Second Secretary, Commercial. But more significantly he left a cloud of doubt behind him, which Kurtz's telephone call next morning was certainly intended to disperse.

"What the hell are you trying to tell me?" he demanded roughly, in English, as soon as Becker had picked up the phone. "You're going to start muddying the nest, then come on home where nobody pays you any attention."

"How is she?" Becker said.

Kurtz's response was perhaps deliberately cruel, for the conversation took place just when he was at his lowest. "Frankie's just fine. Fine in her mind, fine in her appearance, and for some reason beyond me she persists in loving you. Elli spoke to her only the other day and formed the distinct impression that she did not regard the divorce as binding."

"Divorces aren't intended to be binding."

But Kurtz as usual had an answer. "Divorces aren't intended, *period*."

"So how is she?" Becker repeated, with emphasis.

Kurtz had to harness his temper before replying. "If we are speaking of a mutual friend, she is in good health, she is being healed, and she never wants to see you again—and may you remain young for ever!" Kurtz ended with an unbridled shout, and rang off.

The same evening, Frankie rang—Kurtz must have given her the number out of spite. The telephone was Frankie's instrument. Others might play the violin, the harp, or the *shofar*, but for Frankie it was the telephone every time.

Becker listened to her for quite a time. To her weeping, at which she was unequalled; to her cajolements, and her promises. "I'll be whatever you want me to be," she said. "Just tell me and I'll be it."

But the last thing Becker wanted was to invent anybody.

It was not long after this that Kurtz and the psychiatrist decided the time had come to throw Charlie back into the water.

The tour was called A Bouquet of Comedy, and the theatre, like others she had known, served as a Women's Institute and a play school, and no doubt as a polling booth at election times as well. It was a lousy play and a lousy theatre, and it came at the lower end of her decline. The theatre had a tin roof and a wooden floor, and when she stamped, bullet puffs of dust came up between the blocks. She had begun by

taking only tragic parts, because after one nervous look at
her Ned Quilley had assumed that tragedy was what she
wanted; and so, for her own reasons, had Charlie. But she
discovered quickly that serious parts, if they meant anything
to her at all, were too much for her. She would cry or weep
at the most incongruous places, and several times she had to
fake an exit in order to get hold of herself.

But more frequently it was their irrelevance that got to
her; she had no stomach any more—and, worse, no understanding—for what passed for pain in Western middle-class
society. Thus comedy became, after all, the better mask for
her, and through it she had watched her weeks rotate between Sheridan and Priestly and the latest modern genius,
whose offering was described in the programme as a soufflé
flashing with barbed wit. They had played it in York but,
thank God, bypassed Nottingham; they had played it in
Leeds and Bradford and Huddersfield and Derby; and Charlie for one had yet to see the soufflé rise, or the wit flash, but
probably the fault was in herself, for in her imagination she
went through her lines like a punchdrunk boxer who must either slug away or go down for good.

All day long, when she was not rehearsing, she lounged
about like a patient in a doctor's waiting-room, smoking and
reading magazines. But tonight, as the curtain rose once
more, a dangerous sloth replaced her nervousness and she
kept wanting to fall asleep. She heard her voice run up and
down the scale, felt her arm reach this way, her foot step that
way; she paused for what was normally a safe laugh, but
struck instead an uncomprehending quiet. At the same time,
pictures from the forbidden album began to fill her mind: of
the prison in Sidon and the line of waiting mothers along the
wall; of Fatmeh; of the schoolroom in the camp at night,
ironing on the slogans for the march; of the air-raid shelter,
and the stoic faces staring at her, wondering whether she was
to blame. And of Khalil's gloved hand drawing its crude claw
marks in his own blood.

The dressing-room was communal, but when the interval
came, Charlie did not go to it. Instead she stood outside the
stage door, in the open air, smoking and shivering and staring
down the foggy Midland street, and wondering whether she
should simply walk, and keep walking until she fell down or
got hit by a car. They were calling her name and she could

hear slamming doors and running feet, but the problem seemed to be theirs, not hers, and she left them to it. Only a last—a very last—sense of responsibility made her open the door and wander back in.

"Charlie, for Christ's sake! Charlie, what the bloody hell!"

The curtain rose and she found herself once more on stage. Alone. Long monologue, while Hilda sits at husband's desk and pens a letter to her lover: to Michel, to Joseph. A candle burned at her elbow and in a minute she would pull open the drawer of the desk in search of another sheet of paper, and find—"Oh no!"—her husband's unposted letter to his mistress. She began writing and she was in the motel in Nottingham; she stared into the candle flame and saw Joseph's face glinting at her across the table in the taverna outside Delphi. She looked again and it was Khalil, dining with her at the log table in the house in the Black Forest. She was saying her lines and miraculously they were not Joseph's, not Tayeh's, not Khalil's, but Hilda's. She opened the desk drawer and put in a hand, missed a beat, drew out a sheet of handwriting in puzzlement, lifted it, and turned to give the audience their look. She rose to her feet, and with an expression of growing disbelief, advanced to the front of the stage and began to read aloud—such a witty letter, so full of neat cross-references. In a minute her husband, John, would enter left in his dressing-gown, advance upon the desk, and read *her* own unfinished letter to *her* lover. In a minute there would be an even wittier cross-cut of their two letters, and the audience would roll about in delirium, which would turn to ecstasy when the two deceived lovers, each roused by the other's infidelities, fell together in a lecherous embrace. She heard her husband enter, and it was the cue for her to raise her voice: indignation replaces curiosity as Hilda reads on. She grasped the letter in both hands, turned, and took two paces left front in order not to mask John.

As she did so, she saw him—not John but Joseph, quite distinctly, seated where Michel had sat in the centre of the stalls, staring up at her with the same dreadfully serious concern.

*   *   *

At first, she was really not surprised at all; the divide between her inner and outer world had been a flimsy affair at the best of times, but these days it had virtually ceased to exist.

So he's come, she thought. And about time too. Any orchids, Jose? No orchids at all? No red blazer? Gold medallion? Guccis? Maybe I should have gone to the dressing-room after all. Read your note. I'd have known you were coming, wouldn't I? Baked a cake.

She had stopped reading aloud because there was really no point in acting any more, even though the prompter was unashamedly belting out the lines to her and the director was standing behind him waving his arms like someone fighting off a swarm of bees; they were both in her line of vision, somehow, though she was staring at Joseph exclusively. Or perhaps she was imagining them, because Joseph had become so real at last. Behind her, husband John, with no conviction at all, had started inventing lines to cover for her. You need a Joseph, she wanted to tell him proudly; our Jose here will do you lines for all occasions.

There was a screen of light between them—not a screen so much as an optical partition. Added to her tears, it had started to upset her vision of him, and she was beginning to suspect he was after all a mirage. From the wings, they were shouting at her to come off; husband John had marched downstage—clonk, clonk—and taken her kindly but firmly by the elbow as a preliminary to consigning her to the bin. She supposed that in a minute they would pull the curtain on her and give that little tart—what's-her-name, her understudy—the chance of her lifetime. But her concern was to reach Joseph and touch him and make sure. The curtain closed, but she was already walking down the steps to him. The lights went up, and yes it was Joseph, but when she saw him so clearly he bored her; he was just another member of her audience. She started up the aisle and felt a hand on her arm and thought: Husband John again, go away. The foyer was empty except for two geriatric duchesses who presumably were the management.

"See a doctor, dear, I should," said one of them.

"Or sleep it off," said the other.

"Oh leave it out," Charlie advised them happily, using an expression she had never used before.

No Nottingham rain was falling, no red Mercedes waiting to receive her, so she went and stood at a bus-stop, half expecting the American boy to be aboard, telling her to look out for a red van.

Joseph came towards her down the empty street, walking very tall, and she imagined him breaking into a run in order to beat his own bullets to her, but he didn't. He drew up before her, slightly out of breath, and it was clear that someone had sent him with a message, most likely Marty, but perhaps Tayeh. He opened his mouth to deliver it, but she prevented him.

"I'm dead, Jose. You shot me, don't you remember?"

She wanted to add something about the theatre of the real, how the bodies didn't get up and walk away. But she lost it somehow.

A cab passed and Joseph hailed it with his free hand. It didn't stop, but what can you expect? The cabs these days—a law to themselves. She was leaning on him and she would have fallen if he hadn't been holding her so firmly. Her tears were half blinding her, and she was hearing him from under water. I'm dead, she kept saying, I'm dead, I'm dead. But it seemed that he wanted her dead or alive. Locked together, they set off awkwardly along the pavement, though the town was strange to them.

ABOUT THE AUTHOR

JOHN LE CARRÉ is the pseudonym of David Cornwell. Born in 1931, he attended the universities of Berne and Oxford, taught at Eton and later entered the British Foreign Service. He has been described in *The New York Times* as belonging to the select company of such spy and detective story writers as Arthur Conan Doyle, Dashiell Hammett, Raymond Chandler and Ross Macdonald. His first two novels were *Call for the Dead* (1961) and *A Murder of Quality* (1962). His third novel, *The Spy Who Came in from the Cold* (1963), was greeted with great enthusiasm and secured his worldwide reputation. Mr. le Carré is also the author of *The Naive and Sentimental Lover, The Looking Glass War, A Small Town in Germany, Tinker, Tailor, Soldier, Spy* and *The Honourable Schoolboy.*

SPECIAL
MONEY SAVING
OFFER

Now you can have an up-to-date listing of Bantam's hundreds of titles plus take advantage of our unique and exciting bonus book offer. A special offer which gives you the opportunity to purchase a Bantam book for only 50¢. Here's how!

By ordering any five books at the regular price per order, you can also choose any other single book listed (up to a $4.95 value) for just 50¢. Some restrictions do apply, but for further details why not send for Bantam's listing of titles today!

Just send us your name and address plus 50¢ to defray the postage and handling costs.